END GAME

In the crippled city
where time has lost its meaning
and violence is swift and sudden,
a nameless young man with no memory appears . . .
He shares his great strength
in a loving trinity with a young boy
and a haunted, beautiful woman
in that time before the end of time . . .

DHALGREN
by
Samuel R. Delany

Frederik Pohl, four-time Hugo Award-winner, editor of some thirty science fiction anthologies and author of more than forty books, is an acknowledged master of his field.

Each book that bears the crest "A Frederik Pohl Selection" reflects the taste, integrity and discrimination that have made his own works so highly respected by critics and enjoyed by millions of readers.

Frederik Pohl Selections published by Bantam Books

DHALGREN by Samuel R. Delany
HIERO'S JOURNEY by Sterling E. Lanier

DHALGREN

SAMUEL R. DELANY

DHALGREN
A Bantam Book / January 1975
2nd printing

Bantam Books are published by Bantam Books, Inc. Its trade-
mark, consisting of the words "Bantam Books" and the por-
trayal of a bantam, is registered in the United States Patent
Office and in other countries. Marca Registrada. Bantam
Books, Inc., 666 Fifth Avenue, New York, New York 10019.

PRINTED IN THE UNITED STATES OF AMERICA

This book about many things
must be for many people.
Some of them are

Joseph Cox, Bill Brodecky, David
Hartwell, Liz Landry, Joseph
Manfredini, Patrick Muir, John
Herbert McDowell, Jean Sullivan,
Janis Schmidt, Charles Naylor, Ann
O'Neil, Baird Searles, Martin Last,
Bob & Joan Thurston, Richard Vriali,
& Susan Schweers

and

Judy Ratner & Oliver Shank

also

Thomas M. Disch, Judith Merril,
Michael Perkins, Joanna Russ, Judith
Sherwin, & Marilyn Hacker

"You have confused the true and the real."
GEORGE STANLEY/*In conversation*

CONTENTS

I	Prism, Mirror, Lens	1
II	The Ruins of Morning	61
III	House of the Ax	123
IV	In Time of Plague	313
V	Creatures of Light and Darkness	429
VI	Palimpsest	561
VII	The Anathēmata: *a plague journal*	723

DHALGREN

I

to wound the autumnal city.

So howled out for the world to give him a name.

The in-dark answered with wind.

All you know I know: careening astronauts and bank clerks glancing at the clock before lunch; actresses cowling at light-ringed mirrors and freight elevator operators grinding a thumbful of grease on a steel handle; student riots; know that dark women in bodegas shook their heads last week because in six months prices have risen outlandishly; how coffee tastes after you've held it in your mouth, cold, a whole minute.

A whole minute he squatted, pebbles clutched with his left foot (the bare one), listening to his breath sound tumble down the ledges.

Beyond a leafy arras, reflected moonlight flittered.

He rubbed his palms against denim. Where he was, was still. Somewhere else, wind whined.

The leaves winked.

What had been wind was a motion in brush below. His hand went to the rock behind.

She stood up, two dozen feet down and away, wearing only shadows the moon dropped from the viney maple; moved, and the shadows moved on her.

Fear prickled one side where his shirt (two middle buttons gone) bellied with a breeze. Muscle made a band down the back of his jaw. Black hair tried to paw off what fear scored on his forehead.

She whispered something that was all breath, and

1

the wind came for the words and dusted away the meaning:

"Ahhhhh . . ." from her.

He forced out air: it was nearly a cough.

". . . Hhhhhh . . ." from her again. And laughter; which had a dozen edges in it, a bright snarl under the moon. ". . . hhhHHhhhh . . ." which had more sound in it than that, perhaps was his name, even. But the wind, wind . . .

She stepped.

Motion rearranged the shadows, baring one breast. There was a lozenge of light over one eye. Calf and ankle were luminous before leaves.

Down her lower leg was a scratch.

His hair tugged back from his forehead. He watched hers flung forward. She moved with her hair, stepping over leaves, toes spread on stone, in a tip-toe pause, to quit the darker shadows.

Crouched on rock, he pulled his hands up his thighs.

His hands were hideous.

She passed another, nearer tree. The moon flung gold coins at her breasts. Her brown aureoles were wide, her nipples small. "You . . . ?" She said that, softly, three feet away, looking down; and he *still* could not make out her expression for the leaf dappling; but her cheek bones were Orientally high. She *was* Oriental, he realized and waited for another word, tuned for accent. (He could sort Chinese from Japanese.) "You've come!" It was a musical Midwestern Standard. "I didn't know if you'd come!" Her voicing (a clear soprano, whispering . . .) said that some of what he'd thought was shadow-movement might have been fear: "You're here!" She dropped to her knees in a roar of foliage. Her thighs, hard in front, softer (he could tell) on the sides—a column of darkness between them— were inches from his raveled knees.

She reached, two fingers extended, pushed back plaid wool, and touched his chest; ran her fingers down. He could hear his own crisp hair.

Laughter raised her face to the moon. He leaned forward; the odor of lemons filled the breezeless gap. Her round face was compelling, her eyebrows un-Orientally heavy. He judged her over thirty, but the only lines were two small ones about her mouth.

He turned his mouth, open, to hers, and raised his hands to the sides of her head till her hair covered them.

2

The cartilages of her ears were hot curves on his palms. Her knees slipped in leaves; that made her blink and laugh again. Her breath was like noon and smelled of lemons . . .

He kissed her; she caught his wrists. The joined meat of their mouths came alive. The shape of her breasts, her hand half on his chest and half on wool, was lost with her weight against him.

Their fingers met and meshed at his belt; a gasp bubbled in their kiss (his heart was stuttering loudly), was blown away; then air on his thigh.

They lay down.

With her fingertips she moved his cock head roughly in her rough hair while a muscle in her leg shook under his. Suddenly he slid into her heat. He held her tightly around the shoulders when her movements were violent. One of her fists stayed like a small rock over her breast. And there was a roaring, roaring: at the long, surprising come, leaves hailed his side.

Later, on their sides, they made a warm place with their mingled breath. She whispered, "You're beautiful, I think." He laughed, without opening his lips. Closely, she looked at one of his eyes, looked at the other (he blinked), looked at his chin (behind his lips he closed his teeth so that his jaw moved), then at his forehead. (He liked her lemon smell.) ". . . beautiful!" she repeated.

Wondering was it true, he smiled.

She raised her hand into the warmth, with small white nails, moved one finger beside his nose, growled against his cheek.

He reached to take her wrist.

She asked, "Your hand . . . ?"

So he put it behind her shoulder to pull her nearer.

She twisted. "Is there something wrong with your . . . ?"

He shook his head against her hair, damp, cool, licked it.

Behind him, the wind was cool. Below hair, her skin was hotter than his tongue. He brought his hands around into the heated cave between them.

She pulled back. "Your *hands*—!"

Veins like earthworms wriggled in the hair. The skin was cement dry; his knuckles were thick with scabbed callous. Blunt thumbs lay on the place between her breasts like toads.

3

She frowned, raised her knuckles toward his, stopped.

Under the moon on the sea of her, his fingers were knobbed peninsulas. Sunk on the promontory of each was a stripped-off, gnawed-back, chitinous wreck.

"You . . . ?" he began.

No, they were not deformed. But they were . . . *ugly!* She looked up. Blinking, her eyes glistened.

". . . do you know my . . . ?" His voice hoarsened. "Who I . . . am?"

Her face was not subtle; but her smile, regretful and mostly in the place between her brow and her folded lids, confused.

"You," she said, full voice and formal (but the wind still blurred some overtone), "have a father." Her hip was warm against his belly. The air which he had thought mild till now was a blade to pry back his loins. "You have a *mummer—!*" That was his cheek against her mouth. But she turned her face away. "You are—" she placed her pale hand over his great one (Such *big* hands for a little ape of a guy, someone had kindly said. He remembered that) on her ribs—"beautiful. You've come from somewhere. You're going somewhere." She sighed.

"But . . ." He swallowed the things in his throat (he wasn't *that* little). "I've lost . . . something."

"Things have made you what you are," she recited. "What you are will make you what you will become."

"I want something back!"

She reached behind her to pull him closer. The cold well between his belly and the small of her back collapsed. "What don't you have?" She looked over her shoulder at him: "How old are you?"

"Twenty-seven."

"You have the face of someone much younger." She giggled. *"I thought you were . . . sixteen!* You have the hands of someone much older—"

"And meaner?"

"—crueler than I think you are. Where were you born?"

"Upstate New York. You wouldn't know the town. I didn't stay there long."

"I probably wouldn't. You're a long way away."

"I've been to Japan. And Australia."

"You're educated?"

He laughed. His chest shook her shoulder. "One year

4

at Columbia. Almost another at a community college in Delaware. No degree."

"What year were you born?"

"Nineteen forty-eight. I've been in Central America too. Mexico. I just came from Mexico and I—"

"What do you want to change in the world?" she continued her recitation, looking away. "What do you want to preserve? What is the thing you're searching for? What are you running away from?"

"Nothing," he said. "And nothing. And nothing. And . . . nothing, at least that I know."

"You have no purpose?"

"I want to get to Bellona and—" He chuckled. "Mine's the same as everybody else's; in real life, anyway: to get through the next second, consciousness intact."

The next second passed.

"Really?" she asked, real enough to make him realize the artificiality of what he'd said (thinking: It is in danger with the passing of each one). "Then be glad you're not just a character scrawled in the margins of somebody else's lost notebook: you'd be deadly dull. Don't you have *any* reason for going there?"

"To get to Bellona and . . ."

When he said no more, she said, "You don't have to tell me. So, you don't know who you are? Finding *that* out would be much too simple to bring you all the way from upper New York State, by way of Japan, here. Ahhh . . ." and she stopped.

"What?"

"Nothing."

"What?"

"Well, if you were born in nineteen forty-eight, you've got to be older than twenty-seven."

"How do you mean?"

"Oh, hell," she said. "It isn't important."

He began to shake her arm, slowly.

She said: "*I* was born in nineteen forty-seven. And I'm a *good* deal older then twenty-eight." She blinked at him again. "But that really isn't im—"

He rolled back in the loud leaves. "Do you know who I am?" Night was some color between clear and cloud. "You came here, to find me. Can't you tell me what my name is?"

Cold spread down his side, where she had been, like butter.

He turned his head.

"Come!" As she sat, her hair writhed toward him. A handful of leaves struck his face.

He sat too.

But she was already running, legs passing and passing through moon-dapple.

He wondered where she'd got that scratch.

Grabbing his pants, he stuck foot and foot in them, grabbing his shirt and his single sandal, rolled to his feet—

She was rounding the rock's edge.

He paused for his fly and the twin belt hooks. Twigs and gravel chewed his feet. She ran so fast!

He came up as she glanced back, put his hand on the stone—and flinched: the rock-face was wet. He looked at the crumbled dirt on the yellow ham and heel.

"There . . ." She pointed into the cave. "Can you see it?"

He started to touch her shoulder, but no.

She said: "Go ahead. Go in."

He dropped his sandal: a lisp of brush. He dropped his shirt: that smothered the lisping.

She looked at him expectantly, stepped aside.

He stepped in: moss on his heel, wet rock on the ball of his foot. His other foot came down: wet rock.

Breath quivered about him. In the jellied darkness something dry brushed his cheek. He reached up: a dead vine crisp with leaves. It swung: things rattled awfully far overhead. With visions of the mortal edge, he slid his foot forward. His toes found: a twig with loose bark . . . a clot of wet leaves . . . the thrill of water . . . Next step, water licked over his foot. He stepped again:

Only rock.

A flicker, left.

Stepped again, and the flicker was orange, around the edge of something; which was the wall of a rock niche, with shadow for ceiling, next step.

Beyond a dead limb, a dish of brass wide as a car tire had nearly burned to embers. Something in the remaining fire snapped, spilling sparks on wet stone.

Ahead, where the flicker leaked high up into the narrowing slash, something caught and flung back flashings.

He climbed around one boulder, paused; the echo from breath and burning cast up intimations of the cavern's size. He gauged a crevice, leaped the meter, and scrambled on the far slope. Things loosened under his feet. He heard pebbles in the gash complaining down rocks, and stuttering, and whispering—and silence.

Then: a splash!

He pulled in his shoulders; he had assumed it was only a yard or so deep.

He had to climb a long time. One face, fifteen feet high, stopped him a while. He went to the side and clambered up the more uneven outcroppings. He found a thick ridge that, he realized as he pulled himself up it, was a root. He wondered what it was a root to, and gained the ledge.

Something went *Eeek!* softly, six inches from his nose, and scurried off among old leaves.

He swallowed, and the prickles tidaling along his shoulders subsided. He pulled himself the rest of the way, and stood:

It lay in a crack that slanted into roofless shadow.

One end looped a plume of ferns.

He reached for it; his body blocked the light from the brazier below: glimmer ceased.

He felt another apprehension than that of the unexpected seen before, or accidentally revealed behind. He searched himself for some physical sign that would make it real: quickening breath, slowing heart. But what he apprehended was insubstantial as a disjunction of the soul. He picked the chain up; one end chuckled and flickered down the stone. He turned with it to catch the orange glimmer.

Prisms.

Some of them, anyway.

Others were round.

He ran the chain across his hand. Some of the round ones were transparent. Where they crossed the spaces between his fingers, the light distorted. He lifted the chain to gaze through one of the lenses. But it was opaque. Tilting it, he saw pass, dim and inches distant in the circle, his own eye, quivering in the quivering glass.

Everything was quiet.

He pulled the chain across his hand. The random arrangement went almost nine feet. Actually, three lengths were attached. Each of the three ends looped on itself. On the largest loop was a small metal tag.

He stooped for more light.

The centimeter of brass (the links bradded into the

optical bits were brass) was inscribed: *producto do Brazil.*

He thought: What the hell kind of Portuguese is that?

He crouched a moment longer looking along the glittering lines.

He tried to pull it all together for his jean pocket, but the three tangled yards spilled his palms. Standing, he found the largest loop and lowered his head. Points and edges nipped his neck. He got the tiny rings together under his chin and fingered (Thinking: Like damned clubs) the catch closed.

He looked at the chain in loops of light between his feet. He picked up the shortest end from his thigh. The loop there was smaller.

He waited, held his breath even—then wrapped the length twice around his upper arm, twice around his lower, and fastened the catch at his wrist. He flattened his palm on the links and baubles hard as plastic or metal. Chest hair tickled the creasing between joint and joint.

He passed the longest end around his back: the bits lay out cold kisses on his shoulder blades. Then across his chest; his back once more; his belly. Holding the length in one hand (it still hung down on the stone), he unfastened his belt with the other.

Pants around his ankles, he wound the final length once around his hips; and then around his right thigh; again around; and again. He fastened the last catch at his ankle. Pulling up his trousers, he went to the ledge, buckled them, and turned to climb down.

He was aware of the bindings. But, chest flat on the stone, they were merely lines and did not cut.

This time he went to where the crevice was only a foot wide and stepped far off the lip. The cave mouth was a lambda of moon mist, edged with leaf-lace.

The rocks licked his soles. Once, when his mind wandered, it was brought back by his foot in cold water; and the links were warm around his body. He halted to feel for more heat; but the chain was only neutral weight.

He stepped out onto moss.

His shirt lay across a bush, his sandal, sole up, beneath.

He slipped his arms into the wool sleeves: his right wrist glittered from the cuff. He buckled his sandal: the ground moistened his knee.

8

He stood, looked around, and narrowed his eyes on the shadows. "Hey . . . ?" He turned left, turned right, and scratched his collar-bone with his wide thumb. "Hey, where . . . ?" Turning right, turning left, he wished he could interpret scuffs and broken brush. She wouldn't have wandered down the way they'd come . . .

He left the cave mouth and entered the shingled black. Could she have gone along here? he wondered three steps in. But went forward.

He recognized the road for moonlight the same moment his sandaled foot jabbed into mud. His bare one swung to the graveled shoulder. He staggered out on the asphalt, one foot sliding on flooded leather, took a hissing breath, and gazed around.

Left, the road sloped up between the trees. He started right. Downward would take him toward the city.

On one side was forest. On the other, he realized after a dozen slippery jogs, it was only a hedge of trees. Trees dropped away with another dozen. Behind, the grass whispered and shushed him.

She was standing at the meadow's center.

He brought his feet—one strapped and muddy, one bare and dusty—together; suddenly felt his heart beating; heard his surprised breath shush the grass back. He stepped across the ditch to ill-mowed stubble.

She's too tall, he thought, nearing.

Hair lifted from her shoulders; grass whispered again.

She *had* been taller than he was, but not like . . . "Hey, I got the . . . !" She was holding her arms over her head. Was she standing on some stumpy pedestal? "Hey . . . ?"

She twisted from the waist: "What the hell are *you* doing here?"

At first he thought she was splattered with mud all up her thigh. "I thought you . . . ?" But it was brown as dried blood.

She gazed down at him with batting eyes.

Mud? Blood? It was the wrong color for either.

"Go *away!*"

He took another, entranced step.

"What are you *doing* here? Go away!"

Were the blotches under her breasts scabs? "Look, I got it! Now, can't you tell me my . . . ?"

Leaves were clutched in her raised hands. Her hands

were raised *so* high! Leaves dropped about her shoulders. Her long, long fingers shook, and brittle darkness covered one flank. Her pale belly jerked with a breath.

"No!" She bent away when he tried to touch her; and stayed bent. One arm, branched and branching ten feet over him, pulled a web of shadow across the grass.

"You . . . !" was the word he tried; breath was all that came.

He looked up among the twigs of her ears. Leaves shucked from her eyebrows. Her mouth was a thick, twisted bole, as though some footwide branch had been lopped off by lightning. Her eyes—his mouth opened as he craned to see them—disappeared, first one, up there, then the other, way over there: scabby lids sealed.

He backed through stiff grass.

A leaf crashed his temple like a charred moth.

Rough fingers bludgeoning his lips, he stumbled, turned, ran to the road, glanced once more where the twisted trunk raked five branches at the moon, loped until he had to walk, walked—gasping—until he could think. Then he ran some more.

2

It is not that I have no past. Rather, it continually fragments on the terrible and vivid ephemera of now. In the long country, cut with rain, somehow there is nowhere to begin. Loping and limping in the ruts, it would be easier not to think about what she did (was done to her, done to her, done), trying instead to reconstruct what it is at a distance. Oh, but it would not be so terrible had one calf not borne (if I'd looked close, it would have been a chain of tiny wounds with moments of flesh between; I've done that myself with a swipe in a garden past a rose) that scratch.

The asphalt spilled him onto the highway's shoulder. The paving's chipped edges filed visions off his eyes. A roar came toward him he heard only as it passed. He glanced back: the truck's red, rear eyes sank together. He walked for another hour, saw no other vehicle.

A Mac with a double van belched twenty feet behind him, sagged to a stop twenty feet ahead. He hadn't even been thumbing. He sprinted toward the opening door, hauled himself up, slammed it. The driver, tall, blond, and acned, looking blank, released the clutch.

He was going to say thanks, but coughed. Maybe the driver wanted somebody to rap at? Why else stop for someone just walking the road!

He didn't feel like rapping. But you have to say something:

"What you loading?"

"Artichokes."

Approaching lights spilled pit to pit in the driver's face.

They shook on down the highway.

He could think of nothing more, except: I was just making love to this woman, see, and you'll never guess . . . No, the Daphne bit would not pass—

11

It was he who wanted to talk! The driver was content to dispense with phatic thanks and chatter. Western independence? He had hitched this sector of country enough to decide it was all manic terror.

He leaned his head back. He wanted to talk and had nothing to say.

Fear past, the archness of it forced the architecture of a smile his lips fought.

He saw the ranked highway lights twenty minutes later and sat forward to see the turnoff. He glanced at the driver who was just glancing away. The brakes wheezed and the cab slowed by lurches.

They stopped. The driver sucked in the sides of his ruined cheeks, looked over, still blank.

He nodded, sort of smiled, fumbled the door, dropped to the road; the door slammed and the truck started while he was still preparing thanks; he had to duck the van corner.

The vehicle grumbled down the turnoff.

We only spoke a line apiece.

What an odd ritual exchange to exhaust communication. (Is that terror?) What amazing and engaging rituals are we practicing now? (He stood on the road side, laughing.) What torque and tension in the mouth to laugh so in this windy, windy, windy . . .

Underpass and overpass knotted here. He walked . . . proudly? Yes, proudly by the low wall.

Across the water the city flickered.

On its dockfront, down half a mile, flamed roiled smoke on the sky and reflections on the river. Here, not one car came off the bridge. Not one went on.

This toll booth, like the rank of booths, was dark. He stepped inside: front pane shattered, stool overturned, no drawer in the register—a third of the keys stuck down; a few bent. Some were missing their heads. Smashed by a mace, a mallet, a fist? He dragged his fingers across them, listened to them click, then stepped from the glass-flecked, rubber mat, over the sill to the pavement.

Metal steps led up to the pedestrian walkway. But since there was no traffic, he sauntered across two empty lanes—a metal grid sunk in the blacktop gleamed where tires had polished it—to amble the broken white line, sandaled foot one side, bare foot the other. Girders wheeled by him, left and right. Beyond, the burning city squatted on weak, inverted images of its fires.

12

He gazed across the wale of night water, all wind-runneled, and sniffed for burning. A gust parted the hair at the back of his neck; smoke was moving off the river.

"Hey, you!"

He looked up at the surprising flashlight. "Huh . . . ?" At the walkway rail, another and another punctured the dark.

"You going into Bellona?"

"That's right." Squinting, he tried to smile. One, and another, the lights moved a few steps, stopped. He said: "You're . . . leaving?"

"Yeah. You know it's restricted in there."

He nodded. "But I haven't seen any soldiers or police or anything. I just hitch-hiked down."

"How were the rides?"

"All I saw was two trucks for the last twenty miles. The second one gave me a lift."

"What about the traffic going out?"

He shrugged. "But I guess girls shouldn't have too hard a time, though. I mean, if a car passes, you'll probably get a ride. Where you heading?"

"Two of us want to get to New York. Judy wants to go to San Francisco."

"I just want to get *some* place," a whiny voice came down. "I've got a fever! I should be in bed. I *was* in bed for the last three days."

He said: "You've got a ways to go, either direction."

"Nothing's happened to San Francisco—?"

"—or New York?"

"No." He tried to see behind the lights. "The papers don't even talk about what's happening here, any more."

"But, Jesus! What about the television? Or the radio—"

"Stupid, none of it works out here. So how are they gonna know?"

"But— Oh, wow . . . !"

He said: "The nearer you get, it's just less and less people. And the ones you meet are . . . funnier. What's it like inside?"

One laughed.

Another said: "It's pretty rough."

The one who'd spoken first said: "But like you say, girls have an easier time."

They laughed.

13

He did too. "Is there anything you can tell me? I mean that might be helpful? Since I'm going in?"

"Yeah. Some men came by, shot up the house we were living in, tore up the place, then burned us out."

"She was making this sculpture," the whiny voice explained; "this big sculpture. Of a lion. Out of junk metal and stuff. It was beautiful . . . ! But she had to leave it."

"Wow," he said. "Is it like that?"

One short, hard laugh: "Yeah. We got it real easy."

"Tell him about Calkins? Or the scorpions?"

"He'll learn about them." Another laugh. "What can you say?"

"You want a weapon to take in with you?"

That made him afraid again. "Do I need one?"

But they were talking among themselves:

"You're gonna give him that?"

"Yeah, why not? I don't want it with me any more."

"Well, okay. It's yours."

Metal sounded on chain, while one asked: "Where you from?" The flashlights turned away, ghosting the group. One in profile near the rail was momentarily lighted enough to see she was very young, very black, and very pregnant.

"Up from the south."

"You don't *sound* like you're from the south," one said who did.

"I'm not *from* the south. But I was just in Mexico."

"Oh, hey!" That was the pregnant one. "Where were you? I know Mexico."

The exchange of half a dozen towns ended in disappointed silence.

"Here's your weapon."

Flashlights followed the flicker in the air, the clatter on the gridded blacktop.

With the beams on the ground (and not in his eyes), he could make out half a dozen women on the catwalk.

"What—" A car motor thrummed at the end of the bridge; but there were no headlights when he glanced. The sound died on some turnoff—"is it?"

"What'd they call it?"

"An orchid."

"Yeah, that's what it is."

He walked over, squatted in the triple beam.

"You wear it around your wrist. With the blades sticking out front. Like a bracelet."

From an adjustable metal wrist-band, seven blades, from eight to twelve inches, curved sharply forward. There was a chain-and-leather harness inside to hold it steady on the fingers. The blades were sharpened along the outside.

He picked it up.

"Put it on."

"Are you right or left handed?"

"Ambidextrous . . ." which, in his case, meant clumsy with both. He turned the "flower". "But I write with my left. Usually."

"Oh."

He fitted it around his right wrist, snapped it. "Suppose you were wearing this on a crowded bus. You could hurt somebody," and felt the witticism fail. He made a fist within the blades, opened it slowly and, behind curved steel, rubbed two blunt and horny crowns on the underside of his great thumb.

"There aren't too many buses in Bellona."

Thinking: Dangerous, bright petals bent about some knobbed, half-rotted root. "Ugly thing," he told it, not them. "Hope I don't need you."

"Hope you don't either," one said above. "I guess you can give it to somebody else when you leave."

"Yeah." He stood up. "Sure."

"*If* he leaves," another said, gave another laugh.

"Hey, we better get going."

"I heard a car. We're probably gonna have to wait long enough anyway. We might as well start."

South: "He didn't make it sound like we were gonna get any rides."

"Let's just get going. Hey, so long!"

"So long." Their beams swept by. "And thanks." Artichokes? But he could not remember where the word had come from to ring so brightly. He raised the orchid after them. His gnarled hand, caged in blades, was silhouetted with river glitter stretching between the bridge struts. Watching them go, he felt the vaguest flutter of desire. Only one of their flashlights was on. Then one of them blocked that. They were footsteps on metal plates; some laughter drifting back; rustlings . . .

He walked again, holding his hand from his side.

This parched evening seasons the night with remembrances of rain. Very few suspect the existence of this city. It is as if not only the media but the laws of perception themselves have redesigned knowledge and perception to pass it. Rumor says there is practically no power here. Neither television cameras nor on-the-spot broadcasts function: that such a catastrophe as this should be opaque, and therefore dull, to the electric nation! It is a city of inner discordances and retinal distortions.

3

Beyond the bridge-mouth, the pavement shattered.

One live street lamp lit five dead ones—two with broken globes. Climbing a ten-foot, tilted, asphalt slab that jerked once under him, rumbling like a live thing, he saw pebbles roll off the edge, heard them clink on fugitive plumbing, then splash somewhere in darkness . . . He recalled the cave and vaulted to a more solid stretch, whose cracks were mortared with nubby grass.

No lights in any near buildings; but down those waterfront streets, beyond the veils of smoke—was that fire? Already used to the smell, he had to breathe deeply to notice it. The sky was all haze. Buildings jabbed up into it and disappeared.

Light?

At the corner of a four-foot alley, he spent ten minutes exploring—just because the lamp worked. Across the street he could make out concrete steps, a loading porch under an awning, doors. A truck had overturned at the block's end. Nearer, three cars, windows rimmed with smashed glass, squatted on skewed hubs, like frogs gone marvelously blind.

His bare foot was calloused enough for gravel and glass. But ash kept working between his foot and his remaining sandal to grind like finest sand, work its way under, and silt itself with his sweat. His heel was almost sore.

By the gate at the alley's end, he found a pile of empty cans, a stack of newspaper still wire-bound, bricks set up as a fireplace with an arrangement of pipes over it. Beside it was an army messpan, insides caked with dead mold. Something by his moving foot crinkled.

He reached down. One of the orchid's petals snagged; he picked up a package of . . . bread? The wrapper was twisted closed. Back under the street lamp, he balanced it

17

on his fingers, through the blades, and opened the cellophane.

He had wondered about food.

He had wondered about sleep.

But he knew the paralysis of wonder.

The first slice had a tenpenny nailhead of muzzy green in the corner; the second and third, the same. The nail, he thought, was through the loaf. The top slice was dry on one side. Nothing else was wrong—except the green vein; and it was only that penicillium stuff. He could eat around it.

I'm not hungry.

He replaced the slices, folded the cellophane, carried it back, and wedged it behind the stacked papers.

As he returned to the lamp, a can clattered from his sandal, defining the silence. He wandered away through it, gazing up for some hint of the hazed-out moon—

Breaking glass brought his eyes to street level.

He was afraid, and he was curious; but fear had been so constant, it was a dull and lazy emotion, now; the curiosity was alive:

He sprinted to the nearest wall, moved along it rehearsing his apprehensions of all terrible that might happen. He passed a doorway, noted it for ducking, and kept on to the corner. Voices now. And more glass.

He peered around the building edge.

Three people vaulted from a shattered display window to join two waiting. Barking, a dog followed them to the sidewalk. One man wanted to climb back in; did. Two others took off down the block.

The dog circled, loped his way—

He pulled back, free hand grinding on the brick.

The dog, crouched and dancing ten feet off, barked, barked, barked again.

Dim light slathered canine tongue and teeth. Its eyes (he swallowed, hard) were glistening red, without white or pupil, smooth as crimson glass.

The man came back out the window. One in the group turned and shouted: "Muriel!" (It could have been a woman.) The dog wheeled and fled after.

Another street lamp, blocks down, gave them momentary silhouette.

As he stepped from the wall, his breath unraveled the silence, shocked him as much as if someone had called his . . . name? Pondering, he crossed the street toward the corner of the loading porch. On tracks under the awning, four- and six-foot butcher hooks swung gently— though there was no wind. In fact, he reflected, it would take a pretty hefty wind to *start* them swinging—

"Hey!"

Hands, free and flowered, jumped to protect his face. He whirled, crouching.

"You down there!"

He looked up, with hunched shoulders.

Smoke rolled about the building top, eight stories above.

"What you doing, huh?"

He lowered his hands.

The voice was rasp rough, sounded near drunk.

He called: "Nothing!" and wished his heart would still. "Just walking around."

Behind scarves of smoke, someone stood at the cornice. "What you been up to this evening?"

"Nothing, I said." He took a breath: "I just got here, over the bridge. About a half hour ago."

"Where'd you get the orchid?"

"Huh?" He raised his hand again. The street lamp dribbled light down a blade. "This?"

"Yeah."

"Some women gave it to me. When I was crossing the bridge."

"I saw you looking around the corner at the hubbub. I couldn't tell from up here—was it scorpions?"

"Huh?"

"I said, was it scorpions?"

"It was a bunch of people trying to break into a store, I think. They had a dog with them."

After silence, gravelly laughter grew. "You really haven't been here long, kid?"

"I—" and realized the repetition—"just got here."

"You out to go exploring by yourself? Or you want company for a bit."

The guy's eyes, he reflected, must be awfully good. "Company . . . I guess."

"I'll be there in a minute."

He didn't see the figure go; there was too much smoke. And after he'd watched several doorways for several minutes, he figured the man had changed his mind.

"Here you go," from the one he'd set aside for ducking.

19

"Name is Loufer. Tak Loufer. You know what that means, Loufer? Red Wolf; or Fire Wolf."

"Or Iron Wolf." He squinted. "Hello."

"Iron Wolf? Well, yeah . . ." The man emerged, dim on the top step. "Don't know if I like that one so much. Red Wolf. That's my favorite." He was a very big man.

He came down two more steps; his engineer's boots, hitting the boards, sounded like dropped sandbags. Wrinkled black-jeans were half stuffed into the boot tops. The worn cycle jacket was scarred with zippers. Gold stubble on chin and jaw snagged the street light. Chest and belly, bare between flapping zipper teeth, were a tangle of brass hair. The fingers were massive, matted—"What's your name?"—but clean, with neat and cared-for nails.

"Um . . . well, I'll tell you: I don't know." It sounded funny, so he laughed. "I don't know."

Loufer stopped, a step above the sidewalk, and laughed too. "Why the hell don't you?" The visor of his leather cap blocked his upper face with shadow.

He shrugged. "I just don't. I haven't for . . . a while now."

Loufer came down the last step, to the pavement. "Well, Tak Loufer's met people here with stranger stories than that. You some kind of nut, or something? You been in a mental hospital, maybe?"

"Yes . . ." He saw that Loufer had expected a *No*.

Tak's head cocked. The shadow raised to show the rims of Negro-wide nostrils above an extremely caucasian mouth. The jaw looked like rocks in hay-stubble.

"Just for a year. About six or seven years ago."

Loufer shrugged. "I was in jail for three months . . . about six or seven years ago. But that's as close as I come. So you're a no-name kid? What are you, seventeen? Eighteen? No, I bet you're even—"

"Twenty-seven."

Tak's head cocked the other way. Light topped his cheek bones. "Neurotic fatigue, do it every time. You notice that about people with serious depression, the kind that sleep all day? Hospital type cases, I mean. They always look ten years younger than they are."

He nodded.

"I'm going to call you Kid, then. That'll do you for a name. You can be—The Kid, hey?"

Three gifts, he thought: armor, weapon, title (like the prisms, lenses, mirrors on the chain itself). "Okay . . ."

20

with the sudden conviction this third would cost, by far, the most. Reject it, something warned: "Only I'm not a kid. Really; I'm twenty-seven. People always think I'm younger than I am. I just got a baby face, that's all. I've even got some white hair, if you want to see—"

"Look, Kid—" with his middle fingers, Tak pushed up his visor—"we're the same age." His eyes were large, deep, and blue. The hair above his ears, no longer than the week's beard, suggested a severe crew under the cap. "Any sights you particularly want to see around here? Anything you heard about? I like to play guide. What do you hear about us, outside, anyway? What do people say about us here in the city?"

"Not much."

"Guess they wouldn't." Tak looked away. "You just wander in by accident, or did you come on purpose?"

"Purpose."

"Good Kid! Like a man with a purpose. Come on up here. This street turns into Broadway soon as it leaves the waterfront."

"What *is* there to see?"

Loufer gave a grunt that did for a laugh. "Depends on what sights are out." Though he had the beginning of a gut, the ridges under the belly hair were muscle deep. "If we're *really* lucky, maybe—" the ashy leather, swinging as Loufer turned, winked over a circular brass buckle that held together a two-inch-wide garrison—"we won't run into anything at all! Come on." They walked.

". . . kid. The Kid . . ."

"Huh?" asked Loufer.

"I'm thinking about that name."

"Will it do?"

"I don't know."

Loufer laughed. "I'm not going to press for it, Kid. But I think it's yours."

His own chuckle was part denial, part friendly.

Loufer's grunt in answer echoed the friendly.

They walked beneath low smoke.

There is something delicate about this Iron Wolf, with his face like a pug-nosed, Germanic gorilla. It is neither his speech nor his carriage, which have their roughness, but the way in which he assumes them, as though the surface where speech and carriage are flush were somehow inflamed.

"Hey, Tak?"

21

"Yeah?"

"How long have you been here?"

"If you told me today's date, I could figure it out. But I've let it go. It's been a while." After a moment, Loufer asked, in a strange, less blustery voice: "Do you know what day it is?"

"No, I . . ." The strangeness scared him. "I don't." He shook his head while his mind rushed away toward some other subject. "What do you do? I mean, what did you work at?"

Tak snorted. "Industrial engineering."

"Were you working here, before . . . all this?"

"Near here. About twelve miles down, at Helmsford. There used to be a plant that jarred peanut butter. We were converting it into a vitamin C factory. What do you do—? Naw, you don't look like you do too much in the line of work." Loufer grinned. "Right?"

He nodded. It was reassuring to be judged by appearances, when the judge was both accurate and friendly. And, anyway, the rush had stopped.

"I was staying down in Helmsford," Loufer went on. "But I used to drive up to the city a lot. Bellona used to be a pretty good town." Tak glanced at a doorway too dark to see if it was open or shut.

"Maybe it still is, you know? But one day I drove up here. And it was like this."

A fire escape, above a street lamp pulsing slow as a failing heart, looked like charred sticks, some still aglow.

"Just like this?"

On a store window their reflection slid like ripples over oil.

"There were a few more places the fire hadn't reached; a few more people who hadn't left yet—not all the newcomers had arrived."

"You were here at the very beginning, then?"

"Oh, I didn't see it break out or anything. Like I say, when I got here, it looked more or less like it does now."

"Where's your car?"

"Sitting on the street with the windshield busted, the tires gone—along with most of the motor. I let a lot of stupid things happen, at first. But I got the hang of it after a while." Tak made a sweeping gesture with both hands—and disappeared before it was finished: they'd passed into complete blackness. "A thousand people are

22

supposed to be here now. Used to be almost two million."

"How do you know, I mean the population?"

"That's what they publish in the paper."

"Why do you stay?"

"Stay?" Loufer's voice neared that other, upsetting tone. "Well, actually, I've thought about that one a lot. I think it has to do with—I got a theory now—freedom. You know, here—" ahead, something moved—"you're free. No laws: to break, or to follow. Do anything you want. Which does funny things to you. Very quickly, surprisingly quickly, you become—" they neared another half-lit lamp; what moved became smoke, lobling from a window sill set with glass teeth like an extinguished jack-o-lantern—"exactly who you are." And Tak was visible again. "If you're ready for that, this is where it's at."

"It must be pretty dangerous. Looters and stuff."

Tak nodded. "Sure it's dangerous."

"Is there a lot of street mugging?"

"Some." Loufer made a face. "Do you know about crime, Kid? Crime is funny. For instance, now, in most American cities—New York, Chicago, St. Louis—crimes, ninety-five per cent I read, are committed between six o'clock and midnight. That means you're safer walking around the street at three o'clock in the morning than you are going to the theater to catch a seven-thirty curtain. I wonder what time it is now. Sometime after two I'd gather. I don't think Bellona is much more dangerous than any other city. It's a very small city, now. That's a sort of protection."

A forgotten blade scraped his jeans. "Do you carry a weapon?"

"Months of detailed study on what is going on where, the movements and variations of our town. I look around a lot. This way."

That wasn't buildings on the other side of the street: Trees rose above the park wall, black as shale. Loufer headed toward the entrance.

"Is it safe in there?"

"Looks pretty scary." Tak nodded. "Probably keep any criminal with a grain of sense at home. Anybody who wasn't a mugger would be out of his mind to go in there." He glanced back, grinned. "Which probably means all the muggers have gotten tired of waiting and gone home to bed a long time ago. Come on."

Stone lions flanked the entrance.

"It's funny," Tak said; they passed between. "You show me a place where they tell women to stay out of at night because of all the nasty, evil men lurking there to do nasty, evil things; and you know what you'll find?"

"Queers."

Tak glanced over, pulled his cap visor down. "Yeah."

The dark wrapped them up and buoyed them along the path.

There is nothing safe about the darkness of this city and its stink. Well, I have abrogated all claim to safety, coming here. It is better to discuss it as though I had chosen. That keeps the scrim of sanity before the awful set. What will lift it?

"What were you in prison for?"

"Morals charge," Tak said.

He was steps behind Loufer now. The path, which had begun as concrete, was now dirt. Leaves hit at him. Three times his bare foot came down on rough roots; once his swinging arm scraped lightly against bark.

"Actually," Tak tossed back into the black between them, "I was acquitted. The situation, I guess. My lawyer figured it was better I stayed in jail without bail for ninety days, like a misdemeanor sentence. Something had got lost in the records. Then, at court, he brought that all out, got the charge changed to public indecency; I'd already served sentence." Zipper-jinglings suggested a shrug. "Everything considered, it worked out. Look!"

The carbon black of leaves shredded, letting through the ordinary color of urban night.

"Where?" They had stopped among trees and high brush.

"Be quiet! There . . ."

His wool shushed Tak's leather. He whispered: "Where do you . . . ?"

Out on the path, sudden, luminous, and artificial, a seven-foot dragon swayed around the corner, followed by an equally tall mantis and a griffin. Like elegant plastics, internally lit and misty, they wobbled forward. When dragon and mantis swayed into each other, they—meshed!

He thought of images, slightly unfocused, on a movie screen, lapping.

"Scorpions!" Tak whispered.

Tak's shoulder pushed his.

His hand was on a tree trunk. Twig shadows webbed his forearm, the back of his hand, the bark. The figures

24

neared; the web slid. The figures passed; the web slid off. They were, he realized, as eye-unsettling as pictures on a three-dimensional postcard—with the same striations hanging, like a screen, just before, or was it just behind them.

The griffin, furthest back, flickered:

A scrawny youngster, with pimply shoulders, in the middle of a cautious, bow-legged stride—then griffin again. (A memory of spiky, yellow hair; hands held out from the freckled, pelvic blade.)

The mantis swung around to look back, went momentarily out:

This one, anyway, was wearing *some* clothes—a brown, brutal looking youngster; the chains he wore for necklaces growled under his palm, while he absently caressed his left breast. "Come on, Baby! Get your ass in gear!" which came from a mantis again.

"Shit, you think they gonna be there?" from the griffin.

"Aw, sure. They gonna be there!" You could have easily mistaken the voice from the dragon for a man's; and she sounded black.

Suspended in wonder and confusion, he listened to the conversation of the amazing beasts.

"They better be!" Vanished chains went on growling.

The griffin flickered once more: pocked buttocks and dirty heels disappeared behind blazing scales.

"Hey, Baby, *suppose* they're not there yet?"

"Oh, shit! Adam . . . ?"

"Now, Adam, you know they're gonna be there," the dragon assured.

"Yeah? How do I know? Oh, Dragon Lady! Dragon Lady, you're too much!"

"Come on. The two of you shut up, huh?"

Swaying together and apart, they rounded another corner.

He couldn't see his hand at all now, so he let it fall from the trunk. "What . . . what *are* they?"

"Told you: scorpions. Sort of a gang. Maybe it's more than one gang. I don't really know. You get fond of them after a while, if you know how to stay out of their way. If you can't . . . well, you either join, I guess; or get messed up. Least, that's how I found it."

"I mean the . . . the dragons and things?"

"Pretty, huh?"

"What are they?"

"You know what is it a hologram? They're projected from interference patterns off a very small, very low-powered laser. It's not complicated. But it looks impressive. They call them light-shields."

"Oh." He glanced at his shoulder where Tak had dropped his hand. "I've heard of holograms."

Tak led him out of the hidden niche of brush onto the concrete. A few yards down the path, in the direction the scorpions had come from, a lamp was working. They started in that direction.

"Are there more of them around?"

"Maybe." Tak's upper face was again masked. "Their light-shields don't really shield them from anything—other than our prying eyes from the ones who want to walk around bare-assed. When I first got here, all you saw were scorpions. Then griffins and the other kinds started showing up a little while ago. But the genre name stuck." Tak slid his hands into his jean pockets. His jacket, joined at the bottom by the zipper fastener, rode up in front for non-existent breasts. Tak stared down at them as he walked. When he looked up, his smile had no eyes over it. "You forget people don't know about scorpions. About Calkins. They're famous here. Bellona's a big city; with something that famous in any other city in the country, why I guess people in L.A., Chicago, Pittsburgh, Washington would be dropping it all over the carpet at the in cocktail parties, huh? But they've forgotten we're here."

"No. They haven't forgotten." Though he couldn't see Tak's eyes, he knew they had narrowed.

"So they send in people who don't know their own name. Like you?"

He laughed, sharply; it felt like a bark.

Tak returned the hoarse sound that was his own laughter. "Oh, yeah! You're quite a kid." Laughter trailed on.

"Where we going now?"

But Tak lowered his chin, strode ahead.

From this play of night, light, and leather, can I let myself take identity? How can I recreate this roasted park in some meaningful matrix? Equipped with contradictory visions, an ugly hand caged in pretty metal, I observe a new mechanique. I am the wild machinist, past destroyed, reconstructing the present.

4

"Tak!" she called across the fire, rose, and shook back fire-colored hair. "Who'd you bring?" She swung around the cinderblock furnace and came on, a silhouette now, stepping over sleeping bags, blanket rolls, a lawn of reposing forms. Two glanced at her, then turned over. Two others snored at different pitches.

A girl on a blanket, with no shirt and really nice breasts, stopped playing her harmonica, banged it on her palm for spit, and blew once more.

The redhead rounded the harmonica player and seized Tak's cuff, close enough now to have a face again. "We haven't seen you in days! What happened? You used to come around for dinner practically every night. John was worried about you." It was a pretty face in half light.

"I wasn't worried." A tall, long-haired man in a Peruvian vest walked over from the picnic table. "Tak comes. Tak goes. You know how Tak is." Around the miniature flames, reflected in his glasses, even in this light his tan suggested chemicals or sunlamps. His hair was pale and thin and looked as if day would show sun streaks. "You're closer to breakfast time than you are to dinner, right now." He—John?—tapped a rolled newspaper against his thigh.

"Come on. Tell me, Tak." She smiled; her face wedged with deeper shadows. "Who have you brought John and me this time?" while John glanced up (twin flames slid off his lenses) for hints of dawn.

Tak said: "This is the Kid."

"Kit?" she asked.

"*Kid.*"

"K-y-d-d . . . ?"

"-*i*-d."

". . . d," she added with a tentative frown. "Oh, *Kidd.*"

27

If Tak had an expression you couldn't see it.

He thought it was charming, though; though something else about it unsettled.

She rared her shoulders back, blinking. "How are you, Kidd? Are you new? Or have you been hiding out in the shadows for months and months?" To Tak: "Isn't it amazing how we're always turning up people like that? You think you've met everybody in the city there is to meet. Then, suddenly, somebody who's been here all along, watching you from the bushes, sticks his nose out—"

"That's how we met Tak," John said. To Tak: "Isn't it, Tak?"

Tak said: "He's new."

"Oh. Well," John said, "we've got this thing going here. Do you want to explain it to him, Mildred?"

"Well, we figure—" Mildred's shoulders came, officially, forward. "We figure we have to survive together some way. I mean we can't be at each other's throats like animals. And it would be so easy for a situation like this—" He was sure her gesture, at 'this', included nothing beyond the firelight—"to degenerate into something . . . well, awful! So we've set up I guess you'd call it a commune. Here, in the park. People get food, work together, know they have some sort of protection. We try to be as organic as possible, but that's getting harder and harder. When new people come into Bellona, they can get a chance to learn how things operate here. We don't take in everybody. But when we do, we're very accepting." There was a tic somewhere (in him or her, he wasn't sure, and started worrying about it) like a nick in a wire pulled over an edge. "You *are* new? We're always glad when we get somebody new."

He nodded, while his mind accelerated, trying to decide: him? her?

Tak said: "Show him around, Milly."

John said: "Good idea, Mildred. Tak, I want to talk to you about something," tapping his newspaper again. "Oh, here. Maybe you want to take a look at this?"

"What? Oh . . ." You *couldn't* worry so much about things like that! Often, though, he had to remind himself. "Thanks." He took the folded paper.

"All right, Tak." John, with Tak, turned away. "Now *when* are you going to start those foundations for us? I can give you—"

"Look, John." Tak put his hand on John's shoulder as they wandered off. "All you need is the plans, and you can—"

Then they were out of earshot.

"Are you hungry?"

"No." She *was* pretty.

"Well, if you are—come, let's go over here—we start cooking breakfast soon as it gets light. That's not too far off."

"You been up all night?" he asked.

"No. But when you go to bed at sundown, you wake up pretty early."

"I have."

"We do a lot of work here—" she slipped her hands into her back pockets; her jeans, torn short, were bunched high on her thighs—"during the day. We don't just sit around. John has a dozen projects going. It's pretty hard to sleep with people hammering and building and what all." She smiled.

"I've been up; but I'm not tired. When I am, I can sleep through anything." He looked down at her legs.

As she walked, light along them closed and crossed. "Oh, we wouldn't mind if you really wanted to sleep. We don't want to force anybody. But we have to maintain some kind of pattern, you understand."

"Yeah, I understand that." He'd been flipping the newspaper against his own thigh. Now he raised it.

"Why do you go around wearing an orchid?" she asked. "Of course, with the city in the state it's in, I guess it makes sense. And really, we do accept many life styles here. But . . ."

"Some people gave it to me." He turned the rolled newspaper around.

SERIOUS WATER

He let the tabloid fall loose.

SHORTAGE THREATENS

The date said Tuesday, February 12, 1995. "What the hell is *that?*"

She looked concerned. "Well, there's not very many people around who know how to keep things running. And we've all been expecting the water to become a real problem any day. You have no idea how much they used when they were trying to put out the fires."

"I mean the 1995?"

"Oh. *That's* just Calkins." On the picnic table sat a

29

carton of canned goods. "I think it's amazing we have a newspaper at all." She sat on the bench and looked at him expectantly. "The dates are just his little joke."

"Oh." He sat beside her. "Do you have tents here? Anything for shelter?" still thinking: *1995?*

"Well, we're pretty outdoors oriented." She looked around, while he tried to feel the city beyond the leafy, fire-lit grotto. "Of course, Tak—he's promised to give John some simple blueprints. For cabins. John wants Tak to head the whole project. He feels it would be good for him. You know, Tak is so strange. He feels, somehow, we won't accept him. At least I think he does. He has this very important image of himself as a loner. He wants to give us the plans—he's an engineer, you know—and let us carry them out. But the value of something like that isn't just the house—or shack—that results. It should be a creative, internal thing for the builder. Don't you think?"

For something to do, he held his teeth together, hard.

"You're sure you're not hungry?"

"Oh. No."

"You're not tired? You can get in a few hours if you want. Work doesn't start till after breakfast. I can get you a blanket, if you'd like."

"No."

In the firelight, he thought he might count twenty-five years in her firm, clear face. "I'm not hungry. I'm not sleepy. I didn't even know Tak was bringing me here."

"It's a very nice place. It really is. The community of feeling is so warm, if nothing else." Probably only twenty.

The harmonica player played again.

Someone in an olive-drab cocoon twisted beyond the fire.

Mildred's tennis sneaker was a foot from the nearest sleeper's canvas covered head.

"I wish you wouldn't wear that." She laughed.

He opened his big fingers under metal.

"I mean, if you want to stay here. Maybe then you wouldn't have to wear it."

"I don't have to wear it," and decided to keep it on.

The harmonica squawked.

He looked up.

From the trees, light brighter than the fire and green

lay leafy shadows over sleeping bags and blanket rolls. Then ballooning claws and barbed, translucent tail collapsed:

"Hey, you got that shit ready for us?"

A lot of chains hung around his neck. He had a wide scab (with smaller ones below it) on the bowl of his shoulder, like a bad fall on cement. Chains wound around one boot: he jingled when he walked. "Come on, come on. Bring me the fuckin' junk!" He stopped by the fireplace. Flames burnished his large arms, his small face. A front tooth was broken. "Is that it?" He gestured bluntly toward the picnic table, brushed tangled, black hair, half braided, from his shoulder, and came on.

"Hello!" Mildred said, with the most amazing smile. "Nightmare! How have you been?"

The scorpion looked down at her, wet lip high off his broken tooth, and said, slowly, "Shit," which could have meant a lot of things. He wedged between them— "Get out of the—" saw the orchid—"fucking way, huh?" and lugged the carton of canned goods off the table edge against his belly, where ripe, wrinkled jeans had sagged so low you could see stomach hair thicken toward pubic. He looked down over his thick arm at the weapon, closed his mouth, shook his head. "Shit," again, and: "What the fuck *you* staring at?" Between the flaps of Nightmare's cut-down vest, prisms, mirrors, and lenses glittered among dark cycle chain, bright stainless links, and hardware-store brass.

"Nothing."

Nightmare sucked his teeth in disgust, turned, and stumbled on a sleeping bag. *"Move*, damn it!"

A head shook loose from canvas; it was an older man, who started digging under the glasses he'd probably worn to sleep, then gazed after the scorpion lumbering off among the trees.

He saw things move behind Milly's face, was momentarily sure she was going to call good-bye. Her tennis shoe dragged the ground.

Down her lower leg was a scratch.

He frowned.

She said: "That was Nightmare. Do you know about the scorpions?"

"Tak told me some."

"It's amazing how well you can get along with people if you're just nice. Of course their idea of being nice

31

back is a little odd. They used to volunteer to beat up people for us. They kept wanting John to find somebody for them to work over—somebody who was annoying us, of course. Only nobody was." She hunched her shoulders.

"I guess," he offered from the faulted structure of his smile, "you have trouble with them sometimes?"

"Sometimes." Her smile was perfect. "I just wish John had been here. John's very good with them. I think Nightmare is a little afraid of John, you know? We do a lot for them. Share our food with them. I think they get a lot from us. If they'd just acknowledge their need, though, they'd be so much easier to help."

The harmonica was silent: the bare-breasted girl had gone from her blanket.

"How'd you get that scratch?"

"Just an accident. With John." She shrugged. "From one of those, actually." She nodded toward his orchid. "It isn't anything."

He leaned to touch it, looked at her: she hadn't moved. So he lay his forefinger on her shin, moved it down. The scab line ran under his callous like a tiny rasp.

She frowned. "It really isn't anything." Framed in heavy red, it was a gentle frown. "What's that?" She pointed. "Around your wrist."

His cuff had pulled up when he'd leaned.

He shrugged. Confusion was like struggling to find the proper way to sit inside his skin. "Something I found." He wondered if she heard the question mark on his sentence, small as a period.

Her eyebrow's movement said she had: which amused him.

The optical glass flamed over his knobby wrist.

"Where do you get it? I've seen several people wear that . . . kind of chain."

He nodded. "I just found it."

"Where?" Her gentle smile urged.

"Where did you get your scratch?"

Still smiling, she returned a bewildered look.

He had expected it. And he mistrusted it. "I . . ." and the thought resolved some internal cadence: "want to know about you!" He was suddenly and astonishingly happy. "Have you been here long? Where are you from? Mildred? Mildred what? Why did you come here? How long are you going to stay? Do you like Japanese food?

32

Poetry?" He laughed. "Silence? Water? Someone saying your name?"

"Um . . ." He saw she was immensely pleased. "Mildred Fabian, and people *do* call me Milly, like Tak does. John just feels he has to be formal when new people come around. I was here at State University. But I come from Ohio . . . Euclid, Ohio?"

He nodded again.

"But State's got such a damned good Poly-sci department. Had, anyway. So I came here. And . . ." She dropped her eyes (brown, he realized with a half-second memory, as he looked at her lowered, corn-colored lashes —brown with a coppery backing, copper like her hair) ". . . I stayed."

"You were *here* when it happened?"

". . . yes." He heard a question mark there bigger than any in the type-box.

"What . . ." and when he said, ". . . happened?" he didn't want an answer.

Her eyes widened, dropped again; her shoulders sank; her back rounded. She reached toward his hand in its cage, lying between them on the bench.

As she took a shiny blade tip between two fingers, he was aware of his palm's suspension in its harness.

"Does . . . I've always . . . well, could you make an . . ." She tugged the point to the side (he felt the pressure on his wrist and stiffened his hand), released it: A muffled *Dmmmmm*. "Oh."

He was puzzled.

"I was wondering," she explained, "if you could make it ring. Like an instrument. All the blades are different lengths. I thought if they made notes, perhaps you could . . . play them."

"Blade steel? I don't think it's brittle enough. Bells and things are iron."

She bent her head to the side.

"Things have to be brittle if they're going to ring. Like glass. Knives are hard, sure; but they're too flexible."

She looked up after a moment. "I like music. I was going to major in music. At State. But the Poly-sci department was *so* good. I don't think I've seen one Japanese restaurant in Bellona, since I've been in school here. But there used to be several good Chinese ones . . ." Something happened in her face, a loosening, part exhaustion,

33

part despair. "We're doing the best we can, you know . . . ?"

"What?"

"We're doing the best we can. Here."

He nodded a small nod.

"When it happened," she said softly, "it was terrible." "Terrible" was perfectly flat, the way he remembered a man in a brown suit once say "elevator." It's that tone, he thought, remembering when it had denuded Tak's speech. She said: "We stayed. I stayed. I guess I felt I had to stay. I don't know how long . . . I mean, I'm going to stay for. But we have to do something. Since we're here, we have to." She took a breath. A muscle leaped in her jaw. "You . . . ?"

"Me what?"

"What do you like, Kidd? Someone saying your name?"

He knew it was innocent; and was annoyed anyway. His lips began a *Well,* but only breath came.

"Silence?"

Breath became a hiss; the hiss became, ". . . sometimes."

"Who are you? Where are *you* from?"

He hesitated, and watched her eyes pick something from it:

"You're afraid because you're new here . . . I think. I'm afraid, I think, because I've been here . . . an awfully long time!" She looked around the campsite.

Two long-haired youngsters stood by the cinderblocks. One held up his hands, either to warm them, or just to feel heat.

It is a warm morning. I do not recognize any protection in this leafy blister. There is no articulation in the juncture of object and shadow, no fixed angle between fuel and flame. Where would they put their shelters, foundations sunk on ash; doors and windows sinking in cinders? There is nothing else to trust but what warms.

Mildred's lips parted, her eyes narrowed. "You know what John did? I think it was brave, too. We had just finished building that fireplace; there were only a few of us here, then. Somebody was going to light it with a cigarette lighter. But John said, wait; then went off all the way to Holland Lake. That was when the burning was much worse than it is now. And he brought back a brand —an old, dried, burning stick. In fact he had to transfer

34

the fire to several other sticks on the way back. And with that fire—" she nodded where one of the youngsters was now poking at the logs with a broken broom-handle— "he lit ours." The other waited with a chunk of wood in his arms. "I think that was very brave. Don't you?" The chunk fell. Sparks geysered through the grate, higher than the lowest branches.

"Hey, Milly!"

Sparks whirled, and he wondered why they all spoke so loud with so many sleeping.

"Milly! Look what I found."

She had put on a blue workshirt, still unbuttoned. In one hand was her harmonica, in the other a spiral notebook.

"What is it?" Milly called back.

As she passed the furnace, she swung the notebook through the sparks; they whipped into Catherine wheels, and sank. "Does it belong to anybody around here? It's burned. On the cover."

She sat with it, between them, shoulders hunched, face in a concentrated scowl. "It's somebody's exercise book." The cardboard was flaky black at one corner. Heat had stained half the back.

"What's in it?" Milly asked.

She shrugged. Her shoulder and her hip moved on his. He slid down the bench to give her room, considered sliding back, but, instead, picked up the newspaper and opened it—blades tore one side—to the second page.

"Who ripped out the first pages?" Milly asked.

"That's the way I found it."

"But you can see the torn edges, still inside the wire."

"Neat handwriting."

"Can you make out what it says?"

"Not in this light. I read some down by the park lamp. Let's take it over by the fire."

The page he stared at flickered with backlight, the print on both sides visible. All he could make out was the Gothic masthead:

BELLONA TIMES

And below it:

Roger Calkins,
Editor and Publisher.

He closed the paper.

The girls had gone to the fireplace.

He stood, left the paper on the bench, stepped, one

35

after another, over three sleeping bags and a blanket roll. "What does it say?"

Her harmonica was still in one fist.

Her hair was short and thick. Her eyes, when she looked at him directly, were Kelly green. Propping the book on the crook of her arm, with her free hand she turned back the cardboard cover for him to see the first page. Remnants of green polish flecked her nails.

In Palmer-perfect script, an interrupted sentence took up on the top line:

to wound the autumnal city.

> *So howled out for the world to give him a name.*

That made goose bumps on his flanks . . .

> *The in-dark answered with wind.*

> *All you know I know: careening astronauts and bank clerks glancing at the clock before lunch; actresses cowling at light-ringed mirrors and freight-elevator operators grinding a thumbful of grease on a steel handle; student*

She lowered the notebook to stare at him, blinked green eyes. Hair wisps shook shadow splinters on her cheek. "What's the matter with you?"

His face tensed toward a smile. "That's just some . . . well, pretty weird stuff!"

"What's weird about it?" She closed the cover. "You got the strangest look."

"I don't . . . But . . ." His smile did not feel right. What was there to dislodge it lay at the third point of a triangle whose base vertices were recognition and incomprehension. "Only it was so . . ." No, start again. "But it was so . . . I know a lot about astronauts, I mean. I used to look up the satellite schedules and go out at night and watch for them. And I used to have a friend who was a bank clerk."

"I knew somebody who used to work in a bank," Milly said. Then, to the other girl: "Didn't you ever?"

He said: "And I used to have a job in a theater. It was on the second floor and we always had to carry things up in the freight elevator . . ." *These* memories were so simple to retrieve . . . "I was thinking about him—the elevator operator—earlier tonight."

They still looked puzzled.

"It was just very familiar."

"Well, yeah . . ." She moved her thumb over the bright harmonica. "I must have been on a freight elevator, at least once. Hell, I was in a school play and there were lights around the dressing room mirror. That doesn't make it weird."

"But the part about the student riots. And the bodegas . . . I just came up from Mexico."

"It doesn't say anything about student riots."

"Yes it does. I was in a student riot once. I'll show you." He reached for the book (she pulled back sharply from the orchid), spread his free hand on the page (she came forward again, her shoulder brushing his arm. He could see her breast inside her unbuttoned shirt. Yeah) and read aloud:

" '. . . thumbful of grease on a steel handle; student happenings with spaghetti filled Volkswagens, dawn in Seattle, automated evening in L.A.' " He looked up, confused.

"You've been in Seattle and Los Angeles, morning and night, too?" Her green-eyed smile flickered beside the flames.

"No . . ." He shook his head.

"I have. It's still not weird." Still flickering, she frowned at his frown. "It's not about you. Unless you dropped it in the park . . . *You* didn't write it, did you?"

"No," he said. "No. I didn't." Lost (it had been stronger and stranger than any *déjà vu*), the feeling harassed him. "But I could have sworn I *knew* . . ." The fire felt hottest through the hole at his knee; he reached down to scratch; blades snagged raveled threads. He snatched the orchid away: threads popped. Using his other hand, he mauled his patella with horny fingers.

Milly had taken the book, turned to a later page.

The green-eyed girl leaned over her shoulder:

"Read that part near the end, about the lightning and the explosions and the riot and all. Do you think he was writing about what happened *here*—to Bellona, I mean?"

"Read that part at the beginning, about the scorpions and the trapped children. What do you suppose he was writing about *there*?"

They bent together in firelight.

He felt discomfort and looked around the clearing.

Tak stepped over a sleeping bag and said to John: "You people want me to work too hard. You just refuse to understand that work for its own sake is something I see no virtue in at all."

"Aw, come on, Tak." John beat his hand absently

against his thigh as though he still held the rolled paper.

"I'll give you the plans. You can do what you want with them. Hey, Kid, how's it going?" Flames bruised Tak's bulky jaw, prised his pale eyes into the light, flickered on his leather visor. "You doing all right?"

He swallowed, which clamped his teeth; so his nod was stiffer than he'd intended.

"Tak, you *are* going to head the shelter building project for us . . . ?" John's glasses flashed.

"Shit," Tak said, recalling Nightmare.

"Oh, Tak . . ." Milly shook her head.

"I've been arguing with him all night," John said. "Hey." He looked over at the picnic table. "Did Nightmare come by for the stuff?"

'Yep." Brightly.

"How is he?"

She shrugged—less bright.

He heard the harmonica, looked:

Back on her blanket, the other girl bent over her mouth harp. Her hair was a casque of stained bronze around her lowered face. Her shirt had slipped from one sharp shoulder. Frowning, she beat the mouth holes on her palm once more. The notebook lay against her knee.

"Tak and me were up looking at the place I want to put the shelters. You know, up on the rocks?"

"You've changed the location *again?*" Milly asked.

"Yeah," Tak said. "He has. How do you like it around here, Kid? It's a good place, huh?"

"We'd be happy to have you," John said. "We're always happy to have new people. We have a lot of work to do; we need all the willing hands we can get." His tapping palm clove to his thigh, stayed.

He grunted, to shake something loose in his throat. "I think I'm going to wander on."

"Oh . . ." Milly sounded disappointed.

"Come on. Stay for breakfast." John sounded eager. "Then try out one of our work projects. See which one you like. You know, those are some strange streets out there. You don't know what you're gonna find in 'em."

"Thanks," he said. "I'm gonna go . . ."

"I'll take him back down to the avenue," Tak said. "Okay, so long, you guys."

"If you change your mind," Milly called (John was beating his leg again), "you can always come back. You

38

might want to in a couple of days. Just come. We'll be glad to have you then, too."

On the concrete path, he said to Tak: "They're really good people, huh? I just guess I . . ." He shrugged.

Tak grunted: "Yeah."

"The scorpions—is that some sort of protection racket they make the people in the commune pay?"

"You could call it that. But then, they get protected."

"Against anything else except scorpions?"

Tak grunted again, hoarsely.

He recognized it for laughter. "I just don't want to get into anything like that. At least not on that side."

"I'll take you back down to the avenue, Kid. It goes on up into the city. The stores right around here have been pretty well stripped of food. But you never know what you're gonna luck out on. Frankly, though, I think you'll do better in houses. But there you take your chances: somebody just may be waiting for you with a shotgun. Like I say, there's maybe a thousand left out of a city of two million: Only one out of a hundred homes should be occupied—not bad odds. Only I come near walking in on a couple of shotguns myself. Then you got your scorpions to worry about . . . John's group?" The hoarse, gravelly laughter had a drunken quality the rest of Tak's behavior belied. "I like them. But I wouldn't want to stick around them too much either. I don't. But I give them a hand. And it's not a bad place to get your bearings from . . . for a day or two."

"No. I guess not . . ." But it was a mulling "no."

Tak nodded in mute agreement.

This park is alive with darknesses, textures of silence. Tak's boot heels tattoo the way. I can envision a dotted line left after him. And someone might pick the night up by its edge, tear it along the perforations, crumple it, and toss it away.

Only two out of forty-some park lights (he'd started counting) were working. The night's overcast masked all hint of dawn. At the next working light, within sight of the lion-flanked entrance, Tak took his hands out of his pockets. Two pinheads of light pricked the darkness somewhere above his sandy upper lip. "If you want—you can come back to my place . . . ?"

39

5

". . . Okay."

Tak let out a breath—"Good—" and turned. His face went completely black. "This way."

He followed the zipper jingles with a staggering lope. Boughs, black over the path, suddenly pulled from a sky gone grey inside a V of receding rooftops.

As they paused by the lions, looking down a wide street, Tak rubbed himself inside his jacket. "Guess we're about to get into morning."

"Which way does the sun come up?"

Loufer chuckled. "I know you won't believe this—" they walked again—"but when I first got here, I could have sworn the light always started over there." As they stepped from the curb, he nodded to the left. "But like you can see, today it's getting light—" he gestured in front of them—"there."

"Because the season's changing?"

"I don't think it's changed that much. But maybe." Tak lowered his head and smiled. "Then again, maybe I just wasn't paying attention."

"Which way is east?"

"That's where it's getting light." Tak nodded ahead. "But what do you do if it gets light in a different place tomorrow?"

"Come on. You could tell by the stars."

"You saw how the sky was. It's been like that or worse every night. And day. I haven't seen stars since I've been here—moons or suns either."

"Yeah, but—"

"I've thought, maybe: It's not the season that changes. It's us. The whole city shifts, turns, rearranges itself. All the time. And rearranges us . . .." He laughed. "Hey, I'm pulling your leg, Kid. Come on." Tak rubbed his stomach again. "You take it all too seriously." Stepping up the curb, Tak pushed his hands into his leather pockets. "But I'm damned if I wouldn't have sworn morning used to start over there." Again he nodded, with pursed lips. "All that means is I wasn't paying attention, doesn't it?" At the next corner he asked: "What were you in a mental hospital for?"

"Depression. But it was a long time ago."

"Yeah?"

"I was hearing voices; afraid to go out; I couldn't remember things; some hallucinations—the whole bit. It was right after I finished my first year of college. When I was nineteen. I used to drink a lot, too."

"What did the voices say?"

He shrugged. "Nothing. Singing . . . a lot, but in some other language. And calling to me. It wasn't like you'd hear a real voice—"

"It was inside your head?"

"Sometimes. When it was singing. But there'd be a real sound, like a car starting, or maybe somebody would close a door in another room: and you'd think somebody had called your name at the same time. Only they hadn't. Then, sometimes you'd think it was just in your mind when somebody had; and not answer. When you'd find out, you'd feel all uncomfortable."

"I bet you would."

"Actually, I felt uncomfortable about all the time . . . But, really, that was years back."

"What did the voices call you—when they called?"

At the middle of the next block, Tak said:

"Just thought it might work. If I snuck up on it."

"Sorry." The clumsiness and sincerity of Tak's amateur therapy made him chuckle. "Not that way."

"Got any idea why it happened? I mean why you got—depressed, and went into the hospital in the first place?"

"Sure. When I got out of high school, upstate, I had to work for a year before I could go into college. My parents didn't have any money. My mother was a full Cherokee . . . though it would have been worth my life to tell those kids back in the park, the way everybody goes on about Indians today. She died when I was about fourteen. I'd applied to Columbia, in New York City. I had to have a special interview because even though my marks in high school were good, they weren't great. I'd come down to the city and gotten a job in an art supply house—

41

that impressed hell out of them at the interview. So they dug up this special scholarship. At the end of the first term I had all B's and one D—in linguistics. By the end of the second term, though, I didn't know what was going to happen the next year. I mean about money. I couldn't do anything at Columbia *except* go to school. They've got all sorts of extracurricular stuff, and it costs. If that D had been an A, I might have gotten another scholarship. But it wasn't. And like I said, I really used to drink. You wouldn't believe a nineteen-year-old could drink like that. Much less drink and get anything *done*. Just before finals I had a breakdown. I wouldn't go outside. I was scared to see people. I nearly killed myself a couple of times. I don't mean suicide. Just with stupid things. Like climbing out on the window ledge when I was really drunk. And once I knocked a radio into a sink full of dishwater. Like that." He took a breath. "It *was* a long time ago. None of that stuff bothers me, really, any more."

"You Catholic?"

"Naw. Dad was a little ballsy, blue-eyed Georgia Methodist—" that memory's vividness surprised him too— "when he was anything. We never lived down south, though. He was in the Air Force most of the time when I was a kid. Then he flew private planes for about a year. After that he didn't do much of anything. But that was after mom died . . ."

"Funny." Tak shook his head in self-reproach; "The way you just assume all the small, dark-complected brothers are Catholic. Brought up a Lutheran, myself. What'd you do after the hospital?"

"Worked upstate for a while. DVR—Division of Vocational Rehabilitation—was going to help me get back in school, soon as I got out of Hillside. But I didn't want to. Took a joyride with a friend once that ended up with me spending most of a year cutting trees in Oregon. In Oakland I worked as a grip in a theater. Wasn't I telling you about . . . No, that was the girl in the park. I traveled a lot; worked on boats. I tried school a couple more times, just on my own—once, in Kansas, for a year, where I had a job as a super for a student building. Then again in Delaware."

"How far on did you get?"

"Did fine the first term, each place. Fucked up the second. I didn't have another breakdown or anything. I didn't even drink. I just fucked up. I don't fuck up on jobs, though. Just school. I work. I travel. I read a lot. Then I travel some more: Japan. Down to Australia— though that didn't come out too well. Bumming boats down around Mexico and Central America." He laughed. "So you see, I'm not a nut. Not a real one, anyway. I haven't been a real nut in a long time."

"You're here, aren't you?" Tak's Germanic face (with its oddly Negroid nose) mocked gently. "And you don't know who you are."

"Yeah, but that's just 'cause I can't remember my—"

"Home again, home again." Tak turned into a door-way and mounted the wooden steps; he looked back just before he reached the top one. "Come on."

There was no lamp post on either corner.

At the end of the block, a car had overturned in a splatter of glass. Nearer, two trucks sat on wheelless hubs —a Ford pickup and a GM cab—windshields and win-dows smashed. Across the street, above the loading porch, the butcher hooks swung gently on their awning tracks.

"Are we going in the way you came out . . . ?"

The smoke around the building tops was luminous with dawn.

"Don't worry," Tak grinned. "You'll get used to it."

"*I* remembered you being on the *other* side of the . . ." He looked across, again, at the three-foot con-crete platform that stretched beneath the awning along the building opposite.

"Come on." Tak took another step. "Oh— One thing. You'll have to park your weapon at the door." He pointed vaguely at the orchid. "Don't take offense. It's just a house rule."

"Oh, sure. Yeah." He followed Tak up the steps. "Here, just a second."

"Put it behind there." Tak indicated two thick asbestos-covered pipes inside the doorway. "It'll be there when you come back."

He unsnapped the wrist band, slipped his fingers from the harness, bent to lay the contraption on the floor be-hind the pipes.

Tak, already at the head of a dim stairwell, started down.

He stood up and hurried after.

"Fifteen steps." Tak was already invisible below him. "It's pretty dark so you better count."

There was no bannister so he kept one hand on the

wall. His wrist prickled where the orchid's collar had been. Hairs, drying now, pulled, tickling, from his skin. Every other step his bare foot hit the stair edge, heel on gritty marble, ball and toes hanging. Tak's boots thudded below . . . Thirteen . . . fourteen . . . The last step still surprised him.

"Back this way."

He followed through the dark. The cement under his bare foot was very warm.

The steps ahead changed timbre. "Steps up now . . ."

He slowed.

". . . don't get lost."

This time he found a rail.

He could anticipate landings from the variations in Loufer's gait. After the third flight, faint lines near head height indicated doors.

Rhythm is the only thing secure. In this darkness, rising, I recall the Pacific stars. This ritual ascendance goes on in a city that has erased them and blurred its sun out altogether. Iron Wolf has something. I want it without the bother of definitions. The dangerous illumination, the light in the exploding eye, is not for this other city.

"Last flight—"

They had come up nine landings.

"—and here we are."

A metal door grated in its frame.

As Tak stepped before him onto the tarred roof, he turned his head away from the cloud-colored dawn. After darkness, it was still too bright. Face scrunched against the light, he stopped on the sill, one hand on the jamb, the other holding back the ribbed and riveted door.

Smoke lay waist-high on the air.

He relaxed his face, blinking a lot.

Beyond the brick balustrade, roofs and roofs checkered into the mist. The gap, there, must have been the park. Beyond it was a hill, scaly with housing. "Jesus." He squinted in the other direction. "I didn't realize this place was so far from the bridge. I'd just come off it when you called to me down in the street."

Tak chuckled. "No, you'd wandered pretty far."

"I can just get a glimpse—" he stood on tiptoe— "of the river." And lowered himself. "*I* thought it was just two, three blocks away."

44

Tak's chuckle became a full laugh. "Hey, how'd you lose one sandal?"

"Huh?" He looked down. "Oh . . . I was being chased. By dogs." That sounded funny, too; so he laughed. "Yeah, I really was." He picked up his foot, rested it above his knee to examine the caked and calloused sole. The horny edge was cracked both sides. His ankle, knob and hollow, was grit-grey. Heel, ball, instep, and each dusty toe were gun-barrel black. He wiggled his toes: grit ground. "I guess it was—" He looked up frowning—"maybe a couple of days ago—" and put his foot down. "It was about three o'clock. In the morning. It was raining. No cars. So I took a nap on somebody's porch. About five, when it was getting light, I went back out on the road to hitch. But it was still raining. So I figured, hell, I'd go back and catch another hour or two, 'cause there weren't any cars. Only when I got back, there was this damn dog, who'd been sleeping under the porch all the time I'd been snoozing topside. He was awake now. And he started barking. Then he chased my ass down to the road. I ran. He ran. My sandal broke and went into a ditch somewhere—I just about didn't notice. While I was running, this old blue car pulled up—big, old lady driving, with her skinny husband, and the back seat full of children. I jumped in out of the rain, and we drove right across the border, into Louisiana! They were all off to spend the day with some other kid of hers who was at some army base." He stepped from the sill. "Bought me a good breakfast, too." The door creaked closed behind him. "But I guess that's when I first *noticed* I couldn't remember my name. She asked me for it and I couldn't tell her . . . But I don't think I've known it for a long, long time." And he was almost used to the light. "I mean, you don't go around thinking about yourself by your own name, do you? Nobody does—unless somebody calls to you by it, or asks you what it is. I haven't been around people who know me for . . . for a while now. It's just something I haven't thought of for a long time, and somehow it's . . . I guess just slipped my mind." He looked at the tops of his feet again, both filthy, one crossed with straps, one bare. "It doesn't bother me. Missing a sandal, I mean. I go barefoot a lot of the time."

"Like a hippie?"

He shrugged. "Yeah, when I'm in a hippie-type

45

town." Again he looked around the misty horizon. "You sleep up here?"

"Come on." Tak turned. A breeze swung one jacket flap from his belly, pressed the other against him, neck to hip. "That's my house."

It had probably been built as a maintenance shack, put on the roof for tool storage. Bamboo curtains backed recently puttied panes. The door—tar paper had ripped in one place from greyed pine—was ajar.

They walked around a skylight. Tak hit the door with his hand-heel. (Like he expected to surprise somebody . . . ?) The door swung in. Tak stepped inside: click. Lights went on. "Come on, make yourself at home."

He followed the engineer across the sill. "Hey, this is pretty nice!"

Tak stooped to peer into a crackling kerosene heater. "It's comfortable . . . now I *know* I didn't walk out of here and leave this thing going. Someday I'm gonna come back home and find this whole place just a pile of ashes—of course, in Bellona that could happen whether I left it on or not." He stood up, shaking his head. "It gets a little chilly here in the morning. I might as well leave it go."

"Christ, you've got a lot of books!"

Shelves covered the back wall, floor to ceiling, filled with paperbacks.

And: "Is that a short wave setup?"

"Part of one. The rest is in the next room. I could just sit in bed and CQ all over the place—if I could get anything but static. The interference around this place is something terrible. Then, it may be something's wrong with my set. I've got my own power supply: a couple of dozen acid batteries in the back. And a gasoline charger." He stepped to the desk in the corner, shrugged his jacket down the gold rug of his back, and hung it on a wall hook. (He still wore his cap.) Blurred in blond, his forearm bore a dragon, his bicep some naval insignia. On one shoulder, a swastika had been tattooed, then, not very efficiently, removed. "Have a seat." Tak pulled a swivel chair from the desk, turned it around, and sat. Knees wide, he slid his hand under his belt to arrange himself where his genitals bagged the denim. "Take the bed . . . there."

An incongruous fur throw lay on the board floor. An India print draped down over what he thought was a

46

daybed. But when he sat on it, he realized it was just a very thin mattress on the top of some built-out cabinet: or at any rate, just plank. Still, the place looked comfortable. "You're doing a little better than thóse kids in the park."

Tak grinned, took off his cap, and dropped it on the desk blotter. "I guess I am. But then, that's not too difficult." The military short hair jarred with his unshaven jaw.

The desk, except for the cap, was bare.

Shelves above it held binoculars, slide rules, drafting compasses and pens, two pocket calculators, French curves and templates, colored pentels, several cut and polished geodes, a row of ornamental daggers on display stands, a pile of plastic parts boxes, a soldering gun . . .

"Hey . . ." Tak slapped one knee. "I'm gonna make some coffee. Got some canned ham, too. Real good ham. And bread." He stood up and went to a door, hung, like the windows, with tan splints. "You just relax. Take it easy. Take your clothes off and stretch out, if you want." By his boot, the bubbling heater picked out what still glowed in the scuffed leather. "I'll be back in a minute. Glad you like the place. I do too." He ducked through bamboo.

On one wall (he had only glanced till now) were three, yard-high, full color, photographic posters:

On one, some adolescent weightlifter, Germanic as Tak, wearing only boots and a denim jacket with no sleeves, leaned against a motorcycle, stubby hands flat against his naked legs.

On the second, a muscular black, in what could have been Tak's jacket, cap, and boots, stood against some indistinct purple background, legs wide, one fist before his bared thigh, one against his bare hip.

On the third, a dark youth—Mexican or Indian perhaps?—shirtless and shoeless, sat on a boulder under a stark, blue sky, his jeans pushed down to his knees.

Their bared genitals were huge.

The photographs had been taken from crotch level, too, to make them look even larger.

From the other room he heard pans clinking; a cabinet opened and closed.

By the head of the bed, on a table near a tensor lamp, books were piled irregularly:

47

A bunch on the Hell's Angels: Thompson, and Reynolds/McClure; four cheaply bound, two-dollar paperbacks: *Angels on Wheels*, and *Weekend in Hell, a True Story of the Angels as Told by Millicent Brash*—he read the first paragraph of ill-lined type, shook his head, and put it down. A book called *Bike Bitch* was apparently the sequel to (same cover/different author) *Bike Bastard*. Under that was *The Poems of Rimbaud*, with English at the bottom of the pages; then a paperback *Selected Letters of Keats;* next, Dickey's *Deliverance;* a green, hard-cover book of logs and trigonometric functions, place held by a white enamel, circular slide rule. There was sundry science fiction by Russ (something called *The Female Man*), Zelazny, and Disch. The last book he picked up had a purple and gold reproduction of a Leonor Fini for cover: *Evil Companions*. He opened it in the middle, read from the top of the left-hand page to the bottom of the right, closed it, frowning, went to the bamboo, and pushed it aside.

"You ever see one of these in somebody's house before?" Tak thumped the grey cabinet with his elbow. "It's a Micro Wave oven. They're great. You can roast a whole rib roast in ten, twenty minutes. They cost about six hundred dollars. At least that's what the price tag said in the store I lifted this one from. Only I don't like to run it because it uses up so much power. Someday, though, I'm gonna give a dinner party for thirty or forty people. Hold it outside on the roof. For all my friends in the city. I'll knock their eye out with what this thing can do." He turned to the counter.

On two burners of a three-burner camp stove, pale flames from canned heat licked an enameled coffeepot and an iron skillet. Along the back of the counter were several gallons of wine, white and red, and a dozen bottles of whiskeys, liqueurs, and brandies. "This is sort of my work room." Back muscles shifted under hairy flesh. "Probably spend more time here than in the front." More bookshelves here; more shortwave components; a work bench slagged with solder, strewn with spaghetti wire, bits of pegboard in which dozens of small, colorful transistors, resistors, and capacitors had been stuck; several dissembled chassis. A single easy-chair, with stuffing pushing between worn threads across the arms, made the room cluttered. Above the tin sink, the bamboo had been

48

pushed back from the glass. (The putty can stood open on the sill, a kitchen knife stuck in it; the panes were spotless—save a few puttied fingerprints.) Outside, two pairs of jeans and a lot of socks hung from a line. "You looking for the john, Kid? I just use the roof. There's a coffee can upside down outside with a roll of toilet paper under it. There's no drain. Everything goes right over the edge."

"Naw, that's okay." He stepped through. Bamboo clicked and clicked behind him. "I guess here—in a place like Bellona—you can have about anything you want. I mean, you just walk in and take it out of stores and things."

"Only—" Tak put a handful of something in the skillet—"I don't want very much." Steam, hissing, made the room smell, and sound, very good. "Figured while I was at it I'd make us up a full breakfast. I'm starved."

"Yeah . . ." At the pungence of thyme and fennel, the space beneath his tongue flooded. "I guess if you liked you could live here about as well as you wanted." And rosemary . . .

On a cutting board by the stove, a loaf of mahogany-colored bread sat among scattered crumbs. "Fresh food is hard as hell to come by. Meat especially. But there's canned stuff in the city enough to last . . ." Tak frowned back over his hirsute shoulder. "Truth is, I don't know *how* long it'll last. I lucked out on a couple of pretty well-stocked places nobody else seems to have found yet. You'll discover, by and large, people are *not* very practical around here—if they were, I guess they wouldn't be here. But when somebody else eventually does stumble on one of my classified, top-secret, hush-hush food sources, in a place like Bellona you can't very well say, 'Go away or I'll call the cops.' There're aren't any cops to call. Have a piece of bread. Another thing I lucked out on: Ran into this woman who bakes loaves and loaves of the stuff every week; just gives it away to anyone who comes by. For some reason I do not quite understand, she won't use any sugar or salt, so, good as it looks, it takes a bit of getting used to. But it's filling. She lives in the Lower Cumberland Park area—talk about nuts. She's very nice and I'm glad I know her, but she visits all sorts of people, many of whom are simply not in." Tak finished cutting a slice, turned and held it out. "Margarine's over

49

there; haven't found any frozen butter for a while. Good plum preserves, though. Homemade in somebody's cellar last fall."

He took the bread, picked up a kitchen knife, and removed the top from a plastic butter dish.

"That should hold you till breakfast, which—" Tak swirled a spatula in the skillet—"is three minutes off."

Under the jelly and the margarine, bread crumbled on his tongue, oddly flat. Still, it goaded his appetite.

Chewing, he looked through the newspapers piled to one side of the cluttered workbench.

BELLONA TIMES
Saturday, April 1, 1919

BELLONA TIMES
Wednesday, December 25, 1933

BELLONA TIMES
Thursday, December 25, 1940

BELLONA TIMES
Monday, December 25, 1879

The headline for that one:

ROBERT LOUIS STEVENSON
QUITS MONTEREY FOR FRISCO!

"Calkins has a thing for Christmas?"

"That was *last* week," Tak said. "A couple back, every other issue was 1984."

The next half dozen papers went from July 14, 2022, to July 7, 1837 (Headline: ONLY ONE HUNDRED YEARS TILL THE DEATH OF HARLOW!)

"It's a real event when he brings out two papers with consecutive dates. They're never two in a row with the same year. But sometimes he slips up and Tuesday actually follows Wednesday—or do I have that backward? Well, I'm just surprised people don't take bets; trying to pick the next date for the *Times* could be the Bellona equivalent to playing the numbers. Oh, he's got real news in there—articles on evacuation problems, scorpions terrorizing remaining citizens, what's happening

50

in the poorer communities, pleas for outside help—even an occasional personality article on newcomers." Tak gave him a knowing nod. "You read it; but it's the only paper around to read. I read it up here. John, Wally, Mildred, Jommy—they read it down in the park. Still, it makes me incredibly hungry to see a real paper, you know? Just to find out how the rest of the world is getting on without us."

Did Tak's voice veer, once more, toward that unsettling tone? Only by suggestion, he realized, and realized too: The longer he stayed, the less of that tone he would hear. Whatever request for complicity, in whatever labyrinth of despair, it made of the listener, whatever demand for relief from situations which were by definition unrelievable, these requests, these demands could only be made of the very new to such labyrinths, such situations. And time, even as he munched flat bread, was erasing that status. "The rest of the country, it's fine."

Tak turned, with the knife.

He jumped, even though he knew Fire Wolf was only in the midst of some domestic slicing. "Yesterday, I think it was: I got a ride with a guy who had an L.A. paper in his car. Nothing's wrong on the West Coast. Then later, two women picked me up; and they had a Philadelphia paper. The Eastern Seaboard's all okay." He looked down at the papers on the bench again, watched his thick, nail-gnawed fingers grub there, leaving crumbs, margarine tracks, jelly stains. *"This* is the only place where . . ." He shrugged, wondering if Tak took his news as good, bad; or even believed it. ". . . I guess."

"Why don't you pour some coffee?" Tak said.

"Okay." He stepped around the armchair, lifted the enameled pot from the burner; the handle stung his knuckle as he poured.

In the cups, one after another, glistening disks rose, black without translucence.

"We'll eat inside." Above the plates of eggs, ham, and bread, two amber ponies rose on the tray between Tak's gripping thumbs. As Tak turned to the bamboo, the brandies ran with light.

Inside, sitting on the bed again, he lay his plate on his clamped knees till it burned. Lifting it by one edge, then the other, he speared ham chunks from the gravy, or pushed them on his fork with his thumb.

51

"It's amazing what Worcestershire will do for dehydrated eggs," Tak said through a mouthful of food, "Thank God."

He bit a tiny die of garlic; in his stinging mouth the scrambled flavors bloomed; the confusion of tastes recalled many good things, but gave no basic flavor (his plate was half clean already) to which he could fix his tongue.

"Since this is supper as well as breakfast—" seated at the desk, Tak poured himself another glass—"I guess brandy is all right."

He nodded, the amber bulb lost in his outsized fingers. "It's really good." He looked back at his plate and wished there was a vegetable; even some lettuce.

"You have any plans where you'll go?" Tak finished his second pony, poured another, and extended the bottle.

He shook his head to the drink and shrugged at the question.

"You can catch some sleep here."

Idly, he thought: Artichokes. Then he looked at the posters. "You're really into the S and M thing, huh?" He hoped the food in his mouth would muddle the comment.

"Mmm?" Tak's coffee chattered as he sipped. "It depends on who I'm with." He put his cup on the desk, opened the side drawer, reached in: "You ever seen one like this?"

It was an orchid.

The blades, twice as long as his, with greater curve, were brass. On the ornate band, brass leaves, shells, and claws gripped the bases of the damasked knives.

Tak placed the points around his left nipple, pressed, winced—let the weapon drop to his lap. "Not your thing, huh?" In the yellow hair, flushed points ringed his breast. "It's a beautiful object." He smiled, shook his head, and put it back in the drawer.

"Can I put my brandy in my coffee?"

"You can do anything you like."

"Oh, yeah." He spilled the glass over the steaming black. "Uh . . . thanks." He raised the cup. Brandy fumed about his face. A deep breath made his tongue stagger in his throat. "It's a very nice breakfast." Squinting eyes observed his from beyond the cup's bottom.

He drank, set the cup on the floor, thumbed the last of the ham onto his fork; still chewing, he set the plate down by the cup.

"More brandy?"

"No, thanks."

"Come on." Tak poured himself a third glass. "Relax. Take your shirt off."

He had known what was coming since he'd accepted the invitation in the park. Another time, he would have had some feelings about it. But feelings were muted in him; things had drifted to this without his really considering. He tried to think of something to say, couldn't, so unbuttoned the three buttons, pulled the tails from his pants.

Tak raised his eyebrows at the optical chain. "Where'd you get that?"

"On my way here."

"Outside the city?"

"It says 'Made in Brazil' . . . I think."

Tak shook his head. "Bellona has become a city of *strange*—" he burlesqued the word with a drawl—"craftsmen. Ah, the notions that are engineered here! Orchids, light-shields, that chain you're wearing—our local folk art."

"I'm not going to take it off!" The conviction surprised him; its articulation astounded him.

Tak laughed. "I wasn't going to ask you to." He looked down at his chest, ran his forefinger, in the hair, from one pink dot to the next—still visible where he'd pressed the orchid prongs. "You've got some nerve thinking you were *ever* any crazier than anybody else."

His shirt lay beside him on the bed. He pulled his hands together into his lap, fingers and knuckles twisted around one another—scratched his dark, creased stomach with his thumb. "Look, about . . . being nuts." He felt self-righteous and shy, looked at the doubled fist of flesh, hair, horn and callous pressed into his groin; it suddenly seemed weighted with the bones in it. "You're not, and you never have been. That means what you see, and hear, and feel, and think . . . you think that *is* your mind. But the real mind is invisible: you're less aware of it, while you think, than you are of your eye while you see . . . until something goes wrong with it. *Then* you become aware of it, with all its dislocated pieces and its rackety functioning, the same way you become aware of your eye when you get a cinder in it. Because it *hurts* . . . Sure, it distorts things. But the strange thing, the thing that you can never explain to anyone, except another nut, or, if you're lucky, a doctor who has an unusual

53

amount of sense—stranger than the hallucinations, or the voices, or the anxiety—is the *way* you begin to experience the edges of the mind *itself* . . . in a way other people just can't." He pushed his shirt down to the foot of the bed, pushed his sandal free of his foot with his other toes. "You see?" He was far more conscious of the texture of the floorboards with the foot that had been bare.

"All right." Tak spoke gently and appeasingly. "Why don't you take the rest of your clothes off?"

"Look, I'm awfully dirty, man—" He raised his eye. "I probably stink like hell. If you don't want—"

"I know *just* what you stink like," Tak said. "Go on."

He took a breath, suddenly found it funny, lay back on the hard pallet, unhooked his belt, and closed his eyes.

He . heard Tak grunt. One, then another boot, thumped the floor and fell over.

A moment later a warm hip pressed his. Palms and fingers pressed his stomach; the fingers spread. Tak slid his hands to the jeans' waist, tugged.

Heels and shoulders pressed on the hard pad, he raised his buttocks.

Tak slid the jeans down, and—"Jesus Christ, man! What's the matter with you—that stuff all over your dick!"

"What . . . huh?" He opened his eyes, propped his elbows under him, looked down at himself. "What do you . . . ?" Then he grinned. "Nothing's the matter. What's the matter with you?"

"You got dandruff in your crotch?"

"That's not dandruff. I was with a woman. Just before I met you. Only I didn't get a chance to wash."

"Was *she* sick?"

"Naw. Didn't you ever fuck a woman?"

Tak had a strange expression. "I'll be honest: I can count the attempts on the fingers of one hand." He narrowed his already thin mouth.

"If my God-damn *feet* don't turn you off, *that's* sure not going to hurt you!" He reached to brush off his rough groin hair. "It's just like dried . . . come or something." The chain glittered across it. "It happens with some women, when they're very wet. It's nothing wrong." He stopped brushing, let himself back down on his elbows. "I bet it turns you on."

Tak shook his head, then laughed.

"Go on," he said.

Tak lowered his head, looked up once with bright blue eyes: "It turns *you* on, doesn't it?"

He reached down from the hairy shoulder, pressed: "Go on."

Thick arms joined under his waist. Once Tak, twice-full fist between their groins, ground his stubbed chin against his neck. He pushed Tak away; the chunky head rolled down his chest and belly. The heated ring of Tak's mouth fell down his cock; his cock engorged; the ring rose; and fell down again. Tak's forehead butted low on his stomach. He had to cross his ankles and strain, his mouth open, his eyes closed, the chain tightening on his chest. Think of her, it would be easy. (Tak's face pressed glass bits into his groin hair.) The insides of his lids were moon-silvered, run with cracks like branches. A memory of blowing leaves suddenly became hair moving from her face, eyes clamped, mouth taking tiny breaths. He gasped at the welling heat, and came. A moment later Tak raised his head, grunted, "Yeah . . ." and moiled his wet, sensitive genitals.

He clamped his teeth.

Tak elbowed up beside him, turned on his back.

His forehead pressed Tak's arm. From his left eye, Loufer's chest was a heaving meadow. (His right was closed against flesh.) "You want me to do anything?" He didn't feel like doing anything. He was tired.

Tak scooped up his head and pulled it against him.

Chest hair ran between his fingers.

"Bite my tit," Tak said. "The right one. Hard."

"Okay. Where is . . . ? Oh." He gripped the knoblet in his teeth.

Tak pushed his hand to the outsized scrotum, squeezed his fingers to the full, wrinkled flesh. "Go on. Really hard."

Tak's fist fell and fell on his hand heel. It took a long time.

He ground Tak's nipple in his teeth, chin and nose rubbing in hair. He squeezed Tak's testicles a few times, tightening his grip as much as he could; Tak's rhythm quickened. And his own mouth was salty; he didn't want to see if it was blood.

Something hot splattered his hip and rolled down between them. He let go, with teeth and fingers, closed his eyes, and turned over. A heavy arm slid around his chest. Tak's chin knocked his shoulder a few times seeking

55

a position on the thin pillow; he squeezed Tak's forearm, once, leaned sleepily, and comfortably, into the cradle of Tak's body.

And slept.

Now and again, he felt Tak turning and turning on the single bed. Once he awoke fully to a hand rubbing his shoulder; but slept again before the motion halted. At one point he was aware that Tak was not in the bed; at another, felt him climbing back in. Through it all, he had not moved, but lay facing the wall, lids closed, head on his forearm, one knee drawn up, one foot off the mattress bottom, surfacing and submerging in sleep.

Later, he woke with heat behind his groin. As he blinked, sexuality resolved into an urge to pee. He rolled to his back, pushed himself to his elbows.

Loufer, probably unable to get comfortable with two in so cramped a space, sat deep in the swivel chair, knees wide, head lolling forward on one matted shoulder, hands curled on snarled thighs.

Plate on the desk, books scattered on the table; plate and coffee cup on the floor, as well as Tak's boots, his own sandal, and both their pants—the room, before fairly neat, looked disordered.

When he sat up, his foot carried the print spread to the floor. There was no sheet on the mattress pad. Rings of stain overlapped on the ticking. He kicked the cloth loose, looked at the chain fastened on his ankle, spiraling his calf, groin, stomach, and thigh . . . He touched, in the hollow of his collarbone, the catch fastening the chain around his neck. He extended his arm, turned it back and forth: light jumped from glass to glass at the loops there, joined around his wrist. Then he hunched to examine one of the mirrors against his belly: it was silvered on both sides. Bent over, on the bed, he felt his bladder burn.

He stood up, went out the door.

Warm.

Grey.

Smokey gauzes tore on his body as he walked toward the balustrade. He dug two horny fingers at the inner corners of his eyes for sleep grains. The retaining wall hit him mid-thigh. Without looking down, he let his water go. It arched away, perfectly silent, while he wondered if there was any traffic . . .

56

From a building, a block away, astounding billows raised a lopsided tower.

Finished, he leaned across the splattered stone.

The alley was a torrent of grey in which he could see no bottom. Licking his coated teeth, he walked back to the shack, stepped sideways through the tar-papered door: "Hey, you can have your bed back; I'm gonna . . ."

In the shadowed room, Tak's chest rose evenly in a subvocal growl.

"I'm going to go now . . ." but spoke it more softly; he took a few steps toward the naked engineer, asleep in the chair.

Tak's long toes spread the boards. Between his knuckles, a stumpy cock with its circumsized helmet was nearly hidden in hair above a long, heavy scrotum rivaling those on the posters. The single belly crease, just above his navel, smoothed with each breath.

He looked for scab at the nipple; there was none.

"Hey, I'm gonna go . . ." The desk drawer was slightly open; inside, in shadow, brass glinted.

He leaned down to look at Tak's slack lips, the broad nostrils flaring each breath—

And his teeth jarred together. He stepped back, wanted to go forward, stepped back again: his heel hit a coffee cup—cold coffee spread around his foot. He still didn't look away.

In his lowered face, Tak's eyes were wide.

Without white or pupil, the balls were completely crimson.

Mouth still closed, he heard himself make a muffled roar.

His left flank glittered with gooseflesh.

He *did* look again, leaning forward violently, almost hitting Tak's knee.

Loufer continued his quiet breathing, scarlet-eyed.

He backed away, stepped on wet fur, tried to work his throat loose. Gooseflesh, at face, flank, and buttocks, crawled across him.

He was in his pants when he got outside. He stopped to lean on the wall while he fumbled his sandal strap closed. As he sidestepped the skylight, he punched one arm down one woolen sleeve, pulled back the metal door and went into the dark well, working his other fist down the other.

With darkness in his eyes, the red memory was worse than the discovery.

On the third landing, he slipped, and fell, clutching the rail, the whole next flight. And still did not slow. He made it through the corridors at the bottom (warm concrete under his bare foot) on kinesthetic memory. He tore up the bannisterless stair, slapping at the wall, till he saw the door ahead, charged forward; he came out under the awning, running, and almost impaled himself on the dangling hooks.

Averting his face, he swung his arm against them—two clashed, trundling away on their rails. At the same time, his bare foot went off the porch's concrete edge.

For one bright instant, falling, he thought he was going to do a belly-whop on the pavement, three feet down. Somehow, he landed in a crouch, scraping one hand and both knees (the other hand waving out for balance) before he pushed up, to stagger from the curb.

Gasping, he turned to look back up at the loading porch.

From their tracks, under the awning, the four- and six-foot butcher hooks swung.

Blocks away, a dog barked, barked, barked again.

Still gasping, he turned, and started walking toward the corner, sometimes with his sandaled foot on the curb, mostly with both in the gutter.

Nearly there, he stopped, raised his hand, stared at the steel blades that curved from the plain wrist band to cage his twitching fingers. He looked back at the loading porch, frowned; looked back at the orchid on his hand: he felt the frown, from inside; a twisting in his facial flesh he could not control.

He remembered snatching up his pants. And his shirt. And his sandal. He remembered going down the dark stair. He remembered coming up and out on the porch, hitting at the hooks, and falling—

But nowhere in the past moments did he recall reaching behind two asbestos-covered pipes, fitting his fingers through the harness, clamping the collar to his wrist . . .

He reviewed: pants, shirt, sandal, the dark stair—down, across, up. Light from the door; the racketing hooks; his stinging palm.

He looked at his free palm; scraped skin was streaked grey . . . He looked down the block. There were no vehicles anywhere on the street . . .

No. Go back.

Warm concrete under his foot. His sandal clacking. Slapping the wall; coming up. Seeing the doorway. *Seeing* the pipes . . . ! They were on the *left*-hand side of the doorway. The blistered covering was bound with metal bands! On the thicker one, near the ceiling, hadn't there been some kind of valve? And had rushed past them, onto the concrete, nearly skewered himself; hit with his forearm—it was still sore. He was falling . . .

He was turning; missed the curb, staggered, shook his head, looked up.

The street sign on the corner lamppost said *Broadway*.

". . . goes up into the city and . . ." Someone had said that. Tak?

But no . . .

. . . seeing the light. Ran out the door. The hooks . . .

The muscles in his face snarled on chin and cheekbones. Suddenly tears banked his eyes. He shook his head. Tears were on his cheek. He started walking again, sometimes looking at one hand, sometimes at the other. When he finally dropped his arms, blades hissed by one jean thigh—

"No . . ."

He said that out loud.

And kept walking.

Snatched his clothes from the floor, jammed his feet into his pants; stopped just outside the shack (leaning against the tar-paper wall) for his sandal. Around the skylight; one sleeve. Into the dark; the other. Running down steps—and he'd fallen once. Then the bottom flight; the warm corridor; coming up; slapping; he'd seen light before he'd reached the top, turned, and seen the daybright doorway (the big pipe and the little pipe to one side), run forward, out on the porch, beat at the hooks; two trundled away as his bare foot went over. For one bright moment, he fell—

He looked at his hands, one free, one caged; he looked at the rubble around him; he walked; he looked at his hands.

A breath drained, roaring, between tight teeth. He took another.

As he wandered blurred block after blurred block, he heard the dog again, this time a howl, that twisted, rose, wavered, and ceased.

II

Here I am and am no I. This circle in all, this change changing in winterless, a dawn circle with an image of, an autumn change with a change of mist. Mistake two pictures, one and another. No. Only in seasons of short-light, only on dead afternoons. I will not be sick again. I *will* not. You are here.

He retreated down the halls of memory, seething.

Found, with final and banal comfort— Mother?

Remembered the first time he realized she was two inches taller than his father, and that some people thought it unusual. Hair braided, Mother was tolerant severity, was easier to play with than his father, was trips to Albany, was laughter (was dead?) when they went for walks through the park, was dark as old wood. More often, she was admonitions not to wander away in the city, not to wander away in the trees.

Father? A short man, yes; mostly in uniform; well, not that short—back in the force again; away a lot. Where was dad now? In one of three cities, in one of two states. Dad was silences, Dad was noises, Dad was absences that ended in presents.

"Come on, we'll play with you later. Now leave us alone, will you?"

Mom and Dad were words, lollying and jockeying in the small, sunny yard. He listened and did not listen. Mother and Father, they were a rhythm.

He began to sing, "Annnn*nnnn*nnnnnnn*nnnn*nnnn . . ." that had something of the fall of words around. "Annnn*nnn*—"

61

"Now *what* are you going on like that for?"

"Ain't seen your mom in two weeks. Be a good boy and take it somewhere else?"

So without stopping he took his Ann*nnnnnnnn* down the path beside the house where hedge-leaves slapped his lips and tickled them so that he took a breath and his sound snagged on laughter.

ROAR and ROAR, ROAR: he looked up. The planes made ribs across the sky. The silver beads snagged sun. The window wall of his house blinded him so— "*Annnnnnnn* . . ."—he made his noise and gave it the sound of the planes all up and down the street, walking and jogging with it, in his sneakers, and went down the steps at the side of the street, crossed over. His sound buzzed all the mask of his face. Shadows slid over him: he changed sound. Shadows slid away: he changed it back. The sun heated the bony spots above his eyes; that changed it again; and again, when the birds (he had wandered into the woods that lapped like a great tongue five blocks into town; soon he had been in them for a quarter of an hour) collided in the leaves, then flung notes down. One note was near enough; he caught it with his voice and it thrust him toward another. Sun and chill (spring had just started) cuffed and pummeled him and he sang, getting pine needles inside his canvas shoes (no socks) and the back of his neck tickling from hair when the wind came.

He climbed the rocks: his breath made windy pauses in the sound and that was interesting, so that when he reached the top he pushed the leaves away and made each note as low as the green whisper—

Three of the five were naked.

Which stopped him.

And one girl was wearing only a little cross around her neck. The silver tilted on the inner slope of one breast. She breathed.

He blinked and whispered another note.

Silver broke up the sun.

The man still in pants pushed one fist up into the foliage (pants undone, his belt lay free of half its loops, away from his hip), pushed his other hand down to scratch, twisting his hips so that more and more, stretching in the green—

The girl who was darker even than his mother rolled to her side: someone else's yellow hair fell from her back

62

and spread. And her hands on the man's face were suddenly hidden by his hands on hers (in the pile of clothing he recognized another uniform, but blue-black where his father's was green) and she was moving against him now, and there was a grass blade against her calf that slipped first one way, then the other.

He held his breath, forgot he was holding it: then it all came out in a surprising at-once that was practically not a note at all. So he got more air back in his lungs and began another.

"Hey, look!" from the other naked one, on elbows and laughing: "We got company!" and pointing.

So his sound, begun between song and sigh, ended in laughter; he ran back through the brush, pulling a music from their laughing till his was song again. He cantered down the path.

Some boys came up the path (this part of the wood was traveled as any park), thumbs in their jeans, hair all points and lines and slicks. Two of them were arguing (also, he saw as they neared, one of the boys was a girl), and one with carroty hair and small eyes glared at him.

He hunched, intently, and didn't look back at them, even though he wanted to. They were bad kids, he decided. Dad had told him to stay away from bad kids.

Suddenly he turned and sang after them, trying to make the music stealthy and angular till it became laughter again. He had reached the playground that separated the woods from town.

He mixed his music with the shouting from the other side of the fence. He rippled his fingers on the wire and walked and looked through: children clustered at the sliding board. But their scuffle had turned to shouts.

Beyond that were street sounds. He walked out among them and let his song pick them up. Cars, and two women talking about money, and something bang-banging in the big building with the corrugated walls: emerging from that, foot-rhythms. (Men in construction-helmets glanced at him.) That made him sing louder.

He walked up a hill where the houses got bigger, with lots of rock between. Finally (he had been flipping his fingers along the iron bars of the gate) he stopped to really look in (now going Hummmm, and hmmmmm, hmmmm, and hmmmmm) at the grass marked with tile squares, and a house that was very big and mostly glass and brick. A woman sat between two oaks. She saw him, cocked her head curiously, smiled—so he sang for her Ahhhhhhhhh—she frowned. He ran down the street, down the hill, singing.

The houses weren't so big any more.

The ribs of day cracked on the sky. But he didn't look up at the planes this time. And there were lots more people.

Windows: and on top of the windows, signs: and on top of the signs, things that turned in the wind: and on top of those, blue where wind you couldn't see went—

"Hey, watch it—"

He staggered back from a man with the dirtiest wrists he had ever seen. The man repeated: "Watch where you're God-damn going—" to nobody, and lurched away.

He drew his song in till it bubbled around his mouth. He was going to turn and run down the next street . . .

The brick were cracked. A plank had come away from the window.

Trash heaped beside the door.

No wind, and warm; the street was loud with voices and machinery, so loud he could hardly catch rhythm for his song.

His sounds—long and lolling over his tongue now—were low, and he heard them under, not over, the noise.

"Hey, look out—"

"What the—"

"Hey, did you see that—"

He hadn't.

"What are you—"

People turned. Somebody ran past him close, slapping black moccasins on the stone.

"Those bastards from the reservation!"

"That's one of their kids, too."

He wasn't; and neither was his mother—she was from . . . ? Anyway, he tried to sing that too, but was worried now. He turned the corner into an alley crowded with warm-weather loungers.

Two women, bony and delighted, stood in the doorway:

One: "Did you see *that?*"

The other laughed out loud.

He smiled; that changed his sound again.

From the next doorway, fat and ragged, face dirty as the drunkard's wrists, she carried a cloth bag in one fist, with the other beat at the trash. She turned, lumbering in the heap, blinked at him.

His music stuttered, but took it in. He hurried onto the avenue, dodged around seven nuns, started to run, but turned to watch them.

They walked slowly and talked quickly, with sharp small voices. Falls of white broke at breast and knee; black scuffed toes wrinkled white hems.

People stepped around them.

"Good morning, sisters."

Sisters nodded and smiled, probably because it was afternoon. They walked straight, brushing and brushing.

He tried to fit the rhythm of their walk into his music. He glanced around the street, hurried on, making his sounds longer and longer; hurried till he was running and each note took half a block.

Ran around another corner.

And all his breath came hissing between his teeth.

The man's palm lifted, his finger tips stayed down to draw wet lines on the pavement, before he rolled over to show most of the wound. The one standing swayed and sweated. When the woman at the other corner began to call out, "Ohma'god! Ohma'god, he-e-elp!" the standing man ran.

He watched him run, and screamed, a little, twice.

The man on the street was grunting.

Someone running joggled him and he stepped back, with another sound; then he ran too and what had begun as music was now a wail. He ran until he had to walk. He walked until he had to stop singing. Then he ran again: Throat raw, he wailed again.

Once he passed a clutch of unshaven men; one pointed at him, but another put a bottle in the hand shucked with purple.

He ran.

He cried.

He cut across the corner of the woods. He ran some more.

He ran on the wide street under a ribbon of evening. Lights came on like twin necklaces suddenly unrolled down the avenue, traffic and tail beacons between. He shrieked. And fled from the street because people were looking.

This street was more familiar. Noise hurt his throat.

Sharp lights in his eyes; hedges marred with darkness. And he was roaring now—

"For God's sake—!"

He came up hard against her hands! Mother, and he tried to hug her, but she was holding him back.

"Where have you been? What is the *matter* with you, shouting around in the street like that?"

His mouth snapped. Sound to deafen built behind his teeth.

"We've been looking for you nearly half the *day!*"

None of it escaped. He was panting. She took his arm and led him.

"Your father—" who was turning the corner now— "comes home the first time in two weeks, and *you* decide to go running off!"

"There he is! Where did you find him!" and his father laughed and that at least was some sound. But not his.

They received him with scolding affection. But more vivid was the scalding energy he could not release. Wanting to cry, he had been silent, chewed on his knuckles, the heels of his palms, his cuticles, and what was left of his nails.

These memories intact solved little as those riddled with gaps. Still, he raised from them, reassured.

He hunted over them for his name. Once, perhaps, his mother calling, from across a street . . .

No.

And memory was discarded:

How can I say that *that* is my prize possession? (They do not fade, neither those buildings or these.) Rather what we know as real is burned away at invisible heat. What we are concerned with is more insubstantial. I do not know. It is as simple as that. For the hundredth time, I do not know and cannot remember. I do not want to be sick again. I do not want to be sick.

This lithic grin . . . ?

Not on the lions he'd walked between last night with Tak.

Vaguely he thought he'd been wandering toward the river. But somehow chance, or bodily memory, had returned him to the park.

Inside the entrance was ashy grass; dimmed trees forested the crest.

He turned his forefinger in his nostril, put it in his

66

mouth for the salt, then laughed and pressed his palm on the stone jaw; moved his hand. Stain passed between his fingers. The sky—he'd laughed, flung up his head—did not ·look infinitely far; a soft ceiling, rather, at some deceptive twenty, a hundred twenty feet. Oh, yes, laughter was good. His eyes filled with the blurry sky and tears; he moved his hand on the pitted jaw. When he took his palm from the dense braille, he was breathing hard.

No gushing breeze over this grass. His breath was thin, hoarse, suggestive of phlegm and obstacles and veins. Still, he'd laughed.

The sculptor had dug holes for eyes too deep to spot bottom.

He dug his finger in his nose again, sucked it, gnawed it; a gusty chuckle, and he turned through the leonine gate. It's easy, he thought, to put sounds with either white (maybe the pure tone of an audio generator; and the other, its opposite, that was ·called white noise), black (large gongs, larger bells), or the primary colors (the variety of the orchestra). Pale grey is silence.

A good wind could wake this city. As he wandered in, buildings dropped behind him below the park wall. (He wondered what ill one had put it to sleep.) The trees waited.

This park stretches on wracks of silence.

In his mind were some dozen visions of the city. He jogged, jaggedly, among them. His body felt hip heavy. His tongue lay down like a worm in his mouth. Breath in the cavity imitated wind; he listened to the air in his nose since that was all there was to listen to.

In its cage, his fist wilted, loose as a heavy flower.

Mornings after sex usually gave him that I've-been-eating-the-lotus-again, that Oh-all-soft-and-drifty, that hang-over-inside-out where pain is all in the world and the body tingly and good. Delayed? But here it was. The commune? Debating whether to hunt them or avoid them, he found the water fountain.

He spat blood-laced, amber clots. Water tugged them from the pebbly basin. The next were greenish and still gum bloody. He frothed the water, bitter with what was under his tongue, through his teeth and spat and spat till he spat clear. His lips tingled. Yeah, and felt better.

He left the fountain, gazing on grey, his belly cooler, blades whispering at his jeans. Across the damask of doubt and hesitation was unexpected joy like silver.

Something . . . He'd survived.

He pranced on the hill, happily oblivious to heart and bowels and the rest of the obstreperous machinery. This soft, this ecstatic grey, he swung through, in lop-looped chain, tasting the sweet smoke, buoyed on dusty grass.

The long, metallic note bent, broke to another. Someone was playing the harmonica—silver? Artichokes? Curiosity curved through, pressed down his mouth at both corners.

Like some color outside this grey range, music spilled the trees. He slowed and walked wonderingly into them. His feet came down in hushing puddles of grass. He frowned left and right and was very happy. The notes knotted with the upper branches.

In a tree? No . . . on a hill. He followed around the boulders that became a rise. The music came down from it. He looked up among leaf-grey and twig-grey. Picture: the harp leaving the lips, and the breath (leaving the lips) become laughter. "Hello," she called, laughing.

"Hello," he said and couldn't see her.

"Were you wandering around all night?"

He shrugged. "Sort of."

"Me too."

While he realized he had no idea of her distance, she laughed again and that turned back into music. She played oddly, but well. He stepped off the path.

Waving his right hand (caged), grasping saplings with his left (free), he staggered on the slope. "Hey . . . !" because he slipped, and she halted.

He caught up balance, and climbed.

She played again.

He stopped when the first leaves pulled from her.

She raised her apple eyes—apple green. Head down, she kept her lips at the metal organ.

Roots, thick as her arms, held the ground around her. Her back was against a heavy trunk. Leaves hid her all one side.

She wore her shirt. Her breasts were still nice.

His throat tightened. He felt both bowels and heart now; and all the little pains that defined his skin. It's stupid to be afraid . . . of trees. Still, he wished he had encountered her among stones. He took another step, arms wide for the slant, and she was free of foliage—except for one brown leaf leaning against her tennis shoe.

"Hi . . ."

68

A blanket lay beside her. The cuffs of her jeans were frayed. This shirt, he realized, didn't *have* buttons (silver eyelets on the cloth). But now it was half laced. He looked at the place between the strands. Yes, very nice.

"You didn't like the group last night?" She gestured with her chin to some vague part of the park.

He shrugged. "Not if they're going to wake me up and put me to work."

"They wouldn't have, if you'd pretended to be asleep. They don't really get too much done."

"Shit." He laughed and stepped up. "I didn't think so."

She hung her arms over her knees. "But they're good people."

He looked at her cheek, her ear, her hair.

"Finding your way around Bellona is a little funny at first. And they've been here a while. Take them with a grain of salt, keep your eyes open, and they'll teach you a lot."

"How long have you been with them?" thinking, I'm towering over her, only she looks at me as though I'm too short to tower.

"Oh, my place is over here. I just drop in on them every few days . . . like Tak. But I've just been around a few weeks, though. Pretty busy weeks." She looked out through the leaves. When he sat down on the log, she smiled. "You got in last night?"

He nodded. "Pretty busy night."

Something inside her face fought a grin.

"What's . . . your name?"

"Lanya Colson. Your name is Kidd, isn't it?"

"No, my name isn't Kidd! I don't know *what* my name is. I haven't been able to remember my name since . . . I don't know." He frowned. "Do you think that's crazy?"

She raised her eyebrows, brought her hands together (he remembered the remains of polish; so she must have redone them this morning: her nails were green as her eyes) to turn the harmonica.

"The Kid is what Iron Wolf tried to name me. And the girl in the commune tried to put on the other 'd'. But it isn't my name. I don't remember my God-damn name."

The turning halted.

"That's like being crazy. I forget lots of other things.

69

Too. What do you think about that:" and didn't know how he would have interpreted his falling inflection either.

She said: "I don't really know."

He said, after the silent bridge: "Well, you *have* to think something!"

She reached into the coiled blanket and lifted out . . . the notebook? He recognized the charred cover.

Biting at her lip, she began ruffling pages. Suddenly she stopped, handed it to him—"Are any of these names yours?"

The list, neatly printed in ballpoint, filled two columns:

Geoff Rivers	Arthur Pearson
Kit Darkfeather	Earlton Rudolph
David Wise	Phillip Edwards
Michael Roberts	Virginia Colson
Jerry Shank	Hank Kaiser
Frank Yoshikami	Garry Disch
Harold Redwing	Alvin Fischer
Madeleine Terry	Susan Morgan
Priscilla Meyer	William Dhalgren
George Newman	Peter Weldon
Ann Harrison	Linda Evers
Thomas Sask	Preston Smith

"What is this shit?" he asked, distressed. "It says Kit, with that Indian last name."

"Is that your name after all?"

"No. No, it's not my name."

"You look like you could be part Indian."

"My mother was a God-damn Indian. Not my father. It isn't my name." He looked back at the paper. "Your name's on here."

"No."

"Colson!"

"My *last* name. But my first name's Lanya, not Virginia."

"You got anybody in your family named Virginia?"

"I used to have a great aunt Virgilia. Really. She lived in Washington D.C. and I only met her once when I was seven or eight. Can you remember the names of anybody else in your family? Your father's?"

"No."

"Your mother's?"

". . . what they look like but . . . that's all."

"Sisters or brothers?"

". . . didn't have any."

After silence he shook his head.

She shrugged.

He closed the book and searched for speech: "Let's pretend—" and wondered what was in the block of writing below the lists—"that we're in a city, an abandoned city. It's burning, see. All the power's out. They can't get television cameras and radios in here, right? So everybody outside's forgotten about it. No word comes out. No word comes in. We'll pretend it's all covered with smoke, okay? But now you can't even seen the fire."

"Just the smoke," she said. "Let's pretend—"

He blinked.

"—you and I are sitting in a grey park on a grey day in a grey city." She frowned at the sky. "A perfectly ordinary city. The air pollution is terrible here." She smiled. "I like grey days, days like this, days without shadows—" Then she saw he had jabbed his orchid against the log.

Pinioned to the bark, his fist shook among the blades.

She was on her knees beside him: "I'll tell you what let's do. Let's take that off!" She tugged at the wrist snap. His arm shook in her fingers. "Here." Then his hand was free.

He was breathing hard. "That's—" he looked at the weapon still fixed by three points—"a pretty wicked thing. Leave it the fuck alone."

"It's a tool," she said. "You may need it. Just know when to use it." She was rubbing his hand.

His heart was slowing. He took another, very deep breath. "You ought to be afraid of me, you know?"

She blinked. "I am." And sat back on her heels. "But I want to try out some things I'm afraid of. That's the only reason to be here. What," she asked, *"happened to you just then?"*

"Huh?"

She put three fingers on his forehead, then showed him the glistening pads. "You're sweating."

"I was . . . very happy all of a sudden."

She frowned. "I thought you were scared to death!"

He cleared his throat, tried to smile. "It was like a . . .

71

well, suddenly being very happy. I was happy when I walked into the park. And then all of a sudden it just . . ." He was rubbing her hand back.

"Okay." She laughed. "That sounds good."

His jaw was clamped. He let it loosen, and grunted: "Who . . . what *kind* of a person are you?"

Her face opened, with both surprise and chagrin: "Let's see. Brilliant, charming—eight—*four* pounds away from being stunningly gorgeous . . . I like to tell myself; family's got all sorts of money and social connections. But I'm rebeling against all that right now:"

"Okay."

Her face was squarish, small, not gorgeous at all, and it was nice too.

"That sounds accurate."

The humor left it and there was only surprise. "You believe me? You're a doll!" She kissed him, suddenly, on the nose, didn't look embarrassed, exactly; rather as though she were timing some important gesture:

Which was to pick up her harmonica and hail notes in his face. They both laughed (he was astonished beneath the laughter and suspected it showed) while she said: "Let's walk."

"Your blanket . . . ?"

"Leave it here."

He carried the notebook. They flailed through the leaves, jogging. At the path he stopped and looked down at his hip. "Uhh . . . ?"

She looked over.

"Do you," he asked slowly, "remember my picking up the orchid and putting it on my belt here?"

"I put it on there." She thumbed some blemish on the harmonica. "You were going to leave it behind, so I stuck a blade through your belt loop. Really. It *can* be dangerous around here."

Mouth slightly open, he nodded as, side by side, they gained the shadowless paths.

He said: "*You* stuck it there." Somewhere a breeze, without force, made its easy way in the green. He was aware of the smoky odor about them for two breaths before it faded with inattention. "All by yourself, you just found those people in the park?"

She gave him a You-must-be-out-of-your-mind look. "I came in with quite a party, actually. Fun; but after a couple of days they were getting in the way. I mean it's

72

nice to have a car. But if you're rendered helpless by lack of gasoline . . ." She shrugged. "Before we got here, Phil and I were taking bets whether this place really existed or not." Her sudden and surprising smile was all eyes and very little mouth. "I won. I stayed with the group I came in with a while. Then I cut them loose. A few nights with Milly, John, and the rest. Then I've been off having adventures—until a few nights ago, when I came back."

Thinking: Oh—"You had some money when you got here?"—Phil.

"Group I came with did. A lot of good it did them. I mean how long would you wander around a city like this looking for a hotel? No, I had to let them go. They were happy to be rid of me."

"They left?"

She looked at her sneaker and laughed, mock ominous.

"People leave here," he said. "The people who gave me the orchid, they were leaving when I came."

"Some people leave." She laughed again. It was a quiet and self-assured and intriguing and disturbing laugh.

He asked: "What kind of adventures did you have?"

"I watched some scorpion fights. That was weird. Nightmare's trip isn't my bag, but this place is so small you can't be that selective. I spent a few days by myself in a lovely home in the Heights: which finally sent me up the wall. I like living outdoors. Then there was Calkins for a while."

"The guy who publishes the newspaper?"

She nodded. "I spent a few days at his place. Roger's set up this permanent country weekend, only inside city limits. He keeps some interesting people around."

"Were you one of the interesting people?"

"I think Roger just considered me decorative, actually. To amuse the interesting ones. His loss."

She *was* pretty in a sort of rough way—maybe closer to "cute".

He nodded.

"The brush with civilization did me good, though. Then I wandered out on my own again. Have you been to the monastery, out by Holland?"

"Huh?"

"I've never been there either but I've heard some very sincere people have set up a sort of religious retreat. I still can't figure out if they got started *before* this whole

73

thing happened, or whether they moved in and took over afterward. But it still sounds impressive. At least what one hears."

"John and Mildred are pretty sincere."

"Touché!" She puffed a chord, then looked at him curiously, laughed, and hit at the high stems. He looked; and her eyes, waiting for him to speak, were greener than the haze allowed any leaf around.

"It's like a small town," he said. "Is there anything else to do but gossip?"

"Not really." She hit the stems again. "Which is a relief, if you look at it that way."

"Where does Calkins live?"

"Oh, you *like* to gossip! I was scared for a moment." She stopped knocking the stalks. "His newspaper office is awful! He took some of us there, right to where they print it. Grey and gloomy and dismal and echoing." She screwed up her face and her shoulders and her hands. "Ahhhh! But his house—" Everything unscrewed. "Just fine. Right above the Heights. Lots of grounds. You can see the whole city. I imagine it must have been quite a sight when all the street lights were on at night." A small screwing, now. "I was trying to figure out whether he's always lived there, or if *he* just moved in and took it over too. But you don't ask questions like that."

He turned and she followed.

"Where is his house?"

"I think the actual address is on Brisbain South."

"How'd you get to meet him?"

"They were having a party. I was wandering by. Someone I knew invited me in. Phil, actually."

"That sounds easy."

"Ah, it was very difficult. *You* want to go up there and meet Calkins?"

"Well, everything looks pretty scroungy down around here. I could wander up and see if somebody would invite me in." He paused. "Of course, you're a girl. You'd have an easier time, wouldn't you? To be . . . decorative?"

She raised her eyebrows. "Not necessarily."

He glanced at her in time to catch her glancing back. The idea struck him as amusing.

"You see that path behind the soccer posts?"

"Yeah."

"It exits right on to Brisbain North. Which turns into Brisbain South after a while."

"Hey!" He grinned at her, then let his head fall to the side. "What's the matter?"

"I'm sad you're going. I was all set for a dangerous, exciting afternoon, wandering about with you, playing my harmonica for you."

"Why don't you come?"

Her look held both embarrassment and collusion. "I've been."

Hammering sounded behind them.

To his frown, she explained: "One of John's work projects. They've gotten back from lunch. I know there's food left. The guy who does the most of their cooking, Jommy, is a friend of mine; do you want to eat?"

"Naw." He shook his head. "Besides, I haven't decided if I want—"

"Yes, you have. But I'll see you when you get back. Take this." She held out the notebook. "It'll give you something to read on the way."

For a moment he let his face acknowledge that she wanted him to stay. "Thanks . . . all right."

"That's one nice thing about this place," she answered the acknowledgement; "when you come back, I *will* see you." She raised her harmonica to her mouth. "You can't lose anybody here." In the metal, her eyes and nostrils were immense darknesses, set in silvered flesh, cut through, without lid or lash or limit, by green and green. She blew a discord, and walked away.

As he left the eyeless lions, it occurred to him: You can't make that discord on a harmonica.

Not on any harmonica he'd ever had.

2

He'd walked three blocks when he saw, in the middle of the fourth, the church.

Visible were two (of presumably four) clocks around the steeple. Nearing, he saw the hands were gone.

He scrubbed at his forehead with the back of his wrist. Grit rolled between skin and skin. All this soot . . .

The thought occurred: I'm in fine shape to get myself invited into a house party!

Organ music came from the church door. He remembered Lanya had said something about a monastery . . . Wondering if curiosity showed on his face, he stepped carefully—notebook firmly under his arm—into the tiled foyer.

Through a second door, in an office, two of the four spools on the aluminum face of an upright tape recorder revolved. There were no lights on.

It only really registered as he turned away (and, once registered, he had no idea what to do with the image): Thumb-tacked above the office bulletin-board was the central poster from Loufer's wall: the black man in cap, jacket, and boots.

Another door (leading to the chapel itself?) was ajar on darkness.

He stepped back to the sidewalk—

"Hey, there!"

The old man wore maroon bell bottoms, gold-rimmed spectacles; underneath a dull corduroy jacket, a bright red tanktop: beard, beret. He carried a bundle of newspapers under one arm. "How you doing on this pearly afternoon?"

"Hello."

"Now . . . I bet you're wondering what time it is." The old man strained his ropy neck. "Let me see." He gazed at the steeple. "Let me see. That would be about . . .

eleven . . . twenty-five." His head came down in wheezy laughter. "How do you like that, hey? Pretty good trick, huh? (You want a paper? Take one!) It *is* a trick. I'll show you how to do it. What's the matter? Paper don't cost you. You want a subscription?"

"Under your beard . . . where'd you get that thing around your neck?"

"You mean . . ." The old man's free hand moved to the peppery hair that went without break from the top of his chest to his chin. He unfastened the necklace, which fell, like a diamond snake. ". . . this? Where'd you get yours?"

He'd thought collar and cuff hid his own. "On my way here. It says it comes from Brazil."

The old man held the end of the chain close to see: ". . . Japan?" then extended the end for him to look.

On the tab of brass were stamped letters: *ade in Japan*. Before *ade* there was a squiggle undoubtably *m*.

The old man got it around his neck again and finally managed to secure it with one hand.

He looked down at the papers: he could read, just at the old man's crumpled cuff:

BELLONA TIMES
Wednesday, April 1, 1979

NEW BOY IN TOWN!

He frowned at that.

"I didn't see your chain," the man went on, in unrequested explanation. "But you wouldn't have asked if you hadn't got one yourself, now, would you?"

He nodded, mainly to make the geezer continue— an urging not needed.

"I guess it's like a prize for an initiation. Only you didn't know you were being initiated? And that sort of upset you, I bet."

He nodded again.

"My name's Faust," the old man said. "Joaquim Faust."

"Wakeem . . . ?"

"You're pronouncing it right. From your accent, though, I bet you wouldn't put the same letters in it I do."

He reached for Joaquim's extended hand: Joaquim caught his up in a biker shake. "You say—" Joaquim

77

frowned before he let go—"you got yours on your way here? *Outside* Bellona?"

"That's right."

Joaquim shook his head and said, "Mmmmmm," while a roaring that had been gathering seconds now, broke over head. They looked up. Nothing was visible in the haze. The jets lingered disturbingly long, then pulled away. The taped organ sounded soft after it.

"On the clock," Joaquim said. "The front face. That little stub used to be the minute hand. So you can about figure out which way it's pointing."

"Oh. What about the hour?"

Joaquim shrugged. "I left the office around eleven. Least I guess it was eleven. I haven't been gone that long."

"What happened to the . . . hands?"

"The niggers. The first night, I guess it was. When all that lightning was going on. They went wild. Swarmed all over. Broke up a whole lot of stuff around here— Jackson's just down there."

"Jackson?"

"Jackson Avenue is where most of the niggers live. Used to live. You new?"

He nodded.

"See if you can get hold of the paper for that day. People say you never seen pictures like that before. They was burning. And they had ladders up, and breaking in the windows. This guy told me there was a picture of them climbing up on the church. And breaking off the clock hands. Tearing each other up, too. There's supposed to be one set of pictures; of this *big* buck, getting after this little white girl . . . a whole *lot* of stink about them pictures. 'Rape' is the nasty word they didn't use in the paper but rape is what it was. People was saying Calkins shouldn't've printed them. But you know what he did?" Joaquim's twisted face demanded answer.

"No. What?" he ceded, warily.

"He went down and hunted up the nigger in the pictures and had somebody interview him; and he printed *every* thing. Now if you ask me, what he shouldn't have printed was that interview. I mean, Calkins is all interested in civil rights and things. He really is. The colored people in this town had it bad I guess, and he was concerned with that. Really concerned. But that nigger had the dirtiest mouth, and didn't use it to talk nothing but

78

dirt. I don't think he even knew what a newspaper interview was. I mean, I know the colored people got it rough. But if you want to help, you don't print a picture of the biggest, blackest buck in the world messin' up some little blond-headed seventeen-year-old girl, and then runnin' two pages of him saying how good it was, with every other word 'shit' and 'fuck,' and 'Wooo-eeeee', how he's going to get him some more soon as he can, and how easy it's gonna be with no pigs around! I mean not if you want to help—do you? And because of the article, Harrison—his name was George Harrison—is some sort of hero, to all the niggers left over in Jackson; and you'd think just about everybody else too. Which shows you the kind of people we got."

"But *you* didn't see it, though?"

Faust waved that away.

"There's this other colored man up from the South, some civil rights, militant person—a Mr Paul Fenster? He got here right around the time it happened. Calkins knows him too, I guess, and writes about what he's doing a lot. Now I would guess this guy probably has some decent intentions; but how's he going to do anything with all that George Harrison business, huh? I mean it's just as well—" he looked around—"there's not too many people left that care any more. Or that many niggers left in Jackson."

He resolved annoyance and curiosity with the polite question:

"What started it? The riot I mean."

Joaquim bent his head far to the side. "Now you know, nobody has the story really straight. Something fell."

"Huh?"

"Some people say a house collapsed. Some others say a plane crashed right there in the middle of Jackson. Somebody else was talking about some kid who got on the roof of the Second City bank building and gunned somebody down."

"Somebody got *killed?*"

"Very. It was supposed to be a white kid on the roof and a nigger that got shot. So they started a riot."

"What did the paper say?"

"About everything I did. Nobody knows which one happened for sure."

"If a plane crashed, somebody would have known."

"This was back at the beginning. Things were a hell of a lot more confused then. A lot of buildings were burning. And the weather was something else. People were still trying to get out. There were a hell of a lot more people here. And they were scared."

"You were here then?"

Joaquim pressed his lips till mustache merged with beard. He shook his head. "I just heard about the newspaper article. And the pictures."

"Where'd you come from?"

"Ahhhhh!" Faust waggled a free finger in mock reproval. "*You* have to learn not to ask questions like that. It's not polite. I didn't ask nothing about you, did I? I told you my name, but I didn't ask yours."

"I'm sorry." He was taken back.

"You going to meet a lot of people who'll get all kinds of upset if you go asking them about before they came to Bellona. I might as well tell you, so you don't get yourself in trouble. Especially——" Faust raised his beard and put a thumb beneath his choker——"people wearing one of these. Like us. I bet if I asked your name, or maybe your age, or why you got an orchid on your belt . . . anything like that, I could really get your dander up. Now couldn't I?"

He felt the discomfort, vague as remembered pain, in his belly.

"I come from Chicago, most recently. Frisco before that." Faust reached down to hold out one leg of his belled pants. "A grandpa Yippie, yeah? I'm a traveling philosopher. Is that good enough for you?"

"I'm sorry I asked."

"Think nothing of it. I heard Bellona was where it was at. It must be, now. I'm here. Is *that* good enough?"

He nodded again, disconcerted.

"I got a good, honest job. Sold the *Tribe* on the corner of Market and Van Ness. Here I'm Bellona's oldest newspaper boy. Is *that* enough?"

"Yeah. Look, I didn't mean——"

"Something about you, boy. I don't like it. Say——" Eyelids wrinkled behind gold-rimmed lenses——"*you're* not colored, are you? I mean you're pretty dark. Sort of full-featured. Now, I *could* say 'spade' like you youngsters. But where I was comin' up, *when* I was comin' up, they were niggers. They're still niggers to me and I don't mean nothing by it. I want all the best for them."

"I'm American Indian," he decided, with resigned wrath.

"Oh." Joaquim tilted his head once more to appraise. "Well, if you're not a nigger, you must be pretty much in sympathy with the niggers." He came down heavy on the word for any discomfort value it still held. "So am I. So am I. Only they won't ever believe it of me. I wouldn't either if I was them. Boy, I got to deliver my papers. Go on—take one. That's right; there you go." Faust straightened the bundle under his arm. "You interested in rioting niggers—and just about everybody is—" the aside was delivered with high theatricality—"you go look up those early editions. Here's your paper, Reverend." He strode across the sidewalk and handed another paper to the black minister in pavement-length cassock who stood in the church door.

"Thank you, Joaquim." The voice was . . . contralto? There was a hint of . . . breasts beneath the dark robe. The face was rounded, was gentle enough for a woman.

The minister looked at him now, as Joaquim marched down the street. "Faust and I have a little game we play," she—it was she—explained to his bemusement. "You mustn't let it upset you." She smiled, nodded, and started in.

"Excuse me . . . Reverend . . ."

She turned. "Yes?"

"Eh . . ." Intensely curious, he could focus his curiosity on no subject. "What kind of church is this, here?" He settled on that, but felt it hopelessly contrived. What he wanted to ask about, of course, was the poster.

She smiled. "Interfaith, interracial. We've been managing to have services three times a week for a while now. We'd be very happy if you were interested in coming. Sunday morning, of course. Then again, Tuesday and Thursday evenings. We don't have a very large congregation, yet. But we're gathering our flock."

"You're Reverend . . . ?"

"Amy Taylor. I'm a lay preacher, actually. This is a project I've taken on myself. Working out quite well, too, everything considered."

"You just sort of moved into the church and took it over?"

"After the people who were here abandoned it." She did not brush her hands off. She extended one. It might have been the same gesture. "I'm glad to meet you."

81

He shook. "Glad to meet you."

"I hope you come to our services. This is a time of stress for everybody. We need all the spiritual help we can get . . . don't you think?"

Her grip (like Joaquim's) lingered. And it was firmer. "Hey, do you know what day it is?"

She looked down at the paper. "Wednesday."

"But . . . How do you know when it's Sunday."

She laughed. It was very self-assured laughter. "Sunday services happen when the paper says Sunday. Mr Calkins confuses dates, I know. But there's never more than one Sunday every seven days. Or one Tuesday, either. Now, Thursdays slip up. I went to see him about that. A very polite man. And very concerned about what goes on in his city, despite what some people find a trying sense of humor. I had noticed about the frequency of Sundays myself. He explained about Tuesdays; but he held out for arbitrary Thursdays. He quite nicely offered to declare a Thursday any time I asked—if I would give him twenty-four-hour notice." Her perfect seriousness ruptured with a smile. And she dropped his hand. "The whole business *is* funny. I feel as strange talking about it as you must hearing it, I'm sure." Her natural hair, her round, brown face: he liked her. "Will you try and come to our services?"

He smiled. "I'll try." He was even vaguely sorry to lie.

"Good."

"Reverend Taylor?"

Her sparse eyebrows raised as she looked back.

"Does this street go toward . . . Mr Calkins's?"

"Yes, his home is about a mile up. You have to cross Jackson. Two days ago some brave soul had a bus running back and forth along Broadway. Only one bus. But then it doesn't have any traffic to fight. I don't know if it's still going. But that would take you to the newspaper office, anyway. Not his home. I suppose you could walk. I did."

"Thanks." He left her, smiling after him from the doorway. No, he decided. That probably *wasn't* the monastery. He pictured the tape winding and winding as the music dimmed, chord after chord falling from glimmering reels.

Jackson Avenue was a wide street, but the crowded houses, blurred with noon-smoke, were mostly wood. Trolley wires webbing the intersection were down, in a snarl,

82

on the corner pavement. Two blocks off, wreckage fumed. Billows cleared charred beams, then rolled to.

A block in the other direction a heavy figure with a shopping bag paused mid-trek between corner and corner to watch him watching. Though it was an arbitrary Wednesday afternoon, the feel was of some ominous Sunday morning.

3

There is no articulate resonance. The common problem, I suppose, is to have more to say than vocabulary
and syntax can bear. That is why I am hunting in these
desiccated streets. The smoke hides the sky's variety, stains
consciousness, covers the holocaust with something safe
and insubstantial. It protects from greater flame. It in-
dicates fire, but obscures the source. This is not a useful
street. Very little here approaches any eidolon of the
beautiful.

This is what a *good* neighborhood in Bellona looks
like?

The ground floor windows were broken in the white
house there; curtains hung out.

The street was clean.

Bare foot and sandal, bare foot and sandal: he
watched the pavement's grain slip beneath them.

A door beside him stood wide.

He kept walking. Easier to think that all these buildings are inhabited, than that their vacancy gives me li-
cense to loot where I will—not loot. Borrow. Still, it's unnerving.

Loufer had said something about shotguns.

But he was hungry after all and he was going to—
borrow food soon.

He broke a window with a stick he had found wedging
back a garage door, (eight jars of instant coffee on the
kitchen shelf,) and sat at the formica dinette table to
eat a cold can (can-opener in the drawer) of Campbell's
Pepperpot. (Easy!) Marveling between fingerfuls of un-
diluted soup (salty!), he looked from the paper he'd taken
from Faust, to the notebook he'd gotten from Lanya. Made
himself a cup of coffee with hot water—after running
ten seconds, it was steaming and spitting—from the tap.

Finally, he opened the notebook at random and read, in the terribly neat ballpoint:

> It is not that I have no future. Rather it continually fragments on the insubstantial and indistinct ephemera of now. In the summer country, stitched with lightning, somehow, there is no way to conclude . . .

He looked up at creakings. But it was only some slight architectural shift. Nobody, he subvocalized, lives here now. (The kitchen was very clean.) Without particularly understanding what he'd read (or not understanding it, for that matter) the notes by the absent journalist, coupled with the creak, made the back of his neck tingle.

Déjà vu is a thing of the eye.

This was like reading lines that echoed some conversation he might have followed idly once on a crowded street. The book hinted he pay attention to part of his mind he could not even locate.

> lability, not affectation; a true and common trait. But if I tried to write down what I say as I move from speech

He flipped more pages. There was only writing on the right-hand ones. The left-hand ones were blank. He closed the book. He put the coffee cup in the sink, the can in the empty garbage pail: when he caught himself doing it, he laughed out loud, then tried silent justification: he could always stay here, make this place nicer than Tak's.

That made the back of his neck tingle again.

He closed the notebook and, with the paper tucked beside it, climbed back out the window.

He scratched himself on broken glass, but only noticed it a block away when he looked down to see a drop of blood had trickled across the notebook cover, red-brown on the char. He nudged at the new, purple-red scab with the blunt of his thumb, which just made it itch. So he forgot about it and hurried on up Brisbain. It was only . . . a scratch.

Distance? Or destination?

He had no idea what to expect of either. These lawns

85

and facades needed sunlight, or at least light rain, to be beautiful. The corner trees might be clear green. But mist blurred them now.

Odd that the elements of pleasure were so many greys, so much fear, so many silences. That house there, gaping through drear drapes with intimations of rugs still out in July—someone had *lived* there. A Doctor sign hung beside the door of that one: he mulled on the drugs closeted behind the Venetian blinds. Well, maybe on the way back . . .

Charcoal, like the bodies of beetles, heaped below the glittering wall on the far corner. The sharpness of incinerated upholstery cut the street's gritty stink. Through a cellar window, broken, a grey eel of smoke slithered the sidewalk to vaporize in the gutter. Through another, intact, flickerings . . . The singular burning among the dozens of whole buildings was the most uncanny thing he'd seen.

He crossed quickly to the next block.

The loose rhythm of the day carried him through the streets. Once it occurred to him that he was tired. Later, he looked for the tiredness and found it had dispersed, like the eel.

This had to be the Heights.

He trudged on up the sloping street, by a window full of brass: three layers of glass doors in a foyer: the head of a white statue behind a high hedge—all the vulnerable, gloomy elegance bothered him. Break in for another cup of coffee? He wondered why the images of shotguns behind the curtains were stronger here. But laughed at them, anyway.

He moved, and the movement was a rush of sound among his body's cavities. He slapped the paper and bloody notebook on his thigh, thinking of Lanya, of Milly, of John. From his other hip the orchid swung. Chained in points of view, he loped along, an uneasy vandal, suffering for the pillage his mind wreaked among the fabulous facades. He moved, a point of tension, by homes that would have been luxurious in sunlight.

He was not sure why he decided to explore off the avenue.

In the center of the alley was an oak, set in a circle of cobbles, ringed in a decorative fence. His heart beat fast.

He passed it.

The backside of the trunk was ash. Instead of heavy greenery, the rear leaves were shriveled black.

Eyes wide at the vision, he turned as he passed it, to back away. Then he looked at the houses.

On both sides of him walls were sundered on smashed furniture, beams, and piled masonry. The demarcation between lawn and street vanished beneath junk. Twenty feet on, the cobbles were upturned. He felt his face squinch against the destruction.

Bulldozers?

Grenades?

He could not imagine what had caused this. Paving-stones were smashed, loose, or upside down in raw earth, so that he was not even certain where the next street began. Frowning, he wandered in the debris, stepped over a pile of books, vaguely seeking the source of a smoke plume waving fifty feet away, then, suddenly, not seeking it.

He picked up a clock. The crystal flaked out, tinkling. He dropped it and picked up a ballpoint pen, wiped the ashes against his pants, clicked the point in and out. Half under plaster was a wooden chest, slightly larger than an attaché case. With the toe of his sandal, he nudged up the lid. White powder swirled above forks, spoons, and knives bound in grey ribbon, then settled to the purple velvet. He let the lid clack, and hurried to the Avenue.

He practically ran Brisbain's next three blocks, past houses empty and elegant. But now he was aware of lawn poles askew, of shapeless heaps between them, of windows, which, beyond pale curtains, were light as the sky behind them.

He was still clicking the ballpoint pen. So he put it in his shirt pocket. Then, at the next corner, he took it out again and stood very still. If a wind came now, he thought, and caused any sound on this drear street, he would cry out.

There was no wind.

He sat down on the curb, opened to the notebook's first page.

to wound the autumnal city

he read once more. Hastily he turned the page over to the clear side. He looked down the four streets, looked at the corner houses. He sucked a breath through closed teeth, clicked the point out and began to write.

In the middle of the third line, without taking pen off paper, he swept back to cross it all out. Then, carefully, he recopied two words on the next line. The second was "I." Very carefully now, word followed word. He crossed out two more lines, from which he salvaged "you," "spinner," and "pave," dropping them into a new sentence that bore no denotative resemblance to the one from which they came.

Between lines, while he punched his pen point, his eye strayed to the writing beside his:

> *It is our despair at the textural inade-*
> *quacies of language that drives us to heighten*
> *the structural ones toward*

"Annn!" out loud. There was not a pretty word in the bunch. Roughly he turned the notebook back around the paper to avoid distraction.

Holding the last two lines in his head, he looked about at the buildings again. (Why *not* live dangerously?) He wrote the last lines hurriedly, notating them before they dispersed.

He printed at the top: "Brisbain"

Lifting his pen from the "n", he wondered if the word had any other meaning than the name of the Avenue. Hoping it did, he began to recopy, in as neat a hand as he could, what he had settled on. He altered one word in the last two lines ("cannot" became "can't"), and closed the book, puzzled at what he had done.

Then he stood.

Struck with dizziness, he staggered off the curb. He shook his head, and finally managed to get the world under him at the right angle. The back of his legs were cramped: he'd been in a near-foetal squat practically half an hour.

The dizziness gone, the cramps stayed with him for two blocks. As well he felt choked up in his breathing. That put him in touch with a dozen other little discomforts that he had ignored till now. So that it was not for another block after that he noticed he wasn't afraid.

The pulling in the back of his right shin, or the mental disquiet? He gave up pondering the preferable, looked at a street sign, and noticed that *Brisbain N* had become *Brisbain S*.

Click-click, click-click, click-click: realizing what he was doing, he put the pen in his shirt pocket. Along the street, beside him, was a stone wall. The houses across from him, porched and lawned and spacious and columned, all had broken windows.

The car—a blunt, maroon thing at least twenty years old—grumbled up behind.

He'd jumped, in surprise, turning.

It passed, leaving no impression of the driver. But two blocks ahead, it turned in at a gate.

Willow fronds draped the brick above him. Walking again, he ran two fingers along the mortared troughs.

The gate was verdigrised brass, spiked at the top, and locked. Ten yards beyond the bars, the road got twisted up in the shaggiest pines he'd ever seen. The brass plate, streaked pink with recent polish, said: ROGER CALKINS

He looked through at the pines. He looked back at the other houses. Finally he just walked on.

The street ended in brush. He followed the wall around its corner into bushes. Twigs kept jabbing beneath his sandal straps. His bare foot went easier.

In the clearing, someone had piled two crates, one on another, against the brick: children after fruit or mischief?

As he climbed (notebook and paper left on the ground) two women behind the walls laughed.

He paused.

Their laughter neared, became muffled converse. A man guffawed sharply; the double soprano recommenced and floated off.

He could just grasp the edge. He pulled himself up, elbows winging. It was a lot harder than movies would make it. He scraped at the brick with his toes. Brick rasped back at knees and chin.

His eyes cleared the top.

The wall was covered with pine needles, twigs, and a surprising shale of glass. Through spinning gnats he saw the blunt pine tops and the rounded, looser heads of elms. Was that grey thing the cupola of a house?

"Oh, I don't believe it!" an invisible woman cried and laughed again.

His fingers stung; his arms were trembling.

"What the fuck do you think you're doing, kid?" somebody behind him drawled.

Shaking, he lowered, belt buckle catching a mortice once to dig his stomach; his toes hit at the thin ledges; then the crate: he danced around.

And went back against the wall, squinting.

Newt, spider, and some monstrous insect, huge and out of focus, glared with flashbulb eyes.

He got out an interrogative *"Wh . . ."* but could choose no defining final consonant.

"Now you know—" the spider in the middle extinguished: the tall redhead dropped one freckled hand from the chains looping neck to belly—"damn well you ain't supposed to be up there." His face was flat, his nose wide as a pug's, his lips overted, his eyes like brown eggshells set with tarnished gold coins. His other hand, freckles blurred in pale hair, held a foot of pipe.

"I wasn't climbing in."

"Shit," came out of the newt on the left in a black accent much heavier than the redhead's.

"Sure you weren't," the redhead said. His skin, deep tan, was galaxied with freckles. Hair and beard were curly as a handful of pennies. "Yeah, sure. I just *bet* you weren't." He swung the pipe, snapping his arm at the arc's end: neckchains rattled. "You better get down from there, boy."

He vaulted, landed with one hand still on the crates.

The redhead swung again: the flanking apparitions. came closer, swaying. "Yeah, you better jump!"

"All right, I'm down. Okay—?"

The scorpion laughed, swung, stepped.

The chained boot mashed the corner of the notebook into the mulch. The other tore the newspaper's corner.

"Hey, come on—!"

He pictured himself lunging forward. But stayed still . . . till he saw that the pipe, next swing, was going to catch him on the hip—*was* lunging forward.

"Watch it! He's got his orchid on . . . !"

He slashed with his bladed hand; the scorpion dodged back; newt and beetle spun. He had no idea where they were under their aspects. He jammed his fist at the scaly simulation—his fist went through and connected jaw-staggeringly hard with something. He slashed with his blades at the retreating beetle. The spider rushed him. He staggered in rattling lights. A hand caught him against the

90

cheek. Blinking, he saw a second, sudden black face go out under newt scales. Then, something struck his head.

"Hey, he cut you, Spitt, man!" That was the heavy black accent, very far away. "Oh, hey, wow, Spitt! He really cut you. Spitt, you all right?"

He wasn't all right. He was falling down a black hole.

"The mother fucker! I'm going to get him for that—"

He hit bottom.

Pawing across that leafy bottom, he finally found the remnants of a thought: His orchid had been hanging from his waist. No time had he reached down to—

"Are . . . you all right?"

—slip his roughened fingers into the harness, fasten the collar about his knobby wrist . . .

Someone shook him by the shoulder. His hand gouged moist leaves. The other was suspended. He opened his eye.

Evening struck the side of his head so hard he was nauseated.

"Young man, are you all right?"

He opened his eyes again. The throbbing twilight concentrated on one quarter of his head. He pushed himself up.

The man, in blue serge, sat back on his heels. "Mr Fenster, I think he's conscious!"

A little ways away, a black man in a sports shirt stood at the clearing's edge.

"Don't you think we should take him inside? Look at his head."

"No, I don't think we should." The black put his hands in the pockets of his slacks.

He shook his head—only once, because it hurt that much.

"Were you attacked, young man?"

He said, "Yes," very thickly. A nod would have made it cynical, but he didn't dare.

The white collar between the serge lapels was knotted with an extraordinarily thin tie. White temples, below grey hair: the man had an accent that was disturbingly near British. He picked up the notebook. (The newspaper slid off onto the leaves.) "Is this yours?"

Another thick, "Yes."

"Are you a student? It's terrible, people attacking people right out in the open like this. Terrible!"

91

"I think we'd better get inside," the black man said. "They'll be waiting for us."

"Just a minute!" came out with surprising authority. The gentleman helped him to sitting position. "Mr Fenster, I really think we should take this poor young man inside. Mr Calkins can't possibly object. This is something of an exceptional circumstance."

Fenster took dark brown hands from his pockets and came over. "I'm afraid it isn't exceptional. We've checked, now come on back inside."

With surprising strength Fenster tugged him to his feet. His right temple exploded three times en route. He grabbed the side of his head. There was crisp blood in his hair; and wet blood in his sideburn.

"Can you stand up?" Fenster asked.

"Yes." The word was dough in his mouth. "Ah . . . thanks for my—" he almost shook his head again, but remembered—"my notebook."

The man in the tie looked sincerely perplexed. With a very white hand, he touched his shoulder. "You're sure you're all right?"

"Yes," automatically. Then, "Could I get some water?"

"Certainly," and then to Fenster. "We can certainly take him inside for a glass of water."

"No—" Fenster spoke with impatient resignation— "we *can't* take him inside for a glass of water." It ended with set jaw, small muscles there defined in the dark skin. "Roger is very strict. You'' just have to put up with it. Please, let's go back in."

The white man—fifty-   sixty?—finally took a breath. "I'm . . ." Then he jus   led away.

Fenster—forty? forty-fiv   —said, "This isn't a good neighborhood to be in, young fellow. I'd get back downtown as fast as I could. Sorry about all this."

"That's all right," he got out. "I'm okay."

"I really am sorry." Fenster hurried after the older gentleman.

He watched them reach the corner, turn. He raised his caged hand, looked at it between the blades. Was that why they had . . . ? He looked back toward the street.

His head gave a gratuitous throb.

He collected the paper and the notebook, mumbling profanity, and walked out.

They'd apparently gone back through the gate. And

locked it. Mother-fuckers, he thought. The gloom was denser now. He began to wonder how long he'd been away from the park. Four or five hours? His head hurt a lot. And it was getting dark.

Also it looked like rain . . . But the air was dry and neutral.

Brisbain South had just become Brisbain North when he saw, a block away, three people run from one side of the avenue to the other.

They were too far to see if they wore chains around their necks. Still, he was overcome with gooseflesh. He stopped with his hand on the side of a lamp post. (The globe was an inverted crown of ragged glass points, about the smaller, ragged collar of the bulb.) He felt his shoulders pull involuntarily together. He looked at the darkening sky. And the terror of the vandal-wrecked city assailed him: His heart pounded.

His armpits grew slippery.

Breathing hard, he sat with his back to the post's base.

He took the pen from his pocket and began to click the point. (He *hadn't* put the orchid on . . . ?) After a moment, he stopped to take the weapon from his wrist and put it through his belt loop again: moving armed through the streets might be provocative . . . ?

He looked around again, opened his notebook, turned quickly past "Brisbain" to a clean page, halfway or more through.

"Charcoal," he wrote down, in small letters, "like the bodies of burnt beetles, heaped below the glittering black wall of the house on the far corner." He bit at his lip, and wrote on: "The wet sharpness of incinerated upholstery cut the general gritty stink of the street. From the rayed hole in the cellar window a grey eel of smoke wound across the sidewalk, dispersed before" at which point he crossed out the last two words and substituted, "vaporized at the gutter. Through another window," and crossed out *window*, "still intact, something flickered. This single burning building in the midst of dozens of other whole buildings was," stopped and began to write all over again:

"Charcoal, like the bodies of beetles, heaped below the glittering wall. The sharpness of incinerated upholstery cut the street's gritty stink." Then he went back and crossed out "the bodies of" and went on: "From a broken cellar window, a grey eel wound the sidewalk to vaporize at the gutter. Through another, intact, something flickered. This burning building," crossed that out to substitute, "The singular burning in the midst of dozens of whole buildings," and without breaking the motion of his hand suddenly tore the whole page from the notebook.

Pen and crumpled paper in his hand; he was breathing hard. After a moment, he straightened out the paper, and on a fresh page, began to copy again:

"Charcoal, like beetles heaped under the glittering wall . . ."

He folded the torn paper in four and put it back in the notebook when he had finished the next revision. On the back the former owner of the notebook had written:

> . . . *first off. It doesn't reflect my daily life. Most of what happens hour by hour is quiet and still. We sit most of the time*

Once more he made a face and closed the cover.

The mist had turned evening-blue. He got up and started along the street.

Several blocks later he identified the strange feeling: Though it was definitely becoming night, the air had not even slightly cooled. Frail smoke lay about him like a neutralizing blanket.

Ahead, he could see the taller buildings. Smoke had gnawed away the upper stories. Stealthily, he descended into the injured city.

It does not offer me any protection, this mist; rather a refracting grid through which to view the violent machine, explore the technocracy of the eye itself, spelunk the semi-circular canal. I am traveling my own optic nerve. Limping in a city without source, searching a day without shadow, am I deluded with the inconstant emblem? I don't like pain. With such disorientation there is no way to measure the angle between such nearly parallel lines of sight, when focusing on something at such distance.

4

"*There* you are!" She ran out between the lions, crossed the street.

He turned, surprised, at the lamp post.

She seized his hand in both of hers. "I didn't think I would see you again before— Hey! What happened?" Her face twisted in the shadow. She lost all her breath.

"I got beat up."

Her grip dropped; she raised her fingers, brushed his face.

"Owww . . ."

"You better come with me. What in the world did you do?"

"Nothing!" vented some of his indignation.

She took his hand again to tug him along. "You did *some*thing. People just don't get beat up for nothing at all."

"In this city—" he let her lead—"they do."

"Down this way. No. Not even in this city. What happened? You've got to get that washed off. Did you get to Calkins'?"

"Yeah." He walked beside her; her hand around his was almost painfully tight—then, as though she realized it, the grip loosened. "I was looking over the wall when these scorpions got at me."

"Ohhh!" That seemed to explain it to her.

" 'Oh' what?"

"Roger doesn't like snoopers."

"So he sets scorpions to patrol the battlements?"

"I wouldn't be surprised. Sometimes he asks them for protection."

"Hey!" He pulled loose; she swung around. In shadow, her eyes, glaring up, were empty as the lions'. He tried to fix his tongue at protest, but she merely stepped to his side. They walked again, together, not touching, through the dark.

"In here."

"In where?"

"Here!" She turned him with a hand on his arm.

And opened a door he hadn't realized was beside them. Someone in flickering silhouette said, "Oh, it's you. What's the matter?"

"*Look* at him," Lanya said. "Scorpions."

"Oh." Leather jacket, cap . . . and leather pants: long fingers pulled closed the door. "Take him inside. But don't make a big thing, huh?"

"Thanks, Teddy."

There were voices from the end of the hall. The flakes of light on nail-thin Teddy's attire came from candles in iron candelabras.

He followed her.

At the end of the bar a woman's howl shattered to laughter. Three of the men around her, laughing, shed away like bright, black petals: four-fifths present wore leather, amidst scattered denim jackets. The woman had fallen into converse with a tall man in a puffy purple sweater. The candlelight put henna in her hair and blacked her eyes.

Another woman holding on to a drink with both hands, in workman's greens and construction boots, stepped unsteadily between them, recognized Lanya and intoned: "Honey, now where have you been all week? Oh, you don't know how the class of this place has gone down. The boys are about to run me ragged," and went, unsteadily, off.

Lanya led him through the leather crush. A surge of people toward the bar pushed them against one of the booth tables.

"Hey, babes—" Lanya leaned on her fists—"can we sit here a minute?"

"Lanya—? Sure," Tak said, then recognized him. "Jesus, Kid! What the hell happened to *you?*" He pushed over in the seat. "Come on. Sit down!"

"Yeah . . ." He sat.

Lanya was edging off between people:

"Tak, Kidd—I'll be right back!"

He put the notebook and the paper on the wooden table, drew his hands through the shadows the candles dropped from the iron webs, drew his bare foot through sawdust.

Tak, from looking after Lanya, turned back. "You got beat up?" The visor still masked his upper face.

He nodded at Tak's eyeless question.

Tak's lips pressed beneath the visor's shadow. He shook his head. "Scorpions?"

"Yeah."

The young man across the table had his hands in his lap.

"What'd they get from you?" Tak asked.

"Nothing."

"What did they think they were going to get?"

"I don't know. Shit. They just wanted to beat up on somebody, I guess."

Tak shook his head. "No. That doesn't sound right. Not scorpions. Everybody's too busy trying to survive around here just to go beating up on people for fun."

"I was up at the Calkins place, trying to look over the wall. Lanya said he keeps the bastards patrolling the damn walls."

"Now there." Loufer shook a finger across the table. "That's like I was telling you, Jack. It's a strange place, maybe stranger than any you've ever been. But it still has its rules. You just have to find them out."

"Shit," he repeated, indignant at everybody's questioning of the incident. "They beat hell out of me."

"Looks like they did." Tak turned across the table. "Jack, want you to meet the Kid, here. Jack just pulled into town this afternoon. The Kid got in yesterday."

Jack pushed himself forward and reached out to shake.

"Hi." He shook Jack's small, sunburned hand.

"Jack here is a deserter from the army."

At which Jack glanced at Tak with dismay, then covered it with an embarrassed smile. "Ah . . . hello," he said with a voice out of Arkansas. His short-sleeve sportshirt was very pressed. Army shorn, his skull showed to the temple. "Yeah, I'm a God-damn deserter, like he says."

"That's nice," then realized how flip that sounded and was also embarrassed.

"Tak here has been trying to tell me about how to get along in this place," Jack offered: he had either not taken offense, or just not heard. "Tak's a lot smarter than I am, you know. It's pretty funny here, huh?"

He nodded.

"I was gonna go to Canada. But somebody told me about Bellona. Said it was a pretty swinging place, you know? So I thought I'd stop off here. On the way." Now he looked around the bar. The woman howled again: the purple angora had abandoned her. The howl moved predictably once more toward laughter and she sat, alone, shaking her dark red hair over her drink. "I ain't ever seen a place quite like this. Have you?" Jack offered the conversation back to him.

"Oh, I bet you ain't," Tak intercepted. "Now the Kid here, you know, he's my age? You probably would have thought he was younger than you are. Jack here is twenty. Now seriously, how old would you say the Kid here is?"

"Uh . . . oh, I don't know." Jack said, and looked confused.

(He wanted to look at the engineer's shadowed face again, but not yet.)

"Where the hell did you run off to this morning, anyway?"

A dog barked, somewhere in the bar.

About to turn and answer Tak, he looked toward the noise. Claws scrabbled; then, bursting between the legs of the people next to them, the black muzzle and shoulders!

He snatched his arm up from the barking.

At the same time, Lanya arrived: "Hey, come on, girl!"

O‥ ‥ned to watch the beast bark up at their table.

"Come on. Quiet down." Lanya's hand strayed on the shaking head, played on the black snout. "Be quiet! Quiet, now." The dog tried to pull its head away. She grabbed its lower jaw and shook it gently. "What you making so much noise about? Shhhhh, you hear me? Shhhh!" The dog turned its brown eyes from the table, to Lanya, back to the table. Bright pricks from the candles slid on the black pupils. It licked her hand. "There now. Be quiet." In the other was a wad of wet paper towels. She sat down, put them on the table: they trickled on the wood.

Jack's hands were back in his lap.

Tak pushed up his cap; the shadow uncovered his

98

large, blue eyes. He shook his head, and sucked his teeth in general disapproval.

"Come *on*, now," Lanya said once more to the dog. It waited beside the table, panting.

He reached out toward the dark head. The panting stopped. He passed his fingers over the rough hair, the wiry brows. The dog turned to lick the ham of his thumb. "Yeah," he said. "You just be quiet."

"Is Muriel bothering you people?" Purple Angora sucked a sighing breath. "I tell her—" he gestured toward the woman at the bar—"she shouldn't bring her *in* here. Muriel is just not that well trained. She gets so excited. But she *will* bring her in here every night. I hope she hasn't annoyed you."

Lanya reached again to rough the dog's head. "She's an old dear! She didn't bother anybody."

"Well, thank you." Purple Angora bent to drag Muriel back to the bar by the collar. Once he glanced back, frowned at them—

"See if you can wipe some of that stuff off your face," Lanya said, wrinkling hers.

"Huh? Oh, yeah." He picked up a towel and held it to his temple; which stung. Water rolled down.

He rubbed the blood off his cheek. Picked up another towel (the first now purple to the rim) and wiped his face again.

"Hey," Jack said. "I think you're . . ." with a vague gesture.

"Lord—!" Lanya said. "I'll get some more towels."

"Huh? Am I bleeding again?"

Tak took him by the chin and turned his face. "You sure are," and pressed another towel against his head.

"Hey!" He reached across for Lanya's arm. "Look, let me just go to the men's room. I'll fix it up."

She sat again. "Are you sure . . . ?"

"Yeah. I'll be back in a little while." With one hand he held the paper to his face; with the other, he picked up the notebook. ("What happened to him?" Tak was asking Lanya. And Lanya was leaning forward to answer.) He pushed through the people next to them toward where the men's room ought to be.

Behind him, music began, staticy as an old radio; more like somebody's wind-up victrola. He turned in front of the rest room door.

Neon lights had come on in a cage hung up behind

the bar. (The redhead's face (forty-five? fifty?) was soap yellow in the glare:

("Muriel! Now, Muriel, be quiet!"

(The fugitive barking stilled and the Purple Sweater sat up once more.) Through the black curtain stepped a boy in a silver lamé G-string. He began to dance in the cage, shaking his hips, flicking his hands, kicking. His ash-pale hair was flecked with glitter; glitter had fallen down his wet brow. He grinned hugely, open mouthed, lips shaking with the dance, at customers up and down the bar. His eyebrows were pasted over with silver.

The music, he realized through the static, was a medley of Dylan played by something like the Melachrino Strings. The "boy" was anywhere between fifteen and an emaciated thirty-five. Around his neck hung glittering strands of mirrors, prisms, lenses.

He pushed into the bathroom as a big man in an army jacket came out fingering his fly.

He locked the door, put his notebook on the cracked porcelain tank (he'd left the paper on the table), looked at the mirror and said, *"Christ . . . !"*

Tap turned full, the cold water only trickled over the tear-shaped stain. He pulled paper towels, rasping, from their container, and let them soak. Minutes later the sink was awash with blood; the battleship linoleum was speckled with it; but his face was clear of gore and leakage.

Sitting on the toilet, pants around his shins, shirt open, he turned up a quarter-sized mirror on his belly and gazed down at a fragment of his face with an eye in it. Water beaded his eyelashes.

He blinked.

His eye opened to see the drop, pink with dilute blood, strike the glass and spread to the gripping callous.

He let go, took the notebook from the toilet tank, turned it back on his thighs, and took out his pen. The coil pressed his skin:

"Murielle"

He doubted the spelling, but wrote on:

"Seen through blood, her clear eyes . . ." He crossed out "clear" methodically, till it was a navy bar. He frowned, re-read, rewrote "clear", and wrote on. He stopped long enough to urinate and re-read again. He shook his head, leaned forward. His penis swung against cold porcelain. So he wiggled back on the seat; rewrote the whole line.

Once he looked up: A candle by the painted-over window was guttering.

"Remembering," he wrote, "by candle what I'd seen by moon . . ." frowned, and substituted a completely different thought.

"Hey!" Pounding at the door made him look up. "You all right in there, Kid?"

"Tak?"

"You need some help in there? Lanya sent me to see if you'd fallen in. You all right?"

"I'm okay. I'll be out in a minute."

"Oh. Okay. All right."

He looked back at the page. Suddenly he scribbled across the bottom: "They won't let me finish this God-damn" stopped, laughed, closed the book, and put the pen back in his pocket.

He leaned forward on his knees and relaxed: The length and splash surprised him. There wasn't any toilet paper.

So he used a wet towel.

Light glittered on the dancer's hips, his shaking hair, his sweating face. But people had resumed their conversations.

He pushed through, glancing at the cage.

"Well, you certainly *look* a lot better," Lanya said.

Jack said, "Hey, I got you and your girl friend a beer. One for you too, see, because I didn't want you to think . . . well, you know."

"Oh," he said. "Sure. Thanks."

"I mean Tak ain't let me buy anything all evening. So I thought I'd get you and your girl friend a beer."

He nodded and sat. "Thanks."

"Yeah, thanks," Lanya said.

"She's a very nice girl."

Lanya gave him a small Well-what-can-you-do look across the table and drank.

The music growled to a stop in the middle of a phrase; people applauded.

Jack nodded toward the cage, where the dancer panted. "I swear, I never been in a place like this. It's

101

really too much, you know? You got a lot of places like this in Bellona?"

"*Teddy's* here is the one and only," Tak said. "No other place like it in the Western World. It used to be a straight bar back before. Improvement's not to be believed."

"It sure is pretty unbelievable," Jack repeated. "I've just never seen anything like it."

Lanya took another swallow from her bottle. "You're not going to die after all?" She smiled.

He saluted her with his and emptied it by a third. "Guess not."

Tak suddenly twisted in his seat. "Ain't this a bitch! Hot as it is in this God-damn place;" He shrugged out of his jacket, hung it over the bench back, then leaned one tattooed forearm on the table. "Now that's a little more comfortable." He furrowed the meadow of his chest, and looked down. "Sweating like a pig." He slid forward, stomach ridged by the plank, and folded his arms. "Yeah, that's a little better." He still wore his cap.

"Jesus," Jack said, looking around. "They let you do that in here?"

"They'd let me take my pants down and dance on the fucking table," Tak said, "if I wanted. Wouldn't they, Lanya-babes? You tell 'em."

"Tak," Lanya said, "I'd like to *see* that. I really would." She laughed.

Jack said: "Wow!"

The dancer was climbing from the cage down to the bar; he made a joke with somebody below; somebody else gave him a hand, and he leaped lightly away.

At the doorway, a group had just come in.

A couple of men in leather had gone up to a tall black with a khaki shirt: Even by candlelight, sweat stained his shirt flanks. Other black men around wore suits and ties. People were putting tables together.

The redhead's laughter carried her across the bar. She took the black's beam-broad, khaki shoulders. He embraced her; she struggled, still laughing. Muriel barked about their knees.

Sepulchral Teddy, like some leather-sheathed plant, set bottles down, held back chairs. The tall black fell into his seat; his fists cracked open like stone on the table. Others sat around him. He reared back, stretched his arms, and caught the woman in coveralls with one and the sparkling dancer with the other. Everyone laughed. The woman tried not to spill her drink and pushed at the rough, dark head. The dancer squealed: "Ooooo!" His G-string broke. He pulled the cord across his white hip, yanked the whole pouch away, and spun from the circling arm. A black hand smacked the chalky buttocks. The dancer dodged forward, threw back an evil look that ended with a wink, flipped the silver strap over his shoulder, and stalked off, cheek grinding cheek.

"Jesus!" Jack said from the other side of the table.

The rabbity tuft above the dancer's bobbing genitals had been dusted with glitter.

Teddy moved about the joined tables, pouring. Other people were coming up to talk, leaving to drink.

Lanya explained to his puzzled look: "That's George Harrison. Do you . . . ?"

He nodded. "Oh."

"Jesus!" Jack repeated. "You got all sorts of people in a place like this, you know? I mean all kinds. Now that wouldn't happen where I come from. It's—" he looked around—"pretty nice, huh?" He drank more beer. "Everybody's so friendly."

Tak put his boot up on the bench and hung his arm across his knee. "Until they start to tear the place apart." He turned up his bottle to waterfall at his wide mouth. "Hey, you all want to come up to my place? Yeah, why don't you all come on back with me?" He put the beer down. "Jack, Lanya, you too, Kid."

He looked across at her to see if she wanted to go.

But she was drinking beer again.

"Yeah, come on." Tak pointed at her, so that when her bottle came down from her mouth, she looked at the engineer and frowned. *"You*'re not going to sit around *this* place all night and fight off the Horse Women of Dry-gulch Canyon, are you?"

Lanya laughed. "Well, if you really want me, all right."

Tak slapped the table. "Good." Then he leaned over and stage-whispered, "You know she's a real stuckup bitch. Back when she used to hang out here, she wouldn't be caught dead with the likes of me. But after we got to know each other, she turned out not to be so bad." He grinned across the table.

"Tak, I'm *not* stuck up. I *always* spoke to you!"

"Yeah, yeah, so's your old man!" Tak pointed with a

103

thumb. "Is *he* your old man now?" Then he laughed. "Come on. Late supper at Tak Loufer's. Tak Loufer's gonna give a party. Jack, you were saying how hungry you were."

"Gee," Jack said. "I don't know if . . ."

Lanya suddenly turned to him. "Oh, come on! Now, you *have* to come with us. You've just gotten here. Tak wants to show you around." She positively beamed.

"Well . . ." Jack grinned at the table, at Tak, at the candelabra.

"I'll give you something to eat," Tak said.

"Hell, I'm not that—"

"Oh, come on!" Lanya insisted.

(He moved his hands over the notebook, stained with blood and charcoal, to where the newspaper stuck out from the sides . . .) Lanya reached across and laid one fingertip on his gnawed thumb. He looked up. Tak was standing to leave. Jack: "Well, all right," finishing up his beer; Tak pulled his coat from the bench back. Lanya rose.

He picked up the paper and the notebook and stood beside her. Jack and Tak (he remarked again the juxtaposition of sounds) went ahead. She pressed his arm and whispered, "I'd say I just earned my supper, wouldn't you?"

They skirted the Harrison party. "Hey, look a-dere go' ol' I'n' Wo'f!" Harrison grinned up from a hand of cards.

"Go drown yourself, ape," Tak jibed back, "or I'll tell everybody you're holding—"

Harrison pulled his cards away and rumbled into laughter—when suddenly the silver-haired dancer bounced into their midst, G-string mended; he grabbed Lanya's arm. "Darling, *how* do you always manage to leave here with *all* the beautiful men? Come on, everyone! A *big* smile for your mother . . . Fabulous! Can I come too?"

Tak swung his jacket, and the silver head ducked. "Get outa here."

"Oh, now, with that big old hairy chest of hers, she thinks she's just too too!"

But they pushed toward the door.

The red-headed woman and Purple Angora were talking quietly by the wall. Muriel, panting, lay between their feet. The flickering candles kept gouging lines in the woman's yellow face. She was not that made up, he realized as they passed, nor that old. But the roughness of her skin under the unsteady light suggested misplaced artifice. Over her jacket (he had not seen it before and wondered how he had missed it; unless simple profusion had misled him to think it was something else) were loops and loops and loops of the strange chain Faust, Nightmare, the dancer, indeed, he himself, as well, wore.

Muriel barked.

He pushed into the hall, behind Lanya, in front of Jack.

Teddy smiled at them, like a mechanical skull beneath his cap, and held the door.

The very blonde girl at the sidewalk's edge bit at her knuckle and watched them intently.

The cool was surprising.

He had reached down to make sure that the orchid still hung in his belt loop when she said: "Excuse me, I'm terribly sorry to bother you, but was——" her face held its expression unsteadily—"George Harrison . . . in there?" then lost it completely. Her grey eyes were very bright.

"Huh? Oh, yeah. He's inside."

Her fist flew back against her chin and she blinked. Behind him Jack was saying, "Jesus, will you look at *that!*"

"Now that *is* something!" Tak said.

"You say he *is* in there? George Harrison, the big colored man?"

"Yeah, he's inside." At which point Lanya tugged his arm: "Kid, *look* at that! Will you?"

"Huh? What?" He looked up.

The sky—

He heard footsteps, lowered his eyes: the blonde girl was hurrying down the street. Frowning, he looked up again.

—streamed with black and silver. The smoke, so low and limitless before, had raddled into billows, torn and flung by some high wind that did not reach down to the street.

Hints of a moon struck webs of silver on the raveling mist.

He moved against Lanya's shoulder (she too had glanced after the girl), all warm down his side. Her short hair brushed his arm. "I've never *seen* it like that before!" And then, louder: "Tak, has it ever been like that before?"

(Someday I'm going to die, he thought irrelevantly, but shook the thought away.)

"Damn!" Loufer took off his cap. "Not since I been here." He was holding his jacket over his shoulder by one finger. "How do you like that, Jack? Maybe it's finally breaking up."

They started to the corner, still staring.

"That's the first time here I've seen the—" Then Lanya stopped.

They all stopped. He swallowed, hard: with his head back, it tugged uncomfortably at his Adam's apple.

Through one rent, the lunar disk had appeared; then, as the aperture moved with the wind, he saw a *second* moon!

Lower in the sky, smaller, it was in some crescent phase.

"Jesus!" Jack said.

The smoke came together again, tore away.

"Now wait just a God-damn minute!" Tak said.

Once more the night was lit by the smaller, but distinctly lunar crescent. A few stars glittered near it. The smoke closed here, opened there: The gibbous moon shone above it.

Before the bar door another group had gathered, craning at the violated night. Two, pulling a bottle back and forth, came loose, came close.

"What the hell—" The sky cleared again under two lights, crescent and near-full—"is that?" Tak demanded.

Someone else said: "What do *you* think it is, a sun?"

"The moon!" One gestured with his foaming bottle.

"Then what's *that?*"

One pulled the bottle from the other's hand. "That's another . . . that one's George!"

They reeled off, spilling liquor.

In the gathered group, people laughed;

"You hear that, George? You got a God-damn moon named after you!" and out of the laughter and chatter, a louder laugh rose.

Lanya shrugged closer beneath his arm.

"Jesus . . ." Jack whispered again.

"Not according to them," Tak said. "Come on."

"What *is* it?" Lanya asked again.

"Maybe it's some kind of reflection." He flexed his fingers around on her small shoulder. "Or one of those

106

weather balloons. Like they used to think were flying sau-cers."

"Reflected *from* what, *on* to what?" Tak asked.

Flakes of smoke spun over. One or the other, and oc-casionally both moons showed. There was a breeze now. The sky was healing. Over half the sky clouds had already coalesced. Voices came from in the bar doorway:

"Hey, we got a moon! And we got a George!"

"Shine on, shine on harvest George—"

"Oh man, June and George don't rhyme!"

("Tak and Jack do," Lanya whispered, giggled, and pulled her harmonica from her pocket.)

"But *you* remember what he do to that little white girl—"

"Oh, shit, was *that* her name!"

Lanya blew harmonica notes in his ear. He pulled away, "Hey . . . !" and came back to her, perturbed. She reached up and held his forefinger. Something tickled his blunt knuckle. She was brushing her lips across the ruin of his thumb's first joint. The shoutings died behind them. Overhead, the lights blurred in returning clouds. She played lazy music by his chest, following the ex-soldier and the ex-engineer. Her motion pulled him. She paused to tell him, "You smell good."

"Huh? Yeah, I guess I stink," and cringed.

"I mean it. Good. Like a pear somebody's soaked in brandy."

"That's what happens when you bum around for three weeks and can't get a bath." She nuzzled the fork-ing of his arm.

He thought she was funny. And liked her funniness. And realized that it was because she made it easier to like . . . whoever he was; and came out of the thoughts trying not to smile. She played randomly.

He beat the paper and notebook on his thigh, till he remembered John whom he did not like, and stopped.

5

Look for shadow in this double-lit mist. A dark communion in the burning streets between the landscape and the smarting senses suggests more sterile agonies. Clouds out of control decoct anticipation. What use can any of us have for *two* moons? The miracle of order has run out and I am left in an unmiraculous city where anything may happen. I don't need more intimations of disorder. It *has* to be more than that! Search the smoke for the fire's base. Read from the coals neither success nor despair. This edge of boredom is as bright. I pass it, into the dark rim. There is the deceiving warmth that asks nothing. There are objects lost in double-light.

With the jollity of their progress through the night streets, the repeated exclamations and speculations at the twinned satellites, moments into Tak's dark stairway—footsteps pummeling around him, down, across, then pummeling up—he realized he had no memory of the doorway through which they'd just entered out of the night, save the memory of his exit that lingered from the morning.

"A great idea!" Lanya, behind, was breathing heavily. "A Full George party!"

"*If* George was the full one," Tak said. "Excuse me; gibbous."

"How far up do you live?" Jack asked, ahead.

The orchid jogged on his hip. Notebook and newspaper—he'd read none of the paper yet—were still clamped in clammy fingers.

"We'll be there in one more— Nope. I mis-counted," Tak called down. "We're here already! Come on! It's party time!"

Metal creaked on metal.

Both Lanya, behind, and Jack, ahead, were laughing.

Above is light. What else does this city cast up on its cloudy cover, from ill-functioning streetlights, from what leaks tentatively out of badly shaded doors and windows, from flame? Is it enough to illuminate another bright, brief, careening, but less-than-standard body?

6

He put the wine bottle on the roof's thigh-high wall. Below, the street lamp was a blurred pearl. He searched the dense and foggy distances, was lost in them.

"What are you looking at?" She came up, surprising, behind.

"Oh." The night was thick with burnt odors. "I don't know."

She picked up the bottle and drank, "All right," and put it down; then said, "You're looking for something. You've got your eyes all squinched up. You were craning way out and . . . oh, you can't see anything down there for the smoke!"

"The river," he said.

"Hm?" She looked again.

"I can't see the river."

"What river?"

"When I came off the waterfront, across the bridge. This place, it was like two blocks away, maybe. And then, when I first came up here, you could just see the water, as though suddenly the river was a half a mile off. It was right through there. But now I can't see . . ." craning again.

She said: "You couldn't see the river from here. It's nearly . . . I don't know exactly; but it's quite a way."

"I could this morning."

"Maybe, but I doubt it." Then she said: "You were here this morning?"

He said: "There isn't any smoke over there. I can't even make out the lights from the bridge, or anything; even the reflections from the places on the waterfront that're burning. Unless they've gone out."

"If they've gone out, the electricity's gone on somewhere else." Suddenly she pulled her shoulders together, gave a little shiver; sighed, and looked up. And said, eventually: "The moon."

"What?"

"Do you remember," she asked, "when they got the first astronauts to the moon?"

"Yeah," he said. "I saw it on TV. A whole bunch of us were over at my friend's house."

"I missed it, until the next morning," she said. "But it was . . . funny."

"What?"

She pulled her lips in between her teeth, then let them pop. "Do you remember the next time you were outside and you looked up and saw the moon in the sky instead of on television?"

He frowned.

"It was different, remember. I realized that for the last fifty thousand science-fiction novels it had still been just a light hanging up there. And now it was . . . a place."

"I just figured somebody had taken a shit up there, and why weren't they telling." He stopped laughing. "But it was different; yeah."

"Then tonight." She looked at the featureless smoke. "Because there was another one, that you don't know if anybody's walked on, suddenly both of them were . . ."

"Just lights again."

"Or . . ." she nodded. "Something else." Leaning, her elbow touched his arm.

"Hey," Jack said from the doorway, "I think I ˌ ·ᵗᵉʳ go now. I mean . . . maybe I better go." He loo around the roof. The mist had wrapped them in. mean," he said, "Tak's awful drunk, you know? He's sort of . . ."

"He isn't going to hurt you."

Lanya poised her quick laugh at the rim of amuse-ment, started back, and entered the cabin.

He picked up the wine and followed.

"Now here," Tak announced, coming from the bamboo curtain. "I knew I had some caviar. Got it on the first day up here." He grimaced. "Too much, huh? But I like caviar. Imported." He held up the black jar in his left hand. "Domestic." He raised the orange one in his right. His cap was on the desk with his jacket. His head seemed very small on his thick torso. "I got more stuff in there than you can twitch the proverbial stick at." He set the jars down among a dozen others.

111

"Isn't it sort of late . . ." Jack's voice trailed off in the doorway.

"Christ," Lanya said, "what are you going to do with all this junk, Tak?"

"Late supper. Don't worry, nobody goes hungry up at the Fire Wolf's."

He picked up a small jar (cut glass in scarred, horny flesh): ". . . Spiced Honey Spread . . . ?"

"Oh, yeah." Tak arranged the breadboard on the edge of the desk. "I've even tried some of that before. It's good." He swayed above pickled artichoke hearts and caponata, deviled ham, herring, pimento, rolled anchovies, guava paste, pâté. "And another glass of—" He raised the bottle and splashed the liquid around inside. "Jack, some for you?"

"Aw, no. It's getting pretty late."

"*Here* you go!" He pushed the glass into the boy's hand. Jack took it because it would have dropped otherwise:

"Eh . . . thanks."

". . . for me." Tak finished his and poured another. "Come on, everybody, now you help yourselves. You like pimento?"

"Not just by its lonesome," Lanya protested.

"With bread, or . . . cheese, here. Anchovies?"

"Look," Lanya said, "*I'll* do it."

Loufer gestured toward Jack. "Now come on, boy. You said you were hungry. I got all this damn caviar and stuff."

"It's sort of . . ." Behind Jack, smoke filtered across the doorway. ". . . well, late."

"Tak?"

"Hey, Kid, here's a glass for you."

"Thanks. Tak?"

"Yeah, Kid? What can I do for you?"

"That poster."

From the center picture, the tall black glared out into the room, oiled teak belly gleaming under scuffed leather, his fist, a dark and gouged interruption on a dark thigh. The light source had been yellow: that made brass hints in the nappy pubis. The scrotal skin was the color and texture of rotten avocado rind. Between the thighs, a cock, thick as a flashlight haft, hung dusty, black and wormy with veins. The skin of the right knee intimated a marvelous machine beneath. The left ear was a coil of serpents. The brass light barred his leg, his neck, slurred the oil on his nostrils.

"That's the spade who came into the bar, the one they named the moon after."

"Yeah, that's George—George Harrison." Tak took the top off another jar, smelled it, scowled. "Some of the boys at Teddy's got him to pose for that. He's a·real ham. That ape likes to get his picture taken more than just about anything, you know? Long as he doesn't get too drunk, he's a great guy. Ain't he beautiful? Strong as a couple of horses, too."

"Wasn't there something about some pictures in the paper of him . . . raping some girl? That's what the newspaper man told me this morning."

"Oh yeah." Tak put down another jar, drank more of his brandy. "Yeah, that business with the white girl, in the paper, during the riot. Well, like I said: George just likes to get his picture taken. He's a big nigger now. Might as well enjoy it. I would if I was him."

"What *is* this, Tak . . . octopus!" Lanya, with a wrinkled nose, bit. "Sort of tough . . . it *tastes* all right."

"Jesus!" Jack exclaimed. "That's salty!"

"Have some brandy," Tak reiterated. "Spicy food is good with booze. Go ahead. Drink some more."

"You know—" he still considered the poster—"I saw that thing hung up in a church this morning?"

"Ah!" Tak gestured with his glass. "Then you   re down at Reverend Amy's. Didn't you know? She's chief distributor. Where do you think I got my copy?

He frowned at the poster, frowned at Tak (who wasn't looking), frowned at the poster again.

Eyes of ivory, velvet lips, a handsome face poised between an expression disdainful and embarrassing. Was it . . . theatrical? Perhaps theatrical disdain. The background was a horizonless purple. He tried to put this rough face with his memory of the astounding second moon.

"Try this!" Lanya exclaimed. "It's good."

It was. But mumbling through the tasteless crumbs under it, he stepped outside and breathed deep in the thick smoke. He couldn't smell it, but he felt his heart in his ears in a moment, very quick and steady. He searched for either blotted light. A rapist? he thought. An

113

exhibitionist? He is approaching the numinous: gossip; the printed word; portents. Thrilled, he narrowed his eyes to search the clouds for George once more.

"Hey," Lanya said. "How you feeling?"

"Tired."

"I left my blankets and stuff in the park. Let's go back."

"Okay." He started to put his arm around her—she took his hand in both of hers. She cupped his from the wrist, her fingers like orchid blades. Blades closed, and she held his little finger, his forefinger, kissed the horny palm, and would not look at his confusion. She kissed his knuckles, opening her lips, and lay her tongue there. Her breath warmed in the hair on his hand's back.

Her face was an inch away: he could feel the warmth of that too. In his reiterate curiosity, and his embarrassment, he offered, obliquely, "You know . . . the moon?"

She looked at him, still holding his fingers. "What moon?"

"I mean . . . when we saw the two moons. And what you were talking about. Their being different."

"Two moons?"

"Oh, come on now." He lowered his hand; hers lowered with it. "Remember when we came out of the bar?"

"Yes."

"And the night was all messed up and streaked?" He glanced at the enveloping sky, fused and blurred.

"Yes."

"What did you see?"

She looked puzzled. "The moon."

"How—" something awful at the base of his spine— "many?"—clawed to his neck.

Her head went to the side. "How *many?*"

"We were all standing outside the bar, and in the sky we saw . . ."

But she laughed and, laughing, dropped her face to his hand again. When she looked up, she halted the sound to question. "Hey?" And then, "Hey, I'm kidding you . . . ?"

"Oh," he said.

But she saw an answer that confused. "No, really, I'm just kidding. What were you going to say about it?"

"Huh?"

"You were about to say something?"

114

"Naw, it's nothing."

"But . . . ?"

"Don't do that again. Don't kid like that. Not . . . here."

She looked around too when he said that. Then pushed her face against his hand again. He moved his fingers between her lips. "I won't," she said, "if you'll let me do this," and slid her mouth around his wrecked thumb.

As expression releases the indicated emotion, as surface defines the space enclosed, he felt a strange warmth. It grew behind his face and made his breath shush out. "All right," he said, and, "Okay," and then, " . . . Yes," each more definite in meaning, each more tentatively spoken.

Tak pushed the door back hard enough to make the hinges howl. He walked up to the balustrade, fingering his fly and mumbling, "Shit!" saw Lanya and stopped. "Sorry. I gotta take a leak."

"What's the matter with *you?*" she asked the swaying Loufer.

"What's the *matter?* Tonight's trick isn't going to put out. Last night's is all caught up the biggest fag-hag in the city." His zipper hissed open. "Come on, I want to take a leak." He nodded to Lanya. "You can stay here, sweetheart. But he's gotta go away. I got this hangup. I'm piss-shy in front of men."

"Fuck off, Tak," he said, and started across the roof.

She caught up, her head down, making a sound he thought was crying. He touched her shoulder, and she looked up at him in the midst of a stifled giggle.

He sucked his teeth. "Let's go."

"What about Jack?" she asked.

"Huh? Fuck Jack. We're not going to take him with us."

"Oh, sure; I didn't mean . . ." And followed him toward the stairwell.

"Hey, good night, Tak," he called. "I'll see you around."

"Yeah," Loufer said from the cabin door, going in: the hair on his shoulder and the side of his head blazed with back-light.

"Good night," Lanya echoed.

The metal door grated.

A flight into the dark, she asked, "Are you mad at Tak . . . about something?" Then she said: "I mean, he's a sort of funny guy, sometimes. But he's—"

"I'm not mad at him."

"Oh." Their footsteps perforated the silence.

"I like him." His tone spoke decision. "Yeah, he's a good guy." The newspaper and the notebook were up under his arm.

She slipped her fingers through his in the dark; to keep from dropping the notebook, he had to hold her near.

At the bottom of the next flight, she asked, suddenly: "Do you care if you don't know who you are?"

At the bottom of the next, he said, "No." Then he wondered, from the way her footsteps quickened (his quickened to keep up) if that, like his hands, excited her.

She led him quickly and surely through the basement corridor—now the concrete was cold—and up. "Here's the door," she said, releasing him; she stepped away.

He couldn't see at all.

"Just a few stairs." She moved ahead.

He held the jamb unsteadily, slid his bare foot forward . . . onto board. With his other hand, he raised notebook and newspaper before his face, thrust his forearm out.

Ahead and below, she said, "Come on."

"Watch out for the edge," he said. His toes and the ball of his foot went over the board side and dangled. "And those damn meat hooks."

"Huh . . . ?" Then she laughed. "No—that's *across* the street!"

"The hell it is," he said. "When I came running out of here this morning, I nearly skewered myself."

"You must have gotten lost—" she was still laughing—"in the basement! Come on, it's just a couple of steps down."

He frowned in the dark (thinking: There *was* a lamp on this street corner. I saw it from the roof. *Why* can't I see anything . . .) let go the jamb, stepped . . . down: to another board, that squeaked. He still held his arm up before his face, feeling for the swaying prongs.

"One of the corridors in the basement," she explained, "goes under the street and comes up behind a door to the loading porch across from here. The first few

116

times I came to visit Tak, that happened to me too. The first time, you think you're losing your mind."

"Huh?" he said. "Under the . . . street?" He lowered his arm.

Maybe (the possibility came, as relieving as fresh air in these smoke-stifled alleys) he'd simply looked down from the roof on the wrong side; and *that* was why there was no street-light. His semiambidextrousness was always making him confuse left and right. He came down two more board steps, reached pavement.

He felt her take his wrist. "This way . . ."

She led him quickly through the dark, up and down curbs, from complete to near-complete darkness and back. It was more confusing than the basement corridors. "We're in the park, now, aren't we . . . ?" he asked, minutes on. Not only had he missed the entrance, but, at the moment he raised from his reveries to speak, he realized he did not know *how* many minutes on it was. Three? Thirteen? Thirty?

"Yes . . ." she said, wondering why he wondered.

They walked over soft, ashy earth.

"Here," she told him. "We've reached my place."

The trees rustled.

"Help me spread the blanket."

He thought: How can *she* see? A corner of blanket fell across his foot. He dropped to his knees and pulled the edge straight; felt her pull; felt her pull go slack.

"Take all your clothes off . . ." she said, softly.

He nodded, unbuttoned his shirt. He had known this was coming, too. Since when? This morning? New moons come, he thought, and all of heaven changes; still we silently machinate toward the joint of flesh and flesh, while the ground stays still enough to walk, no matter what above it. He unbuckled his pants, slipped out of them, and looked up to notice that he *could* see her a little, across the blanket, a blot moving furiously, rustling laces, jeans—a sneaker fell in grass.

He pushed off his sandal and lay down, naked, on his back, at the blanket's edge.

"Where are you . . . ?" she said.

"Here," but it sounded, shaking the mask of his face, more like a grunt.

She fell against him, her flesh as warm as sunlight in the dark, slipped on top of him. Her knees slid between his. Happily, his arms enclosed her; he laughed, and rocked her to the side, while she tried to find his mouth with hers, found it, pushed her tongue into it.

A heat, whose center was just behind his groin, built, layer around layer, till it seemed to fill him, knees to nipples. The bone behind her crotch hair moved on his hip while she clutched his shoulders—but he did not get an erection.

They rocked, kissed; he touched, then rubbed her breasts; she touched, then rubbed his hands rubbing her; they kissed and hugged, five? ten minutes? He grew apologetic. "I guess this isn't . . . well, I mean for you . . ."

Her head pulled back. "If you're worried about it," she said, "you've got toes, a tongue . . . fingers . . ."

He laughed—"Yeah."—and moved down: his feet, then his knees, went off the blanket into grass.

With two fingers, he touched her cunt. She reached down to press his hand against her. He dropped his mouth; she spread her fingers, her hair pressed out between them.

The odor, like a blow against his face, brought back —was it from Oregon?—an axe blade's first hack in some wet pine log. He thrust out his tongue.

And his cock dragged against the blanketing; the tenderer oval pushed forward in the loose hood.

She held his head, hard, with one hand; held his two fingers, hard against her hip, with her other.

He mapped the folds that fell, wetly out, with his tongue; and the grisly nut in the folded vortex, and the soft, granular trough behind it. She moved, and held her breath for half a minute, gasped, held it again; gasped. He let himself rub against the blanket, just a little, the way he used to masturbate when he was nine. Then he crawled up onto her; both her hands, thrust between her thighs, caught his cock: he pushed into her. Her arms fought from beneath him, to lock suddenly and tightly, on his neck. Holding her shoulders, he pushed, and retreated, and pushed again, slowly; pushed again. Her hips rolled under his. Her heels walked up the blanket, ankles against his thighs.

Finally, she clutched his fist, like a rock or a root-knob, too big for her fingers, first out from them— hunching and hunching, he pressed the back of her hand into grass; between her spread fingers, grass blades tickled his knuckles—then, as he panted and fell, and panted, she dragged it by jerks, to the blanket; dragged up the blanket; and finally held it against her cheek, her mouth, her chin.

His chin, wet and unshaven, slipped against her throat. He remembered how she had sucked his thumb before and, taking a curious dare, opened his fingers and thrust three into her mouth.

The realization, from her movement (her breaths were loud, long, and wet beside him, the underside of her tongue between his knuckles hot), that it was what she had wanted, made him, perhaps forty seconds after her, come.

He lay on her, shuddered; she squeezed his shoulders.

After a while, she practically woke him with: "Get off. You're heavy."

He lifted his chin. "Don't you . . . like to be held afterwards?"

"Yes." She laughed. "You're still heavy."

"Oh," and he rolled—taking her with him.

She squealed; the squeal became laughter as she ended up on top of him. Her face shook against his, still laughing. It was like something she was chewing very fast. He smiled.

"*You*'re not heavy," he said, and remembered her saying she was four or eight pounds overweight; it certainly wasn't with fat.

In the circle of his arms, she snuggled down; one hand stayed loose at his neck.

The contours of the ground were clear beneath his buttocks, back, and legs. And there was a pebble (or something, (under the blanket?) under his shoulder (or was it a prism on his chain) . . . there . . .

"You all right?"

"Mmm-hm." He got it into a depression in the ground; so it didn't bother him. "I'm fine."

He was drifting off, when she slid to his side, knees lapped with his shins, head sliding to his shoulder. She moved one hand on his belly beneath the chain. Her breath tickled the hair at the top of his chest. She said: "It's the kind of question you lose friends for . . . But I'm curious: Who do you like better in bed, Tak or me?"

He opened his eyes, looked down at what would be the top of her head; her hair brushed his face. He laughed into it, shortly and sharply: "Tak's been telling tales?"

"Back at the bar," she said, "while you were in the john." Actually, she sounded sleepy. "I thought he was joking. Then you said you'd been there in the morning."

"Mmmm." He nodded. "What did he say?"

"That you were cooperative. But basically a cold fish."

"Oh." He was surprised and felt his eyebrows, and his lower lip, raise. "What do *you* think?"

She snuggled, a movement that went from her cheek in his armpit (he moved his arm around her), down through her chest (he could feel one breast slide on his chest; one was pressed between them so tightly he wondered if it wasn't uncomfortable for her), to her hips (his cock rose from between his thighs and fell against his belly), to her knees (he clamped his together around hers) to her feet (he pushed his big toe between two of hers: and she held it). "Intense . . ." she said, pensively. "But I like that."

He put his other arm around her. "I like you better," and decided that he did. Suddenly he raised his head from the blanket, looked down at her again: "Hey . . . Do you have any birth-control stuff?"

She began to laugh, softly at first, her face turned into his shoulder, then out full, rolling away from him to her back, laughing in the dark.

"What's so funny?" He felt the length where she'd been as cold now as it had been warm.

"Yes. I *have* taken care of the birth-control . . . 'stuff,' as you put it." Her laughter went on, as light as leaf tipping leaf. "It's just your asking," she told him at last, "sounds so gallant. Like manners from another age and epoch. I'm not used to it."

"Oh," he said, still not quite sure he understood. And, anyway, he felt himself drifting again.

He wasn't sure if he actually slept, but came awake later with her arm moving sleepily against his; aroused, he turned to her, and at his movement, she pulled herself half on top of him: she had been lying there, already excited.

They made love again; and fell into sleep like stone —till one or the other of them moved; and once more they woke, clinging.

So they made love once more; then talked—about love, about moons ("You can't see them at all now," she

120

whispered. "Isn't that strange?"), about madness—and then made love again.

And slept again.
And woke.
And made love.
And slept.

Beginning in this tone, for us, is a little odd, but such news stands out, to your editor's mind, as *the* impressive occurrence in our eccentric history. Ernest Newboy, the most notable English-language poet to emerge from Oceana, was born in Auckland in 1916. Sent to school in England, at twenty-one (he tells us) he came back to New Zealand and Australia to teach for six years, then returned to Europe to work and travel.

Mr Newboy has been three times short-listed for the Nobel Prize, which, if he receives it, will make him one in a line of outstanding figures in the twin fields of diplomacy and letters which includes Asturias, St-John Perse, and Seferis. As a citizen of a comparatively neutral country, he has been visiting the United States at an invitation to sit on the United Nations Cultural Committee which has just adjourned.

Ernest Newboy is also the author of a handful of short stories and novellas, collected and published under the title *Stones* (Vintage Paperback, 434 pp., $1.95), including the often anthologized long story, *The Monument*, a disturbing and symbolic tale of the psychological and spiritual dissolution of a disaffected Australian intellectual who comes to live in a war-ravaged German town. Mr Newboy has told us that, though his popular reputation rests on that slim volume of incisive fiction (your editor's evaluation), he considers them essentially experiments of the three years following the close of the War when he passed through a period of disillusionment with his first literary commitment, poetry. If nothing else, the popularity of *Stones* and *The Monument* turned attention to the three volumes of poems published in the thirties and forties, brought together in *Collected Poetry 1950* (available in Great Britain from Faber and Faber). To repeat something of a catch-phrase that has been echoed by various critics: While writers about him caught the despair of the period surrounding the War, Newboy, more than any other, fixed it in such light that one can lucidly see in it the genesis of so much of the current crisis. From his early twenties, through today, Newboy has produced occasional, literary, and philosophical essays to fill several volumes. They are characterized by a precise and courageous vision. In 1969 he published the book-length poem *Pilgrimage*, abstruse, surreal, often surprisingly humorous, and, for all its apparent irreverence, a profoundly religious work. After several more volumes of essays, in 1977 the comparatively brief collection of shorter poems written in the thirty-odd years since the War, *Rictus*, appeared.

A quiet, retiring, scholarly man, Newboy has traveled for most of his life through Europe, North Africa, and the East. His work is studded with images from the Maori and the many cultures he has been exposed to and explored, with his particular personal insight.

Newboy arrived in Bellona yesterday morning and is indefinite about the length of his stay. His comment to us when asked about his visit was, after a reticent smile: "Well, a week ago I wasn't intending to come here at all. But I suppose I'm happy I did."

We are honored that a man with such achievement in English letters and a figure of such world admiration should.

"What are you doing?" she mumbled, turning from his side.

"Reading the paper." Grass creased his elbows. He had wiggled free of the blanket as far as his hips.

"Did it come out yet?" She raised her head in a haze of slept-in hair. "It isn't that late?"

"Yesterday's."

She dropped her head back. "That's the trouble with sleeping out. You can't do it past five o'clock in the morning."

"I bet it's eight." He spread the wrinkled page bottom.

"What—" opened her eyes and squinted—"you reading about?"

"Newboy. That poet."

"Oh, yeah."

"I met him."

"You did?" She raised her head again, then twisted, tearing blankets from his leg. "When?"

"Up at Calkins'."

She pulled up beside him, hot shoulder on his. Under the headline, NEW BOY IN TOWN, was a picture of a thin white-haired man in a dark suit with a narrow tie, sitting in a chair, legs crossed, looking as though there were too much light in his face. "You saw him?"

"When I got beat up. He came out and helped me. From New Zealand; it sounded like he had some sort of accent."

"*Told* you Bellona was a small town." She looked at the picture. "Hey, how come you didn't get inside then?"

"Somebody else was with him who raised a stink. A spade. Fenster. He's the civil rights guy or something?"

She blinked at him. "You really *are* out meeting everybody."

"I wish I hadn't met Fenster." He snorted.

"I told you about Calkins' country weekends. Only he has them seven days a week."

"How does he get time to write for the paper?"

She shrugged. "But he does. Or gets somebody to do it for him." She sat up to paw the blankets. "Where did my shirt go?"

He liked her quivering breasts.

"It's under there." He looked back at the paper, but did not read. "I wonder if he's ever had George up there?"

"Maybe. He did that interview thing."

"Mmmm."

Lanya dropped back to the grass. "Hell. It *isn't* past five o'clock in the morning. You know damn well it isn't."

"Eight," he decided. "Feels like eight-thirty," and followed her glance up to the close smoke over the leaves. He looked down again, and she was smiling, reaching for his head, pulling him, rocking, by the ears, down: He laughed on her skin. "Come on! Let me go!"

She hissed, slow. "Oh, I can for a while," caught her breath when his head raised, then whispered, "Sleep . . ." and put her forearm over her face. He lost

125

himself in the small bronze curls under her arm, and only loosened his eyes at faint barking.

He sat, puzzled. Barking pricked the distance. He blinked, and in the bright dark of his lids, oily motes exploded. Puzzlement became surprise, and he stood.

Blankets fell down his legs.

He stepped on the grass, naked in the mist.

Far away a dog romped and turned in the gap between hills. A woman followed.

Anticipatory wonder caught in the dizzy fatigue of morning and sudden standing.

The chain around his body had left red marks on the underside of his forearms and the front of his belly where he'd leaned.

He got on his pants.

Shirt open over tears of jewels, he walked down the slope. Once he looked back at Lanya. She had rolled over on her stomach, face in the grass.

He walked toward where the woman (the redhead, from the bar) followed behind Muriel.

He fastened one shirt button before she saw him. She turned on sensible walking shoes and said, "Ah, hello. Good morning."

Around her neck, the jewels were a cluttered column of light.

"Hi." He pulled his toes in in the grass, shy. "I saw your dog last night, at that bar."

"Oh yes. And I saw you. You look a little better this morning. Got yourself cleaned up. Slept in the park?"

"Yeah."

Where candlelight had made her seem a big-boned whore, smoke-light and a brown suit took all the meretricious from her rough, red hair and made her an elementary-school assistant principal.

"You walk your dog here?"

An assistant principal with a gaudy necklace.

"Every morning, bright and early . . . um, I'm going to the exit now."

"Oh," and then decided her tentativeness was invitation.

They walked, and Muriel ran up to sniff his hand, nip at it.

"Cut that out," she demanded. "Be a good dog."

Muriel barked once, then trotted ahead.

"What's your name?" he asked.

"Ah!" she repeated. "I'm Madame Brown. Muriel went over and barked at you last night, didn't she? Well, she doesn't mean anything by it."

"Yeah. I guess not."

"About all you need now is a comb—" she frowned at him—"and a towel, and you *will* be back in shape." She released her shrill and astounding laughter. "There's a public john over there where I always see the people from the commune going to wash up." Then she looked at him seriously. "You're *not* with the commune there, are you?"

"No."

"Do you want a job?"

"Huh?"

"At least you're not a long-hair," she said. "Not *very* long, anyway. I asked you if you wanted a job."

"I wear sandals," he said, "when I put anything on my feet at all."

"That's all right. Oh, heavens, *I* don't care! I'm just thinking of the people you'd be working for."

"What kind of work is it?"

"Mainly cleaning up, or cleaning out I suppose. You *are* interested, aren't you? They'll pay five dollars an hour, and those aren't the sort of wages you can sneeze at in Bellona right through here."

"Sure I'm interested!" He swallowed in surprise. "Where is it?"

They approached twin lions. Madame Brown put her hands behind her back. Muriel brushed the hem of her skirt. The glut of chain and glass could catch no glitter in this light. "It's a family. Do you know where the Labry Apartments are?" To his shaking head: "I guess you haven't been here very long. This family, now, they're nice, decent people. And they've been very helpful to me. I used to have my office over there. You know there was a bit of confusion at the beginning, a bit of damage."

"I heard about some of it."

"A lot of vandalism. Now that it's settled down some, they asked me if I knew some young man who would help them. You mustn't take the long-hair thing seriously. Just clean yourself up a little—though it probably isn't going to be very clean work. The Richards are fine people. They've just had a lot of trouble. We all have. Mrs Richards gets easily upset by . . . anything strange. Mr Richards perhaps goes a little too far in trying to protect her. They've got three very nice children."

He pushed his hair from his forehead. "I don't think it's going to grow too much in the next couple of days."

"There! You *do* understand!"

"It's a good job."

"Oh, it is. It certainly is." She stopped at the lions as though they marked some far more important boundary. "That's the Labry Apartments, up on 36th. It's the four hundred building. Apartment 17-E. Come up there any time in the afternoon."

"Today?"

"Certainly today. If you want the job."

"Sure." He felt relief from a pressure invisible till now through its ubiquitousness. He remembered the bread in the alley: its cellophane under the street lamp had flashed more than his or her fogged baubles. "You have an office there. What do you do?"

"I'm a psychologist."

"Oh," and didn't narrow his eyes. "I've been to psychologists. I know something about it, I mean."

"You do?" She touched the lion's cheek, not leaning. "Well, I think of myself as a psychologist on vacation right now." Mocking him a little: "I only give advice between the hours of ten and midnight, down at Teddy's. That's if you'll have a drink with me." But that mocking was friendly.

"Sure. If the job works out."

"Go on over when you get ready. Tell whoever's there that Mrs Brown—Madame Brown is the nickname they've given me at Teddy's, and since I saw you there I thought you might know me by it—that Mrs Brown told you to come up. Possibly I'll be there. But they'll put you to work."

"Five dollars an hour?"

"I'm afraid it isn't that easy to find trustworthy workers now that we've got ourselves into this thing." She tried to look straight up under her eyelids. "Oh no, people you can trust are getting rarer and rarer. And you!" Straight at him: "You're wondering how I can trust you? Well, I've seen you before. And you know, we really are at that point. I begin, really, to think it's too much. Really too much."

128

"Get your morning paper!"

"Muriel! Oh, now Muriel! Come back here!"

"Get your morning— Hey, there, dog. Quiet down. Down girl!"

"Muriel, come back here this instant!"

"Down! There. Hey, Madame Brown. Got your paper right here." Maroon bells flapping, Faust stalked across the street. Muriel danced widdershins about him.

"Hello, old girl."

"Good morning there," Madame Brown said, "It *is* about time for you to be along, Joaquim, isn't it?"

"Eleven-thirty, by the hands on the old church steeple." He cackled. "Hi there, hi there young fellow," handing one paper, handing another.

Madame Brown folded hers beneath her arm.

He let his dangle, while Faust howled to no one in particular, "Get your morning paper," and went on down the street. "Bye, there, Madame. Good morning. Get your paper!"

"Madame Brown?" he asked, distrusting his resolve. She was looking after the newspaper man.

"What are those?"

She looked at him with perfect blankness.

"I've got them." He touched his chest. "And Joaquim's got a little chain tight around his neck."

"I don't know." With one hand, she touched her own cheek, with the other, her own elbow: her sleeve was some cloth rough as burlap. "You know, I'm really not sure. I like them. I think they're pretty. I like having a lot of them."

"Where did you get them?" he asked, aware he broke the custom Faust had so carefully defined the day before. Hell, he was still uneasy with her dog, and with her transformation between smoke and candlelight.

"A little friend of mine gave them to me." She had the look, yes, of someone trying not to look offended.

He shifted, let his knees bend a little, his toes go, nodded.

"Before she left the city. She left me, left the city. And she gave me these. You see?"

He'd asked. And felt better for the violence done, moved his arms from the shoulder . . . his laughter surprised him, broke out and became huge.

Over it, he heard her sudden high howl. With her

fist on her chest, she laughed too, "Oh, yes!" squinting.
"She did! She really did. I was never so surprised in all
my life! Oh, it was funny—I don't mean funny peculiar,
though it certainly was. Everything was, back then. But
it was funny ha-ha-ha. Ha-ha-ha-haaaaa." She shook
the sound about her. "She—" almost still—"brought them
to me in the dark. People shouting around out in the
halls, and none of the lights working. Just the flickering
coming around the edge of the shades, and the terrible
roaring outside . . . Oh, I was scared to death. And she
brought them to me, in handfuls, wound them around
my neck. And her eyes . . ." She laughed again, though
that cut all smile from him. "It *was* strange. She wound
them around my neck. And then she left. There." She
looked down over the accordion of her neck, and picked
through the loops. "I wear them all the time." The accordion opened. "What do they mean?" She blinked at
him. "I don't know. People who wear them aren't too
anxious to talk about them. I'm certainly not." She
leaned a little closer. "You're not either. Well, I'll respect
that in you. You do the same." Now she folded her hands.
"But I'll tell you something: And, really, there's no reason
behind it, I suppose, other than that it seems to work.
But I *trust* people who have them just a little more than
those who don't." She shrugged. "Probably very silly.
But it's why I offered you that job."

"Oh."

"I suspect we share something."

"Something happened," he said, "when we got them.
Like you said. That we don't like to talk about."

"Then again, it could be nothing more than that we
happen to be wearing the same . . ." She rattled the longest
strand.

"Yeah." He buttoned another button. "It could be."

"Well. I'll drop in on you at the Richards' later in
the afternoon. You *will* be there?"

He nodded. "Four hundred, on 36th Street . . ."

"Apartment 17-E," she finished. "Very good. Muriel?"

The dog clicked back from the gutter.

"We'll be going now."

"Oh. Okay. And thanks."

"Perfectly welcome. Perfectly welcome. I'm sure."
Madame Brown nodded, then ambled down the street.
Muriel caught up, to circle her, this time diesel.

He walked barefoot through the grass, expectation and confusion bobbling. Anticipation of labor loosened tensions in his body. At the fountain, he let the water spurt in his eyes before he flooded and slushed, with collapsing cheeks, water between filmed teeth. With his forearm he blotted the tricklings, squeegeed his eyelids with rough, toad-wide fingers, then picked up his paper, and, blinking wet lashes, went back up to the trees.

Lanya still lay on her belly. He sat on the drab folds. Her feet, toes in, stuck from under the blanket. An olive twist lay over the trough of her spine, shifting with breath. He touched her wrinkled instep, moved his palm to her smooth heel. He slid his first and second finger on either side of the tendon there. The heel of his hand pushed back the blanket from her calf, slowly, smoothly, all the way till pale veins tangled on the back of her knee. His hand lay on the slope of her thigh.

Her calves were smooth.

His heart, beating fast, slowed.

Her calves were unscarred.

He breathed, and with it was the sound of air in the grass around.

Her calves had no scratch.

When he took his hand away, she made some in-slumber sound and movement. And didn't wake. He opened today's paper and put it on top of yesterday's. Under the date, July 17, 1969, was the headline:

MYSTERIOUS RUMORS, MYSTERIOUS LIGHTS. Would your editor *ever* like some pictures with this one! We, unfortunately, were asleep. But from what we can gather, shortly after midnight last night—so far twenty-six versions of the story have come in, with contradictions enough to oblige our registering an official editorial doubt—the fog and smoke blanketing Bellona these last months was torn by a wind at too great an altitude to feel at street level. Parts of the sky were cleared, and the full —or near full—moon was, allegedly, visible—as well as a crescent moon, only slightly smaller (or slightly larger?) than the first!

The excited versions from which we have culled our own report contain many discrepancies. Here are some: The full orb was the usual moon, the crescent was the intruder.

The crescent was the real moon, the full, the impostor . . . a young student says that, in the few minutes

131

these downright Elizabethan portents were revealed, he made out markings on the full disk that prove it was definitely not *our* moon.

Two hours later, someone came into the office (the only person so far who claims to have caught any of this phenomenon through an admittedly low-power telescope) to assure us the full disk definitely was *the* moon, while the crescent was bogus.

In the six hours since the occurrence (as we write, into the dawn), explanations offered the *Times* have ranged from things so science-fiction-y we do not pretend to understand their arcane machinery, down to the all-purpose heat lightning and weather balloon, perennial explanation for the UFO.

I pass on, as typical, one comment from our own Professor Wellman, who was observing from the July gardens with several other guests: "One, we all agreed, was nearly full; the other was definitely crescent. I pointed out to the Colonel, Mrs Green, and Roxanne and Tobie, who were with me, that the crescent, which was lower in the sky, was convexed *away* from the bright area of the higher moon. Moons do not light themselves; their illumination comes from the sun. Even with *two* moons, the sun can only be in *one* direction from them both; no matter which phases they are in, if they are both visible in the same quarter of the sky, *both* should be light on the *same* side—which was not the case here."

To which your editor can only say that *any* "agreement," "certainty," or "definiteness" about these moons are cast into serious doubt—unless we are prepared to make even *more* preposterous speculations about the rest of the cosmos?

No.

We did not see it.

Which leaves us, finally, in this editorial position: We are *sure* something happened in the sky last night. But to venture what it was would be absurd. Brand new moons do not appear. In the face of the night's hysteria, we should like to point out, quietly, that whatever happened is explicable: things are—though this, admittedly, is no guarantee we shall ever have the explication.

What seems, both oddly and interestingly, to have been agreed on by *all* who witnessed, and must therefore be accepted by all who did not, is the name for this new light in the night: George!

The impetus to appelation we can only guess at; and what we guess at we do not approve of. At any rate, on the rails of rumor, greased with apprehension, the name had spread the city by the time the first report reached us. The only final statement we can make with surety: Shortly after midnight, the moon and something called George, easy enough to mistake for a moon, shone briefly on Bellona.

"What are you doing," she whispered through leaves, "now?"

Silent, he continued.

She stood, shedding blankets, came to touch his shoulder, looked down over it. "Is that a poem?"

He grunted, transposed two words, gnawed at his thumb cuticle, then wrote them back.

"Um . . ." she said, "do you mean making a hole through something, or telling the future?"

"Huh?" He tightened his crossed legs under the notebook. "Telling the future."

"A-u-g-*u*-r."

"Whoever wrote this notebook spells it different on another page." He flipped pages across his knees to a previous, right-hand entry:

A word sets images flying from which auguries
we read . : .

"Oh . . . he *did* spell it right." Back on the page where he had been writing, he crossed and recrossed his own kakograph till the bar of ink suggested a word beneath half again as long.

"Have you been reading in there?" She kneeled beside him. "What do you think?"

"Hm?"

"I mean . . . the guy who wrote that was strange."

He looked at her. "I've just been using it to write my own things. It's the only paper I've got and he leaves one side of each page blank." His back slumped. "Yeah. He's strange," but could not understand her expression.

Before he could question it with one of his, she asked, "Can I read what you're doing?"

He said, "Okay," quickly to see what it would feel like.

"Are you sure it's all right?"

"Yeah. Go on. It's finished anyway."

He handed her the notebook: his heart got loud; his tongue dried stickily to the floor of his mouth. He contemplated his apprehension. Little fears at least, he thought, were amusing. This one was large enough to joggle the whole frame.

Clicking his pen point, he watched her read.

Blades of hair dangled forward about her face like orchid petals, till—"Stop that!"—they flew back.

They fell again.

He put the pen in his shirt pocket, stood up, walked around, first down the slope, then up, occasionally glancing at her, kneeling naked in leaves and grass, feet sticking, wrinkled soles up, from under her buttocks. She would say it was silly, he decided, to show her independence. Or she would Oh and Ah and How wonderful it to death, convinced that would bring them closer. His hand was at the pen again—he clicked it without taking it from his pocket, realized what he was doing, stopped, swallowed, and walked some more. *Lines on Her Reading Lines on Her* he pondered as a future title, but gave up on what to put beneath it; that was too hard without the paper itself, its light red margin, its pale blue grill.

She read a long time.

He came back twice to look at the top of her head. And went away.

"It . . ."

He turned.

". . . makes me feel . . . odd." Her expression was even stranger.

"What," he risked, "does that mean?" and lost: it sounded either pontifical or terrified.

"Come here . . . ?"

"Yeah." Crouching beside her, his arm knocked hers; his hair brushed hers as he bent. "What . . . ?"

Bending with him, she ran her finger beneath a line. "Here, where you have the words in reverse order from the way you have them up here—I think, if somebody had just described that to me, I wouldn't have found it very interesting. But actually reading it—all four times —it gave me chills. But I guess that's because it works

135

so well with the substance. Thank you." She closed the notebook and handed it back. Then she said, "Well don't look so surprised. Really, I liked it. Let's see: I'm . . . delighted at its skill, and moved by its . . . well, substance. Which is surprising, because I didn't think I was going to be." She frowned. "Really, you . . . *are* staring something fierce, and it makes me nervous as hell." But she wouldn't look down.

"You just like it because you know me." That was also to see what it felt like.

"Possibly."

He held the notebook very tight, and felt numb.

"I guess—" she moved away a little—"somebody liking it or not doesn't really do you any good."

"Yeah. Only you're scared they won't."

"Well, I did." She started to say more, didn't. Was that a shrug? Finally, she looked from beneath the over-hanging limbs. "Thank you."

"Yeah," he said almost with relief. Then, as though suddenly remembering: "Thank *you!*"

She looked back, confusion working through her face toward some other expression.

"Thank you," he repeated, inanely, palms pressing the notebook to his denim thighs, growing wet. "Thank you."

The other expression was understanding.

His hands worked across each other like crabs, crawled round himself to hug his shoulders. His knees came up (the notebook dropped between them) to bump his elbows. A sudden, welling of . . . was it pleasure? "I got a job!" His body tore apart; he flopped, spread-eagle, on his back. "Hey, I got a job!"

"Huh?"

"While you were asleep." Pleasure rushed outward into hands and feet. "That lady in the bar last night; she came by with her dog and gave me this job."

"Madame Brown? No kidding. What kind of job?" She rolled to her stomach beside him.

"For this family. Named Richards." He twisted, be-cause the chain was gnawing his buttocks. Or was it the notebook's wire spiral? "Just cleaning out junk."

"Well there's certainly enough junk—" she reached down, tugged the book loose from beneath his hip —"around Bellona to clean out." She lay it above his head, propped her chin on her forearms. "A pearl," she mused. "Katherine Mansfield once described San Francisco, in a letter to Murray, as living on the inside of a pearl. Because of all the fog." Beyond the leaves, the sky was darkly luminous. "See." Her head fell to the side. "I'm literate too."

"I don't think—" he frowned—"I've ever heard of Katherine . . . ?"

"Mansfield." Then she raised her head: "Was the reference in the thing you wrote, to that Mallarmé poem . . ." She frowned at the grass, started tapping her fingers. "Oh, what *is* it . . . !"

He watched her trying to retrieve a memory and wondered at the process.

"*Le Cantique de Saint Jean!* Was *that* on purpose?"

"I've read some Mallarmé . . ." He frowned. "But just in those Portuguese translations Editora Civilizaçáo put out . . . No, it wasn't on purpose I don't think . . ."

"Portuguese." She put her head back down. "To be sure." Then she said: "It *is* like a pearl. I mean here in Bellona. Even though it's all smoke, and not fog at all."

He said: "Five dollars an hour."

She said: "Hm?"

"That's what they're going to pay me. At the job."

"What do you want with five dollars an hour?" she asked, quite seriously.

Which seemed so silly, he decided not to insult her by answering.

"The Labry Apartments," he went on. "Four hundred, Thirty-Sixth Street, apartment seventeen-E. I'm supposed to go up there this afternoon." He turned to look at her. "When I come back, we could get together again . . . maybe at that bar?"

She watched him a moment. "You want to get together again, don't you." Then she smiled. "That's nice."

"I wonder if it's late enough to think about going over there?"

"Make love to me once more before you go."

He scrunched his face, stretched. "Naw. I made love to you the last two times." He let his body go, glanced at her. "You make love to *me* this time."

Her frown fell away before, laughing, she leaned on his chest.

He touched her face.

Then her frown came back. "You washed!" She looked surprised.

137

He cocked his head up at her. "Not very much. In the john down there, I splashed some water on my face and hands. Do you mind?"

"No. I wash, myself, quite thoroughly, twice—occasionally even *three* times a day. I was just surprised."

He walked his fingers across her upper lip, beside her nose, over her cheek—like trolls, he thought, watching them.

Her green eyes blinked.

"Well," he said, "it's not something I've ever been exactly famous for. So don't worry."

Just as if she had forgotten the taste of him and was curious to remember, she lowered her mouth to his. Their tongues blotted all sound but breath while, for the . . . fifth time? Fifth time, they made love.

The glass in the right-hand door was unbroken.

He opened the left: a web of shadows swept on a floor he first thought was gold-shot, blue marble. His bare foot told him it was plastic. It *looked* like stone . . .

The wall was covered with woven, orange straw— no, the heel of his palm said that was plastic too.

Thirty feet away, in the center of the lobby—lighting fixtures, he finally realized—a dozen grey globes hung, all different heights, like dinosaur eggs.

From what must have been a pool, filled with chipped, blue rock, a thin, ugly, iron sculpture jutted. Passing nearer, he realized it wasn't a sculpture at all, but a young, dead tree.

He hunched his shoulders, hurried by.

The "straw"-covered partitioning wall beside him probably hid mailboxes. Curious, he stepped around it.

Metal doors twisted and gaped—like three rows, suddenly swung vertical (the thought struck with unsettling immediacy), of ravaged graves. Locks dangled by a screw, or were missing completely. He passed along them, stopping to look at one or another defaced nameplate, bearing the remains of *Smith, Franklin, Howard* . . .

On the top row, three from the end, a single box had either been repaired, or never prised: *Richards: 17-E*, white letters announced from the small, black window. Behind the grill slanted the red, white and blue edging of an airmail envelope.

He came out from the other side of the wall, hurried across the lobby.

One elevator door was half-open on an empty shaft, from which drifted hissing wind. The door was coated to look like wood, but a dent at knee level showed it was black metal. While he squatted, fingering the edge of the depression, something clicked: a second elevator door beside him rolled open.

He stood up, stepped back.

There were no lights in the other car.

Then the door on the empty shaft, as if in sympathy, also finished opening.

Holding his breath and his notebook tight, he stepped into the car.

"17" lit his fingertip orange. The door closed. The number was the only light. He rose. He wasn't exactly afraid; all emotion was in super solution. But anything, he understood over his shallow breath, might set it in fantastic shapes.

"17" went out: the door opened on dimness.

At one end of the beige hall, an apartment door stood wide; grey light smoked through. At the other, in the ceiling-globe, at least one bulb worked.

He passed 17-B, 17-C, 17-D, nearing the globe.

After the third ring, (and practically a minute between) he decided to leave: And walk down the steps, because the pitch dark elevator was too spooky.

"Hello . . . ? Who is it . . . ?"

"Madame—Mrs Brown sent me."

"Oh." Things rattled. The door rasped on two inches of chain. A woman perhaps just shy of fifty, with shadowed hair and pale eyes, looked at him above the links. "You're the young man she said she'd send to help?"

"Yeah."

"Oh," she repeated. "Oh," closed the door and opened it again without the chain. "Oh."

He stepped in on green carpet. She stepped back to look at him; he began to feel uncomfortable, and dirty, and nervous.

"Edna told you what we wanted?"

"Cleaning," he said. "You've got some junk to move?"

"And moving—"

Two thuds, and two men's loud laughing was joined by a woman's.

They both looked down at the Acrolan.

"—to an apartment higher up in the building," she said. "The floors, the walls of these buildings are so thin,

139

Everything goes through. Everything." When she looked up, he thought: Why is she so uncomfortable . . . am I making her uncomfortable? She said, "We want you to help clear out the place upstairs. It's on the nineteenth floor, at the other end of the hall. It has a balcony. We thought that would be nice. We don't have a balcony in this apartment."

"Hey, Momma, is—"

He recognized her when she was half into the hall. "Yes, June?"

"Oh . . ." which wasn't recognition, though she held the wall and blinked at him. Her yellow hair swung to hit her shoulders. She frowned by the green wall, just paler than the carpet. "Is Bobby here?"

"I sent him down for some bread."

"Oh," again, and into her room.

"I'm," pausing till he looked back at her, "Mrs Richards. My husband, Arthur, will be here very soon now. But come in, and I'll explain just what we want done."

The living room was all picture windows. Beyond half-raised Venetian blinds, a hill of patchy grass rolled between several brick high-rises.

"Why don't you sit—" her finger fell from her chin to point—"there."

"I didn't get a chance to wash too well, this morning, and I'm pretty messy," then realized that was just the reason she'd picked that particular chair. "No thanks."

"You're living . . . ?"

"In the park."

"Sit down," she said. "Please. Please sit down."

He sat, and tried not to pull his bare foot behind sandal.

She balanced at the edge of the L-shaped couch. "19-A where we want to move is, well frankly, a mess. The apartment itself is in good condition, the walls, the windows—so many windows got broken. We wrote to Management. But I wouldn't be surprised if they've lost the letter. Everything's so inefficient. So many people have left."

A rattling, with thumps, moved outside in the hall: Then, someone punched the door!

While he tried to fix his surprise, tattered whispers outside raveled with laughter.

Mrs Richards sat straight, eyes closed, small knuckles against her stomach, her other hand mashing the couch.

The loose flesh between the ligaments over her collar pulsed either with slow heart beats or quick breathing.

"Ma'am . . . ?"

She swallowed, stood up.

They punched again: he could see the chain shake.

"Go away!" Her hands were claws now. "Go away! I said go away!"

Footsteps—three or four pair, one, high heels—chattered to echo.

"Mother . . . ?" June rushed in.

Mrs Richards opened her eyes, her mouth, and took a breath. "They've done that—" turning to him—"twice today. Twice. They only did it once yesterday."

June kept raising her knuckle to her mouth. Behind her the wall was covered with rough green paper, shelves of plants in brass pots, unwaterably high.

"We're going to move into another apartment." Mrs Richards took another breath and sat. "We wrote to Management. We haven't got an answer, but we're going to anyway."

He put his notebook on the table beside the chair and looked at the door. "Who are they?"

"I don't know. I don't know; I don't care. But they're about—" she paused to pull herself together —"about to drive me mad. I think they're . . . children. They've gotten into the apartment downstairs. So many people have left. We're going to move upstairs."

June kept looking over her shoulder. Her mother said: "It must be very difficult for you, living in the park."

He nodded.

"You've known Mrs Brown a while? It's nice of her to send somebody to help. She goes out, meets people. Myself, I just don't feel safe walking around the city."

"Mother hardly ever goes out," June said, very fast, yet still with the hesitancy he remembered from last night.

"It isn't safe, and I don't see any reason for a woman to take that sort of chance. Perhaps if I were someone else I wouldn't feel that way." She smiled. Her hair was salted brown, recently and simply done. "How long can you work?"

"As long as you want, I guess."

"I mean how many hours? Today?"

"The rest of the day, if you want. It's pretty late now. But I'll come earlier tomorrow."

"I'm talking about the light."

"Light?"

"The lights aren't working in most of the apartments."

"Oh, yeah. Well, I'll work till it gets dark. What time is it now?"

"The clocks." Mrs Richards turned up her hands. "The clocks have stopped."

"Your electricity's out?"

"All except one outlet in the kitchen. For the refrigerator. And that goes off too sometimes."

"In the hall, there's a light on. And the elevator's working. You could run a cheater in."

Mrs Richards looked puzzled.

"An extension cord. From the hall light, into your apartment. That would give you some electricity."

"Oh." Lines deepened in her forehead. "But then we'd lose the hall light, wouldn't we? We have to have some light in the hall. That would be just too—"

"You get a double socket. You put a bulb in one and run a cord from the other, under the door."

"From the hall?"

"Yeah. That's what I was talking about."

"Oh." She shook her head. "But the hall lights aren't on our utilities bill. Management wouldn't be very happy about that. They're strict here. You see, the hall lights, they're on another—" Her hands fluttered—"meter. I don't think we could do that. If someone saw . . ." She laughed. "Oh no, this isn't that kind of place."

"Oh," he said. "Well, you're moving. So I guess you don't have to. The apartment you're going to has electricity?"

"One of the things we have to find out. I don't know yet." Her hands went back together in her lap. "Oh, I *hope* it does!"

"I'll work till it gets dark, Mrs Richards."

"Very good. Oh, yes, that'll be fine. At least you'll be able to get started today."

"Maybe you better ask your husband about the extension cord. I could do it for you. I used to be a super."

"Did you?"

"Yeah. And I could do it, no trouble."

"I will . . ." She pinched at her skirt, noticed, then smoothed it. "But I don't think Management would go along with that. Oh no, I don't think so at all."

142

The door bell rang twice.

"That's Bobby!" from June.

"*Ask* who it is!"

"Who is it?"

Muffled: "Me."

The chain rattled loose.

"Okay, I got your—"

June interrupted him: "You know they came back and did it again! You didn't see anybody, in the halls, did you?"

"No . . . ?" Bobby's questioning was toward the living room. "Who's he?"

Bobby (fourteen?) was holding a loaf of bread too tightly. Around his left wrist, in a bright bracelet, were half a dozen loops of the optical chain.

"Come in, Bobby. This is a young man Edna Brown sent over."

"Gee." Bobby stepped into the living room. Blond as his sister, where her features suggested shyness, his sharper nose, his fuller mouth hinted belligerence. Under his arm was a newspaper. "Are you just living out in the street, huh?"

He nodded.

"You want to use the bathroom or wash or something?"

"Bobby!" from June.

"Maybe," he said.

Mrs Richards laughed. "Isn't it rather difficult for you, and dangerous?"

"You . . . have to keep your eyes open." That sounded inane enough.

"We'll go upstairs and look around."

"I wanna stay and read the—"

"We'll go together, Bobby. All of us."

"Oh, Bobby," June said, "come *on!*"

Bobby stalked through the living room, threw the paper at the coffee table, said, *"Okay,"* and went into the kitchen. "I have to put the bread away first."

"Well, *put* it away," Mrs Richards said. "Then we'll go."

"I could only find half a loaf," Bobby called.

"Did you *ask* for a whole one?" Mrs Richards called. "I'm sure if you asked them politely for a whole loaf, they would have tried to find one for—"

"There wasn't anybody in the store."

"Oh, *Bobby*—"

"I *left* the money."

"But you should have waited for somebody to come back. Suppose someone had seen you going out. *They* wouldn't have known you'd—"

"I did wait. Why do you think I was gone so long. Hey, this has got mold in it."

"Oh, *nooo*," Mrs Richards cried.

"Not a *lot*," from the kitchen. "Just a little spot on one corner."

"Does it go all the way through?"

"It's on the second slice. And the third—"

"Oh stop tearing in it!" Mrs Richards exclaimed, punched the cushion, stood, and followed her son into the kitchen. "Let me see."

Perhaps it was the discomforting lucidity centered in the recapitulation: he said to June: "Last night, did you ever find—?"

Cellophane rattled from the kitchen.

By the door frame, June's eyes widened in recognition—finally. Her forefinger brushed her lips awkwardly for silence, brushed, and brushed again, till it wiped all meaning from the gesture.

She blinked.

The cellophane rattled.

Bobby came out, sat in front of the coffee table, and pulled the paper onto his lap. When he saw his sister, he cocked his head, frowning, then looked back at the paper, while June's hand worked down the front of her sweater to her lap.

"It's through," announced Mrs Richards. "All the way through. Well, it isn't very large. Beggars can't be choosers." She came into the living room. "We can cut it out, and all have sandwiches with little rings in them. We *are* all beggars till this thing gets straightened out, you know. Are you reading that again?"

Mrs Richards put a fist against her hip.

Bobby did not look up.

"What is it talking about today?" in a gentler tone. The fist dropped.

Bobby read on.

He said, "That whole business last night, with the moons."

"What?"

144

June offered, "I . . . I told you, Mother. Last night, when I went out—"

"Oh, yes. And I told you, June, I didn't like that. I didn't like that at all. We'd better go upstairs. Bobby?" who only grunted.

"Some people said they saw two moons in the sky." He stood up from his chair. "They named one of them George," and didn't watch June but the back of Bobby's head; and knew June reacted anyway.

"Two moons in the sky?" Mrs Richards asked. "Now who said they saw that?"

"Calkins doesn't say," Bobby mumbled.

"The guy who wrote the article didn't see them," he told Mrs Richards.

"Two moons?" Mrs Richards asked again. "June, when you came in, you didn't say anything about—"

June had left the room.

"June! June, we've got to go upstairs!"

"Do I *have* to come too?" Bobby asked.

"Yes, you *have* to!"

Bobby folded the paper loudly.

"June!" Mrs Richards called again.

He followed mother and boy to the door, where June waited. While Mrs Richards opened first the upper, then the lower, at last the middle lock, June's eyes, perfectly round, swept his, implored, and closed.

"*There* we are."

All blinking for different reasons, they entered the hall. He followed till Mrs Richards announced, "Now," and continued, "I want you—what *is* your name?—to walk up in front."

It was surprisingly easy to say, "Kidd," as he stepped around the children.

"Pardon?" Mrs Richards asked.

"Kidd. Like Captain Kidd."

"Like Billy the Kid?" Bobby asked.

"Yeah."

"Neither of them were too terribly nice people," said June.

"The Cisco Kid," Bobby said. Then, with raised eyebrows and small smile, droll as an adult of thirty: "Pow, pow . . . ?"

"Bobby, stop!"

He walked with Mrs Richards. Her heels clunked; his sandal lisped, his bare foot hardly whispered.

As they reached the elevators there was noise above. They looked at the stairwell door with its wire-webbed glass and *EXIT* in red letters across it. Trundling footsteps grew louder—

(His hand pressed against his leg, across one turn of chain.)

—grew louder still, till shadows crossed the glass. The footsteps, dropping below, softened.

Mrs Richards' hand, grey as twigs from fire, hung against the wall by the elevator bell. "Children," she said. "It must be children. They run up and down the stairs, in the hall, banging on the walls, the doors. They don't show themselves, you know. That's because they're afraid." Her voice, he realized, was hoarse with terror. "They're afraid of us. They don't have to be. We're not going to hurt them. I just wish they wouldn't do that. That's all. I just wish they wouldn't."

Two separate elevators opened.

From one a man said, "Oh," a little gruffly. "Honey. It's you. Scared me to death. Where're you going?"

From the other came a faint wind, from a long way up or a long way down.

"Arthur! Oh, Arthur, this is Kidd! Edna Brown sent him to help. We're taking him to see the new apartment."

He shook the large, moist hand.

"Pleased," Arthur Richards said. The closing door *k-chunked* his shoulder, retreated, then tried to close again.

"Edna sent him over to help us with the cleaning and the moving."

"Oh. Edna coming over later?"

"She said she'd try this afternoon, Mr Richards."

K-chunk.

"Good. Hey, let's get in this thing before it knocks me down." Mr Richards guffawed. His white collar made folds in his fleshy neck. His hair was so pale, possible white was lost in the gloom. "Sometimes I think this thing doesn't like me. Come in."

K-chunk.

They ducked before the door swung them into darkness.

"19" hung, orange, on the black.

"Arthur," Mrs Richards said in the humming dark, "they've been running in the hall, again. They came and beat on the door. Twice. Once this morning, and once right after Kidd came. Oh, I was *so* glad he was there!"

"That's all right, honey," Mr Richards reassured. "That's why we're moving."

"Management has just got to do something. You say you *have* been down to the office and told them?"

"I've been down. I told them. They said they're having difficulty right through here. You've got to understand that, sweetheart. We're all having difficulty."

June breathed beside him. She was the closest person to him in the elevator.

"You'd know how upsetting it was if you ever heard it, Arthur. I don't see why you can't take a day off of work. Just so you'd know."

"I'm sure it's upsetting."

The door opened; in the hall he could see two ceiling globes were working.

Mrs Richards looked across her husband's chest. "They wouldn't do it if Arthur was home."

"Where do you work, Mr Richards?" he asked as they got out.

"MSE . . . Maitland Systems Engineering. Honey, I wish I could take off from work. But things are even more confused there than they are here. This just isn't the time for it. Not now."

Mrs Richards sighed and took out a key. "I know, dear. You're sure Management said it would be all right?"

"I told you, honey, I got the key from them."

"Well, they never answered my letter. They answered in two days when I wrote them last year about the plaster in June's bedroom." The key went in with a sound like gravel. "Anyway—" she looked across Mr Richards' chest again—"this is where we're going to move to."

She strode into the pale blue room through rattling mountains of brown paper. "The lights," she said. "Try the lights."

Mr Richards and June and Bobby waited in the doorway.

He stepped inside, flicked the switch.

The ceiling light flared, went *Pppp!*, and out.

June, behind him, let a small cry.

"That's only the bulb. At least you have some power."

"Oh, we can fix that," Mr Richards said and came inside. "Come on, kids. Get inside now."

June and Bobby squeezed through shoulder to shoulder, but remained sentinel at the jambs.

"What else has to go beside this paper?"

"Well." Mrs Richards righted a cane bottom chair. "There're the other rooms, furniture and stuff." Brown paper roared about her shins. "All sorts of junk. And the dirt. And then of course, we'll have to move our things."

Blinds, fallen from one fixture, dangled their crushed aluminum slats to the floor. "Just take those all down. It'll be a nice apartment when it's clean."

"Did you know the people who lived here before?"

"No," Mrs Richards said. "No. We didn't know them. Now all you have to do is clean these out." She walked into the kitchen and opened a broom closet. "Mop, pail, *Spic-n'-span*. Everything." She came back. "There's all *sorts* of things in the other rooms."

"What were they doing with all this paper?"

"I dunno," Bobby said uneasily from the doorway.

Stepping into the lichenous leaves, his bare foot came down on wood, wire, glass: *krak!* He jerked his foot, kicking away paper.

The break in the cover-glass went through both faces: framed in black wood, husband and wife, bearded and coiffed, posed in nineteen-hundred clothing. He picked it up from the papers. The loose glass ground.

"What's that?" Mrs Richards asked, stepping around more overturned furniture.

"I guess I broke it," trying to feel, without looking, if he had cut his foot.

Between the parents, in matching sailor suits, a sister and her two brothers (one younger, one older) looked serious and uncomfortable.

"It was just lying on the floor."

Mrs Richards took it from him. The hanging-wire rattled on the cardboard backing. "Isn't that something. Who do you suppose *they* are?"

"The people who lived here before—?" June stepped up, then laughed. "Oh, it couldn't be. It's so *old!*"

"Daddy," Bobby said from the doorway.

"Yes?"

"I think Kidd wants to use the bathroom."

June and Mrs Richards both turned.

"I mean," Bobby said, "he's just been living in the park, and stuff; he's real dirty."

Mrs Richards sucked her teeth and June only just did not say, "Oh, *Bobby!*"

Mr Richards said, "Well . . ." smiling, and then, "Um . . ." and then, "Well . . . sure."

"I am sort of scroungy," he admitted. "I could use a washup, after I finish work up here."

"Sure," Mr Richards repeated, heartily. "I've got a razor you can use. Mary'll give you a towel. Sure."

"In *this* room—" Mrs Richards had leaned the photograph against the wall and was trying to open a door now—"I don't know *what* they put in this room."

He went to take the knob. Something scraped as he shoved the door in a few inches. A few inches more and he could peer: "Furniture, ma'am. I think the whole room is filled up with furniture."

"Oh, dear . . ."

"I can squeeze in there and get it out."

"Are you sure—?"

"Why don't you all just go downstairs? I can get started on this. It's got to be neat and clean. It's a mess now. There's not too much you have to show me."

"Well, I suppose . . ."

"Come on, Mary. Let the boy get to work."

He went back to the front room and began to push the paper over to one side of the room.

"Bobby, come on back from there. I don't want you getting in trouble."

"*Mom*ma . . ."

The door closed: . . . the boy? Well, he was used to having his age misjudged. (Where do they want me to put this crap!) He turned around and, with his sandal, stepped on something else. He kicked back paper: a kitchen fork.

He put his notebook on the chair Mrs Richards had set right, and began to fold the wrapping paper to yard-square packets. Out there on the balcony, he could toss it over. Shit-colored angel flakes? And the furniture: crash! No, can't do that very well. Drag all that junk to the elevator, drop a traveling furnished room to the cellar. Punch around in the basement dark with it? Beating on the wall, thumping on the floor? Not that either. Put it all on one side of the room, sweep and scrub, then all to the other. Burn it in the middle? What *does* she expect?

At any rate, in ten minutes, half the floor was clear.

On the black (with white marbling) vinyl, he'd already uncovered a saucer filmed with dried coffee; *Time* with a wrinkled cover he recognized from several years back; some paint-crusted rags—

The knock made him jump.

June called, "It's just me . . ."

When he opened the door, she stepped in with a bottle of Coke in one hand, in the other a plate with a sandwich. The sandwich had a hole at one side. She thrust them out and said: "Please, don't say anything about last night, at the bar! Please! Please?"

"I didn't say anything to your mother." He took plate and bottle. "I wasn't going to get you in trouble."

"They don't know anything *about* that . . . ! The paper had the pictures, but they didn't have my name . . . though everybody knows it anyway!"

"All right—"

"They looked at them, Mother and Daddy. They looked at them and they didn't recognize me! Oh, I thought I was going to die . . . I cried. Afterward, Oh . . ." She swallowed. "Mother . . . sent that up to you. She thought you might be hungry. *Please* don't say anything?"

"I won't," and was annoyed.

"It was like you were playing with me. That was awful!"

He took a drink. "*Did* you find him, George Harrison?" It was bubbly but tepid.

She whispered, "No . . ."

"What did you want him for?"

Her totally vulnerable look made him grin.

He put the plate down on the chair, considering whether to accept what so resembled once rejected; then he took the sandwich and tore through the hole with his teeth. Spam. And mayonnaise. "He was in there. You shouldn't've run off. He came out just a minute later." He swallowed. "Hey, you want a picture of him?"

"Huh?"

"I can get you a picture of him, if you want, not like they had in the newspaper."

"No. I don't want a picture of him. What kind of picture?"

"Big full-color poster. Buck naked."

"No!" She dropped her head. "You *are* playing with me. I wish you wouldn't. It's just awful."

"Hey, I just . . ." He looked from sandwich to bottle.

He wasn't hungry, but had eaten in complicity. Now he wished he hadn't. He said: "If you play by yourself, you're just going to lose. If I play with you, maybe you'll . . . have a chance."

Her hair swung; she looked up, with a confusion he paid her the compliment of assuming feigned.

"Tomorrow I'll get you the—"

"You were supposed to wait for me," Bobby said from the doorway. "Mom said we were supposed to come up here together . . . Gosh, you almost got this room clean."

June made shoulder motions which Bobby did not exactly ignore; neither did he respond. Instead, he said, "You got that stuff around your neck. Like this." He held up his bright wristlet.

"Yeah." He grinned. "Bet you won't tell me where you got yours."

Bobby looked more surprised than he'd expected. "I told Mom and Daddy that I just found them."

June said, petulantly, "You shouldn't wear them."

Bobby put his hands behind his back and *humphed*, as though this were an exchange from a frequent argument.

"Why shouldn't he?"

Bobby said, "She thinks terrible things happen if you wear them. She's scared. She took hers off."

June glared at him.

"You know what I think?" Bobby said. "I think even worse things happen to people who wear them for a while and *then* take them off!"

"I didn't take it off."

"You did!"

"I didn't!"

"You did!"

"It *wasn't* mine! And you shouldn't have said you found it. I bet *really* bad things happen to people who *steal* them."

"I didn't steal it!"

"You did!"

"I didn't!"

"You did!"

"Oh . . . !" In sibling frustration she flung her hands out to end the antiphon.

He took another bite of pulpy bread; swallowed it with warm Coke: bad idea. He put both down.

151

"I'm going back!" Bobby said. "You better come too. We're supposed to be together." And marched out the door.

She waited. He watched.

Her hand moved in the side folds of her skirt, started to come up. Then she raised her head.

"Maybe you better—"

"Oh, he's going to go exploring." Contempt?

"Why do you want to find . . . George?"

She blinked. A word lost itself in breath. "I . . . I have to. I *want* to!" Her hands tried to raise, each one, in turn, holding the other down. "Do you know him?"

"I've seen him."

For all her light-eyed, ash-like blondness, her expression was incredibly intense. "You just . . . live out there?"

"Yeah." He examined her face. "So far I haven't needed a . . ." Intense, but it told him little. " . . . I haven't been here anywhere near as long as you have." He forced his shoulders down; they'd hunched to fend something he had not even consciously acknowledged an attack. "I hope you find him." It wasn't an attack; it was just that intensity. "But you've got a lot of competition."

"What . . . ?" Her reaction to his realizing it was to suddenly lose all of it. "What do you want?" She sounded exhausted, looked as if she would repeat it with no voice at all. "Why . . . did you come here?"

"To clean up . . . I don't know why. To play, maybe. Why don't you let me clean up? You better go back downstairs." He picked up another paper and folded it, growling and flapping, to manageable size.

"Oh . . ." And suddenly she seemed just a very young girl again. "You're just . . ." She shrugged; and left.

He finished the paper, put the revealed junk in the kitchen, up-righted more furniture, and thought about this family.

They filled his mind while he finally shouldered into the packed room; he reached innumerable decisions about them which he lost to scraping chair legs, collapsing bridge tables, drawers that would not fit in their chiffoniers. One thought, however, remained surfaced for the time it took to move five pieces into the swept front room: Trying to stay sane under that sort of madness drives us nuts. He contemplated writing it in his note-

152

"Bobby, Arthur, *both* of you! This isn't enough light to read by; you'll ruin your eyes."

"Bobby, put your book down. You heard your mother. You read too much anyway."

"Arthur, he can't read too much. It's just his *eyes*." She went back into the kitchen.

On top of the bookcase by Mr Richards' chair (neither he nor Bobby had ceased their reading) between an edition of *Paradise Lost* that said "Classics Club" and something thick by Michener, was a volume, thinner than both, with white letters down a black spine: *"Pilgrimage/ Newboy."* He pulled the book loose. The candles flaked light across the cover. "Did Mrs Brown ever come?" He turned the book over. From the case, black ceramic lions looked somewhere else and glistened. The back blurb was only three uninformative lines. He looked at the front again: *Pilgrimage* by Ernest Newboy.

"She'll be here by the time we eat. She always is." June snickered, waiting for Father or Mother to object. Neither did. "That's by that poet they told about in the paper. Bobby got it for Mother from the bookstore yesterday."

He nodded. "Ma'am?" He looked in the kitchen door. "May I look at this?"

"Certainly," Mrs Richards said, stirring, at the stove.

He went into the bathroom; probably laid out the same as the one he'd peed all over upstairs. Two candles on the back of the toilet tank put two flecks on each tile; and there was another candle up on the medicine cabinet.

He turned the taps, sat on the toilet top, and, with Newboy on his notebook, read at the "Prologemena."

The water rushed.

After a page he skipped, reading a line here, a verse paragraph further on. At some he laughed out loud.

He put down the book, shucked his clothing, leaned over the rim and lowered his chained, grimy ankle. Steam kissed the sole of his foot, then hot water licked it.

Sitting in the cooling tub, chain under his buttocks, he had scrubbed only a minute before the water was grey and covered with pale scalings.

Well, Lanya had said she wouldn't mind.

He let that water out, and ran more over his feet, rubbing the gritty skin from his insteps. He'd known he was dirty, but the amount of filth in the water was amazing. He soaked and soaped his hair, rubbed his arms and chest with the bar till the chain tore it. He grounded the balled washrag beneath his jaw, and then lay back with his ears under water, to watch the isle of his belly shake to his heart beat, each curved hair a wet scale, like the shingled skin of some amphibian.

Sometime during all this, Madame Brown's high laughter rolled into the hall; and a little on, her voice outside the door; "No! No, you can't go in there, Muriel! Someone's taking a bath."

He let out the water, and lay back, exhausted and clean, occasionally wiping at the tub-line of grit, wider than Loufer's garrison. He pressed his back against porcelain. Water trapped there poured around his shoulders. He sat, wondering if one could will oneself dry. And, slowly, dried.

He looked at his shoulder, peppered with pores, run with tiny lines he could imagine separated each cell, fuzzed with dark down. He brushed his mouth on his skin, licked the de-salted flesh, kissed it, kissed his arm, kissed the paler place where veins pushed across the bridge from bicep to forearm, realized what he was doing, with scowling laughter, but kissed himself again. He pushed to standing. Drops trickled the back of his legs. He was dizzy; the tiny flames wobbled in the tiles. He stepped out, heart knocking to the sudden effort.

He toweled roughly at his hair, gently at his genitals. Then, on his knees, he did a slightly better job washing away the hairs and grit and flaky stuff still on the bathtub bottom.

He picked up his pants, shook his head over them; well, they were all he had. He put them on, combed his moist hair back with his fingers, tucked in his shirt, buckled on his sandal, and came out into the hall. Behind his ears was cool, and still wet.

"How many baths did you take?" Mr Richards asked. "Three?"

"Two and a half." Kidd grinned. "Hello, Ma— Mrs Brown."

"They've been telling me how hard you've worked."

Kidd nodded. "It's not that bad. I'll probably finish up tomorrow. Mr Richards? You said you had a razor?"

"Oh yes. You're sure you don't want to use my electric?"

"I'm used to the other kind."

"It's just you'll have to use regular soap."

156

"Arthur," Mrs Richards called from the kitchen, "you have that mug of shaving soap Michael gave you for Christmas."

Mr Richards snapped his fingers. "Now I'd forgot. That was three years back. I never did open it. Grew a beard since too. I had a pretty good-looking beard for a while, you know?"

"It looked silly," Mrs Richards said. "I made him shave it off."

Back in the bathroom, he lathered his jaw, then scraped the warm foam away. His face cooled under the blade. He decided to leave his sideburns half an inch longer. Now (in two distinct stages) they came well below his ears.

For a moment, holding a hot washcloth across his face, he contemplated the patterns inside his eyes against the dark. But like everything in this house, they seemed of calculated inconsequence.

From the kitchen: "Bobby, *please* come in and set the table. *Now!*"

Kidd went into the living room. "Bet you'd hardly recognize me," he said to Madame Brown.

"Oh, I don't know about that."

"Dinner's ready," Mrs Richards said. "Kidd, you and Bobby sit back there. Edna, you sit here with June."

Madame Brown went over and pulled out her chair. "Muriel, stay down there and be good, hear me?"

He squeezed between the wall and the table—and took some tablecloth with him.

"Oh, dear!" Madame Brown lunged to grab a tottering brass candlestick. (In suddenly bared mahogany, the reflected flame steadied.) By candlelight her face had again taken on that bruised-eyed tawdriness she had last night in the bar.

"Jesus," Kidd said. "I'm sorry." He pulled the cloth back down across the table and began to straighten silverware. Mrs Richards had put out a profusion of forks, spoons, and side plates. He wasn't sure if he got all of them in the right place or which were his or Bobby's; when he finally sat, two fingers lingered on the ornate handle of a knife; he watched them rubbing, thick with enlarged knuckles and gnawed nails, but translucently clean. After baths, he reflected, when you're still alone in the john, is the time for all those things you don't want people around for: jerking off, picking your nose and

157

eating it, serious nail biting. Was it some misguided sense of good manners that had kept him from any of these here? His thoughts drifted to various places he'd indulged such habits not so privately: seated at the far end of lunch counters, standing at public urinals, in comparatively empty subway cars at night, in city parks at dawn. He smiled; he rubbed.

"Those were my mother's," Mrs Richards said, on the other side of the table. She set down two bowls of soup for Arthur and Madame Brown, then went back to the kitchen. "I think old silver is lovely—" her voice came in—"but keeping it polished is awfully difficult." She came out again with two more bowls. "I wonder if it's that—what do they call it? That sulfur dioxide in the air, the stuff eating away all the paintings and statues in Venice." She set one in front of Kidd and one in front of Bobby, who was just squeezing into place—more plates and silverware slid on the wrinkling cloth; Bobby pulled it straight again.

Kidd took his fingers from the tarnished handle and put his hand in his lap.

"We've never been to Europe," Mrs Richards said, returning from the kitchen with bowls for her and June. "But Arthur's parents went—oh, years ago. The plates are Arthur's mother's—from Europe. I suppose I shouldn't use the good ones; but I do whenever we have company. They're so festive— Oh, don't wait for me. Just dig in."

Kidd's soup was in a yellow melmac bowl. The china plate beneath bore an intricate design around its fluted lip, crossed by more intricate scratches that might have come from cleanser or steel wool.

He looked around to see if he should start, caught both Bobby and June looking around for the same purpose; Madame Brown had a china bowl but every one else's was pastel plastic. He wondered if he, or Madame Brown alone, would have merited the spread.

Mr Richards picked up his spoon, skimmed up some soup.

So he did too.

With the oversized spoon-bowl still in his mouth, he noticed Bobby, June, and Madame Brown had all waited for Mrs Richards, who was only now lifting hers.

From where he sat, he could see into the kitchen: other candles burned on the counter. Beside a paper

158

bag of garbage, its lip neatly turned down, stood two open Campbell's cans. He took another spoonful. Mrs Richards has mixed, he decided, two, or even three kinds; he could recognize no specific flavor.

Under the tablecloth edge, his other hand had moved to his knee—the edge of his little finger scraped the table leg. First with two fingers, then with three, then with his thumb, then with his fore-knuckle, he explored the circular lathing, the upper block, the under-rim, the wing bolts, the joints and rounded excrescences of glue, the hairline cracks where piece was joined to piece—and ate more soup.

Over a full spoon, Mr Richards smiled and said, "Where's your family from, Kidd?"

"New York—" he bent over his bowl—"State." He wondered where he had learned to recognize this as the milder version of the blunt What-nationality-*are*-you? which, here and there about the country, could create unpleasantnesses.

"*My* people are from Milwaukee," Mrs Richards said. "Arthur's family is all from right around the Bellona area. Actually my sister lived down here too—well, she did. She's left now. And so has all of Arthur's family. It's quite strange to think of Marianne and June—we named our June after Arthur's mother—and Howard and your Uncle Al not here any more."

"Oh, I don't know," Mr Richards said; Kidd saw him preparing to ask how long he'd been here, when Madame Brown asked: "Are you a student, Kidd?"

"No, ma'am," realizing it was a question whose answer she probably knew; but liked her for asking. "I haven't been a student for a while."

"Where were you in school, then?" Mr Richards asked.

"Lots of places. Columbia. And a community college in Delaware."

"Columbia University?" Mrs Richards asked. "In New York?"

"Only for a year."

"Did you like it? I've spent a lot of time—Arthur and I have *both* spent a lot of time—thinking about whether the children should go away to school. I'd like for Bobby to go to some place like Columbia. Though State, right here, is very good."

"Especially the poly-sci department," Kidd said. Mr

Richards and Madame Brown spooned their soup away from them. Mrs Richards, June, and Bobby spooned theirs toward them. One, he remembered, was more correct; but not which. He looked at the ornate silverware handles, diminishing in size either side of his plate, and finally simply sank his spoon straight down in the soup's center.

"And of course it's a lot less expensive." Mrs Richards sat back, with a constrained laugh. "Expense is always something you have to think about. Especially today. Here at State—" (Four more spoonfuls, he figured, and the soup would be too low for his compromise technique.) Mrs Richards sat forward again. "You say, the poly-sci department?" She tipped her soup bowl toward her.

"That's what someone told me," Kidd said. "Where's June going to go?"

Mr Richards tipped his away. "I don't know whether June has thought too much about that."

Mrs Richards said: "It *would* be very nice if June wanted to go to college."

"June isn't too, what you'd call, well, academic. June's sort of my old-fashioned girl." Mr Richards, tipping his bowl, apparently couldn't get enough; he picked it up, poured the last drops into his spoon, and set it down. "Aren't you, honey?"

"Arthur, really . . . !" Mrs Richards said.

"It's very good, dear," Mr Richards said. "Very good."

"Yes, ma'am," Kidd said. "It is," and put his spoon on his plate. It wasn't.

"I'd like to go to college—" June smiled at her lap— "if I could go someplace like New York."

"That's silly!" Mr Richards made a disparaging gesture with his soup spoon. "It was all we could do to keep her in high school!"

"It just wasn't very interesting." June's bowl—pink melmac—moved, under her spoon, to the plate's rim. She centered it again. "That's all."

"You wouldn't like New York," Mr Richards said. "You're too much of a sunshine girl. June likes the sun, swimming, outdoor things. You'd wither away in New York or Los Angeles, with all that smog and pollution."

"Oh, Daddy!"

"I think June ought to apply to the Junior College next term—" Mrs Richards turned in mid-sentence from

160

husband to daughter—"to get some idea if you liked it or not. Your marks weren't *that* bad. I don't think it would be such a terrible idea to try it out, at the Junior College."

"Mom!" June looked at her lap, not smiling.

"Your mother went through college," Mr Richards said, "I went through college. Bobby's going to go. If nothing else, it's a place to get married in."

"Bobby reads more than June," Mrs Richards explained. "He reads all the time, in fact. And I suppose he *is* more school-minded."

"That Junior College is an awful place," June said. "I hate everybody who goes there."

"Dear," Mrs Richards said, "you don't know *every-body* who goes there."

Kidd, with his middle finger, was exploring the counter sinking about some flathead screw, when Madame Brown said:

"Mary, how close are we to the second course? Arthur up there looks like he's about to eat the bottom of his bowl."

"Oh, dear me!" Mrs Richards pushed back in her chair. "I don't know what I'm thinking of. I'll be right in—"

"You want any help, mom?" June said.

"No." Mrs Richards disappeared into the kitchen. "Thank you, darling."

"Pass me your soup plates, everybody," June said.

Kidd's hand came up from under the tablecloth to join his other on the china plate to pass it—but stopped just below the table lip. Knuckles, fingertips, and two streaks on the back of the hand were smudged black.

He put his hand down between his legs and looked around.

Anyway, people were keeping their plates and just passing their bowls. He passed his with one hand, his other between his knees. Then the other joined it and he tried, without looking, to rub his fingers clean.

Mrs Richards came in with two steaming ceramic bowls. "I'm afraid we're vegetarian tonight." She went out, returned with two more. "But there's nowhere to get any meat that you can trust," and returned again.

"You do that nice tunafish casserole," Mr Richards called after her. "That's very good."

"Ugh," Bobby said.

161

"Bobby!" June said.

"Yes, I know, Arthur." Mrs Richards returned with a gravy boat, set it on the table, and sat. "But I just feel so funny about fish. Wasn't it a couple of years back all those people *died* from some canned tuna that had gone bad? I just feel safer with vegetables. Though Lord knows, they can go bad too."

"Botulism." Bobby said.

"Really, Bobby!" Madame Brown laughed, a hand against her sparkling chains.

"Oh, I don't think we're doing so badly. Mashed potatoes, mushrooms, carrots—" Mrs Richards indicated one and another of the bowls—"and some canned egg-plant stuff I've never tried before. When I went to that health-food restaurant with Julia—when we were in Los Angeles?—she said they always use mushrooms and egg-plants in place of meat. And I've made a sauce." She turned to her husband, as though to remind him of something. "Arthur . . . ?"

"What?" Then Mr Richards too seemed to remember. "Oh, yes . . . Kidd? Well, we've taken up this little habit of having a glass of wine with our meals." He reached down beside his chair, brought up a bottle, and set it beside the candle at his end of the table. "If it isn't something that appeals to you, you're perfectly welcome to have water—"

"I like wine," Kidd said.

Mrs Richards and Madame Brown had already passed their wine glasses up. So Kidd did too; though the water glass at the head of his knife seemed the better size for wine drinking as he was accustomed to it.

Mr Richards peeled away gold foil, pulled loose the plastic stopper, poured, passed back the glasses.

Kidd sipped; it was almost black in candlelight. At first he thought his mouth was burning—the wine was bubbly as soda pop.

"Sparkling burgundy!" Mr Richards grinned and doffed his glass. "We haven't tried this one before. 1975. I wonder if that's a good year for sparkling Burgundy?" He sipped. "Tastes okay to me. Cheers."

The candle flame staggered, stilled. Above and below the ornate label, green glass flickered.

"I put a little wine in the gravy," Mrs Richards said. "In the sauce, I mean—it was left over from last night's

162

bottle. I like to cook with wine. And soy sauce. When we went to Los Angeles two years ago for Arthur's conferences, we stayed with the Harringtons. Michael gave Arthur that shaving soap. Julia Harrington—she's the one who took me to that Health Food restaurant—made absolutely *everything* with soy sauce! It was very interesting. Oh, thank you, Arthur."

Mr Richards had helped himself to mashed potatoes and now passed the dish. So had Madame Brown.

Kidd checked his fingers.

The rubbing had not removed any dirt; but it had divided it fairly evenly between both hands; the rough strips of nail back on the wide crowns were once more darkly ringed, as though outlined, nub and cuticle, with pen. He sighed, served himself when the dishes passed him, passed them on, and ate. His free hand back beneath the tablecloth, found the table leg, again explored.

"If you're not a student," Madame Brown asked, "what do you put down in your notebook?—none of us could help noticing it."

It was inside, on the table by the chair; he could see it beyond her elbow. "I just write things down."

Mrs Richards hung her hands by the fingertips on the table edge. "You write! You're going to be a writer? Do you write poetry?"

"Yeah." He smiled because he was nervous.

"You're a poet!"

Mr Richards, June, and Bobby all sat back and looked. Mrs Richards leaned forward and beamed. Madame Brown reached down with some silent remonstrance to Muriel.

"He's a poet! Arthur, give him some more wine. Look, he's finished his glass already. Go on, dear. He's a poet! I think that's wonderful. I should have known when you took that Newboy book."

Arthur took Kidd's glass, refilled it. "I don't know too much about poetry." He handed it back with a smile that, on a college football player, would have purveyed sheepish good will. "I mean, I'm an engineer . . ." As he took his hand away, wine splashed on the cloth.

Kidd said, "Oh, hey, I—"

"Don't worry about that!" Mrs Richards cried, waving her hand—which knocked against her own glass. Wine splashed the rim, ran down the stem, blotched the linen. While he wondered if such a thing were done on pur-

163

pose to put strangers at ease (thinking: What an uncomfortably paranoid thought), she asked: "What do you
think of him? Newboy, I mean."

"I don't know." Kidd moved his glass aside: through
the base, he could see the diametric mold line across the
foot. "I only met him once."

At the third second of silence, he looked up, and decided he'd said something wrong. He hunted for the
proper apology: but, like a tangle of string with a lost
end, action seemed all loop and no beginning.

"You *know* Ernest Newboy? Oh, Edna, Kidd's a *real*
poet! And he's helping us, Arthur! I mean, move furniture
and things." She looked from Mr Richards to Madame
Brown, to Kidd. "Tell me—" She spilled more wine—
"is Newboy's work just—wonderful? I'm sure it is. I
haven't had a chance to read it yet. I just got the book
yesterday. I sent Bobby down to get it, because of that
article in the *Times*. We have this very nice little book-
and-gift shop down the street. They have just everything
like that— But after the article, I was afraid they were
going to be all out. I think it's *very* important to keep up
with current books, even if it's just bestsellers. And I'm
really interested in poetry. I really am. Arthur doesn't
believe me. But I do—I really *do* like it."

"That's just because you went to that coffee shop
with Julia in Los Angeles where they were reading that
poetry and playing that music."

"And I *told* you, Arthur, the evening we came back,
though I don't pretend I understood it all, I liked it *very*
much! It was one of the most—" she frowned, hunting for
the right description—"*exciting* things I've . . . well, ever
heard."

"I don't know him very well," Kidd said, and ate more
mushrooms; that and the eggplant weren't bad. The
mashed potatoes (instant) were pretty gluey, though. "I
just met him . . . once."

"I'd love to meet him." Mrs Richards said. "I've never
known a real writer."

"Mike Harrington wrote a book," Mr Richards ob-
jected. "A very good book, too."

"Oh, Arthur, that was an instruction manual . . . on
stresses and strains and the uses of a new metal!"

"It was a very *good* instruction manual." Mr Richards
poured more wine for Madame Brown and himself.

"Can I have some?" Bobby said.

"No," Mr Richards said.

"How long have you been writing poetry?" Madame Brown asked, helpfully.

Kidd looked up to answer—Madame Brown was waiting with a forkful of well-sauced eggplant, June with one of carrots; Mrs Richards had a very small fluff of potato on the tine tips of her fork—when it struck him that he didn't know. Which seemed absurd, so he frowned. "Not very . . ." *long*, he'd started to say. He had a clear memory of writing the first poem in the notebook, seated against the lamp post on Brisbain Avenue. But had he ever written any poems before? Or was it something he'd wanted to do but never gotten around to? He could see not remembering *doing* something. But how could you not remember not doing something? ". . . for very long," he finally said. "Just a few days, I guess," and frowned again, because that sounded silly. But he had no more surety of its truth or falsity than he had of his name. "No, not very long at all." He decided that was what he would say from now on to anyone who asked; but the decision simply confirmed how uncertain he was of its truth.

"Well I'm sure—" there was only one more fluff of mashed potatoes on Mrs Richard's plate—"they must be very good." She ate it. "Did Mr Newboy like them?"

"I didn't show them to him." Somehow silverware, glasses, sideplates, and candles didn't seem right for talking about scorpions, orchid fights, the invisible Calkins and the belligerent Fenster—

"Oh, you should," Mrs Richards said. "The younger men in Arthur's office are always bringing him their new ideas. And he says they've been coming up with some lulus lately—didn't you, Arthur? Arthur's always happy to talk to the younger men about their new ideas. I'm sure Mr Newboy would be happy to talk to you, don't you think, Arthur?"

"Well," Mr Richards reiterated, "I don't know too much about poetry."

"I'd certainly like to see some of what you'd written," Madame Brown said and moved Mrs Richards' wine glass away from her straying hand. "Maybe some day you'll show us. Tell me, Arthur—" Madame Brown looked over joined fingers—"what *is* going on át Maitland, now? With everything in the state it's in, I'm amazed when I hear of *any*thing getting done."

165

She's changing the subject! Kidd thought with relief. And decided he liked her.

"Engineering." Mr Richards shook his head, looked at Mrs Richards— "Poetry . . ." changing it, rather bluntly, back. "They don't have too much to do with one another."

Kidd decided to give it a try himself. "I met an engineer here, Mr Richards. His name was Loufer. He was working on . . . yeah, converting a plant. It used to make peanut butter. Now it makes vitamins."

"Most people who like poetry and art and stuff," Mr Richards adhered, "aren't very interested in engineering—" Then he frowned. "The vitamin plant? That must be the one down at Helmsford."

Kidd sat back and saw that Madame Brown did too.

Mrs Richards' hands still spasmed on the table.

Mr Richards asked: "What did you say his name was?"

"Loufer."

"Don't think I know him." Mr Richards screwed up his face and dropped his chin over the smooth gold-and-mustard knot of his tie. "Of course I'm in Systems. He's probably in Industrial. Two completely different fields. Two completely different professions, really. It's hard enough to keep up with what's going on in your own field, what your own people are doing. Some of the ideas our men do come up with—they're lulus all right. Like Mary says. Sometimes *I* don't even understand them—I mean, even when you understand *how* they work, you don't really know *what* they're for. Right now I'm just back and forth between the office and the warehouse— lord only knows what I'm supposed to be doing."

"Just keeping up," Madame Brown said, and leaned one elbow on the table. As she moved, the candle flame drifted back and forth across her left eye. "At the hospital, it was all I could do to read two or three psychology bulletins a week, what with the behaviorists and the gestaltists—"

"Peaches?" said Mrs Richards, leaning forward, knuckles like two tiny mountain ranges on the table edge. "Would anyone like some peaches? For dessert?"

Maybe, Kidd thought, she really *did* want to talk about poetry—which would be fine, he decided, if he could think of anything to say. His own plate was empty of everything except the sauce-and-mashed-potato swamp.

"Sure."

He watched the word hang over the table, silence on both sides.

"I don't want any!" Bobby's chair scraped.

Both candlesticks veered.

"Bobby—!" Mrs Richards exclaimed, while June caught one and Mr Richards caught the other.

Bobby was off into the living room. Muriel barked and ran after him.

"I'll have some, dear." Mr Richards sat back down. "Let him go, Mary. He's all right."

"Muriel? Muriel!" Madame Brown turned back to the table and sighed. "Peaches sound lovely. Yes, I'll have some."

"Yes, please, Mother," June said. Her shoulders were rather hunched and she was still looking at her lap, as though considering something intensely.

Mrs Richards, blinking after her son, rose and went in the kitchen.

"If I went to school," June blurted, looking up suddenly, "I'd go into psychology—like you!"

Madame Brown, slightly flattered, slightly mocking, turned to June with raised brows. Mocking? Or, Kidd wondered, was it simply surprise.

"I'd like to work with . . . mentally disturbed children—like you!" June's fingertips were over the table edge too, but tightly together, and even, so that you'd have to count to find where right fingertips ended and left began.

"In my job, dear, at the hospital—" Madame Brown lifted her glass to sip; as she bent forward, loops of optic chain swung out like a glittering bib, and back—"I have more to do with the disturbed parents."

June, now embarrassed by her outburst, was collecting plates. "I'd like to . . . to help people; like a nurse or a doctor. Or like you do—" Kidd passed his over; it was the last—"with problems in their mind."

He dragged his hands back across the cloth (spotted with sauce, soup, pieces of carrot, the purple wine blot) and let them fall into his lap.

Mrs Richards' place was nearly as messy as his own.

"I know it's a cliché—" Madame Brown shook her head—"but it really is true. The parents need the help far more than the children. Really: they bring their totally demolished child to us. And you know what they want in the first interview? It's always the same: they want us to say, 'What you should do is beat him.' They come in with some poor nine-year-old they've reduced to a state of numb, inarticulate terror; the child can't dress itself, can't talk above a whisper, and then only in some invented language; it soils its clothing, and the only coherent actions it can make are occasional attempts at murder or, more frequently, suicide. If I said to them, 'Beat her! Hit him!' they would glow—*glow* with delight. When they discover that we want to take the children *away* from them, they're indignant! Under all the frustration and apparent concern, what they actually come hoping is that we will say, 'Yes, you're handling it all marvelously well. Just be a little firmer!' The reason I'm successful at my job at all—" Madame Brown touched June's shoulder and leaned confidentially—"as all I *really* do is pry the children loose from their parents—is because what *I'm* saying, underneath all my pleasant talk about how much better it would be for the rest of the family if they let little Jimmy or Alice come to us, is: Wouldn't it be ever so much more fun to work on one of your other children for a while? Wouldn't it be ever so much more interesting to fight someone with a little more strength left than this poor half-corpse you've just brought in. Why not clear the field and start in on little sister Sue or big brother Bill? Or maybe each other. Try to get an only child away from its parents once they've driven it practically autistic!" Madame Brown shook her head. "It's very depressing. I really think, sometimes, I'd like to change my field—do individual therapy. That's what I've always been interested in, anyway. And since there's nobody at the hospital now anyway—"

"But don't you need licenses, or special examinations to do that, Edna?" Mrs Richards asked from the kitchen. "I mean, I know it's your profession, but isn't fiddling with people's minds dangerous? If you don't know what you're doing?" She came in with two long-stemmed dessert dishes, gave one to Madame Brown, and one to Mr Richards. "I read an article—" She paused with her hands on the back of her chair—"about those encounter group things, I think they call them? Julia Harrington was going to one of those, two years ago. And the minute I read that article, I cut it out and sent it to her—it was just terrifying! About all those unskilled people leading them and how they were driving everybody *crazy!* Touching each other all over, and picking each other up in the

168

air, and telling each other about *every*thing! Well, some people just couldn't take it and got very seriously ill!"

"Well I—" Madame Brown began some polite protest.

"*I* think it's all poppycock," Mr Richards said. "Sure, people have problems. And they should be put away where they can get help. But if you're just indulging yourself, somebody telling you to straighten up and fly right may be what you need. A few hard knocks never hurt anybody, and who's in a better position to give out a few than your own parents, I say—though I've never lifted a hand to my own." Mr Richards lifted his hand, palm out, to his shoulder. "Have I, Mary? At least not since they were big."

"You're a very good father, Arthur." Mrs Richards came back from the kitchen with three more dessert glasses clutched together before her. "No one would ever deny that."

"You kids just be glad your parents are as sane as they are." Mr Richards nodded once toward Bobby's (empty) chair and once toward June's; she was just sitting down in it after taking the plates into the kitchen. She put a cut glass bowl, filled with white, on the white cloth.

"Here you are," Mrs Richards said, passing Kidd his fruit.

In its long-stemmed dessert dish, the yellow hemisphere just cleared the syrup.

Kidd looked at it, his face slack, realized his lips were hanging a little open, so closed them.

Beneath the table, he clutched the table-leg so tight a band of pain finally snapped along his forearm. He let go, let out his breath, and said: "Thank you . . ."

"It's not terribly exciting," Mrs Richards said. "But fruit has lots of vitamins and things. I made some whipped cream—dessert topping, actually. I *do* like real cream, but this was all we could get. I wanted to flavor it almond. I thought that would be nice. With peaches. But I was out of almond extract. Or vanilla. So I used maple. Arthur, would you like some? Edna?"

"Lord, no!" Madame Brown waved the proffered bowl away. "I'm heavy enough as it is."

"Kidd, will you?"

The bowl came toward him between the candles, facets glittering. He blinked, worked his jaw slowly inside the mask of skin, intent on constructing a smile.

He spooned up a white mound—with the flame behind it, its edges were pale green.

Madame Brown was watching him; he blinked. Her expression shifted. To a smile? He wondered what his own was. It was supposed to be a smile too; it didn't *feel* like one . . .

He buried his peach.

White spiraled into the syrup.

"You know what I think would be lovely?" Mrs Richards said. "If Kidd read us one of his poems."

He put half his peach in his mouth and said, "No," swallowed it, and added, "thanks. I don't really feel like it." He was tired.

June said, "Kidd, you're eating with the whipped cream spoon."

He said: "Oh . . ."

Mrs Richards said, "Oh, that's all right. Everybody's had some who wants some."

"*I* haven't," Mr Richards said.

Kidd looked at his dish (a half a peach, splayed open in syrup and cream), looked at his spoon (the damasking went up the spoon itself, streaked with cream), at the bowl (above the faceted edges, gouges had been cut into the heaped white).

"No, that's all right," Mr Richards said. Glittering, the bowl moved off beyond the candle flames. "I'll just use my spoon here. Everybody makes mistakes. Bobby does that all the time."

Kidd went back to his peach. He'd gotten whipped cream on his knuckles. And two fingers were sticky with syrup. His skin was still wrinkled from the bath. The gnawed and sucked callous looked like he imagined leprosy might.

Arthur Richards said something.

Madame Brown answered something back.

Bobby ran through the room; Mrs Richards yelled at him.

Arthur Richards said something else.

Cream, spreading through the puddle in the bottom of his dish finally met glass all the way around. "I think I'm going to have to go soon." He looked up.

The gold knot of Mr Richard's tie was three inches lower on his shirt.

Had he loosened it when Kidd was not looking? Or did he just not remember? "I have to meet somebody before it gets too late. And then . . ." He shrugged: "I want to get back here to work early tomorrow morning."

"Is it that late?" Mrs Richards looked disappointed. "Well, I guess you need a good night's sleep after all that furniture-moving."

Madame Brown put her linen napkin on the table. (Kidd realized he had never put his in his lap; it lay neatly, by the side of his stained and spotted place, a single drop of purple near the monogrammed R.) "I'm feeling a little tired myself. Kidd, if you could wait a minute, I wish you'd walk with me and Muriel. Is there coffee, Mary?"

"Oh, dear . . . I didn't put any up."

"Then we might as well go now. Kidd is anxious. And I certainly don't want to be out on the streets any later than I have to."

Downstairs, somebody laughed; the laughter of others joined it, till suddenly there were a series of thumps, like large furniture toppling, bureau, after bedstead, after chiffonier.

Kidd got up from the table—held the cloth in place this time. His arm still hurt. "Mr Richards, were you going to pay me now, or when I finished the whole job?" Getting that out, he was suddenly exhausted.

Mr Richards leaned back in his chair. His fists were in his suit coat pockets; the front chair legs lifted. "I imagine you could use a little right now." One hand came out and up. A bill was folded in it; he'd been anticipating the request. "Here you go."

"I worked about three and a half hours, I guess. Maybe four. But you can call it three if you want, since I was just getting started." He took the dark rectangle; it was a single five-dollar bill, folded in four.

Kidd looked at Mr Richards questioningly, then at Madame Brown, who was leaning over her chair, snapping her fingers for Muriel.

Mr Richards, both hands back in his pockets, smiled and rocked.

Kidd felt there was something else to say, but it was too difficult to think of what. "Um . . . thank you." He put the money in his pants pocket, looked around the table for June; but she had left the room. "Good night, Mrs Richards." He wandered across green carpet to the door.

Behind him, as he clicked over lock after lock—

171

there were so *many*—Madame Brown was saying: "Good night, Arthur. Mary, thanks for that dinner. June . . . ? June . . . ?" she called now—"I'm on my way, dear. See you soon. Good night, Bobby—Oh, he's back in his room. With that book I bet, if I know Bobby. Muriel, come along, sweetheart. Right with you, Kidd. Good night again."

The smoke was so thick he wondered if the glass were opaque and he only misremembered it as clear—

"Well—" Madame Brown pushed open the cracked door—"what do you think of the Richards after your first day on the job?"

"I don't think anything." Kidd stretched in the overthick night. "I'm just an observer."

"I take that to mean you've thought a great deal but find it difficult, or unnecessary, to articulate." Muriel clicked away down the cement walk. "They are perplexing."

"I wish," Kidd said, "he'd paid me for the whole day. Of course, if they're feeding me and stuff—" another highrise loomed before them, tier on tier of dark windows—"five dollars an hour is a lot." Smoke crawled across the facade. He had thought about them, of course; he remembered all his mulling while he worked in the upstairs apartment. And—again she was right—he'd certainly reached no synopsizable conclusion.

Madame Brown, hands behind her back, looked at the pavement, walked slowly.

Kidd, notebook before him in both hands (He'd almost forgotten it; Madame Brown had brought it to him at the door), looked up and could make out practically nothing. "You're still working in that hospital?"

"Pardon me?"

"That mental hospital, you were talking about." Walking revived him some. "With the children. Do you still go there every day?"

"No."

"Oh."

When she said nothing more, he said:

"I was in a mental hospital. For a year. I was just wondering what happened with—" he looked around at building faces whose wreckage was hidden behind night and smoke; he could smell smoke here—"with yours."

"You probably don't want to know," she said, walk-

172

ing a few more steps in silence. *"Especially* if you were in one. It wasn't pleasant." Muriel spiraled back and away. "You see, I was with the hospital's social service department—you must have gathered that. Lord, I got twenty-two phone calls at home in two hours about evacuation procedures—the phone went dead in the middle of the last one. Finally, we just decided, even though it was the middle of the night, we'd better go to the hospital ourselves—my friend and I; you see, I had a little friend staying with me at the time. When we got there—walking, mind you—it was just incredible! You don't expect doctors around at midnight in a place as understaffed as that. But there was not one orderly, one night nurse, one guard around! They'd just gone, like that!" She flung up her hand, in stark dismissal. "Patients were all up in the open night wards. We let out everybody we could. Thank God my friend found the keys to that incredible basement wing they first shut down fifteen years ago, and have been opening up and shutting down regularly—with not a bit of repair!—every three years since. You could see the fires out the windows. Some of the patients wouldn't leave. Some of them couldn't—dozens were logy in their beds with medication. Others were shrieking in the halls. And if all those phone calls about evacuation did anything besides scare off whatever staff was around, I'm sure I didn't see it! Some rooms we just couldn't find keys to! I broke windows with chairs. My friend got a crowbar, and three of the patients helped us break in some of the doors— Oh, yes: did I mention somebody tried to strangle me? He just came up in his pajamas, while I was hurrying down the second floor corridor, grabbed me, and started choking. Oh, not very seriously, and only for about two or three minutes, before some other patients helped me get him off—apparently, as I discovered, it takes quite a bit of effort to really choke somebody to death who doesn't want to be choked. And, believe me, I didn't. But it was a doozer. I was recovering from *that* in the S.S. office, when she came in with these." He heard Madame Brown finger the chains around her neck: it was too dark to see glitter. "She said she'd found them, wound them around my neck. You could see them flashing in flickers coming from outside, around the window shades." Madame Brown paused. "But I told you about that . . . ?" She sighed. "I also told you that was when she left . . . my friend.

173

Some of the rooms, you see, we *just* couldn't get into. We tried—me, the other patients, we tried! And the patients on the inside, trying just as hard! Christ, we tried! But by then, fire had broken out in the building itself. The smoke was so thick you could hardly—" She took a sudden breath. Did she shrug? "We had to leave. And, as I said, by that time, my little friend had left already."

He could see Madame Brown beside him now.

She walked, contemplating either the past or the pavement.

Muriel wove ahead, barked, turned, ran.

"I went back once," she said at last. "The next morning. I don't want to go again. I want to do something else . . . I'm a trained psychologist! Social service was never really my forte. I don't know if the patients who got out were finally evacuated or not. I assume they were; but I can't be sure." She gave a little humph. "Perhaps that has something to do with why I don't leave myself."

"I don't think so," Kidd said, after a moment. "It sounds like you—and your friend—were very brave."

Madame Brown humphed again.

"It's just—" he felt uncomfortable, but it was a different discomfort than at the table—"you made it sound, when you were talking about it at dinner, like you still worked there. That's why I asked."

"Oh, I was just making conversation. To keep Mary entertained. When people take the trouble to bring out the best in her, she's quite a handsome woman; with quite a handsome soul—even if the quotidian surface sits on it a bit askew. I imagine some people find that hard to see."

"Yeah." He nodded. "I guess so." Half a block ahead, Muriel was a shifting dollop of darkness. "I thought—" on the curb, he scraped his heel—"Hey, watch . . . !" He staggered. "Um. I thought you said they had *three* children."

"They do."

They crossed the damp street. On cool pavement, his heel stung.

"Edward, the oldest, isn't with them now. But it isn't a subject I'd bring up. Especially with Mary. It was very painful for her."

"Oh." He nodded again.

174

They stepped up another curb.

"If nothing's functioning around here," Kidd asked, "why does Mr Richards go in to work every day?"

"Oh, just to make a showing. Probably for Mary. You've seen how keen she is on appearances."

"*She* wants him to stay home," Kidd said. "She's scared to death!—I was pretty scared too."

Madame Brown considered a few moments. "Maybe he does it just to get away." She shrugged—it was light enough to see it now. "Perhaps he just goes off and sits on a bench somewhere."

"You mean he's scared?"

Madame Brown laughed. "Why wouldn't he be?" Muriel ran up, ran off. "But I think it's much more likely he simply doesn't appreciate her. That isn't fair of me, I know; but then, it's one of those universal truths about husbands and wives you really don't have to be fair with. He loves her, in his way." Muriel ran up again, leapt to Madame Brown's hip. She roughed the beast's head. Satisfied, it ran off again. "No, he *must* be going somewhere! Probably just where he says he is. To the office . . . the warehouse . . ." She laughed. "And *we've* simply got far too poetic an imagination!"

"I wasn't imagining anything." But he smiled, "I just asked." In the light from a flickering window, a story above them, he saw, through faint smoke, she was smiling too.

Ahead, Muriel barked.

And what have I invested in interpreting disfocus for chaos? This threat: The only lesson is to wait. I crouch in the smoggy terminus. The streets lose edges, the rims of thought flake. What have I set myself to fix in this dirty notebook that is not mine? Does the revelation that, though it cannot be done with words, it might be accomplished in some lingual gap, give me right, in injury, walking with a woman and her dog, to pain? Rather the long doubts: That this labor tears up the mind's moorings; that, though life may be important in the scheme, awareness is an imperfect tool with which to face it. To reflect is to fight away the sheets of silver, the carbonated distractions, the feeling that, somehow, a thumb is pressed on the right eye. This exhaustion melts what binds, releases what flows.

Madame Brown opened the bar door for him.

Kidd passed by vinyl Teddy, the bill in his fist. But

while he contemplated offering her a drink, someone came screaming across the bar; Madame Brown screamed back; they staggered away. He sat down at the counter's end. The people whose backs he had seen along the stools, as he leaned forward, gained faces. But no Tak; nor any Lanya. He was looking at the empty cage when the bartender, rolled sleeves tying off the necks of tattooed leopards, said, "You're a beer drinker, ain't you?"

"Yeah." He nodded, surprised.

The bottle clacked the scarred counter board. "Come on, come on! Put it away, kid."

"Oh." Wonderingly, he returned the money to his pocket. "Thanks."

Under a haystack mustache, the bartender sucked his teeth. "What do you think this place is, anyway?" He shook his head, and walked off.

His hand had wandered to his shirt pocket to click the pen. He frowned down, paused above some internal turning: he opened the notebook, held his pen in the air, plunged.

Had he ever done this before? he wondered. With pen to paper and the actual process occurring, it was as though he had never done anything else. But pause, even moments, and it was as if not only had he never done it, but there was no way to be sure that he ever would again.

His mind dove for a vision of perfected anger while his hand crabbed and crossed and rearranged the vision's spillage. Her eyes struck a dozen words: he chose one in the most relevant tension to the one before. Her despair struck a dozen more; he grubbed among them, teeth clamped against what cleared. And cleared. So gazed at the cage again till the fearful distractions fell, then turned to her. An obtuse time later, he raised his hand, swallowed, and withdrew.

He jabbed the pen back in his pocket. His hand dropped, dead and ugly on the paper. His tongue worked in the back of his mouth while he waited for energy with which to copy. Sounds resolved from the noise. He blinked, and saw the pyramided bottles against the velvet backing. Between his fingers he watched the curling inkline peeled off from meaning. He reached for the beer, drank a long time, put down the bottle, and let his hand drop on the paper again. But his hand was wet . . .

He took a breath, turned to look left.

"Eh . . . hello, there," from his right.

He turned right.

"I thought it might be you when I was on the other side of the bar." Blue serge; narrow lapels; hair the color of white pepper. "I really am glad to see you again, to know you're all right. I can't tell you how upset that whole experience left me. Though that must be a bit presumptuous: *you* were the one who was hurt. It's been a long time since I've had to move through such suspicion, such restraint." The face was that of a thin, aged child, momentarily sedate. "I'd like to buy you a drink, but I was told that they don't sell the drink here. Bartender?"

Walking his fists on the wood, the bartender came, like some blond gorilla.

"Can you put together a tequila sunrise?"

"Make my life easy and have a beer."

"Gin and tonic?"

The bartender nodded deeply.

"And another for my friend here."

The gorilla responded, forefinger to forehead.

"Hey, I'm sort of surprised," Kidd volunteered into the feeling of loss between them, "to see you in here, Mr Newboy."

"Are you?" Newboy sighed. "I'm out on my own, tonight. I've a whole list of places people have told me I must see while I'm in town. It's a bit strange. I gather you know who I . . . ?"

"From the *Times*."

"Yes." Newboy nodded. "I've never been on the *front* page of a newspaper before. I've had just enough of that till now to be rather protective of my anonymity. Well, Mr Calkins thought he was doing something nice; his motives were the best."

"Bellona's a very hard place to get lost in." What Kidd took for slight nervousness, he reacted to with warmth. "I'm glad I read you were here."

Newboy raised his peppered brows.

"I've read some of your poem now, see?"

"And you wouldn't have if you hadn't read about me?"

"I didn't buy the book. A lady had it."

"Which book?"

"*Pilgrimage*."

Now Newboy lowered them. "You haven't read it carefully, several times, all the way through?"

He shook his head, felt his lips shake, so closed his mouth.

"Good." Newboy smiled. "Then you don't know me any better than I know you. For a moment I thought you had an advantage."

"I only browsed in it." He added: "In the bathroom."

Newboy laughed out loud, and drank. "Tell me about yourself. Are you a student? Or do you write?"

"Yes. I mean I write. I'm . . . a poet. Too." That was an interesting thing to say, he decided. It felt quite good. He wondered what Newboy's reaction would be.

"Very good." Whatever Newboy's reaction, surprise was not part of it. "Do you find Bellona stimulating, making you produce lots of work?"

He nodded. "But I've never published anything."

"Did I ask if you had?"

Kidd looked for severity; what he saw was a gentle smile.

"Or are you interested in getting published?"

"Yeah." He turned half around on his stool. "How do you get poems published?"

"If I could really answer that, I would probably write a lot more poems than I do."

"But *you* don't have any problems now, about getting things in magazines and things?"

"Just about everything I write now—" Newboy folded his glass in both hands—"I can be sure will be published. It makes me very careful of what I actually put down. How careful are you?"

The first beer bottle was empty. "I don't know." He drank from the second. "I haven't been a poet very long," he confessed, smiling. "Only a couple of days. Why'd you come here?"

"Pardon?" There was a little surprise there; but not much.

"I bet you know lots of writers, famous ones. And people in the government too. Why did you come here?"

"Oh, Bellona has developed . . . an underground reputation, you call it? One never reads about it, but one hears. There are some cities one must be just dying to visit" In a theatrical whisper: "I hope this isn't one of them." While he laughed, his eyes asked forgiveness.

Kidd forgave and laughed.

"I really don't know. It was a spur of the moment thing," Newboy went on. "I don't quite know how I did it.

I certainly wasn't expecting to meet anyone like Roger. That headline was a bit of a surprise. But Bellona is full of surprises."

"You're going to write about it here?"

Newboy turned his drink. "No. I don't think so." He smiled again. "You're all safe."

"You *do* know a lot of famous people though, I bet. Even when you read introductions and flyleaves and book reviews, you begin to figure out that everybody knows everybody. You get this picture of all these people sitting around together and getting mad, or friendly, probably screwing each other—"

"Literary intrigues? Oh, you're right: It's quite complicated, harrowing, insidious, vicious; and thoroughly fascinating. The only pastime I prefer to writing is gossip."

He frowned. "Somebody else was talking to me about gossip. Everybody around here sort of goes for it." Lanya was still not in the bar. He looked again at Newboy. "She knows your friend Mr Calkins."

"It is a small city. I wish Paul Fenster had felt a little less—up tight?" He gestured toward the notebook. "I'd enjoy seeing some of your poems."

"Huh?"

"I enjoy reading poems, especially by people I've met. Let me tell you right away, I won't even presume to say anything about whether I think they're good or bad. But you're pleasant, in an angular way. I'd like to see what you wrote."

"Oh. I don't have very many. I've just been writing them down for . . , well, like I say, not long."

"Then it won't take me very long to read them—if you wouldn't mind showing them to me, sometime when you felt like it?"

"Oh. Sure. But you *would* have to tell me if they're good."

"I doubt if I could."

"Sure you could. I mean I'd listen to what you said. That would be good for me."

"May I tell you a story?"

Kidd cocked his head, and found his own eager distrust interesting.

Newboy waved a finger at the bartender for refills. "Some years ago in London, when I was much younger than the time between then and now would indicate, my Hampstead host winked at me through his sherry glass

179

and asked if I would like to meet an American writer staying in the city. That afternoon I had to see an editor of an Arts Council subsidized magazine to which my host, the writer in question, and myself all contributed. I enjoy writers: their personalities intrigue me. I can talk about it in this detached way because I'm afraid I do so little of it myself now, that, though I presumptuously feel myself an artist at all times, I only consider myself a writer a month or so out of the year. On good years. At any rate, I agreed. The American writer was phoned to come over that evening. While I was waiting to go out, I picked up a magazine in which he had an article —a description of his travels through Mexico—and began the afternoon's preparation for the evening's encounter. The world is small: I had been hearing of this young man for two years. I had read his name in conjunction with my own in several places. But I had actually read no single piece by him before. I poured more sherry and turned to the article. It was impenetrable! I read on through the limpest recountings of passage through pointless scenery and unfocused meetings with vapid people. The judgments on the land were inane. The insights into the populace, had they been expressed with more energy, would have been a bit horrifying for their prejudice. Fortunately the prose was too dense for me to get through more than ten of the sixteen pages. I have always prided myself on my ability to read anything; I feel I must, as my own output is so small. But I put *that* article by! The strange machinery by which a reputation precedes its source we all know is faulty. Yet how much faith we put in it! I assumed I had received that necessary betrayal and took my shopping bag full of Christmas presents into London's winter mud. The editor in his last letter had invited me, jokingly, to Christmas dinner, and I had written an equally joking acceptance and then come, two thousand miles I believe, for a London holiday. Such schemes, delightful in the anticipation and the later retelling, have their drawbacks in present practice. I'd arrived three days in advance, and thought it best to deliver gifts in time for Christmas morning and allow my host to rejudge the size of his goose and add a plum or so to his pudding. At the door, back of an English green hall, I rang the bell. It was answered by this very large, very golden young man, who, when he spoke, was obviously American. Let me see how nearly I can remember the conversation. It contributes to the point.

"I asked if my friends were in.

"He said no, they were out for the afternoon; he was babysitting with their two daughters.

"I said I just wanted to leave off some presents, and could he please tell them to expect me for dinner, Christmas day.

"Oh, he said. You must be—well, I'm going to be coming to see you this evening!

"I laughed again, surprised. Very well, I said, I look forward to it. We shook hands, and I hurried off. He seemed affable and I gained interest in the coming meeting. First rule of behavior in the literary community: never condemn a man in the living room for any indiscretion he has put on paper. The amount of *charity* you wish to extend to the living-room barbarian because of his literary excellence is a matter of your own temperament. My point, however, is that we exchanged no more than seventy-five or a hundred words. Virtually I only heard his voice. At any rate, back at Hampstead, as sherry gave way for redder wine, I happened to pick up the magazine with the writer's article. Well, I decided, I shall give it one more chance. I opened it and began to read." Newboy glared over the rim, set down the glass without looking at it and pressed his lips to a slash. "It was lucid, it was vivid, it was both arch and ironic. What I had taken for banality was the most delicate satire. The piece presented an excruciating vision of the conditions under which the country struggled, as well as the absurdity of the author's own position as American and tourist. It walked that terribly difficult line between grace and pathos. And all I had heard was his *voice!* It was retiring, the slightest bit effeminate, with a period and emphasis oddly awry with the great object of fresh water, redwoods, and Rockies who spoke with it. But what, simply, had happened was that now I could *hear* that voice informing the prose, supplying the emphasis here or there to unlock for me what previously had been as dense and graceless as a telephone directory. I have delighted in all of this writer's work since with exquisite enjoyment!" Newboy took another sip. "Ah, but there is a brief corollary. Your critics here in the States have done me the ultimate kindness of choosing only the work of mine *I* find interesting for their discussions, and those interminable volumes of hair-splitting which insure a university position for me when the Diplomatic Service exhausts my passion for tattle, they let by. On my last trip to your country I was greeted with a rather laudatory review of the reissue of my early poems, in one of your more prestigious literary magazines, by a lady whom modesty forbids me to call incisive if only because she had been so generous with her praise. She was the first American to write of me. But before she ever did, I had followed her critical writings with an avidity I usually have only for poets. A prolific critic of necessity must say many absurd things. The test is, once a body of articles has passed your eye, whether the intelligence and acumen is more memorable than the absurdity. I had never met her. To come off a plane, pick up three magazines at the airport, and, in the taxi to the hotel, discover her article halfway through the second was a delight, a rarity, a pleasure for which once, in fantasy, I perhaps became a writer. And *at* the hotel, she had left a letter, not at the desk, but in my door: She was passing through New York, was in a hotel two blocks away, and wanted to know if I would meet her for a drink that evening, assuming my flight had not tired me out. I was delighted, I was grateful: what better creatures we would be if such attention were not so enjoyable. It was a pleasant drink, a pleasant evening: the relation has become the most rewarding friendship in the years since. It is rare enough, when people who have been first introduced by reputation *can* move on to a personal friendship, to remark it. But I noted this some days later, when I returned to one of her articles: Part of the measured consideration that informed her writing came from her choice of vocabulary. You know the Pope couplet: *When Ajax strives some rock's vast weight to throw,/The line too labours and the words move slow.* She had a penchant for following a word ending in a heavy consonant with a word that began with one equally heavy. In my mind, I had constructed a considered and leisurely tone of voice which, even when the matter lacked, informed her written utterances with dignity. Using the same vocabulary she wrote with, I realized, on the evening we met, she speaks extremely rapidly, with animation and enthusiasm. And certainly her intelligence is as acute as I had ever judged it. But

182

though she has become one of my closest friends, I have lost practically all enjoyment in reading her. Even as I re-read what before has given me the greatest intellectual pleasure, the words rush together in *her* vocal pattern, and all dignity and reserve has deserted the writing; I can only be grateful that, when we meet, we can argue and dissect the works before us till dawn, so that I still have some benefit of her astounding analytical faculty." He drank once more. "How can I possibly tell if your poems are good? We've met. I've heard you speak. And I have not even broached the convolved and emotional swamp some people are silly enough to call an objective judgment, but merely the critical distortion that comes from having heard your voice." Newboy waited, smiling.

"Is that a story you tell to everybody who asks you to read their poems?"

"Ah!" Newboy raised his finger. "*I* asked *you* if I might be *allowed* to read them. It is a story I have told to several people who've asked me for a judgment." Newboy swirled blunted ice. "Everyone knows everyone. Yes, you're right." He nodded. "I wonder sometimes if the purpose of the Artistic Community isn't to provide a concerned social matrix which simultaneously assures that no member, regardless of honors or approbation, has the slightest idea of the worth of his own work."

Kidd drank his beer, resentful at the long-windedness but curious about the man indulging it.

"The aesthetic equation," Newboy mused. "The artist has some internal experience that produces a poem, a painting, a piece of music. Spectators submit themselves to the work, which generates an inner experience for them. But historically it's a very new, not to mention vulgar, idea that the spectator's experience should be identical to, or even have anything to do with, the artist's. That idea comes from an over-industralized society which has learned to distrust magic—"

"You're here!" Lanya seized his arm. "You look so bright and shiny and polished. I didn't recognize you!"

He pulled her against his shoulder. "This is Ernest Newboy," glad of the interruption. "This is my friend Lanya."

She looked surprised. "Kidd told me you helped him up at Mr Calkins'." She and Newboy shook hands across Kidd's chest.

"I'm staying there. But I was let out for the evening."

"I was there for days but I don't think I ever got a night off."

Newboy laughed. "There is that to it, yes. And where do you stay now?"

"We live in the park. You mustn't look astonished. Lots of people do. It's practically as posh an address as Roger's, today."

"Really? Do the two of you live there together?"

"We live in a little part all by ourselves. We visit people. When we're hungry. Nobody's come to visit us yet. But it's better that way."

Newboy laughed again.

Kidd watched the poet smile at her banter.

"I wouldn't trust myself to hunt you out of your hidden spot. But you must certainly come and see me, some day during the afternoon." Then to Kidd: "And you can bring your poems."

"Sure." Kidd watched Lanya be delightedly silent. "When?"

"The next time Roger decides it's Tuesday, why don't you both come around? I promise you won't have the same problem again."

He nodded vigorously. "All right."

Mr Newboy smiled hugely. "Then I'll expect you." He nodded, still smiling, turned, and walked away.

"Close your mouth." Lanya squinted about. "Oh, I guess it's okay. I don't see any flies." Then she squeezed his hand.

In the cage, neon flickered. Music rasped from a speaker.

"Oh, quick, let's go!"

He came with her, once glanced back: the back of Newboy's blue serge was wedged on both sides with leather, but he could not tell if the poet was talking or just standing.

"What have you been doing all day?" he asked on the cool street.

She shrugged closer. "Hanging out with Milly. I ate a lot of breakfast. Jommy is cooking this week so I really had more than I wanted. In the morning I advised John on a work project. Kibitzed on somebody's Chinese Checker game. After lunch I took off and played my harmonica. Then I came back for dinner. Jommy is a love, but dull. How was your job?"

184

"Strange." He pulled her close. (She brushed his big knuckles with her small ones, pensive, bending, removed.) "Yeah, they're weird. Hey, Newboy asked us up there, huh?" She rubbed her head against his shoulder and could have been laughing.

Her arm moved under his hand. "Do you want this back now?"

"Oh. Yeah. Thanks," and took the orchid, stopping to fix the longest blade in his belt loop. Then they walked again.

He did not demand a name. What does this confidence mean? Long in her ease and reticence, released from an effort to demand and pursue, there is an illusion of center. Already, presounded, I am armed with portents of a disaster in the consciousness, the failure to suspect, to inspect. Is she free here, or concerned with a complex intimacy dense to me? Or I excuse myself from her, lacking appellation. Some mesh, flush, terminal turned here through the larynx's trumpet. The articulate fear slips, while we try to measure, but come away with only the perpetual angle of distortion, the frequency of an amazed defraction.

In the half—or rather four-fifths dark, the lions looked wet. He brushed his right knuckles against the stone flank in passing: It was exactly as warm as Lanya's wrist, brushing his knuckles on the left.

How does she find her way? he wondered, but thirty steps on realized he had anticipated the last dark turn himself.

Distant firelight filigreed through near leaves. Lanya pushed them aside and said, "Hi!"

A shirtless man, holding a shovel, stood knee deep in a . . . half-dug grave?

Another man in a denim shirt, unbuttoned, stood on the lip. A young woman in a serape, her chin balanced on both fists, sat on a log, watching.

"Are you still at this?" Lanya asked. "You were *this* far along when I was here this morning."

"I wish you'd let me dig," the young woman said.

"Sure," the bare-chested man with the shovel said. He shook blond hair from his shoulders. "Just as soon as we get it going."

The woman dropped her fists between her patched knees. Her hair was very long. In the distant light it was

185

hard to see where its color was between bronze and black.

"I wonder where John gets the ideas for these projects," the man in the denim shirt on the lip said. "I was just as happy running off to squat in the bushes."

The guy with the shovel made a face. "I guess he's worried about pollution. I mean, *look* at all this!" The shovel blade swung.

But other than the dozen people standing or sitting over near the flaming cinderblocks, Kidd could see nothing outside the bubble of night the flames defined.

"Can you actually see what you're doing there?" Lanya asked.

"Enough to dig a God-damn latrine!" The shovel chunked into earth again.

"You know," the one on the lip said, "I could be in Hawaii right now. I really could. I had a chance to go, but I decided I'd come here instead. Isn't that too fucking much?"

As though she'd heard this too many times, the woman on the log sighed, palmed her knees, stood up, and walked off.

"Well, I really could." He frowned after her, then back at the pile of dirt. "Did your old lady really want to dig?"

"Naw." Another shovelful landed. "I don't think so."

Slap-slap, slap-slap, slap-slap went a rolled *Times* against a thigh. John walked up, cutting out more light.

Chunk-shush, chunk-shush went the shovel.

"They're digging it awfully close to where everybody stays," Kidd said to Lanya, "for a latrine."

"Don't tell me," Lanya said. "Tell them."

"I've been wondering about that too," John said, and stilled his paper. "You think we're digging it too close, huh?"

"Shit," the one who wanted to be in Hawaii said and glared at Kidd.

"Look," Kidd said, "you do it your way," then walked off.

And immediately tripped over the foot of somebody's sleeping bag. Recovering himself, he just missed another's head. Millimeters beyond the circle of darkness were chifferobes, bureaus, easy-chairs, daybeds, waiting to be moved from here, to there, to someplace else . . . He blinked in the fireplace's heat and put his hands in his back pockets. Standing just behind three others, he watched the curly-headed boy (Jommy?) wrestle a barrel— "Isn't this great, man? Oh, wow! Look at this. When we found this, I just didn't believe it— It's flour. Real flour. And it's still good. Oh, hey thanks, Kidd. Yeah, push it this . . . yeah, this way." —around the end of the picnic table.

"Here?" Kidd asked, and grunted. The barrel weighed two hundred pounds at least.

"Yeah."

Others stepped back a little more.

Both grunting now, Kidd and Jommy got it in place.

"You know," Jommy said, standing back, smiling, and wiping his forehead, "if you're hungry around here, man, you should ask for something to eat."

Kidd tried to figure out what that referred to when Milly and Lanya walked up. "It's awfully nice to see you here again and helping out," Milly said, passing between Kidd and the fire. The hot places just above his eyes cooled in her shadow. She passed on.

Lanya was laughing.

"Why'd we come here?" he asked.

"I just wanted to talk to Milly for a moment. All done." She took his hand. They started walking through the blanket rolls and sleeping bags. "We'll go sleep back at my spot, where we were last night."

"Yeah," he said. "Your blankets still there?"

"If nobody moved them."

"Hawaii," somebody said ten feet off. "I don't know why I don't take off for there right now."

Lanya said: "John asked me if you wanted to take charge of the new commune latrine work project."

"Jesus—!"

"He thinks you have leadership qualities—"

"And a feeling for the job," he finished. "I've got enough work to do." Blinking away after-images of fire-light, he saw that the blond-haired guy with no shirt now, stood on the lip, shoveling dirt back in the hole.

He moved with her into dark.

Once more he wondered how she found her way. Yet once more, in the dark, he stopped first when he realized they had arrived.

"What are you doing?"

"I hung the blanket up over a limb. I'm pulling it down."

"You can see?"

"No." Leaves roared. Falling, the blanket brushed his face. They spread it together. "Pull down on your left . . . no, your right corner."

Grass and twigs gave under him as he lurched to the center on his knees. They collided, warm. "You know the Richards?" Artichokes . . .

He frowned.

She lay down with him, opened her fist on his stomach. "Um?"

"They're stark raving twits."

"Really?"

"Well, they're stark. They're pretty twitty too. They haven't started raving, but that's just a matter of time. Why do I have this job, anyway?"

She shrugged against him. "I thought, when you took it, you were one of those people who has to have one."

He humphed. "Tak took one look at me and decided I'd never worked in my life. I *don't* need the money, do I?"

She put her hand between his legs. He let his legs fall open and put his own hand on top, thick fingers pressing between her thin ones. "I haven't needed any yet." She squeezed.

He grunted. "You wouldn't. I mean, people like you. You get invitations places, right?" He looked up. "He's a systems engineer, she's a . . . housewife, I guess. She reads poetry. And she cooks with wine. People like that, you know, it's funny. But I can't imagine them screwing. I guess they have to, though. They've got kids."

She pulled her hand away, and leaned up on his chest. "And people like us." Her voice puffed against his chin. "Screwing is the easiest thing to imagine us doing, right? But you *can't* think of us with kids, can you?" She giggled, and put her mouth on his, put her tongue in his mouth. Then she stiffened and squeaked, "Owww."

He laughed. "Let me take this thing off before I stab somebody!" He raised his hips and pulled his orchid from the belt loops, pulled his belt out.

They held each other, in long lines of heat and cool. Once, on his back, naked, under her, while his face rubbed her neck, and he clutched her rocking buttocks, he opened his eyes: light came through the jungle of their hair. She halted, raising. He bent back his head.

188

Beyond the trees, striated monsters swayed.

The scorpions passed, luminous, on the path below.

More trees cut out their lights, and more, and more.

He looked up at her and saw, across the top of her breasts, the imprint of his chain, before darkness. Then, like a two-petaled flower, opened too early at false, fugitive dawn, they closed, giggling, and the giggling became long, heavy breaths as she began to move again. After she came, he pulled the corner of the blanket over them.

"You know, he tried to cheat me out of my money."

"Mmm." She snuggled.

"Mr Richards. He told Madame Brown he'd pay me five dollars an hour. Then he just gave me five for the whole afternoon. You know?" He turned.

When he pushed against her leg she said, "For God's sakes, you're still all hard . . ." and sucked her teeth.

"He did. Of course they fed me. Maybe he'll settle up tomorrow."

But she took his hand and moved it down him; again meshed, their fingers closed on him and she made him rub, and left him rubbing. She put her head down on his hip, and licked and nipped his knuckles, the shriveled scrotal flesh. He beat, till her hair on his thighs was nearly lost in some vegetative horror, then grunted, "Okay . . ." His fist hit her face three times, before he let her take him. She slid her arms behind his hip, put her legs around his, while he panted and let go of her hair.

Anxiety lost outlines beneath glittering fatigue. Once he did something like wake to her back against his stomach. He reached beneath her arm to hold her breast, the nipple a button on his palm. She took his thumb as gently, he realized, as she possibly could, in case he slept.

So he slept.

There was grey light after a while. On his back, he watched leaves appear in it. Suddenly he sat, in one motion, to his knees. He said:

"I want to be a poet. I want to be a great, famous, wonderful poet."

As he looked toward the hem of darkness beneath grey streakings, something caught in his stomach. His arms began to shake; he was nauseated; and his head throbbed; and throbbed; and throbbed. He opened his mouth and breathed roughly through it. He shook his

189

head, felt his face shaking, and dragged his breath back in. "Wow," he said. The pain receded, and let him smile. "I don't think they . . . *make* poets as great as I want to be!" That only came out as a hoarse whisper. Finally he rose, naked, to a squat and looked back at her.

He thought she would have slept through: her head was propped on her hand. She watched him.

He whispered. "Go back to sleep."

She pulled the blanket across her arm and put her head down.

He turned for his shirt, took the pen. He opened the notebook to what he had written at the bar. Cross-legged on the blanket's edge, he readied to recopy. The paper was blued with halfdawn. While he contemplated the first word, distractions of book jackets, printed praise, receptions by people who ranged from Richards to New-boys— The twig under his ankle brought him back. He shook his head again, shifted his ankle, again bent to re-cast fair copy. His eyes dropped in a well of *Time* maga-zine covers, ("Poet Refuses Pulitzer Prize"), the audience's faces as he stood on Minor Latham's stage where he had consented to give a rare reading. He hauled himself back before the fantasies' intensity hit pain. Then he laughed, because he had still not re-copied a word. He sat a while more, unable to write for thinking, amused at his lack of control, but bored with its obvious lesson.

Self-laughter did not stop the fantasies.

But neither could the fantasies stop self-laughter.

He looked in the lightening sky for shapes. Mist bellied and folded and coiled and never broke. He lay back beside her, began to rub her under the blanket. She turned to him and hid in his neck when he tried to kiss her. "I don't think I taste very good," she murmured. "I'm all sleepy—" He licked her teeth. When he put his thumb in her cunt, she began to laugh through the kiss, till she caught her breath at his cock and another finger. His knees outside of hers, he swung his hips. His wet hand held her shoulder, his dry one her hair.

Later, he woke again with his arms tight around her, the blanket wound around them from rolling. The sky was lighter. "You know, I shouldn't go back to that God-damn job," he said. "What do I need a job for, here?"

"Shhh," she said. "Shhhhhh," and rubbed his shaven cheek. "Now shhhhhh."

He closed his eyes.

190

"Yes, who is it?" with a timbre of complaint.

"It's Kidd. Look, if it's too early, I'll come back—"

The chain rattled.

"No. No. It's all right." Mrs Richards, in a green bathrobe, opened the door.

"Isn't anybody up yet? I didn't know how early it was."

"It's all right," Mrs Richards repeated. "It's probably about eight." She yawned. "Would you like some coffee?"

"Thanks, yes. Can I use your bathroom." He stepped by before she finished her sleepy nod. "You know you got a letter in your mailbox, airmail?"

"I thought the boxes were broken."

"Your box is okay." He paused with his hand on the bathroom door jamb. "And there's a letter in it."

"Oh dear!"

He had already lathered for shaving before he registered her voice's despair.

June, in blue slacks and a pink sweater, a daisy embroidered near the collar, brought full coffee cups to the table as he sat. "Good morning."

"Were you up?"

"In my room. I'm always the early riser in this family. What have you been doing since yesterday?"

"Nothing. This morning, before I came here, I copied out a poem I wrote last night."

"Read it to me?"

"No."

She looked disappointed. "I guess I wouldn't want to read anything I wrote to other people either."

He held his cup in both hands, sipping.

"Is that strong enough for you?" Mrs Richards asked from the kitchen doorway. "I've got the jar of instant right here."

"It's fine." Black coffee hung in his mouth's emptied center, losing heat.

"Is Bobby up yet?" Mrs Richards asked from the kitchen.

"I heard him moving. What about Daddy?"

"Let your father sleep, dear. He had a hard day yesterday."

June asked: "Do you want some more coffee?"

He shook his head, and with his movement the bitter taste spread over her yellow hair, the plants in their brass pots, the plastic handles on the green drapes' pull. He smiled and swallowed it all.

Apartment 19-B was open, abandoned and perfectly ordinary:

Appliances in the kitchen, bathmat over the tub edge, the beds unmade. And there was not one book. Well, it would hold furniture.

The legs of the easy chair roared in the hall. Silly, he mulled in the echo. Why don't I ask them where they want it. Fuck—! Tilt the chair to get it in.

The chair roared; the daybed mattress on its side *Sssssssss*ed. He left it leaning against the flowered couch, and went back out into the hall for the chifferobe.

Two elevator doors opened. From one came wind, from the other, Mr Richards. "Hi, there. Thought I'd stop up before I went out." His tie dropped, severe and indigo, between worsted lapels. "What are you doing with all the junk?"

Kidd worked his feet on sandal sole and vinyl tile. "I . . . well, I was putting it in the apartment down the hall."

Mr Richards walked past him, looked into 19-B. "It doesn't matter too much." He looked back. "Does it?"

They went together into 19-A.

"I figure I can get all this stuff out by tonight, Mr Richards." Kidd was relieved there was no protest. "Then I'll get the floors and everything mopped. I'll have it really nice. She'll like it. I'll do a good job."

Mr Richards frowned up at the dead bulbs.

"If you'd rather, I could take the stuff into the cellar." Relaxed enough to offer, he knew the offer would be refused.

"Only if you want." Mr Richards took a breath, and came in. His cordovan ground on the piled glass. He looked down. "Don't see any need. To take it all the way to the cellar. I don't know what's in that cellar, anyway." Not moving his foot, he looked at the remaining furniture. "She'll like it. Yes." He took his hand from his pocket. "Why don't you get your other shoe on, boy? You'll cut your foot all to hell."

"Yes, sir."

Mr Richards stepped away from the sweepings, shook his head.

"Mr Richards——?"

"You know, I've been thinking——" Mr Richards fingered his collar at his heavy neck; he might once have been a heavy man—"I mean if it's a good idea for us to move. For Mary. What do you think? She takes to you, you know. That's good. I was wondering what Edna was going to send us. She has some funny friends. Wondered about you too, until I saw you out from under all that dirt. But you seem like a nice kid. What do you think?"

"Your downstairs neighbors are pretty rough."

"Do you think it'll do any good, coming up here?"

It occurred to him to accuse: *You don't.* But he shrugged.

"What do you think? Go on. You can tell me. The situation we're all in now, we have to *make* ourselves be honest. I'll admit, it's hard for me. But you try."

"Why do you stay in the city?"

"Do you think she'd go? No, we live here: she wouldn't be able to do it." Then a breath that had been held in him broke away painfully. Mr Richards raised his thumbs to his belt. "Do you know, in here, in this house, I almost have the feeling that none of it's real? Or just a very thin shell."

Kidd wanted to frown. But didn't. *Honest,* he thought.

"Mary lives in her world of cooking and cleaning and the children. I come home. And nothing looks . . . I can't describe it. A man's home is supposed to be—well, a place where everything is real, solid, and he can grab hold. In our home, I just don't know. I come in from that terrible world, and I'm in some neverland I just don't believe in. And the less I believe in it, the more it slips. I think it's me, sometimes. Mary's always been a strange woman; she hasn't had it that easy. She tries so hard to be . . . well, civilized. We *both* do. But what with this . . ." He nodded toward the open balcony doors. Outside, layers of mist pulled from mist. "She's got imagination. Oh, that she's got, all right. It was the thing I first saw in her. My work, well, it's interesting. But it doesn't require that much what you'd call creativity. At least you probably wouldn't think so. But we get things done. Still, I *like* to come home to somebody who's got all sorts of ideas, reads books and things. But——" Mr Richards' hands rubbed at his hips, searching for pockets—"suddenly you begin to feel she's changing the world into her own ideas. She doesn't go out, now; but who could blame her. And once you get inside the door, it's all hers."

"She keeps a nice house," Kidd offered.

"Oh, she does much more than that. She keeps us too. We all say things for her, you notice? Everybody who comes in there. She projects this . . . well, nervousness. And then you start to try and figure out what she wants you to say; and you say it. At first so you won't get her upset. Then, out of habit. You don't think so?"

"I don't . . . well, not much."

"You do, unless you just fit into it naturally. She used to always like musicians. And suddenly everybody who came to see us was a musician, or remembered that they used to play in the high school band, or something. And that was fine until she had some people over to play some chamber music stuff—" He raised his head and laughed. "That was funny. They were terrible. Mary and I laughed about it for weeks." He lowered his chin. "But that was the end of the music. Now—well, she's been reading that fellow you were talking about—"

"Ernest Newboy?" Kidd resolved not to mention meeting him again.

"Yeah. And you're here. Once she tried to get interested in engineering. I brought home a few of our younger men. And their wives. I brought the ones who had the ideas—like she said. That didn't last too long." He shook his head. "But she makes it all go her way. Which would be fine if I thought . . . thought that it was real. That if I touched anything, it wouldn't just crumble, like eggshell, like plaster. You think I should talk to Edna?" He smiled: his hands found his pockets, finally, and sank in them. "Maybe it is just me." He looked around the room again. "I hope moving does some good."

"Is Mrs Richards happy?"

"Not as happy as I'd like to see her. You know we used to have another—well, that's none of your affair. I won't put it on you. I've gone on too long already."

"That's okay."

"Better go. Have to be in the office by ten and the warehouse by eleven thirty."

"Hey, Mr Richards?"

Mr Richards turned in the doorway.

"You've got a letter in your mailbox. Airmail."

"Ah!" Mr Richards nodded. "Thanks." He went out.

"—and Mr Richards?" When there was no answer, he went to the hall. Both elevators were closed.

He put his hand in his pocket and felt the moist, crushed bill. He shook his head and started to work a dresser toward the door. Three feet, and he decided to take the drawers out.

After he'd moved furniture for a long time, he went out on the balcony. On the building across, smoke coiled. The mist to his right was bright as ivory. When he looked down, the top of a tree was just visible in pooling haze.

He moved the final large pieces of furniture; then, two at a time, he lugged off the cane-bottom chairs. On the last lay the notebook.

He rubbed his shirt pocket, wondering if he should take a break. The pen slipped under the cloth. He looked at the emptied room. In the doorway was the pail, the mop, the soap box. He moved his teeth on one another, took up the book and sat.

He wrote slowly. Every little while he looked sharply up, toward the door, and even toward the window. Eight lines later he put the pen in his pocket. The already enlarged front knuckle of his left middle finger was sore and dented from the pen. He yawned, closed the book, and sat for a while watching the fog stretch and constrict. Then he tossed the book on the floor, stood up, and carried his chair into 19-B.

He used a piece of cardboard for a dustpan, and carried the sweepings into the other apartment. Finding no can, he dumped them into a bureau drawer. Back in the kitchen, he clanked the pail into the sink. The water crashed on the zinc, swirled up in suds; crashing diminished to roaring, muffled more and more in foam.

"I just don't know what I was thinking of!"

"It's all right, ma'am. Really—"

"I just don't know what's the matter with me. Here they are—"

"That's all right, Mrs Richards."

"Right in the icebox." She swung the door back. "See. I made them. I really did."

Three sandwiches, each with corner hole, lay on a plate.

He laughed. "Look, I believe you."

"I made them. Then I thought I'd send June and

Bobby up. Then I thought again, Oh no, it must be too early for lunch; so I put them in the icebox. And then—" She closed the icebox door halfway—"I forgot about them. You could eat them now."

"Thank you. That's fine. All I wanted to tell you is I got the furniture all out, and the back two rooms mopped, and the back bathroom."

"Take them." She opened the door again. "Go ahead. Go inside and eat. Oh!" The icebox door slammed and just missed knocking the plate from his hand. "Coffee! You'll want coffee. There, I'll start the water. Go on. I'll be in in a minute."

Maybe she is mad (he thought and went into the living room), too.

He sat on the L-shaped couch, put the plate on the coffee table, and peeled up the bread corners, one after the other: peanut butter and jelly, spam and mustard, and—? He stuck his finger in it, licked: Liver pâté.

He ate that one first.

"Here you are!" She put down his cup and sat on the other leg of the L, to sip her own.

"It's very good," he mumbled with a full mouth, joggled the sandwich demonstratively.

She sipped a while more. Then she said: "You know what I want?"

"Mmm?"

She looked down at the notebook lying on the couch and nodded. "I want you to read me one of your poems."

He swallowed. "Naw, I should go upstairs and finish mopping. Then clean up the kitchen. You can start getting your stuff together, and I'll take some of it up this evening."

"Tomorrow!" she cried, "Oh, tomorrow! You've been working terribly hard. Read me a poem. Besides, we don't have a thing ready."

He smiled and contemplated murder.

And here, he thought, it would be so much easier to get away with . . . "I don't think you'd like them."

Hands together in her lap, she leaned forward: "Please."

He dragged the book into his lap (like I was covering myself, he thought. I could kill her). "All right." Something tickled the underside of his thigh. It was sweat catching on the chain that bound him. "I'll read . . ." He opened the book, coughed: "This one." He took a breath,

196

and looked at the paper. He was very hot. The chains across his back pulled: he was hunching his shoulders. When he opened his mouth, for a moment he was sure no voice would come.

But he read.

He dropped word after word into the room's silence. Meaning peeled away from his voice and raveled.

Sounds he had placed together to evoke a tone of voice mis-sounded. The mouth's machinery was too clumsy to follow what his eye knew. He read each word, terribly aware how the last *should* have fallen.

Once he coughed.

For one phrase he grew quieter, easier. Then, frantically, at a place where his voice closed out a comma, he wondered, Why did I choose this one! I should have chosen *any* one except this!

Hoarsely he whispered the last line, and put one hand on his stomach to press away the small pain. He took some more deep breaths and sat back. The back of his shirt was sopping.

"That was lovely."

He wanted to and didn't laugh.

". . . Lost inside your eye . . ." she misquoted. No, paraphrased.

His stomach tightened again.

"Yes, I liked that very much."

He arched his fingers there, and said: "Thank you."

"Thank *you*. I feel . . ."

He thought: I'm too tired to kill anyone.

". . . feel that you have given me something of yourself, a very precious thing."

"Uhh." He nodded vaguely. Tension finally forced the laugh: "You just like it because you know me." With the laugh, some of the tiredness went.

"Definitely." She nodded. "I don't know any more about poetry than Arthur does. Really. But I'm glad you read it. For the trust."

"Oh." Something more terrifying than the possibility of murder happened in him. "You really are?" A cold metallic wire sewed somewhere, taking small stitches. "I better get back up to finish the mopping." He began to move on the couch, preparing to stand.

"I'm very glad you read that poem to me."

He stood. "Yeah. Sure. I'm glad you . . . liked it," and hurried for the door. It closed behind him far too loud. In the hall, his face heating, he thought: She was going to say something else to me! What else was she going to . . . ? He hurried to the elevator.

In 19-B he filled the pail again, kicked off his sandal, and slushed the mop in suds. Foam, mop-strands and water returned him to varied beaches. He mopped angrily, remembering waves.

The water slopped his feet. It had been warm when he put it in the pail. Each stroke wet the baseboard further along.

They're cheating me, he thought and twisted the mophead. Among failing suds the water was black. I've got to tell them, he thought, that I *know* it. At least *ask* them why they're not paying me what they said. Of course they didn't say it to me. Not that I need the money, even . . . That made him even angrier.

He sloshed up more beaches in his mind, moving from room to room.

I don't have a name, he thought. Tides and tides rolled from the tangled cords. These things I'm writing, they're not *descriptions* of anything. They're complex names. I don't want her to believe what they say. I just want her to believe I said them. Somewhere (Japan? Yeah . . .) I walked up the wharf from where the little boats were tied and the black rocks gave out to sand. And everything, even the sand slipping back under my feet, looked miles away like it used to all the time when I was tired, when I was a kid. One of the other fellows from the ship called to me. What did he call me? And how could I have possibly answered?

His eyes stung; he sniffed for the detergent smell.

Or was the smoke thicker? He wiped his face on his cuff.

In the hall, people laughed: footsteps. A door closed.

Gooseflesh enveloped him. His next heartbeat shocked loose his breath; he breathed. Perhaps ten seconds later he realized how tightly he was holding the handle. He laid the mop on the floor, went to the open door, and looked into the . . . empty hall. For at least a minute.

Then he got the mop and began to work again.

They're cheating me! he thought to replay the familiar. The tone was wrong. To think words set off pricklings.

More water.

His hands, soaked and soaked again, were translucent, the yellow all out of the horn, flesh white and ragged around the fragment nails and swollen crowns. Yeah, leprosy. He recalled Lanya sucking his middle finger with something like relief. What she liked was funny. Especially what she liked in him. Her absence mystified.

Slopping suds over recollected sands, he tried to hallucinate her face. It dissolved in water. He scrubbed the balcony sill, and backed into the room, swinging cords from side to side.

Confront them about his salary? Yes! Images of gifts for her. But he had not seen one store open; not *one!* Do they talk salary, he pondered, and I talk wages just to keep up?

But we *haven't* talked!

The inside of his mouth held much more room than the room. As he mopped, he seemed to stagger, shin-deep in tongue, bumping his knees on teeth, and his head against wet, palatal rugae, grasping for an uvula to steady himself. He flopped the mop in the water again, eyes a-sting, and passed his arm across his face; the blunted chain raked his cheek. Energies searched through the mechanic of his body for points to wreck changes. The rhythm and slosh lopped talk out of the brain. "I live in the mouth . . ." he had been mumbling over and over, he realized as he stopped it. Stopping, he mopped harder at the swirling floor.

"You . . . ?"

He blinked at June in the doorway.

". . . didn't get . . . ?"

He grunted interrogatively.

"You said you were going to get me a . . . picture of . . ." Her knuckle made its habitual strike at her chin.

"Huh? But I thought you didn't . . ."

Her eyes beat, banal and wild. Then she ran from the door.

"Hey, look, I'm sorry! I didn't think you . . ." thought about running after her, sucked his teeth, shook his head, didn't, and sighed.

In the kitchen, he changed the dirty water in his pail for clear, then dry-mopped as much as possible of the flood.

He worked methodically. Every once in a while he made a sound of disgust, or shook his head. Finally he got to swiping after his own footprints. Which was futile; you just made more.

Balancing on one foot in the doorway, he fumbled at his sandal. Leather and wet flesh: He might as well throw it away. But the tab slipped into the buckle. He picked up his notebook and clacked to the elevator.

Half a minute later, the door opened (from the door beside it, where he did not want to look, came hissing wind); he stepped in. The thought, when he recalled it later, seemed to have no genesis:

He did not press seventeen.

"16" glowed before his falling finger in the falling car.

4

No bell-box was on the door.

Cloth or paper covered the hole inside.

Jaw clamped, he knocked; clamped tighter when something inside moved.

The door swung back. "Yeah?" Hot grease clattered.

Behind the man in the undershirt, the girl came forward, her features disappearing to silhouette before the hurricane lamp on the wall.

"What'cha want?" the man asked. "You want something to eat? Come on in. What'cha want?"

"No, I just was . . . well." He made himself grin and stepped inside. "I just wanted to know who was here."

"You wanna eat, you can." The girl behind the man's shoulder floated back far enough to take light on a cheek bone.

Against the wall people slept in iron bunks. Men sat on the mattresses on the floor. The lantern-light cast down hard blacks to their left.

The door swung behind Kidd. When it slammed, only one looked up.

Against the wall leaned a motorcycle with a day-glo gas tank. In one corner stood a dressmaker's mannequin, splashed with red paint, head twisted to the side, and looped with rounds of greasy chain (but none of the kind Kidd wore under his shirt and pants).

"I been doing work for the people upstairs. I was just wondering who was down here." The room smelled stale, and the cooking odor brought him momentarily back to a filthy fried-food stand where he had not been able to finish eating in waterfront Caracas. "That's why I came down."

Somewhere the sound of water ceased. Wet, blond hair dripping down his shoulders, a boy walked, naked, into the room, picked up a pair of black jeans. Glistening, he balanced on one leg. He glanced at Kidd, grinned: then his foot, bunioned, hammer-toed, and mostly ankle (with a dog's choke chain wrapped three times around it), went into the denim.

"The people upstairs?" The man shook his head, chuckling. "They must be somethin', all the shit that comes down here. What they do to each other all the time? Hey, you want to smoke some dope? Smokey, get our friend here some dope. Get me some too." The girl moved away. "You like dope, man, don't'cha?"

Kidd shrugged. "Sure."

"Hey, yeah. I thought you looked like you did." He grinned and hooked his thumbs over his beltless jeans; his first finger joints were tattooed *love* and *hate*. Between thumb and forefinger on the left was a large, red 13. "The noise that comes down here out of that place; was he beatin' her up last night?"

"Huh?" Kidd asked. "I thought you made all the damn noise."

Someone else said: "Oh, man, there was all sorts of crying and stuff comin' down."

And someone else: "Look, Thirteen; what come up from this place must be pretty weird too sometimes."

The second voice was familiar. Kidd looked for it:

Sitting on the bottom bunk, out of the light, was the newspaper carrier, Joaquim Faust—who now raised a finger in greeting. "How you doing, kid?"

Kidd gave back a bewildered smile.

There was someone in the bed Faust sat on.

Smokey returned with a glass jar, a plastic hose and ass bowl in the rubber stopper.

Thirteen took it from her. "God-damn water pipe, and you think somebody would fill it up with water—or wine or something. That's nice too, you know? Creme de Menthe or like that." He shook his head. "Nobody's got time." On the wall he struck a wooden match. "Some *good* hash, man." He pursed his lips on the rubber tube. The flame suddenly inverted over the brass. The bottle swirled with grey. "Here you go!" he mouthed, with tucked chin.

Kidd took the warm glass and sucked sweet, chalky smoke.

The arch of air grew solid beneath his sternum: breath held, palate tight, somewhere after ten seconds he felt sweat on the small of his back. "Thanks . . . !" Smoke exploded from his nose.

The pipe had gone to others.

"What kind of work you doing?"

"Hey, Thirteen, he gonna eat?" somebody called from the kitchen.

Through the doorway Kidd saw an enamel stove licked with burn marks.

The boy from the shower stooped to buckle his boots. "Give you a hand in a second." He tucked his cuffs into the boot tops, and stood. Scratching his wet belly, he ambled inside and asked, "What is that shit, anyway?"

"I've been moving furniture around for them, upstairs." Kidd said. "Thirteen—that's you?"

Thirteen raised his tattooed hand, then snapped his fingers. "Sure. Come on in, come on inside and sit." The girl passed Thirteen the water pipe and he extended it toward Kidd. "And have another toke."

Kidd drew in another chest full, and passed the pipe to someone else who wandered by.

Holding in the hash, Kidd noticed the mirror on the side wall, the end table with the crumpled antimacassar lingering from previous occupancy. He coughed: *"How—"* plosive with smoke—"long have you guys been down here?" What covered the door hole was the framed photograph of mother, father, and three children in their dated sailor suits, with the cracked coverglass.

"Too—" Thirteen exploded smoke of his own—"much. Somebody left that in the hallway, you know?"

He nodded.

Thirteen went on, "I just been here a couple of weeks. I mean in *this* place. Guys in and out here all the time. I don't even know how long I been in the city. Months, maybe. Cool. You?"

"Days." He looked again to Faust.

Faust was looking intently at the shape in the blanket.

Thirteen looked too, shook his head. "She got messed up, you know? I think she's got an infection or something. Course, it could be bubonic plague for all I know." He jabbed Kidd with his elbow. "Long as you're healthy, Bellona is great. But there's no doctors or nothing, you know?"

"Yeah. That must be bad."

203

From the kitchen; "What did you put in this shit, huh?"

"Will you stop bitching? Half of it's from last night."

"Then I know half of it won't kill me."

"Here, *do* something huh! Scrape that." A kitchen knife growled over metal.

"This place used to be all scorpions." Thirteen nodded toward the bed. "That's when she came here; she decided to be a member. Which is fine if you can do it. Guys get messed up like that too. But now she got an infection . . . If that's what it is."

Smokey returned with the waterless pipe, waiting at Thirteen's shoulder.

Kidd took it, sucked; Thirteen nodded approval.

"You . . . guys . . . are . . . ?" Kidd loosed smoke-spurts between his words.

"—Scorpions? Shit, no . . . Well, you know." He scrunched his face, with an appropriate hand joggle. "I don't intend to be, again, ever; and Denny in there," he thumbed at the boy from the shower who passed by the kitchen door, "ain't exactly on active duty any more." And that one's Denny, Kidd thought.

Thirteen took the pipe, sucked, and went off into a coughing fit.

"Hey, will she be all right?" Kidd asked, coming to the bed.

Faust made some noncommittal lip movement, lost in beard. "Somebody ought to take care of this girl." He kneaded his maroon and raveled knee.

She she she "She asleep?" sleep sleep. The hash was coming on. Sleep.

The olive landscape, mountains of shoulder and hip, was immobile.

Nobody there. Pillows?

Faust moved over for him.

Kidd sat on the bed's edge, warm from Faust.

"Isn't there a doctor *any* place in the city?" all over the city, city?

Faust's wrinkles shifted around on his face. "These sons of bitches wouldn't know if there was. I can't figure out whether to let her sleep or make her eat."

"She must be pretty tired if she can sleep through all this noise," Thirteen said. Coming up, Smokey handed the pipe to Faust, who closed his wrinkled eyelids when he sucked. When he. When.

"Maybe," Kidd suggested, "you better let her sleep. Save some food for when she wakes up," akes, akes.

"That—" Thirteen shook a tattooed finger—"is brains at work, Joaquim. Which are in short supply around here . . . Man!" He shook his head, turned away.

"Maybe," Faust nodded.

Kidd wondered whether it was Faust or the hash that muddled the meaning.

"Here."

He looked up for the pipe. Pipe. Plate? A plate of. Denny, face and chest still wet, stood in front of him, holding out a plate in a white, bath-wrinkled hand.

"Oh, thanks."

Faust took the other one.

"You ain't got no fork?" Denny asked.

"No." It was rice, it was onions, it had string beans in it, and corn. "Thanks." He looked up and took the fork. Water tracked on the white arm, shimmered in adolescent chest-hair, broken with acne.

Thirteen said, "You gotta give people *food*, you know? I mean, to be peaceable." Behind him, Smokey, plate just under her chin, ate eagerly.

It had meat in it too. Hash brought edges out from the grease that transformed the odor. He ate. And those were . . . nuts? No. Crisp potatoes. As the tastes staggered in his mouth, a muffled man's voice said something? something like, "Stop it! Now, *stop* it!" and a woman's wail rose toward the metallic.

He looked around, wondering which other room they were in.

Faust glanced at the ceiling.

So did Thirteen. "See what I'm talking about?" He sucked his teeth and shook his head. "They really go on up there."

The wail, which began to balk now toward sobbing, could have been either June or Mrs Richards. He had not realized before four for how alike their voices were.

Frowning, he ate more of the greasy rice (Bacon grease? Well, at any rate, bacon) and listened to forks tick tin.

Denny ate on one of the mattresses on the floor, back to Kidd: The marble knobs of vertebrae disappeared under the corn-colored hair which dried, lightened, curled.

Thirteen came from the kitchen at the rap on the door. "Hey, it's Nightmare!" Thirteen stepped back on

205

his sudden shadow. "Sweetheart, you just made hash time! And have something to eat for dessert."

It and the blazing apparition in the doorway went out.

"Come on in." Thirteen stepped back again. "What can we do for you?"

The tickings had stopped.

"I'm looking—" Nightmare stepped forward, jingling—"for mother-fuckers who want to run." He pushed away the tangled braid from his shoulder; his hand stayed to massage the heavy muscle below the scratches, favoring that arm. "I'm not even gonna ask you, Thirteen. You're chicken shit." He nodded toward Faust. "Ain't she got out of the fuckin' bed yet?" Faust jammed another fork of rice somewhere into his beard and shook his head.

Thirteen stepped back to one side of the door, Smokey to the other.

Nightmare walked forward between them. His lips pulled from his broken tooth and his face creased with something like concern. Then he shook his head.

Kidd thought how many different meanings could reside in one gesture. The thought prickled through his stuttering ering ing mind. Nightmare—his eyes were the grey-green of wet, wet clay—looked at him. And blinked.

"You staring like you got toothpicks propping up your eyelids again," Nightmare said, grimacing. "Every time I seen you. Which is twice. I don't like that."

Confused, Kidd looked at his plate.

"I ain't gonna *do* anything about it," Nightmare went on. "I'm just telling you I don't like it, understand? I mean I like to make things clear."

He looked up again.

Nightmare laughed, a short, rough thing happening in his nose. "Okay, now. Which of you cocksuckers wants to run? Hey, Denny, wrap something around your neck and come on."

"I ain't finished eatin'," Denny said from the floor.

Nightmare grunted and stepped over him. Denny ducked.

"Hey, is that shit any good?"

Kidd hesitated in glistening sheets of clarity. Then he held out his plate and fork, and watched Nightmare warily decide to take the dare.

The scorpion took the fork in his fist, swept through the mixture, spilling some, and, fork still in his mouth, chewed, with grains about his lips. Still chewing, he grinned. "Hey, that's okay." As he handed Kidd back the fork, Thirteen broke the tensions that, with the hash, had almost grown visible about the room.

"Well, have a God-damn plate, will you? Here, Nightmare, I'll get you some. Hey—" he turned to Smokey—"take him some hash, while I get him something to eat."

Nightmare sat down on the bed, between Faust and Kidd, leg against Kidd's leg, arm against Kidd's arm. The figure under the blanket behind them didn't move. Nightmare sucked the pipe. He let out, with his smoke, "Now you want to tell me what you lookin' for, kid, all the time?"

"Man, he's higher than the World Trade Center's flagpole." Thirteen handed Nightmare a tin plate and a spoon. "I been pumping hash in him all evening. What you wanna do all this heavy shit to his head for?"

Nightmare took the plate but waved Thirteen away with the spoon. "No, this is friendly. The kid and me, we know each—"

Faust, finished with the last of his rice, suddenly put his plate on the floor, stood, picked up his paper, and marched toward the door.

"Hey, where *you* going?" Nightmare said.

"Thanks for the meal," Faust mumbled to Thirteen without stopping.

"Hey, mother-fucker, so *long!*" Nightmare bellowed into the wake of ice.

The door swung open for Faust.

"Good *bye!*" Nightmare flipped his arm: the door slammed; the flung spoon clattered the picture frame.

The picture swung.

Nightmare laughed. Ice flushed away in the blow-torch of his hilarity.

Thirteen, first dubiously, then in full-throated hoarseness, laughed with him.

"Toss me back my fuckin' spoon!" Nightmare howled between landslides of laughter.

It came back underhand from Thirteen. "Now what's the old man all upset about, huh Smokey? He's crazy, ain't he?" and looked over his shoulder as Smokey nodded corroboration.

Nightmare had caught his spoon and now leaned toward Kidd. "He's all fucked up in the head, you know?

Cause he thinks I messed up the bitch." He pointed the spoon at the form under the blanket. "I didn't mess her up. She got caught fightin' fair. I wasn't even around. Shit." He swiped food into his mouth. "You know—" grains fell—to his wrist, to his jeans, to the scarred parquet—"some of these sons of bitches didn't *want* no bitches whatsoever in the business?" He down stabbed the air with his spoon. "Keep 'em away! Keep 'em out of here! They just gonna mess up the works!" With a malicious grin he looked around the room at the people leaning on the walls, sitting on the mattresses, or on the other bunks. Three among the dozen of them were girls, Kidd saw: but the lamplight was harsh and full of shadow. Nightmare's clay-colored eyes came back and caught his. "Then some of the bitches got together and beat the *shit* out of a couple of brothers . . . !" He reared back, heavy arms shaking. More food spilled from his plate. "Well, since I was boss-man, I said come right on in, ladies, and do your thing! Shit, I been livin' off bitches since I was ten, so it ain't no news to me what they can do." He came forward again, his weight-lifter's shoulder flattened to Kidd's, and whispered conspiratorially: "When you knee 'em in the nuts, a bitch don't go down quite so fast, either." Which he thought was very funny and laughed again. "Good people to have on your side." He took another mouthful, and made another large gesture with his spoon; grains scattered. "Magnificent shit!" he said with his mouth full. "Magnificent! Which of you fine young ladies is responsible?" He swung his lowered head around, mimicking an exaggerated politeness.

A heavy girl, in a blue sweatshirt, standing by the mannequin said, "It was one of the guys . . . Denny helped."

"Hey, Denny!" Nightmare's small, boomerang chin jounced.

Denny looked up, still eating.

"I should throw this mother-fucker at you!" Nightmare jerked the plate back to his shoulder. Kidd jerked aside. But Nightmare returned the plate to his lap, and laughed loudly and wetly.

Denny hadn't even flinched.

"People are very funny," Nightmare pronounced, recovering, nodding over another mouthful. "The ladies had their problems." He thumped his thumb against his ster-

208

num among rattling links. "I had mine too—some of the brothers just weren't interested in having *no* white people involved *no* how."

Kidd glanced around the room again; everyone in the room looked white.

Nightmare saw him glance and lifted a finger: "Now don't get your idea from this. Thirteen here runs the Lily White Rest Home for Depraved and Indigent A-heads; but the true brotherhood is of a much deeper hue."

"God *damn*, Nightmare," Thirteen said from the door. "Why are you always going on like that? We get spades here. There was—" he began to snap his tattooed fingers—"what's-his-name . . . ?"

Nightmare waved in the air. "Tokens! Mere tokens." The nails on his beefy fingers were overlong and crested black as an auto mechanic's. " 'Cause I'm white," he said out of the side of his mouth to Kidd, "these racist bastards here will let me come around to look for replacement troops. Well, mother-fuckers, I'd come around here even if I was black as George! And I'll *keep* coming around till both moons fall out of the sky and the sun comes up backwards!" He looked at Kidd directly. "And we're getting a few, too—though these shitheads would give up a nut before they'd admit that just a *few* of them even *like* it better living over there and being scorpions than hanging around this behavioral sink!" His hand, which was still up before him, returned to hold the edge of his plate, about to slide off. "Yes, the ladies had to beat some heads." He glanced back at the figure behind them in the blankets: "And some of the ladies, indeed, got *their* heads beat. Well, I had to beat some heads too, to attain my present status—and though I am now *quite* satisfied with my current position in the community, I would not be surprised if *my* head eventually took some beating too." He turned back, dark hair falling in tangles from his shoulder, and made a face. "Sisterhood . . . Brotherhood . . . *very* powerful stuff, man!" Grimacing, he shook his head. "Very powerful. Hey—?" once again at Denny. "Denny, you gonna run? We need you tonight. You run it good, boy."

"I dunno." Denny didn't turn. "Lemme finish my dinner, huh?"

Nightmare laughed again, looked around the room. "He's gonna come. How you like that, the little bastard's

209

gonna come! I don't think I'd even take any of the rest of you cocksuckers. Denny? It's a good run with us, ain't it? Go on, tell 'em."

"Yeah," Denny said with his mouth full, then swallowed: "It's a good run, okay?"

"Now you see; *these* mother-fuckers all think I want to be the daisy in a field of black orchids" (lower:)— "though we have two or three of those; and no problems with 'em. But since I been boss-man, I take whoever wants in and knows their business." He nodded to Kidd. "I'd even take you, and you ain't no nigger . . . what?" He leaned back, narrowed his eyes, and raised a hand like an artist at a picture: "A half-blood American Indian on your . . . father's side? 'Course, the light's a little dim . . ."

Kidd grinned. "On my mother's."

Nightmare grinned back, shrugged. "Well, you still got more meat on you than most of these sad-assed A-heads."

A frustrated laugh came from across the room. Thirteen said: "Nightmare, *why* are you always down on us like that? You got us out as racists, and chauvinist pigs, and speed freaks to boot. We ain't had no speed around here for I don't know how long."

Nightmare bounced on the bed with delight, the back of his wrist against his forehead, miming a distressed belle. "Me!" in falsetto. "Me?" even higher. "Me, down on *speed?* I'm just waiting for you racist, chauvinist pigs to get some *more!*"

Smokey said: "That blond Spanish guy hasn't been around with any for a long time . . . I sort of wonder where he went."

Somebody else said: "He probably burned the whole city."

Thirteen began laughing again, moved across the room, laughing. Others moved too.

Nightmare turned back to Kidd. "How'd you like that idea, goin' on a scorpion run?" It must have suddenly struck him as funny; he guffawed, snorting, shook his head, and brushed rice grains from his chin with his fist. "You'd picked yourself a nice shiny orchid last time I saw you. What would you do in a real garden party, huh, kid?" Two more spoonfuls and Nightmare's plate was empty. Holding it between both thumbs and forefingers, he opened his knees and dropped it. "You think about that, running. Maybe that's what you're looking for, huh? Let me tell you something." He fingered among the chains around his neck, held up the thin brass one with its round and triangular glasses, and shook it. "You're a fool to wear yours where anybody can see it, kid." Glass glittered, harsh in white lantern light.

Why why "Why? You got yours on around your neck," nd your neck our eck ck. He hadn't been aware that his shirt was half open.

"Just shut up and listen now. Smokey over there. I know she's got one. But you don't see *her* with it out and waving it, now?"

"You know," Kidd said, "I figured two people who saw each other with . . . these: well, they'd sort of trust each other, you know? Because they'd . . . know something about each other," and wondered if Madame Brown had arrived upstairs for dinner.

Nightmare frowned. "Say, he's got a brain, you know?" He glanced at Thirteen. "The kid ain't that stupid. But I'll tell you: You look at this and you know something about me. I look at that and I know something about you. Well, what are we gonna do with what we know, huh? I'll tell you what you'll do with it. You'll use it to put the longest, sharpest blade on that orchid of yours, soon as I ain't lookin, between that rib, and that rib." His finger suddenly ger suddenly turned to enly his ly jab Kidd's his side. "And don't think for one second I wouldn't do the same thing to you. So I don't trust anybody I see with one at all." He pressed his lips to make a little pig's snout and nodded, mocking sagesse. "Hey, just look at Denny!"

Finished with his food, Denny had walked over to the mannequin. He took up a heavy chain loop from it, draped dark links around his own neck.

"I told you Denny'd run with me. Okay, man. You know when, you know where. Lemme get out of this freak hole. I gotta hunt some more." He stood and lumbered over the mattresses. "I knew you'd come through, Denny. Hey?" He frowned at Thirteen. "Do something with her," and gestured back toward the bed.

"Yeah, sure, Nightmare." Thirteen opened the door for him. When he closed it, he looked back at Denny. Smokey at his shoulder blinked in anticipation.

"Hey, man," Thirteen said slowly after seconds of silence, "are you still into that shit?"

Denny put another chain around his neck. It rattled on the one already there.

Thirteen swung up his hands and grunted. "Come on, Denny, I thought you were gonna stay out of all that. All right, all right. It's your ass."

Upstairs a woman was laughing, and the laughter grew, ghter grew, laughter: "Stop it! Stop it will you?" in Mr Richards' harsh voice. "Just stop it." op it, ghter grew ew.

"Look, I'm gonna have to get back to work." Kidd stood up. "Thanks for the food, you know? And the dope. It's good stuff."

Denny put on another loop, and Thirteen said, "Oh, yeah, sure." He seemed as disappointed at Kidd's leaving as Mrs Richards always was. "Come on down again and smoke some more dope. Don't mind Nightmare. He's crazy, that's all."

"Sure." Kidd went to the door, opened it.

The moan stopped him: hesitant, without vocal color, it came on behind. He started to turn, but his eyes stalled on the mirror. In it he could see practically the whole room:

On the bed where he had been sitting, she had pushed herself up to her elbow. The blanket slipped down, and she turned a face, wet as Denny's from the bath. It was puffed, bruised. Though her temples trickled with fever, the sound, as she swayed, came from the driest tissue.

She blinked on balls of scarlet glass.

The door clapped behind him. After ten steps, he released his breath. Then he dragged back air, rasping with something like sobbing, something like laught er aughter sobb ter bing er.

"Excuse me."

"Yes?"

"Reverend Taylor?"

"What can I do for you?"

On the shelf behind the desk, tape-spools turned. Organ music gentled in the shadowed office. "I . . . well, somebody told me I could get those pictures—posters here. Of George," he explained, "Harrison."

"Oh yes, certainly." Her benign smile as she pushed herself away from the desk, made him, holding his notebook in the church foyer, absolutely uncomfortable. "Just reach over for the latch there and it'll open."

He pushed through the waist high door. His bare foot left tile and hit carpet. He looked around the walls; but they were covered with shelves. The bulletin board was a shale of notices and pamphlets.

The poster was down.

"Now which picture would you like?" She opened the wide top drawer.

He stepped up: it was filled with eight-by-ten photographs of the rough-featured black man. Reverend Taylor stood up and spread a disordered pile of pictures across more pictures. "We have six of these. They're very nice. I'm afraid I haven't got them arranged though. I just had to dump them in here. Let's see if I can pull out a complete set—"

"Oh. I think maybe—"

She paused, still smiling.

The pictures in the drawer were all, full-head photos.

"No." His embarrassment hove home. "You probably don't have the ones I was looking for, ma'am. Somebody told me he'd gotten one from you, and I guess . . . well, I'm sorry—"

"But you said posters, didn't you?" She closed the drawer and her eyes, a comment on her own misunderstanding. "Of course, the posters!" She stepped around the desk and the toes of her shoes beat at the hem of her robe. "We have two, here. There's a third in preparation, since that article in Mr Calkins' paper about the moon."

Behind the desk were portfolio-sized cardboard boxes. Reverend Taylor pulled one open. "Is this what you want?"

"Really, I'm pretty sure you don't have—"

Harrison, naked and half-erect, one hand cupping his testicles, leaned against some thick tree. The lowest branches were heavy with leaves. Behind him, a black dog—it could have been Muriel—sat in the dead leaves, lolling an out-of-focus tongue. Sunset flung bronzes down through the browns and greens. "It was done with a backdrop, right down in the church basement," she said. "But I think it's rather good. Is that the one you want?"

213

"No . . ." he said, too softly and too quickly.

"Then it must be *this* one."

She flipped over a handful to let him see.

"Yeah—yes. That's it," and was still astounded with the memory.

She peeled the poster from its identical twin and began to roll it up. "It had to be. Until the new one comes in—" as jacket, genitals, knees, boots and background purple rose into the white roll turning in dark fingers—"these are all we ·have. Here you go. I'll get you a rubber band." She stepped to the desk.

"Hey," he said, putting belligerent stupidity in front of his disconcerted astonishment, "why do you—" He stopped because the idea came, interrupting his question, clearly and without ambiguity, to request the other poster as well. "—why do you have stuff like this here? I mean to give away."

Only later did it occur to him that her ingenuous surprise must have been as calculated to disarm as his naiveté. When she recovered from it, she said, "They're very popular. We like to be up to date, and posters are being used a lot . . . they were done for us free, and I suppose that's the main reason. We've given out quite lots of the first one you saw. That one," she pointed to the one he held, "isn't in quite as much demand."

"Yeah?"

She nodded.

"What I mean is, why . . ."

She picked up a rubber band from the desk and stretched her fingers inside it to slip it over his roll. The band pulled in the fingertips: he thought a moment of his orchid. With deliberation, as though she had reached a decision about him, she said, "The poor people in this city—and in Bellona that pretty well means the black people—have *never* had very much. Now they have even less." She looked at him with an expression he recognized as a request for something he could not even name. "We have to give them—" she reached forward—"something." The red rubber snapped on the tube. "We have to." She folded her hands. "The other day when I saw you, I just assumed you were black. I suppose because you're dark. Now I suspect you're not. Even so, you're still invited to come to our services." She smiled brightly again. "Will you make an effort?"

"Oh. Yeah." He doffed the poster: He'd realized

214

before he probably would not come to a service. Now he resolved never to return at all. "Sure. What do I owe you for—this." One hand, in his pocket, he fingered the crumpled bill.

"It's free," she said. "Like everything else."

He said, "Oh." But his hand stayed on the moist note.

In the foyer he stepped around the dumpy black woman in the dark coat too heavy for the heat. She blinked at him suspiciously from under her black hat, pulled up her shopping bag, and continued toward the office door. Between what Nightmare had said earlier and what Reverend Taylor had just said, he found himself wondering, granted the handful he'd seen, just where all the black people in Bellona *were*. The poster under his arm, he hurried into the evening.

"Hello!" Mrs Richards said, eyes both wide and sleepy. She held her bathrobe at the neck. "Come in, Kidd. Come in. I didn't know what happened to you yesterday. We were expecting you to come back down. And eat with us."

"Oh. Well, when I got finished, I just thought . . ." He shrugged and entered. "You got coffee this morning?"

She nodded and went off to the kitchen. He followed her, letting his notebook flap his leg. She said, "The way you left, I thought there might have been something wrong. I thought perhaps you weren't going to come back at all."

He laughed. "I just went upstairs and finished my work. Then I went back to the park. I mean, you don't have to feed me. I do the work. You pay me for it, what you told Mrs Brown you would. That'll be okay."

"Of course," she said from the kitchen.

He went into the dining room and sat. "Coffee, I mean. And a sandwich, and letting me use your bathroom and stuff. That's nice. I appreciate it. But you shouldn't put yourself out." He was talking too loud. More softly: "You see?"

June, in pink slacks and robin's-egg sweater, a bird appliquéd near the neck, came to the door.

"Hey . . ." he said, quietly. "I have something for you. Upstairs, in nineteen."

"What—" then caught herself and mouthed: "What is it?"

He grinned and pointed up with his thumb.

June looked confused. Then she called: "I'll help you with the coffee, Mom."

"That's all right, dear." Mrs Richards came in with a tray, a pot, and cups. "If you want to bring in a cup for yourself. Darling?" She sat the tray down. "Aren't you drinking too *much* coffee?"

"Oh, Mother!" June marched into the kitchen and returned with a cup.

He liked putting his hands around the warming porcelain while the coffee went in.

"I did something, you know, perhaps I ought not to have." Mrs Richards finished pouring and spoke carefully. "Here, I'll bring it to you."

He sipped and wished it wasn't instant. His mind went off to some nameless spot on the California coast, carpeted with rust-colored redwood scraps and the smell of boiled coffee while a white sun made a silver pin cushion in the tree tops, and fog wrapped up the gaunt trunks—

"Here." Mrs Richards returned and sat. "I hope you don't mind."

June, he saw, was trying to hold her cup the same way he did.

"What is it?" On blue bordered stationery, in black, calligraphic letters, Mrs Richards had written out his poem.

"I've probably made all sorts of mistakes, I know."

He finished reading it and looked up, confused. "How'd you do that?"

"It stayed with me, very clearly."

"All of it?"

"It's only eight lines, isn't it? It sticks very persistently in the mind. Especially considering it doesn't rhyme. Did I make any terrible mistakes?"

"You left out a comma." He slid the paper to her and pointed.

She looked. "Oh, of course."

"You just remembered it, like that?"

"I couldn't get it out of my mind. I haven't done anything awful, have I?"

"Um . . . it looks very nice." He tried to fix the

216

warmth inside him, but it was neither embarrassment, nor pride, nor fear, so stayed un-named.

"You may have it." She sat back. "Just stick it in your notebook. I made two copies, you see—I'm going to keep one for myself. Forever." Her voice broke just a little: "That's why I was so worried when I thought you weren't coming back. You really go and sleep out in the park, just like that, all alone?"

He nodded. "There're other people there."

"Oh, yes. I've heard about them. From Edna. That's . . . amazing. You know you haven't told me yet, is it all right that I remembered your poem; and wrote it down?"

"Eh . . . yeah." He smiled, and wished desperately she would correct that comma. "Thanks. You know, we can start moving stuff up today. You got everything all ready down here?"

"We can?" She sounded pensive. "You mean you've got it all ready."

"I guess I should have come back last night and told you we could start today on the moving."

"Arthur—" who stood at the door, tie loose—"Kidd says we can move today. By the time you come home, dear, we'll all be upstairs."

"Good. You really are working!" When Mr Richards reached the table, Mrs Richards had his cup poured. Standing, he lifted it. The cup's reflection dropped away in the mahogany, stayed vague while he drank, then suddenly swam up like a white fish in a brown pool to meet the china rim that clacked on it. "Gotta run. Why don't you get Bobby to give you a hand with the little stuff? Exercise'll do him some good."

"Beds, and things like that . . ." Mrs Richards shook her head. "I really wonder if we shouldn't get somebody else, to help."

"I can get everything up there," Kidd said. "I'll just take the beds apart."

"Well, if you're sure."

"Sure he can," Mr Richards said. "Well, I'm on my way. Good-bye." In his fingers, the knot rose up between his collar wings, wobbled into place. He turned and left the room. The front door slammed.

Kidd watched the amber rim make nervous tides on the china, then drank the black sea. "I better go on upstairs and get last-minute things cleaned up. You can

217

start putting things out. I'll be down in about fifteen minutes." He clinked his cup in his saucer, and went out.

"Where is it?" June called from the door.

He closed the broom closet on the mop and pail. "Over there, leaning against the wall."

When he came in, she was staring at the white roll in its red rubber band; her fist floated inches under her chin. "You're sure that's a picture of . . ."

"George," he said, "Harrison. Look at it."

She picked up the roll.

On the floor he saw the stack of her father's computer magazines she had brought up as excuse.

She rolled the rubber band toward the end, but stopped. "Where did you get it?"

"You wouldn't believe me if I told you. They got them all over." He wanted to avoid the specific answer. "There's a woman minister who just gives him away." He sighed. "At a church."

"Have you seen . . . him, again?"

"No. Aren't you gonna open it?"

"I'm afraid to."

The simplicity with which she said it surprised and moved him. The fog outside the windows was almost solid. He watched: she stood, head slightly bent, and still.

"Does Madame Brown know about you and George—"

Her "No!" was so quick and soft (her head whirled) he stiffened.

"She goes to that bar too. She knows him," he said. "That's why I was wondering."

"Oh . . ." so less intense.

"She was in there the night you stopped me to ask about him."

"Then it's good I didn't go in. She might have . . . seen." June closed her eyes, too long for blinking. "If she had seen me, that would have been just . . ."

Her blonde energies were to him terrible but dwindling things. "Why—I still don't understand—are you so hung up on him? I mean, I know about what . . . happened. And I mean, that doesn't matter to me. But I . . ." He felt his question confused among hesitations, and stopped it.

She looked vulnerable and afraid. "I don't . . . know. You wouldn't understand—" then even vulnerability fell away—"if *I* told you. They named that . . . moon after him!"

He pretended not to stare. "Enough other people are after him too, I guess. That's why they have those, huh? Open it."

She shook her head with small, quick movements. "But they don't know . . ." Unable to look at him longer, she looked down at the roll. "I know more than they do."

"Hey," he asked to fill the discomforting silence, "what *did* happen between you?"

"Go read about it in the *Times*." She looked up.

He searched for the belligerence he'd heard: her raised features held none of it.

"The night the . . . black people had the riot? I was out, just walking around. There was lightning. And that immense thundering. I didn't know what had happened. And then it . . . I didn't even see the man with the camera until— It's just like it showed in the paper!"

"Oh," which gave her none of what she'd requested.

She walked toward the door. Just before she reached it, she finished removing the rubber band and unrolled the poster.

"Is that him?" he asked, thinking it would be friendly rhetoric but hearing a real request.

The movement of the back of her head as she looked here and there became nodding. She glanced back. "Why . . . did they make . . . these?"

"I guess some other people felt the same way about him you do. I was talking, last night, with some friends. This girl I stay with: she's maybe a few years older than you are. And this guy. He's an engineer, like your father. We were talking, in a bar, about whether I should give that to you."

Her face began worry on itself.

"I didn't tell them your name or anything. They took it very seriously, you know? More seriously than I did, at first. They didn't laugh at you or anything."

". . . What did they say?"

"That it was up to me, because I knew you. That some bad things could happen, or some good things. You like it?"

She looked again. "I think it's the most horrible thing I've ever seen."

He was angry, and swallowed to hold it. "Tear it up and throw it down the elevator shaft, then . . . if you

219

want." He waited and wondered if her shaking head was confusion or denial. "I'd keep it if I were you."

"Hey, what's that?" From the way Bobby ran into the room, Kidd thought he would burst through the poster like a clown through a paper hoop.

June crashed the edges together. "It's a picture!" The white backing wrinkled against her thighs.

"What's it a picture *of?*"

"It isn't anything *you'd* be interested in!"

"D'you find it up here in a closet?" Bobby asked Kidd, walking into the room. "I bet it's a naked lady. I've seen pictures of naked ladies in school before."

June sucked her teeth. "Oh, really!"

"Come on. Let me see."

"No." June tried to roll the paper. Bobby peered, and she whipped around. "It isn't *yours!*"

"Oh, I don't want to see your old naked lady anyway. Hey, you really got the place cleaned up, Kidd. We gotta carry everything up here?"

"Yeah."

"We got an awful lot of stuff in our house." Bobby looked dubious.

"We'll make it."

June finished rolling the crinkled poster, picked up her magazines, and started down the hall to the back of the apartment.

"I'm just gonna sneak in and look at it when you're not there!" Bobby called.

At the hall's end a door closed loudly.

"Come on," Kidd said. "Leave your sister alone. Let's go downstairs and move some furniture."

"Naw!" Bobby complained, though he started to the door with Kidd. "She'd tell on *me* if she caught *me* with a picture of a naked lady."

They went out.

"You tell on her," Kidd said, "they'll take it away and you'll never see it."

"*Is* it a naked lady?" Bobby asked, wonderingly.

"Nope. It's not." Kidd rang the elevator bell.

"What is it?"

"A naked man."

"Aw, come on!" Bobby began to laugh as the elevator doors rolled open and stepped forward.

"*Hey*, boy! This one!" Kidd grabbed Bobby's shoulder.

The wind hissed.

"Oh, wow!" Bobby stepped back, then shrugged from Kidd's grip on his shoulder. "Hey, *I* almost . . . !" He shook his head.

"You better watch yourself. Come on."

They stepped into the other elevator.

The door pulled darkness around them.

Bobby, still breathing hard, pushed "17".

"Does June always tell on you?"

"Sure, she does . . . well, not always."

"What's the last thing she didn't tell on you about?"

"What do you want to know for?"

"Just curious."

The door opened. Bobby, revealed beside him, had one hand around his chained wrist, stroking the clumsy beads.

"I can't decide," Mrs Richards announced when they walked in, "whether we should take the big things up first or the little things. I really haven't arranged this very well in my head. I assumed because we were moving inside the building, it wouldn't be any trouble."

"I want my old room!"

"What do you mean, dear? We're moving into a *new* apartment."

"It's just the same as this one; only backward. And it's blue. I want my old room."

"Of course, darling. What room did you *think* you were going to have?"

"I just wanted to make sure." Bobby marched off down the hall. "I'll start putting my stuff together."

"Thank you, dear."

"I'll start with the couch and the beds and things, Mrs Richards. They're the hardest; but once they're up, you'll really be moved in, just about, you know?"

"All right. But the beds, they're so big!"

"I'll take them apart. You got a hammer and screwdriver?"

"Well, all right. I guess if you're going to get them upstairs, you have to. I'm just feeling guilty that I didn't organize this thing any better. Now you want a screwdriver. And a hammer. You're sure you'll be able to put them back together?"

Mrs Richards was pulling off the bedding as he came back from the kitchen with the tools. "You see,

221

ma'am," he explained, hoisting off the mattress, "these big beds, the frames just come off the headboards." Even so, as soon as he got to work, he realized five full-sized beds, to dismantle, move, and reassemble, would take at least two hours.

He'd been working for one when (Mrs Richards herself had already made several trips) he heard Bobby and June out in the front room. He put down his screwdriver as Bobby said: "You didn't tell on me about this . . . and Eddie; so I won't tell about your old picture."

Kidd walked out of the bedroom and stopped by the living room door.

June, her back to him, was reaching into the sideboard. Silverware clashed in her hands. She turned with the bunched, heavy spoons and forks.

"Only," Bobby continued by the bookshelf, "you shouldn't have taken yours off." *This* and *yours* apparently referred to the optic chain that bound his wrist; he was holding his arm up to show his sister. "Eddie took his off, and you remember what happened."

"I was just scared," June protested. "Because of all that other stuff. If you hadn't stolen that one from Eddie, he wouldn't have—"

"I didn't steal it!"

"He didn't give it to you, did he?"

"I didn't steal it," Bobby insisted. "If you say I stole it, I'll tell them about your bad picture—"

"It isn't bad!"

"Of course it's bad; if it wasn't bad, you'd let me see it."

"Hey," Kidd said.

Both children looked.

"Eddie's your brother, isn't he? What happened to Eddie, anyway."

Both looked at each other.

The silverware recommenced clanking.

Bobby moved his palm over his beaded wrist.

"Okay," Kidd said. "I guess it isn't really any of my business."

"He went away," June said.

"He ran away from home," Bobby said. "Only—"

"—he came back a couple of times," June said. "And did terrible things. It wouldn't have been so hard on Mommy if he hadn't kept coming back like that."

222

"Daddy said he was gonna kill him if he ever came back like that again—"

"Bobby!"

"Well, he did. And Mommy screamed—"

"Look, it isn't any of my business," Kidd concluded. "Once we have all the kitchen stuff upstairs, your mother can start getting ready for dinner—in your new apartment." Which sounded perfectly inane. He wondered where Eddie was—

"We don't know," Bobby said in a way that, once, in the mental hospital, when someone did the same thing, made Kidd go around for ten hours thinking all the other patients could read his mind, "where Eddie is now. He said he was going to another city. I wanted to go with him. But I was scared."

June looked more and more uncomfortable.

"Come on," Kidd said, "take the silverware. And Bobby, you start on those books. We'll have everything up but the rugs by the time your father gets home."

He got most of the disassembled stuff into the hall, a couple of times thinking that the thumping, banging, and scraping might be causing as much unrest in Thirteen's place as any running in the halls or banging on the doors had caused in the Richards'.

He loaded springs and headboards into the elevator —the empty shaft, whose door apparently opened at whatever floor the car beside it stopped, hissed blandly by his side.

The ride up in the dark, with only bed springs, the orange number "19" before him, and his own harsh breath, was oddly calming.

"They should have the padding in the elevators when people are moving furniture," Mrs Richards, waiting for him in the upper hall, admonished. "Well, there's no one to get it out for us. There's nothing we can do."

In the new apartment (an hour later), he had reassembled the frames and, going from room to room, put the springs on—he was sitting on the last spring, staring at the folded mattress on the floor when Mrs Richards came in carrying a small night-table against her chest, its legs stuck forward like four horns. "You know, I didn't *believe* you were actually going to get them up here?" she exclaimed. "You really have been working like a madman! You should take a rest, I think."

He said, "Yeah, I'm resting," and smiled.

She put the table down, and he noticed her distraught expression. For a moment he thought she'd taken offense at his flip answer. But she said: "They were back, just a moment ago. Downstairs. Running in the halls, making that terrible noise!"

Kidd frowned.

"I am so happy to be out of there . . ." Mrs Richards shook her head, and for a moment he thought she was going to cry. "I'm so happy! Really, I was practically afraid to take this—" her fingers swayed on the night table's carved corner—"out of there. And carry it up here. But we've done it. We've moved! We've . . . done it!"

He looked about the room, at the folded mattress, at the night table, at the dresser out from the wall. And the rugs were still downstairs.

"I guess we have . . ." He frowned. "Just about."

A bubble grew at the caldron's rim, reflecting both their faces, one front, one profile, tiny and distant.

Jommy's spoon handle, circling the soup, passed: the bubble broke.

Kidd, still panting, asked, "You seen Lanya?"

"Sure." Jommy's face was wider ear to ear than from chin to forehead. "She was right over there talking to Milly—*hey*, before you run off again! Will you two be back for dinner?" He rested the spoon on a black pipe, crusted with burnt grease, sticking from the cinderblocks.

"I guess so. I took off before the lady at my job could get a chance to feed me."

Soup ran down the granular grey, bubbled and popped. "Good." Grinning, Jommy went back to stirring. His khaki shirt sleeve, rolled loosely up his thin arm, swung: the shirt was about three sizes too big. "It'll be ready about time it gets dark. Lanya knows, but I guess I gotta tell you again: Now come and eat, any time you want, you hear? John and Milly won't mind . . ."

But Kidd was crossing the worn grass, among sleeping bags, rolled or airing; knapsacks and pack-braces scattered the clearing, lay piled around the picnic bench, or leaned beneath the trees.

She wasn't among the dozen spectators to the Chinese Checker game between the squat, dark-haired man who sat crosslegged behind the board and rocked with his elbows on his knees, and a tall, freckled woman with

224

crew-cut hair, who wore much Southwestern silver under and over her denim shirt; her belt was silver and turquoise. As her long freckled fingers, heavy with blue-stoned rings, moved and moved back over the marbles, Kidd saw her nails were bitten badly as his own.

. A girl who looked at first like nothing but a mop squatted (two threadbare knees poked up either side) to paw through the cardboard carton of colored string— what was left of John's "loom" project.

Another girl (her hair was the color of a car he recalled, whose owner said he'd just had it painted "Mediterranean Gold") sat on a dented brass drum, lacing a high-topped shoe—the kind with hooks in place of the last dozen eyes. Her pants leg was rolled up above a very red knee. A bearded boy stood beside her, talking and grinning, occasionally pushing his own bushy hair back from an earlobe pierced with a gold cross. His sneaker, on top of the drum, was wedged against her thigh. The drum itself held clay, cracked away from the side and shot with crevices—that was Milly's "pottery" project.

Milly herself, or Lanya, were not there . . .

Harmonica notes tangled with the smoky leaves above. He looked up. More music—but not from above. Just far away. And from which—?

He looked around the clearing again, charged off into the brush . . . which dumped him on another park path, sloping up toward silver notes. He started after them, wondering at how little of the park he'd actually explored.

The music moved away.

Notes bent like blues, and slid, chromatically, from mode to austere mode. It was as if her major influences, (he grinned) were late Sonny Terry and early Stockhausen.

At the top of the rise, he saw them at the bottom: Milly's bare legs below her denim shorts, Lanya's jeans; Milly's heavy red hair shook as she gazed around; Lanya's, scrap bronze, bent to her harp. Shoulder to shoulder, the two girls disappeared around a turn.

He started to run after them, anticipated dialogue filling his mouth: Hey, I just about got the Richards into their new apartment! All the big stuff is up, so Mrs Richards gave me the rest of the day off. Tomorrow morning, I take up the rugs and we put the furniture . . .

Two steps, and erupting through it was the sudden

225

and inexplicable urge to—follow, to observe, to overhear! What he *wanted* to do, he realized, was watch
Lanya when she was not watching him.

The path curved right.

To the right, he pushed into the brush—making a
lot of noise. Well, if they discovered him, he was discovered. He was still curious.

The music halted; were they talking?

That path had sloped down; the ground he pushed
over sloped up. Was he going to come out on them after
all?

A sharp drop stopped him.

Beyond rocks and a few trees grown crookedly on
the slope, the path lay sixteen feet below. Which meant,
he figured, they'd come around the bend right there—and
see him.

They came around the bend—and didn't.

One hand above, he hooked a slender branch; bare
foot flat, sandal on its toe, he waited, a smile ready behind
his face to push forward when they noticed him. Would
he get some snatch of conversation (possibly even about
him) before they looked up and saw?

". . . perfectly terrified," Milly said in a tone neither
flip nor rhetorical.

"There isn't anything to be terrified of," Lanya said.
"I'd think, with the rumors of rape and violation going
around, you'd be fascinated to meet the man himself and
get a look."

"Oh, the rumors are fascinating enough," Milly said,
"in a perfectly horrible way—"

"And the man is rather nice—" Lanya turned her
harmonica, examining it as she walked—"despite the rumors. Don't you find reality *more* fascinating than a
flicker of half truths and anxiety-distorted projections?"

The two young women passed beneath. He imagined
his reflection sliding across her harmonica; her eyes starting up—

"In principle," Milly said. "In practice, when the
rumors get to a certain point, I'm willing to let the
whole business alone and go off exploring in the opposite
direction. Suppose the reality turns out to be *worse* than
the rumors?"

"Oh, really . . . !" Lanya raised her harmonica,
played. "You're going to chicken out, again, aren't you?"
She played another snatch.

"Someday," Milly said, pensively, "I wish you'd play a piece from one end to the other. The snatches are awfully nice."

(Kidd looked after them.)

Lanya looked at her harmonica. "I guess that's because I never play for anybody else."

"You should," Milly said. "I mean, everybody hears it anyway. Sometimes, all those little pieces, pretty as they are, practically give me a headache because they aren't connected to each other."

"I'll try," Lanya said. "And *you* should not try to avoid the subject. Are you going to chicken out?"

"Look," Milly said, "going to *meet* George Harrison was *your* idea. I just said it might be interesting to talk to him."

"But I've *already* met George," Lanya said. "I've talked to him lots of times, I told you. Going to *meet* him was *your* idea; I just said I'd make introductions."

"Oh, you know everyone," Milly said; her hair shook. And then, ". . ." which was maddeningly beyond ear shot. Lanya's answer was another burst of music, that went on as they disappeared around the next turn; after a few wrong notes, the tune halted.

Kidd crab-walked down the dirt, stepped from behind the last bush, and looked where the girls had been.

The mention of George Harrison left a funny feel. A subterranean frown battled the inner smile still behind his face. His cheek twitched, his lips moved to shape vowels from no languages he spoke. Again he was tempted to run after them. But his curiosity had shifted a thumb's width toward anxiety.

The path, apparently, wound back the other way.

Perhaps he could cut through again, overtake them once more—? Speculation became resolution. He crossed into the bushes, again climbing; he scrambled over a stretch of rock, pushed forward through leaves. Ten feet away, fifteen—a long note from Lanya's harmonica, a flicker of Milly's bright hair! He crouched, cheek and one palm against bark. His bare boot, over a root, rocked him unsteadily.

Through dull leaves, he could just make them out.

There was another musical sound—not her harmonica, but their two laughters.

"Okay," he heard Lanya say, "we'll do it that way—if you want."

227

"Oh, yes," Milly cried. "Let's!"

"It's silly." Lanya laughed. "But all right. He's there every afternoon, almost. All right, we'll do it that way, but only because you're my . . ."

They were further away, so he heard less this time —except their laughter, leaving. What, he wondered, were they going to do *what* way, that involved George Harrison? Were they going to see him *now*—? Suddenly he was convinced they were. Their interchange, like schoolgirls planning a prank, upset him. What prank, he wondered, do two women sanely play on a man who'd just molested a girl only a few years younger than themselves? He remembered the obscene poster. He remembered his glimpse of Harrison at the bar.

He stood again, took three loping steps through the brush, the worried laugh to stop them with, ready in his throat. (Thinking: Hey, what kind of crazy idea have you two nuts gotten into your—)

A root caught his sandal toe and spun him out on the concrete. He almost fell. Pushing up from one knee, he turned. And was suddenly confused.

Which way had they come from?

Which way had they gone?

He'd only glimpsed them this time. In both directions the path curved the same way . . . His faulty left-right orientation, always worse under strain—the plague of the ambidextrous, a doctor had once explained—gave way completely. Well, he'd come from *that* side of the road. He darted into the other, hoping to catch the path again and head them off.

The growth—of course—was thicker. The slope here was so steep he had to scrabble with hands as well as feet. Thinking: When was the last time I saw sunlight a golden flutter in bright green? The sky, flickering through, was the color of iron. The leaves, each in a caul of ash, were like grey velvet scraps, or dead mice.

Pebbles rolled underfoot. No, he thought, they *can't* be going to see George Harrison now! For all he knew, the conversation had changed subject completely between the first turn and the second.

And where the hell was the third? Trees cleared to high boulders. He skirted one and, leaning on it, vaulted down a small drop, brushed aside brush—

Across flat rock (a section had been filled with cement to level it) was a building of black stones, rounded

228

and the size of heads, webbed in white mortar. Above the building's several wings rose a square tower with a crenellated balcony of the same black stone. The building was not large; the tower was not quite three stories. The vaulted windows, paned with pebbled glass, deeply recessed, were so thin he would have had trouble climbing out.

A waist-high wall of stone went along two sides of a large, informal courtyard in front of the building.

On the corner, wearing black-framed glasses, work-shoe heels wedged in a deep tenon, elbows on the knees of soiled khaki coveralls, and reading the *Times*, sat George Harrison.

Kidd squatted.

Leaves flicked up the image.

Knuckles mashed in dirt, Kidd leaned forward.

Leaves tickled his cheek.

Kidd was afraid; Kidd was fascinated. Whatever caused both left him clammy-handed.

George took off his glasses, put them in his shirt pocket, slid from the wall and, work shoes wide and fist-heels up, stretched. Khaki creases fanned from flank to shoulder.

(Squatting, watching; curiosity and alarm resolved into a sort of self-righteous, silent mumble: Okay, fun is fun, but what sort of prank *were* they up to?)

George's face twisted under a metal sky so low the city's fires had scorched and marred it like an aluminum pot-bottom.

Beyond a break in the wall (which, Kidd realized only from her gait, had steps below it) Lanya—hair, nose, chin, shoulders—emerged. "Hey, George," she said. "You're back here again this afternoon? City life too much for you?"

Milly (*had* she chickened out?) was not with her.

"Hu'?" the aspiration voiced and the vowel voiceless; George turned as she gained the top step. "Y'com'-ba'" (*back* or *by*, Kidd wasn't sure) "heah too?" The *t* was nearly a *d*, and the final vowel was a strangely breathy one from which the lips made no recovery, but hung heavy and open from teeth Kidd could see, even from here, were large, clean, and yellow. How, Kidd wondered, could this mauled and apocopated music be fixed to a page with roman letters and standard marks of elision? He decided: It can't. "You taking an afternoon stroll, yeah?" George laughed and nodded. "I hear you playing before, and I think: She gonna come by" (or *was* it "back"?) "here maybe say hello." -

"Hello!" Lanya laughed too, and put her harmonica in her own shirt pocket. "I don't always come by," Lanya said. (She, he realized, had mis-heard *gonna,* with its almost unstopped *g* and *n*'s loose as *l*'s, as *always.*) "I saw you here a couple of days ago, but the last time we said hello was in the bar. Why *do* you come out here in the park every afternoon?"

"To look at the sky . . ." George shrugged. "To read the paper."

(Kidd's ankle stung from squatting. He slid his foot over—twigs crackled. But George and Lanya didn't hear.)

"Last time I was at the bar—" (Kidd listened to the melodious inflection that catapulted the broad bass into the tenor at *I* and *bar:* Irony? yes. But italics, he thought, would brutalize it to mere sarcasm.)—"I didn't even get a chance to say hello. You just running out of there with your friends." George looked up at the sky again. "Can't see nothing in all that mess. Can't see nothing at all."

"George," Lanya said, leaning back against the wall, finger tips in her jean pockets and tennis shoes crossed, "this is the sort of question you lose friends over, but—" Kidd remembered when she'd used the same phrase with him—"I was curious, so I figured I'd just ask. What *did* happen with you and that girl there was suppose to be all the pictures of in the papers?"

"You know—" George paused to stick his tongue way down inside his cheek, and turned half around with his hands in his pockets—"the first time somebody asked me that, I was mad as shit! But you ain't gonna lose you no friends 'cause too many other people done asked me now."

Lanya said quickly: "I was asking because my old man knows her and he's been—"

George's face took a strange expression.

"—been telling me something about her . . . That's all." Lanya's face, after a moment, mirrored it as if in attempt to understand it. (Kidd felt his own face twitch.)

After a few seconds, George said: "Well, I got me an answer."

"What is it?"

In the khaki pockets, George's knuckles became a row of rounded points.

230

"Well, now I done raped this little white gal, right? I told the papers, right out, that's what I done." He nodded, like a man agreeing with the obvious—then glanced at Lanya, as though considering the new fact she brought. "Now there's rape and there's rape." George's hands came free. "You walking along one night and some guy jump—" George lunged, crouching—"out and grab you—" (Kidd, in the leaves, pulled back.) Lanya blinked—"and pull you into some alley and tie you up and other than that he don't touch you, but he pull his thing out and Wank! Wank! Wank!—"crouching, Harrison swung his fist up and down at his groin. (Kidd's jaw and buttocks clamped; Lanya, still leaning back on the wall, hands in her pockets, watched George's mime.)—"and Oh it's so good and Wow-wee that's gooood shit and *Ohhhh*—*!*" George stood, threw up his head, then let it fall slowly to the side with the end of the exhalation. His head came back up: "If he get one drop— *one*—" The fist rose with forefinger toward veiled heaven —"one drop on your *handbag* . . . that is lying there three feet away—" the fist fell—"in this state, that's rape! Even though his pecker ain't touched you . . . just dribbled on your handbag, like I say, see?" George nodded and considered: "And suppose some little girl who is seventeen years, three hundred and sixty-four days and twenty-three hours and fifty-five minutes old, she come up and say, 'Oh, honey, I want it *so* bad! Give it to me, give it to me, baby! Oh, please!'" George's long head went back again, wobbling side to side. "And she throw herself on the ground and pull down her panties and rubbing herself all up and down—" in a jogging crouch, he dragged his forearms up and down between his legs, pale nails on black fingers clawing toward the ground— "and moaning Oh, baby, do it to me, do it to me, I want it so bad! and you damn fool enough not to wait five minutes before you say—" George stood, punched the air—"*Yeah*, baby!" Both hands went slowly back to his pockets. "Well, that's rape too—"

"Wait a minute, George." Lanya said. "If you're walking home at nine o'clock and somebody behind you grabs you by the throat and bangs your head into a wall and hisses he'll knife you if you scream or don't do what he says— No, wait a minute; listen! And you're pissing in your pants in little squirts while he cuts you once on the arm and twice on the leg just so you see he's serious

231

and then tells you to spread your legs and gives you a black eye when you shake your head, because you're so scared you don't think you can, so you bunch up your skirts, while he's got your ear between the blade and his thumb and he keeps twisting and it's bleeding down your neck already and he tries to pull you open with his hand and pokes and prods you with a half-hard dick and slaps you a few times because you're not doing it right—no, don't stop me; we're talking about rape, now—and when he's got it about a half inch in you, he shoots, and while he's panting and it's dripping down your leg, you finally get a chance to run, and when he lunges after you, he trips and drops the knife, shouting he's gonna kill you now, he's gonna kill you, and for the next four days you can't walk right because of what he did inside you with his fingers, and in court—because they *do* catch him—a lawyer spends six hours trying to prove that you gave him some come-hither look or your hem was too high or your tits were too big, but they put him away anyway: only next week, they ask you to change schools because you're not a good influence any more . . . Now while you're telling me all this, don't forget, that's *also* rape!" Lanya's forefinger speared the air; she leaned back once more.

"Well," George said, "it is. Yes . . . that ever happen to you?"

"A friend of mine." Lanya put her hands back in her pockets.

"Here in Bellona?"

"There aren't any schools in Bellona you can be asked to change. No, it was before. But you men have a strange idea of the way the world works."

"Now you," George said, "are trying to make me think about something, right?"

"You think enough to bounce up and down here like a damn monkey and tell me a lot of bullshit. I asked you what happened. Tell me it's none of my business, if you want. But don't give me that."

"Well just maybe," George said, "you got a funny idea too if you think this is something I *didn't* think about." He looked at Lanya; a smile lurked behind his face. "You ask me a question, see, and you don't wanna hear my answer? The whole point, see, is rape is one pot with a lot of different kinds of stew in it. Some of them

232

is tastier than others." George narrowed his eyes: "How you like it?"

"What?" Lanya asked.

"You like it rough, with fighting and beating and scratching and crying—" George leaned toward her, looking out of one eye, one hand between them, one fingertip wagging faster and faster—"and moaning No, no, don't do it, please, don't do it, but crawling back for more between trying to get away and a few yesses slipping out every once in a while between the scratching and the biting?"

"That's the way you like it?"

"Yeah!" George stood back. His fist closed. (In the dirt, Kidd's opened.) "You know what I tell my women? 'Hit me! Go on, fight me! I'm gonna take it, now. I'm gonna take it, see. And you see if you can keep me from takin' it.' Then we do it—anywhere. In an alley, in a stairway, on a roof, in a bed . . ." George's brows lowered. "That the way you like it?"

"No," Lanya said. "That's not me. I'd rather do some of the taking myself."

The black hand turned up its lighter palm. One shoulder shrugged. "Then you and me—" George began to chuckle—"we just gonna have to stay like we is; friends. 'Cause any other way, we just wouldn't get along. Now I been liking it like that a long time, honey. And when you like it that way, when you do it that way, then you think about it; and you learn about it. And one of the things you learn is which women likes it that way too. Now you can't tell all the time, without askin'; and some like it more than others. But you learn." George's eyes narrowed again. "Now you really want to know what it was like, with her and me?"

Lanya nodded. (Kidd's chin tapped a leaf that swung down and up to tap it back.) "I asked."

"There it was, you see—" George's shoulders hunched —"all dark in the middle of the day and lightning rolling easy and slow overhead and the flames licking up and the smoke licking down and people screaming, running, rioting, bricks falling in the street and glass breaking behind me—I turned to see: And there she was, just staring. At me. People going past her every which way, and her the only still one on the street, looking like she was about to eat the back of her own hand, all pressed up

233

against her mouth like that, and from the way she was looking at me, I—knew! I knew what she wanted and I knew how she wanted it. And I knew I wanted it too." One hand was back in George's pocket. "Now I'll tell you, that ain't something you know all *that* often. But when you do, you can either say 'Shit man,' and walk away. Or, 'I know what I know!' Now, you an' me, we wouldn't get along." The chuckle ran out into a sound too low to hear. George breathed. "But her and me, *we* got along!" He suddenly turned, took a step, and halted as though his great body had been struck. *"Shit,* we got along!" He turned back. "I ain't got along with nobody that well since I was twenty-eight years old and that's been more than ten years! We was in this alley, and there was this light flashing on and off, on and off; and people would run in, run out, and we just didn't *care!* Or maybe that made it better, that there wasn't nothing they could do, or that they wanted to do." Suddenly he looked down, laughed: "I remember one old woman with a shopping bag full of empty old tin cans come running in and seen us and started shouting bloody murder and running in and out, and screaming 'Get off that poor little white girl, nigger! You do that, they gonna kill us, they gonna kill us for sure!'" George shook his head. "The light, I guess, was this guy taking his pictures; I don't know if I really seen him or not. He wasn't there when I finished. I stood up, see, and she was lying there, still reachin' for it, you know?" Once more he shook his head, laughed once more: both meant something different from when he'd done them moments before. "Like I say, she weren't no more than seventeen. And she got hit and she got punched and she got thrown around and she was yelling and screaming, 'No, no, oh, don't, oh please don't.' So I guess it was rape. Right? But when we finished—" George nodded—"she was reaching for it. She wanted some more, awful bad." He tapped the air with a concluding forefinger. "Now that's a very interesting kind of rape. It's the kind they always have in the movies. It's the kind your lawyer friend was trying to make this other thing into. And when it gets to the law courts, it's a pretty *rare* kind. But it's the one they all afraid of—especially between little-bitty white girls and big, black niggers."

"Well," Lanya said, "it still sounds a little strange. Okay, it's not my thing. But what do you think, say, about the guy I was telling you about, who did that to my friend?"

"I think," George said, "I know a little bit more about him than you do. And I think if he'd maybe come talked to somebody like me first, we could have maybe worked somethin' out where he didn't have to go and get himself and some little girl in trouble. About him or the girl, I don't think nothing; I don't know them. But I think what you told me about is very," and George dropped his chin, "very, very sad."

Lanya took a breath. "I'm just still wondering about the girl. I mean the one you were with . . . Do you even know her *name?*"

"Well, after I was finished, we did not exactly introduce ourselves." Suddenly George scowled. "Look, you try and understand this. I don't *give* a shit about the bitch! I really don't. And suppose I did? Suppose, afterward, I'd done said, 'Oh, hey baby, that was *so* fine, let's you and me get married and live all happily ever after so we can just take care of one another every night!' What she gonna say? 'You *crazy*, nigger!' I mean a couple of times I tried that, and it don't work. That ain't *her* thing. That ain't mine. She ain't interested in me neither. She interested in what she *thinks* about me. And that's fine by me. She know my name—it was in the paper. I gave it to them for free, too. I told them I ain't ashamed of nothing I done, I like it like that, and I'm gonna do it again, any time, any place. And believe me, that's *all* she wants to know!" George's scowl relaxed. "Afterward, people was gossiping around and saying her name was June or something like that. You say your old man know her? What he say about her?"

"About," Lanya said, "what you just did." She pressed her lips, considering. Then she said, "She's looking for you, George. I saw her once, come up to ask my old man after you. She wants to find you again."

George's laugh launched high as Madame Brown's and, with his rocking head, tumbled down into its easy bass. "Yeah . . . ! *Yeah*, she looking for me! She just circling and circling around me, getting in closer and closer—" George's forefinger circled on the air, spiraled in—"just circling and circling, closer and closer, like the moon around the sun!"

Something (though Kidd was not sure what it was)

struck Lanya as funny and she laughed too. "George, you've got your images mixed up! *You're* supposed to be the moon; not her. Besides, the moon doesn't circle around the sun!"

"Well," George said, "maybe it *usually* don't, but *this* is Bellona, and you ain't got no way to tell what's gonna happen here!" His laugh grew, fell away; he came out of it with a serious expression. "You see, I been around, I know some things. How old are you? Twenty-three?"

"On the head," Lanya said. "You should be guessing in a fair."

"Well I'm old enough to be your daddy—"

"You're old enough to be June's daddy too." Lanya said. "Do you have any children?"

"I got five of them I know about," George said, "and one of them off a white woman, too, young lady. Green-eyed, mustard-headed—" George screwed his face —"*ugly* little motherfucker! Well, maybe he ain't so ugly. And I got one of them as old now as her momma was when I first stuck it to her, too." George cocked his head the other way. "And that ain't nowhere near as old as the little girl we was talking about. None of the five of them is here in Bellona. But I tell you, if I was to see that oldest girl of mine, standing on the corner, looking at me like that little white girl was looking—I don't care if she my kin or not, I'd do the same fuckin' thing. Now you believe it!"

"George," Lanya said, "you are incorrigible!"

"Well, sometimes you look pretty funny yourself, Miss Anne! Look—" George got back his explanatory tone—"what it is, is that women wants it just exactly like men do. Only nobody wants to think about that, you know? At least not in the movies. They pretends it don't exist, or they pretends it's something so horrible, making all sorts of death and destruction and needless tragedy and everybody getting killed, that it might just as well not exist—which is the same thing, you see?"

"Yes," Lanya said, "I'd noticed. George, people are scared of women *doing* anything to get what they want, sex or anything else. Christ, you men are presumptuous bastards. If I was telling you how blacks really are the way you're telling me about women, you'd organize a sit-in!"

"Well," George said, "I just didn't know if you went to the movies that much so's you'd know."

After a moment, Lanya asked: "What do you think's gonna happen when you two finally do meet again, George?"

George's eyebrows, darker crescents on an iron-black face (the tarnished light erased all browns and reds), rose. "Well, she gonna get closer, and closer, just circling—" one hand traced its spiral while the other waited for it at the spiral's center—"and circling, and closer and closer, till—" George's cupped palms smashed; Kidd blinked; his back muscles cramped—"Blam! And the sky gonna go dark and the lightning gonna go roll over the night, wide as a river and slow as the sea, and buildings gonna come toppling and fire and water both gonna shoot in the air, and people gonna be running and screaming in the streets!" George winked, nodded. "Gonna be just like last time."

"I think," Lanya said, "you've got your images mixed again." She came away from the wall and ambled a few steps across the stone. "You're doing just what the movies are doing—making it into something terrible and frightening."

"*That's* the problem—like I say: You see I *like* it like the movies. But when we get together again, *we* just gonna be doing our thing. *You* all is the ones who gonna be so frightened the city gonna start to fall down around your head." George's head went to the side. He grinned. "See?"

"Not quite." Lanya grinned back. "But let it ride. Okay, what are you gonna do afterward?"

"Same as before, I guess. Blam! and excuse me, ma'am, and then be on my way. And then it starts all over . . ." Once more that oblique expression came to George's face. "You say your old man . . . is she all right? I mean is she okay and all?"

"Yeah," Lanya said. "I guess so."

George nodded. "Yeah . . . somebody told me back in the bar you done got yourself a new boy friend. That's nice."

Where, Kidd wondered, was Milly?

"Things get around." Lanya smiled, and Kidd had an image of her suddenly snatching her harmonica to fling up some fusillade of notes to hide her embarrassment.

237

Only she didn't look embarrassed. (He remembered wanting to overhear Lanya and Milly discussing him; the prospect of a discussion of him with George left him vaguely uncomfortable.) Fingers hooked over her pocket rim, Lanya *was* toying with her harmonica. "Yeah. I don't know if I'd say I got him; how about getting?"

"Well, you sure get yourself some winners! That last one . . ." George shook his head.

"What did you think of Phil, George?" The subject, almost as uncomfortably, had changed.

"*I* thought he was crazy!" George said. "I thought he was a stuckup, up-tight, tight-assed asshole— Smart? Oh, he was smart as a whip. But I'm still glad to see you shut of him." George paused; his brows wrinkled. "Though I guess maybe you ain't . . . ?"

"I don't know." Lanya's lowered eyes suddenly rose. "But that's easier to say if you got a new one, isn't it?"

"Well—" George's laugh came out surprising and immense—"I guess it is. Say, when you gonna bring your old man on down to Jackson and say hello?"

"Well, thanks," Lanya said. "Maybe we'll come down . . . if we don't see you in the bar, first."

"Gotta check your new old man out," George said. "First, see, I thought maybe you'd got involved with one of them faggot fellas up at Teddy's. God damn, sometimes I think there ain't nobody in the city no more ain't a faggot but me."

"Is that a standard male, heterosexual fantasy?" Lanya asked. "I mean, to be the only straight man around when all the others are gay?"

"I ain't got nothing against faggots," George said. "You seen them pictures them boys made of me? Something, huh? Some of my best friends is—"

"George!" Lanya held up her hand, her face in mock pain. "Come on, don't say it!"

"Look—" George's gestures became sweepingly gallant—"I just like to make sure all my friends is taken care of. If you wasn't getting none, see, I was gonna volunteer to make an exception in my standard methods of procedure and fit you in my list. We got to watch out for our friends? Now, don't we?"

"That's sweet of you," Lanya said. "But I'm royally taken care of in that department."

And Kidd, gloriously happy, put his other knee on the ground and sat back. A thought, circling below articu-

238

lation, suddenly surfaced, dripping words: They *know* each other . . . were the first that fell off it; more followed, obscuring clear thought with lapped, resonant rings. He remembered the poster. It was the same man, with the same, dark, rough face (the face was laughing now), the same body (the khaki coverall was mostly too loose but now and again, when a leg moved so or a shoulder turned, it seemed about to tear at arm or thigh), that he'd seen reproduced, bared, black, and bronze-lit.

"Well, then—" George made a slate-wiping motion —"everything's fine! You two come on down. I'd like to meet this guy. You pick 'em pretty interesting."

"Okay." Lanya said: "Well, I guess I'm gonna be on my way. Just stopped in to say hello."

Now, Kidd thought, now Milly is going to jump out and . . . ?

"Okay. I see you," George said. "Maybe later in the bar."

Now . . . ?

"So long." Lanya turned around and started down the steps.

George shook his head, went back to the wall— glanced after her once—picked up the newspaper and while he shook it out, speared two fingers at his breast pocket for his glasses. He got them on the third try.

Harmonica notes twisted up like silver wires in the haze.

Kidd waited half a dozen breaths, realizing finally he had misjudged Lanya's and Milly's intentions. Milly *had*, apparently, chickened out. Again he wondered from what. Backing into thicker brush, he stood with cramping thighs and, ignoring them, circled the court. The ground sloped sharply. This time, if he could overtake her on the path, he would not hide—

The music wound in the smoke toward some exotic cadence that, when achieved, slid it into a new key where the melody defined itself along burbling triplets till another cadence, in six measures, took it home.

He came out on the side of the steps. Small branches tugged his hips and shoulders, swished away.

Lanya, at the bottom of the flight, ambled onto the path, dragging her music after like a silver cape.

And she had almost completed the song. (He had never heard her play it through.) Its coda hauled up the end in one of those folk suspensions that juxtapose two unrelated chords to hold a note from one above the other and make chaos of it. Starting down the steps behind her, he got chills, not from fear or confusion, but from the music's moment which sheered through mouse-grey mist glimmering in the leafy corridor.

He tried to walk silently, twice stopped entirely, not to break the melody before its end.

He was on the bottom step. She was fifteen feet ahead.

The melody ended.

He hurried.

She turned, lips together for some word that began with "m." Then her eyes widened: "Kidd—?" and she smiled. "What are you doing here—?" and took his hand.

"I was spying on you," he said, "and George."

She raised an eyebrow. "You were?"

"Yeah." They walked together. "I liked your song."

"Oh . . ."

He glanced over.

She was more embarrassed, he realized, by his over-hearing the music than the conversation. While he was wondering what to offer her to atone, she managed to say:

"Thank you," softly, "though."

He squeezed her hand.

She squeezed his.

Shoulder to shoulder, they walked up the path, while Kidd's mind turned and sorted and wondered what hers turned and sorted. He asked, suddenly: "The person you were telling George about, who got raped—was that Milly?"

Lanya looked up, surprised. "No . . . or let's say that I'd rather not say."

"Huh? What does *that* mean, no or you'd rather not say?"

Lanya shrugged. "I just mean Milly probably wouldn't want me to say, one way *or* the other."

Kidd frowned. "That doesn't make sense."

Lanya laughed, without letting it out, so that it was only an expression, a breath through her nose, her head shaking. She shrugged again.

"Look, just give me a simple answer, was she or—?"

"Now you look," Lanya said: "You're a very sweet man, and I know you're not doing it on purpose, it's just the habit men get into of trying to undermine anything that goes on between two women. But stop it."

He was confused.

She asked: "Okay."

Confused, he agreed. "Okay."

They wandered on. The song, etched on memory, filigreed, in memory, the silent, present trees. The sky had deepened to a color that could be called blue, in leaf-shaped flakes among them.

Confused, he was still happy.

At the commune clearing, Milly, with Jommy at the furnace, turned, saw them, and ran over. "Lanya, Kidd—" and to Lanya: "Did you tell him?"

Lanya said: "No. I didn't, yet . . ."

"Oh, Kidd, I'm afraid—" Milly took another breath; she had been running more than just from the furnace. "I'm afraid I was spying on the two of you most of the way back here." She laughed. "You see, *we* decided *I* was going to hide in the bushes and overhear Lanya and George—"

"Huh?" Kidd said.

Lanya said: "He's not so bad after all—"

"Kidd?" Milly said. "Oh—you mean George! No, of course he isn't . . ." Back to Kidd: "*I* was going to come out and join Lanya again on the path back from the Weather Tower—" then it wasn't the monastery; but he'd pretty well decided it couldn't have been—"when I saw you pop out on the steps, thirty seconds before I was going to!"

He said to Lanya: "Then you were expecting . . . ?" The half-dozen questions in his mind were halved again when Milly said:

"I couldn't keep close enough to hear *every*thing you were saying. If I had, I would have made too much noise. I just cut straight through and caught the paths on the snake-turns. Oh, Lanya, it *is* a lovely song! Really, you've got to play it for other people. See, you *can* play it all the way through. I told you you could. You knew *I* was listening, and you got through it. Just don't let people embarrass you . . . Kidd—?" Milly frowned. "You look so confused, Kidd!" Suddenly she hugged him; red hair brushed dry against his face. He nearly stumbled. "Really, I'm sorry!" She released him, put her hand on Lanya's shoulder. "I didn't mean to spy. But *you* knew I was there . . ." She looked imploringly at Lanya. "I just couldn't resist!" And she laughed.

He blinked; he smiled. ". . . that's all right." The memory of the melody came again; it had not been a private moment he'd overheard, but one meant for a friend. Had that, he wondered, given it its beauty? Lanya was laughing too.

So he laughed with them.

At the furnace, Jommy banged his ladle on the caldron. "Come on! Soup's ready! Come and get it!"

About the clearing, with mess-pans and mess-pots, crocks and tin cups and bowls, two dozen people gathered at the fire.

"Come on, let's eat," Lanya said.

"Yes, you *too*, Kidd!" Milly said. "Come on."

He followed the girls toward the crowd. A thin, ginger-haired spade with gold-rimmed teeth gave him a dented enamel soup plate. "I got two, man. You can take this one." But when he reached the front, at the furnace, for his ladle-full, it was John (with swinging vest and eye-glasses full of flame), not Jommy, who served. The sky was almost dark. Though firelight lay coppery against Milly's hair, he could not make out, on either bare leg, as he followed Milly and led Lanya out among the crowd, trying to balance his bowl, that scratch.

Dusk had come quickly—and lingered, holding off dark. They sat on the rumpled blankets at Her Place. He squinted up between lapped leaves while the sky drizzled powdery rubbings, gritty and cool.

"One more day's work at the Richards, and I'll have them moved."

"You've . . . well, you've got a name now. And a job. Are you happy?"

"Shit—" He stretched out on his back and felt beneath him twigs, creases, pebbles, and the beaded chain around him. "I haven't even decided how to spell it. And they still haven't paid me more than that first five dollars."

"If they don't pay you—" she stretched out too— "why do you go back?"

He shrugged. "Maybe they know if they gave me my money, I wouldn't come." He shrugged again. "It doesn't matter. Like I told Madame Brown, I'm just an observer. They're fun to watch." Thinking: Someday I'm

242

going to die. He glanced at her: "Do you know, I'm afraid of dying. A lot."

"Hm?"

"I am. Sometimes, when I'm walking around, I think maybe my heart is going to stop. So I feel it, just to make sure it's going. Which is funny, because if I'm lying down, about to go to sleep, and I can hear my heart going, I have to move into another position, or I get scared—"

"—that it might stop and you'll hear it?" she asked.

"Yeah."

"That happens to me sometimes. When I was fifteen, in boarding school, I sat on the edge of the main building roof for a long time and thought about committing suicide."

"I've never wanted to kill myself," he said. "Never in my life. Sometimes I thought I was going to—because I'd gotten some crazy compulsion, to jump off a building or throw myself under a train, just to see what dying was *like*. But I never thought that life wasn't worth living, or that there was any situation so bad where just sitting it out wouldn't fix it up—that's if I couldn't get up and go somewhere else. But not wanting to kill myself doesn't stop me thinking about death. Say, has this ever happened to you? You're walking along a street, or sitting in a room, or lying down on the leaves, or even talking to people, and suddenly the thought comes—and when it comes, it comes all through you like a stop-action film of a crystal forming or an opening bud: 'I am going to die.' Someday, somewhere, I will be dying, and five seconds after that, I will be dead. And when it comes it comes like—" he smashed cupped palms together in the air so sharply she jumped—"that! And you know it, know your own death, for a whole second, three seconds, maybe five or ten . . . before the thought goes and you only remember the words you were mumbling, like 'Someday I will die,' which isn't the thought at all, just its ashes."

"Yes . . . yes, that's happened to me."

"Well, I think all the buildings and the bridges and the planes and the books and the symphonies and the paintings and the spaceships and the submarines and . . . and the poems: they're just to keep people's minds occupied so it doesn't happen—again." After a while he said: "George Harrison . . ."

She said: "June Richards . . ." and glanced at him. When he said nothing, she said: "I have this picture, of us going down to the bar one night, and you saying, 'Hey, man, come on with me. I want you to meet a friend of mine,' and George says, 'Why sure!'—and he probably would, too; he knows how small the world is he's acting moon for—so you take him, in all his big, black, beautiful person up to that pink brick high-rise with all the broken windows and you get a-hold of Miss Demented-sweetness-and-light, and you say, 'Hey, Lady, I've just brought you His Midnight Eminence, in the flesh. June, meet George. George, meet June.' I wonder what they'd talk about—on her territory?"

He chuckled. "Oh, I don't know. He might even say, Thank you. After all, she made him what he is today." He blinked at the leaves. "It's fascinating, life the way it is; the way everything sits together, colors, shapes, pools of water with leaves in them, reflections on windows, sunlight when there's sun, cloudlight when it's cloudy; and now I'm somewhere where, if the smoke pulls back at midnight and George and the moon are up, I might see two shadows instead of one!" He stretched his hands behind him on the blanket. He knocked something—which was his orchid, rolling across his notebook cover.

"When I was at Art School," she said, "I remember an instructor of mine saying that it was only on days like you have here that you know the true color of anything. The whole city, all of Bellona, it's under perpetual north light."

"Mmm," he said.

What is this part of me that lingers to overhear my own conversation? I lie rigid in the rigid circle. It regards me from diametric points, without sex, and wise. We lie in a rigid city, anticipating winds. It circles me, intimating only by position that it knows more than I want to. There, it makes a gesture too masculine before ecstatic scenery. Here, it suggests femininity, pausing at gore and bone. It dithers and stammers, confronted by love. It bows a blunt, mumbling head before injustice, rage, or even its like ignorance. Still, I am convinced that at the proper shock, it would turn and call me, using those hermetic syllables I have abandoned on the crags of a broken conscience, on the planes of charred consciousness, at the entrance to the ganglial city. And I would raise my head.

"You . . ." he said, suddenly. It was dark. "Are you happy, I mean, living like that?"

"Me?" She breathed a long breath. "Let me see . . . before I came here, I was teaching English to Cantonese children who'd just arrived in New York's Chinatown. Before that, I was managing a pornographic bookstore on 42nd Street. And before that, for quite a while, I was a self-taught tape-jockey at WBAI, FM, in New York, and before that, I was doing a stint at her sister station KPFA, in Berkeley, Cal. Babes, I am *so* bored here that I don't think, since I've come, I've ever been more than three minutes away from some really astonishing act of violence." And suddenly, in the dark, she rolled against him.

"Gotta run." *Click*. The tie knot rose.

"Hey, Mr Richards?" Kidd put down his own cup.

"Yes, Kidd?" Mr Richards, already in the doorway, turned back. "What do you want?"

Bobby spooned at his frosted cereal. There was no milk. June traced a column in the Friday, October 24, 1985 *Times* with her forefinger. It was several weeks old.

"I want to know about my money."

"You need some more? I'll have some for you when I get home this evening."

"I want to know how much I'm getting."

"Hm?"

"Oh. Well, we'll have to figure that out. Have you been keeping track of how long you've been working each day?"

"More or less," Kidd said. "Madame Brown told me you were going to give me five bucks an hour."

Mr Richards took the door knob. "That's pretty high wages." He shook his head, thoughtfully.

"Is that what you told her?"

The knob turned. "We better talk about it later on this evening." The door closed on his smile.

Kidd turned back to Mrs Richards.

She sipped, eyes flickering above the china rim.

"I mean that's what you told her, isn't it?"

"Five dollars an hour is quite high. For unskilled labor." The cup lowered to her chin.

"Yeah, but not for furniture movers. Look, let me go downstairs and finish bringing up the rugs and the clothes. It's only going to take another half-dozen trips.

245

I'll be through before you get started on lunch." Kidd got up too noisily and went to the door.

Bobby's spoon, silent the exchange, crunched again.

June's eyes had stayed down, but once more her finger moved.

From the doorway Kidd glanced back at her (as moments before her father had glanced back at him) and tried to set her against George's and Lanya's conversation of the previous afternoon. But, with blonde head bent over the paper at the edge of dark wood—blonde and pink reflection fuzzed in the polish—she seemed as at home among the fluted, white china cups, the brass pots of plants, the green rugs, the blue flowered drapes, her mother, her brother, the wide windows, or the green wallpaper with its paler green florals.

Down on seventeen, he came into the apartment (unchained, unlocked) and thought: Why didn't we take the rugs up *first?* That was silly, not to have taken the rugs up. Like mottled eels (the underpad, a smaller darker eel, printed with a design that, till now, he'd only seen on corrugated ceilings) the rugs lay against the living room wall. Outside the window, pale leviathans swam. Piles of books sat on the floor.

Pilgrimage was on top of one.

For the third—or was it the fourth? Or the fifth?—time he picked it up, read at random pages, waiting to be caught and driven into the work. But the receptivity he tried to bring was again and again hooked away by some pattern of shadow on the bare vinyl tile, some sound in the apartment below, some itch in his own body: and there went all his attention. Though his eye moved over the print, his place and the print's sense were lost: At last he lay the book back on the pile, and put a book from another pile on top, as though—and wondered why he thought of it this way—the first book were his own.

He stood up—he had been squatting—and gazed around: still to be moved were bridge tables from the back storage closet, folding chairs with scrolled arms, green cushions, and black metal hinges; and toys from Bobby's room, scattered among them. A set of four nest tables was crowded with small, bright breakables.

He wandered down the hall (there was the carton of papers from Mr Richards' den) and turned into Bobby's room. Most of what was left was evidence of the older brother who'd once shared it: a handkerchief that had fallen out of a bureau drawer yesterday, showing the monogram: EGR; propping the closet door were three small cartons with *Eddy* written across them in magic marker; on the floor was the Bellona High School Yearbook. Kidd picked it up and paged through: Edward Garry Richards (*Soccer team, G.O. Volunteer,* "The Cafeteria Staff's favorite two years running . . .") was *Camera Shy*.

He lay the book down on the boxes, wandered across the hall into June's room: on the window sill was the tepee of an empty matchbook and a white plastic flower pot still filled with earth which, June had told him yesterday, had once grown a begonia her aunt Marianne had given her two Easters ago.

In memory he refurnished the space with the pieces he'd taken upstairs the previous day and tried to pull back, also from memory, the image of June that had come to him in George's overheard converse. Memory failed at a sound outside.

Kidd stepped back into the hall as Bobby came from the living room; he grunted, over an armful of books, "I'm taking these upstairs."

"Why don't you take about half of them?"

"Maybe—" two books fell—"I better."

June came in: "Oh, hey, I'll take some of those . . ." They divided the stack, left.

Where, he wondered as the door closed (the unlatched chain swung and swung over green paint), is my notebook? Of course; down the hall in what had been the back bedroom, from when he'd stopped in this apartment out of habit when he'd first come in the morning: He had momentarily forgotten that the Richards were living in nineteen now.

In the back bedroom another file box stood off center in the middle of the floor.

The notebook was on the window sill. Kidd walked up to it, looked at the worn, smeared cardboard. Outside, small darknesses moved below the mist. What, he thought, should I say to Mr Richards about my money? Suppose Mr Richards comes back this evening and doesn't bring up the subject? Kidd considered writing down alternative opening lines and rehearsing them for Mr Richards' return. No. No, that's exactly the wrong way! It's almost nine o'clock, he thought, and too smoky to tell people from shadows at seventeen stories.

Something thumped; a girl cried out. A second thump, and her pitch changed. A third—it sounded like toppling furniture—and her cry swooped. A fourth ended it.

That was from the apartment below.

Breaking glass, much nearer, brought his eyes from the floor.

Kidd went to the living room.

Mrs Richards, kneeling over something shattered, looked up and shook her head. "I . . ."

He stopped before her restrained confusion.

". . . I dropped one of the—"

He could not tell what the figurine had been.

"So thin—these walls are so very thin. Everything comes through. I was so startled . . ." By the nest tables, she picked faster in the bright, black shards, white matt overside.

"I hope it wasn't anything you really—" but was halted by his own inanity.

"Oh, that's all right. Here, I've got it all." She stood, cupping chips. "I heard that awful . . . and I dropped it."

"They were going on pretty loud." He tried to laugh, but before her gaze, he let the laugh die in breath. "Mrs Richards, it's just noise. You shouldn't let yourself get so upset about it."

"What are they *doing* down there? Who *are* they?"

He thought she might crush the ceramic between her palms. "They're just some guys, some girls, who moved into the downstairs apartment. They're not out to bother you. They think the noises from up here are pretty strange too."

"Just moved in? How do you mean, they *just* moved in?"

He watched her expression lurch at fear, and not achieve even that. "They wanted a roof, I guess. So they took it over."

"Took it *over?* They *can't* come in here and take it over. What happened to the couple who lived there before? Management doesn't know things like this are going on. The front doors used to be closed at ten o'clock, every night! And locked! The first night they started making those dreadful sounds, I sent Arthur out for one of the guards: Mr Phillips, a very nice West Indian man, he's always in front of our building till one in the morning. Arthur couldn't find him. He'd gone away. All the

248

guards. And the attendants for the garage. I want you to know I put that in my letter to Management. I certainly did." She shook her head. "How can they just come in and take it over?"

"They just . . . Ma'am, there aren't any more guards, and nobody was living there; they just moved in. Just like you're moving into nineteen."

"We're not *just* moving in!" Mrs Richards had been looking about. Now she walked into the kitchen. "I *wrote* Management. Arthur went to see them. We got the key from the office. It isn't the same thing at all."

Kidd followed Mrs Richards around the stripped kitchen.

"How do *you* know nobody was living there? There was a very nice couple downstairs. She was Japanese. Or Korean or something. He was connected with the university. I didn't know them very well. They'd only been here six months. What happened to *them?*" She looked back, just before she went into the dining room again.

"They left, just like everybody else." He still followed.

She carried the broken things, clacking, down the rugless hall. "I think something awful happened to them. I think those people down there did something awful. Why doesn't Management send some new guards?" She started into Bobby's room, but changed her mind and continued to June's. "It's dangerous, it's absolutely, terribly dangerous, without guards."

"Mrs Richards?" He stood in the doorway while she circuited the room, hands still cupped. "Ma'am? What are you looking for?"

"Someplace to throw—" she stopped—"this. But you took everything upstairs already."

"You know you could just drop it on the floor." He was impatient and his impatience embarrassed him. "I mean you don't live here any more."

After the silence in which her expression became curious, she said, "You don't understand the way we live at all. But then, you probably think you understand all too well. I'm going to take this out to the incinerator."

He ducked back as she strode through.

"I don't like to go out in the hall. I don't feel safe—"

"I'll take it out for you," he called after her.

"That's all right." Hands still together, she twisted the knob.

When the door banged behind her, he sucked his teeth, then went and got his notebook from the window. The blue-rimmed stationery slid half out. He opened the cover and looked at her even letters. With his front teeth set, he took his pen and drew in the comma. Her ink was India black; his, dark blue.

Going back to the living room, he stabbed at his pocket several times. Mrs Richards came in with a look of accomplishment. His pen caught. "Mrs Richards, do you know, that letter's still down in your mailbox?"

"What letter?"

"You've got an airmail letter in your mailbox. I saw it again this morning."

"All the mailboxes are broken."

"Yours isn't. And there's a letter inside it. I told you about it the first day I came here. Then I told Mr Richards a day later. Don't you have a mailbox key?"

"Yes, of course. One of us will go down and pick it up this afternoon."

"Mrs Richards?" Something vented still left something to come.

"Yes, Kidd?"

His teeth were still set. He sucked air and they opened. "You're a very nice woman. You've really tried to be nice to me. And I think it's a shame you have to be so scared all the time. There's nothing I can do about it, but I wish there was."

She frowned; the frown passed. "I don't suppose you'd believe just how much you have done."

"By being around?"

"Yes. And also by being, well . . ."

He could not interpret her shrug: "Mrs Richards, I've been scared a whole lot of my life too. Of a lot of things that I didn't know what they were. But you can't just let them walk all over you—take over. You have to—"

"I am moving!" Her head bobbed in emphasis. "We are moving from seventeen-B to nineteen-A."

"—do something inside yourself."

She shook her head sharply, not looking. "And you are very presumptuous if you think you are telling me something I don't know." Now she looked up. "Or your telling me makes it any easier."

Frustration drove the apology. "I'm sorry." He heard his own reticence modify it to something else.

Mrs Richards blinked. "Oh, I know you're just trying to . . . *I* am sorry. But do you *know* how terrible it is to live inside here—" she gestured at the green walls—"with everything slipping away? And you can hear everything that goes on in the other rooms, in the other apartments? I wake up at night, and walk by the window, and I can see lights sometimes, moving in the smoke. And when the smoke isn't so heavy, it's even worse, because then the lights look like horrible things, crawling around . . . This has got to stop, you know! Management must be having all sorts of difficulty while we're going through this crisis. I understand that. I make allowances. But it's not as though a bomb had fallen, or anything. If a bomb had fallen, we'd be dead. This is something perfectly natural. And we have to make do, don't we, until the situation is rectified?" She leaned forward: "You don't think it *is* a bomb?"

"It isn't a bomb. I was in Encenadas, in Mexico, just a week or so ago. There was nothing about a bomb in the papers; somebody gave me a lift who had an L.A. paper in his car. Everything's fine there. And in Philadelphia—"

"Then you see. We just have to wait. The guards will be back. They will get rid of all these terrible people who run around vandalizing in the halls. We have to be patient, and be strong. Of course I'm afraid, I'm afraid if I sit still more than five minutes I'll start to scream. But you can't give in to it, any more than you can give in to them. Do you think we should take kitchen knives and broken flower pots and run down there and try to scrape them out?"

"No, of course not—"

"I'm not that sort of person. I don't intend to become that sort. You say I have to do something? Well, I have moved my family. Don't you think that takes a great deal of . . . inner strength? I mean in *this* situation? I can't even let myself assess how dangerous the whole thing really is. If I did, I wouldn't be able to move at all."

"Of course it's dangerous. But I go out. I live outside in it; I walk around in it. Nothing happens to me."

"Oh, Edna told me how you got that scab on your face. Besides, you are a man. You are a young man. I am a middle-aged woman."

"But that's all there is now, Mrs Richards. You've got to walk around in it because there isn't anything else."

"It will be different if I wait. I know that because I *am* middle-aged. You don't because you're still very young."

"Your friend Mrs Brown—"

"Mrs Brown is not me. I am not Mrs Brown. Oh, are you just *trying* not to understand?"

He gathered breath for protest but failed articulation.

"I have a family. It's very important to me. Mrs Brown is all alone, now. She doesn't have the same sort of responsibilities. But you don't understand about that; perhaps in your head, you do. But not inside, not really."

"Then why don't you and Mr Richards take your family out of all this mess?"

Her hands, moving slowly down her dress, turned up once, then fell. "One can retreat, yes. I suppose that's what I'm doing by moving. But you can't just give up entirely, run away, surrender. I *like* the Labry Apartments." Her hands pulled together to crush the lap of her dress. "I like it here. We've lived here since I was pregnant with Bobby. We had to wait almost a year to get in. Before that, we had a tiny house out in Helmsford; but it wasn't as nice as this, believe me. They don't let just anyone in here. With Arthur's position, it's much better for him. I've entertained many of his business associates here. I especially liked some of the younger, brighter men. And their wives. They were very pleasant. Do you know how hard it is to make a home?"

His bare heel had begun to sting, just from the weight of standing. He rocked a little.

"That's something that a woman does from inside herself. You do it in the face of all sorts of opposition. Husbands are very appreciative when it works out well. But they're not that anxious to help. It's understandable. They don't know how. The children don't even appreciate. But it's terribly necessary. You must make it your own world. And everyone must be able to feel it. I *want* a home, here, that looks like my home, feels like my home, is a place where my family can be safe, where my friends —psychologists, engineers, ordinary people . . . poets— can feel comfortable. Do you see?"

He nodded.

He rocked.

"That man Calkins, the one who runs the *Times*, do

252

you think he has a home? They're always writing articles about the people who're staying with him, visiting with him, those people he's decided are important. Do you think I'd want a place like that? Oh, no. This is a real home, a place where real things happen, to real people. You feel that way, I know you do. You've become practically part of the family. You are sensitive, a poet; you understand that to tear it all apart, and set it up again, even on the nineteenth floor: that's taking a desperate chance, you see? But I'm doing it. To you, moving like this is just a gesture. But you don't understand how important a gesture can be. I cannot have a home where I hear the neighbors shrieking. *I* cannot. Because when the neighbors are shrieking, I cannot maintain the peace of mind necessary for *me* to *make* a home. Not when that is going on. Why do you think we moved into the Labry? Do you know how I thought of *this* moving? As a space, a gap, a crack in which some terrible thing might get in and destroy it, us, my home. You have to take it apart, then put it back together. I really felt as though some dirt, or filth, or horrible rot might get in while it was being reassembled and start a terrible decay. But here—" once more she waved her hand—"I couldn't live here any more."

"But if everything *outside* has changed—"

"Then I have to be—" she let go her skirt—"stronger inside. Yes?"

"Yeah." He was uncomfortable with the answer forced. "I guess so."

"You guess?" She breathed deeply, looking around the floor, as if for missed fragments. "Well, I *know*. I know about eating, sleeping, how it must be done if people are going to be comfortable. I have to have a place where I can cook the foods I want; a place that looks the way I want it to look: a place that can be a real home." Then she said: "You do understand." She picked up another ceramic lion from the nest tables. "I know you do."

He realized it was its twin that had shattered. "Yeah, Mrs Richards but—"

"Mom?" June said over the sound of the opening door. She glanced hesitantly between them. "I thought you were going to come right back up. Is that my shell box?" She walked to the cluster of remaining furniture. "I didn't even know we still had it in the house."

"Gee," Bobby said from the doorway. "We've almost got everything upstairs. You want me to take the television?"

"I don't know why," June said. "You can't get any picture on it any more; just colored confetti. You better let Kidd take the teevee. You help me carry the rug."

"Oh, all right."

June dragged the carpet roll by one end. Bobby caught the other.

"Are you sure the two of you can manage that?" Mrs Richards asked.

"We got it," June said.

It came up like a sagging fifteen-foot sausage between them. They maneuvered across the room—Mrs Richards slid the nest tables back, Kidd pushed aside the television —June going forward and Bobby going backward.

"Hey, don't back me into the damn door," Bobby said.

"Bobby!" his mother said.

June grunted, getting the rug in a firmer grip.

"I'm *sorry*." Bobby hugged the rug under his arm, reached behind him for the door knob. *"Darn* door . . . Okay?"

"You got it all right?" June asked; she looked very intense.

"Uh-huh." Bobby nodded, backing out into the hall.

June followed him: the edge of the rug hissed by the jamb. "Just a second." She shoved the door with her foot; and was through.

"All right, but don't push me so fast," Bobby repeated out in the echoing corridor.

The door swung to.

"Mrs Richards, I'll take the television . . . if you want?"

She was stepping here and there, searching.

"Yes. Oh. Certainly, the television. Though June's right; you can't see anything on it. It's terrible the way you get to depend on all these outside things: Fifty great empty spots during the evening when you wish a radio or something were there to fill them up. But the static would just be awful. Wait. I could take the rest of these things off the tables, and you could carry them up. Once we get the front room rug down, I'm going to try putting that end table beside the door to the balcony. That's what I really like up there, the balcony. When we came here, we applied for an apartment with a balcony but we couldn't get it then. I'm going to split these up and put them on either side of—"

Out in the hall, June screamed: a long scream he could hear empty her of all breath. Then she screamed again.

Mrs Richards opened her mouth without sound; one hand shook by her head.

He dashed between the television and the tables, out the door.

June, dragging one hand against the wall, backed up the hall. When he caught her shoulder, the scream cut and she whirled. "Bobby . . . !" That had almost no voice at all. "I . . . I didn't see the . . ." Shaking her head, she motioned down the hall.

He heard Mrs Richards behind him, and ran three more steps.

The rug lay on the floor, the last foot sagging over the sill in to the empty elevator shaft. The door nudged it, went *K-chunk,* retreated, then began to close again.

"Mom! Bobby, he fell in the—"

K-chunk!

"No, oh my dear God, no!"

"I didn't see it, mom! I didn't! I thought it was the other—"

"Oh, God. Bobby, no he couldn't—"

"Mom, I didn't know! He just backed into it! I didn't see—"

K-chunk!

Kidd hit EXIT with both palms, vaulted down the flight, came out on sixteen, sprinted to the end of the hall, and beat the door.

"All right, all right. What the fuck you—" Thirteen opened for him—"banging so hard for?"

"A rope . . . !" Kidd was gasping. "Or a ladder. You guys got a rope? And a flashlight? The boy from upstairs, he just fell down the elevator shaft!"

"Oh, wow . . . !" Thirteen stepped back.

Smokey, behind his shoulder, opened her eyes very wide.

"Come on! You guys got a light and a ladder? And a rope?"

A black woman with hair like two inches of Brillo with hints of rust, shouldered Smokey aside, stepped around Thirteen: "Now what the fuck is going on, huh?"

Around her neck hung some dozen chains, falling between her breasts between the flaps of a leather vest laced through its half-dozen lowest holes. Her thumb hooked a wide, scuffed belt; her wrists were knobby, the back of her hands rough. Dark skin rounded above the belt and below the vest bottom.

"A boy just fell down the God-damn elevator shaft!" Kidd took another breath and tried to see past the crowd that had gathered at the door. "Will you bastards get a ladder and a rope and a light and come on! Huh?"

"Oh, hey, man!" The black woman looked over her shoulder. "Baby! Adam! Denny, you had that line! Bring it out here. Some kid fell down the shaft." She turned back. "I got a light." A brown triangle of stain, that looked permanent, crossed her two, large, front teeth. "Come on!"

Kidd turned away and started back down the hall.

He heard them running behind him.

As he ducked into the stairwell, Denny's voice separated from the voices and footsteps around it: "Fell down the *elevator!* Oh, man," and a barking laugh. "All right. All right, Dragon Lady—I'm with you."

Sudden light behind him flung his shadow before him down the next flight. At the landing he glanced back:

The bright scales, claws, and fangs careened after him, striated and rigid as a television image from a monster film suddenly halted in its projector: it was the dragon he'd seen his first night in the park with Tak. He could tell because griffon and mantis glimmered just behind, and sometimes through it. Bleached out like ghosts, the others clustered down, streaked with sidelight. Kidd ran on, heart hammering, breath scoring his nasal roof.

He fell against the bottom door; it sagged forward. He staggered out. The others ran behind. Harsh light lay out harsh shadow, dispersing the lobby's grey as he crossed.

"How do you get down into the fucking basement?" He hammered the elevator bell.

"The downstairs is locked," Thirteen said. "I tried to get in when we first got—"

Both elevator doors rolled open.

Dragon Lady, light extinguished, swung around him into the one with the car, wrenched away the plate above the buttons: The plate clattered on the car floor as she did something with switches. "Okay, I got both doors locked open."

Kidd looked back—the two other apparitions swayed forward among the others standing—and called: "Where's the rope?" He held the other jamb and leaned into the breezy shaft. Girders rose by hazy brick. "I can't see too much." Above and in the wind a voice echoed:

Oh, no! He's down there! He must be terribly hurt!

And another:

No, Mom, come back. Kidd's down there. Mom, please!

Bobby, Bobby, are you all right? Please, Bobby! Oh, dear God!

Kidd strained to see: the vaguest suggestion of light up in the distance—was it some upper, open door? "Mrs Richards!" His shout vaulted about the shaft. "You get back from that door!"

Oh, Bobby! Kidd, is he all right? Oh, please, let him be all right.

Mom, come back, will you?

Then lights around him moved forward, harshening the brick, the painted steel. On the shaft wall shadows of heads swung; some grew, some faded; new shadows grew.

"You see anything?" Dragon Lady asked, crowding his shoulder. "Here." Her arm came up, hooked his. "Lean on out further if you want."

He glanced back at her.

She said, her head to the side: "I ain't gonna let you fall, motherfucker!"

So he hooked up his arm. "Got me?"

"Yeah."

Their elbows made a hot, comfortable lock.

He leaned forward, swaying into the dark. She let him slowly out.

The other lights had filled the door, flushing the shaft with doubled shadows.

"You see anything in there?" which was not Dragon Lady's voice but Denny's.

The junk down there: On darkness like velvet, cigarette packages, chewing-gum papers, cigarettes and cigarette butts, match books, envelopes and, there to one side, heaped up . . . the glitter in it identified the wrist. "Yeah, I can see him . . . I think."

257

*Can you see where he is? Bobby? Bobby, Kidd, can
you see him? Oh, my God, he fell all that way! Oh, he
must be hurt, so badly! I can't hear him. Is he unconscious? Oh, can't you see where he is yet?*

Momma, please, please come back from here!

Behind him, Dragon Lady said with soft brutality:
"Christ, I wish that bitch would shut the fuck up!"

"Look, man," Thirteen said, behind them, "that's
her *kid* down there!"

"Don't 'man' me, Thirteen," Dragon Lady said; and
Kidd felt her grip—well, not loosen so much as shift,
about an inch; his shoulder tensed. "I *still* wish she'd keep
quiet!"

"I' brought the crowbar," somebody said. "And a
screwdriver. Do you need a crowbar or a screwdriver?"

"After that fall," Dragon Lady said, "there can't
be too much left of him. He gotta be dead."

"Shit, Dragon Lady," Thirteen said, "his *Momma's*
right up there!"

"I said: He's gotta be dead! You heard me?"

Mom, come on!

*Can you see him down there? I can't see anything.
I can't hear anything. Oh, Bobby, Bobby! Can you hear
your mommy? Please, Bobby!*

The grip suddenly sagged; for a moment Kidd
thought he was falling—Dragon Lady, still holding, had
leaned in behind him. Her voice roared about his ears.
"YOUR SON IS DEAD, LADY!" And Kidd was pulled
away. "Come on, let's get you back."

Thirteen, with an unhappy expression, shook his
head.

Denny, up front now, gripped a length of wound
clothes line. "You want to get him up? You take the rope.
We'll hold you while you go down."

Kidd took hold of the doubled 'end, ducked his head
through, and hooked his arms over. (Griffon and Mantis
flanked the door.) Thirteen, Denny, and Dragon Lady
were handing out the other end among them.

"You just hold on," Kidd said. "I'll climb down."
He got onto his knees at the sill, holding the edge (one
rough hand lost in griffon light), dropped one leg down,
then the other. The shaft at his back was cool. He could
not tell if the wind came from above or below. He went
over the edge, had to keep away from the wall first with
his knee, then with his foot.

"You all right?" Denny asked, legs wide, fists close.

Kidd grunted, pulling on the ropes, taut around his back (pushing something glass into his back) and taut under his arms: "Yeah." The slanted bar of the door mechanism slid under his bare foot. His sandal toe scraped metal.

Swaying at either side of the door, the apparitions loomed, luminous.

Once he called; "You can lower it a little faster than that. I'm okay."

"Sorry," which was Thirteen, catching his breath; and the rope.

His shin scraped the basement door-sill. His bare foot hit something and slipped, in either grease or blood.

He turned, while the rope sagged around him, and looked at the—he had to be dead.

The shaft was momentarily silent, except for wind.

Finally Dragon Lady called down: "You still okay . . . ?"

"Yeah." Kidd took a breath. "I'll tie the rope around him. You can haul him up." He slipped the rope from under his arms, pulled it over his head, but left it around one shoulder; he stepped forward on the oozy filth, stooped, and tugged a leg from where it had wedged between two blackened bumper plates.

". . . *is* he alive?" Thirteen called.

Kidd took another breath. "Naw." He pulled at the arm, got a grip around the chest, which was all soft against him. His own shirt front soaked immediately. Blood dribbled along his forearm. Standing, he dragged the body back a step. A foot caught, pulled free; the leg fell back against his thigh—his thigh wet, warm, to the knee. Dragging it, limp, reaching for the rope, he thought: Is this what turns on blood and blade freaks? He thought of Tak, he thought of George, hunted in himself for any idle sexuality: he found it, disconcertingly, a small warmth above the loins that, as he bared his teeth and the rope slid through his sticky hand, went out. "Let me have another couple of feet!" Well, he had found it before in auto wrecks, in blue plush, in roots, in wet wood with the bark just stripped.

Rope dropped over his shoulder; the voices eighteen floors up came again:

Oh, Mom—

259

Is he all right? Kidd, have you found him yet? Bobby? Bobby, can you hear me at all?

Oh, Mom, you heard—

Bobby, are you all right?

He got the rope around the chest, got a clumsy knot done—like trying to do it with your hands in glue—that *maybe* would hold. Bobby sagged against Kidd's knees, heavy enough to make his bare foot slide backward. "Okay!" He tugged the rope.

He could see it run across the sill above him, go taut, and slow. The weight lifted from against him. A sneaker dragged across his foot, thumped against the door, and swung away again, and raised, dripping on his cheek. He smeared at his face with the heel of his hand and stepped back.

"Jesus Christ . . . !" from a girl at the doorway silenced everything but the wind and the reverberating voice:

Bobby, Bobby, please, can you hear me at all?

Another boy said: "Hey, wow . . . !"

Then, Denny's nervous laugh: "Oh, man, that's a mess . . . !"

Dragon Lady said, "All right, I'm untying him here—you get that rope down to the kid."

Standing on the bottom of the shaft, his bare heel wedged against one caked girder that crossed the bumper plates, Kidd stared up. For a moment he thought the elevator car descended at him. But it was a trick of light from the flanking beasts, both of whom swayed and flickered at the edge of sight.

The rope fell at him. He grabbed it with one hand, then the other. Someone pulled it; it rasped his coated palms. "Hey . . . !" It went slack again.

Dragon Lady leaned in, the rope wrapped around one fist. "You got it now?"

"Yeah." Once more he shrugged it over his head, under his arms. "Got it."

They tugged him up.

When his head reached the sill, Denny and somebody else were on their knees, catching him around under the armpits. The sill scraped his chin, his chest.

Smokey simply put her hand over her mouth and stepped back behind Thirteen.

Kidd crawled over, got to his feet, moved a few steps forward. The others fell back.

260

"God damn!" Dragon Lady shook her head, eyes wide, and rolled the rope against her thigh. "God . . . !"

Denny, with a funny smile, stepped back, black-lined nails moving over his chest. "Wow, you really . . ." He shook back pale hair, seemed to be considering several things to say. "You look just about as bad as . . ." He glanced at the floor.

"Uh . . ." Thirteen said, "we got some clothes up at the place. You wanna look through them for something? To change into, well, that's . . . all right."

"Oh, yeah . . ." Kidd looked down at blood, on himself, on the floor. It didn't run. It looked like jellied paste. "Thanks." He looked at the thing on the floor too, while wind and the woman's voice made torrents in the shaft. "I better get . . . him upstairs."

Bobby's shirt had ripped across the back. The flesh that wasn't torn was purple.

"You could make a sling, or something," Thirteen offered. "Hey, do we got any more of that canvas stuff?"

Someone he didn't recognize said: "We threw it out."

Kidd sucked his teeth, stopped, got his arms under Bobby's shoulders, tugged him over. One eye, open, had burst. The face, as though it had been made of clay, was flattened across one quarter.

Thirteen, glancing up the shaft, said: "Dragon Lady, why you want to go hollering up at her about her kid's dead?"

"Because," Dragon Lady said, "if *I* was his mother, *I*'d want to *know!*"

"But suppose he *was* still—"

"Man," Dragon Lady said, "that ain't like gettin' dumped out a two story window. That's seventeen, eighteen flights!"

Kidd wedged his hand under the knees, stood, unsteadily, stepped back.

"*Watch* it!" Denny grabbed Kidd's shoulder. "You don't want to go down there *again*, now, do you?"

Kidd said: "Make the elevator go!" In his arms, the body was heavy, not so warm, and dripped less.

"Huh?" from Dragon Lady, who was coiling up the rope. "Oh, yeah!" She swung into the car, did something else to the switches above the buttons.

The door started to close. She stopped it with her forearm. (*K-chunk.*)

Denny stepped back as Kidd carried Bobby inside.

261

"Baby, Adam, you go on up with the others," Dragon Lady said from the back of the car.

But Kidd, turning to face the door as it rolled to, could not tell which of the people standing behind Thirteen and Smokey she addressed: their light shields had been extinguished.

A moment into darkness, he heard Dragon Lady's hand move among her chains; and the car filled with light. "So you can see what you're doing," the dragon said. "Here, I'll push the floor. Which one? Seventeen?"

"Yeah." He nodded, stepped aside.

The car rose.

The dragon beside him, he realized, was bigger than the elevator. Since it was light, he would have expected walls and ceiling to cut off that side claw, the top of that head. The effect, however, was that those places in the blue, enameled walls and ceiling seemed transparent, and the claw and the head shone through. The apparition was reflected on four sides.

Standing there, shifting the weight in his arms—Kidd had to shift it several times—he noticed the striations, like a muzzy image on some vertical television screen, raced to the left if he swayed right; if he swayed left, they raced right. Kidd said: "I don't think you should get out with me."

The dragon said: "I wasn't planning to."

He shifted the weight again, looked down at it, and thought: It smells . . . it has a specific smell. And there was an annoying piece of paper—he glanced down over the knees; was it a match book?—stuck to his bare foot.

Why, Kidd thought, why am I standing here with this armful of heavy, heavy meat, filthy with blood . . . ? Then something raked inside his face; his throat clamped, his eyes teared. Either fear or grief, it extinguished as quickly as the lust that had momentarily raked inside his loins.

He blinked, again shifted his weight to the sandaled foot. The bare one stuck to the floor.

Beside him the swayings and motions that might tell him Dragon Lady's thoughts were hidden in light.

He shifted back the other way. His sandal stuck too.

The car slowed; the door opened.

Mrs Richards' fist rose to strike her chin. The gesture was a stronger version of June's.

Mrs Richards stepped back, and back again.

June caught her mother's arm.

Mrs Richards closed her mouth and her eyes and began to shake. High brittle sobs suddenly crackled the silence.

"You better take your mother upstairs," Kidd said and stepped, after his grotesque shadow, into the hall.

June's head whipped back and forth between him and her mother, till an edge of shadow swept over his. It was not him she was staring at, but the bright apparition in the closing elevator.

"I'll put him in the old apartment."

"Bobby's . . . ?" June whispered, and smashed back against the wall to avoid him as he passed.

"Yeah, he's dead."

Behind him Mrs Richards' crying changed pitch.

The other elevator door, against the rolled carpet, went *K-chunk, K-chunk, K-chunk* . . .

He shouldered into seventeen-B. Put the boy in his own . . . ? Kidd walked down the hall, turned into the bare room. One of Bobby's hands (the one with the chain, all stained) struck and struck his shin. All he had to do was look at what he lugged not to be sad.

He tried not to drop it on the floor, lowered it, almost fell; and dropped it. He pulled at the bent leg; it . . . bent again, at the wrong place. So he stood up.

Christ, the blood! He shook his head, and peeled his shirt from stomach and shoulders. Starting for the door, he unbuckled his pants and, holding them with one hand— they dropped to his thighs—stepped into the hall.

Mrs Richards, standing in the middle of the hall, began to shake her head and cry again.

He scowled and pulled his pants up. He'd been heading for the bathroom but, exposed to her astonished grief, he was thrown back to the moment of sexual response at the shaft bottom. Shit, he thought: "Ma'am, why don't you go upstairs. There's nothing you can do. Being here won't make you feel . . . any better. June . . . ?"

June half hid behind her mother.

". . . why don't you take her upstairs." Suddenly he didn't want to be there at all. "Look, I've got to go get some—something." Holding his pants closed, he went past them into the living room, picked up his notebook and, holding it in front of his lap, stalked out the door.

Thirteen said, "I guess she's taking it pretty rough," and stepped back to let him in.

263

"Shit." Dragon Lady glanced at the ceiling.

The sound of crying, high and stifled, dripped into the room like something molten.

"Why don't she shet up!" Dragon Lady said.

"Look, man—" Thirteen started.

"I know, I know. Somebody just asked me if I wanted a glass of wine. Well I sure as shit do. Baby? Adam? You bringing that damn wine?"

"You said," Kidd began, "you had some clothes?"

"Oh yeah. Sure. Come on in."

Denny, who was resting a glass jug on the crook of his arm, said, "I think he wants to use the bathroom."

"Yeah, you want to wash up. Tub's a mess, but you can use it if you want. What's the matter?"

"Nothing." But Denny's last sentence had caused gooseflesh more unpleasant than either grief or terror. "Yeah, I better wash up."

"Down the hall. It don't have no fuckin' windows. I'll get a lantern." Thirteen lifted one from a nail in the wall.

Kidd followed him into the john.

In the swaying lantern light, he saw a line of rust along the middle of the tub to the drain. The enamel had flaked here and there from black patches. "We had to put a fucked-up scorpion in here a couple of nights back —name was Pepper—and he'd put something in his arm he shouldn't have. Put him in the bathtub with his spurs on, and he tried to kick holes in it." Lantern high in one hand, Thirteen bent and picked up a screw from the tub bottom, looked at it, shrugged. "Use any of those towels you want. We don't got no washcloths." He put the lantern down on the back of the toilet.

Kidd put the notebook on the seat-top, turned on the water and picked up the soap: Flakes of rust had dried into it.

With a grey towel (torn) he swabbed the bottom of the tub. There was no stopper, so he rolled it up and plugged the drain, then got in before the water had covered the bottom.

"Do you want something to drink?" a girl called through the door.

"Yeah."

While he sat, scrubbing at his face, he could hear the crying upstairs. He wondered if she were moving from room to room.

The girl came into the bathroom with a white cup in her hands. She wore jeans, was heavy, and had a cheerful face that was trying to look very serious. "Here you are. That poor boy." She bent down, spilling curly hair from her shoulder and put the cup on the tub edge. She had loose, heavy breasts under a blue sweatshirt. "That must have been *aw*ful!"

Her voice was breathy, and he thought she probably giggled a lot. The thought of her giggling made him smile. "It wasn't nice."

"You live upstairs?" she asked.

Perhaps she was seventeen. "I just work there. You know if you keep on staring at me like that, I'm gonna get all excited."

She giggled.

He leaned back in the tub. "See, I told you."

"Oh . . ." She gestured mock frustration, left—she had to push past Denny who stood in the door now. He gave a sharp, short laugh. "You really got yourself messed up, huh, kid?"

"Yeah, well. I guess we couldn't leave him down there."

"I guess not." Denny came in and sat on the toilet cover, picked up the notebook. "Hey, kid? This yours?"

He nodded, only realizing now that Denny's "kid" had neither capital *K* or extra *d*. Kidd grinned and picked up the mug. (Around him the water ran brown. The match book from his foot floated under the spigot.) When he sipped, his mouth burned. "Shit, what is this?"

"Whisky," Denny said, looking up. "You want wine, we got wine. But I thought maybe you'd want something good and strong. I mean after . . ." His hair swung in pale blades.

"That's fine."

"You write all this?"

"Yeah. Leave it alone."

"Oh." Quickly Denny put it on the floor between his boots. He rubbed two fingers on his naked chest a while. Then he glanced up and said, "She's really going on, huh? I guess that's cause she's his momma?"

Kidd nodded and ground his knuckles in the soap. "I got all that junk off my face?"

"Nope. On the side, under your chin."

He lathered there. The lantern showed the suds gone tan.

Denny gestured. "What you got a hard-on for?"

"Your scrawny ass hanging over the back of your pants."

"Yeah?" Denny grinned. "Be the best piece you ever had."

But when Kidd sloshed the lather off his face, Denny was still looking at it. "How'd your run go?" Kidd asked.

"With Nightmare?"

"Yeah."

"It was a fuck-up." Denny shrugged. "We didn't get nothing. Time before was really good. Next time be good too."

"What you guys run after?" Kidd drank some more, and rubbed the rusty soap on his stomach.

"You all that interested in scorpion shit?"

Kidd shrugged. The soap bobbed away.

Denny nodded. "You interested, you ask Dragon Lady."

"Not that interested." He retrieved it, pushed it between his toes.

"You ask her, she'll tell you if she thinks you wanna know. Dragon Lady, she likes you." Suddenly Denny stood. "So does Nightmare. I'll be back in a second."

Kidd took another drink, and fell to scrubbing again. His nails were lined—ruined rim and bitten cuticle—with brown. He dunked his head, rubbed it, lifted it; dark streaks wormed from the drippings.

"Here you go, kid." Denny came back in with an armful of clothing and sat down again on the toilet. "Now we got *this* pair of pants; and this pair—naw, that's pretty raunchy. I guess these'll fit you. Nice belt, too. I dunno who left all this shit. You think there'd be a shirt in here, you know."

"I thought scorpions didn't wear shirts." Kidd stood up in the loud water to soap his groin.

Denny glanced at him once more. "Shit, I better keep my ass out of your way. You want a black leather vest? That'd look good on you, kid, you know? Scorpions just wear vests, usually. You seen the one I got?"

"How old are you?"

"Eh . . . sixteen," followed with a questioning glance.

Fifteen, Kidd decided. "I'm practically a dozen years older than you. Stop calling me kid."

"Huh? You are?"

"Yeah. Now throw me that other towel." As he

caught it, the door crashed back. Dragon Lady lurched in, dark face twisted, stained teeth bared, shaking a fist with one finger up. "Look, when you go back upstairs, you tell that bitch to cut it out, you hear? It's driving me up the fuckin' wall! God damn, I know it's her kid, but—well, Jesus Christ, she been whining up there a fuckin' hour!" She looked at the ceiling and bellowed: "I mean, go out and take a *walk,* lady!"

"Dragon Lady . . ." Denny's interruption seemed to take in none of the scorpion's rage.

"We dragged the cocksucker up there for her! She keep it up, I'm gonna go up there and beat the shit out of her, if you don't quiet her down!"

Anger and the cold air: his erection, anyway, was gone: "The *walls* are thin." He rubbed himself with the bunched towel.

"Dragon Lady?"

"What do you want?"

"The . . . Kid was asking about the run."

Kidd sensed the hesitant disobedience was some acquiescence to previous commitment. But he could not be sure whether the newly implied capital was respectful or mocking.

"Yeah?" Dragon Lady's anger was quickly exhausted.

"Look, lemme out of here and see what I can do upstairs," Kidd said. "We'll talk about it some other time." He wished Mrs Richards would quiet too.

"Oh, yeah. Sure. Try and shut her up, huh?" Dragon Lady backed out again.

"You don't want the vest?" Denny still pawed in the heap.

The crying suddenly rose in pitch. Outside, Dragon Lady said, "God damn!"

"Yeah, I want the fucking vest." Kidd stepped from the tub, reached down, and drained the whisky. Twin warmths of agreement and alcohol turned through him.

Denny, still sitting, was bent almost double, as he sorted the clothing. His belt loops tugged his jeans below his buttocks' crevice.

Kidd sucked his teeth again and toweled his groin. "What's she here for, anyway?"

"Dragon Lady?" Denny glanced up, unbending.

"Yeah."

"You remember when you were here last time, Nightmare was collecting us for the run?" Denny shrugged and fell back to sorting. "Well, she's bringing us back, I guess."

"Oh."

The door opened again. The girl stood there, with a plastic cup this time. "Oh," she said. "I didn't know you were . . ." That was to Denny who didn't look up. So she said to Kidd, "Denny told me I should bring you another glass after fifteen minutes. Did you finish the first one?"

"You don't give a fuck whether he finished it or not," Denny said, still bent over. "Just give it to him."

"I'm finished."

She blinked rapidly, while they exchanged mug for cup. Then, without glancing at Denny, she left. Kidd drank some more, then put the cup on the tub edge. "Thanks."

Denny still didn't say anything, almost as though embarrassed.

In black jeans and leather vest, Kidd went into the front room.

"Oh, man!" Dragon Lady was saying. "This is just too much—"

The crying was louder here.

"Dragon Lady," Smokey said, tugging at the tassels of her macramé belt, "*why* do you shout things up there like that? It . . . it isn't necessary!"

"Well," Dragon Lady said, thumb hooked around hers, "if I was making that big a fool of myself, after about an hour, I don't know as how I wouldn't appreciate somebody telling me to cut it out—like they meant it!"

Which Smokey seemed to think was funny; Thirteen's reaction, though, was silent, hand-throwing frustration. He moved, almost protectively, between the two women; Smokey didn't seem to mind.

"Look," Thirteen said, with settling gestures of the palms, "if your neighbor, I mean your own *neighbor* is going through that, you're just obliged, *obliged*, see, to put up with—"

Dragon Lady threw her glass. It missed Thirteen. Smokey ducked too. "Hey, watch . . ." Thirteen shouted. Pieces of glass rocked on the floor. Wine licked down the wall. Smokey just blinked and looked like she didn't know whether to be amused or angry.

268

But Dragon Lady launched into doubled-over laughter. "Oh, Thirteen . . . Thirteen, you are so—" Chains swung, flung back around her neck as she stood. "You are *so* chicken shit!" She laughed again.

Maybe, Kidd thought, scorpions just yelled loud, laughed a lot, and threw things.

"Baby!" Dragon Lady shouted. "Adam! We gonna get out of here, soon . . ."

"Good-bye," Kidd said, at the door, and went. The girl in the blue sweatshirt who had brought him the whiskey was the only one who said "good-bye". Somehow, though, he was sure it was time to leave. In the hall, it occurred to him he hadn't even noticed if the sick girl were still in her bunk or not.

5

He carried the nest tables into nineteen-A.

Mrs Richards stood in the middle of the room.

"Um," he said, "I thought I'd bring these, uh, up with me. Since I was coming. You said you wanted them by the . . ." then went and put them by the balcony door.

"Your clothes," she said. "I was going to give you some of my . . . son's clothes."

"Oh. I got these . . ." They were all black, too.

Her hands gripped one another beneath her breasts. She nodded.

"Is June all right?"

She kept nodding.

"I thought I heard you downstairs, but when I went in, you'd already gone up."

The nodding continued till suddenly she averted her face.

"I'll go bring the rest of the stuff up, ma'am."

He returned with rugs over each shoulder, and dumped them. Mrs Richards was out of the room. On his next trip (he'd considered Bobby's toys, but decided he'd better leave those down there) she passed through and did not look at him. Three more trips and everything (toys too: he took them to Bobby's room and put them in the closet right away) was up.

He sat on the easy chair and opened his notebook. A rusty line still ringed the gnawed lozenges of his nails. He took his pen (clipped to a buttonhole in the vest now) and turned pages. He was surprised how few empty ones were left. He turned to the last and realized pages had been torn out. Their remains feathered inside the coil. The cover was very loose. Half a dozen of the holes in the cardboard had pulled free. He turned back to the furthest-front free page and clicked his pen point.

Then, slowly, he lost himself in words:

Both legs were broken. His pulped skull and jellied hip . . .

He paused; he re-wrote:

Both legs broken, pulp-eyed, jelly-hipped . . .

Only somewhere in there his tongue balked on unwanted stress. He frowned for a way to remove a syllable that would give the line back its violence. When he found it, he realized he had to give up the *ed*'s and re-order three words; what was left was a declarative sentence that meant something else entirely and made his back crawl under the leather vest, because, he recognized irrelevantly, it was far more horrifying than what he had intended to describe. The first conception had only approached the bearable limit. He took a breath, and a clause from the first three lines, to close the passage; and, writing it, saw only one word in it was necessary, so crossed out the others.

Mrs Richards came into the room, circled it, searching, saw him: "You're writing. I didn't mean to disturb your . . . writing."

"Oh, no." He closed the book. "I'm finished." He was tired. But he was finished.

"I thought perhaps you were writing some sort of . . . elegy. For . . ." and dropped her head.

"Oh. No . . ." he said, and decided "Elegy" was the title. "Look, you've got everything up here. Maybe I should just go on and leave."

"No." Mrs Richards' hand left her neck to reach for him. "Oh, you mustn't go! I mean you haven't talked to Arthur about your pay, have you?"

"Well, okay." He sat back.

Mrs Richards, all exhausted nervousness, sat across the coffee table from him.

He asked: "Where's June?"

"She's in her . . ." ended by vague gesture. She said, "It must be awful for you."

"It's worse for you." He was thinking: Her son's clothes? She couldn't have meant Bobby, we weren't anywhere near the same size. Edward's? "Mrs Richards, I can't even say how sorry I—"

She nodded again, chin striking her knuckles. "Oh, yes. You don't have to. I understand. You went down there and brought him—" in the pause he thought she was going to cry—"back. How can *I* say thank you for that? You went down there. I saw you when you brought him up. How can I say—"

"It's all right, Mrs Richards. Really." He wanted to ask her about the structure of light that had been in the elevator car with him; and could think of no way. Momentarily he wondered, maybe she hadn't seen it. But moved his jaws on one another to dispel those implications. "I don't have to wait here, for Mr Richards. I can catch him another time. You might want to be alone with him when . . ."

The disorganized movements of her face stopped. "Oh no, I want someone here! Please stay, stay for me! That would be—" she began to look around in the seat of her chair—"the kindest thing. You could do."

"All right."

What she looked for, she did not find. "I want somebody with me. I need somebody." She stood. "With me here." Again, she circled the room. "It's so strange, I haven't the faintest idea what I'll say. I wish I could phone him; on the phone it would be so much easier. But I just have to wait. He'll come in the door. And I'll say, Arthur, this afternoon, June backed Bobby into the elevator shaft and he fell down seventeen flights and killed himself . . ." She looked into the kitchen, crossed the room, looked down the hall.

"Are you *sure* you wouldn't feel better if I went?" He wanted to go, could not conceive her wanting him to remain, even though she waved her hand at him, even though she said:

"Please. You have to stay."

"Yes, ma'am. I will."

She came back to her chair. "It doesn't feel like we live here. The walls are blue. Before they were green. But all our furniture, it's all in the proper place."

"The rugs aren't down yet," he suggested. Well, it filled the silence.

"Oh, no. No, I don't think it's the rugs. It's the feeling. It's the feeling of trying to make a home. A home for my husband and my . . ." Then she pressed her lips together and dropped her head.

"Look, Mrs Richards, why don't you go in and lie down or something till Mr Richards gets back? I'll put the rugs down," and thought abruptly: That's what she wanted me to say; so *I'll* have to tell him!

272

Who told the damn kids to take the rugs up anyway? And couldn't remember whether it was him or her.

But she shook her head. "I couldn't sleep now. No. When Arthur comes back . . . no." The last was calm. She put—pushed her hands into her lap. Bobby's pile of books still sat in the corner . . . Kidd wished he had put them away.

She stood.

She walked the room once more.

Her motions began definitively but lost focus in a glance—first out the balcony doors, next into the dining room, now toward the hall.

She stopped behind her chair.

"Arthur," she said, followed by what sounded more like a comma of address than of apposition, "he's outside."

"Ma'am?"

"Arthur is outside, in that." She sat. "He goes out every day. I can watch him from the window turn down Forty-Fourth there and disappear. Into the smoke. Like that." Outside the balcony door, buildings were blurred. "We've moved." She watched the fog for the length of five breaths. "This building, it's like a chessboard. Now we occupy a different square. We had to move. We had to. Our position before was terrible." Smoke pulled from the window, uncovering more smoke—"But I didn't know the move would cost so much."—and more. "I am not prepared for this. I'm really not. Arthur goes out there, every day, and works in Systems. Maitland Systems Engineering. Then he comes home." She leaned forward. "Do you know, I don't believe all that out there is real. Once the smoke covers him, I don't believe he goes anywhere. I don't believe there's anyplace to go." She sat back. "I don't think I believe there ever was. I'm very much in love with that man. And I'm very much in awe of him. It frightens me how much I don't understand him. I often suspect that he isn't happy, that going out to work every-day in that—" she shook her head slightly—"that it doesn't give him anything real, the inner things he needs. Whatever it is he does out there, it frightens me. I picture him going to a great empty building, filled with offices, and desks, and work benches, and technician shops, and drafting tables, and filing cabinets, and equipment closets —no people. He walks up and down, and looks into the open office doors. I don't think he opens the closed ones.

273

Sometimes he straightens a pile of papers on some-body's desk. Sometimes he looks through a pile of circuit plans, but he puts them back, neatly. That's all. All day. With no one else there. Do you think any of the windows are broken? Do you think he sometimes turns on a light switch and only one of those long fluorescent tubes flickers, faintly orange at one end? There's something wonderful about engineering, you know. I mean, you go in and you solve problems, you make things, with your hands, with your mind. You go in, and you have a problem to work with, and when you've finished solving it, you've . . . well, done something with real, tangible results. Like a farmer who raises a crop; you can see that it's there. You don't just push a button, again and again, or put endless piles of paper in the proper drawers. Engineers are very wise. Like farmers. They can also be very dense and stubborn. Oh, I don't know what's out there, where he goes to do every day. He won't talk about it. He used to. But not now. I don't know where he goes, every morning. If he walked around the streets all day, I could tell that. That's not it. But whatever it is, it isn't good for him. He's a good man. He's more than a good man; he's an intelligent man. Do you know he was hired right out of his class in college? Oh, they were doing that a lot a few years ago. But it wasn't as common as all that when we were in school. He needs . . . something—I'd seem like a silly woman if I said 'worthy of him.' But that's what I mean. I've never understood what was out there." She looked again through the balcony doors. "I've suspected, oh, I've suspected that whatever was there wasn't really what he needed, what would make him—happy? Oh, I learned a long time ago you don't look for that. But the thing you do try for—excellence? Contentment? Oh no, oh no: not in a great empty office building, where the lights don't work, where the windows are broken, where there aren't any people."

"There're probably people there," Kidd said, uncomfortably. "Probably a skeleton staff. Madame Brown and I were talking about that. It's probably like at . . . the Management office."

"Ah." Her hands met in her lap. "Yes." She sat back. "But I'm only telling you how it feels. To me. When the smoke thins, I can look across at the other buildings. So many of the windows are broken. Maybe the maintenance men in Arthur's office have already started putting in new panes. The maintenance is always better in a place of business. Well, there's more money involved. I just wonder when we can expect some sort of reasonable return to normal here. There's a certain minimum standard that must be kept up. They should send somebody around, if only to let us know what the situation is. Not knowing, that's the worst. If I did know something, something for sure about plans for repairing the damages, for restoring service, lights, and things, when we could expect them to start . . ." She looked oddly annoyed.

"Maybe they will," he suggested, "send somebody around."

"You'd think they would. We have had trouble with them before; there was a huge crack, it opened up in June's ceiling. It wasn't our fault. Something upstairs leaked. It took them three months to send somebody. But they answered my letter right away. Meanwhile, I just have to muddle, muddle on. And every morning I send Arthur out of here, out into that." She nodded. "That's the crime. Of course I couldn't keep him back; he wouldn't stay. I'd tell him how dangerous I thought it was out there, all the awful things I'm afraid might happen, and he'd— Oh, I wish he'd laugh. But he wouldn't. He'd scowl. And go. He goes away, every morning, just disappears, down Forty-Fourth. The only thing I can do for him is try and keep a good home, where nothing can hurt him, at least here, a happy, safe and—"

He thought she'd seen something behind him, and was about to turn around. But her expression went on to something more violent than recognition.

She bent her head. "I guess I haven't done that very well. I haven't done that at all."

He wished she would let him leave.

"Mrs Richards, I'm going to see about that stuff in the back." He thought there was some stuff in the back still to be put in place. "You just try and take it easy now." He got up, thinking: When I come back I can put down the living-room rug.

There's nothing I can do, he justified, to sponge up her grief. And I *can't* do nothing.

He opened the door to Bobby's room where the furniture had still not been put against the walls.

And June's fists crashed the edges of the poster together.

"Hey, I'm sorry . . . I didn't realize this was your—"

275

But it *was* Bobby's room. Kidd's apologetic smile dropped before her astounded despair. "Look, I'll leave you alone . . ."

"He was going to *tell!*" she whispered, wide-eyed, shaking her head. "He *said* so! But I swear," and she crushed the poster altogether now. "I *swear* I didn't do it on purpose . . . !"

After a few moments, he said, "I suppose that's the first thing that would have occurred to anybody else in his right mind. But I didn't even think of it till just now." Then—and was afraid—he backed out of the room and closed the door, unable to determine what had formed in her face. I'm just an observer, he thought, and, thinking it, felt the thought crumple like George's poster between June's fists.

Walking toward the living room, he envisioned her leaping from the door, to bite and rake his back. The doors stayed closed. There was no sound. And he didn't want to go back to the living room.

Just as he came in, the lock ratched, and the hall door pushed open. "Hello, guess who I found on the way up here?"

"Hi, Mary." Madame Brown followed Mr Richards in.

"Honey, what in the world is that mess down in the lobby? It looks as though somebody—"

Mrs Richards turned around on the couch.

Mr Richards frowned.

Madame Brown, behind him, suddenly touched her hand to her bright, jeweled chains.

Mrs Richards squeezed the fabric of her skirt. "Arthur, this afternoon Bobby . . . June—*Bobby*—!"

His eyelids, snapped wide enough to pain the sockets. He rolled, scrabbling on snarled blankets and crushed leaves, flung his hands at her naked back. Had he nails, he would have torn.

"Unnnh," Lanya said and turned to him. Then, "Hey—" because he dragged her against him. "I know," she mumbled beside his ear, moving her arms inside his to get them free, "you want to be a great and famous—"

His arms shook.

"Oh, hey—!" Her hands came up across his back, tightened. "You were having bad dreams! About that boy!"

276

He shook his head beside hers.

"It's all right," she whispered. She got one hand high enough to rub the back of his shoulder. "It's all right now. You're awake." He took three rough breaths, with stomach-clenched silences between, then let go and rolled to his back. The red veil, between him and the darkness, here, then there, fell away.

She touched his arm; she kneaded his shoulder. "It was a really bad dream, wasn't it?"

He said, "I don't . . . know," and stopped gasping. Foliage hung over them. Near the horizon, blurred in fog, he saw a tiny moon; and further away, another! His head came up from the blanket—went slowly back:

They were two parklights which, through smoke, looked like diffuse pearls. "I can't remember if I was dreaming or not."

"You were dreaming about Bobby," she said. "That's all. And you scared yourself awake."

He shook his head. "I shouldn't have given her that damned poster—"

Her head fell against his shoulder. "You didn't have any way to know . . ." Her hand dropped over his chest; her thigh crossed his thigh.

"But—" he took her hand in his—"the funny *lack* of expression Mr Richards got when she was trying to tell him how it happened. And in the middle of it, June came in, and sort of edged into the wall, and kept on brushing at her chin with her fist and blinking. And Mrs Richards kept on saying, 'It was an accident! It was a terrible accident!' and Madame Brown just said 'Oh, Lord!' a couple of times, and Mr Richards didn't say anything. He just kept looking back and forth between Mrs Richards and June as though he couldn't quite figure out what they were saying, what they'd done, what had happened, until June started to cry and ran out of the room—"

"It sounds awful," she said. "But try to think about something else—"

"I am." He glanced at the parklights again; now there was only one. Had the other gone out? Or had some tree branch, lifted away by wind, settled back before it. "About what George and you were saying yesterday—about everybody being afraid of female sexuality, and trying to make it into something that wreaks death and destruction all about it. I mean, I don't *know* what

Mr Richards would do if he found out his sunshine girl was running around the streets like a bitch in heat, lusting to be brutalized by some hulking, sadistic, buck nigger. Let's see, he's already driven one child out of the house with threats of murder—"

"Oh, Kidd, *no* . . ."

"—and the sounds that come out of that apartment when they don't think anybody's listening are just as strange as the ones that come up from Thirteen's, believe me. Maybe she's got good reason not to want her old man to know, and if Bobby was threatening, in that vicious way younger brothers can have, to show the poster to her parents, well maybe just for an instant, when she was backing him down the hall, and the door rolled open, from some sort of half-conscious impulse, it was easier to shove—or not even to shove, but just not say anything when he stepped back toward the wrong—"

"Kidd," Lanya said, "now come *on!*"

"It would be just like the myth: her lust for George, death and destruction! Only—only suppose it *was* an accident?" He took another breath. *"That's* what frightens me. Suppose it was, like she said, *just* an accident. She didn't see at all. Bobby just backed into the wrong shaft door. That's what terrifies me. That's the thing I'm scared of most."

"Why?" Lanya asked.

"Because . . ." He breathed, felt her head shift on his shoulder, her hand rock with his on his chest; "Because that means it's the city. That means it's the landscape: the bricks, and the girders, and the faulty wiring and the shot elevator machinery, all conspiring together to *make* these myths true. And that's crazy." He shook his head. "I shouldn't have give her that poster. I shouldn't. I really shouldn't—" His head stopped shaking. "Mother-fucker still hasn't paid me my money. I was going to talk to him about it this evening. But I couldn't, then."

"No, it doesn't sound like the most propitious time to bring up financial matters."

"I just wanted to get out of there."

She nodded.

"I don't *want* the money. I really don't."

"Good." She hugged. "Then just forget about the whole thing. Don't go back there. Let them alone. If people are busy living out myths you don't like, leave them do it."

He raised his hand above his face, palm up, moving his fingers, watching them, black against four-fifths black, his arm muscle tiring, till he let his knuckles fall against his forehead. "I was so scared . . . When I woke up, I was so *scared!*"

"It was just a dream," she insisted. And then: "Look, if it *really* was an accident, your bringing that poster didn't have anything to do with it. And if she *did* do it on purpose, then she's so far gone there's no way you could possibly blame yourself!"

"I know," he said. "But do you think . . ." He could feel the place on his neck her breath brushed warmly. "Do you think a city can control the way the people live inside it? I mean, just the geography, the way the streets are laid out, the way the buildings are placed?"

"Of course it does," she said. "San Francisco and Rome are both built on hills. I've spent time in both and I'm sure the amount of energy you have to spend to get from one place to the other in either city has more to do with the tenor of life in each one than whoever happens to be mayor. New York and Istanbul are both cut through by large bodies of water, and even out of sight of it, the feel on the streets in either is more alike than either one than say, Paris or Munich, which are only crossed by swimmable rivers. And London, whose river is an entirely different width, has a different feel entirely." She waited.

So at last he said. "Yeah . . . But thinking that live streets and windows are plotting and conniving to make you into something you're not, that's crazy, isn't it?"

"Yes," she said, "that's crazy—in a word."

He slid his arm around her and could smell her wake-up breath, cuddling her. "You know, when I pulled him out, blood all over me, like a flayed carcass off a butcher hook . . . you know, I had half a hard-on? That's too much, huh?"

She reached between his legs. "You still do." She moved her fingers there; he moved in her fingers.

"Maybe that's what I was dreaming about?" He laughed sharply. "Do you think that's what I was—?"

Her hand contracted, released, moved forward, moved back.

He said: "I don't think that's going to do any good . . ."

Against his chest he felt her shrug. "Try."

Not so much to his surprise, but somehow against his will, his will ceased, and it did.

I let my head fall back in this angry season. There, tensions I had hoped would resolve, merely shift with the body's machinery. The act is clumsy, halting, and without grace or reason. What can I read in the smell of her, what message in the code of her breath? This mountain opens passages of light. The lines on squeezed lids cage the bursting balls. All efforts, dying here, coalesce in the blockage of ear and throat, to an a-corporal lucence, a patterning released from pleasure, the retained shadow of pure idea.

The leaf shattered in his blunt fingers: leaf and flesh—he ground the flakings with his roughened thumb —were the same color, a different texture. He stared, defining the distinction.

"Come on." Lanya caught up his hand.

Flakes fluttered away (some he felt cling); notebook under his other arm, he stood up from where he'd been leaning on the end of the picnic table. "I was just thinking," Kidd said, "maybe I should stop off at the Labry's and try to collect my money."

"And keep Mr Newboy waiting?" Lanya asked. "Look, you said you *got* them all moved!"

"I was just thinking about it," Kidd said. "That's all."

A young man with a high, bald forehead and side hair to his naked shoulders sat on an overturned wire basket, one sandal resting over the other. He leaned forward, a burned twig in each hand. They had smudged his fingers. "I take these from you crossed," he said to a girl sitting Indian fashion on the ground before him, "and give them to you crossed."

The girl's black hair was pulled back lacquer tight, till, at the thong whipped a dozen times around her pony tail and tied, it broke into a dozen rivulets about the collar of her pink shirt: her sleeves were torn off; frayed pink threads lay against her thin arms. With her own smudged fingers, she took the twigs. "I take these from you—" she hesitated, concentrated—"uncrossed and I give them to you—" she thrust them back—"uncrossed?"

Some spectators in the circle laughed. Others looked as bemused as she did.

"Nope. Got it wrong again." The man spread his feet, sandal heels lining the dirt, and drew them back against the basket rim. "Now watch." With crossed wrists he took the sticks from her: "I take these from you . . . uncrossed—" his wrists came apart—"and I give them back to you . . ."

John, scratching under the fringed shoulder of his Peruvian vest with one hand and eating a piece of bread with the other, came around the furnace. "You guys want some more?" He gestured with the slice, chewing. "Just go take it. You didn't get here till we were already half-way through breakfast." Gold-streaked hair and gold wire frames set off his tenacious tan; his pupils were like circles cut from the overcast.

Kidd said: "We had enough. Really."

In the basket on which the bald man sat ("I take these from you uncrossed and I give them to you . . . crossed!" More laughter.) a half dozen loaves of bland, saltless bread had been brought over by two scorpions who had taken back two cardboard cartons of canned food, in exchange.

Kidd said: "You're sure that's today's paper?" which was the third time he'd asked John that over the last hour.

"Sure I'm sure." John picked the paper up off the picnic table. "Tuesday, May 5th—that's May-day, isn't it?—1904. Faust brought it by this morning." He folded it back, began to beat it against his thigh.

"Tell Milly when she gets back thanks again for the clean shirt." Lanya tucked one side of the rough-dried blue cotton under her belt. "I'll bring it back later this afternoon."

"I will. I think Milly's laundry project—" John mused, beating, munching—"is one of the most successful we've investigated. Don't you?"

Lanya nodded, still tucking.

"Come on," Kidd said. "Let's get going. I mean if this is really Tuesday. You're sure he said Tuesday now?"

"I'm sure," Lanya said.

("Nope, you're still doing it wrong, now watch: I take them from you crossed and I give them to you un-crossed." His fingers smudged to the second knuckle and bunched at the base of the charred batons, came forward. Hers, smeared equally, hesitated, went back to fiddle with one another, started to take them again. She said: "I just don't get it. I don't get it at all." Fewer laughed this time.)

"So long," Kidd said to John, who nodded, his mouth full.

They made their way through the knapsacks.

"That was nice of them to feed us . . . again," he said. "They're not bad kids."

"They're nice kids." She brushed at her clean, wrinkled front. "Wish I had an iron."

"You really have to get dressed up to go visit Calkins' place, huh?"

Lanya glanced appraisingly at his new black jeans, his black leather vest. "Well, you're practically in uniform already. I, unlike you, however, am not at my best when scruffy."

They made their way toward the park entrance.

"What's the laundry project?" he asked. "Do they have some place where they pound the clothes with paddles on a rock?"

"I think," Lanya said, "Milly and Jommy and Wally and What's-her-name-with-all-the-Indian-silver found a laundromat or something a few days ago. Only the power's off. Today they've gone off to find the nearest three-pronged outlet that works."

"Then when did the one you have on get done?"

"Milly and I washed a whole bunch by hand in the ladies' john yesterday, while you were at work."

"Oh."

"Recording engineer to laundress," Lanya mused as they passed through the lion gate, "in less than a year." She humphed. "If you asked him, I suspect John would tell you that's progress."

"The paper says it's Tuesday." Kidd moved his thumb absently against the blade of his orchid he'd hooked through a side belt loop; inside it, the chain harness jingled, each step. "He said come up when the paper said it was Tuesday. You don't think he's forgotten?"

"If he has, we'll remind him," Lanya said. "No, I'm sure he hasn't forgotten."

He could press his thumb or his knuckles against the sharp edges and leave only the slightest line, that later, like the other cross-hatches in the surface skin, filled with dirt; but he could hardly feel it. "Maybe we'll avoid any run-ins with scorpions today," he said as they crossed from Brisbain North to Brisbain South. "If we're lucky."

"No self-respecting scorpion would be up at this hour of the morning," Lanya said. "They all sleep till three or four, then carouse till dawn, didn't you know?"

"Sounds like the life. You been in Calkins' place before, you keep telling me. It'll be okay?"

"If I hadn't been in there before—" she slapped her harmonica on her palm—"I wouldn't be making this fuss." Three glistening notes. She frowned, and blew again.

"I think you look pretty good scruffy," he said.

She played more notes, welding them nearly into melody, till she changed her mind, laughed, or complained, or was silent, before beginning another. They walked, Lanya strewing incomplete tunes.

His notebook flapped his hip. (His other hand was petaled in steel, now.) He swung, in twin protections, from the curb. "I wonder if I'm scared of what he's going to say."

Between notes: "Hmm?"

"Mr Newboy. About my poems. Shit, I'm not going to see him. I want to see where Calkins lives. I don't care what Mr Newboy says about what I write."

"I left three perfectly beautiful dresses there, upstairs in Phil's closet. I wonder if they're still there."

"Probably, if Phil is," he said from within his protections.

"Christ, no. Phil hasn't been in the city for . . . weeks!"

The air was tingly and industrial. He looked up on a sky here the color of clay, there the color of ivory, lighter over there like tarnished tin.

"Good idea," Lanya said, "for me to split. I got you." Slipping her hand between blades, she grasped two of his fingers. Even on her thin wrist, turned, the blades pressed, rubbed, creased her skin—

"Watch out. You're gonna . . ."

But she didn't.

Over the wall hung hanks of ivy.

At the brass gate, she said, "It's quiet inside."

"Do you ring?" he asked, "or do you shout?" Then he shouted: "Mr Newboy!"

She pulled her hand gingerly away. "There used to be a bell, I think . . ." She fingered the stone around the brass plate.

"Hello . . . ?" from inside. Footsteps ground the gravel somewhere behind the pines.

"Hello, sir!" Kidd called, pulling the orchid off, pushing a blade into a belt-loop.

Ernest Newboy walked out of shaggy green. "Yes, it is Tuesday, isn't it." He gestured with a rolled paper. "I just found out half an hour ago." He did something on the inside of the latch plate. The gate clanked, swung in a little. "Glad to see you both." He pulled it open the rest of the way.

"Isn't the man who used to be a guard here anymore?" Lanya asked, stepping through. "He had to stay in there all the time." She pointed to a small, green booth, out of sight of the sidewalk.

"Tony?" Mr Newboy said. "Oh, he doesn't go on till sometime late in the afternoon. But practically everybody's out today. Roger decided to take them on a tour."

"And you stayed for us?" Kidd asked. "You didn't have to—"

"No, I just wasn't up to it. I wouldn't have gone anyway."

"Tony . . ." Lanya mulled, looking at the weathered paint on the gate shed. "I thought his name was something Scandinavian."

"Then it must be somebody else now," Mr Newboy said. He put his hands in his pockets. "Tony's quite as Italian as you can get. He's really very nice."

"So was the other one," Lanya said. "Things are always changing around here."

"Yes, they are."

They started up the path.

"There're so many people in and out of here all the time I've given up trying to keep track. It's very hectic. But you've picked a quiet day. Roger has taken everyone down town to see the paper office." Newboy smiled. "Except me. I always insist on sleeping late Tuesdays."

"It's nice to see the place again," Lanya consented. "When will everybody be back?"

"I would imagine as soon as it gets dark. You said you'd stayed here before. Would you like to wait and say hello to Roger?"

"No," Lanya said. "No. I was just curious."

Mr Newboy laughed. "I see."

The gravel (chewing Kidd's calloused foot) turned between two white columned mock-temples. The trees gave way to hedges; And what might have been an orchard further.

"Can we cut across the garden?"

"Of course. We'll go to the side terrace. The coffee urn's still hot I know, and I'll see if I can find some tea cakes. Roger keeps telling me I have the run of the place, but I still feel a little strange prying into Mrs Alt's kitchen just like that—"

"Oh, that's—" and "You don't have—" Kidd and Lanya began together.

"No, I know where they are. And it's time for my coffee break—that's what you call it here?"

"You'll love these!" Lanya exclaimed as they stepped through the high hedge. "Roger has the most beautiful flowers and—"

Brambles coiled the trellis. Dried tendrils curled on splintered lathe. The ground was gouged up in black confusion here, and here, and there.

"—What in the world . . ." Lanya began. "What *happened?*"

Mr Newboy looked puzzled. "I didn't know anything had. It's been like this since I've been here."

"But it was full of flowers: those sun-colored orange things, like tigers. And irises. Lots of irises—"

Kidd's foot cooled in moist ground.

"Really?" Newboy asked. "How long ago were you here?"

Lanya shrugged. "Weeks . . . three weeks, four?"

"How strange." Mr Newboy shook his head as they crossed the littered earth. "I'd always gotten the impression they'd been like this, for years . . ."

In a ten-foot dish of stone, leaves rotted in puddles.

Lanya's head shook. "The fountain used to be going all the time. It had a Perseus, or a Hermes or something in it. Where did it get to?"

"Dear me," Newboy squinted. "I think it's in a pile of junk behind the secretary cottage. I saw something like that when I was wandering around. But I never knew it had anything to do with the fountain. I wonder who's been around here long enough to know?"

"Why don't you ask Mr Calkins?" Kidd said.

"Oh, no. I don't think I would do that." Mr Newboy looked at Lanya with bright complicity. "I don't think I would do that at all."

285

"No," said Lanya, face fallen before the desolation, "I don't think so."

At the brim's crack, the ground, oozy under thin grass, kept their prints like plaster.

They passed another vined fence; a deal of lawn, and, higher than the few full trees, the house. (On a rise off to one side was another house, only three floors. The secretary cottage?)

Set in the grass a verdigrised plate read:

MAY

From the five fat, stone towers—he sought a sixth for symmetry and failed to find it—it looked as though a modern building of dark wood, glass, and brick had been built around an old one of stone.

"How many people does he have here?" Kidd asked.

"I don't really know," Mr Newboy said. They reached the terrace flag. "At least fifteen. Maybe twenty-five. The people he has for help, they're always changing. I really don't see how he gets anything done for looking after them. Unless Mrs Alt does all that." They climbed the concrete steps to the terrace.

"Wouldn't you lose fifteen people in there?" Kidd asked.

The house, here, was glass: inside were maple wall panels, tall brass lamps, bronze statuary on small end-tables between long couches covered in gold velvet, all wiped across with flakes of glare.

"Oh, you never feel the place is crowded."

They passed another window-wall; Kidd could see two walls covered with books. Dark beams inside held up a balcony, flanked with chairs of gold and green brocade; silver candlesticks—one near, one far off in shadow—bloomed on white doilies floating on the mahogany river of a dining table. "Sometimes I've walked around thinking I was perfectly alone for an hour or so only to come across a party of ten in one of the other rooms. I suppose if the place had a full staff—" dried leaves shattered underfoot—"it wouldn't be so lonely. Here we are."

Wooden chairs with colored canvas webbing sat around the terrace. Beyond the balustrade the rocks were licked over with moss and topped by birches, maples and, here and there, thick oaks.

"You sit down. I'll be right back."

Kidd sat—the chair was lower and deeper than he thought—and pulled his notebook into his lap. The glass doors swung behind Newboy. Kidd turned. "What are you looking at?"

"The November garden." Arms crossed, Lanya leaned on the stone rail. "You can't see the plaque from here. It's on top of that rock."

"What's in the . . . November garden?"

She shrugged a "nothing." "The first night I got here there was a party going on there: November, October, and December."

"How many gardens does he have?"

"How many months àre there?"

"What about the garden we first came through?"

"That one," she glanced back, "doesn't have a name." She looked again at the rocks. "It was a marvelous party, with colored lights strung up. And a band: violins, flutes, and somebody playing a harp."

"Where did he get violins here in Bellona?"

"He did. And people with lots and lots of gorgeous clothes."

Kidd was going to say something about Phil.

Lanya turned. "If my dresses are still here, I know exactly where they'd be."

Mr Newboy pushed through the glass doors with a teawagon. Urn and cups rattled twice as the tires crossed the sill. The lower tray held dishes of pastry. "You caught Mrs Alt right after a day of baking."

"Hey," Kidd said. "Those look good."

"Help yourself." He poured steaming coffee into blue porcelain. "Sugar, cream?"

Kidd shook his head; the cup warmed his knee. He bit. Cookie crumbs fell and rolled on his notebook.

Lanya, sitting on the wall and swinging her tennis shoes against the stone, munched a crisp cone filled with butter-cream.

"Now," Mr Newboy said. "Have you brought some poems?"

"Oh." Kidd brushed crumbs away. "Yeah. But they're handwritten. I don't have any typewriter. I print them out neat, after I work on them."

"I can probably decipher good fair copy."

Kidd looked at the notebook, at Lanya, at Mr Newboy, at the notebook. "Here."

Mr Newboy settled back in his seat and turned

through pages. "Ah. I see your poems are all on the left."

Kidd held his cup up. The coffee steamed his lips.

"So . . ." Mr Newboy smiled into the book, and paused. "You have received that holy and spectacular wound which bleeds . . . well, poetry." He turned another page, paused to look at it not quite long enough (in Kidd's estimate) to read it. "But have you hunkered down close to it, sighted through the lips of it the juncture of your own humanity with that of the race?"

"Sir . . . ?"

"Whether love or rage," Mr Newboy went on, not looking up, "or detachment impels the sighting, no matter. If you don't do it, all your blood is spilled pointlessly . . . Ah, I suppose I am merely trying to reinvest with meaning what is inadequately referred to in art as Universality. It *is* an inadequate reference, you know." He shook his head and turned another page. "There's no reason why all art should appeal to all people. But every editor and entrepreneur, deep in his heart of hearts is sure it does, wants it to, wishes it would. In the bar, you asked about publication?" He looked up, brightly.

"That's right," Kidd said with reserve and curiosity. He wished Newboy would go on, silently, to the poems.

"Publishers, editors, gallery owners, orchestra managers! What incredible parameters for the creative world. But it is a purgatorially instructive one to walk around in with such a wound as ours. Still, I don't believe anybody ever enters it without having been given the magic Shield by someone." Newboy's eyes fell again, rose again, and caught Kidd's. "Would you like it?"

"Huh? Yeah. What?"

"On one side," intoned Newboy with twinkling gravity, "is inscribed: 'Be true to yourself that you may be true to your work.' On the other: 'Be true to your work that you may be true to yourself.' " Once more Newboy's eyes dropped to the page; his voice continued, preoccupied: "It is a little frightening to peer around the edge of your own and see so many others discarded and glittering about in that spiky landscape. Not to mention all those naked people doing all those strange things on the tops of their various hills, or down in their several dells, some of them—Lord, *how* many?—beyond doubt out of their minds! At the same time—" he turned another page—"nothing is quite as humbling, after a very little while, as realizing how close one has already come to dropping it a dozen times oneself, having been distracted—heavens, no!—not by wealth or fame, but by those endless structures of logic and necessity that go so tediously on before they reach the inevitable flaw that causes their joints to shatter and allow you passage. One picks one's way about through the glass and aluminum doors, the receptionists' smiles, the lunches with too much alcohol, the openings with more, the mobs of people desperately trying to define good taste in such loud voices one can hardly hear oneself giggle, while the shebang is lit by flashes and flares through the paint-stained window, glimmers under the police-locked door, or, if one is taking a rare walk outside that day, by a light suffusing the whole sky, complex as the northern aurora. At any rate, they make every object from axletrees to zarfs and finjons cast the most astonishing shadows." Mr Newboy glanced up again. "Perhaps you've followed some dozen such lights to their source?" He held the page between his fingers. "Admit it—since we are talking as equals—most of the time there simply wasn't anything there. Though to your journal—" he let the page fall back to what he'd been perusing before—"or in a letter to a friend you feel will take care to preserve it, you will also admit the whole experience was rather marvelous and filled you with inadmissible longings that you would be more than a little curious to see settle down and, after all, admits. Sometimes you simply found a plaque which read, 'Here Mozart met da Ponti,' or 'Rodin slept here.' Three or four times you discovered a strange group heatedly discussing something that happened on that very spot a very long time by, which, they assure you, you would have thoroughly enjoyed had you not arrived too late. If you can bear them, if you can listen, if you can learn why they are still there, you will have gained something quite valuable. 'For God's sakes, put down that thing in your hand and stay a while!' It's a terribly tempting invitation. So polite themselves, they are the only people who seem willing to make allowances for your natural barbarousness. And once or twice, if you were lucky, you found a quiet, elderly man who, when you mumbled something about dinner for him and his slightly dubious friend, astounded you by saying, 'Thank you very much; we'd be delighted.' Or an old woman watching the baseball game on her television, who, when you brought her flowers on her birthday, smiled

289

through the chain on the door and explained, 'That's very sweet of you boys, but I just don't see anyone now, any more, ever.' Oh, that thing in your hand. You do still have it, don't you?"

"Sir, maybe if——?"

Newboy moved his hand, looked back down. "It starts out mirrored on both sides: initially reassuring, but ultimately distracting. It rather gets in the way. But as you go on, the silvering starts to wear. Now you can see more, and more, directly through. Really——" Newboy glanced up quickly, then returned his eyes to the page—— "it's a lens. The transition period is almost always embarrassing, however. While you are still being dazzled with bits of your own reflection, you have begun to suspect that it might, after all, be one-way glass—with a better view afforded from *out there!* Still, once used to it, you find the view more interesting. With only a little practice, you get so you can read both legends at once, without having to stop what you're doing to turn the thing around. Oh, and how many, many times you came close to clashing into someone you thought buck-naked only to find his Shield had grown transparent as your own. You become chary of judging too quickly who still has, and who has discarded, his. And when some youngster, glitteringly protected, through malice or, worse, some incomprehensible vision of kindness, shouts up at the dreadfully stark crag on which you happen to be panting, or down into the fetid ravine from which you are manfully trying to clamber with only one arm free, 'You're naked, don't you understand?' you may, momentarily, squint to make sure the double legend is still etched before you, but you are not liable to waste much energy setting him straight unless your own vision of kindness is as incomprehensible as his. There are more important things to do. As best you can, you go about doing them. But things still interrupt: now your eyes are deviled by a recurrent, polychrome flash. You try to ignore it. But its frequency increases. From habit, you check the cut runes to make sure. But, frankly, during the moments of illumination, it is practically impossible for you to read them, much less decide whether they still contain sense. The thing you have been baring, not to mention staring through all this time, has become an immense prism." Newboy leaned back now, his eyes somewhere on the underside of the balcony. "Did I say the first transition

290

was embarrassing? This one is monstrous. And it is the same fear: one-way glass! If only you didn't remember all those other, endless, elderly ladies with their water-color sets, the old men with their privately printed poems, whom one had, out of politeness, brought flowers for or invited out to dinner, as well, even though their heads were wrapped in tin foil and they babbled ceaselessly about Poetry and Truth. After all, they were nice in a useless sort of way, which is, after all, the only way to be truly nice. You even could discern two or three of the proper letters among the foil folds, admittedly cut from cardboard and taped there with sticking plaster. Are all these humbling fireworks some sort of cruel second childhood, a defect in the eye: You begin to suspect, as you gaze through this you-shaped hole of insight and fire, that though it is the most important thing you own—never deny that for an instant—it has not shielded you from anything terribly important. The only consolation is that though one could have thrown it away at any time, morning or night, one didn't. One chose to endure. Without any assurance of immortality, or even competence, one only knows one has not been cheated out of the consolation of carpenters, accountants, doctors, ditch-diggers, the ordinary people who must do useful things to be happy. Meander along, then, half blind and a little mad, wondering when you actually learned—was it before you began? —the terrifying fact that *had* you thrown it away, your wound would have been no more likely to heal: indeed, in an affluent society such as this, you might even have gone on making songs, poems, pictures, and getting paid. The only difference would have been—and you learned it listening to all those brutally unhappy people who did throw away theirs—and they do, after all, comprise the vast and terrifying majority—that without it, there plainly and starkly would have been nothing there; no, nothing at all."

Newboy fixed his eyes on Kidd's. Kidd smiled and felt uncomfortable. Then he felt belligerent, which maybe tainted the smile. He was going to say, Do you always rap like this when somebody . . .

The notebook suddenly slipped from Newboy's knees. The poet bent, but Kidd snatched it up first.

Its back cover had fallen open. Kidd frowned at the final block of handwriting that ran off the page bottom:

. . . *The sky is stripped. I am too weak to write*

much. But I still hear them walking in the trees; not speaking. Waiting here, away from the terrifying weaponry, out of the halls of vapor and light, beyond holland and into the hills, I have come to

"Do you . . ." Kidd's hand fell on the page. He looked up slowly.

The chain snaked around his wrist up his arm. It crossed his belly, his chest, between the vest flaps. "Do you think that's what they mean?"

"Pardon me?"

Kidd hooked his thumb beneath the chain and pulled it. "These. Do you think that's what they're supposed to mean?"

Mr Newboy laughed. "I haven't the faintest idea! You have them. I don't. I've *seen* people with them, here, but no. No. I was just *using* them. Oh, no! I would never presume to say what they meant."

Kidd looked down again. "Do you always go on like that to people who bring you poems?" he asked, with nowhere near the belligerence he had intended: He grinned.

Newboy was still laughing. "Go on." Newboy waved his hand. "You read some of them to me now." He sat forward, took another sip, then put his cup down. "No, really, I want to hear some of them out loud."

"All right," Kidd said, expecting to feel resentment, but experiencing a different anxiety altogether. He noted, with concern, once more, the number of pages left with free sides.

"Read the one about the dog-thing. I liked that one." *"Murielle?"*

Newboy nodded, hands together in his lap.

Kidd turned toward the front of the book.

He began to read.

Breathlessness left about the third line. Somewhere, something like enjoyment bloomed under his tongue and, rather than tripping it, somehow made it more sensitive, so that, without pause he realized how the vowels in both *loom* and *flow* took off from the same point but went different places. He found his face hollowing for the more resonant tones. He let them move the muscles about his mouth till staccato *t*'s and *k*'s riddled the final line and made him smile.

"Lovely," Newboy said. "In a rather horrifying way. Read the one in front of it."

He read, and lost himself in the movements of his

mouth, till a momentary convocation in the ear stunned him into a shriller voice. Then the long sounds quieted the answer.

"There are two voices in dialogue in that one, aren't there," Newboy commented at the finish. "I didn't pick it up just glancing at it."

"Huh? Oh, yeah. Maybe I should set them apart on the page—"

"No, no!" Mr Newboy sat up and motioned. "No, believe me, it isn't necessary. It would be perfectly clear in a page of print. It was my attention reading, believe me. Just go on."

He read.

What had come to him as images (among which he had pecked with tongue tip and pen point) returned, shocked, luminous—sometimes more, sometimes less luminous than memory, but so rich he thrust them out with his tongue to keep from trying to eat them.

"It's so much fun," Newboy said, "that you enjoy your own poems so much. Have you ever noticed how free verse tends to turn into iambic pentameter all by itself? Especially by people who haven't written much poetry."

"Sir?"

"Well, it's only nautral. It's the natural rhythm of English speech. You know, when the line goes ba-*da*, ba-da, ba-da, ba-da, ba-da? Oh, now don't sit there and look confused. Read some more. I'm not going to get pedantic again. I am enjoying this. Really."

Kidd was happily embarrassed. His eyes dropped—to the page. Kidd read; turned; read . . . Several times he thought he must be going on awfully long. But Newboy motioned for another, and once asked to hear both versions ("I saw that you had two when I was looking through . . ." and, after the earlier version: "Well, most of your revisions are in the right direction.") and had him reread several more. More confident, Kidd chose others now, went back to one he had left out, then skipped ahead, gathering some enjoyment that was not pride, was greatest when he was least aware of the man eating cookies before him, was a supportive pattern in the caverns under the tongue.

He stopped to glance at Newboy—

The poet was frowning at something not him.

Lanya said (in a voice that made Kidd turn, frown-

293

ing) ten feet down the terrace: "I . . . I didn't mean to interrupt." It was blue, it was shredded, it was silk.

"What's that?"

"My . . . dress." She came forward carrying it over her arm. "I looked upstairs in the Observatory Wing . . . for my dress, while you were reading. Christ, it's a mess up there!"

Mr Newboy frowned. "I didn't even know anybody was staying there."

"It doesn't look like anybody is," she said, "now."

"Is that on the third floor?"

Lanya nodded.

"Roger said something about not using that section —the doors were closed, weren't they? I thought it was something about plumbing repairs."

"They were closed but they weren't locked." Lanya said. "I just went right in. They were using it when I was here—I was just looking for the room Phil and I stayed in. But . . . the carpets have been pulled up off the floor; and torn. It looks like somebody yanked the light fixtures out of the ceiling, with about a foot of plaster each. In the bathroom off our bedroom, the sink's just sitting in the middle of the floor, and all that lovely blue Victorian tilework has been smashed. There're two holes in the wall that look like they've been put there with a battering ram—and somebody's slashed all the mattresses!" She looked down at the shredded material. "And my dress. It was balled up in a corner of the closet . . . the clothes bars were all pulled down and the clothes hook had been hammered back and bent or something." She held the dress up. "Somebody had to *do* this—it looks like somebody's been at it with a razor! But what in the world *for?*"

"Oh, dear!" Mr Newboy said. "Why, that's perfect-ly—"

"I mean it doesn't matter," Lanya said. "About the dress. When I left it, I didn't think I was coming back for it. But why in the *world*—?" She looked at Kidd, at Newboy. Suddenly she said, "Oh, hey—I didn't mean to interrupt!" She pulled the dress together into a ball, leaned back against the balustrade. "Please, go on. Don't stop reading, Kidd—"

Kidd said, "Let's go up and take a look at—"

"No," Lanya said, surprisingly loud.

294

Newboy blinked.

"No, I really don't want to go back up there."

"But . . . ?" Kidd frowned.

"Roger did ask us all not to go in that wing," Newboy said, uncomfortably. "But I had no idea it was—"

"I closed the doors." Lanya looked at the blue silk in her fist. "I should have left this up there."

"Maybe some wild party got out of hand?" Kidd asked.

Lanya said: "It didn't look like any party to me."

Newboy, Kidd suddenly saw (and realized at the same time that Lanya saw it too) was upset. Lanya's response was: "Is the coffee hot? I think I'd like a cup."

"Certainly." Newboy stood, went to the urn.

"Go on, Kidd," Lanya said. "Read another poem," as Newboy brought her the cup.

"Yes." The elderly poet, collecting himself, returned to his chair. "Let's hear another one."

"All right." Kidd paged through: they were all in some conspiracy to obliterate, if not Lanya's news itself, at least its unsettling effect. And he's got to live here, Kidd thought. There were only three more poems.

After the second, Lanya said: "That one's one of my favorites." Her hand moved over torn blue, folded over the wall.

And he read the third. "So now," Kidd said, primarily to keep something going, "you've got to give me *some* idea of what you think of them, whether they're good or bad," a thought which hadn't occurred to him once since he'd come; only previous mental rehearsal brought it out now.

"I thoroughly enjoyed hearing you read them," Newboy said. "But for anything else, you simply have to say to yourself, with Mann: I cannot know, and you cannot tell me."

Kidd smiled, reached for three more cookies on the tea-wagon, tried to think of something else.

Newboy said: "Why don't we take a stroll around the grounds? If it were a bright sunny day, it would be quite spectacular I'm sure. But it's still nice, in an autumnal sort of way."

Lanya, who was looking into her cup, suddenly raised her eyes. "Yes, that's an idea. I'd like that."

And that, Kidd realized, was Newboy's kindness to

Lanya. Somehow after her initial confidence, a moodiness had surfaced, but she had jumped to dispel it with movement and converse.

She put down her saucer, got down from the balustrade.

Kidd started to ask her: "Are you gonna take your ... ?"

But obviously she wasn't.

What, he wondered as they walked along the terrace and turned down the low steps, would be the emotional detritus from the violence upstairs in himself? But, as he wondered, Lanya, at the bottom step, took hold of his little finger in a hot, moist grip.

They walked across grass till rock rose from under it.

They climbed stone steps. They crossed a bridge with wrought railings.

A waterfall rushed beside them, stilled beneath them.

"This is *April*," Mr Newboy informed them from the plaque in the bridge's center.

They crossed it.

The corner bit Kidd's heel.

"You must know these quite well," Newboy said to Lanya.

"Not really. But I like them." She nodded.

"I've always meant to ask Roger why he has *September* and *July* in each other's place."

"Are they?" Lanya asked. "I must have walked around here fifty times and never noticed!"

They left the bridge to stroll under huge-leafed catalpas, past bird baths, past a large bronze sundial, tarnished brown and blank of shadow.

Stone benches were set out before the hedges in *August*.

Beyond the trees he could see the lawns of *September*. They passed through high stone newels where a wrought iron gate was loose from the bottom hinge, and, finally, once more, they were on the gravel driveway curving through great, squat evergreens.

Mr Newboy walked them to the front gate. By the green guard-shack, they exchanged Good-bye's, So-long's, I really enjoyed myself's, You must come again, and more good-bye's, during which, Kidd felt, as the gate-latch clanked behind them, each person had spoken one time too many.

He turned on the sidewalk to take Lanya's hand, sure she would bring up the shattered Observatory Wing the moment silence settled.

They walked.

She didn't.

After a dozen steps she said, "You want to write, don't you?" which, he realized, was what this compulsion to articulation was.

"Yeah," he said. "I guess I'll stop off at the bar, maybe do something there."

"Good," she said. "I'm going back to the park, first. But I'll come by Teddy's later."

"Okay."

She ambled beside him, shoulder brushing his, sometimes looking at the houses beside them, sometimes at the pavement before them, sometimes glancing up at the willow-lapped wall.

He said: "You want to go off and play your harmonica, don't you?" knowing it by the same pattern of silent cues she had known his desire. He put his arm around her shoulder; their walks fell into sync.

"Yes."

He thought his own thoughts, occasionally glancing to wonder what hers were.

Silent on the circuit of the year, speech is in excess of what I want to say, or believe. On the dismal air I sketch my own restraint, waking, reflexively, instant to instant. The sensed center, the moment of definition, the point under such pressure it extrudes a future and a past I apprehend only as a chill, extends the overlay of injury with some retentive, tenuous disease, the refuse of brick-and mortar-grinding violence. How much more easily all machination were such polarized perception to produce so gross an ideal.

Speech, the notebook's owner had written across from the page where Kidd wrote now, *is always in excess of poetry as print* . . .

"Hello."

He looked up from the counter (in the cage the silver dancer bowed to thin applause and flicked through the black curtain), then down as the dog gave a short bark.

"Muriel—!"

"Hello, Madame Brown. I haven't seen you in a while."

"Odd: I haven't seen you either." She laughed, high to low. "God, this place is dead tonight. May I sit down? You can pretend to buy an old woman a drink."

"Sure—"

"But I'm interrupting your work."

He shrugged. "I'm sort of at a stopping point."

As Madame Brown sat, the bartender brought her usual and replaced Kidd's beer. "What are you writing. Another poem?"

"A long one. It's in the natural rhythm of English speech."

She raised her eyebrow, and reflexively he closed the book; then wished he hadn't. "How are Mr and Mrs Richards, and June?"

"Oh." She flattened her knuckles to the wood. "Like always."

"They like their new place?"

She nodded. "I was over there for dinner night before last. But this evening they're having other guests, apparently. It was quite amusing to watch Mary try and make sure I didn't just accidentally drop around tonight." She didn't laugh. "Oh, yes, they're quite settled in now." She sat back. "I wish there were some more people. The city soaks them up; or maybe people are just . . . leaving?"

Kidd put the orchid on the cover of his book where it balanced on the three longest prongs.

"I guess you have to carry that around, don't you." Madame Brown laughed. "Perhaps I ought to get one. Perhaps I've just been very lucky in this dangerous city?"

From opposite sides he moved his hands together till his blunt fingertips bumped in the cage, and the blade points tugged back the skin between, burning now, about to cut. "I've got to go back to see them." He separated his fingers a little. "About my money."

"You haven't been paid?"

"Five dollars, the first day." He looked at her. "That morning I met you in the park, you said they'd told you they'd pay five an hour."

She nodded and said something softly. He thought he heard ". . . poor kid," but could not tell if "poor" were preceded by "you" or followed by comma and capital.

"*How* did they tell you?"

She looked at him questioningly.

"What did they say to you, exactly?"

She turned her frown to her glass. "They told me that if I found a young man who might help them with their moving, I should tell him they would pay him five dollars an hour."

"Mr Richards?"

"That's right."

"It's one of the reasons I took the job. Though, lord knows, you don't need it here. But I guess they knew what they were doing, then?"

"You should have spoken to him. He'd have given you some—thing."

"I want him to give me what he said he was going to —shit, I couldn't ask him that last day."

"Yes, it would have been a little odd."

"I'm going to have to go back and talk to him, I guess." He opened his notebook. "I think I'm going to write some more now, ma'am."

"I *wish* there were more people here." She pushed back from the bar.

"Well, it's early."

But she wasn't listening.

He went through the pages till he found: . . . *as print is in excess or words. I want to write; but can fix with words only the desire itself. I suppose I should take some small comfort in the fact that, for the few writers I have actually known, publication, in direct proportion to the talent of each, seems to have been an occurrence always connected with catastrophe. Then again, perhaps they were simply a strange group of . . .*

"Ba-da," he whispered and turned over the notebook to the blank page, "ba-da, ba-da, ba-da, ba-da."

The letter was still in the mailbox.

Among the bent and broken doors, red, white, and blue edging crossed this one, intact grille. He thought he could see the inking of a return address. I can pretend, he thought, it says Edward Richards, from a hotel in Seattle, Washington, off Freemont Avenue, on Third. He could make some things appear like that, when it was this dim . . . He turned and went to the elevator.

Someone, at least, had mopped the lobby.

He pressed the button.

Wind hissed from the empty shaft. He stepped into the other.

He'd come out in the pitch-dark hall before—as the door went *k-chunk*—he realized habit had made him push seventeen, not nineteen. He scowled in the dark and walked forward. His shoulder brushed a wall. He put out his hand and felt a door. He walked forward till he felt another.

Then he stopped—because of the smell. He scowled harder.

By the time he reached the next door (three, four doors on that side of the hall?) the odor was nauseous and sharp. "Jesus . . ." he whispered; his breath echoed.

He made himself go on.

The next door, which had to be the Richards' old apartment, swung in under his hand. The stench made him reel and lose kinesthetic focus. He hurried back, twice banging walls, one with his left shoulder, one with his right.

He was wondering how long it would take him to feel for the elevator bell . . .

K-chunk . . . k-chunk . . . k-chunk. One of the doors had caught on something. Between *k-chunks*, reminiscent of his own breath, came wind.

He paused, disoriented in the putrid dark. The left elevator door? The right? Then fear, like the lightest forefinger, tickled his shoulder. He nearly bent double, and staggered against the wall; which was not a wall, because it gave.

Inside the exit door, he caught the bannister, and stumbled down.

Faint light greyed the glass a flight below. Gulping fresh breath, he came out in the hall of sixteen. One bulb burned at the far end.

His next gulp checked explosive giggles. Kidd shook his head. Well, what the fuck were they *supposed* to do with it? He started down the hall, grinning and disgusted. Still, then why did I go to all that to drag it up?

When he knocked on the door, rattlings suggested it was opened. When he pushed it in, a girl caught her breath. "Hey, who's home?" he asked.

"Who . . . who is it?" She sounded afraid and exhausted. The window let in dark blue over the iron bunks, piles of clothing, an overturned stool.

300

"It's the Kid." He was still grinning.

"They're all gone," she said, from the muddle of blankets. "There's just me. Please . . . they're all gone."

"I'm not going to do anything." He stepped in.

She pushed herself up on her elbow, brushed hair back from her face and blinked bruised eyes.

"You're . . . the one who was sick?"

"I'm better," she whined. "Really, I'm better. Just leave me alone."

"Thirteen, and the others? How long have they been gone?"

She let herself fall, sighing.

"Are they coming back?"

"No. Look, just—"

"Do you have food and things?"

"Please . . . yes, I'm all right. They split a couple of days ago. What do you want?"

Because he had once feared her, he stepped closer. "Don't you have any light?"

"Lights, huh?" Plurality and inflection baffled him. "Look, I'll be all right, just go away. Lights? Over there . . ." She gestured toward the mannequin.

He went to see what she pointed at. "Has Faust been coming to check you out? He was all worried about you last time I was here." Bald plaster breasts were snaked with chain.

"Yeah, he comes. Look around the neck." That was further instruction. "Some guy left them. He ain't gonna come back." She coughed. "They don't got no battery."

He lifted the heavy links from the jointed neck. The smile was paint streaked and chipped under one eye. "Lights? Light shield?" The thing linked to the bottom clicked on the plaster chin, nose, forehead.

"All right. Now just go, will you?"

"It doesn't have a battery?"

She only sighed, rustled her covers.

"All right, if you say you're okay, I'll go." Something in him . . . thrilled? That's what he'd heard people say. The fear was low, the physical reaction runneled and grave. He dared the mirror:

Her bunk was filled with shadow and crumpled blankets.

"All right," he repeated. "Good-bye. Tell Thirteen or Denny if they come back—"

She sighed; she rustled. "They're not coming back."

301

So he shut the door behind him. Ominous: but what would he have had her tell? He put the chain around his neck. A blade snagged the links. He pulled his bladed hand away.

Light shield?

The thing linked to the bottom was spherical, the diameter of a silver dollar, black, and set with lenses. The heavy links crossed the brass chain and glass bits. He ran his thumb around the back of his vest, shrugged the lapels closed, and walked up the hall.

The elevator opened.

Rising in the dark, "19" suspended orange at eye level, he thought about batteries and rubbed his naked stomach.

At the Richards' new apartment door he heard voices. A woman, neither Mrs Richards nor June, laughed.

He rang.

Carpet-muffled heels approached.

"Yes?" Mrs Richards asked. "Who is it?" The peek-hole clicked. "It's Kidd!"

The chain rattled, the door swung back.

"Why, come in! Bill, Ronnie, Lynn; this is the young man we were telling you about!" Air from the opened balcony doors beat the candle flames: light flapped through the foyer. "Come in, come in. Kidd, some friends of Arthur's . . . from work. Arthur? They came over for dinner. Would you like some coffee with us? And dessert?"

"Look, if you're busy, just let me talk to Mr Richards a minute?"

"Kidd?" Mr Richards called from the dining room, "come on in, will you?"

Kidd sought for an expression, but finding nothing adequate for his impatience, came, patiently, inside; he settled on a frown.

Mrs Richards' smile was perfect.

Kidd went into the dining room.

The woman sitting next to Mr Richards was doing something with her earring. "You write poems, Mary told us. Are you going to read us some?"

"Huh? Oh. No, I didn't bring any."

The man across from her took his leather-patched elbows from the tablecloth. "That's a rather dangerous looking thing you did bring."

"Oh." Kidd looked at the orchid. "Well, it's almost dark out." He snapped the band open, shucked the finger harness, while the people up and down the table chuckled.

From where he stood, the flame at the white wax taper tip covered June's left eye. She smiled.

"Here," Mrs Richards said behind him. "Here's a chair. Move down a little bit, Sam. Pour him a cup of coffee, Arthur."

"What do you think I'm doing, honey," Mr Richards said with total affability.

A large woman in brown corduroy began to talk again with the man on her left. The cup passed from hand to hand to hand.

The woman in the green dress smiled, but couldn't keep her eyes (pale grey) from flicking at the steel cage he had set on the corner of the tablecloth. She put the cup beside it. Mrs Richards held the back of her chair, about to sit. "Really, just like I was telling you, Kidd absolutely saved our lives. He was such a help. We were beginning to think of him as part of the family."

At the other end of the table, a large man rubbed one finger against his nose and said, "Mary, you've been about to bring in that dessert for fifteen minutes now, and I'm on my second cup of coffee."

Mrs Richards laughed. "I *have* been talking on. Here, I'll bring it in right now."

"June," Mr Richards said from his end of the table, "go help your mother."

June, her small fists whispering in white taffeta, rounded the table for the kitchen.

The man beside the woman in green leaned around her and said, "Mary's just been going on all about you and your poems. You just live downtown, near the park?"

"Yeah," he said. "Where do you live?"

"Ah-ha." Still leaning forward he fingered the collar of his sports shirt. "Now, that's a very good question." His nails were not clean and the side of the collar was frayed. "That's a very good question indeed." He sat back, still laughing.

Still plucking at her earring, the woman at Mr Richards' right said, "You don't look like a poet. You look more like one of those people they're always writing about in the *Times*."

"Scorpions?" said the very blond man (tweed and

303

leather elbow patches) over his clasped hands. "His hair isn't long enough."

"His hair *is* long," insisted the earring plucker.

"Long *enough*," explained the blond man and turned to look for a napkin fallen by June's vacated chair.

Kidd grinned at the woman. "Where do you live?"

She stopped plucking, looked surprised. "Ralph and I used to be out on Temple. But now we've been staying—" and stopped because somebody said something on her other side, or may have even elbowed her.

"You like it better there?" Kidd asked, vaguely curious as to where Temple was.

"If you can like anything in Bellona, right now!"

Mrs Richards entered with a large glass bowl.

"What is that?" the man on Madame Brown's left asked, "jello?"

"No, it *isn't* jello!" Mrs Richards set the bowl before Mr Richards. "It's wine jelly." She frowned at the purple sea. "Port. The recipe didn't mention any sugar. But I think that was probably a mistake, so I put some in, anyway."

Beside Mrs Richards, June held a bowl heaped with whipped cream, glossy as the taffeta. Wrapped around one wrist, glittering in the candlelight . . . No, Kidd thought, she *wouldn't* have taken them off the . . . But the idea made him grin.

"Do you want to serve that, Arthur?"

At his corner Kidd contemplated being belligerently nice to the woman with the earring. But she was too far away. He turned to the woman beside him in green. "You work with Mr Richards?"

"My husband used to," she said and passed him a white-capped dessert dish.

He ate a spoonful: maple.

"I," he said and swallowed, "have to talk to Mr Richards about some money. You like it here?"

"Oh, it's a very nice apartment. You moved all the furniture for them, they told us."

He smiled, nodded, and decided he just couldn't take grape jello with maple flavored whipped cream.

The man beside the woman leaned around again: "I didn't really work with Arthur. I used to work for Bill over there who used to do statting for MSE—where Arthur works. So Lynn and me, we just came along."

"Oh," Lynn said deprecatingly while Kidd drank

304

coffee, "we just have to extend ourselves, you know, while all this is going on."

"That's what I'm doing; that's what I'm doing. A bunch of us have gotten together, you see. We're living together in . . . well, we're living together. I mean we were just about to get chased out of our house. By some guys with those things, you know?" The man pointed to the orchid. "But today, I'd wear one if I had it."

"No, you wouldn't!" Lynn insisted. "You wouldn't."

"It's pretty rough," Kidd said.

"The way we got together," Lynn went on to explain, "it's much better for the children. You see?"

"Yeah, sure!" He'd heard her suddenly helpless tone and he responded to it.

"What's there around here to write poems about?" That was her husband again. "I mean, nothing ever happens. You sit around, scared to go outside. Or when you do, it's like walking into a damn swamp."

"That's the whole thing," Lynn acknowledged. "Really. In Bellona, I mean, now. There's nothing to do."

From her father's side, June said: "Kidd writes lovely poems." Under the candles, shadows doffed in the cream.

"Oh, yes," Mrs Richards affirmed, setting down dishes of jelly before the large woman in corduroy and the blond man in tweeds. "Kidd, you will read something to us, won't you?"

"Yes," Mr Richards said. "I think Kidd should read a poem."

Kidd sucked his teeth with annoyance. "I don't have any. Not with me."

Mrs Richards beamed: "*I* have one. Just a moment." She turned and hurried out.

Kidd's annoyance grew. He took another spoonful of jello; which he hadn't wanted. So drank the rest of his coffee. He hadn't wanted that either.

"Here we are!" Mrs Richards cried, returning; she slipped the blue-edged paper before him.

"Oh," Kidd said. "I forgot you had this one."

"Go on, read it."

"Better be good," said blond and tweedy, affably enough. "Otherwise Ronnie will run the other way every time she sees you on the street because she thinks you're a—"

"I don't *go* out on the streets," Ronnie said. "I want to hear what kind of poems you write. Go on."

A man who wasn't Mr Richards said, "I don't know very much about poetry."

"Stand up, Kidd," Mr Richards said, waving a creamy spoon. "So we can hear you."

Kidd stood and said as dumbly as possible, "Mr Richards, I just came to see you about getting my money for the work I did," and waited for reaction.

Mr Richards moved his shoulders back and smiled. Somewhere—outside in the hall?—a door closed.

Mrs Richards, holding the edge of the table and smiling, nodded: "Go on, Kidd."

Ronnie said to Mrs Richards: "He wants his money: He's a pretty practical poet." Though she spoke softly, everyone laughed.

He looked down at Mrs Richards' copy of his poem, and drew his tongue back from his teeth for the first word.

In the hall, a man screamed, without words or inflection; footsteps, some dull thuds—the scream changed pitch at each of them.

Kidd started reading. He paused at the third line, wanting very much to laugh, but didn't look up.

Footsteps: running voices arguing—a lot of them.

Kidd kept reading till he reached Mrs Richards' omitted comma.

Lynn, beside him, let out a little cry. From the corner of his eye, he saw her husband take her arm. Somebody banged on the wall outside with what sounded like a crowbar. And the screaming cracked to a hysterical, Mexican accent: "Oh, come on, please, come on lemme 'lone. Don't fool 'round like that—No! C'mon, c'mon—No. Don' please—"

Kidd read the last lines of his poem and looked up.

The crashes had moved from the wall to the door, and fell with timed, deliberate thuds. Within the crash, as though it were an envelope of sound, he could hear the chain rattle, the hinges jiggle, the lock click.

As he looked around the table, the thought passed with oblique idleness: They look like I probably do when somebody's eyes go red.

Outside, above the shouting, somebody laughed.

Kidd's own fear, dogged and luminous and familiar

enough to be almost unconscious, was fixed somewhere in the hall. Yet he didn't want to laugh. He still wanted to giggle.

Out there, someone began to run. Others ran after.

A muscle on the back of Kidd's thigh tensed to the crashing. He smiled, vaguely, confused. The back of his neck was tickly.

Someone's chair squeaked.

"Oh, for God's sake, why don't they—" and, where rhythm predicted the next crash, only her word fell: "—stop!"

Footsteps lightened, tumbled off down steps, retreated behind banged doors.

Kidd sat down, looked at the guests, some of whom looked at him, some who looked at each other; the woman in corduroy was looking at her lap; Mrs Richards was breathing hard. He wondered if anyone liked his poem.

"They do that around here too, huh?" Sam forced, jocularly.

Then a woman Kidd could not really see at the table's end spilled coffee.

"Oh, I'll get a rag!" Mrs Richards screamed, and fled the room.

Three people tried to say nothing in particular at once.

But when Mrs Richards returned with a black and white, op-art dishtowel, one voice detached itself, a hesitant baritone: "For God's sakes, can't we do something about that? I mean, we've got to do something!"

Of several feelings, the only sharp one Kidd felt was annoyance. "Mr Richards?" he said, still standing, "Mr Richards? Can I talk to you now?"

Mr Richards raised his eyebrows, then pushed back his chair. June, beside him, surprisingly concerned, touched her father's arm, . . . restrainingly? protectively? Mr Richards brushed her hand away and came down the table.

Kidd picked up his orchid and went out into the hall.

The woman in corduroy was saying, "When you can *think* of something to do, will you *please* let me know what it is. You'll have my cooperation one hundred per cent. One hundred per cent, believe me."

At the door Kidd turned. "We should get this five

dollars an hour business settled now, don't you think, Mr Richards, because it'll just—"

Mr Richards' slight, taut smile broke. "What are you trying to do, huh?" he demanded in a whisper. "What are you trying to do? I mean five dollars an hour, you must be crazy!"

Mrs Richards, still holding the dishtowel, drifted up behind her husband's shoulder, blinking, in perfect imitation of Smokey with Thirteen.

"I mean just what are you trying to do?" Mr Richards went on. "We don't have any money to give you, and you better understand that."

"Huh?" because it seemed absurd.

"Five dollars an hour?" Mr Richards repeated. "You *must* be crazy!" His voice was insistent, tense and low. "What does somebody like you need that kind of money for, anyway? It doesn't cost anything to live in this city— no food bills, no rent. Money doesn't mean anything here any more. What are you trying to do . . . ? I've got a wife. I've got a family. MSE hasn't had a payroll for months. There hasn't even been anyone in the damn office! I've got to hold on to what I have. I can't spend that kind of money now, with everything like this. I can't—"

"Well, isn't that what you told—?" He was angry. "Oh shit. Look, then why don't you . . ." Then he reached around to his pocket.

Mr Richards' eyes widened as the orchid Kidd held flicked by him.

But Kidd only dug at his pocket. "Then why don't you keep this too?" Mr Richards swayed when the moist, green knot, bounced off his shirt and fell to the floor, unfolding like paper on fire.

Kidd turned the lock and pulled the door open. The chain stopped it—*ratch!*—at two inches.

Mrs Richards, immediately beside him, fumbled with the catch. A step into the hall, he looked back to show them his disgust.

The astonishment Mr Richards returned him, as Mrs Richards with varied bitternesses at her eyes, closed the door on it, was unexpected, was satisfying, was severed with the door's clash.

He counted the fifteen, paint-chipped dents before he decided (someone was laughing inside again) to go.

In the elevator, he dropped, ruminating. Once he looked up to wrinkle his nose at a faint putrescence. But dropped on. Echoing in the shaft, with the wind, were footsteps from some stairwell, were voices.

There was no one in the lobby.

Satisfied?

His annoyance, at any rate.

But all the vague and loose remains roiled and contended for definition. "Ba-da ba-da ba-da?" he asked. "Ba-da ba-da," he answered, sitting. It listed like oil on turbulence. At last Ba-da ba-da ba-da? formed around the fragments of a question, but Ba-da ba-da fit no worded answer. He flexed his fingers on the pen point till they ached, then went back to struggling with the recalcitrant quantities of sound overlapping their sense. He reread some dozen alternate lines for the beginning of one section: with the delight of resignation, he decided, with the change of a "This" to a "That", on his initial version.

A candle on the high windowsill cast the batteryless projector's swinging shadow across the notebook opened on his naked thigh.

Someone knocked just at the point he discovered he was copying, in quick, cramped letter, the same line for the fourth time (his mind had meandered on). "Are you in there?" Lanya asked.

"Huh?" He looked up at the door's layered scrawl. "Yeah. I'm coming out now." He stood and pulled his pants up from around his shins, pulled the flush chain.

"He said you were in there." She nodded toward the bartender when Kidd opened the door. "Come on."

"Huh? Where?"

She smiled. "Come on." She took his hand.

"Hey," he called, passing the bar. "You wanna keep this for me again?"

The bartender leaned over for the notebook. "In the usual place, kid." He reached up and stuck it through the cage bars.

She paused at the door to ask, "How did it go with the Richards?"

"I gave him back his fucking five bucks."

Her confusion suddenly went in laughter. "That's too much! Tell me what happened." And she tugged him on into the hallway and out to the street.

"What happened?" she asked again, shrugging her shoulder into his armpit. They walked quickly down the

309

block. When she turned to glance at him, her hair tickled his arm.

"He didn't want to pay me. They were having a dinner party or something there. So I gave him back what he gave me already, you know?" He rubbed his chest underneath his vestflap. At his hip, the orchid's harness jingled. "You know their kid, the little boy, they just left him . . ." He shook his head against hers. "Hell, I don't want to talk about that. Where we going?"

"To the park. To the commune."

"Why?"

"I'm hungry, for one thing."

"Just as well I'm not talking."

She hurried him across the street, into an ocean of smoke and evening. He tried to smell it, but his nostrils were numb or acclimated. The lions gaped in the blur with stony, astonished protest. They neared the foggy pearl of a functioning street light. "This morning," Lanya said, "after you went away to write, some people said that there had been some new fires at the other end of the park!"

"Smoke's sure thicker."

"Down there," she nodded, "before, I thought I could see it flickering. And it hadn't even gotten dark yet."

"There couldn't be any fires in the park," he announced suddenly. "The whole thing would just burn up, wouldn't it? It would either all burn or it wouldn't."

"I guess so."

"Did they send anybody to check? Maybe they should get some people down there to dig one of those things, a breakfront." Breakfront? and heard the word resonate with images of a charred forest, where years back he had tramped with a cannister of water strapped to his shoulders, hand pumping from the brass nozzle into sizzling ash. "Maybe you and John and his people could go."

She shrugged under his arm. "No, really, I'd rather not go down there . . ."

From her voice he tried to reconstruct what it told him of her expression, and remembered her sitting on the stone railing with arms full of torn blue silk.

"You're scared to death!"

Her head turned abruptly in question or affirmation. "Why?"

She leaned her head forward and surprised him by reiterating, "Come on," quietly, sharply.

His bare foot went from concrete to grass.

The night billowed and sagged: habit guided them through a maze of mist.

He saw quivering fires.

But they were from the commune's cinderblock furnace. People moved silently, listlessly before flame.

Perched along the picnic table, in a variety of army jackets, paisley shirts, and grubby tank-tops, young people stared through stringy hair. Someone dragged a sleeping bag in front of the fire. Shadow: pale, hairy skin; black leather: Tak stood back from the fire, arms folded, legs wide. The ornate orchid of yellow metal hung from his belt. Three scorpions stood behind him, whispering.

One was the red-headed, freckled black who had pipe-whipped him at Calkins; the other two were darker. But his initial start was followed by no more uneasiness. Somebody swaggered past with a cardboard carton of tin cans, crumpled cellophane wrappers, paper cups. He realized (very surprised) he was very high. Thought swayed through his mind, shattered, sizzled like water in hot ash. It's the smoke, he thought frantically. Maybe there's something in this fog and smoke. No . . .

John walked by the fire's edge, bald chest glistening between his vest, stopped to talk with Tak; they bent over Tak's weapon. Then, at John's wrist:—brass leaves, shells, claws: from the ornamented wrist band the overlong yellow blades of the orchid curved down around John's fingers. He was making motions from the elbow as if he would have beat his leg were his hand un-armed.

Tak grinned and John moved away.

Kidd blinked, chill and unsteady. There was Lanya— she had moved from his side—talking with some of the people around the table. Isolate questions pummeled inarticulately. A muscle twitched in his flank, and he was terribly afraid of it. He stepped, brushing shoulders with someone who smelled of wine. The fire put a hot hand against cheek, chest, and arm, leaving the rest of him cool.

Milly shook her hair somewhere in the shadow of a tree: bloody copper shingles rattled her shoulders.

Why were they here? Why did they mill here? His inner skull felt tender and inflamed. Watch them, listen to them, put together actions and conversation snatches:

311

He searched the screen where perception translated to information, waiting for somebody to dance, to eat, to sing. He wished Lanya had told him why they had come. But he was very tired. So he moved around. Someday I'm going to die, he thought irrelevantly: But blood still beat inside his ear.

He stepped backward from the heat, and backward again. (Where was Lanya?) But was too distraught to turn his head. Everything meant, loudly and insistently, much too much: smoke, untwirling over twigs; the small stone biting his heel; the hot band from the fire across his lowered forehead; the mumblings around him that rose here, fell there.

Milly stood a few feet in front of him, bare legs working to a music he couldn't hear. Then John crashed down, crosslegged in the leaves, beside her, fiddling absently with the blades around his hand.

A while ago, he realized, he had thought once again: Please, I don't want to be sick again, please, but had hardly heard the thought go by, and could only now, disinterestedly, discern the echo.

Something, or one, was about to emerge into the clearing—he was sure; and was equally sure that, naked and glistening, it would be George! It would be June!

"Isn't this stupid," someone Kidd couldn't see was saying, "when I could be in Hawai—?"

Tongue tip a pink bud at the corner of his lips, John stared at Milly's shifting calves. He raised his bladed hand (a reflection crossed his chin), and, with a sharp, downward sweep, cut.

Milly gasped, bit off the gasp, but made no other sound. She did not step, she did not even look.

Astounded, Kidd watched blood, in a torrent wide (the thought struck irrelevantly amidst his terror) as a pencil run down her heel.

IV

"Look, leave me alone . . ."

"Come on; come—"

"Tak, will you get your fuckin' hands—"

"I'm not after your tired brown body. I just want to get you to the bar where you can sit down."

"Look, please I'm . . ."

"You're *not* drunk; you say you're *not* stoned or anything, then you damn well better sit down and relax!" Tak's beefy hand clamped his shoulder. (Kidd took three more unsteady steps.) "You were staggering around there like you were half in some sort of trance. Now come on with me, sit down, have a drink, and get yourself together. You sure you didn't take anything?"

The ornate orchid at Tak's belt clashed the simple one at Kidd's.

"Hey, look! Just come on and leave me alone . . . Where's Lanya?"

"She's more likely to find you at Teddy's than wandering around out in the dark. *You* come on."

In such colloquy they made their hesitant way from park to bar.

Kidd swayed in the doorway, looking at rocking candle flames, while Tak argued with the bartender:

"Hot brandy! Look, just take your coffee-water there, in a glass with a shot of . . ."

June? Or George?

Paul Fenster looked up from his beer, three people down (Kidd felt something cold but manageable happen

313

in his belly at the recognition), and came over to stand behind Tak; who turned with two steaming glasses.

"Huh . . . ?"

"So. I've found somebody here I know." Fenster was buttoned halfway up the chest in a red, long-sleeve shirt. "I didn't think I was, and it's my first night back."

"Oh." Tak nodded. "Yeah. How you doing? Hey, I gotta bring a friend a drink. Um . . . Come on." Tak lifted the brandy glasses over some woman's shoulder, stepped around some man. Fenster raised his chin, watching.

Tak came across to Kidd. Fenster came behind.

"Here's your brandy. This is Paul Fenster, my favorite rebel-who-has-managed-to-misplace-his-cause."

"That's what you think." Fenster saluted with his beer bottle.

"Well, he didn't misplace it, actually. It went somewhere else when he wasn't looking. Paul this is the Kid." (Kidd wondered if he were projecting Tak's lack of enthusiasm.) "Come on over and sit down."

"Hello." Kidd nodded toward Fenster, who wasn't looking at him, hadn't heard him, apparently did not recognize him. Well, he didn't feel like talking anyway, so could be amused at Fenster's obliqueness.

"Come on, come on." Tak headed them toward a booth, glanced apprehensively at Kidd again.

Gesturing with his bottle, Fenster continued: "Oh, there's a cause all right! Maybe you've lost ninety-five per cent of your population, but you're still the same city you were before—"

"*You* weren't *here*, before." Tak sat at the outside edge of the seat, so that Fenster had to sit across the table. Then Tak slipped over, making room for Kidd, who noted the whole maneuver and wondered if Fenster had.

Kidd sat. Tak's leg immediately swung against his in warm, if unwanted, reassurance.

"That's not what I mean," Fenster said. "Bellona was . . . what? Maybe thirty per cent black? Now, even though you've lost so many people, bet it's closer to sixty. From my estimate, at any rate."

"All living in harmony, peace, and brotherly love—"

"Bullshit," Fenster said.

"—with the calm, clear, golden afternoon only occa-

314

sionally torn by the sobs of some poor white girl dishonored at the hands of a rampaging buck."

"What are you trying to do, show off for the kid there?" Fenster grinned at Kidd. "I met Tak here the first day I got to Bellona. He's a really together guy, you know? He likes to pretend he's short on brains. Then he lets you hang yourself." Fenster still hadn't recognized him.

Kidd nodded over his steaming glass. The fumes stung; he smiled back and felt ill.

"Oh, I'm the God-damn guardian of the gate. I've spoken to more people on their first day in this city than you could shake a stick at." Tak sat back. "Let me clue you. It's the people I take time to speak to again on the third, fourth, and fifth day you should watch."

"Well, you're still kidding yourself if you think you don't have a black problem here."

Tak suddenly sat forward and put his worn, leather elbows on the table. "You're telling me? What I want to know is how you're going to do anything about it sitting up there on Brisbain Avenue?"

"I'm *not* at Calkins' any more. I've moved back to Jackson. Down home again."

"Have you now? Well, how did your stay work out?"

"Hell—I guess it was nice of him to invite me. I had a good time. He has quite a place up there. We got into a couple of talks. Pretty good, I think. He's an amazing man. But with that constant weekend bash going, thirty-eight days a month it looks like, I don't know how he has time to take a leak, much less write half a newspaper every day, and run what's left of the God-damn town. I outlined a couple of ideas: a switchboard, a day-care center, a house-inspection program. He says he wants to cooperate. I believe him . . . as much as you can believe anybody, today. Since there's as little control around here as there is, I wouldn't be surprised if he gets more done than you'd expect, you know?"

Tak turned his hands up on the table. "Just remember, nobody voted him up there."

Fenster sat forward too. "I've never been that down on dictators. Long as they didn't dictate me." He laughed and drank more beer.

Brandy sips dropped in hot knots to Kidd's stomach and untied. He moved his leg away from Tak's. "Did you

315

talk to him about that Harrison article?" Kidd asked Fenster.

"George Harrison?"

"Yeah."

"Hell, that's just a whole lot of past noise. There're real problems that have to be dealt with now. Have you ever *walked* up Jackson Avenue?"

"I've crossed it."

"Well, take a good look around it, talk to the people who live there before you go on to me about any of that George Harrison horseshit."

"Paul here doesn't approve of George." Tak nodded deeply.

"I don't approve or disapprove." Fenster clinked his bottle on the wood. "Sadism simply isn't my bag. And I don't hold with anybody committing rape on anybody. But if *you* want to associate with him, that's your problem, not mine. I think making all that to-do over it is the worst sort of red-herring."

"If you're back down on Jackson, then you got him for a nextdoor neighbor; so you're more or less stuck with associating with him, huh? I just have to be friendly in the bar." Suddenly Tak slapped the table edge: "You know what the problem is, Paul? George is *nicer* than you."

"Huh?"

"No, I mean: I know you both, I like you both. But I like George more."

"Hell, man, I seen those posters Reverend Amy's giving out. I know what you guys in here like—"

"No," Tak said. "No, you're missing the point."

"Like hell I am— Hey, you know?" Fenster turned to Kidd. "Have you ever *read* those articles, the ones in the issue about the riot, and the other issue with the interview?"

"Huh? No, but I heard about them."

"Tak hasn't read them either."

"I've heard enough about them," Tak echoed.

"But here's the point. Everybody's heard about the articles. But since I've been here, I've only talked to one person who actually says he read them."

"Who?" Tak asked.

"George Harrison." Fenster sat back and looked satisfied.

Kidd tilted his brandy. "I met somebody who read them."

316

"Yeah?" Fenster asked. "Who?"

"The girl he screwed. And her family. Only they didn't recognize her in the pictures." From something that happened on Fenster's face without destroying the smile, Kidd decided maybe Fenster wasn't so bad after all.

"You met her?"

"Yeah." Kidd drank. "You probably will too. Everybody keeps telling me how small the city is. Hey, Tak, thanks for the drink." He started to stand.

Tak said, "You sure you're all right, Kidd?"

"Yeah. I feel better." He nodded at Fenster, then walked, relieved, to the bar.

When Jack said, "Hey, how you doing?" Kidd started. His relief, the shallowest of things, vanished.

"Hello," he said. "Fine. How you been?"

"I been fine." Jack's shirt was wrinkled, his eyes red, his cheeks unshaven. He looked very happy. "I just been fine. How are you? And your girl friend?"

"I'm fine," Kidd repeated, nodding. "She's fine."

Jack laughed. "That's great. Yeah, that's really great. Say, I want you to meet a friend of mine. This is Frank." Jack stepped back.

"Hello." With a high, bald forehead and neck-length hair, Frank had apparently decided to grow a beard perhaps a week ago: *I give them to you crossed, I take them uncrossed* . . . yes, that was who it was. Only he had put on a green shirt with milky snaps instead of buttons; and washed his hands.

"This," Jack explained to Frank, "is the friend of Tak's I was telling you about who writes the poems. Only I can't remember his name."

"Kidd," Kidd said.

"Yeah, they call him the Kid." Jack continued his explanation. "Kid, this is Frank. Frank was in the army, and he writes poems too. I was telling him all about you, before. Wasn't I?"

"Yeah, I've seen you around the park." Frank nodded. "Jack was telling me you were a poet?"

Kidd shrugged. "Yeah. A little."

"We been drinking," Jack continued his explanation, "all afternoon."

"And it's night now." Frank grinned.

"This God-damn city. If you wanna stay drunk, it sure is the place to come. You can buy drinks at the God-damn bars and you don't have to pay no money.

317

Or anything. And anyplace you go, people always got stuff to smoke or to drink. Jesus." He burped. "I gotta go water the garden. Be back in a minute." He stepped away and headed for the john.

Kidd felt a wave of disorientation, but the phrases he'd prepared before broke through: "You been looking out for nature boy?"

"He's sort of looking out for me," Frank said. "We're both army deserters. Him, a little more recently. Only I think Jack's getting homesick."

Kidd swallowed. "For the army?" And felt better.

Frank nodded. "I'm not. I left about six months ago. Happy I'm here. I'm getting a chance to write again, and it's a pretty together place."

"You," and at the reiteration he felt toward Frank sudden, surprising, and total distrust, "write poems?" So he smiled.

Frank smiled back and nodded over his glass: "Well, I've been sort of lucky about getting things published, really. The book was just an accident. One of the west coast little magazines puts out good editions of people who contribute. I was lucky enough to get selected."

"You mean you have a book?"

"No copies in Bellona." Frank nodded. "Like I said, even that was an accident."

"You been writing a long time, then."

"Since I was fifteen or sixteen. I started in high school; and most of what you write back then is crap."

"How old are you now?"

"Twenty-five."

"Then you've been one for a long time. A poet. I mean it's your job, your profession."

Frank laughed. "You can't make a living at it. I taught for a year at San Francisco State, till I went into the army. I like to think of it as a profession, though."

Kidd nodded. "You got a lot of poems in magazines and things?"

"Three in the *New Yorker* about a year ago. Some people think that's my crowning achievement. Two in *Poetry, Chicago,* before that. There're a few others. But those are the ones I'm proud of."

"Yeah, I used to read that magazine a lot."

"You did?"

"It's the one that used to have the little curlicue horse a long time ago? Now it just has funny pictures on it. I read it every month in the library, at school. For years."

Frank laughed. "Then you're doing better than I am."

"I've seen the *New Yorker*," Kidd said. "But I never read it."

Frank's expression changed slightly and noncomittally.

"And I've never published any poems at all," Kidd said. "Anyplace. I've only been a poet a little while. A couple of weeks. Since I came here. You probably know a lot more about it than I do."

"About getting things published?"

"That too. I mean about writing them, though. It's hard."

"Yes, I guess it can be."

"It's about the God-damned hardest thing I've ever done."

Frank laughed and rubbed his young beard. "Sometimes. You've . . . only been writing—poems, for a few weeks? What made you start?"

"I don't know. What made you?"

"I suppose," and Frank nodded again, "I had to."

"Do you—" Kidd paused a moment, considering the theft—"do you find Bellona stimulating, making you produce work?"

"About as much as anyplace else, I guess. Maybe a little less, because you have to spend so much time scuffling, you know? I was working on a few short things. But I lost my notebook a few weeks back."

"Huh?"

Frank nodded. "Since then I haven't written anything. I haven't had time."

"Hey, you lost your notebook!" Discomfort broached fear. "Christ, that must be . . ." Then his feelings centered. Kidd leaned over the bar. "Hey, can I get the notebook! Huh? Come on! You want to give me the notebook, please!"

"All right," the bartender said. "All right, I'll get it. Simmer down. You guys ready for another—"

"The notebook!" Kidd knocked the counter with his fist.

"All right!" Sucking his teeth, the bartender pulled it from the cage and flopped it on the bar. "*Now* do you want another drink?"

"Oh. Yeah," Kidd said. "Sure."

Besides blood, urine, mulch, and burn marks, there were rings from the bottles he had set haphazardly on the cover. He opened it in the middle. " . . . This isn't yours, is it?"

Frank frowned. "You found this?"

"Yeah. It was in the park."

Geoff Rivers   Arthur Pearson
Kit Darkfeather   Earlton Rudolph
David Wise . . .   Phillip Edwards . . .

Kidd looked over Frank's shoulder and read the listed names, till Frank turned the page.

"Hey, what you doin'?" Jack said behind them. "You showing Frank here your poetry writing?"

Kidd turned around. "Just this notebook I found, filled up with somebody's writing."

"Frank's pretty smart." Jack nodded. "He knows about all sorts of shit. He taught history. In a college. And he cut out on the army too."

"Lots of us have," Frank said, not looking up. "The ones with any sense go to Canada. The rest of us end up here." He turned a page.

"You been having a good time?" Jack put his hand on Kidd's shoulder. "This is the place to have a good time, you know?"

"Fine time," Kidd said. "But I haven't seen you around. Where you been staying?"

"Stayed on a few days with Tak." Jack's hand rose and fell. "He kicked me out after a week when I wouldn't let him suck on my peter no more."

Across the bar Loufer, his cap low on his ears, still talked earnestly with Fenster.

Jack's hand fell again. "They got *girls* in this city! Frank knows this whole house. Full of girls. Real nice girls. We was over there, and . . ." His grin widened toward ecstasy. "They like Frank a lot." He screwed up his face. "I think that's 'cause he's growin' a beard and things. Or maybe taught in a college."

"They liked you okay," Frank said, still not looking up. "They just didn't know you."

"Yeah, I guess they just didn't know me well enough, yet."

"Say?" Frank looked up now. "You wrote all this—?"

320

"Yeah—well, no. I mean most of it was written in there when I found it. That's why I wanted to know if it was yours."

"Oh," Frank said. "No. It's not mine."

Kidd turned from under Jack's hand. "That's good. Because when you said you had lost your notebook, you know, I just thought . . ."

"Yeah," Frank said. "I see."

"We're gonna go out and look for some more girls," Jack said. "You wanna come along?"

"Jack thinks there's safety in numbers," Frank said.

"No. No, that's not it," Jack protested. "I just thought he might want to come and help us look for some girls. That's all. Maybe we can go back to that house?"

"Hey, thanks," Kidd said. "But I got to hang around here for a while."

"The Kidd here's got his own old lady," Jack said in knowing explanation. "I bet he's waiting on her."

"Hey, I'm . . . sorry it's not your notebook," Kidd told Frank.

"Yeah," Frank said. "So am I."

"We see you around," Jack said, while Kidd (smiling, nodding) wondered at Frank's tone.

Absently rubbing the paper (he could feel the pen's blind impressions), he watched them leave.

Bumping shoulders with them, Ernest Newboy came into the bar. Newboy paused, pulling his suit jacket hem, looked around, saw Fenster, saw Kidd, and came toward Kidd.

Kidd sat up a little straighter.

"Hello, there. How've you been for the past few days?"

The small triumph prompted Kidd's grin. To hide it he looked back at the book. The poem Frank had left showing, had been tentatively titled:

LOUFER

In the margin, he had noted alternates: *The Red Wolf, The Fire Wolf, The Iron Wolf.* "Eh . . . fine." Suddenly, and decisively, he took his pen from the vest's upper button hole, crossed out LOUFER, and wrote above it: WOLF BRINGER. He looked up at Newboy. "I been real fine; and working a lot too."

"That's good." Newboy picked up the gin and tonic

the bartender left. "Actually I was hoping I'd run into you tonight. It has to do with a conversation I had with Roger."

"Mr Calkins?"

"We were out having after-dinner brandy in the October gardens and I was telling him about your poems." Newboy paused a moment for a reaction but got none. "He was very impressed with what I told him."

"How could he be impressed? *He* didn't read them."

Newboy doffed his gin. "Perhaps what impressed him was my description, as well as the fact that—how shall I say it? Not that they are *about* the city here—Bellona. Rather, Bellona provides, in the ones I recall best at any rate, the décor which allow the poems to . . . take place." The slightest questioning at the end of Newboy's sentence asked for corroboration.

More to have him continue than to corroborate, Kidd nodded.

"It furnishes the décor, as well as a certain mood or concern. Or am I being too presumptuous?"

"Huh? No, sure."

"At any rate, Roger brought up the idea: Why not ask the young man if he would like to have them printed?"

"Huh? No, sure." Though the punctuation was the same, each word had a completely different length, emphasis, and inflection. "I mean, that would be . . ." A grin split the tensions binding his face. "But he hasn't seen them!"

"I pointed that out. He said he was deferring to my enthusiasm."

"You were *that* enthusiastic? He just wants to put some of them in his newspaper, maybe?"

"Another suggestion I made. No, he wants to print them up in a book, and distribute them in the city. He wants me to get copies of the poems from you, and a title."

The sound was all breath expelling. Kidd drew his hand back along the counter. His heart pounded loudly, irregularly, and though he didn't think he was sweating, he felt a drop run the small of his back, pause at the chain—"You must have been pretty enthusiastic—" and roll on.

Newboy turned to his drink. "Since Roger made the suggestion, and I gather you would like to go along with

322

it, let me be perfectly honest: I enjoyed looking over your poems, I enjoyed your reading them to me; they have a sort of primitive vigor that comes very much from a pruned sort of language that, from looking at the way you revise, at any rate, you've apparently done quite a bit of work to achieve. But I haven't lived with them by any means long enough to decide whether they are, for want of a simple term, good poems. It's very possible that if I just picked them up in a book store, and read them over, read them over very carefully too, I might easily not find anything in them at all that interested me."

Kidd frowned.

"You say you've only been writing these for a few weeks?"

Kidd nodded, still frowning.

"That's quite amazing. How old are you?"

"Twenty-seven."

"Now there." Mr. Newboy pulled back. "I would have thought you were much, much younger. I would have assumed you were about nineteen or eighteen and had worked most of your life in the country."

"No. I'm twenty-seven and I've worked all over, city, country, on a ship. What's that got to do with it?"

"Absolutely nothing." Newboy laughed and drank. "Nothing at all. I've only met you a handful of times, and it *would* be terribly presumptuous of me to think I knew you, but frankly what I've been thinking about is how something like this would be for you. Twenty-seven . . . ?"

"I'd like it."

"Very good." Newboy smiled. "And the decision I've come to is, simply, that so little poetry *is* published in the world it will ill behoove me to stand in the way of anyone who wants to publish more. Your being older than I thought actually makes it easier. I don't feel quite as responsible. You understand, I'm not really connected with the whole business. The idea came from Mr Calkins. Don't let this make you think ill of me, but for a while I tried to dissuade him."

"Because you didn't think the poems were good enough?"

"Because Roger is not in the business of publishing poetry. Often unintentionally, he ends up in the business of sensationalism. Sensationalism and poetry have nothing to do with one another. But then, your poems are not sensational. And I don't think he wants to make them so."

323

"You know, I was just talking to another poet, I mean somebody who's been writing a long time, and with a book and everything. He's got poems in *Poetry*. And that other magazine . . . the *New Yorker*. Maybe Mr Calkins would like to see some of his stuff too?"

"I don't think so," Mr Newboy said. "And if I have one objection to the whole business, I suppose that's it. What would you like for the name of your book?"

The muscles in Kidd's back tightened almost to pain. As he relaxed them, he felt the discomfort in the gut that was emblematic of fear. His mind was sharp and glittery. He was as aware of the two men in leather talking in the corner, the woman in construction boots coming from the men's room, of Fenster and Loufer still in their booth, of the bartender leaning on the towel against the bar, as he was of Newboy. He pulled the notebook into his lap and looked down at it. After the count of seven he looked up and said, "I want to call it—*Brass Orchids*."

"Again?"

"*Brass Orchids*."

"No '*The*' or anything?"

"That's right. Just: *Brass Orchids*."

"That's very nice. I like that. I—" Then Newboy's expression changed; he laughed. "That really *is* nice! And you've got quite a sense of humor!"

"Yeah," Kidd said. "Cause I think it takes some balls for me to pull off some shit like that. I mean, *me* with a book of poems?" He laughed too.

"Yes, I *do* like that," Newboy repeated. "I hope it all works out well. Maybe my hesitations will prove unfounded after all. And any time you want to get us copies of the poems, in the next few days, that'll be fine."

"Sure."

Newboy picked up his glass. "I'm going to talk to Paul Fenster over there for a while. He left Roger's today and I'd like to say hello. Will you excuse me?"

"Yeah." Kidd nodded after Newboy.

He looked at his notebook again. With his thumb, he nudged the clip on the pen out of the spiral where he had stuck it, and sat looking at the cover: click-click, click-click, click.

He lettered across the cardboard: *Brass Orchids*. And could hardly read it for dirt.

Brushing to the final pages (pausing at the poem called *Elegy* to read two lines, then hurrying past), he

324

felt a familiar sensation: at the page where he'd been writing before, listening for a rhythm from his inner voice, he turned to strain the inner babble—

It hit like pain, was a pain; knotted his belly and pushed all air from his lungs, so that he rocked on the stool and clutched the counter. He looked around (only his eyes were closed) taking small gulps. All inside vision blanked at images of glory, inevitable and ineffably sensuous till he sat, grinning and opened mouthed and panting, fingers pressing the paper. He tore his eyelids apart, the illusory seal, and looked down at the notebook. He picked up the pen and hastily wrote two lines till he balked at an unrevealed noun. Re-reading made him shake and he began automatically crossing out words before he could trace the thread of meaning from sound to image: he didn't want to feel the chains. They drew across him and stung.

They carried pain and no solution for pain.

And incorrectly labeled it something else.

He wrote more words (not even sure what the last five were) when once more his back muscles sickled, his stomach tapped the bar edge, and inside the spheres of his eyes, something blind and luminous and terrifying happened.

Those women, he thought, those men who read me in a hundred years will . . . and no predicate fixed the fantasy. He shook his head and choked. Gasping, he tried to read what he had set down, and felt his hand move to X the banalities that leached all energy: ". . . pit . . ." There was a word (a verb!), and watched those on either side suddenly take its focus and lose all battling force, till it was only flabby, and archaic. Write: he moved his hand (remember, he tried to remember, that squiggle is the letters ". . . tr . . ." when you go to copy this) and put down letters that approximated the sounds gnawing his tongue root. "Awnnn . . ." was the sound gushing from his nose.

Someday I am going to . . . it came this time with light; and the fear from the park, the recollections of all fear that stained and stained like time and dirt, page, pen, and counter obliterated. His heart pounded, his nose ran; he wiped his nose, tried to re-read. What *was* that squiggle that left the word between ". . . reason . . ." and ". . . pain . . ." indecipherable?

The pen, which had dropped, rolled off the counter

and fell. He heard it, but kept blinking at his scrawl. He
picked the notebook up, fumbled the cover closed, and
the floor, hitting his feet, jarred him forward. "Mr Newboy . . . !"

Newboy, standing by the booth, turned. ". . . yes?"
His expression grew strange.

"Look, you take this." Kidd thrust the notebook
out. "You take this now . . ."

Newboy caught it when he let-it go. "Well, all
right—"

"You take it," Kidd repeated. "I'm finished with
it . . ." He realized how hard he was breathing. "I mean
I think I'm finished with it now . . . so—" Tak looked up
from his seat—"you can take it with you. Now."

Newboy nodded. "All right." After a slight pause,
he pursed his lips: "Well, Paul. It was good seeing you.
I'd hoped you'd have gotten up again. You must come
sometime soon, before I leave. I've really enjoyed the
talks we've had. They've opened up a great deal to me.
You've told me a great deal, shown me a great deal, about
this city, about this country. Bellona's been very good for
me." He nodded to Tak. "Good meeting you." He looked
once more at Kidd, who only realized the expression
was concern as Newboy—with the notebook under his
arm—was walking away.

Tak patted the seat beside him.

Kidd started to sit; halfway, his legs gave and he
fell.

"Another hot brandy for the Kidd here!" Tak hollered, so loud people looked. To Fenster's frown, Tak
simply shook his grimacing head: "He's okay. Just had a
rough day. You okay, Kidd?"

Kidd swallowed, and did feel a little better. He
wiped his forehead (damp), and nodded.

"Like I was saying," Tak continued, as blond arms
with inky leopards set Kidd a steaming glass, "for me,
it's a matter of soul." He observed Fenster across his
knuckles, continuing from the interruption. "Essentially,
I have a black soul."

Fenster looked from the exiting Newboy. "Hum?"

"My *soul* is black," Tak reiterated. "You know what
black soul is?"

"Yeah, I know what black soul is. And like hell you
do."

326

Tak shook his head. "I don't think you understand—"

"You can't have one," Fenster said. "I'm black. You're white. You can't have a black soul. I say so."

Loufer shook his head. "Most of the time you come on pretty white to me."

"Scares you I can imitate you that well?" Fenster picked up his beer, then put the bottle back down. "What is it that all you white men suddenly want to be—"

"I do *not* want to be black."

"—what *gives* you a black soul?"

"Alienation. The whole gay thing, for one."

"That's a passport to a whole area of culture and the arts you fall into just by falling into bed," Fenster countered. "Being black is an automatic cutoff from that same area unless you do some fairly fancy toe-in-the-door work." Fenster sucked at his teeth. "Being a faggot does *not* make you black!"

Tak put his hands down on top of one another. "Oh, all right—"

"You," Fenster announced to Loufer's partial retreat, "haven't wanted a black soul for three hundred years. What the hell is it that's happened in the last fifteen that makes you think you can appropriate it now?"

"Shit." Tak spread his fingers. "You can take anything from me you want—ideas, mannerisms, property and money. And I can't take anything from you?"

"That you *dare—*" Fenster's eyes narrowed—"express, to me, surprise or indignation or hurt (notice I do not include anger) because that is exactly what the situation is, is why you have no black soul." Suddenly he stood—the red collar fell open from the dark clavicle—and shook his finger. "Now you live like that for ten generations, then come and ask me for some black soul." The finger, pale nail on a dark flesh, jutted. "You can have a black soul when I *tell* you you can have one! Now don't bug me! I gotta go pee!" He pulled away from the booth.

Kidd sat, his finger tips tingling, his knees miles away, his mind so opened that each statement in the altercation had seemed a comment to and/or about him. He sat trying to integrate them, while their import slipped from the tables of memory till Tak turned to him with a grunt, and with his forefinger hooked down the vizor

327

of his cap. "I have the feeling—" Tak nodded deeply—
"that in my relentless battle for white supremacy I have,
yet once again, been bested." He screwed up his face.
"He's a good man, you know? Go on, drink some of that.
Kid, I worry about you. How you feeling now?"

"Funny," Kidd said. "Strange . . . okay, I guess." He
drank. His breath stayed in the top of his lungs. Something dark and sloppy rilled beneath.

"Pushy, self-righteous." Tak was looking across to
where Fenster had been sitting. "You'd think he was a
Jew. But a good man."

"You met him on his first day here too," Kidd said.
"You ever ball him?"

"Huh?" Tak laughed. "Not on your life. I doubt he
puts out for any one except his wife. If he has one. And
even there one wonders. Anyplace he's ever gone, I'll
bet he's gotten there over the fallen bodies of love-sick
faggots. Well, it's an education, on both sides. Hey, are
you *sure* you didn't take some pill you shouldn't have, or
something like that? Think back."

"No, really. I'm all right now."

"Maybe you want to come to my place, where it's
a little warmer, and I can keep an eye on you."

"No, I'm gonna wait for Lanya." Kidd's own
thoughts, still brittle and hectic, were rattling so hard it
was not till fifteen seconds later, when Fenster returned to
the table, he realized Tak had said nothing more, and
was merely looking at the candlelight on the brandy.

Voiding his bladder had quenched Fenster's heat. As
he sat down, he said quite moderately, "Hey, do you see
what I was trying to—"

Tak halted him with a raised finger. "Touché, man.
Touché. Now don't bug *me*. *I'm* thinking about it."

"All right." Fenster was appeased. "Okay." He sat
back and looked at all the bottles in front of him. "After
this much to drink, it's all anybody can ask." He began to
thumb away the label.

But Tak was still silent.

"Kidd—?"

"Lanya!"

2

Wind sprang in the leaves, waking her, waking him beneath her turning head, her moving hand. Memories clung to him, waking, like weeds, like words: They had talked, they had walked, they had made love, they had gotten up and walked again—there'd been little talk that time because tears kept rising behind his eyes to drain away into his nose, leaving wet lids, sniffles, but dry cheeks. They had come back, lay down, made love again, and slept.

Taking up some conversation whose beginnings were snarled in bright, nether memories, she said: "You *really* can't remember where you went, or what happened?" She had given him time to rest; she was pressing again. "One minute you were at the commune, the next you were gone. Don't you have any idea what happened between the time we got to the park and the time Tak found you wandering around outside—Tak said it must have been three hours later, at least!" He remembered talking with her, with Tak in the bar; finally he had just listened to her and Tak talk to each other. He couldn't seem to understand.

Kidd said, because it was the only thing he could think: "This is the first time I've seen real wind here." Leaves passed over his face. "The first time."

She sighed, her mouth settling against his throat.

He tried to pull the corner of the blanket across his shoulders, grunted because it wouldn't come, lifted one shoulder: it came.

The astounded eye of leaves opened over them, turned, and passed. He pulled his lips back, squinted at the streaked dawn. Dun, dark, and pearl twisted beyond the branches, wrinkled, folded back on itself, but would not tear.

329

She rubbed his shoulder; he turned his face up against hers, opened his mouth, closed it, opened it again.

"What is it? Tell me what happened? Tell me what it is."

"I'm going . . . I may be flipping out. That's what it is, you know?"

But he *was* rested: things were less bright, more clear. "I don't know. But I may be . . ."

She shook her head, not in denial, but wonder. He reached between her legs where her hair was still swive-sticky, rubbed strands of it between his fingers. Her thighs made a movement to open, then to clamp him still. Neither motion achieved, she brushed her face against his hair. "Can you talk to me about it. Tak's right—you looked like you were *drugged* or something! I can tell you were scared. Try to talk to me, will you?"

"Yeah, yeah, I . . ." Against her flesh, he giggled. "I can still screw."

"Well, a lot, and I love it. But even that's sort of . . . sometimes like instead of talking."

"In my head, words are going on all the time, you know?"

"What are they? Tell me what they say."

He nodded and swallowed. He had tried to tell her everything important, about the Richards, about Newboy. He said, "That scratch . . ."

"What?" she asked his lingering silence.

"Did I say anything?"

"You said, 'The scratch.'"

"I couldn't tell . . ." He began to shake his head. "I couldn't tell if I said it out loud."

"Go on," she said. "What scratch?"

"John, he cut Milly's leg."

"Huh?"

"Tak's got an orchid, a real fancy one, out of brass. John got hold of it, and just for kicks, he cut her leg. It was . . ." He took another breath. "Awful. She had a cut there before. I don't know, I guess he gets his rocks off that way. I can understand that. But he cut—"

"Go on."

"Shit, it doesn't make any sense when I talk about it."

"Go on."

"Your legs, you don't have any cut on them." He
330

let the breath out; and could feel her frowning down in her chest. "But he cut her."

"This was something you saw?"

"She was standing up. And he was sitting down. And suddenly he reached over and just slashed down her leg. Probably it wasn't a very big cut. He'd done it before. Maybe to someone else. Do you think he ever did it to anyone else——?"

"I don't know. Why did it upset you?"

"Yes . . . no, I mean. I was already upset. I mean because . . ." He shook his head. "I don't know. It's like there's something very important I can't remember."

"Your name?"

"I don't even . . . know if that's it. It's just—very confusing."

She kept rubbing till he reached up and stopped her hand.

She said: "I don't know what to do. I wish I did. Something's happening to you. It's not pretty to watch. I don't know who you are, and I like you a lot. That doesn't make it easier. You've stopped working for the Richards; I'd hoped that would take *some* pressure off. Maybe you should just go away; I mean you should leave . . ."

In the leaves, the wind walked up loudly. But it was his shaking head that stopped her. Loudly wind walked away.

"What were they . . . why were they all there? Why did you take me there?"

"Huh? When?"

"Why did you take me there tonight?"

"To the commune?"

"But you see, you had a reason, only I can't understand what it was. It wouldn't even matter." He rubbed her cheek until she caught his thumb between her lips. "It wouldn't matter." Diffused anxiety hardened him and he began to press and press again at her thigh.

"Look, I only took you there because—" and the loud wind and his own mind's tumbling blotted it. When he shook his head and could hear again, she was stroking his thick hair and mumbling, "Shhhhh . . . Try and relax. Try and rest now, just a little . . ." With her other hand, she pulled the rough blanket up. The ground was hard under shoulder and elbow.

331

He propped himself on them while they numbed, and tried out memory.

Suddenly he turned to face her. "Look, you keep trying to help, but what do you . . ." He felt all language sunder on silence.

"But what do I really feel about all this?" she saved him. "I don't know—no, I do." She sighed. "Lots of it isn't too nice. Maybe you're in really bad shape, and since I've only known you for a little while, I should get out now. Then I think, Hey, I'm into a really good thing; if I worked just a little harder I might be able to do something that would help. Sometimes, I just feel that you've made *me* feel very good—that one hurts most. Because I look at you and I see how much you hurt and I can't think of anything to do."

"He . . ." he dredged from flooded ruins, "I . . . don't know." He wished she would ask what he meant by "he," but she only sighed on his shoulder. He said, "I don't want to scare you."

She said, "I think you do. I mean, it's hard not to think you're just trying to get back at me for something somebody else did to you. And that's awful."

"Am I?"

"Kidd, when you're off someplace, working, or wandering around, what *do* you remember when you remember me?"

He shrugged. "A lot of this. A lot of holding each other, and talking."

"Yeah," and he heard a smile shape her voice, "which is a lot of the most beautiful part. But we do other things. Remember those too. That's cruel of me to ask when you're going through this, isn't it? But there's so much you don't see. You walk around in a world with holes in it; you stumble into them; and get hurt. That's cruel to say, but it's hard to watch."

"No." He frowned at the long dawn. "When we went up to see Newboy, did you like——" and remembered her ruined dress while he said:

"At Calkins'—did you have fun?"

She laughed. "You didn't?" Her laugh died.

Still, he felt her smile pressed on his shoulder. "It was strange. For me. It's easy sometimes to forget I've got anything to do other than . . . well, this."

"You talked about an art teacher once. I remember

that. And the tape editing and the teaching. You paint too?"

"Years ago," she countered. "When I was seventeen I had a scholarship to the Art Students' League in New York, five, six years back. I don't paint now. I don't want to."

"Why'd you stop?"

"Would you like to hear the story? Basically, because I'm very lazy." She shrugged in his arms. "I just drifted away from it. When I was drifting, I was very worried for a while. My parents hated the idea of my living in New York—I had just left Sarah Lawrence, again, and they wanted me to stay with a family. But I was sharing an awful apartment on Twenty-Second Street with two other girls and going part time to the League. My parents thought I was quite mad and were very happy when I wanted to go to a psychiatrist about my 'painting block'. They thought he would keep me from doing anything really foolish." She barked a one-syllable laugh. "After a while, he said what I should do is set myself a project. I was to make myself paint three hours each day—paint anything, it didn't matter. I was to keep track of the time in a little twenty-five cent pad. And for every minute under three hours I didn't paint, I had to spend six times that amount of time doing something I didn't like—it was washing dishes, yes. We had decided that I had a phobia against painting, and my shrink was behaviorist. He was going to set up a counter unpleasantness—"

"You had a phobia about dishwashing too?"

"Anyway." She frowned at him in the near dark. "I left his office in the morning and got started that afternoon. I was very excited. I felt I might get into all sorts of areas of my unconscious in my painting that way . . . whatever that meant. I didn't fall behind until the third day. And then only twenty minutes. But I couldn't bring myself to do two hours of dish washing."

"How many dishes did you have?"

"I was supposed to wash clean ones if I ran out of dirty ones. The next day I was okay. Only I didn't like the painting that was coming out. The day after that I don't think I painted at all. That's right, somebody came over and we went up to Poe's Cottage."

"Ever been to Robert Louis Stevenson's house in Monterey?"

333

"No."

"He only rented a room in it for a couple of months and finally got thrown out because he couldn't pay the rent. Now they call it *Stevenson's House* and it's a museum all about him."

She laughed. *"Any*way, I was supposed to see the doctor the next day. And report on how it was going. That night I started looking at the paintings—I took them out because I thought I might make up some work time. Then I began to see how awful they were. Suddenly I got absolutely furious. And tore them up—two big ones, a little one, and about a dozen drawings I'd done. Into lots of pieces. And threw them away. Then I washed every dish in the house."

"Shit . . ." He frowned at the top of her head.

"I think I did some drawing after that, but that's more or less when I really stopped painting. I realized something though—"

"You shouldn't have done that," he interrupted. "That was awful."

"It was years ago," she said. "It was sort of childish. But I—"

"It frightens me."

She looked at him. "It was years ago." Her face was greyed in the grey dawn. "It was." She turned away, and continued. "But I realized something. About art. And psychiatry. They're both self-perpetuating systems. Like religion. All *three* of them promise you a sense of inner worth and meaning, and spend a lot of time telling you about the suffering you have to go through to achieve it. As soon as you get a problem in any one of them, the solution it gives is always to go deeper into the same system. They're all in rather uneasy truce with one another in what's actually a mortal battle. Like all self-reinforcing systems. At best, each is trying to encompass the other two and define them as sub-groups. You know: religion and art are both forms of madness and madness is the realm of psychiatry. Or, art is the study and praise of man and man's ideals, so therefore a religious experience becomes just a brutalized aesthetic response and psychiatry is just another tool for the artist to observe man and render his portraits more accurately. And the religious attitude I guess is that the other two are only useful as long as they promote the good life. At worst, they all try to destroy one another. Which is what my psychia-

334

trist, whether he knew it or not, was trying, quite effectively, to do to my painting. I gave up psychiatry too, pretty soon. I just didn't want to get all wound up in any systems at all."

"You like washing dishes?"

"I haven't had to in a long, long time." She shrugged again. "And when I have to now, actually I find it rather relaxing."

He laughed. "I guess I do too." Then: "But you shouldn't have torn up those paintings. I mean, suppose you changed your mind. Or maybe there was something good in them that you could have used later—"

"It was bad if I wanted to be an artist. But I wasn't an artist. I didn't want to be."

"You got a scholarship."

"So did a lot of other people. Their paintings were terrible, mostly. By the laws of chance, mine were probably terrible too. No, it wasn't bad if I didn't want to paint at all."

But he was still shaking his head.

"That really upsets you, doesn't it? Why?"

He took a breath and moved his arm from under her. "It's like everything you—anybody says to me . . . it's like they're trying to tell me a hundred and fifty other things as well. Besides what they're saying direct."

"Oh, perhaps I am, just a bit."

"I mean, here I am, half nuts and trying to write poems, and you're trying to tell me I shouldn't put my faith in art or psychiatry."

"Oh *no!*" She folded her hands on his chest, and put her chin there. "I'm saying *I* decided not to. But I wasn't nuts. I was just lazy. There is a difference, I hope. And I *wasn't* an artist. A tape editor, a teacher, a harmonica player, but not an artist." He folded his arms across her neck and pushed her head flat to its cheek. "I suppose the problem," she went on, muffled in his armpit, "is that we have an inside and an outside. We've got problems both places, but it's so hard to tell where the one stops and other takes up." She paused a moment, moving her head. "My blue dress . . ."

"That reminds you of the problems with the outside?"

"That, and going up to Calkins'. I don't mind living like that—every once in a while. When I've had the chance, I've always done it rather well."

335

"We could have a place like Calkins'. You can have anything you want in this city. Maybe it wouldn't be as big, but we could find a nice house; and I could get stuff like everybody else does. Tak's got an electric stove that cooks a roast beef in ten minutes. With microwaves. We could have anything—"

"That—" she was shaking her head—"however, is when the inside problems start. Or start to become problems, anyway. Sometimes, I don't think I have any inside problems at all. I think I'm just giving myself something to worry about. I'm not scared of half the things half the people I know are. I've gone lots of places, met lots of people, had lots of fun. Maybe it is all a matter of getting the outside problems solved. Another not nice thing: When I look at you, sometimes I don't think I have a right to think I have any problems, inside or out."

"Don't you want to *do* anything? Change anything; preserve anything; find any . . ." He stopped because he felt distinctly uncomfortable.

"No." She said it very firmly.

"I mean, maybe that would make it easier to solve some of the outside problems, anyway. You know, maybe you'd feel happier if you could get another dress."

"No," she repeated. "I want wonderful and fascinating and marvelous things to happen to me and I don't want to do anything to make them happen. Nothing at all. I suppose that makes you think I'm a superficial person . . . no, you're too intelligent. But a lot of people would."

He was confused. "You're a marvelous, deep, fascinating person," he said, "and therefore you should be world-famous this instant."

"For twenty-three, I'm famous enough, considering I haven't done anything. But you're right."

"How are you famous?"

"Oh, not really famous. I just have lots of famous friends." She rolled her head once more to her chin. "It said in that article that Newboy had been nominated three times for the Nobel Prize. I know three people who've actually won it."

"Huh?"

"Two in the sciences, and Lester Pearson was a good friend of my uncle and would come spend weeks with us at my uncle's summer place in Nova Scotia. The one in chemistry was very pleasant—he was only twenty-nine

336

—and connected with the university. We were very close for a while."

"You went out on dates and things. With all your famous friends?"

"No, I hate that. I never go on dates. These are people I met and I talked to and I liked talking to, so I talked to again. That's all."

"I'm not famous. Would you be happy in a place like Calkins', living with me?"

"No."

"Why not? Just because I'm not famous?"

"Because you wouldn't be happy. You wouldn't know what to do there. You wouldn't fit." Then he felt all her muscles, thigh to shoulder, tighten on him. "That isn't *true!* I'm being awful." She sucked her teeth. "Do you know, I was *terrified* to go up to Roger's with you. It had nothing to do with what *I* was wearing: I thought you'd behave dreadfully—you'd either Ooooh and Ahhh the whole afternoon to death, or you'd shut up and be a big silent hole in the day."

"You think I've never been in any nice places before?"

"But you *weren't* like that," she said. "That's the point! You were perfectly fine, you had a good time, and I'm sure Mr Newboy enjoyed it. If anyone spoiled it, it was me with my silly dress. And I'm a mean, small, petty person for worrying about such things in the first place." She sighed. "Do I get points at all for keeping it to myself this long?" She sighed again. "No, I guess not."

He blinked at the wild sky and tried to comprehend: he could follow her logic, though the emotions behind it confused.

After a while she said: "I grew up in some awfully big houses. Some were almost as big as Roger's. When I was at boarding school, once, my uncle said I could have some kids to the summer place for my birthday. It came on a long weekend and they said I could have ten kids up from Thursday night till Sunday afternoon. There was one boy at the Irving School—the boys' school next to ours— named Max, whom I thought was just great. He came from a poor—well, poorish family. He was on scholarship. He was intelligent, sensitive, gentle . . . and gorgeous—I was probably in love with him! I would have been perfectly happy to take him off for the weekend all by himself. But

337

I had to plan a party: so I planned it all for him. I got two girls who just loved to listen to intelligent boys talk— I wasn't a very good listener at the time, and Max *could* go on. I invited this perfectly dreadful colored boy who Max said he'd admired because he was second on the debating team and never did *anything* wrong. I scoured four schools for the most marvelous and charming people —people who would entertain him, complement him, offer just the right contrast. No two people from the same clique, you know, who would stick together and make a little indigestible dumpling in the stew. The weekend was dreadful. Everyone had a fabulous time, and for the next two years kept asking me when I was going to do it again. Except Max. The plane ride, the horses, the boats, the maids, the chauffeurs, they were just too much for him. All he said the whole four days was, 'Thank you,' and, 'Gosh.' About forty-four times each. Oh, I guess we were just very young. In another couple of years he would probably have been a socialist or something and might have attacked the whole thing. That would have been fine! I had people there who could have argued. At least there would have been communication. I don't know—maybe I'm still young." Suddenly she turned over. "I could be the older woman in an eighteenth century French novel right now." She turned back. "Twenty-three! Isn't that awful? And they say the twentieth century has a youth hangup." She giggled against his chest.

"You want to hear a story from me, now?"

"Hm-hm." He felt her nod.

"About when I was twenty-three. Your age."

"Sure thing, gramps. That's about three years after you got out of the mental hospital?"

"No, it's about going to nice places." He frowned. "One summer I was working up and down the gulf coast, as a header on the shrimp boats."

"What's a header?"

"He washes dishes and pulls the heads off the shrimp. Anyway, I'd just gotten fired in Freeport and was waiting around to get on another boat—"

"Why'd you get fired?"

"I got seasick. Now shut up. Anyway, I was sitting in front of this café, which was about the only thing there to do, when these two guys in black Triumphs came hauling around the dust. One yells, Did I know where he could get a traveler's check cashed in this God-damn town. I'd

338

been there three days, so I told him where the bank was. He told me, Get in, and I showed him and his friend where to go. We got to talking: he was in law school up in Connecticut. I told him about going to Columbia. He got his check cashed and asked if I wanted to come along with them—which was better than two bucks a night I didn't have, so I said, Yeah. A whole bunch of kids were staying out on this island just off the coast."

"Like the commune?"

"One of the kids' fathers was head of a land development company down there. The company had moved the fisherman who lived on the island someplace else, built a bridge to the mainland, dug a canal, and built a whole bunch of hundred-and-fifty-thousand, two-hundred-thousand dollar homes, lawns in the front, swimming pool on one side, garage on the other, and boat house in the back on the canal so you could get your boat out to sea. They were all for the executives of Dow Chemical, who just about owned the city. So prospective buyers could check them out first, the houses were furnished, the freezers were filled with steaks, the closets stocked with liquor, towels in the bathrooms and all the beds kept made. The executives could bring their families in for a weekend to try out the house before they bought it. On Monday, a truck would come by with maids, carpenters, plumbers, and supplies to replace anything that had been used up, to clean out the mess, and fix anything broken. There wasn't anybody on the island, so the doors had all been left open. The kid's father had told him since he was in the area, why didn't he stay there. So the kid, with about twenty of his friends—they went from about seventeen to twenty-five—had moved in. They'd start on one house, drink up all the liquor, eat up the food, destroy the furniture, break the windows, tear up everything they could, then move on to another one. On Monday the maids, carpenters, and plumbers would fix the damages. I stayed with them for two weeks. I'd pick out a room, lock the door, and read most of the time, while all the noise went on outside. Every once in a while, you know, I'd come out to get something to eat—wade through the beer cans in the kitchen, scrape the grease out of some pan and fry a piece of steak. Then I'd go down to the swimming pool maybe if it wasn't too bad and, if there wasn't too much furniture floating in it, or bottles, or broken glass around, I'd swim a while. Pretty

339

soon, when it would get too crowded, I'd go back to my room. There'd be people screwing in my bed, or somebody would've gotten sick all over the bureau. Once I found some little girl sitting in the middle of the floor, out of her head—cocaine all *over* the rug, and that is a *lot* of cocaine: she'd pulled down the drapes and was cutting paper-dolls out of them. So I'd take my book and go lock myself in another room. A couple of days after I got there, the two guys who'd brought me suddenly decided to fly back to somewhere else. They gave me the keys to the Triumphs and said I could have them. I don't even know how to drive. One of them had got the front smashed in by now, but the other one was still good. The police came twice. The first time the kids told them to go fuck themselves and said they were supposed to be there, and the police went away. The second time, I thought it was better I split. When the shit came down, I wouldn't have any rich Texas relatives to run home to. There was one girl there who said she'd buy me a ticket into Houston if I would fuck her and stay on more than five minutes."

"*No* . . ." Lanya giggled against his neck.

"She bought me a bus ticket and a pair of jeans and a new shirt."

Her giggling turned to laughter. Then she looked up. "That isn't really true, is it?" Her smile tried to force through the dawn light.

After a second he said, "Naw. It isn't. I mean I screwed her and she bought the bus ticket for me. But she didn't put it that way. It just makes a better story."

"Oh." She put her head down again.

"But you see, I know about nice places. How to act in them. You go in, and you take what you want. Then you leave. That's what they were doing down there. That's what I was doing up at Calkins'."

Once more she balanced on her chin.

He looked down over his.

She was frowning. "I think you have that absolutely ass backward. But if it makes you, in your own delightfully naive way, polite and charming, I guess . . ." She put her head down again, and sighed. "But I wouldn't be surprised if there turned out to be one or two people who came up to my party in Nova Scotia who were also down in Texas a few years later at . . . yours."

He glanced at her again and chuckled.

Mist made mountains above the trees, made waves that broke, and fell and did not reach them.

His chest was damp from her cheek. She turned her head, tickling him with hair. A leaf, surprising as shale, struck his forehead and made him look up at the half-bare branches. "We shouldn't be trying to do it like this. We're dirty. It's uncomfortable. Soon it's going to get colder, or start raining, or something. Like you said, the commune is sort of a drag. You sit around and watch them waste whatever they have and then you finish up the leavings. We'll get a place—"

"Like the Richards?" she asked, in a tired voice.

"No. No, not like that."

"You think you'd like to put together something like Roger's place?"

"It doesn't have to be all that spectacular, huh? Just somewhere that was ours, you know? Maybe something like Tak's got."

"Mmmm," she said. Then once more she raised her head up on her chin. "You should go to bed with Tak again."

"Huh? Why?"

"Because he's a nice person. And he'd enjoy it."

He shook his head. "Naw, he's not my type. Besides, he catches them when they first get here. I don't think he's interested in anything more than the first taste, you know?"

"Oh." She put her head down again.

"You trying to get rid of me," he asked, "like you always think I'm trying to do with you?"

"No." After a while she asked, "Does it ever bother you that you make it with both men and women?"

"When I was fifteen or sixteen it used to bug hell out of me. I guess I worried about it a lot. By the time I was twenty, though, I noticed that no matter how much worrying I did, it didn't seem to have too much effect on who I ended up in bed with. So now I don't worry. It's more fun that way."

"Oh," she said. "Glib. But logical."

"Why'd you ask?"

"I don't know." He moved her to the side. She reached down to touch his hip. Moved her hand across his hip. "I fooled around a few times in boarding school. With girls, I mean. Sometimes, you know, I felt maybe I

341

was a little strange because I didn't do it more. But I've just never been turned on to girls, sexually."

"Your loss," he said, and pulled her shoulder against his.

She turned to taste his neck, his chin, his lower lip. "What you were telling me happened . . ." she said between her tongue's dartings ". . . at the Richards' tonight . . . must have been . . . awful."

"I'm not going back there." He nipped her. "Ever. I'm not ever going back."

"Good . . ."

Then, from a small movement down her body, he recognized some new thought had come to her mind. "What?"

"Nothing."

"What is it?"

"It isn't anything. I just remembered you told me you were twenty-seven years old."

"That's right."

"But once I remember, just in passing, you mentioned you were born in nineteen forty-eight."

"Yeah?"

"Well, that's impossible . . . hey, what's the matter? You're going all gooseflesh."

As well, behind his rigid loins was a slab of pain. He pushed against her. The edge of the blanket, caught under them, rubbed across his shoulder as he rocked, till she tugged them free, and made a sound, caught his neck. He held his hips up, probing. She moved her hands down his back, pushed him down, thrust up her tongue under his. He made love taking great, gasping breath. She took many small ones. Wind wandered back and cooled his running shoulders.

After a laboring release, seething, he relaxed.

How jealous I am of those I have known afraid to sleep for dreaming. I fear those moments before sleep when words tear from the nervous matrix and, like sparks, light what responses they may. That fragmented vision, seductive with joy and terror, robs rest of itself. Gratefully, sunk in nightmare, where at least the anxious brain freed from knowing its own decay can flesh those skeletal epiphanies with visual and aural coherence, if not rationale: better those landscapes where terror is experienced as terror and rage as rage than this, where either is merely a pain in the gut or a throb above the eye, where a nerve spasm in the shin crumbles a city of bone, where a twitch in the eyelid detonates both the sun and the heart.

"What are you staring at?" Lanya asked.

"Huh? Nothing. I was just thinking."

Her hand moved on his chest. "About what?"

"About sleep . . . and I guess poetry. And being crazy."

She made a small sound that meant "go on."

"I don't know. I was remembering. Being a kid and things."

"That's good." She moved her hand, made that small sound again. "Go on . . ."

But with neither fear nor anguish, he felt he had nowhere to go.

He came out of sleep to lights and the stench of burning.

The luminous spider above him blinked off: the redhead lowered (and as he did, Kidd recognized him) one hand from the chains hanging to his belly. In the other, this time, was a slat from an orange crate.

An iridescent beetle disappeared from a sudden black face (also familiar) above a vinyl vest, shiny as his former carapace.

The arched pincers of a scorpion collapsed: "Hey," Nightmare said, "I think they're about awake."

Kidd's arms were around Lanya. She moved her face against his neck; then moved it again, sharper, deliberate now, conscious.

Two dozen scorpions (most were black) stood in a ring against the grey morning.

Kidd recognized Denny between one bony, brown shoulder and a fleshy black one.

Then the redhead swung his stick.

Lanya shouted—he felt her jerk against his shoulder. She also caught the end of the slat.

She got to her knees, still holding the stick, her eyes were wide; her cheek kept hollowing.

Kidd pushed up to his elbows.

The redhead started to move his end of the stick back and forth.

"Cut that shit, Copperhead." Nightmare hit the stick with his knuckles.

"I just wanted to make sure they were awake," the

343

redhead said. "That was all I want to do. That's all." He pulled the stick.

Lanya let go.

Nightmare squatted slowly before her, resting his wrists on his torn knees, with heavy hands, drooping between, balanced by muscle-builder forearms.

"Man," Lanya said, "if you're trying to scare hell out of us, you've about succeeded."

Kidd didn't feel scared.

Lanya, sitting back on her heels, held her left arm with her right hand, moving her thumb over the knob of her elbow.

Kidd pushed the blanket from his legs and sat up cross-legged.

Naked in the chained circle, he figured, was better than half covered.

"I got better things to do than scare you, Lady. I just wanna talk."

She took a breath, waiting.

"How's he doin'?" Nightmare bobbed his head toward Kidd.

"What?"

"You doin' pretty well with him?"

"Say what you want to say," she said, and touched Kidd's knee. She was scared; her fingers were icy.

Nightmare's forehead, large pores and heavy creases, creased more. "The other one. You got rid of the other one, huh? That's good." He nodded.

"Phil . . . ?"

"I didn't have much use for . . . Phil? That was his name, huh?" Nightmare's smile moved his lips more to the side then it curved them. "Guess you didn't either. So you don't have to worry now. What about it? I asked you before." Suddenly he ducked his head and, from his thick neck—the half-braided hair falling from it—lifted a loop of chain.

It wasn't the optical one.

Reaching forward, Nightmare placed it around Lanya's neck. His fists hung from it like clock weights. The half-inch links creased her breasts at the nipples. One fist went up, one down.

"*Hey*, man . . ." Kidd said.

Copperhead flipped the stick against his hand, watching Kidd.

Kidd looked up: the leopard-freckled, bearded and

344

redheaded spade was taller and narrower than Nightmare and, for all Nightmare's barbell muscles, looked stronger.

Nightmare's fists stopped, one on Lanya's belly, one on her breast: he watched her.

She watched back, her jaw flexing. She took her hand from Kidd's knee, put both fists around the chain, up near her neck, and ran them down, so that her left one pushed Nightmare's high one away. "Take it off," she said. "I told you once, I don't want it."

A thin, dark woman in the circle, bare breast pushing aside her vest flap and chains, shifted her weight. Someone else coughed.

"What about him?" Nightmare said and didn't look at Kidd. "What you gonna do when we take him? This one's comin' with us, Lady."

"What do you guys . . . ?" Kidd stopped. Anger, fascination, and a third feeling he couldn't name braided together from his brain base into his belly and below.

"Take it off," Lanya said. "I don't want it."

"Why?"

"I just want to stick to my guns. I don't that often." Then she gave a funny laugh. "Beside, your costume designer's cruddy."

Nightmare snorted. A few people in the circle laughed too. "What about yours?" somebody else said. But Nightmare lifted the chain. Scraps of her hair fell from the links.

Then the scorpion swiveled, boot toes tearing grass. "Here." The chain went over Kidd's head. Nightmare's eyes were traced with coral. His vest had apparently come apart at one, scarred shoulder and was laced now with rawhide.

Nightmare began to pull the chain.

Cold links slid down Kidd's right nipple. Nightmare's fist came up against his left breast, warm and rough. "Okay?" Nightmare squinted. There was something wrong with his eyes' focus, Kidd realized, irrelevantly.

"What am I supposed to do with it?" Kidd said. "What is all this supposed to mean?"

"Don't mean nothin'." Nightmare let go. "You can take it and throw it in Holland Lake if you want." Then he rocked back and stood. "I'd keep it if I were you."

The circle broke.

Nightmare at their head, big shoulders rocking, big arms swinging, the scorpions filed away. A few glanced back. Ten feet off, a girl who could have been white or black, and a tall black boy began to laugh loudly. Then, as though inflated too fast to follow, an iguana ballooned luminously, translucent in the grey-light. Then a peacock. Then a spider. The scorpions wandered into the trees.

"What the fuck," Kidd asked, "was that about?" He felt his neck where there were three chains now: the optic, the projector, and this new one—the heaviest.

"Nightmare gets it in his head sometimes that he wants certain people . . ."

The timbre of her voice made him look.

". . . get certain people into his nest." Scrabbling in the blanket, she came up with her harmonica, put it down and scrabbled some more.

"He wanted you before, huh? What's with Phil?"

"I told you, he was my boy friend for a while before I met you."

"What was he like?"

"He was a black guy, sort of bright; sort of nice, sort of square. He was here checking out scenes, about like you are . . ." Her voice muffled for the last words. He looked again: her head was coming out the top of her shirt while she tugged the bottom down over her shaking breasts. "He couldn't really make Calkins' thing that well. He couldn't make Nightmare's either."

The edge of the blanket was tented with the orchid beneath. Reaching for it, Kidd noticed nearly an acre of charred grass across the meadow. Smoke wisped along the edges. That hadn't been there. He frowned. It hadn't.

"People liked him down at the commune, I guess. But he was one of those people you get tired of pretty quick." He heard the fly of her jeans rasp. "Nightmare's funny. It's sweet of him to ask, I suppose, but I'm just not the joining kind. With anyone."

Kidd slid his hand into the orchid's harness, clicked it closed. The burning smell was very strong. He spread his chewed and enlarged knuckles, flexed his scarred and blunted fingers—

—tickling his shoulder.

He sprang up, whirling, and crouched.

The leaf rolled down his shoulder fluttered against his knee, spun on to the ground. Gasping, and with thudding heart, he looked up the leaning trunk, over the great bole at the stump of some thick, major branch, at bare

346

branches and branches hung with ragged tan, at crossed twigs like shatter lines on the sky.

Moisture sprung on his body and he grew cold.

"Lanya . . . ?"

He looked around at the clearing, and then back at the blanket. She hadn't had time to put her sneakers on!

But her sneakers were gone.

He circled the tree, frowning, looking out at the charred grass and the other trees, looking back at this one.

With orchid and chains, he was suddenly far more aware of his nakedness than when he had awakened with Lanya at the center of the scorpion ring.

She's gone back down to the commune, he thought. But why off just like that? He tried to recall the funny quality that had been in her voice. Anger? But that's silly. He touched the chain Nightmare had placed around his neck. That's silly.

But he stood there a long time.

Then—and his whole body moved with a different rhythm now—he stepped toward the tree, stepped again; stepped a third time, and the side of his foot pressed a root. He leaned forward, his knee against the bark, his thigh, his belly, his chest, his cheek. He closed his eyes and stretched his chained arm high as he could and pressed his fingers on the trunk. He breathed deep for the woody smell and pushed his body into the leaning curve. Bark was rough against the juncture at penis and scrotum, rough on the bone of his ankle, the back of his jaw.

Water was running out the corners of both his eyes. He opened them slightly, but closed them quickly against distortions.

With his weaponed hand—the urge came and went, like a flash bulb's pulsing after-image, to jam the orchid pholem deep—gently he moved his blades across the bark. Turning his hand this way and that; listening to the variated raspings, again and again he stroked the tree.

When he pushed away, the bark clung to his chest hair, his crotch hair. His ankle stung. So did his jaw. He rubbed his palm across his face to feel the mottled imprint; could see it along the flesh of his inner arm, stopping at the loops of chain to continue on the other side.

He went back to the blanket and pulled his vest from the folds. His feelings sat oddly between embarrassment

347

and the greatest relief. Unused to either, the juxtaposition confused him. Still wondering where she'd gone, he pulled up his pants, then sat to strap on (wondering why he still bothered) his one sandal.

He began to search the blanket. He looked under the folds, lifted it to see beneath, frowned and finally searched the whole area.

After fifteen frustrating minutes, he gave up and started down the slope. It was only when he reached the door of the park rest rooms (it had been locked before but someone had broken it open so that the hasp still dangled by one screw) he remembered he had already given the notebook, last night, to Newboy.

3

The pipes yowled, started to knock.

A trickle spilled the porcelain, crawled like a glass worm through the light lozenges from the window high in the concrete. He put his orchid in the next sink and scrubbed hard at his hands, wrists, and forearms, then bent to drink. He washed some more till his bladder warmed.

He urinated into the drain in the middle of the floor. Under his stream the loose grate chattered.

At the sink he wet his fists and ground them in his armpits. Again and again he wiped his neck. He filled his cupped hands, sloshed his face, and cupped them to fill again. Bark crumbs flecked him, neck to knee. He brushed them, rubbed them, washed them away. (Pants and vest were across another sink.) He put his foot in the bowl. Water ran between the ligaments. He rubbed; the porcelain streaked black and grey. Laboriously, fingers tingling, he washed away all the dirt except what callous had taken permanently. He wet and rubbed his legs to the thigh, then began the other foot. With dripping hands he kneaded his genitals; they shriveled at cold water.

Once the trickle gave out.

A minute later, the pipes recommenced yowling. The stream, slightly stronger, started once more.

Water gathered in the hair behind his testicles, dribbled his legs. He ran his hands over his head. His hair was greasy. With his hand's edge, he squeegeed as much as possible from arms, legs, and sides. The muddy puddle where he stood reached the drain: plonk-plonk, plonk-plonk, plonk-plonk.

Someone around in the stalls coughed.

The labored ablutions had dissolved all verbal thought. But his brain was super-saturated with the stuff of thinking. The cough—repeated, and followed by a clearing throat—set thought forming.

Someone very old and ill?

He used his left pant leg to blot dry groin, belly, and back. He dressed, put the orchid in his belt, and even went outside to walk his feet dry. He put on his sandal, came back in—he had made a mess, he realized—and went around the dividing wall hiding the johns.

Not old, the guy certainly looked sick.

Cowboy boots, turned in, rested on their sides. One sole, pulled free, showed toes crusty as Kidd's own before washing. Sitting on the toilet ring, head against the empty paper dispenser, face strung with ropey hair, bare ribs and wrinkled belly hung with chain—among them a spherical shield projector. "You okay?" Kidd asked. "You look like you're—"

"Unnnn. . . ." The white scorpion moved his head and, though he sat both feet on the floor, swayed like a drunken cyclist on a high wire. "Naw. Naw, I'm not sick . . ." The long nose cut the shaking hair. Beside the nose a rimmed eye blinked its purple lid. "Who . . . who you?"

"Who're you?" Kidd countered.

"Pepper. I'm Pepper. I ain't sick." He put his head back against the dispenser. "I just don't feel well."

Kidd felt a small, sharp sadness; as well, an urge to laugh. "What's the matter?"

Pepper suddenly shook the hair from his eyes and was almost still. "Who you run with?"

Kidd frowned.

"Ain't you a scorpion?" Pepper gestured with a hand whose nails were graphite spikes. "Guess you run with Dragon Lady."

"I don't run," Kidd said. "With anybody."

Pepper squinted. "I used to be with Nightmare's nest." The squint became curious. "You with Dragon Lady now? What did you say your name was?"

On a ludicrous impulse, Kidd stuck his thumb in his pocket, put his weight on one hip. "Some people been calling me the Kid."

Pepper's head went back the other way. Then he laughed. "Hey, I heard of you." His gums were rimmed with rot and silver. "Yeah, Nightmare, he said something about the Kid. He was talkin' to Dragon Lady when she

350

was over. I heard 'em talking. Yeah." His laugh broke; he laid his head back against the wall and moaned. "I don't feel real well."

"What'd you hear?" Within surprise, Kid (Kidd decided) reflected on the smallness of the city.

Pepper raised only his eyes; "Nightmare," and lowered them. "He told her you was around, that he thought you was . . ." He coughed: the sound, weak, still tore things inside. His hands, upturned, shook on his thighs, shook when he coughed: ". . . till she went away."

Which made fairly little sense; so he asked: "You been in here all night?"

Cough. "Well, I ain't gonna stay out *there* in the dark!" Pepper's hand gathered enough strength to indicate the doorway.

"You can find yourself a clump of brush, get inside where nobody can see. It's pretty warm out, and it's more comfortable than sleeping on the can. Get yourself a blanket for the night—"

"Man, there're *things* out there." At first Pepper's face seemed seized with pain. But he was just squinting. "That's what you do, huh? Yeah, you must be pretty brave. Like Nightmare told her."

Which made equally little sense. "How come you're not with Nightmare? I saw him this morning, with his gang. Dragon Lady wasn't with him."

"Naw," Pepper said. "Naw, she ain't gonna be with him now. They had a fight, see. Oh, Jesus, was that one bloody garden party!" This time Pepper's "pain" was memory.

"What was it about?" Kid asked.

Pepper's head came forward, hair strings swinging. "You see those scars on Nightmare's shoulder? You seen them scars?" He tried to nod. "Oh, I guess it's blown over now, and they almost friendly. But she got her own nest again, somewhere over in Jackson I heard. And they ain't gonna be together too much any more, I don't think." His head fell back, and he repeated: "I ain't feeling too well."

"What's the matter with you?"

"I dunno. Maybe I ate something bad. Or I got a cold maybe."

"Well, does it hurt in your stomach, or is your head stopped up?"

"I told you, I don't know why."

351

"What hurts?"

Pepper shook back hair and sat up again. "How can I tell you what hurts till I know what's wrong?"

"How can anybody know what's wrong till you say what—"

Pepper lurched upright.

Kid started to catch him.

But Pepper didn't fall. Scrubbing at his face with his fist and snuffling, he said, "I been staying with Bunny, but I think she threw me out. Maybe we better go back there and find out, huh?" He let go of the side of the stall. "I think I'm feeling a little better. You know Bunny?"

"I don't think so."

"She dances over in that freak joint, *Teddy's.*"

"You mean the little silver-haired guy?"

"She's pretty together. A nut. But together." Pepper lurched forward. "I wish I had a God-damn drink of water."

"Come on around to the sink."

Pepper passed unsteadily, staggered around the partition.

Kid followed.

Pepper spun one of the taps and jerked his hand back when the pipes began their complaint. ". . . nothing's coming out," he ventured.

"Give it a second."

When the trickle had gone on half a minute, Pepper grimaced. "Shit, that ain't big enough to drink." He turned again and staggered for the door. "God *damn* I wish I had some water."

Kid, in amused frustration, turned off the tap and went out. Pepper was wandering up the slope.

Kid watched for a few steps, then turned down toward the commune.

"Hey!"

He looked back. "What?"

"Ain't you coming with me?"

His amusement diminished to minuscule. "No." Minuscule, it still made him wait Pepper's reaction.

"Hey, then." Pepper returned, his stagger now loosened to a bow-legged jounce. "Maybe I better come on with *you,* huh?"

Kid started walking: *Not* the reaction he'd wanted.

Pepper caught up. "Look, we go where you going, then we go where I'm going, huh? That's fair."

"There's a water fountain."

"Naw, naw, man! You're in a rush. I don't wanna hold you up none."

Kid sighed, came to a decision, and bellowed, "GET THE FUCK OUT OF HERE!"

Pepper stopped, blinking.

Kid took a breath and walked on, shaking his head. I don't like to yell at people, he thought. And then, smiling: That isn't true—I just don't get much chance.

He came to the trees at the edge of the clearing.

The cinderblocks on the near side of the fireplace had been pushed over. Smoke dribbled into the air. Ashes greyed the grass.

There were no people.

Ten feet from the picnic table lay the torn sleeping bag that nobody used because somebody had been sick in it one night and fouled it with puke and diarrhea.

Puzzled, he walked to the furnace, between tin cans and package wrappers. (On the picnic bench, someone had overturned a carton of garbage.) With his sandal, he scraped away cinders. Half a dozen coals turned up red spots, which pulsed, wavered and went out.

"Lanya?"

He turned, waiting, for her answer, uncomfortable at any noise in this ringed, misty clearing. Even at the height of the project period, there were usually half a dozen people at the fire. A torn blanket lay under the bench—but it had been there all week. The sleeping bags and blanket rolls usually piled haphazard by trees and behind the firewood were gone.

"Lanya!"

A decision to move? But she would have known about that and told him. Save for the overturned cinderblocks of the furnace wall, there were no marks of violence; only junk and disorder. He had come here with her to eat . . . how many times? He had been quiet and observed his own measured politeness. Momentarily he fantasized that his reserve and preoccupation had been so unbearable to them that they had all, with Lanya cooperating, schemed to abandon him, suddenly and silently. He would have pondered it more than a moment had the idea not urged him to giggle; frowning still seemed more appropriate.

"Lanya?"

He turned to squint among the trees.

When the figure hiding in the brush realized it had

353

been seen, it—it was Pepper—stepped hesitantly forward. "You're looking for somebody down here, hey?" Pepper craned to look left, then right. "I guess they all gone away, you know?"

Kid sucked his teeth and scanned the clearing again, while Pepper judged distances.

"I wonder why they all went away, huh?" Pepper stepped nearer.

Kid's annoyance with Pepper's presence was absorbed in his discomfort at Lanya's absence. He hadn't been that long washing. Wouldn't she have waited—?

"Where you think they all went?" Pepper advanced another step.

"Well if you don't know, *you're* no use."

Pepper's laugh was hoarse, light, and infirm as his cough. "Why don't you come on with me to Bunny's? She lives right behind the bar. I mean, if you can't find your friend down here. Get something to eat. She don't mind none if I bring friends over. She says she likes them long as they're nice, you know? You ever seen Bunny dance?"

"A couple of times." Kid thought: She might have gone over to the bar.

"I never have. But she's supposed to be good, huh? All sorts of weird people hang out in that place. I'm scared to go in."

"Come on." Kid looked once more: And she was not there. "Let's go."

"You coming? Good!" Pepper followed him for a dozen steps. Then he said, "Hey."

"What?"

"It's shorter if we go this way."

Kid stopped. "You say Bunny lives right behind *Teddy's?*"

"Uh-huh." Pepper nodded. "This way, through here."

"Okay. If you say so."

"It's a lot shorter," Pepper said. "A whole lot. It really is." He started, still stiff-legged, into the trees.

Kid followed, doubtful.

He was surprised how soon they reached the park wall; it was just over a hill of trees. The path down to the lion gate must have been more curvy than he'd thought.

Pepper scrambled up the wall, wheezing and grimacing. "You know," he panted from the far side as Kid crouched to vault, "Bunny is a guy, you know? But she likes to be called 'she'."

Kid sprang, one hand on the stone. "Yeah, yeah, I know all about it."

Pepper stepped back as Kid landed on the pavement. "You know," he said, as Kid bounced up right, "you're like Nightmare."

"How?"

"He yells a lot. But he don't mean it."

"I'm not gonna yell at you again," Kid said. "I may break your head. But I'm not gonna yell."

Pepper grinned. "Come on this way."

They crossed the empty street.

"You meet a new person, you go with him," Kid mused, "and suddenly you get a whole new city." He'd offered it as a small and oblique compliment.

Pepper only glanced at him, curiously.

"You go down new streets, you see houses you never saw before, pass places you didn't know were there. Everything changes."

"This way." Pepper ducked between buildings not two feet apart.

They sidled between the flaking boards. The ground was a-glitter from the broken windows.

Pepper said, "Sometimes it changes even if you go the same way."

Kid recalled conversations with Tak, but decided not to question Pepper further, who didn't seem too good with abstractions. In the alley, Kid stopped to brush the glass off his bare foot.

"You okay?" Pepper asked.

"Callous like a rock."

They walked between the gaping garages. A blue car—'75 Olds?—had been driven through a back wall: snapped boards and sagging beams, scattered glass, skid marks across the roadway. The car was impaled in broken wood to its dangling door. Who, Kid wondered, had been injured in the wreck, who had been injured in the house? Hanging over the sill of another smashed window was a blue telephone receiver—hurled out in fear or fury? Accidentally dropped or jarred?

"Uhn." Pepper gestured with his chin toward an open door.

As they walked the dark corridor, Kid smelled traces of something organic and decayed, which was about to

355

remind him of—when he remembered what, they had already come out on the porch.

Somebody in workman's greens and orange construction boots, on a high ladder against the corner lamp post—it was a woman he had noticed his first night in the bar—was unscrewing the street sign.

Metal ground metal; HAYES ST came out of its holder. From the ladder top she picked up 23RD AVE, inserted it, and began to screw the bolts.

"Hey?" Kid was both amused and curious. "Which one of those is right?"

She frowned back over her shoulder. "Neither one, honey, far as I know."

But Pepper was crossing toward the unmarked, familiar door. Kid followed, looking around the street, estranged by smoky daylight. "I don't think I've ever been here this time of day before."

Pepper just grunted.

The door they entered was two from the bar entrance.

At the top of the steps, Pepper blocked the cracks of light and thumped with the back of his hand.

"All right, all right. Just a second, dear. It isn't the end of the world—" the door swung in—"yet." Around Bunny's thin neck a white silk scarf was held by a silver napkin ring. "And if it is, I certainly don't want to hear about it at this hour of the morning. Oh, it's you."

"Hi!" Pepper's voice mustered brightness and enthusiasm. "This is a friend of mine, the Kid."

Bunny stepped back.

As Kid walked in, Bunny pointed a knuckly, manicured finger at Pepper. "It's his teeth, actually."

Pepper gave his stained and pitted grin.

"Peking Man—do you know about Peking Man? Peking Man *died* of an ulcerated tooth." Bunny brushed back bleached, silken hair. "Show me a boy with bad teeth and I just feel so sorry for him, that I—well, I'm not responsible. Pepper, darling, *where* have you been?"

"Jesus, I'm thirsty," Pepper said. "You got something to drink? You couldn't get a God-damn drink of water in the God-damn park."

"On the sideboard, dear. It hasn't moved."

Pepper poured wine from a jug with an ornate label first into a handle-less cup, then a jelly jar.

"Have *you* any idea where he was? I know *he's*
356

not going to tell me." Bunny dodged while Pepper handed Kidd the jar.

"You get the glass 'cause you're company."

"You could have poured one for me too, dear. But you're famous for not thinking of things like that."

"Jesus Christ, sweetheart, I thought you had one already working. I really did." But Pepper made no move to pour another.

Bunny raised exasperated eyebrows and went to get a cup.

Pepper doffed his. "You don't tell her where I was. That's for me to know and her to find out." He finished his wine and went for seconds. "Go on, have a seat. Sit down. Bunny, did you throw me out of here last night?"

"The way you were carrying on, doll, I should have." Bunny ducked under Pepper's elbow and, cup on finger tips, returned. "But I didn't get a chance. Have you ever noticed that about people who are dumb in a particular way? In-*sen*-si-tive—" Bunny's eyes closed on the antepenultimate— "to everything. Except one second before catastrophe: Then they split. Oh, they know when *that's* coming all right. I guess they have to. Otherwise they'd be dead. Or missing an arm, or a head, or something." Bunny's eyes narrowed at Pepper (who, on his third cup already, turned to the room, a little more relaxed). "Darling, I could have killed you last night. I could have committed murder. Did I throw you out? If I did, you wouldn't be here now. But I'm calmer today."

Kid decided not to ask what Pepper had done.

"Go on," Pepper said. "Sit down. On the couch. That's where I sleep, so it's okay. She sleeps in there."

"My boudoir." Bunny gestured toward another room, where Kid could see a mirror and a dressing table with bottles and jars. "Pepper's very eager to clear that up with all his new friends. Yes, do have a seat."

Kid sat.

"Oh, there've been a *few* times—but you were probably too high to remember those—when you've turned into quite a tiger. Pepper, darling, you shouldn't be so *concerned* about what other people think."

"If I cared what he thought, I wouldn't 'a brung him in here," Pepper said. "You want some more wine, Kid, just take it. Bunny don't mind."

"Actually—" Bunny stepped back into the boudoir

357

door—"Pepper is a part of that tragic phenomenon, the Great American Un-screwed. A lot of talk about how much he *wants* to, but if you want my opinion, I don't think Pepper has gone to bed with anything in all his twenty-nine years that didn't just roll him over in his sleep. And God forbid he wake up!"

"I don't talk about doin' anybody I ain't never done," Pepper said, "which is more'n I can say for you. Why don't you lay off?"

From the couch, Kid said: "I just came around to see if somebody was in Teddy's. I want to—"

"Well, take a look, if you like." Bunny unblocked the door. "But I doubt it. In here. Where you can see."

Wondering, Kid got up and walked past Bunny into the second room. Though nothing was out of place, it gave the impression—with three chairs, a bed, a dozen pictures on the wall, from magazines (but all framed)—of clutter. Oranges, reds, purples, and blues massed in the bedspread. Yellow plastic flowers hung over the back of a pink ceramic dove. Interrupting the floral wallpaper was a black curtain.

"In there."

Kid stepped around a grubby, white vinyl hassock (everything had speckles of silver glitter on it) and pushed back black velvet.

Through cage bars, he saw upturned stools clustering the counter. Under a skylight he had never noticed before—this *was* the first time he had seen the place during the day—the empty booths and tables looked far more rickety: the whole room seemed larger and shabbier.

"Is the bartender there?" Bunny asked.

"No."

"Then they aren't even open."

Kid dropped the curtain.

"Isn't that convenient? I just run right out there and do my thing, then run right back in here, and am shut of you all. Come on back inside. Don't run away." Bunny motioned Kid into the living room. "I really think scorpions are perfectly fascinating. You're the only really effective enforcement organization in the city. Pepper, what was the name of your friend with all the ugly muscles and that lovely, broken . . . ?" Bunny nudged his upper lip with his forefinger ". . . This one here?"

"Nightmare."

"Fascinating boy." Bunny glanced at Kid. "He's old

358

as I am, dear, but I still consider him very young. (Really, you must sit down. I'm the only one who's allowed to wander around and make everyone nervous.) You scorpions do more to keep law and order in the city than anyone else. Only the good and the pure in heart dare go out on the street after dark. But that's the way, I suppose, the law has always worked. The good people are the ones who live their lives so that they don't have anything to do with whatever law there is anyway. The bad ones are the ones unfortunate enough to become involved. I rather like the way it works here, because, since you *are* the law, the law is far more violent, makes much more noise, and isn't everywhere at once: so it's easier for us good people to avoid. Are you sure you wouldn't like some more wine—?"

"I told him to get it when he wants it."

"*I'll* get it for him, Pepper. You may not be a gentleman, but *I* am a lady." Bunny plucked the jar from Kid's hands and went to fill it and another cup. "Just an old-fashioned girl, too shy to dive into the rushing river of worldly fame, too late for the mouse-drawn pumpkin to take me to the ball, too old for Gay Lib—not to mention Radical Effeminism!" Bunny couldn't have been more than thirty-five, Kid thought. "Not in body, mind you. Just in spirit. Ah, well . . . I have the consolations of philosophy —or whatever the hell you call it."

Kid sat down on the couch beside Pepper.

Bunny returned with the brimming jelly glass. "When you let your little light shine, what great and luminous beast do you become?"

"I'm not a scorpion."

"You mean you just like to dress up that way? And wear a shield around your neck? Mmmm?"

"Somebody gave me these clothes when I got my others messed up." Kid took the jar and picked up his projector at the end of its chain. "This doesn't have a battery or something. I just found it."

"Ah, then you're not really a scorpion *yet*. Like Pepper, right? Pepper *used* to be a scorpion. But his battery's run down."

"I guess that's what it is." Pepper rattled the links of his shield among his other chains. "I gotta get hold of another one and see."

"Pepper used to be the most charming bird of paradise. Red, yellow, and green plumes—one could almost

359

ignore its relation to the common parrot. Then he began to flicker, more and more, splutter, grow dim. Finally—" Bunny's eyes closed—"he went totally out." They opened. "He hasn't been the same since."

"Where could you pick up one? A battery, I mean."

"Radio store," Pepper said. "Only the guys have about stripped all the places around here. A department store, maybe. Or maybe somebody's got an extra one. Nightmare's got a lot, I bet."

"How exciting, to anticipate your glowing aspect, to puzzle over what you'll turn out to be."

"Inside here—" Pepper snapped his shield apart— "they got a little thing in here that's supposed to be what it is. But it just looks like a whole lot of colored dots to me. The battery goes in there." He picked at the mechanism with a grey nail—"This one . . ."—and pried loose a red and white striped oblong with blue lettering: *26½ Volts D. C.*, below a colophon of gathered lightning. "This one ain't worth shit." He flipped it across the room.

"Not on the floor, Pepper love." Bunny picked up the battery and put it on a shelf behind some porcelain frogs, vases of colored glass, and several alarm clocks. "Tell me, Kid, now that you've found *me,* just who *were* you looking for?"

"A girl. Lanya. You know her: You spoke to her one night in the bar when George Harrison was there."

"Oh, yes: She-who-must-be-obeyed. And you were with her. Now I *do* remember you. That was the night they made George the new moon, wasn't it? The way that poor man has driven all those silly dinge-queens out of their flippy little minds is just *terrible!"*

Kid turned his jar. "He has a pretty heavy fan club."

"More power to him, I say." Bunny raised the cup overhead. "But if George is the New Moon, darling, *I* am the Evening Star."

Pepper loosed his consumptive giggle.

"I want to go out and look for her," Kid said. "If she comes into Teddy's after it opens, will you give her a message for—"

"'I can't think of any reason why I should. She has a *much* easier time getting hers than I do getting mine. What do you want me to tell her?"

"Huh? Just that I was around looking for her, and that I'll be back."

360

"Smile."

"What?"

"Grin. Like this." Bunny's bony face became a death mask around bright, perfect teeth. "Let's see an expression of ecstatic happiness."

Kid twisted his lips back quickly and decided this was his last politeness.

To Kid's leer, Bunny returned a wistful grin. "You just don't seem to have any special points of attraction. Actually, I'd put you rather low down on my list. It's completely personal, you understand. I suppose I can afford to tell your girl friend you're looking for her. I will if I see her."

"Everybody's somebody's fetish," Kid said. "Maybe I still got hope?"

"*That's* what I keep telling Pepper. But he just won't believe me."

"I believe it." Pepper said from his end of the couch. "You just won't believe you ain't mine."

"Oh, I don't think I'm revealing any embarrassing secrets when I say that you can be very sweet and affectionate once you relax. No, Pepper is just terribly uncomfortable at the idea that anyone could find *him* attractive. It's that simple."

"It ain't happened that often so I'm what you'd call used to it." Pepper squinted into the bottom of his cup, rocked up to his feet, and walked to the counter. He gave Bunny a passing nudge on the arm with his elbow. "Bunny's a good guy, but she's a nut."

"Ow!" Bunny rubbed the spot, but grinned after Pepper.

Kid grinned too and tried not to shake his head.

"Why are you two here now, anyway?" Bunny asked. "What are the scorpions doing today? Shouldn't you be out working?"

"You trying to kick me out again?" Pepper stooped to open a cabinet and took out another jug which he put on the counter beside the one now empty.

Kid saw four more gallons and decided to leave after this glass. "Where was Nightmare's gang off to this morning?"

"You said you saw them. How many were there?"

"Twenty, twenty-five maybe," Kid said.

"Maybe he's gonna pull that Emboriky rip-off today. How you like that?"

361

"Oh, *no!*" Bunny put the cup down—"Oh well."—then picked it up again, to sip pensively.

"He's been talking about it for a month, but he wants a whole damn army."

"Why's he need so many people?" Kid asked. "What's Emboriky?"

"Big downtown department store."

"Lovely things," Bunny said sadly. "Perfectly lovely things. I mean it isn't just your run of the mill five-and-dime. I just wish I could have some of their stuff in here. Give some class to this place. Oh, I hate to think of you guys clomping around in all that beautiful stuff."

"Nobody's gotten to it before?"

"Guess not," Pepper said.

"Maybe just a little," Bunny explained. "But you see, now it's 'occupied.' Some kid got killed back a little while ago trying to break in."

"Killed?"

"Somebody leaned out the third-story window," Pepper said, "and shot the mother-fucker dead." He laughed. "A couple of other people got shot at, who were just passing by. But they didn't get hurt."

"Perhaps it's Mr Emboriky, protecting his worldly goods." Bunny contemplated the cup bottom, looked over at the fresh gallon, but thought better. "I wouldn't blame him."

"Naw, naw," Pepper said. "It's a whole bunch in there. Nightmare's one of the people who got shot at. He said shots came from lots of places."

Bunny laughed. "Imagine! Two dozen sales clerks valiantly holding off the barbarian hordes! I hope those poor children don't get hurt."

"You think it's the sales clerks?" Pepper asked.

"No." Bunny sighed. "It's just whoever got to the Gun Department in Sporting Goods first."

"Nightmare's got this real thing about it. He really wants to get in there and see what's going on. I guess I would too if somebody'd shot at me out the third-story window."

"*You?*" Bunny exploded at the ceiling. "You'd be back here with your head under the pillow so fast! Why aren't you out there with them now? No, no, that's all right. I'd rather have you here safe and sound. If you got your ass full of buckshot, I just know it would be for something stupid."

"I think getting your ass full of buckshot is pretty stupid for any reason."

"Fine!" Bunny pointed an admonishing finger. "You just stick to that idea and keep momma happy. *One* honorable man!" Bunny's hand returned to the cup. "Yea, even for the want of one honorable man. Or woman— I'm not prejudiced. That's really what Bellona needs." Bunny regarded Kid. "You look like a sensitive sort. Haven't you ever thought that? Lord knows, we have everything else. Wouldn't it be nice to know that somewhere around there was one good and upright individual —one would do, for contrast."

"Well, we've got Calkins," Kid said. "He's a pillar of the community."

Bunny grimaced. "Darling, he *owns* that den of iniquity in there where I display my pale and supple body every evening. Teddy just runs it. No, Mr C won't pass, I'm afraid."

"You got that church person," Pepper offered.

"Reverend Amy?" Bunny grimaced again. "No, dear, she's sweet, in her own strange way. But that's absolutely *not* what I mean. That's the wrong feeling entirely."

"Not *that* church," Pepper countered. "The *other* one, over on the other side of the city."

"You mean the monastery?" Bunny was pensive as Pepper nodded. "I really don't know that much about it. Which speaks well for it, I'm sure."

"Yeah, someone mentioned that to me once," Kid said, and remembered it was Lanya.

"It would be nice to think that, somewhere inside its walls, a truly good person walked and pondered. Can you *imagine* it? Within the city limits? Perhaps the abbot or the mother superior or whatever they call it? Meanwhile the scorpions play down at the Emboriky."

"Maybe if you went to the monastery, somebody'd shoot at you too."

"How sad," Bunny looked at the jug again. "How probable. That wouldn't make me happy at all."

"Where is this place?" Kid asked; with the memory occurred the fantasy that Lanya, with her curiosity about it, might have gone there.

"I don't actually know," Bunny said. "Like everything else in town, you just hear about it until it bumps into you. You have to put yourself at the mercy of the geography, and hope that down-hills and up-hills, work-

363

ing propitiously with how much you feel like fighting and how much you feel like accepting, manage to get you there. You'll find it eventually. As we are all so tired of hearing, this is a terribly small city."

"I heard it's on the other side of town," Pepper said. "Only I don't even know which side of town this is."

Kid laughed and stood up. "Well, I'm gonna go." He drained the wine, and tongued the bitter aftertaste. Wine first thing in the morning, he pondered. Well, he'd done worse. "Thanks for breakfast."

"You're going to *go?* But honey, I have enough in here for brunch, lunch, high tea, and *dinner!*"

"Come on," Pepper said. "Take another glass. Bunny don't mind the company."

"Sorry." Kid moved his jar from Bunny's reach. "Thanks." He smiled. "I'll come back another time."

"I'll only let you go if you promise me." Bunny suddenly reached for Kid's chest. "No, no, don't jump. Mother's not going to rape you." Bunny put a finger beneath the chain that crossed Kid's belly. "We have something in common, you and I." With the other hand, Bunny lifted the white silk to show the optical chain around a slim, veined neck. "Nightmare and I. Madame Brown and Nightmare. You and Madame Brown. I wonder if I betray it by mentioning it." Bunny laughed.

Kid, unsure why, felt his cheeks heat and the rest of his body cool. I can't have absorbed the custom of reticence so completely in so little time, he thought. And still wanted anxiously and urgently to leave.

Bunny was saying, "I'll tell your girl friend what you said if I see her. You know even if you did have one of those . . . ahem, smiles I find just too irresistible, I'd still deliver your message. Because then, you see, I'd want you to like me, and to come back. Doing something you wanted me to do would be one way to get that. Just because I'm not a good person—" Bunny winked—"you mustn't think I'm a bad one."

"Yeah. Sure. Thanks." Kid tugged away from Bunny's finger. "I'll see you."

"Good-bye!" Pepper called from the counter where he'd gone for more wine.

Now the street sign said FILBERT and PEARL.
The ladder and the lady in greens were gone.

364

He pondered and compared directions, dismissed the park, looked where the mist was thickest (down "Pearl"), and walked. Lanya? remembered his calling, an echo in the dim, an after image on the ear. Here? In this city? He smiled, and thought about holding her. He sorted his dubious recollections, wondering where he was going. It's only, he thought, when we're stripped of purpose that we know who we are.

His missing name was a sudden ache and, suddenly, he wanted it, wanted it with the same urge that had made him finally accept the one Tak had given. Without it he could search, survive, make word convections in somebody else's notebook, commit fanciful murder, strive for someone else's survival. With it, just walking, just being might be easier. A name, he thought, is what other people call you. And that's exactly where it's important and where it's not. The Kid? He thought: I'm going to be thirty in a mouthful of winter and sun. How unimportant then that I can't remember it. How important what my not being able to remember it means. Maybe I'm somebody famous? No, I do remember too well what I've done. I wish I felt cut off, alone, an isolate society of one, like everybody else. Alienation? That isn't what it's about. I'm too used to being liked.

Damn! He wished he had his notebook; but before the feeling, as he listened, no word rose to begin the complex fixing. Fingering the blades at his waist, hearing, not feeling, an edge rasp his calloused thumb, he turned another corner.

Car motors were so unfamiliar that he was frightened, until he actually saw the bus. It hauled itself around the corner and into the whitewashed stop-markings. *Clap-clap,* the doors. He looked at the balding driver squinting out the windshield as if for traffic.

Why not, he thought, and climbed the worn rubber steps.

"You got a transfer?"

"Hey, I'm sorry. If you need fare or something—" He stepped back.

But the driver motioned him on. "This is a transfer point. I thought you had a transfer, maybe. Come on." *Clap-clap:* the bus rocked forward.

An old man slept in the back seat, hat down, collar up.

A woman in the front sat with her hands crossed on

365

the top of her pocketbook. A younger woman with a large natural stared out the window. A boy with a smaller one sat nervously just behind the back door, toeing one sneaker with the other.

A couple—he with knees wide, sunk in the seat with his arms folded, his face set belligerently, she with legs together, her face registering something between fear and boredom—were making a point of not looking at him.

Simultaneously he realized that there was no seat from which he could watch everybody, and that he was the only non-black on the bus. He decided to give up the old man and took the next to the last seat.

Where am I—but wouldn't think: going? He looked over the bars on the seat backs to the blunt nose and lips, the sharp chin, profiled below the brillowy ball.

He watched the buildings she watched go headlong in goalless motion.

She blinked.

He was only nervous at the turnings, and had to quell the absurd impulse to go ask the driver where the bus was headed. The headlong, with its implication of easy return, was safe. The bus turned again, and he tried to enjoy being lost: but they were going parallel to their first route.

They passed a deserted street construction. Only one of the saw-horses had been broken. But from a truck with a flat tire, coils of cable had spilled the pavement.

He let his stomach untense, marveling that these disaster remnants still excited.

After the smashed plate glass of an army-navy surplus store came movie marquees: no letters at all on the first, a single R on the second; the one line on the next, he had time to reconstruct was "Three Stars says the Times." On the next R, O, and T were stacked on top of one another; E, Q, and U were followed by a space of three letters and then a Y. Contemplating messages, he fingered for the spiral wire of his notebook, but only bumped his knuckle on blades.

On a billboard, some six by sixteen feet, George Harrison, naked, in near silhouette before a giant lunar disk, craned his head to search or howl or execrate the night. The black, only recognizable by a highlight here and there, stood at the left; the right of the poster was filled with night-time forest.

Kid turned half around in his seat to watch it, then turned back to the bus in time to see the others turn. He put his fists on the seat between his parted thighs, and leaned, grinning and hanging his neck from slung shoulders.

ECK N W'S

S R   OGS

ND

T E G TTA Y

announced the next marquee. He looked at broken store windows—in one was a pile of naked dummies. The street widened and once smoke rolled by so that he could make out no letters at all upon the final marquee of the strip.

Where am I going? he thought, thinking they were just words. Then the echoes came: his back chilled, his teeth clicked, then opened behind closed lips, staggered and jogged by the engine. He looked for shadows and found none in the dim bus, on the pale street. So searched what highlights his own body sensation cast in the nervous matrix. None there: in which to hunt a recollection of her face mottled and incomplete as though lit through leaves. He tried to laugh at his loss. Not because of this, oh no. It's the wine: Christ, he thought, where did they all go? The old man behind him moaned in his sleep.

He looked out the window.

Up the sand-colored wall, gold letters (he read it bottom-to-top first):

E
M
B
O
R
I
K
Y'
S

Only one show window was shattered: boards had been nailed across it. Two others were covered with canvas. A crack in another zagged edge to edge.

Kid pulled the frayed ceiling cord, then held on to the bar across the back of the seat before him till the bus, a block later and somewhat to his surprise, stopped. He jumped off the back treadle to the curb and turned; through the dirty window, he saw the couple who had not looked at him when he'd gotten on, stopped looking at him now. The bus left.

He was standing diagonally across from the five, six, seven, eight story department store. Uneasily, he backed into a doorway. (People with guns, hey?) He felt for his orchid—looked at it. It was a very silly weapon. People shooting out the windows? Several, higher up, were open. Several more were broken. Across the street a gutter grill waved a steamy plume. Why, he thought, get out here? Maybe the people in there have all gone and he could just cross the street and—the skin of his back and belly shriveled. Why *had* he gotten off here? It had been in response to some un-named embryo feeling, and he had leapt out of the bus, following it to term. But now it was born; and was terror.

Cross the street, mother-fucker, he told himself. You get up close to the building and they can't see you out the windows. This way somebody can just aim out and pick you off if they got a penchant for it. He told himself some other things too.

A minute later, he walked to the opposite corner, a sidestep for the fire hydrant, stopped with his hand against the beige stone, breathing long, slow breaths and listening to his heart. The building took up all the block. There were no show windows down the side alley. Save from the front door, there was no place from the store he could be seen. He looked across the avenue. (From what letters still remained on that broken glass, it must have been a travel agency. And down there . . . ? Some kind of office building, perhaps? Burn marks lapped great carbon tongues around the lower stories.) The street looked so wide—but that was because there were no cars at either curb.

He started down the alley, running his hand on the stone and occasionally glancing up for the imaginary gunman to lean out a window and blast straight down.

There's nobody in there, he thought.

There's nobody coming up behind me—

At the end of the block something—moved? No, it was a shadow between two parked trucks.

"Hey," somebody said directly across the alley in a voice just under normal. "What the fuck you think you doin', huh?"

He bruised his shoulder on the wall, then came away, rubbing it.

A thick shoulder pushed from behind a metal door across the alley. "Don't get excited." Half of Nightmare's face emerged. Kid could see half the mouth speaking: "But when I count three, you get your ass over here so fast I wanna see smoke. One. Two . . ." The visible eye rose to look somewhere up the department store wall, looked back down. "Three."

Nightmare caught Kid's arm, and the memory of traversed pavement was battered out by bruises on his back, knee, and jaw—"Hey, man, you don't have to—" as Nightmare snatched him through the quarter-opened doorway.

He was in four-fifths darkness with a lot of people breathing.

"God damn," Nightmare said. "I mean Jesus Christ."

He said, "You don't have to break my head," softer than he'd started to.

Somebody very black in a vinyl vest, laughed loudly. For a moment he thought it was Dragon Lady, but it was a man.

Nightmare made some disgusted sound. The laugh cut off.

Nightmare's scarred shoulder (it was the first thing Kid saw as his eyes cleared of the dark) hid half of Denny's face as the door had hidden half of Nightmare's. The other faces were darker. "You don't think so?" Nightmare still held Kid's arm. With his other hand, he grabbed Kid's hair—"Hey!"—and marched him around 180 degrees: Kid's face came up against wire, behind some dirty glass, and behind that was—

"Now look up there."

Kid focused outside the dirty window on the second story of the department store.

"You lookin' good?"

—was a window where gold letters arched: *New Fashions.* And behind them, a man, with a rifle in one hand, scratched his thin neck under the too large collar of his blue sports shirt, then ambled on.

"Now what—" with sweetness—"the hell are you

369

doing here?" Nightmare yanked Kid's head back from
the window before he let go. "Come on. Tell me now."

"I just—" pain sat in him blankly as anxiety—"was
coming by and—" Pain subsided.

"I should break your head open, you know?"

"Hey, man, you—"

"Shut up, Copperhead," Nightmare said.

The big, bearded, redhead spade leaned in the corner.
"—you don't have to do that," he finished. "I'll do it
for you, if you want." He nodded at Kid in damped
recognition. "Give 'im to me."

"Fuck off." Nightmare waved a peremptory fist.
"You just come by, huh? We been planning this three
months and you just come by?"

"Well, Pepper told me you guys were maybe down
here—"

Nightmare sucked some more. "We been *planning*—"

"I got him," Denny said. "Let him go with us. He
won't hurt nothing. I'll tell him what to do."

Nightmare glanced questioningly over his shoulder.

"Sure," Denny insisted.

In his corner, Copperhead turned his stick up behind
his arm.

"He can go with my group," Denny repeated. "He
won't get in the way."

Kid thought, unsure: Three against two.

Once more Nightmare flung round his fist; and
growled.

"Come on," Denny said. "You come with me."

"You don't let him mess up anything!" Nightmare
admonished with his chin.

"Yeah. The Kid'll be okay."

"He'd better be."

"He's a good guy, Nightmare. Come on, you said
he was a good guy yourself."

Nightmare growled once more.

Kid stepped by him, tried and failed not to look
at Copperhead. Copperhead blinked and started to smile.
Kid decided it was worth his life to fail at anything
among them again.

Denny clapped Kid's arm. "Let's go." He looked
around and, louder: "You guys, let's go."

Some dozen (safer . . .) clustered; and they were
walking through another door, following Denny. The hall
of some sort of warehouse? Maybe the back corridor of

another store? He looked at the faces around him. The real black guy in vinyl looked up from Kid's orchid, blinked, looked away; he wore one too, but in a leather strap.

"Here," Denny said, primarily to Kid. "We just wait here. You follow us when we go. Don't worry."

They stopped before another door. A window on one side showed the Emboriky's sandy wall.

Denny looked over the scorpions with him.

Kid thought: They top Pepper, I guess.

Denny folded his arms, leaned beside the window, occasionally looked out.

Like Copperhead's little blond brother.

They have a plan, Kid thought, caught in it.

I am not thinking of Lanya.

One on wet leather, one on grit, his feet tingled. How did I get here? Did I choose to come? I want to control these people. (The tingling reached his head, subsided.) I chose. Observe and go, easy with them. He would ask Denny the details of the plan—began to tingle; so didn't. Observe? But his mind twisted in. Well. What did he think? Nightmare, with all his unreciprocity, he liked. Copperhead was efficient and detestable, a combination intriguing because, in his experience, it was unusual. Denny? Astounded, he realized: Denny had given him the clothes he wore, had first lopped the obtrusive *d* from his name, and now had him in custody. He squinted at two of the black guys leaning by the window (Denny glanced at Kid, at the floor, out the window) in webbed shadow. Nightmare's lieutenant . . . He tried to review the faces left at the hall's end; there were more than three women in the group. Prompted by the bus ride, he mused on Fenster's population percentages: What percentage were black? George? Waiting, chained and flowered (he'd seen half a dozen knives), I don't want to individualize them. Rather deal in their mass than texture. (Priest, Anthrax, Lady of Spain—these names had already been whispered around him: Devastation, Glass (the black in vinyl), California, Filament, Revelation (blond as Bunny but with brutally red skin), Angel, Dollar, D-t.) Fight that. Some two dozen strung down this grey in grey, waiting: there are probably more here who have killed by accident than by intent. That makes them dangerous. What do they become?

"That thing work?" Denny pointed to Kid's shield.

371

"No battery."

Denny shook his head, aping Nightmare's disgust. "You stay with me, then."

Either the people or the situation is boring. But either the situation or the people are intriguing. I cannot fix the distinction. Nor, having chosen, would it be useful. Again, I am somewhere where the waiting is more instructive than initial or terminal action. Not thinking of Lanya entails: Her green blinking when something I do surprises her, her expression (it always seems sad) seconds before laughter when something I do amuses. Is this like forgetting a name? I want to be among these people. (*Where* would *she* have gone?) It is difficult, because it grosses so little, to consider that I don't want to be with her. But these, who chew their teeth and shuffle, and engage in interesting waiting: what *is* their plan? Not so much afraid of what I don't know about what they do; the cool, absorptive fear I used to feel before stealing books and comics from corner kiosks, shoplifting small compasses and ornamental bullets from army-navy surplus stores.

A long time later, a long way away, someone whistled.

While Denny said, "Come on," everybody moved.

The doors flapped.

They ran across the street; scorpions were running up the alley. "In here!" was steps down and a metal door in the Emboriky's side. Kid thought: Grains struggling through the stricture of an hour-glass. He watched Denny three steps before him, paused when Denny paused (at the bottom of more steps) quickened after him (Worlds within worlds: I am in a different world.) At the first landing, Denny motioned the others ahead, glanced to make sure Kid was still behind him (Plans, completed and synchronized, sketched floor layouts, schedules for the changing guard—he hadn't seen anyone who looked that intelligent), then pulled a heavier chain from his neck and wound two lengths around his fist. "This way." The others' footsteps faded above them as they went from the army drab stairwell through a doorway.

Kid pulled his orchid from his belt loop (the loop, worn from the blade, snapped) and fitted his wrist into the harness. "What's in here?"

"Nothin'," Denny said. "I hope."

The short hall ended on a room full of cardboad

372

boxes. (The wrapping paper in Apartment 19-B. Why?) They had fallen from half-stacked shelves, they covered the floor; they had been pushed into piles and had fallen again.

"What are we doing, huh?" Kid asked.

"Keeping our asses out of trouble," Denny said. "They wanna run around and get shot at, you got more brains than that. The store's eight stories high. Covers the whole block. We figure there's maybe ten, fifteen people in here. I think we're on the mezzanine." He glanced back again. "I hope."

They stepped out into darkness that became three-quarter dark. Kid sniffed. Something had burned in here too. His arm brushed hanging plastic. They snuck through racks of shower curtains, into bathmats and accessories.

"Sure this is the mezzanine?"

"The railing should be over there."

"You been in here before?"

"Keep it down," Denny said. "No. But I talked to somebody who has."

"What—" Kid whispered: "What is Nightmare trying to do in here?"

Denny looked back again. "You think he knows? This is a run!"

They reached towels. By an overturned counter, they walked across mounds of terrycloth. The cool, charred dark stopped at a glass balcony rail with a brass bar. There was light up from below; leaning out ("Hey, watch it," Denny said, "somebody might be down there.") Kidd could not see its source.

There're people in here, Kid thought. There're people in here, walking around with guns! He looked over the balcony, down at counters and the paths between where grey ribbons of light lay over riotous indistinguishables.

Some one, some two scorpions ran out among them.

Denny took Kid's shoulder.

Three more, like mazed mice, zagged through the aisles.

"Hey, what the hell do you people think you're—" shouted by somebody who sounded like he was in a stairwell.

Five heads, deployed among lingerie and watchbands, swiveled. Two of the scorpions went on like flash bulbs— a rooster and some sort of baby dinosaur.

Kid pulled back from the light. Denny was looking up, suddenly aware that they both now had shadows swinging across the ceiling.

"Douse your God-damn lights!" which was Nightmare.

The gun-clap filled the double story. The echo settled.

Some flat reflex that held neither fear nor excitement took him back from the rail (for a moment he saw Denny's excited, frightened face) among the dark displays. Then Denny was behind him.

"Hey, they got in! Hey, they God-damn got in—"

"Mark?" A woman. "Mark? Mark, what's down there . . ."

"You get back! Did they get in? You didn't see—"

Echo botched all meaning in a fourth, fricative voice. Someone nearer tried to interrupt: "What are you—? Why don't you—? Hey, look . . ."

"I saw their lights! For God's sakes, I saw their lights! Somebody called out, too. I saw . . ."

Draped plastic dragged Kid's shoulder. And the woman standing behind it shook the rifle at them, said, "Hhhhhhhhaa . . ." and started walking backward.

Mutually, Kid thought, paralyzed with terror.

But Denny wasn't paralyzed. He grabbed his shield projector and disappeared in light.

Neither was the woman. She staggered backward, in the sudden glare and fired somewhere between them. The rifle gave a breathy *crack*, and Kid recognized her green dress: it was the woman, Lynn, he'd sat next to, his last visit to the Richards'. Now, squinting, and screaming, she held up the rifle to block the light. On the handle, lit by Denny's shield, in four-color decalcomania, Red Rider smiled at Little Beaver, surrounded by a yellow lariat. The air-pump rattled. A bee-bee in the eye, he mused: And lunged.

He thought she would throw the gun at him.

But she held it, and when she didn't let go on the second jerk (the blades of the orchid clicked on the barrel he grasped), he turned it hard and kicked her. She jerked her twisted hands away, shook them, turned. He smacked her shoulder with the rifle butt, and she dodged in darkness.

He turned, mainly to see what Denny was:

A ten-foot blob of light, colorful and disfocused, ran into itself like an amoeba erupting.

It went out, and Denny's hand came down from his neck. Kid pushed the bee-bee gun at him. "What the hell," he whispered, "are you supposed to be?" The fear made him laugh.

Waving the gun, they stalked through the mezzanine shadows.

"Huh?"

"Your shield."

"Oh. About a month ago, something happened to it. I shorted something, I guess, and the projection grid—it's plastic—melted or something. So it comes out like that. I sort of like it."

"What did it used to be?" They turned past bolts of fabric.

Denny gave a confidential whisper. "A frog."

With the woman, Kid thought all of a sudden, did that really happen?

People were screaming again. Below, Nightmare cried, "Hey, man, look at that!" and his excited laugh.

They went into a stairwell: it was pitch-black. Three steps down Kid said, "Wait up—"

Half a flight down, Denny asked, "What happened?"

"My sandal strap broke. I lost my sandal." Listening to Denny's breathing, Kid felt around with his feet, on the step above, on the one below.

Denny suddenly stopped panting and said, "Hey, thank you."

"I can't find it," Kid said. "Thanks for what?"

"I guess you saved my life."

"Huh?"

"That woman. She would have shot me if she got a chance."

"Oh." Kid's toes stubbed the wall. "It wasn't anything. She would have shot me too." He thought: a bee-bee gun? Fifteen-year-old Denny was very young all of a sudden. "Damn thing's got to be around here somewhere."

"Lemme make a light," Denny said and made one.

Kid moved to see if his sandal was under his shadow. "Maybe it fell over . . ." He glanced across the bannister. "Look, never mind . . . put that out, will you." The luminous amoeboid collapsed. The stairwell filled up with darkness, to his eyes, and over. "Can you hear anything?"

The pulsing blot on the black said, tentatively, "No."

"Come on then." Kid started down.

"Okay," was whispered in front of him.

—shot me if she got a chance: would she have if she recognized me? Or would I have wrested the rifle if I hadn't recognized her? (He collided softly with Denny's shoulder.) He thinks I saved his life. What—because he saw light—are they doing out there? Shoulders bumping, they walked into the silent first floor.

Denny stepped between racks of twilit tweed and corduroy.

Kid glanced at the figure standing just beyond the doorway beside him (which was, of course, a dressing mirror, in a wooden stand, slightly tilted so that the reflected floor sloped) and—in a gym locker-room, that opened onto the field, someone had once thrown snow at his naked back.

Looking, he re-experienced (and remembered) the moment from that Vermont winter. Then forgot it, looking at the reflection, trying to recall, now that he had stared for a third, a fourth, a fifth second what had struck him first. He raised his hand (the reflected hand raised), turned his head a little (the head turned a little) took a breath (the reflection breathed); he touched his vest (the reflection touched its khaki shirt) then suddenly raised his hand to knuckle his chin (the reflection's knuckle dug into its full, black beard) and blinked (its eyes blinked behind black plastic glass frames).

The pants, he thought, the pants are the same! There was a white thread snaking across the black denim of his thigh. He (and the reflection) picked it warily away, suddenly arching his naked toes on the carpet (the tips of the black engineer boots flexed), then once more raised his hand toward the glass. He opened his fingers (reflected fingers opened), the string dropped (the string dropped).

Between gnarled knuckles and gnawed nails he looked at the smooth undersides of fingers thinner than his own. (He's taller than I am, Kid thought inanely, taller and stockier.) He reversed his hand, to look at his own palm: the yellowed callous was lined and lined again, deep enough for scars. Between his fingers he saw the backs of fingers with only the slightest hair, only the

376

faintest scar above the middle knuckle and a darkening at the left of the first joint. The reflection's nails, though without moons save the thumbs, were long as his adolescent dreams, and only slightly dirty. He glanced down at the other hand. Where his was caged in blades, the reflection held—his notebook? But the correspondence (he recalled the church clock with its broken hands) was too banal for relief. Wanting to cry, he gazed full at the face, which, mirroring him twitch to twitch, for all its beard and glasses (and a small brass ring in one ear!) gazed* back, with confusion, desperation, and sadness.

The combination was terrifying.

"Hey," somebody said, "what you staring at?" grabbed the top of the mirror from the back, and yanked it down. It swiveled between its posts. The lower rim struck kid's shins.

Kid reeled.

"You pickin' your pimples?" Copperhead grinned across the glass, flat now like a table.

Astonished and angry, Kid lunged forward and brought his free fist down against the mirror's near edge. The far rim tore from Copperhead's loose fingers, scraped his chest, cracked his chin. The mirror drifted down again.

Roaring and clutching his jaw, Copperhead danced between the clothing racks. "Now what the fuck did you . . . Arggg! Oh, my fuckin' tongue, I think I bit . . . Ahhhh! . . ." The third time he looked up, he just blinked.

Kid gulped air.

A triangle of glass slipped from the frame, broke again on the rug. Beyond shatter lines he saw himself, barefoot and beardless, gasping and rubbing the chains on his chest. At his hip the orchid flickered. Some feet behind, Denny, holding something in his arms, watched.

Kid turned in quarter-light.

"I got some . . ." Denny looked at Copperhead, who rubbed and glowered. "Over there, they got shoes and boots and things. I brought you—" he hefted the armful —"these."

"Huh?"

" 'Cause you lost your shoe." Denny looked at Copperhead again.

Kid said: "You pickin' your pimples now?" Then he laughed. Started, it raced at hysteria. He was frightened.

377

A laugh, he thought, is a lot of clotted barkings. He laughed and leaned against a table covered with shirts, and motioned Denny to come.

"You only wear the right one, huh?" Denny dumped the shoes—boots mostly—on the table.

Kid picked up two, three—they were all right ones. He laughed harder, and Denny grinned.

"What are you guys making all the God-damn noise for?" Nightmare called across the aisle. "Will you cut the God-damn hollering?"

Kid choked back both his laughter and his fear, picked out a moccasin boot of soft, rough-out black.

Denny watched gravely while Kid, holding the edge in one hand—waving his orchid for balance—pushed in his foot.

Denny said, "That's the one I liked too."

Kid laughed again. Denny, higher, sharper, laughed too.

"I guess we scared them all upstairs," one girl said to Nightmare.

"You bastards over here making enough noise to scare anybody," Nightmare said.

"Hey," Kid said, "if I broke any of your teeth, I'm sorry. But don't fuck with me any more, hear?"

Copperhead mumbled and rubbed his scantly bearded jaw.

"All this shit going down, and the two of you got into it?" Nightmare rubbed his shoulder.

"Nightmare," Denny said, "the Kid saved my life. Upstairs, up on the balcony. Somebody came at us with a gun, shot at us as close as you are to me. The Kid just grabbed the barrel and pulled it away."

"Yeah?"

A heavy scorpion behind Nightmare said: "Somebody was shootin' down here too."

"You goin' around savin' peoples' lives?" Nightmare said. "You got guts in you after all. Told you he was a good kid."

Kid flexed his toes. The boot gave like canvas. Fear kept lancing, looking for focus, found one: he felt vastly embarrassed. A bee-bee gun, he thought, from some scared woman I ate dinner with, read a poem to! He put his booted foot on the floor.

Denny looked hugely happy.

Nightmare pushed Copperhead's head to the side to

378

examine it. "I wouldn't mess with the Kid if I was you. First time I saw him, I didn't like him either. But I said: If I ain't gonna kill him, I ain't gonna mess with him. That'd be best."

Copperhead pulled away from Nightmare's inspection.

"There was something about him," Nightmare went on. "You nasty, Copperhead, but you dumb. I'm tellin' you this 'cause I'm smarter than you and I thought you'd like to know how to act. The Kid's smarter than you too."

Behind teeth clamped and filled with tongue, Kid thought: does he want him to kill me, huh?

"He just grabbed the gun," Denny repeated. "By the barrel. And pulled it away."

"I'm gonna carry this on back to the place," another white scorpion said, lugging a marble slab on which crouched a large, brass lion; the blacks all seemed so silent, a reversal of his usual experience. The lamp shade kept striking the boy's pimpled, unshaven chin. "I always wanted one of these."

"You carry it," Nightmare said. "I ain't gonna help you. Let's get out of here."

"There're still people up there with guns?" Copperhead took his hand from his jaw to gesture at the dark mezzanine.

"Kid scared 'em away," the black called D-t said.

Nightmare turned and bellowed so loud his knees and elbows bent: *"All right, mother-fuckers! Here we are! You wanna shoot us, go on!"* He glanced around at the others and giggled. *"God damn it, go on, pick us off!"* He started forward.

The unshaved, pimpled scorpion hefted the lion up on his belly, turned his chin away to avoid the shade, and followed.

"You up there, you better get us now! Come on, you mangy mother-fuckers, you chicken-shit assholes! You ain't gonna get another chance!"

This, Kid thought walking between a tall, thin black (named Spider) and the heavy one (called Cathedral: Kid slowed to let Copperhead get a step ahead of them so he could see him), is insane. Laughter: only a fragment blurted. Two of the others looked at him. Grinning, Kid shook his head.

"You up there, you better shoot!" Nightmare bawled at the mezzanine railing. *"You don't, you some real*

379

scroungy cocksuckers!" He unscrewed his face and said to Priest, who walked next to him:

"I heard you over on the other side, hollering. What were you doing?"

"There was somebody in there. I don't think he had a gun. I chased him up the——"

"You better do it now, you son of a bitch!" Nightmare turned back to the guy beside him. "Yeah? . . . *Do it, you do it, cocksucker, if you're gonna do it, do it now!"*

"——chased him up the stairs."

Lady of Spain had kicked in the board bottom of a display case. Copperhead looked up, with consternation and surprise, and put his boot through the glass case in front of him, first the top shelf, then the bottom, then once on the other end; glass and watches scattered the rug. Gasping, he loped to the next. *Crash!* and *crash!* and *crash-crash-crash!* All their eyes, Kid noted (trying to recall what it meant), are red glass.

Another thin black frowned toward Kid, his lids narrowing over blank crimson balls. He looked about Denny's age.

"You real chicken-shit up there, you know!"

CRASH-CRASH!

"You ain't worth shit, god damn it!"

CRASH!

"Eat my shit . . . !" Nightmare looked around and smiled. *"Up your ass! . . . Fuck you!"*

Lady of Spain pushed a whole case over; it smashed into the one behind it. She grinned at Copperhead who didn't see; others laughed.

"They got the door locked." Someone jiggled the handle.

"Here you go . . ." Nightmare said, grabbing for the lion.

"Hey, no——"

Glass exploded over the pavement. The grey street was momentarily obscured by myriad bright prisms. "Come on!"

Kid stepped gingerly across the shards, remembering: On broken glass, go flatfooted.

The white, unshaven scorpion stood (among others moving) looking at his lamp. The marble base was in two pieces, the shade crushed. Finally he stooped, caught up the injured object—a marble chip fell but the cracked base stayed amazingly together—and shuffled on, kicking glass.

"Come on . . ." Denny tugged Kid's arm.

Kid started walking again.

"A God-damn bus!" which hove around the corner. "How do you like that!"

Some stood in the street now, waving their arms.

The bus pulled to the curb. Nightmare at their head, they crowded between the folding doors. Shoulders collided. Through them, Kid saw the bald, black driver's worried face.

"You gonna take us *home!*" the thin black was saying, while the others tried to push past. "Now that's convenient, brother! You gonna take us—!"

"AHHHH—!" shrill and directly into Kid's ear.

Kid flinched and turned (A gun crack? *There!*) and grabbed the scorpion opening and closing his mouth and falling. Hooking the post by the front seat with the elbow of his bladed arm, Kid swung the wounded youth inside. As he fell, the unshaven guy (and some others) no longer holding his lion, clambered over them—"Watch it—!" Crouched at the top of the bus steps, Kid saw the crushed lamp shade leaning against the sill. He grabbed the socket stalk, wrenched the whole thing up into the bus and as the doors closed he heard *ping-CRACK!* The bus was moving: *ping-CRACK!*

He stood—everyone else was crouched in seats or between them.

Even the driver was hunkering over his wheel.

Outside, Kid saw the figure in a third story window of the sandstone wall (right beside the gold *i* in *Emboriky*)—sighting along the rifle, eye to the finder.

The broken marble cut at his shin, joggling. Thirty pounds? As he pulled the lion up onto his forearm (so not to blunt his orchid which stuck from underneath) the bus lurched. "Here." The stubbled face turned up from the seat and blinked. "Here."

The scorpion wrapped his arms around it—the shade came completely off and joggled around the post— dropped his face, then raised it, at the gasping.

Kid turned, holding the back of the seat.

Denny stopped at the feet of the wounded scorpion.

A woman in a grey hat, jammed against the window next to Nightmare, said, "Oh dear! Oh, he's terribly

381

hurt—" then put both hands flat against the pane when Kid looked at her, and began to cry. Then she stopped, faced forward again with her eyes closed.

From a rear seat: "Say . . ."

No one said.

". . . what *happened* to you guys?"

No one answered.

Kid took off his orchid and poked a prong around for his belt loop till he saw (remembering) it had broken. So he hung it from his chain and squatted.

"Annnnnnnn—waa! They got my . . . arm. I . . . Annnn!"

Denny looked up: his very blue eyes were bloodshot.

"Annnnnn—ah. Awww? . . . Oh, hey. Awwwee . . !"

Warm blood touched Kid's toes and spread.

"You want to make a tourniquet or something . . ." Denny suggested.

"Awwwwwwww—Ahhh . . ."

"Yeah."

"Here!" The colored girl in the front seat leaned forward holding a scarf, and almost dropped it when Kid reached. The scorpion panted like a woman in childbirth while Kid tightened the looped cloth on the handle of a knife one of the others gave him. "You gotta loosen it," he told Spider who was helping. "Every five minutes or so. So he doesn't get gangrene or something." Then he sat back on his heels, jogging with the bus. The driver looked back, then turned a corner.

Nightmare, forearms across his knees, was watching them with interest. "You really into this hero bit. Tourniquet, huh? That's pretty good. Yeah, I like that."

Kid stood, about to look disgusted: pain shot up his calves from the minutes spent crouched. So he didn't look anything, walked to Denny's seat, and sat.

Across the aisle, the old man with his head in his coat collar, who had been on the bus when it had been going in the other direction, pretended to sleep.

"You okay?" Denny asked. "You look . . ."

Kid turned to the boy (two others, a scorpion and a passenger, were just turning away): Denny rubbed beneath his nose, blinked his blue—

The memory of crimson eyes in the *Emboriky's* lobby made Kid open his mouth: the eyes that watched now, intently and compassionately, became horrible as the discovered significance of what he had forgotten. Sur-

382

prise blotted another memory—he felt it fade from his mind, struggled to keep it, failed—of something passed in a looking glass. What could he have seen in a mirror? Himself? Nothing else? I'm mad, he thought: like echo, *This is insane,* he had said there. Stripped of context— what *had* happened in the department store?—he shook before what it could have signified. Why did I say, *This is insane?* Something shook in him. His head waggled.

"Kid . . . ?" which Kid was desperately aware was not his name.

Denny's hand had been on his forearm. He knew because now it moved away. Released, he tried to remember having been held, fixed by the warmth that was fading, had faded. Denny rubbed his upper lip again.

Breathing heavily, Kid sat back in the jogging seat.

Outside, movie marquees passed in cryptic cavalcade.

Under high, electric notes, low, wet ones burbled and troughed and erupted. A metallic chord; another metallic chord. Between them: tape-hiss.

Kid cleared his throat; it became a cough.

"Yes?" Reverend Tayler held her pencil by both ends. "Can I help you?"

"I'm hungry," Kid said. "Um . . ." He pulled his hands from the half-door's sill. "Some . . . somebody told me you used to have a free supper here?"

"Oh, we discontinued that some time back—" Behind her, like revolving eyes, the spools turned.

Kid took a breath. "Yeah, I know . . ."

"Did you fall . . . or hurt yourself?"

"Huh? No, I . . . no."

"You're just hungry?"

"Yes, ma'am."

"Really, we're not providing that service any longer, you see. It was far too . . ." Now she let her eyes drop, sucked her teeth, and considered: "Well, perhaps coffee? And . . ." She looked up. "Maybe there's something . . . and you can sit down for a little while."

"Yes, ma'am."

Wheels and swivel roared and squeaked through the music as she pushed away her chair. "Come with me." She stepped to the door, fluttering black robes.

He stepped back while she came through, followed her across the vestibule—"Now, you understand I'm not establishing a tradition. Just this once: I am *not* opening up the Evening Aid Program again. This is for you tonight. Not for your friends tomorrow."—and down a stairway.

"Yes, ma'am."

At the bottom, Reverend Tayler turned on a caged worklight hung on a nail. A high windowsill, level with the street outside, went from blue to black. The heavy cord curved up the steps. "Let's see what we have."

Columns fanned thick shadows across the basement auditorium. Folding chairs were stacked by one wall. A half-collapsed sofa sat by another. Before the closed curtains of a stage was an upright piano, its works bare.

"We're having a service this evening in the chapel upstairs. In just a little while. Maybe if you feel up to it, you can come upstairs to the chapel and join us."

Another high window was open. The slight gust made him look instead of answer. Three leaves jittered to the sill's edge; one spun, before falling. It ticked down the wall, clicked on the piled chairs, to stop at the scuffed linoleum, like an erratic tick-tocking at last run down.

"In here." Reverend Tayler waited by another door.

Inside, she snapped on another worklight.

Across a long, newspaper-covered table, Kid saw a wall hung with pots, potato mashers, colanders, and shelves stacked with thick, church-kitchen crockery. "We were able to get bread for a while, I mean in large quantities. So we could make tinned meat sandwiches—that's when we had Evening Aid. But we lost our source. Without the staff of life, such a program dries up quickly. Beans take too long to cook and I didn't have the help for it." From a wall cabinet she took a can dotted with white paper where the label had been removed. "Beef stew."

He took it from her.

"Taking the labels off," she explained to his questioning expression, "is one minor way to discourage pilfering. I don't like to put locks on things. Snoopers look in on shelves full of blank cans, and don't know whether it's rat poison, motor oil, or green peas. I just have to remember what's where." She tried to look sly. "I have my own system. You must know how these camp stoves work if you've been here any length of time . . . ?"

"Yeah," wondering whether he should explain that he'd learned, however, on a camping trip when he was twelve.

"The urn there is hot. I keep it going all day. I'm sure I'm drinking too much coffee. Can I more or less leave you on your own? I've got to get back to my notes."

"Sure. Thank you, ma'am."

"Wash things up; and let me know when you leave?"

He nodded.

At the kitchen door, she frowned, dark and broad. "You're sure you didn't have some sort of accident? I mean, you're all smudged up there on the side."

"Huh? . . . oh, I'm all right now. Really."

Setting her lips at a blunt, black roundness, she nodded curtly, and left.

Looking over the pans and pots, he thought: *No can-opener,* and panicked.

It lay beside the stove.

He twisted and twisted till the last metal scollop popped, and the can-top, lapped with gravy, began to sink. He looked at the stove, at the can; then something happened in his gut. He went in with fingers, shoved grease, meat, and vegetable chunks into his mouth, licked cold gravy from his hand, wiped what ran on his chin with his forefinger and sucked that.

His stomach bubbled, clamped twice, hard, and he had a mouthful of gas still tasting of Bunny's wine. Anticipating nausea, he stopped, for several deep breaths. Then he took the can out, sat on the sagging sofa, and pushed his hand back into the ragged ring.

He chewed and licked and swallowed and sucked and licked.

When the coppered inside was clean except for the bottom corner for which his middle finger had been too thick, he returned to the kitchen, rinsed the can, and let black coffee steam into it from the urn's plastic spigot. Hot tin between his hands made him aware of his dry left, his sticky right.

Back on the couch, holding it between his knees, he watched the steam and grew sleepy, tasted (hot, bitter) some, decided he didn't want it, and let his eyes close . . .

"Yes, he's right here," Reverend Tayler was saying.

Kid blinked awake. He *had* put the coffee on the arm of the sofa before he drifted off.

"I don't think he's feeling too—oh."

Kid took the can in his fist to hide behind sipping—tepid.

"Ah," said Mr Newboy. "Thank you."

Kid set the coffee on the arm again.

"Ah," Reverend Tayler repeated, but in such a different tone Kid only identified the similarity seconds later, "you got yourself something to eat?"

"Yes, ma'am."

"Good." Reverend Tayler beamed at Newboy, swept

around him, and said, disappearing, "You'll excuse me. I must get back."

"I'm terribly glad I found you!" Mr Newboy carried a briefcase before him, with naked eagerness on his face.

"What'd you want?" Kid's body still tingled from sleep. "How did you know I was here?"

Newboy hesitated before the couch (Kid glanced at the plush and thought: It is pretty dusty), sat. "Just another evidence of the smallness of the city. Your friend in the bar—the big, blond man—"

"Tak?"

"—Yes, that's him. He saw you getting off a bus and coming in this direction. He thought you'd eventually get to Teddy's. When you didn't, I decided to wander over here in case you were still around. I'd never seen this place. And I'm going to be leaving Bellona, soon. Tomorrow morning, actually."

"Oh," Kid said. "He just saw me? . . . and you're leaving? Hey, that's too bad." Fighting the tingling and the sluggishness, he pushed himself up and started toward the kitchen. "You want some coffee, Mr Newboy?"

"Thank you," Newboy said, and called, "Yes."

"What—" through the doorway—"did you want to see me about?"

In the white crock, the coffee ploshed and plopped. Outside Mr Newboy was unsnapping his case.

"I don't know where the milk and sugar is."

"I take it black."

Kid released the plastic spigot, moved a second cup under for himself, (the stuff in the can: cold) and carried them, out to the couch, the foreknuckles of both hands burning.

"Oh, thank you."

"What—" sitting next to Newboy—"did you want to see me about?"

"Well. I thought you'd like to take a look at these." Wide ribbons of paper came up from the plaid lining. "And these." Now a sheaf of black paper. "And this. This is the cover."

On thick, textured paper, were the centered letters:

BRASS
ORCHIDS

He took the—"Oh, my hands aren't too clean . . ."
"Go on, this is just a sample."

—took the cover which suddenly curved down as he held it by the corner, propped it with his other hand and read again:

BRASS
ORCHIDS

"And those are the galleys, which you have to look over." Mr Newboy indicated the papers lying now across Kid's knee. "Fortunately, it isn't too long. Thirty-six pages, I believe. Counting cover. There may be some awful mistakes. It'll be printed on slightly better paper than that. I'd argued for a larger typeface—"

BRASS
ORCHIDS

"—but Roger explained, something I suppose we're all aware of, that here in Bellona we often have to make do."

"Oh, yeah." Kid looked up and let the title of his book embed that part of his consciousness reserved for reality, while he expunged it from the part called dream. The transition came easy, but with a firmness and inevitability he associated with comprehending violence. He was joyous, and upset, but could just distinguish that the reactions were contiguous, not consequent.

"These are the illustrations. Again, we have Roger's sense of theatricality to contend with. I'm not at all sure they're in good taste. Frankly, I don't think poetry needs illustration. But he asked me to show them to you: the decision is yours, ultimately."

He was about to say, They're all black, when he caught glintings in the matt stock.

"They're black ink on black paper," Mr Newboy explained. "The only way you can really see them is to hold them up to the light and look at them from the side. Then the light catches on the ink. Roger feels that since the poems take so much of their imagery from the city, he's used some of what he feels are the most striking pictures from his newspaper. But he's printed them this way —I don't believe there's been any effort to correlate particular pictures with particular poems."

Kid nodded. "That's a good idea." He tilted another picture to catch, in sudden silverpoint, burning buildings, people gaping, and one child, in the foreground, leering into the camera. "Oh, yeah!" He laughed, and looked through the others.

"Have you any idea when you'll be able to look over the proofs? *The Times* is notorious for typos. Your book was set on the same machinery."

"I could do it now." Kid put down the pictures and picked up the galleys. "How many pages did you say it was?"

"Thirty-six. I went over it once myself against your notebook—we'd rather hoped for a typescript; and when you pushed that into my hands, that evening, I was a bit worried. But your fair copies are very neat. You know, you have at least four completely distinct handwritings?"

"It's never been too good."

"But your printing's perfectly legible." Newboy pawed in the case. "Here . . ." He gave Kid the notebook.

It fell open in Kid's hands:

Poetry, fiction, drama—I am only interested in . . .

Kid turned back the book to the page with his poem (a middle draft of *Elegy*), then picked up the galleys. Moving ribbon from ribbon on his lap, saw, printed, ELEGY go by, and caught his breath. The letters were so much sharper and more serene than ink on notebook paper.

He let a random line of print tug his eyes across. Words detonated memories intense enough to blot the fact that they were not his—or, at least, this wasn't . . . or . . . Behind his lips the teeth hung open; now his lips pulled apart. He took a silent breath. My poem, he thought, terribly excited, terribly happy.

"I couldn't help reading some of your notes. I've always found it amusing, writers pouring out pages and pages of analysis on why they can not write—lord knows I've done it myself."

"Huh?"

"There were many, many places where I found your aesthetic analysis let me into some of the more difficult things you were trying to do in the actual work." Mr Newboy picked up his coffee cup. "You have a fascinating critical mind, and quite a bit of insight into the problems of the poem. It made me feel closer to you. And of course, the most important thing, is that the poems themselves deepen considerably in the light of your—"

Kid's head was shaking. "Oh . . ." He closed his

mouth again, opened it, with a moment's urge, luminous in its strength, to allow misconception to become deception.

Newboy paused.

Blinking through the after urge, the pause indicating he was already found out (he pawed his fragmented memory for some previous intent to deceive, to support him in what he wished to reveal), said: "All that other stuff—hey, I didn't write that."

Newboy's grey head went a bit to the side.

"I just found the notebook." The desperation of embarrassment subsided, his heart was left hammering heavily and slowly. "It was all filled up with writing, but just on one side of the page. So I used the other sides for . . . my stuff." A final pulse of heat behind his eyes.

"Oh," Newboy said trying to retain his smile, "this is embarrassing. You didn't write those journal sections?"

"No, sir. Only the poems."

"Oh, I . . . well, I guess . . . oh, really I am sorry." Newboy let the smile become laughter. "Well, I really feel that, once more, I've made myself look quite silly."

"You? No," Kid said, and discovered himself angry. "I should have said something. I just didn't think of it when I gave it to you that evening. Really."

"Of course," Mr Newboy said. "No, I simply mean your poems are your poems. They exist of themselves. In the same way nothing I could say about them is going to change what they are, nothing you could say—or anything I mistakenly *thought* you said—is going to change that either."

"You think that's true?"

Newboy pursed his lips. "Actually, I don't know whether it's true or not. But truly I don't see how any poet can write who doesn't think so."

"Why are you going away, Mr Newboy?" Kid had begun the question to make a connection: But now it seemed equally apt for severing one, and Newboy's embarrassment and his own confusion seemed better left. "Can't you work here very well? Bellona doesn't stimulate you?"

Newboy accepted the severance, acknowledging his acceptance with another sip. "In a way, I suppose you're right. Every once in a while something comes along to remind me that I am—though not as often as I would sometimes like—after all, a poet. What is it Mr Graves says?

All poetry is about love, death, or the changing of the seasons. Well, here the seasons do not change. So I'm leaving." Behind coiled steam, the grey eyes gleamed. "After all. I'm only a visitor. But circumstances seem to have contrived to change that status with a rapidity thoroughly disquieting." He shook his head. "I've met some very pleasant people, seen some fascinating things, had a wealth of rich experiences—just the way the city was represented to me. I certainly haven't been disappointed."

"But not all of the things that happened to you were pleasant?"

"Are they ever? No, Roger has arranged to get me as far as Helmsford. There some people can take me to Lakesville. There's still transportation there. I can get a bus across to the airport at Pittsblain. Then—back to civilization."

"What was so unpleasant here?"

"Not the least was my initial meeting with you."

"At Teddy's?" Kid was surprised.

Newboy frowned. "Outside the wall, in back of Roger's."

"Oh. Oh, yeah. That." He sat back a little on the couch. The projector rolled between his vest flaps. He did not glance down, and felt uncomfortable.

"Inside those walls, I'm afraid," Newboy pondered, "are all the intrigues and personality clashes that—well, that one might imagine at a place like Roger's. And they are beginning to bore me." He sighed. "I suppose such things have driven me from one city to another all my life. No, I can't say Bellona was misrepresented. But even for me, at my age, not all of its lessons have been kind."

"Jesus," Kid said. "What's been happening at—"

"There are, if I can oversimplify," Newboy went on (Kid took a long breath and picked up his coffee), "two concepts of the artist. The one gives all to his work, in a very real way; if he does not produce volumes, at least he goes through many, many drafts. He neglects his life, and his life totters and sways and often plummets into chaos. It is presumptuous of us to judge him unhappy: or, when he is obviously unhappy, to judge the source of it. Be thankful for him, he lends art all its romance, its energy, and creates that absolutely necessary appeal to the adolescent mind without which adult maturation is impossible. If he is a writer, he hurls his words into the

391

pools of our thought. Granted the accuracy of the splashes, the waves are tremendous and glitter and flash in the light of our consciousness. You Americans—not to mention the Australians—are extraordinarily fond of him. But there is another concept, a more European concept—one of the few concepts Europe shares with the Orient—that includes Spenser and Chaucer, but excludes Shakespeare, that includes the Cavaliers and the Metaphysicals, but bypasses the Romantics: the artist who gives his all to life, to living within some sort of perfected ideal. Sometime in his past, he has discovered he is . . . let us say, a poet: that certain situations, certain convergences of situations—usually too complicated for him to understand wholly, as they propitiously juxtapose conscious will with unconscious passion —they something-between-cause-and-allow a poem. He dedicates himself to living, according to his concepts, the civilized life in which poetry exists because it is part of civilization. He risks as much as his cousin. He generally produces fewer works, with greater intervals between them, and constantly must contend with the possibility that he will never write again if his life should so dictate —a good deal of his civilized energies must go toward resigning himself to the insignificance of his art, into the suppression of that theatrical side of his personality of which ambition is only a small part. He stands much closer to the pool. He does not hurl. He drops. Accuracy is again all-important: there are some people who can hit bull's eye from a quarter of a mile while others cannot touch the target at ten feet. Given it, the patterns and ripples this sort of artist produces can be far more intricate, if they lack the initial appearance of force. He is much more a victim of the civilization in which he lives: his greatest works come from the periods art historians grossly call 'conducive to aesthetic production.' I say he stands very close to the pools; indeed, he spends most of his time simply gazing into them. Myself, I rather aspire to be this second type of artist. I came to Bellona to explore. And I find the entire culture here—I cannot be kind—completely parasitic . . . saprophytic. It infects— even inside Roger's carefully closed estate. It's not conducive to my concept of the good life, therefore, if only tertiarily, it damages all my impulses toward art. I would like to be a good person. But it's too difficult here. I suspect that's cowardly, but it's true."

The coffee, prompting a memory that would not resolve, was again cold in his mouth. "Mr Newboy—" he swallowed and was pensive—"do you think a bad person can be a good poet? . . . or is that a silly question?"

"Not if you're essentially questioning yourself. I mean, we *suspect* Villon went on to murder and died by the noose. But—and what a dreadfully unpopular notion —he might just as well have simply been writing about the strange people he knew around him; and, when they got him into trouble, gave up his bad company, abandoned writing, changed his name, and went on to die a peaceful burger in another town. From a perfectly practical point of view—and one would have had to have written fairly well to appreciate the practicality—I would imagine the answer is that it would be quite difficult. But it would be absurd of me to pronounce it impossible. Frankly, I don't know."

When Kid looked up, he was surprised to see the elderly gentleman smiling straight at him.

"But that question is just your natural idealism speaking." Newboy turned a little on his cushion. "All good poets tend to be idealistic. They also tend to be lazy, acrimonious, and power-crazed. Put any two of them together and they invariably talk about money. I suspect their best work tries to reconcile what they are with what they know and feel they should be—to fit them into the same universe. Certainly those three are three of my own traits, and I know they often belong as well to some very bad men. Should I triumph over my laziness, however, I suspect I would banish all feeling for economical expression which is the basis of style. If I overcame my bitterness, beat it out of my person for good, I'm afraid my work would lose all wit and irony. Were I to defeat my power-madness, my craving for fame and recognition, I suspect my work would become empty of all psychological insight, not to mention compassion for others who share my failings. Minus all three, we have work only concerned with the truth, which is trivial without those guys that moor it to the world that is the case. But we are wandering toward questions of doing evil versus the capacity for doing evil, innocence, choice, and freedom. Ah well, during the Middle Ages, religion was often able to redeem art. Today, however, art is about the only thing that can redeem religion, and the clerics will never forgive us that."

393

Newboy glanced at the ceiling and shook his head. Dulled organ music came from the stair. He looked down into his case.

"I guess what I want to know, really—" Kid's thumb had stained the galley margin: momentary panic. "Do you think these—" and four fingers marked the paper in a sweep—"that these are any good?" There will be other copies, he thought to ease himself. There will be. "I mean, really."

Newboy sucked his teeth and put the case on the floor against his knees. "You have no realization what an absurd question that is. Once, when I used to find myself in this situation, I would always answer 'no' automatically, 'I think they're worthless.' But I'm older, and I realize now all I was doing was punishing people who asked such questions for their stupidity, and was only being 'honest' in the most semantically vulgar sense. I really cannot think about poetry in such absolute terms as 'good' and 'bad', or even in the more flexible terms you'd probably be willing to accept in their place: 'well done' or 'badly done'. Perhaps it is because I suffer from all the aesthetic diseases of the times which cause the worthless to be praised and the worthy to be ignored. Well, they have ravaged all ages. But you must leave open the possibility that poetry means far too much to me to vulgarize it in the way you are asking me to do. The problem is essentially one of landscape. I've already made it clear, I hope, that I, personally, have enjoyed the particular complex of interchange between you and your poems, both as I have perceived it and, to my personal embarrassment, misperceived it. If you think my distance insulting, dwell on the complexities in it. But let me pose an example. You know of Wilfred Owen?" Newboy did not wait for Kid's nod. "Like many young men, he wrote his poems during the War; he seems to have hated that war, but he fought in it, and was machine-gunned to death while trying to get his company over the Sambre Canal when he was younger than you. He is generally considered, in English, the greatest war poet. But how is one to compare him to Auden or O'Hara, Coleridge or Campion, Riding or Roethke, Rod or Edward Taylor, Spicer, Ashbery, Donne, Waldmen, Byron or Berrigan or Michael Denis Browne? As war— the experience or the concept—stays a vital image, Owen will stay a vital poet. If war were to be both abolished and forgotten, then Owen would become a minor figure,

394

interesting only as a purely philological point in the development of the language, as an influence on more germane figures. Now your poems wrap themselves around and within this city as Cavafy's twist and refract about pre-World War Two Alexandria, as Olson's are caught in the ocean light of mid-century Gloucester, or Villon's in medieval Paris. When you ask me the worth of these poems, you are asking me what place the image of this city holds in the minds of those who have never been here. How can I presume to suggest? There are times, as I wander in this abysmal mist, when these streets seem to underpin all the capitals of the world. At others, I confess, the whole place seems a pointless and ugly mistake, with no relation to what I know as civilization, better obliterated than abandoned. I can't judge because I am still in it. Frankly I will not be able to judge once out of it, for the bias that will remain from once having been a visitor."

Kid, halfway through the second poem in proof, looked up at the silence.

"The worth of our work?" (Kid dropped his eyes and continued reading.) "People who do not create are always sure that on some inchoate level the creator knows it. But the roster of Nobel laureates I have come so near to joining three times now is cluttered with mediocre writers who have neither elegance nor depth, readability nor relevance: lauded during their lifetimes, they died, I'm sure, convinced they had substantially advanced their languages. Your Miss Dickinson died equally convinced no one would ever read a word she wrote; and she is one of the most luminous poets your country has produced. An artist simply cannot trust any public emblem of merit. Private ones? They are even more misleading."

Kid turned over the next galley. "You're talking to yourself." Eyes down, he wondered what expression was on Newboy's face.

"Most certainly," Newboy said after a longish pause.

"You're really that scared your own stuff isn't any good."

Newboy paused.

In the pause, Kid considered looking up but didn't.

"When I'm not actually working, I have no choice: I *must* consider it worthless. But when I'm engaged in it, writing, revising, shaping and polishing, by the same process, I have to consider it the most important thing in the world. And I'm very suspect of any other attitude."

Kid looked up now: the expression leaving Newboy's face was serious. But laughter marks were replacing it. "Ah, when I was a young man, as young as I once thought you were, I recall I labored with incredible diligence over a translation of *Le Bateau ivre*. Here I am at the respectable, if a bit garrulous, threshold of old age, and last night, in the front library at Roger's, after everyone else had gone up, I sat there working—by hurricane lanterns: the electricity is off in that wing now—on *Le Cimetière marin*. The impulse was thoroughly the same." He shook his head, still laughing. "Have you found any mistakes?"

"Um," Kid said. "Not in the first three sheets."

"I spent yesterday and most of today checking it against your fair copy. I've put a couple of queries here and there. You'll get to them as you go through."

"Where?"

"The first one's near the front." Newboy set down his cup and leaned over Kid's shoulder. "Next sheet. There. It's the poem you had the loose copy of it on blue paper just stuck in the notebook. It looked like somebody else had written it out for you. Did you perhaps intend a comma in the third line? I checked it back with the version in your notebook, and neither one has it. Except for the phrasing, I wouldn't have—"

"The copy in the notebook has a comma, doesn't it?" Kid frowned and flipped handwritten pages. His eyes stumbled among words, trying not to be caught between any two, till he found the notebook page. "It's not there." He looked up. "I *thought* I put one."

"Then you *did* intend it. Here, use my pencil. Just cross out the question mark I put by the line. I had a feeling you might—what's the matter?"

"I thought I had a comma there. But I didn't."

"Oh, I'm always discovering I've left out words I was sure I wrote down in first draft—"

"You . . ."

Mr Newboy started to question, grew uncomfortable with that, so returned his eyes to the line.

". . . just read it and knew I'd wanted one there?"

Newboy began to say several things, but stopped (after a little nod) before voice, as if curious what silence would affect.

Two emotions clawed the inside of Kid's skull. The fear, as it rose, he questioned: Is this some trick of autonomic nerves that causes the small of my back to dampen, my heart to quicken, my knees to shake like motors; it was only a comma, the smallest bit of silence that I have misplaced—only a pause. I am quaking like Teddy's candles. The joy, mounting over, obliterating, and outdistancing it, was at some sensed communion. (Newboy had known!) To restrain it, Kid told himself: Between two phrases like that, why shouldn't Newboy be able to tell? He lowered his head to read on: his eyes filled with water and the emotion tore through such logic. And the darkness under. He anticipated their collision to make some wave. But like two swirls of opposite spin, they met—and canceled. He blinked. Water splashed from his lashes across the back of his hand.

There had been a recurrent pain on the back of his right shoulder that, three or four years ago, had intrigued him because it would be a pulsing annoyance for hours or even days and then would, in a second, vanish: no proddings or contortions could recall it. He hadn't for years, till now.

Tensing his shoulders, he read the next poem, and images set to at the backs of his eyes, their substance and structure familiar, their texture alien, alien and grave. He kept blinking, to finish the line in his mind; eyes opened to finish it on the page, where it demanded new bulbs. Boxes of glass ticked their clear covers on stunned marvels. Things were safe, and that was so horrifying his heart was pulsing in the little pit at the base of his throat as though he were swallowing rock after rock. "Mr Newboy?"

"Mmm?" Papers shuffled.

Kid looked over.

Newboy was going through the illustrations.

"I don't think I'm gonna write any more poems."

Newboy turned another black page. "You don't like them, reading them over?"

Kid peeled off the next paper ribbon. The first two words of the first line of the first poem were transposed—

"Here!" Mr Newboy offered his pencil. "You found a mistake?" He laughed. "Now see, you *don't* have to write quite so hard as that! Wait! You'll tear the paper!"

Kidd unhunched his shoulder, unbent his spine, and let his fingers relax about the yellow shaft. He breathed again. "They're going to fix that, aren't they?"

"Oh, yes. That's why you're looking it over now."

Kid read, and remembered: "The parts I like,

397

well . . ." He shook his head, with pursed lips. "They just don't have anything to do with me: somebody else wrote them, it seems, about things I may have thought about once. That's pretty strange. The parts I don't like—well, I can remember writing those, oh yeah, word by word by word."

"Then why aren't you going to write any—?"

But Kid had found another mistake.

"Here," Newboy said. "Why don't you lay the galleys on your notebook so you can write more easily."

While Kid passed the halfpoint of the next galley, Newboy mused: "Perhaps it's good you're not going to write any more: you'd have to start considering all these dull things like your relation to your audience, the relation between your personality and your poetry, the relation between your poetry and all the poetry before it. Since you told me you weren't responsible for those notes, I've been trying to figure out whether it just happened or whether you were making a conscious reference: You managed to reproduce, practically verbatim, one of my favorite lines from Golding's translation of the *Metamorphosis*."

"Mmm?"

"Are you familiar with it?"

"It's a big green and white paperback? That's the one Shakespeare used for some of his plays. I only read about the first half. But I didn't take any lines from it, at least not on purpose. Maybe it just happened?"

Mr Newboy nodded. "You amaze me. And when you do, I suspect I'm rather a smaller person for having such petty notions in the first place. Well, the line I was referring to was from the last book anyway. So you hadn't gotten to that one yet. Tell me, who *do* you think should read your poems once they're published?"

"I guess people who . . . well, whoever likes to read poetry."

"Do you?"

"Yeah. I read it more than I read anything else, I guess."

"No, that doesn't surprise me."

"You know, in bookstores for the schools I used to go to, or down in the Village in New York, or in San Francisco, they got whole sections for poetry. You can read a lot of it there."

"Why poetry?"

Kid shrugged. "Most poems are shorter than stories."

Newboy, Kid saw, was suppressing a laugh. Kid felt embarrassed.

"And you're not going to write any more?"

"It's too hard." Kid looked down. "I mean if I kept it up, I think it would kill me, you know? I never did it before, so I just didn't understand."

"That's sad—no, I can be more honest than that. It's frightening for one artist to see another one, any other one turn away from art."

"Yeah." Kid's eyes came up. "I know. I really know that. And I wish—I wish I didn't frighten you as much as I do. What is it? What's the matter with you, now?"

"Nothing." Newboy shook his head.

"I wish I didn't," Kid repeated. "The last poem . . ." Kid began to turn through the galleys. "What did you think of that one, I mean compared to all the rest of them?"

"The one in meter? Well, it isn't finished. We printed it up to where you broke off. That's another thing I wanted to query about—"

"How do you like what there is?"

"Frankly, I didn't think it was as strong as many of the others. When I went back over it the fourth or fifth time, I began to see that the substance of it was probably on its way to a great deal of richness. But the language wasn't as inventive. Or as clean."

Kid nodded. "The rhythm of natural speech," Kid mused. "I had to write it. And it was pretty bad, wasn't it? No, I don't think I'll write any more. Besides, I'm probably never going to have another book published . . . ?" He raised an eyebrow at Newboy.

Newboy, lips pursed, considered. "I could say that I sincerely don't believe that should be a consideration. Or that, as I remember it, it was something like eleven years between my first and second book of poems. Or that I think you're asking for confirmation of something that really doesn't have anything to do with poetry."

"What else could you say?"

Newboy's lips unpursed. "I could say, 'Yes, possibly you won't.' "

Kid grinned quickly and went back to correcting.

"It's very silly to commit yourself to something like that, if you're going to write or not. If you wrote those, you will write more. And if you promise yourself you won't, you'll just be very unhappy when you break the promise. Yes, a good part of me doesn't like the idea of an artist giving up art. But this is another part of me talking. Believe me."

Kid's mind was on Lanya.

He pulled it away, to reflect on: Golding's *Metamorphosis*. He'd seen the book on a dozen shelves in a dozen bookstores, picked it up as many times, read the back cover, the first page of the introduction, flipped through three or four pages, unable to read more than three or four lines on each. (The same thing, he realized, had happened with *Pilgrimage*.) The first *half*? He'd been unable to read a whole page! Poetry, he thought. If it makes me start lying to a guy like this, I should stop writing it.

Kid corrected the last half-dozen sheets in silence drenched with vision. He flipped them, rattling like dry feathers, together.

He leaned on the couch arm (he breathed gently: but felt breath's coolness only on the left side of his upper lip) and looked at the paper over his lap. I've just corrected the last half-dozen sheets, he thought: his upper arms were bone tired. Pains pulsed in his finger joints. He loosened his grip on the pencil.

The title-page, he noticed now, read:

BRASS
ORCHIDS
BY

He started to smile; the muscles of his mouth blocked it.

Mr Newboy, gone to the kitchen, returned now with another steaming cup.

"I guess—" the smile broke through—"you better take the 'by' off the title page."

"Ah," Mr Newboy raised his chin. "That does bring up a sort of strange subject. I talked to your friend Mr Loufer. And he told me about—"

"I mean it's okay," Kid said. "I think it would be a good idea if it came out with no name. Anonymously."

"Mr Loufer said that you're—rather picturesquely—called 'the Kid' by many of your friends?"

"That would look pretty stupid," Kid said. " 'Poems by the Kid.' I think it would be better with nothing."

400

Somewhere beneath the thing inside that made him smile, there was the beginnings of embarrassment. He sighed, still smiling.

Gravely, Mr Newboy said: "If you really feel that way, I'll tell Roger. Are you finished looking them over?"

"Yeah."

"That was quick. How were they?"

"Uh, fine. I mean not that many mistakes."

"That's good."

"Here."

"Oh, are you sure you wouldn't like to keep the notebook?"

It was opened back in the middle. Kid lowered the papers to his lap. To avoid the feeling of confusion he let his eyes take the page's opening lines:

> *Poetry, fiction, drama—I am interested in the arts of incident only so far as fiction touches life; oh no, not in any vulgar, autobiographical sense, rather at the level of the most crystalline correspondence. Consider: If an author, passing a mirror, were to see one day not himself but some character of his invention, though he might be surprised, might even question his sanity, he would still have something by which to relate. But suppose, passing on the inside, the character should glance at his mirror and see, not himself, but the author, a complete stranger, staring in at him, to whom he has no relation at all, what is this poor creature left . . . ?*

Newboy was saying, "You're all sure now that you don't want to write again. But be certain, inspiration will come, arriving like one of Rilke's angels, so dazzled by its celestial journey it will have completely forgotten the message entrusted to it yet effectively delivering it merely through its marvelous presence—"

"Here!" Kid thrust out galleys and notebook. "Please take it! Please take it all. Maybe . . . I mean, maybe you'll want to check something else." He watched his extended hands sway to his thumping heart.

"All right," Newboy said. "No, you keep the notebook. You just may want it again." He took the papers, and hefted his case against his hip. "I'll take these back to Roger this evening." The papers rustled down in the case. "I probably won't be seeing you again. I really don't know how long the printing will take. I wish I could see the whole project through." He snapped a last snap. "I'm sure he'll send me a copy when it's done—however your mail system works here. Good-bye." His hand came forward. "I've really enjoyed the time we've spent together, the talks we've had. Do say good-bye to your little girl friend for me?"

Kid shook. "Yes, sir. Um . . . thank you very much." The notebook was on the floor, one corner over Kid's bare foot.

Newboy walked to the steps.

"Good-bye," Kid repeated into the silence.

Newboy nodded, smiled, left.

Kid waited for the disturbing memory to flicker once more. His heart quieted. Suddenly he picked up his and Newboy's coffee cup and went into the kitchen.

Seconds after he began to rinse them in the sink, he noticed how firm the water pressure was. He ran his forefinger around the crock rim. The water hissed on the enamel.

Somebody struck a dissonance on the piano.

Curious, Kid turned off the water. The cups clinked on the sideboard. As he crossed the floor, one of the boards squeaked: he had wanted to be completely quiet.

At the darker end of the auditorium, someone in work clothes stood before the brass innards. The orange construction shoes and the coveralls momentarily recalled the woman on the ladder changing the street signs.

The figure turned and walked to the couch. " 'Ey . . ." A heavy, flattened voice, a slight nod and slighter smile: George Harrison picked up an old *Times,* and lowered himself to the couch, crossed his legs, and opened the tabloid-size paper.

"Hello." Kid heard faint organ music.

"Y's'pos'd' be i' 'eah?" Harrison looked from behind the paper.

The natural rhythm of English speech; no, Kid thought, it *is* impossible.

"You *sure* you supposed to be in here?" George repeated.

"Reverend Tayler brought me down." (It would be stupid, he decided, even to try.)

" 'Cause if you *ain't* suppose to be in here, she gonna get mad." Harrison smiled, a mottled ivory crescent between his lips' uneven pigment. "Seen you in the bar."

"That's right." Kid grinned. "And you're in those posters all over town."

"You séen them?" Harrison put down the paper. "You know, them fellows what make them is a little—" he joggled his hand—"you know?"

Kid nodded.

"They good though. They good guys." He shook his head, then pointed at the ceiling. "She don't want no scorpion around here. You sure you're supposed to be in here. Don't matter to me, she said okay."

"I was hungry," Kid said. "She said I could get something to eat."

"Oh." Harrison turned on the couch. His green jumpsuit was open to the waist, over a banlon shirt with a raveled collar. "You come for the service?"

"No."

"Ain't no scorpion come to the damn service anyway. What you fellows dress up all that shit for?" Harrison laughed, but shook a finger. "It's. cool, it's cool."

Kid looked at the large, lined knuckles and thought of the cracks in black earth. "What kind of service is it?"

"I just come because she say I should please come, so, you know, I come here sometimes." Harrison shook his head. "From Jackson, that's where—" and something Kid couldn't follow—"see?"

Though he didn't, Kid nodded. Then he became curious and asked, "What did you say?"

"In Jackson. You know what Jackson is?"

"Yeah, sure."

But Harrison was laughing again.

He, Kid reflected, *is becoming a god,* to see what emerged from his tone of thought. Kid's inner eye was alive with visions of June.

But George stood, dropping his paper. White leaves opened and fell, one on the couch, several on the floor. "You the one they call the Kid. Yeah?"

Kid was terrified, and felt stupid for not knowing why.

"They talk about you. I heard about you. I heard what they said." The finger shook again. "You the one that don't know who he is. I heard them."

"Nobody around here got anything to do except talk," Kid said. "You know that? You know what I mean about that?"

403

The black hand went down against the coverall. The green wrinkled. "So you don't like it here?"

"Yeah," Kid said. "I like it . . . don't you?"

Harrison nodded, his cheek filled with his tongue. "You ever come over in the Jackson?" The tongue flicked the lips.

"I've walked through."

"You know any black people live over there?"

"No. Well, Paul Fenster . . ."

"Oh, yeah."

"But I don't know where he lives."

"You come over there and see me sometime, huh?"

"Huh?" Kid was not sure he had caught any of the last words bundled in that voice with a nap longer than velvet.

"I say 'You come pay a visit on me.' "

"Oh. Yeah. Thanks." Kid was bewildered. Searching that, he found two questions about things that rhymed which flooding embarrassment blocked. So he narrowed his eyes instead.

"Kid—" she called from the stairs behind him. Then, in a completely different voice: "George—hi there, babes!"

Kid turned. "Hey—!"

George called over him, "Hey there—" and then with a narrowing expression. "Say, this ain't your old man, is it? The guy I been hearing all that talk about over in the bar—well, say! Now the last time I seen your old lady, you know I tell her to bring you down and pay a visit to me, you hear?"

Lanya came down the steps; George walked toward them.

"Now see," Lanya said, "I haven't seen you since the park."

"If I got to invite you twice, I guess I got to invite you twice," George said, starting up. "Got to go see me the Reverend now, though. One of you drag the other on down, now." George nodded toward Kid.

"Um . . . thanks," Kid said, nodded back.

"See you around," George said.

"Sure," said Lanya. They passed. George's response was a falsetto, "Ooooooooo," which broke and became trundling laughter. Laughter rolled beneath the ceiling like smoke. George mounted into it.

At the bottom of the stairs Lanya said, "Where've you been?" and blinked four or five times more than he thought she would have, in the silence.

"I . . . I couldn't find you this morning. I looked for you. I couldn't find you. At the commune, or down at the bar. What happened? Where did everybody go?"

Her eyes questioned. Her lips moved on one another, did not open.

"You want some coffee?" he asked out of discomfort, turned and went into the kitchen. "I'll go get you some coffee. It's all ready, inside."

At the urn, he picked up a cup, pulled the lever. "Did you see Tak too? How'd you know I was here?" Amber bubbles burst at the rim; black liquid steamed. "Here you—" He turned and was surprised that she was right behind him.

"Thank you." She took the cup. Steam flushed before her lowered eyes. "I saw Tak." She sipped. "He said you might be here. And that Mr Newboy was looking for you."

"He just left. He had my book. The galleys, for the poems. The type's all set."

She nodded. "Tell me what you've been doing."

"It was a pretty funny day." He poured coffee for himself, deciding as he did he had already had too much. "Really funny. After you went off, I looked for you. And I couldn't find you anywhere. I stopped in the john to wash up. When I got down to the camp site, I couldn't find you. And everybody'd run off." He put his hand on her shoulder; she smiled faintly. "I got in with some scorpions this afternoon . . . this evening. That was pretty strange. A guy got shot. We were on the bus, and he was bleeding. And I kept on thinking, what are they going to do with him? Where are they going to take him? There isn't any doctor around. We even had his arm in a tourniquet. I couldn't take it. So I just got off the bus. And came here. Because I was hungry. I hadn't had anything to eat all day except a God-damn pint of wine for breakfast."

"You ate here?" She looked by both his shoulders. "That's good."

"What did you do?"

She was wearing a white blouse, clean but unironed, that he had not seen before. As she walked beneath the

405

bulb, he saw her jeans were new enough to show the crease. "You pick up some clothes this afternoon?" He followed her into the bare auditorium.

"Yesterday. I found them in a closet of the place where I'm staying now."

"You *have* been busy, huh? You found a house an' all?"

"About three days ago."

"Jesus," Kid said, "when did you get time to do that? I didn't think I let you alone long enough to go to the damn bathroom, much less find a house——"

"Kid . . ." She turned on the word to lean against the sofa arm. In the hall, shrill echoes returned. "Kid," much more softly, "I haven't seen you in *five* days!"

"Huh?" The heel on the floor and the heel in his boot prickled. Prickling rose up his legs, spread about his thighs. "What do you mean?"

"What do you mean what do I mean?" She spoke clumsily, breaking through three tones of voice. "Where have you *been?*" Retreating from the clumsiness, her voice was left only with hurt. "Why did you go away? What did you do all this time?"

Little things clawed between his buttocks, mounted rib by rib, perched on his shoulder to nip at his neck so he had to drop his chin. Lines of perspiration suddenly cooled. "You're kidding with me, aren't you? Like with the moons?"

She looked puzzled.

"The night when the moons first came out, and later we were talking about them; you pretended that there had just been one, and that I had been seeing things. You're fooling with me like that now?"

"No!" She shook her head, stopped it in the middle of a shake. "Oh, no . . ."

His cheeks felt like pincushions.

"Kid, what *happened* since the last time you saw me?"

"We woke up, when those sons of bitches were standing around us, right?"

She nodded.

"Then you went away, and I . . . well, I hung around for a little while, and then I went down to the john to wash up. I guess I took an awful long time. I should have hurried . . . But there was this guy there, Pepper, a scorpion." The prickling had left his feet: it felt as though

406

he were being poured full of cold water. It rose behind his knees. "Pepper and me, we went down to the camp site, only it had been abandoned."

"John and Milly didn't move the commune till the day after I saw you last; they thought it would be safer."

"Then we went to Teddy's to look for you. Only it wasn't open yet. And I had a lot of wine with Bunny— you know the guy who dances there. I gave him a message for you."

She nodded. "Yes, he gave it to me . . . the day before yesterday!"

"No," he said. "Because I gave it to him this morning." The water reached his loins, poured into his scrotum; his scrotum shriveled. "Then I went out, and ended up at that department store downtown. That's where I met the other guys, and we broke into the place. There were people living in there. We got out. But they shot one of the guys. We just got him out of there, on the God-damn bus that happened to be coming along!"

"That happened *two* nights ago, Kid! Some of the scorpions came into the bar and wanted to know if anybody knew where they could get a doctor. Madame Brown went with them, but she came back in about ten minutes. Everybody was talking about it all yesterday."

"He was bleeding and moaning on the floor of the bus!" The water roared around in Kid's chest, then filled the column of his neck, fountained inside his head. "I got off the bus, and I came—" He choked, and for a moment thought he would drown. "—came here." The water reached his eyes, (and the work bulb grew knitting needles of light); he brushed it away, before more of it rolled down his face, no longer cold, but hot.

He kept rubbing at his eyes with one hand.

Something burned the knuckles of the other: coffee had slopped over.

He raised his cup and sucked the bitter liquid from his skin.

"Oh, give that here!" She took his cup from him and put them both down on the sofa arm. "I'm *not* fooling you!"

His hand, lost with nothing to hold, hung like something torn from among roots and still clumped with earth.

Lanya took it, pressed the knuckles to her mouth. "I'm not kidding you at all. That morning, in the park, when Nightmare woke us up was five days ago. And I haven't seen you since!"

At her touch, he found himself ponderously calm, and kept trying to determine if the submarine silence that filled him hid anger or relief.

"Look, you said Mr Newboy was here with the galleys. You can't set type on a whole book overnight, can you?"

"Oh . . ."

"When we were all talking about you, last night in the bar, he came looking for you with them then, too."

"Talking about me?" He wanted to pull his hand away, but felt embarrassed.

"About you and the scorpions. They said you saved somebody's life."

"Huh?"

She took his other hand now; the familiar gesture only made him less comfortable.

The hurts among her small features and his own made something ugly between them. He raised his hands and pulled her to him, to squeeze it away. She came up against him with her arms crossed over her belly, and there was a hard thing over one breast—her harmonica. She moved her head against his chest. "Oh, for God's sakes," she whispered.

"I'm not fooling you either!" He didn't sound, he thought, nearly as desperate as he felt. "I saw you this morning. I . . . I thought I saw you this morning."

"You've been running around with the scorpions all week. Everybody thinks you're some kind of hero or something."

"What'd you think?" Her hair brushed his moving chin.

"Shit. That's what I thought: 'Shit.' You want to go off in that direction. Fine. But I don't feel like getting messed up in anything like that. I really don't."

"This afternoon," he said. "I mean it was by accident I found them. And I didn't save anybody's life. That was just . . ."

"Look at you," she said, not moving away. "You're dressing like them; you're hanging out with them. I mean go on: If that's what you want, go on. But it's not my scene. I can't go there with you."

"Yeah, but . . . Hey, look. You: you say you've got a house and all. Where are you staying now?"

408

"Would you mind," she said softly, "if I didn't tell you?" But opened her arms and put them around him. "Just for a while?" The harmonica corner cut his chest.

He wondered could she feel the anger inside him, pulsing under her hands. "I," he said, "saw you this morning."

She pulled back, all his anger on her face. "Look!" She made fists at her hips. "Either you're lying to me for some kooky reasons I don't even want to know about, and I shouldn't have anything to do with you, right? The night before I saw you last, you lost three hours. Now you've lost five days. Maybe you really are crazy. Maybe I shouldn't have anything to do with you! That's pretty irrational, isn't it? I haven't seen you in five days and Christ, am I angry at you!"

"Then why the fuck were you looking for me!" He turned and stalked down the hall, a great bubble about to burst inside his ribs.

At the piano, he realized Harrison must have opened the curtains on the low stage. The backdrop—and there were stands with photographer's floods—showed a painted moon, some seven feet across, and indications around it of trees.

He turned at the apron, surprised again to find her behind him. "Why did you come?"

"Because this is the first time I've known where you were. I didn't *know*. . . ." She gasped. "I didn't know if you were all right. You didn't come back. I thought maybe you were angry at me for something. You used to always come back. And suddenly, for all that time, instead of you, all I got was what people were saying about you. You and the scorpions, you and the scorpions." Something spent itself in her eyes. The lids lowered on the shadowed green. "Look, so far we haven't had one of those 'I'll-follow-you-anywhere' relationships. I still haven't made up my mind if that's where I want to go. And I just get a little nervous when I find myself thinking I might. That's all."

"A week." He felt his face twist. "What the hell did I do for . . . five days? When did I . . ." He reached for her.

Her face crashed against his, hitting his mouth, but she pushed her tongue against his, and was holding tight to the back of his neck. He kept trying to pull her even closer, leaning against the stage.

409

He loosed one hand to dig between them, till he could pull the harmonica from her blouse pocket. It rattled on the stage behind them.

"You're not going to hurt anyone," she said once. "You're not going to hurt me. I know that. You're not."

The hysteria with which she made love to him on that dark stage was first furious, then funny, (wondering if someone was going to walk in, and excited by the idea); he lay on his back while she bucked above him, clutching his shoulders, wondering should he feel this way. But the sound she was making that he'd thought was crying cleared to laughter. Her buttocks filled his hands, and he dug between them.

She reared too high, and lost him to the annealing chill. While she reached for him, he rolled her to her side. Legs in the clutch of denim, he crawled down to the sweaty corner of her blouse and pushed his tongue through her salty hair. She lifted a knee to let it fall wide. After she came, (he had worked his pants free of one foot) he straddled her, pushed his penis into her again, lowered his belly to her belly, his chest to her chest, his wet face against the crumpled shoulder of her blouse, and began long final strokes, while her arms tightened on his back.

Coming burned his loins (he remembered the spilled coffee) and left him exhausted and still burning (he remembered how it felt after masturbating when all you started off with was a piss-on), and exhaustion won. Lakes of sweat cooled around his body. She nodded in the crook of his shoulder, where he knew his arm would numb soon, but didn't feel like doing anything about it. He slid his hand down his own chest, till his fingers caught in the transverse chain, beneath angular shapes.

Times' voices in agon? Who wants to hear hunchbacks and spastics haggle? Even, if there are no others in concert. We should not be lying here, cooling, half naked, half asleep. A good reason to do it. I am still angry at her. I am still angry. Would she have it I choose scorpions all for negative reasons? Have they been a surround? No: it is better to accept the inevitable with energy. Well then, if I have not chosen up till now, now I choose. That is freedom. Having chosen, I am free. Somewhere in my memory is a moon that gives odd light. It is safer here—

He woke: which was suddenly arriving in that space

between the boards and the touch of eyelid against eyelid, the weight of his loose fist on his pelvis and the boards pressing his backside.

She's gone, he thought, with her harmonica to sit on the couch and play. He listened to the music from the other end of the hall.

But you can't make that discord on a harmonica.

He opened his eyes and rolled to his side (the batteryless projector clacked onto the floor at the end of the rattling chain) and frowned.

The sound was much further away than he'd thought; and was organ music.

She's gone . . . ?

Kid stood to pull his pants around on his leg.

The harmonica was not on the backdrop curving down over the floor.

He pushed his foot into his pants legs, sweaty in blotches. He picked up his vest, his orchid, and walked down the steps at the stage edge. Booted foot and bare left their alternative prints in the dust.

Also, his notebook was not in front of the couch.

At the room's center, he stopped to swallow something filling his throat. The sound with it was almost a sob.

Upstairs the organ played on. And there were voices, mumbling and growing and diminishing. It was silly to think she was upstairs. He put the orchid in his belt and shrugged up his vest as he climbed the steps.

A dozen black men and women milled from the chapel into the vestibule, from the vestibule into the street. Two women walking together glanced at him curiously. A man in a narrow-brimmed hat smiled at him and vanished. Others looked less friendly. The voices turned and blurred like smoke, or prickled with laughter that melted with the next dozen ambling by the closed office.

"Lovely service, don't you think . . ."

"She ain't gonna talk about all that stuff next time too, is she, 'cause I . . ."

"Didn't you think it was a lovely service . . ."

He stepped among them to leave. Somebody kicked his bare heel twice, but he racked it to accident and didn't look. Outside, the evening was purple grey; smoke blunted the facades across the street.

Only a few white people passed through the trape-

411

zoid of light across the sidewalk. A woman with a flowered scarf tied around her head followed an older man, talking earnestly with a black companion; and a heavy guy, blond, in a shirt with no collar that looked as if it were made of army blanket planted himself before the door, while brown and darker faces passed around him. Now a gaunt girl, with freckles on her tan cheeks and brick-red hair, reached him. The two whispered together, walked into the darkness.

Kid waited by the door, watching the worshippers, listening to the tape. People strolled away. Some voices lingered, till the owners followed their shadows into the night. The dwindling crowd made him feel lost. Maybe he should duck back in to tell Reverend Tayler he was leaving.

Studs bright in scuffed leather, shadows slipping across his shaggy, blond stomach, cap pushed back off the yellow brush, Tak Loufer stepped out, looked at Kid with a single highlight in one shadowed eye, and said, "Hey, you still around here? I sent two people over looking for you. But I thought you'd be gone by now."

5

"What are *you* here for?"

Tak held up a paper roll. "Completing my poster collection. You been keeping yourself away from us a while? We were worried about you."

"Shit!" fell from the residue of anger. "You wanted to suck on my dick some, maybe? Come on. It's all slicked up with pussy juice. You like that, right?"

"Nigger pussy?"

"Huh?"

"Were you screwing a colored girl? And with the clap?"

"What are you talking about?"

"If it wasn't black meat and a little runny, I'm not interested. Since I had you last time, boy, I've gone on to levels of perversion you haven't thought about. What's the matter with you, anyway? You out of it again? Why don't you come up and tell me about it while I get drunk."

"Aw, shit . . ." Not wanting to, Kid put his hands in his pocket and his head down in the night's chalky stench; they walked together to the curb.

"Your girl friend find you?"

Kid grunted.

"Did you have a fight or something? The last few times I spoke to her, I got the impression she was sort of getting ready for one."

"Maybe we did," Kid said. "I don't know."

"Ah, one of those?"

"She said you saw me get off a bus?"

"Yeah. Earlier this evening. I was down at the corner. I was going to call to you, but you turned first, down toward here."

"Oh."

A light moved in a window.

413

Fire, Kid thought. The flickering made him uneasy. He tried to imagine the whole block, the church and the buildings around it, conflagrated.

"I think somebody lives there," Tak said. "It's just candles." They stepped off the curb.

"Where are we?" Kid asked when they stepped up again. "I mean, Tak . . . what *is* this place? What happened here? How did it get like this?"

"A good question," Tak answered over tapping boot heels. "A very good one. For a while, I thought it was international spies—I mean, maybe the whole city here was just an experiment, a sort of test-out plan to destroy the entire country. Maybe the world."

"You think it's something like *that?*"

"No. But it's comforting to consider all this the result of *something* organized. On the other hand, it could just be another ecological catastrophe. Maybe somebody filled in our swamp by mistake."

"What swamp?"

"By every big city there's always some sort of large swamp nearby, usually of about the same area. It keeps the smog down, supplies most of the oxygen, and half a dozen other absolutely essential things. New York has the Jersey Flats, San Francisco, the whole mudded-out Oakland edge of the Bay. You fill the swamp in, the smog goes up, the sewage problem gets out of hand, and the city becomes unlivable. No way to avoid it. I think it's fair to say most people would find this unlivable."

Kid sniffed. "We sure got enough smog." The blades at his belt tickled the hair on his inner forearm. The chain that wrapped him had worked down so that it tugged across the back of his left hip at every other step. He reached under his vest and moved it with his thumb. "Do you think that's what happened to Bellona?" Some day I'll die, turned irrelevantly through his mind: Death and artichokes. Heaviness filled his ribs; he rubbed his chest for the reassuring systolic and diastolic thumps. Not that I really think it might stop, he thought: only that it hasn't just yet. Sometimes (he thought), I wish I couldn't feel it. (Someday, it will stop.)

"Actually," Tak was saying, "I suspect the whole thing is science fiction."

"Huh? You mean a time-warp, or a parallel universe?"

414

"No, just . . . well, science fiction. Only real. It follows all the conventions."

"Spaceships, ray-guns, going faster than light? I used to read the stuff, but I haven't seen anything like that around here."

"Bet you don't read the new, good stuff. Let's see: the Three Conventions of science fiction—" Tak wiped his forehead with his leather sleeve. (Kid thought, inanely: He's polishing his brain.) "First: A single man can change the course of a whole world: Look at Calkins, look at George, look at you! Second: The only measure of intelligence or genius is its linear and practical application: In a landscape like this, what other kind do we even allow to visit? Three: The Universe is an essentially hospitable place, full of earth-type planets where you can crash-land your spaceship and survive long enough to have an adventure. Here in Bellona—"

"Maybe that's why I don't read more of the stuff than I do," Kid said. He had had his fill of criticism with Newboy; the noise was no longer comforting. "Wasn't there a street lamp working on this block?"

Tak bulled out the end of his sentence: "—in Bellona you can have anything you want, as long as you can carry it by yourself, or get your friends to."

"It's funny, not that many people have that much."

"A comment on the paucity of our imaginations—none at all on the wonders here for the taking. No—it's a comment on the limits of the particular mind the city encourages. Who wants to be as lonely as the acquisition of all those objects would make them? Most people here have spent most of their time someplace else. You learn something from that."

"You've got more than practically anybody else I know," Kid said.

"Then you know very few people."

"Except Mr Calkins." Kid thought about the Richards. "And I don't know him." But Tak had seen Mr Newboy earlier. Tak would know his book was set.

"There's a whole range between," Tak said. "You've limited your acquaintances to the people who don't want very much. Essentially a religious choice, I suppose. All things considered, I'd say it was a wise one. There *are* a thousand people—perhaps—in this city."

"I did meet one family who—"

415

"There are many others. And most of them, as Paul Fenster keeps reminding us, are black."

"George Harrison just told me I should come over and visit him in Jackson."

Tak beat the darkness with his poster. "There! The whole thing. Paul will tell you, but George will show you, if you give him half a chance." Now Loufer sighed. "I'm afraid I'm still pretty much a verbal type. I'd just as soon be told."

"And look at posters."

"And read books. Preferably science fiction. But like I say, Bellona is terribly hospitable. You can have your fantasy and . . . well, besides eating it too, you can also feel just a bit less like you're depriving anyone else of theirs. Home again."

Kid looked around with blunt thumbs of darkness on his eyes. "We are? Tak, *didn't* there used to be a street light working at the end of your block?"

"Went out a few days ago. This way. Watch out for the steps. There's all sorts of junk around."

Some of it rolled beneath Kid's flexible leather sole. Soft darkness turned hard. The echo from the sound of breath and footsteps changed timbre.

They went through the hall, went downstairs, went up.

"First time you were up here," Tak laughed, "I made you park your weapons at the door. Boy, I don't know how some people put up with me."

The roof door opened on distant, flesh-colored light. Where the streets had been hopelessly black, the roof was dusted with nightlight.

Like two giant hieroglyphs, over-printed and out of register, the bridge's suspension cables rose to twin cusps, then dropped in smoke. No more than one row of buildings away, night water took up the glitter of both street lamps and redder quavering fires. "Hey, it's so close . . ."

Before him, above the city, shapes unfurled out over the water. He could not see the far shore. It could even have been a sea he gazed at, save for the bridge . . . Above, sky-bits seemed to clear, their clarity, however, unconfirmed by stars.

"How come it's so close?" He turned from the wall, as the light came on in the shack.

Tak had already gone inside.

416

Kid looked at the warehouses, at the waters between. Joy, sudden and insistent, twisted the muscles of his mouth toward laughter. But he held the sound in with tiny pantings. What swelled inside was made of light. It burst—he blinked and the backs of his lids were blinding—and left a great wave of trust washing inside. Not that I *trust* that trust for a moment, he thought, grinning. But it was there, and pleasant. He went into the shack. "It's ... it's so clear tonight."

A tiny solitaire of sadness gleamed in the velvet folds of good feeling.

"Last time I was up here, Lanya was with me."

Tak just grunted and turned from his desk. "Have some brandy." But he smiled.

Kid took the glass and sat on the hard bed. Now Tak unrolled the poster:

George Harrison as the moon.

"You got all three now." Kid sipped, with hunched shoulders.

George in cycle drag was still above the door.

George in the forest had replaced the Germanic youth.

Tak rolled his chair to the wall and climbed onto the green cushion. Corner by corner he tugged loose "Spanish boy on the rocks". "Hand me the staple gun?"

The first poster swayed to the floor.

Ch-klack, ch-klack, ch-klack, ch-klack, the new moon replaced it.

Kid sat down again and regarded the three aspects of George over the rim of his glass while Tak got down from the chair. "I . . ." Kid's voice sounded hollow and made something deep in his ear tickle so that he grinned. "You know, I lost five days?" He slid his fingers around the glass till the nubs butted.

"Where—" Tak put down the stapler, took up the bottle and leaned back against the desk, hands locked on the green neck; the base put a crease in his stomach— "—or would you be telling me if you knew—did you lose them?"

"I don't know."

"You look pleased enough about it."

Kid grunted. "A day now. It takes about as long as an hour used to when I was thirteen or fourteen."

"And a year takes about as long as a month. Oh yes, I'm familiar with the phenomenon."

"Most of the time in my life is spent lying around getting ready to fall asleep."

"That one has been mentioned to me before, but I'm not conscious of it myself."

"Maybe, somehow, for the last few days, I've just missed out on the sleeping part. There's hardly any change in light around here from morning to evening anyway."

"You mean the *last* five days are the ones you can't remember?"

"Yeah, what have I been up to, anyway? Lanya . . . said everybody was talking about it."

"Not everybody. But enough, I suppose."

"What were they saying?"

"If you lost those days, I can see why you'd be interested."

"I'd just like to know what I've been doing."

Brandy splashed inside the bottle to Tak's laughter. "Maybe you've traded the last five days for your name. Quick, tell me: Who are you?"

"No." Kid hunched his shoulders more. The feeling that he was being played with wobbled like an unsteady ball on some slanted rim, rolled into the velvet pouch. "I don't know that either."

"Oh." Tak drank from the bottle, set it back on his belly. "Well, I thought it was worth a try. I suspect it isn't something to be harped on." The brandy swayed. "What have you been doing for the last week? Let me see."

"I know I was with the scorpions—I met this guy named Pepper. And he turned me on to this department store they were going to try and . . . rip off, I guess."

"So far I'm with you. There was supposed to have been some shooting there? You were supposed to have saved one guy by fighting off somebody with a gun, bare-handed. You were supposed to have busted a mirror over the head of another guy who acted up with you—"

"Under his chin."

"That's it. Copperhead told me about that himself. And then when another cat named Siam got shot—"

"Was that his name?"

"—when Siam got shot, you pulled him off the street and got him into the bus."

"And you saw me get out of this bus earlier this evening."

418

"Copperhead told me about it a couple of days back."

"Only it happened to me this afternoon, God damn it!" Ashamed, he blinked at his hands. "That's all they said happened? I mean there wasn't anything else?"

"Sounds to me like enough."

"What happened to Siam?"

Tak shrugged. Brandy splashed. "Somebody went to see about him, I remember, from the bar."

"Madame Brown?"

"I think that's who it was. But I haven't heard anything else. For somebody who doesn't remember where he's been, you seem to know as much about it as I do." Tak reached over, dragged the chair to the desk, and sat. He started to put the bottle on the desk, but halted to take a final drink. "You do remember all the things I just told you about actually happening?"

Kid nodded at his lap. "I've just lost the time, then. I mean, I've lost days before—thought it was Thursday when it was Friday."

"All we thought, really, was that you'd deserted us to become a full-fledged scorpion. It was cool with me. You sure look like that's what happened. You got your lights and everything."

Kid focused on the lensed ball hanging against his stomach. "It doesn't work. It needs a new battery."

"Just a second." Tak opened a desk drawer. "Here you go." He tossed.

Kidd caught it in both hands: bunched lightning on red and blue.

"Turn yourself on sometime."

"Thanks." Wanting to talk longer, he put the battery in his pocket, noting the cloth was frayed enough at the bottom seam to feel flesh through it with his fingers. "Tak, you really think you got the city figured out?"

"Me?"

"You were telling me how it follows those conventions—"

Tak laughed, and wiped his mouth with his wrist. "No, not me. I don't understand anything about it. I'm a God-damn engineer. I take a plug; I put it in one socket; and it works. I put it in another one; and it doesn't. I go into an office building and one elevator works, and only the lights on the top floor. That's impossible, by anything

419

I know about. I go down a street: buildings are burning.
I go down the same street the next day. They're still
burning. Two weeks later, I go down the same street and
nothing looks like it's been burned at all. Maybe time is
just running backward here. Or sideways. But that's impossible too. I make my forage trips out to the warehouses, or some of the stores, and sometimes I can get
in, and sometimes I can't, and sometimes I have trouble, and sometimes I don't; and sometimes I take my
shopping bag into a store and clear off a shelf of canned
goods, and come back to that same store again a week
later—I mean I think it's the same damn store—and that
shelf is just as full as the first time I saw it. To my mind,
that's also impossible."

"Sometimes the morning light starts over here," Kid
said. "Sometimes it starts over there."

"Who told you about that?"

"You did. First day I got here."

"Oh." Tak lifted the bottle. "Oh, yeah. That's right.
You got a pretty good memory for some things."

"I remember lots of things: Some of it, so sharp it . . .
hurts sometimes. All this fog, all this smoke—sometimes
it'll be sharper and clearer than what you see in front of
you. And the rest of it—" he looked up again and noticed Loufer's discomfort—"just isn't there." Kid laughed,
which made Loufer chew harder on what was in the back
of his mouth. "Why do you stay in Bellona, Tak?"

"I gather your friend Ernest Newboy is leaving tomorrow. I don't know. Why do you?"

"I don't know."

"I mean, considering what you've been going through,
maybe Bellona isn't the best place for you." Tak leaned
forward, stretching the bottle out.

"Oh," Kid said. "Here." He held out his glass; Tak
refilled it.

"You were talking about the first night I met you.
Remember back then, I asked you why you'd come here,
and you said you had a purpose for coming?"

"That's right."

"Tell me what it is."

And once, in South Dakota, he had dropped a quarter into a pool that turned out to be much deeper than
he'd thought. He had watched the coin spin and dull and
vanish beyond the edging of leaves. Now a thought vanished from his mind, and the memory of the lost quarter

420

was all he had to describe the vanishing. "I . . . I don't know!" Kid laughed and pondered all the other things he might do; laughing seemed best. "I don't . . . remember! Yeah, I know I had a reason for coming here. But I'll be God damned if I can tell you what it was!" He leaned back, then forward, caught the brandy that was about to spill his glass in his mouth, and gulped it. "I really can't. It must have been . . ." He looked at the ceiling, suspending his breath for recollection. "I can't remember . . . remember that, either!"

Tak was smiling.

"You know, I had it with me; I mean, the reason." Kid swung out his hands. "I was carrying it around, in the back of my head, you know? Like on a back shelf? And then I just reached for it, to take it down, only I guess I knocked it over. I saw it fall off and disappear. I'm hunting around in my mind, but I can't . . . find it." He stopped laughing long enough to feel the annoyance that had begun to grow. "Bellona's not a bad place for me." Stated reasonably and smilingly, it was still annoyance. "I mean, I got a girl friend; I've met all sorts of people, some pretty nice—"

"Some not so nice?"

"Well, you learn. And I got a book. *Brass Orchids*, you know, my poems; it's all finished! They got galleys on it."

Tak still smiled, nodding.

"And you say people are talking about me like I'd done something great. Leave? You think I'm not going to go mad in some other city? There I might not have all these extras." Kid put the glass down, punched the air, and leaned back on the wall. "I . . . like it here? No. I want to see some sun. Sometimes I want to reach up and peel off all that sky. It looks like the cardboard they make egg crates out of, you know? Just peel it, in great, flapping strips. I wonder where Lanya went." He frowned. "You know, maybe I don't have a girl friend any more. And the book is finished with; I mean it's all written and in type; and I don't want to do any more." He turned his fist on his forefinger. "And even if they say I'm a hero, I didn't really do anything." He looked at the posters: just pictures, yet thinking that opened both their mocking and their harrowing resonances; he looked away. "Something isn't . . . finished here. No." The denial made him smile. "It's me. At least part has to do with me. Or maybe

421

George. Or June . . . It would almost *look* like every-thing was finished, wouldn't it? And maybe it's time to leave? But that's what lets me know I shouldn't. Because there're no distractions. I can look in and see. There's so much I don't know." The laughter filled his mouth, but when he let it out, it was only breath from a smile. "Hey, you want to blow me? I mean . . . if you'd like to, I'd like it."

Tak frowned, put his head to the side. But before he spoke, his own rough laugh exploded: "You *are* a nervy bastard!"

"I don't mean just suck my dick. I'd make love with you. I've done it before, with guys."

"I never doubted it a minute." Tak laughed again. "And no, I don't want to suck your dick, pussy or no. Where do you come off with that idea?"

But something inside had released. Kid yawned huge-ly and explained, with the end of it muddling his words, "Lanya said I should go to bed with you again; she thought you'd like it."

"Did she, now?"

"But I said you were only interested in first tastes." Looking at Loufer, he suddenly realized behind the blond jocularity there was embarrassment, so looked at his lap again. "I guess I was . . ." *right* was mauled by another yawn.

"Oh, look. Why don't you just lie down and go to sleep. What I want to do is drink about three more shots of brandy and read a God-damn book or something."

"Sure." Kid lay belly down on the pallet, and jiggled around so the chains and prisms and projector did not bite his chest.

Tak shook his head, turned around in his chair, and stretched for the second shelf over the desk. A book fell. Tak sighed.

Kid grinned and moved his mouth down into the crook of his arm.

Tak drank some more brandy, folded his arms on the desk and began to read.

Kid looked for the sadness again, but it was now neatly invisible among dark folds. Hasn't turned a page for ten minutes, was his last amused thought before he closed his eyes and—

"Hey."

Kid, lying on his back, grunted, "Huh?"

422

Tak scratched his naked shoulder and looked perturbed. Kid thought: *Now* he's going to—?

"I'm afraid I gotta kick you out."

"Oh . . ." Kid squinted and stretched, in muffled and mechanical protest. "Yeah, sure." Behind the bamboo curtains were streaks of light.

"I mean a friend of mine came over," Tak explained, "and we'd sort of like . . ."

"Oh, yeah . . ." Kid closed his eyes tight as he could, opened them, and sat up while the chains rattled down his chest, and blinked:

Black, perhaps fifteen, in jeans, sneakers and a dirty white shirt, the boy stood by the door, blinking on balls of red glass.

Kid's back snarled with chills; he made himself smile. From some other time came the prepared thought: Such distortion tells me nothing of him, and is only terrifying because so much is unknown of myself. And the autonomic nerves, habituated to terror, nearly made him scream. He kept smiling, nodded, got groggily to his feet. "Oh, sure," he said. "Yeah, I'll be on my way. Thanks for letting me crash."

Passing through the doorway, he had to close his eyes, again, tight as possible, then look, again, hopeful that the crimson would vanish for brown and white. They will think I'm still half asleep! he hoped, hoped desperately, his boot scraping the roof's tar-paper. Morning was the color of dirty toweling. He left it for the dark stair. Shaking his head, he tried not to be afraid, so thought: Ousted for someone younger and prettier, wouldn't you know. Well—beneath the lids the eyes were glass and red! He reached a landing, swung round it, and remembered the nervous woman with skirts always far too long for the season, who had been his math instructor his first term at Columbia: "A true proposition," she had explained, rubbing chalky fingertips hard on one another, "implies only other true propositions. A false one can imply, well, anything, true, false, it doesn't matter. Anything at all. Anything . . ." As if the absurd gave her comfort, her perpetual tone of hysteria had softened momentarily. She left before the term's completion. He hadn't, damn it!

Nine flights down he walked the warm hall. Twelve steps up? Thirteen he counted this time, stubbing his toe on the top one.

Kid came out on the dawn-dim porch hung with hooks and coiled with smoke. He jumped from the platform, still groggy, still blinking, still filled with the terror for which there was no other way to deal with save laughter. After all, he thought, ambling toward the corner, if this burning can go on forever, if beside the moon there really *is* a George, if Tak kicks me out for a glass-eyed spade, if days can disappear like pocketed dollars, then there is no telling. Or only the telling, but no reasoning. He hooked his thumbs in his pockets where the material was already fraying, and turned the corner.

Between the warehouses, clearing and fading in moving smoke, the bridge rose and swung out into oblivion.

Among the consorted fragments of his curiosity, the thought remained: I should have at least made him give me a cup of coffee before I went. He cleared his sticky throat, and turned, expecting the suspension cables any moment to fade forever, while he (forever?) wandered the smelly waterfront that somehow never actually opened on water.

This wide avenue had to lead onto the bridge.

Kid followed it for two blocks around a dark, official building. Then, beyond a twist of figure-eights and cloverleafs, the road rolled out between the suspensors, over the river.

He could only see as far as the start of the second span. The mist, among folds and tendrils, condensed the limits of vision. Foggy dawns should be chill and damp. This one was grit dry, tickled the back of his arms and the skin beneath his neck with something only a breath off body temperature. He walked up the edge of the road, thinking: There are no cars, I could run down the middle. Suddenly he laughed loudly (swallowing phlegm caught there in the night) and ran forward, waving his arms, yelling.

The city absorbed the sound, returned no echoes.

After thirty yards he was tired, so he trudged and panted in the thick, dry air. Maybe all these roads just go on, he theorized, and the bridge keeps hanging there. Hell, I've only been going ten minutes. He walked beneath several overpasses. He started to run again, coming around a curve to the bridge's actual entrance.

The roads' lines between the cables began a dozen perspective V's, their single vertex lopped by fog. Slowly, wonderingly, he started across toward the invisible

424

shore. Once he went to the rail and looked over through the smoke to the water. He looked up through girders and cables past the walkway toward the stanchion tower. What *am* I doing here? he thought, and looked again into the fog.

The car was back among the underpasses half a minute while its motor got louder. Maroon, blunt, and twenty years old, it swung out onto the gridded macadam; as it growled by, a man in the back seat turned, smiled, waved.

"Hey!" Kid called, and waved after him.

The car did not slow. But the man gestured again through the back windshield.

"Mr Newboy!" Kid took six running steps and shouted: "Good-bye! Good-bye, Mr Newboy!"

The car diminished between the grills of cable, hit the smoke, and sank like a weight on loose cotton. A moment later—*too* soon, from his own recollection of the bridge crossed by foot—the sound of the motor ceased.

What was *that* sound? Kid had thought it was some wind storm very far away. But it was the air rushing in the cavern of his mouth. *Good-bye, Mr Ernest Newboy,* and added with the same good will, *you're a tin Hindenburg, a gassy Nautilus, a coward to the marrow of each metatarsal. Though it would embarrass you to Hollywood and Hell, I hope we meet again. I like you, you insincere old faggot; underneath it all, you probably like me.* Kid turned and looked at the shrouded city, like something crusty under smoke, its streets stuck blind in it, its colors pearled and pasteled; so much distance was implied in the limited sight.

I could leave this vague, vague city . . .

But, holding all his humor in, he turned back toward the underpass. Now and again his face struck into grotesque. Where is this city's center? he wondered, and walked, left leg a little stiff, while buildings rose, again, to receive him.

Free of name and purpose, what do I gain? I have logic and laughter, but can trust neither my eyes nor my hands. The tenebrous city, city without time, the generous, saprophytic city: it is morning and I miss the clear night. Reality? The only moment I ever came close to it was when, on the moonless, New Mexican desert, I looked up at the prickling stars on that hallow, hollow dark. Day?

425

It is beautiful, there, true, fixed in the layered landscape, red, brass, and blue, but it is distorted as distance itself, the real all masked by pale defraction.

Buildings, bony and cluttered with ornament, hulled with stone at their different heights: Window, lintel, cornice and sills patterned the dozen planes. Billows brushed down them, sweeping at dusts they were too insubstantial to move, settled to the pavement and erupted in slow explosions he could see two blocks ahead—but, when he reached, they had disappeared.

I am lonely, he thought, and the rest is bearable. And wondered why loneliness in him was almost always a sexual feeling. He stepped off the sidewalk and kept along the loose line of old cars—nothing parked on this block later than 1968—thinking: What makes it terrible is that in this timeless city, in this spaceless preserve where any slippage can occur, these closing walls, laced with fire-escapes, gates, and crenellations are too unfixed to hold it in so that, from me as a moving node, it seems to spread, by flood and seepage, over the whole uneasy scape. He had a momentary image of all these walls on pivots controlled by subterranean machines, so that, after he had passed, they might suddenly swing to face another direction, parting at this corner, joining now at that one, like a great maze—forever adjustable, therefore unlearnable—

When the heavy man ran into the street, Kid first recognized the green-drab, wool shirt with no collar. Lumbering from the alley sidewalk, he saw Kid, headed for him. The man had been one of the white men at the church last night.

The fleshy face, red and sweat-flecked, shook above pumping fists. The top of the head was blotchy under a haze of yellow; on the forehead the hair lay out like scrap brass.

Suddenly Kid started to move backward. "Hey, watch it—"

"You—!" The man lunged. His fingers caught among, and tugged at, Kid's chains. "You are the one who . . ." At the Mexican accent Kid rifled his wounded memory. "When I was . . . you didn't . . . no? You, please . . . don't . . ." the man panted through wet lips. His eyes were bloodshot coral. "Oh, please, don't you . . . you were in there, yes? I . . . I mean you fool around like that, they gonna . . ." His mouth compressed; he looked across the street, looked back. "You . . . Oh, the Kid!" and

426

yanked his hand from tangled links while Kid thought: No, he didn't say 'the Kid,' he maybe said 'the kid,' or even 'they did.' The man was shaking his head: "No, you gonna . . . Hey, don't do that . . ."

"Look," Kid said, trying to take his arm. "You need some help? Here, let me—"

The man jerked away, nearly fell, began to run.

Kid took two steps after him, stopped.

The blond Mexican tripped on the far sidewalk, pushed up from his knee, and made it into the alley.

Circling Kid's mind was the Mexican voice in the hall at the Richards'; various mentions by Thirteen; amphetamine-psychosis? And then the thought, clear and overriding:

He was . . . crazy!

Something cascaded, tickling like a line of insects, across his stomach. For a moment he mistook it for a chill of recognition; indeed, real chills ignited a moment after.

But the optic chain had parted, probably under the man's tugging, and fallen down over his belt.

Kid picked up the loose end, found the other hanging across his chest—it had parted between lens and prism—and pulled the thin brass together. On one end still hung a tiny, twisted link. With great, stubby fingers, nearly numb inside their callous, he tried to get it closed. He stood in the street, pinching, twisting, sometimes holding his breath, sometimes letting it all out suddenly with a mumbled "Shit . . ." or "Fuck . . ." His armpits slipped with the sweat of concentration. His heels, one on leather, one on pavement, stung at different heats. His chin stayed tucked into his neck: he squinted in the dawn light, turning once so that his own, edgeless shadow slid from his fumbling nubs. It took practically ten minutes to fix.

And you could still tell which link had parted.

When he was finished, he was very depressed.

V

When he had walked for several minutes, turned several corners, and the several tensions in his neck and back had ceased (he could think words now without striking up hysterical images on the screens of all five senses), he pissed in the middle of the street, hoping someone might pass and, with his fly half open and his fingers under his belt, walked again and asked himself: Now just what is the problem with seeing an occasional red eyeball, hey? It is: If I'm hallucinating *that*, how do I tell if anything else is real? Maybe half the people I see aren't there—like that guy who just ran up? What's he doing in my world? Some fragment of Mexico, recreated out of smoke and fatigue? How do I know there isn't a chasm in front of me I've hallucinated into plain concrete? (The entrance to the bridge . . . when I first came off it, was all broken and piled . . . with concrete . . . ?) Put the whole thing up to dreaming? When I was seventeen or eighteen I stopped that. Five days!

I am mad again, he thought. Tears brimmed. He swallowed in a tightened throat. I don't want to be. I'm tired, I'm tired and horny, I'm so tired I can't make sense out of any of it and my mind won't work right half the time I try. I'm thirsty. My head's all filled with kapok coffee wouldn't clear. Still, I wish I had some. Where am I going, what am I doing, stumbling in this smoking graveyard? It's not the pain; only that the pain keeps going on.

He tried to let all his muscles go and stepped aimlessly from sidewalk to gutter, his mouth dryer and dryer

429

and dryer. Well, he thought, if it hurts, it hurts. It's *only* pain. All right (he looked at blurred house tops above the trolley wires), I've chosen, I'm here.

To come upon the monastery? Yes, now, wherever it was, what ever. Walls and white buildings? Syllables to mumble away the meaning? He had passed nothing that could possibly have been one. The streets were strewn with refuse, months old, dried, and odorless: feces gone pale and crumbly, ossified fruit rind, old papers, once wet and now crinkly dry.

He prodded the folds of his consciousness for sadness: the crystal had deliquesced to chalky powder.

. . . she look like? he thought, and was too tired to panic. Her name, what was that?

Lanya: and he saw her short hair, her green eyes, and she was not there.

One of the street signs was marred with filth and scratchings; the other was an empty frame. He turned into the alley because of the beats; for seconds he could not figure what had happened—a row of tree trunks on the narrow sidewalk, each in a metal fence, had burned to charred spikes. Wonderingly, Kid started down the street, not wide enough for two cars.

Denny sat on the fender of a lopsided auto, a-straddle the smashed headlight, drumming two fingers on the bent rim. Kid walked toward him, wondering when to speak . . .

"Hey, how're you!" Denny's surprise became delight. "What you doin' here?" He banged with all his knuckles once and stopped. "What you doin' huh?"

"Just taking a walk. Trying to get my cock sucked. Or something. Only nobody's out."

"Huh?" Denny looked puzzled, and then—to Kid's surprise—embarrassed. He flipped one finger three times on the chrome, then looked up again with his lips tight. "The downtown end of the park has got queers all over it, all day and all night. You know the part with the paths?"

"No."

"Well it does." Denny flipped his finger once more. "If you been walking around all night, you couldn't've been looking very hard."

"I was at this guy's house," Kid explained. "I thought he was gonna do me, but somebody else came over and

430

he kicked me out. What are you doing out this hour of the morning?"

Denny nodded toward one of the unpainted buildings. "I'm staying in there now." Behind dirty window glass, the brass lion leered, pinioned on his brass stalk. The shade was gone. The socket held a broken bulb neck.

On the other side of the street, a white curtain moved in a window almost as dirty. Two black faces pressed together, looked till Kid stared directly. The curtain dropped.

"You want to get your cock sucked? Come on." Denny, with three fingers tucked under the rim, was looking straight down. "I'll blow you."

"Huh?"

When Denny neither moved nor said anything else, Kid started to laugh. "Hey . . ." He stepped on the sidewalk, hit his thighs in imitation of Denny's drumming, then stepped back into the street. "Are you being funny . . . ?"

Denny looked up. "No."

"Now suppose I took you up on that . . ." Kid said, trying to make it a joke; it wasn't. So he said: "You want to . . . ?" Things that made the obscure obvious by overturning overturned.

"Yeah." Denny scratched his chest among rattling chains. "Go on, take it out. Right here, mother-fucker." He shook his head. "I'll do you right here. You want me to show you I mean it? Right here?"

Kid glanced at the window curtain. "Sure, but those spades, they're staring out the damned window."

Denny let out his held breath. "I just told *you;* you think I give a fuck if *they* know?"

What he'd began as banter was suddenly uncomfortable, because though all the actions were predictable, the feelings were not. "Hey, you know maybe you just better let the whole thing . . ."

Denny leaned his head and glanced to the side with a concentrated expression—the look, Kid thought, of someone in a game of go trying to decide if a long-contemplated move, now made, was, after all, right.

"We'd have to find someplace," Kid said. "A doorway, or inside or something. I don't want to do it right here." Fifteen? Kid thought. He's out of his head; this kid is a fucking nut.

Denny got down from the headlight and slid most of his fingers in his back pockets. "You come on with me."

Kid caught up to him on the unpainted steps. "Is this Nightmare's place?" He put his hand on Denny's small, warm shoulder.

Denny looked back. "Used to be." His vest, showing rough-out leather, then scuffed tanning, swung against his ribs. "Just about anybody stays there now. Even Thirteen's been crashing there. The way he goes on, you'd think he was gonna make it his new place."

Kid frowned. "What . . . happened to his old one?"

Denny frowned back. "Well, everybody's moved around since . . ." He nodded. "The kids in the commune, they all went to the other side of the park. Dragon Lady moved her bunch up this side of Cumberland. And Thirteen couldn't stay in that damn apartment no more . . . but you was there." Denny's frowned questioned Kid's.

"Why . . . ?" Kid asked, because there was no answer he could supply.

"The smell," Denny said, "for one thing," and went up the steps.

Kid followed. "Oh, yeah. That . . ." which made sense; but not the whole shifting and rearrangement during the robbed duration. The whole tape of reality which he had been following had somehow overturned. It still continued; he still followed. But during some moment when he had blinked, days had elapsed and everything right had shifted left: Everything left was now right. "Hey, the last time you saw me, how long was I with——?"

"Shhh," Denny said. "Everybody's asleep." He pushed open the door. "It ain't even six o'clock in the morning, I bet."

And Kid suddenly did not want an answer. He asked instead in a softer voice: "Then what are you doing up?"

"I get up real early some times." Denny grinned back over his shoulder as Kid followed him down the hall. "Sometimes I sleep all day, too. You can do that here . . . but then I'm up all night."

By the hall baseboard, tight, black hair shocked from the end of a sleeping bag. Beyond a doorway, on a couch, a naked man with red hair all over his tan, freckled back—it *was* Copperhead—slept with a very blond girl wedged between himself and the couch back. Over his bare ankle, Kid could see her sandal, the neatly

432

rolled cuff of her jeans. Her arm, pale from the sleeve of a navy pea-jacket, moved up the torn upholstery, then fell. Someone in another room stopped snoring, cleared his throat, coughed, was silent.

Denny glanced around. "You wanna do it in the bathroom?"

"No." Kid struck Denny's shoulder with his hand's heel. "I don't want to do it in the bathroom!" While Denny blinked, curious, the bathroom door at the end of the hall opened and Smokey walked out, sleepy, in nothing but jeans, her fly hanging open. With neither shielding nor greeting, she passed.

Leaning against the water tank, Kid saw the splotched dummy looped in chain—before the door swung to.

"I'm in here."

Which is where the Harley had been moved.

"How come you get a room all by yourself . . . ?" Kid asked, realizing with the last word that three of the bundles among the shovels (why shovels?), pipes, lumber, and canvas, were people in sleeping bags.

Someone had built a loft.

Three steps up the ladder, Denny looked back over his shoulder. "You come up."

Denny's boots went over the edge. Kid climbed. The planks (they gave some with his hands and knees) were strewn with blankets. The size of a double bed, the platform was without pillow or mattress. "I keep all my shit up here," Denny explained, pushing himself back among wrinkled cloth. By his left hand was an army compass, a green shirt (with gold trim) fresh pressed and wrapped in plastic, a dagger whose handle was a ball-in-claw, and a gaming case on whose outside were long, alternately black and black-outlined triangles for backgammon.

Kid crawled forward through army drab and a weave of paler green rippled through with an electric-blanket cord. In the window that rose above the platform, a mottled shade let tan light on the tangle. He pulled his feet under him to sit and realized his arm was shaking. "How come you don't have half a dozen people sleeping up here with you?"

"I tell 'em to get the fuck out." Denny's hands lay knotted in his lap.

A zodiacal poster hung on the wall: Scorpio. And

another of Koth, the Dark Angel. "It's sort of nice up here," Kid whispered. His throat was tight. I'm scared of him, he realized. And I like him. "Get the rest of your clothes off."

"Why?"

Kid let out a breath. "Nothing." He thumbed open the top button and tugged down his zipper. "Go on." He pulled his penis and testicle free of the closing V of brass teeth and let his shoulders relax against the plywood wall.

The ceiling would not let Denny stand. With hunkered back and crouched knees, the boy walked across the bedding, his arms swinging like a skinny blond ape. And fell. Kid flexed his knee under Denny's hand. Denny's hair swung forward, brushed Kid's belly.

His mouth is cold! Kid thought, and pulled his hand away a little sharply. Then he realized that it was only that the boy's lips were wet. Heat covered his thickening penis. He bent his knees and clamped them on Denny's thin flanks. He pushed his hand down his stomach, through moving hair. Saliva in his wiry groin was already cool. "That's good. Make it wet." His fingers butted the base. He pushed back Denny's hair, suddenly bending (and failing) to see the flattened cheeks, the distended mouth. The hair fell back. He cupped the back of Denny's neck. An image of the corpse in the shaft made him let his breath; he wished it hadn't. An equally surprising urge to smack the bobbing head away. Kid grunted, "Unn . . ." and then again, "Unn . . ." and had to close his eyes at the sensation. He pressed his palm against the warm ear. The head moved up and his penis was cold.

"Is it okay?" Denny asked.

"Yeah . . ."

Heat fell down it like a loose ring. His scrotal sack loosened between his thighs, then shriveled when spit ran down his leg, inside his pants. The moving head shook Kid's arm to the shoulder. He reached for Denny's shoulders. Denny tightened his fingers on Kid's thigh, let go, let himself be pulled up to lay with his chest on Kid's, a clutch of chain and crushed vest between them.

Denny's face was hard and amazed. "What you want?" All the small muscles of chin, cheek, and jaw were visible.

Kid rubbed Denny's back. "I want you to take the rest of your fucking clothes off." Denny's skin was hot and dusty dry.

With his other hand, Kid reached between them to move his cock, caught between creased denim.

Denny jerked back to his knees, took a breath, and began to unzip his pants. Kid thought: he doesn't want me to touch his dick. Something like anger gathered in his stomach.

Denny said softly and hoarsely, "You don't have to take yours off." He worked his jeans back beneath his knees, stopped to pull handfuls of chain from his neck.

Kid scratched his belly. Denny stopped all motion, his eyes caught Kid's groin. Something happened in Kid's throat and to his mouth that it was easy to think was fear, was easier to think desire.

Kid's cock, hardening, rolled up his thigh.

Denny's throat released the little air he tried to hold.

"Take your pants off . . ." Kid checked anger against desire. Checking only spilled the anger into his voice. "Go on . . ." Desire remained, a heavy heat under his stomach.

Denny sat back to pull off his boots. On the right, the outer half of the heel was worn to the leather. He pulled the left off more quickly. Loops of chain fell around his ankle. The knob of bone divided three strands from four: a dog's choke collar, wrapped several times. Denny leaned back to pull his pants off.

Kid looked at Denny's hands, Denny's feet, Denny's groin. His own back, against the wall, was slightly stiff. Denny, changing the texture of his movements, now began to fold his jeans, not looking at Kid. To relieve his shoulders, Kid sat forward. Then he reached out and pulled the jeans out of Denny's hands and tossed them in the corner with the boots and blankets. Denny's expression, as his eyes sought something other than Kid's, moved from confusion to belligerence.

Kid smiled, and the smile became the soft laughter for a house full of sleepers. "Come on."

Denny pushed himself forward. Then he said hoarsely: "That's pretty funny I should freak out now, ain't it?" The dry, hot skin brushed Kid's, pressed Kid's, a hand between their shoulders: heel hard, four light pressures and the length of thumb. Kid looked down at where the black-lined nails touched him. He reached around Denny's shoulders to cover the boy's fingers with his own. *Child's?* he thought. And then, with concern: Why has this child brought me here? He tightened both arms across Denny's back: Denny was shivering. "Hey . . ." Kid

435

rubbed the boney stalk of Denny's spine down to where the flesh thickened and became soft. Then up. Then down. "Hey, cut that out. What's the matter?"

Denny still shook. "Nothing."

I'm afraid. And I want to stop this. Shit, no! "Come on, then. You try to relax." Kid worked further from the wall across the piled blankets. Holding Denny on top, he made a rocking motion. Denny turned his face away so that the side of Kid's face was all a-brush with yellow.

"If we just lay around like—"

One of the people under the loft turned over. And Denny stopped breathing for the count of three; then went on:

"—like this, we ain't never gonna do nothing."

Go on and do what you want then, was anger. With the sentence in his mouth unsaid, Kid realized: I'm twelve years older than him. He said, "Get down there and suck it," which, at the scrambling over his chest and stomach and the welling heat in his groin, he knew *was* lust. He reached for the hair and hunched shoulders between his legs. With his leg, he rolled Denny over on his side, pushing and pushing. Denny held Kid's thighs. Their congress was intense and diligent, till Denny, not holding him, was hammering near Kid's hip. "Okay . . ." Kid panted, and let the boy go. A quarter toward orgasm, Kid hunkered down to press his hard groin on a hip, a thigh, something.

"Hey . . ." Breathing hard, Denny lay on his back. He raised his hand, glistening knuckles, strung with grey mucous. "I guess I came." He grinned. "What am I gonna do with this stuff?"

"Eat it," Kid said. "That what you usually do?"

"Yeah." Denny looked back up at the ceiling and put his fore knuckle in his mouth, turned his hand to lick the heel.

Kid put his arm, moist with effort, across Denny's thin, hard chest, still dry, and rubbed on the bony hip. Denny took his two middle fingers out of his mouth. "You didn't come yet?"

"Nope."

"Go . . . go on and do what you want."

Yeah, Kid thought, that's anger. He laughed.

"When I was little," Denny said and pressed the back of his hand against his open mouth, "there were these two brothers who were the strongest kids in my neighborhood. I used to want to be like them. And once they told me they were so strong because they used to eat each others' come. I didn't even know what they were talking about then. I hadn't even ever jerked off, you know?" Denny turned to look at Kid. "I guess it's protein or something. You do it too?"

Kid shook his head. "No."

"Then how'd you know?"

Kid shrugged. "You just looked like you were somebody who might."

"What's that mean?"

"I don't know." Kid squeezed the tight muscle under the tissuey skin of Denny's arm. "Maybe it's because you're strong. Like they said." He put his leg over Denny's, then suddenly sat. He felt his hair brush the ceiling and hunched. "You like that, hey?"

Denny grinned again, and held Kid's cock in his slick hand. Kid started to rock. Denny said, "You like girls?"

Kid was surprised. "Yeah."

"You wanna fuck a girl?"

"Why don't you just open your mouth? Or turn over, huh?"

"Just a second. Lemme up—"

"Hey, look, all you gotta—" But Denny struggled up. Kid let himself be pushed away, annoyed and curious.

"I'll be right back," Denny whispered, dropping over the edge of the board. Kid sighed and pushed his hand down between his legs. I may be crazy, he thought, but this one's nuts! He reached under his shoulder and pulled flat a fold of blanket. Look over the edge . . . ? No. He stared at the ceiling that had brushed his head. Former owners had painted the cracked plaster white without spackle.

People came into the room.

She said, "Where?"

Denny said, "Up there, on my bed. Go on."

The platform shook as someone started up the ladder. Kid looked. Her curly hair, confused with sleep, her astounded eyes, her smiling mouth cleared the edge. She said, "Um . . ." then giggled, and then, "Hello."

"Go on up," Denny's voice urged.

She looked back down. "I am." She came over the edge and crawled forward, breasts swinging out against her arms, in against one another.

She had once brought him whiskey in the bathtub when he had been fouled with blood. "Hey!" Kid said, "how're you?" She smiled again and pulled herself to sit cross-legged, with lots of dark hair in the triangle of heel, heel, and groin.

Denny came up too, leaned on his forearms, grinning. I am being used, Kid thought. For what, I am not sure.

"So what are we supposed to do now?" Kid asked.

"He likes to get his dick sucked," Denny said.

The girl reached out, with the tip of her tongue in her teeth.

"Hey!" Kid said to Denny, *"You* get on up here!"

Denny's expression went momentarily blank. Then he scrambled up onto the platform. The girl giggled again, and suddenly fell against him. "Hey . . ." Kid caught her, and while she laughed, he scraped his shoulder on the wall and hit his elbow. She didn't let go his penis.

Denny tried not to giggle and was saying, "Come on, now. Be quiet . . ." He had scooted to the corner, and rocked and hugged his knees.

"Hey . . ." Kid said again and moved a boot (Denny's) from under his shoulder. Something in the midst of the pressure tickled his chest. He looked down. She had her face against him: it was her eyelash opening and closing. "Hey," he said a third time, and caught his hands in her curly hair and pulled her head back.

She just said, "Annnn . . . !" He kissed her. She grabbed his shoulders up near his neck and pushed back with her tongue. He held himself up with his left hand, mashed the softness of her shoulder with his right, of her breast, of her belly. When he pushed his middle fingers against the flesh folded in her cunt, she swung up her knee, with shaking calf and thigh. The entrance was soft. Inside his fingers found a sloppy firmness that slowly gave and grew softer. She made lots of little noises, and her hand on his penis became maddening as feathers. Trying (and succeeding) not to take his tongue out of her mouth, he moved around her, crawling over her large thighs, and wedged himself between them. He pulled out to go in again, and opened his eyes to find hers wide and staring toward Denny. But they came back to his, and at the same time she swung her legs up around him like hot pillows. He dug in her with penis and tongue, yet something changed gears inside him; he let it slow, and from

438

the slowness build. Curious himself, he looked up with jogging sight. Denny, moved forward to his knees, with cantilevered cock, his mouth slightly open, and closing— mumbling things too soft to hear.

Kid turned his face against hers and momentarily saw himself surrounded by soft, by wet, by warm. He thrashed out in it, and came; a single, intense spasm that left her rolling under him and sucking at his mouth, the hard place between the mashed breasts pressing against his. Not felt since sometime far back in adolescence, he wanted violently to be free of physical contact. He rolled from her, feeling silly, while she caught her breath and the cold slapped his sweaty thighs and stomach—as he knew it had slapped hers. That wasn't it either. On his back he worked himself against her again; she made no protest, but turned to push her face against him. "Hey . . ." He raised one arm to slide it beneath her head. "Hey, come here." With the other, he motioned to Denny.

Denny stretched his legs out and slid over. Kid caught him around the shoulder. Denny lay down, put his leg over Kid's, his cock a small bar across Kid's hip. "You didn't come, did you?" Kid asked her.

"Um," she said, surprised, and blinked at him. He tugged at Denny without looking at him. "I shot my load and your girl friend hasn't had hers yet. Get down there and do something about it."

"Huh?" He felt Denny push himself up on one elbow.

Kid licked her nose. She squinted. "I want to watch you eat my come out of her pussy," which was patently untrue. *That's* what I'm being used for! He wanted to watch her face; her eyes were half-closed, glistening slivers between the lashes. Her upper lip brushed and brushed the lower. Denny's neck was two hard bands with a valley between. Kid pulled it forward. "Go on, do it."

Denny grunted his protest. The girl suddenly looked surprised.

Kid clamped his hand on Denny's neck, in time to see fear below the protest. "Go on, mother-fucker. Or I'll bust your head open!"

Denny swallowed and dropped his face.

Kid closed his fingers in the yellow hair, pushed the bobbing head and rocked it, less roughly than he thought he should.

She said, "Oh . . ." once and moved her leg. He looked at her: she kept the surprised expression. Inches away from her face, he questioned her with his eyes (she wouldn't answer), kissed her gently, harder, till at last she closed her eyes—tight—and began to gasp. He felt her hand touch and avoid his in Denny's hair, so let go (but pressed his leg against the boy's back) while he kissed her. He caressed her limp, long breast, rolling on her ribs. A heavy girl of . . . seventeen? Eighteen? Older than Denny; still a child. Her soft tongue blunted on his hard one. He held himself away from her, touching her only with hand and mouth. Once her hands hit his at his arched belly, returned to Denny's hair, and he heard the boy gasp. Denny was flexing on the wrinkled blankets as his head rocked and wobbled. "Unn . . ." she said, "Unn . . . Unnn . . . Unn . . ." Then she squealed and clutched him.

Kid dropped on her, gathering what was soft about her sides between his hands and elbows.

"Get your fucking knee off my head," Denny said.

With the tips of her fingers, she climbed Kid's back, and sighed, and tightened her hands in their climbing.

Denny pulled free of their legs and flopped against Kid.

"How you, sloppy-face?" Kid put his arm around Denny. The boy buried his chin, already cold, in Kid's shoulder. "Do you do this to everybody who drops by for a blow job in the morning?"

"It's *her* idea," Denny said.

She giggled and said, "It is *not!*"

Kid felt the boy's groin against his hip, "Denny's still got a hardon," he told the girl. "You want to take him on front and center?"

She raised her hand and laughed again. "Sure. But he won't do that."

Kid turned to Denny. "You don't like to fuck?" He was thirsty. But you have to ask for something to drink later . . .

"I guess not," Denny said. "I mean it won't stay up . . ." It came out with sudden, adolescent gravity. ". . . see?" And it was softening.

"His tongue sure stays up, hey?" Kid said. The girl rubbed the side of his knee with hers.

Kid rubbed back, reached between Denny's legs.

"Hey, what are you . . ."

440

"Woops!" Kid said. "It's up again. Come on, I want to see you try."

The girl rolled on her back. "He won't do it."

"You shut up."

"I think he should." She folded her hands under her breasts. "But he keeps saying he's gay."

"Why don't you lay off me?" Denny said.

"I got a hand full of your dick." He moved his fingers so that Denny's crotch hair rubbed the ring of knuckle, forefinger, and thumb. "It's hard now."

"Denny . . . ?" the girl said and uncrossed her hands.

Wrapped between ham and heel, Denny's cock bobbed but did not wilt. "Don't worry," Kid said, "I won't let go of it."

"Shit," Denny said and pushed himself up. "Okay, but it won't work." Denny's knee hit Kid's stomach.

"Uhhh . . ."

Denny's hands landed on Kid's chest. "Hey, you let go!"

"So? You still got a hardon. You sure that's the only thing you're worried about?" Kid sat up and put one hand on Denny's hip, and rubbed the boy's buttocks with the other, moved his hand between them, to hair and loose scrotal flesh. Denny's skin was still brick dry. His own and the girl's (one soft thigh spread under his calf) were moist. She moved and made a sound like moaning; could have been mouthed laughter; even protest.

Kid put one hand on her belly, pressed a finger in a crease. He moved his hand onto her hair and mirrored her moan with his voice.

A muscle in Denny's thigh moved on Kid's wrist. The testicles lay on his palm. Kid brushed the undershaft with his fingers. "You like that?" He held the penis, moved his hand out to cover the circumcised head, back so that thick flesh moved under innards rigid as dry sponge. "You just think about the rest of my load in there, what you ain't got on your face. You won't lose it . . . yeah!" because his other hand, spreading the third and fourth finger, pressed and she gave, wet with mucus. "Go on . . ."

Denny lowered himself. The muscle in his thigh shook till his knee slipped on the blanket.

"His dick and my two fingers in your pussy," Kid said. "They can't *all* give out at once. Hey, look at him hump!"

Her hand lay loose: small fingers on white palms

441

where the sweat was shiny as mica. The fingers moved to
close and did not close, moved to open and did not:
she touched Denny's shoulders as his pale hair curled
against her face. Kid felt the boy shake, the cock sliding
on his knuckles. He took his hand from between them to
hold himself up. Denny's body flattened on her larger
one beneath. Kid prodded between them again. "Hey,
boy . . . there you go. You like that, huh?" He balanced
himself to rub her arm, and felt a muscle twitch in her
shoulder. "You like it too, don't you?" On the seventh or
eighth motion, he could again move his middle finger
knuckle deep in her beside Denny's scrotal sack which,
having shriveled tight as possible, now unwrinkled on his
palm. Denny backed up to push. Her hand jerked on
his shoulder. Kid could not see her face. Denny pushed
again and her counterpush beneath him made her legs
sway. They're so silent, he thought, and caught his breath;
his own cock was tight and tense and hard enough to
hurt. He moved his hand from between them, and lay
down beside them, pressed himself against them, his dick
along the flexing crevice between, one arm across Denny's
back, the other around the top of her head. Denny did
not break rhythm. Kid nuzzled between their faces, trying
to kiss her, but she would not turn toward him. Denny's
breath was loud as an engine. "Hey, you fuck that
shit . . ." Kid whispered. "You bust that pussy wide open,
cocksucker! Bury him in pussy, bitch!" Denny was a motion against his right hip; against his left, her hip thrust
and shook under Denny's falling, and falling, and falling
faster. So he moved his hand down between Denny's
buttocks; felt the first sweat on the dry body. Denny
pushed harder. She had raised her far leg around his
thighs, and was panting. Kid reached over her calf, thinking, maybe she won't like that, and between Denny's legs,
moving down a few inches so he could cup balls; Denny
growled, and he was going to take his hand away, but the
growl articulated, "Yeah . . . ! That's right. Go on . . ."
He jabbed his hand forward and she, beneath, jerked in
a way that should have had a cry with it. Denny pushed
and pushed and pushed and pushed and stopped pushing,
while she went on, and let out all his air. "Jesus Christ . . ."
muffled against her neck. His ass relaxed. Then he began
to pant.

Kid rubbed his neck, and Denny laughed against her,

442

reached up to brush his hair from her face. She was panting too.

"Hey?" Kid brushed her cheek with his knuckle. Her wide eyes locked his. "You make it this time?" With his other hand, he pushed his cock down against her thigh. "I can go again."

She flashed an uncertain smile. "I'm okay."

"Shit!" Kid let his head drop with a bark of laughter. "I'm tired, that's what I am." He closed his eyes, and a breath later heard them making movements. His own groin, still engorged, was numbing. I bet I'm going to wake up with cramps under my balls, he thought, and didn't care. Denny touched his shoulder, tugged a little. So he rolled back against them. Denny made another breathy sound, and hugged Kid tightly, suddenly pushed his face against Kid's neck. "Hey . . . !" He caught the boy, who was giggling all panty like a puppy (like her, he remembered, when she had first fallen against him). He moved his hand down the hard flank till his knuckles touched her softer one. "Go to sleep or something." Denny took his face away, and Kid worked his arm beneath her neck (her hair was much crisper than the boy's, and the back of her neck was moist and hot; his own, moist and cooling) and felt comfortable enough to let himself drift. Drifting, he realized how loud Denny's breath was and listened for hers. It was slower and farther away. Then, after a time that might have been sleep, it was faster. He reached for her, only brushed her, he thought: A strangeness, hey, and beautiful. His lips, drying, had adhered to one another. They tore apart with the breath and the mumbled word: beautiful. Released, he fell away into sleep.

He woke in annoyance that turned immediately to pleasure. Somebody was blowing him. He grinned on the darkness of his lids, reached down through three levels of thought. Lanya? No, this other girl. His hand glanced from bone under soft hair to hit the hard, tight shoulder. Denny grunted.

"What you doing?" Kid asked. He rolled his head left, then right on the creased blanket, then again with his eyes open. The girl was gone.

Denny said, "You were asleep all the time with a God-damn hardon. I was just—" Kid locked his fingers in Denny's hair and pulled his head down.

443

"That's what you started doing and *you* ain't finished me yet."

Denny dropped his mouth again.

Kid moved one fist out in the blanket beside his face, hoping it was still warm from her. One fantasy memory of Denny's face between her legs and his penis thrust between them . . . he moved from fantasy and lay, with his mouth opened, his head back, each muscle loosening; Denny held Kid's balls while he sucked; and that felt good. Kid held the boy's sides with his legs. And came. It was something like hot oil poured in cotton (cotton into flame; flame, out beneath water. Water and ashes and ashes washed through him); "Come on up here."

Denny lay down on Kid's chest.

Kid rubbed his back, dry and papery as before. He wanted to say thanks, but decided it would be silly, so he squeezed Denny's shoulder instead.

"Your come tastes different from mine," Denny said.

"Yeah?" Kid closed his eyes.

"It's more, you know, liquid. And there's more of it."

"I'm bigger than you."

"And it's more bitter."

"You know," Kid said, "you're a pretty funny little guy. Where'd your girl friend go?"

"She got—"

Somebody came into the room, moved something below them, turned.

Kid looked down across the blanket as a nondescript top-of-a-head left through the doorway.

"—got up a little while ago and went out." Denny's fist uncurled on Kid's shoulder.

"Oh. You two do this a lot?"

"Huh?"

"Drag people into bed all the time?"

"Not like this."

"Like how?"

"I don't know. It's her idea, most of the time. She's my best friend here."

Kid nodded, his chin tapping the top of Denny's head. "Is she a scorpion too?"

"Naw. She's not a member. Not like Filament. Or Lady of Spain. She just likes to hang around with them." He shifted. "I mean us. I bring guys around for her sometimes. As long as she lets me watch. A couple of times I

444

messed around with the guys, just a little. But not like
. . . well, what *we* did."

"You like messing around with her too?"

Denny shrugged. "I don't know. I guess so. But I
never done that before. I mean get inside."

Kid laughed.

"Sometimes she'd tell me I should, but I never did. It
just embarrassed me, you know? I couldn't keep it hard,
I mean before."

"Oh." Kid tried not to smile, even though Denny
could not see it.

"I can get guys for her two or three times a week,
sometimes. She says she don't wanna be one guy's girl
friend."

"She likes two at a time? I can dig it."

"Maybe." Denny moved a little. "We do anything
together, any old crazy thing, you know? If I told her to
do something real crazy, like go up in an old building
where there might be people hiding with guns, she'd do it.
We found all sorts of junk. In old buildings. There's lots
of stuff around."

Kid crossed his arms over Denny's back; the warm
mouth brushed his chest.

"I like to watch her make it with guys," Denny said.
"When I blew you, were you thinking about her?"

"You'd like that, wouldn't you? No, I wasn't. I mean
only a little at first."

"I don't care what you were thinking about," Denny
said. "You think you know an awful lot about what I
like, huh?"

Now Kid shrugged. "I think I like you. How's that?"
Relaxing from the shrug, he began to laugh. "You want to
suck it, sit on it, that's fine by me. Now you're going to
turn around and run off and look all scared and wide-eyed
at me every time we see each other from now on, huh?
But I want to make love to you, sometime. Just you."

"Like I was a girl?"

Kid sighed. "Yeah. If you want to put it that way."

"I'd like that."

"I know you would." He cuffed the back of Denny's
head with his hand.

"When you jerk off, do you do that like what I did?"

"Huh?"

"You know. Eat it."

445

"Oh. No. I've tasted my own a couple of times. Hell, I guess I ate it once or twice, just to see."

"I do it all the time," Denny said, with resolve. "How did you know I did?"

"I've just known other people who did that too, and ... well. I don't know."

"Oh."

"Is she going to come back?" Kid asked.

Denny shrugged.

"Oh," Kid said again and thought he'd been saying that a lot. So he closed his eyes.

He listened for people moving around the house, thinking it must be growing late in the morning. Something—Denny's elbow—hit the side of his head, and he realized he was waking up after drifting off again.

He opened his eyes and pushed himself to sitting position. Denny lay curled away from him. Kid breathed deeply; his head was heavy with the detritus of pleasure. He rubbed his shoulder and it tingled, paused at the chain that crossed the hair on his chest. It still held: from a very long time ago, a waking and a sleeping and a waking, he recalled the blond Mexican who had surprised him in the street. Kid frowned, and began to reach around for his clothes.

He had to go to the bathroom, for one thing. His head ached slightly, and his mouth tasted like unflavored gelatin, solid around tongue and teeth. He looked for his pants, stopped, put his hand on Denny's buttock. A face, he thought, hatcheted on the obstetric line. Cheeks, he thought, sucked in with astonishment. If you hang around, I'm going to tear it up. Denny rubbed his nose and was probably awake but not moving.

Kid pulled on his pants, dragged his vest and his boot over the edge of the platform. The people in the sleeping bags were still there. Bending to put on his vest, he found his flanks sore; he leaned on the jamb to put on his boot, and for the first time in a while wished he had a second. (A vision of his own hands crumbling dirt between them, the dirt falling on water.) He stepped into the hallway.

The tan shade and the warmth in Denny's loft had intimated a false summer.

The sky beyond a dirty window pane high on the hall wall was stormy. The bathroom door opened: not Thirteen's girl friend, but Thirteen himself. His long hair was bushy from sleep. "Hey I didn't know you was around here?" Thirteen nodded heavily, his voice roughened by fatigue. "Ain't seen you in a couple of days." Kid went into the bathroom and while he urinated, busied himself not thinking about when the last time he had actually seen Thirteen was. He ground his fist against his sore side and reflected: it probably isn't possible to really fuck yourself to death. Punching his tongue into bitter corners of his mouth, he squinted out the window. Stormy?

Incredible suspensions in the dry air, and he moved between them, dribbling and/or blowing out all holes. He waited for some bright precipitate. His water splashed and silenced. He massaged his limp genitals, not with desire, but rather to press some feeling back. His knuckles got wet, and he looked down wondering if it were urine or final mucus. Pleasure can be an appalling business, he thought and buttoned his pants.

In the hallway, he stood sucking his salty fingers until he realized what he was tasting, wondered why he was doing it, and remembered Denny. He grinned: a psychologist had once called him a maddening combination of lability and willfulness.

Then she walked into the hall without seeing him, and opened the front door. He took his fingers from his mouth, recognized her curly hair, tried to envision her full shoulders beneath the blue sweatshirt she now wore.

She went down the steps.

Curious, he walked to the door. If she turns around, he thought, her eyes will be red, hey?

She stopped by the car, prying beneath the bent rim with one finger, looking absently down the block; looked back at him.

The little chill was all anticipation.

She blinked surprised brown eyes at him, from a face that could have been angry.

"Hey," he said, and smiled at her from the top of the steps, which became more and more difficult to do before her blank blinking, except in confusion. In confusion, smiling, he walked down. "I missed you when you cut out." There are some storms, he thought beneath the mangled sky, it's easier to walk into.

"Sure," she said as he came down the steps. "I bet you did." Her fingers kept moving on the broken glass.

"If you keep that up, you're going to cut your—"

"There's something funny about you," she said with

447

a look of distaste. "That was funny, or queer, or some-thing."

"Look," he said, "you're not going to call *me* names," and realized he did not know what hers was. That brought him crashing through his embryo anger till he was much closer to her than he'd wanted to be: his fingers against his leg were trying to take the same position as hers. His face pulled to mimic hers.

"When he was . . . was with me, that was all between you and him. I might as well not have been there!"

"When I was with you, that was all between you and him. I might as well have been beating my meat," and felt, saying it, the comparison was unfair. "He says you're his best friend. What is it? He thinks he's doing it for you, you think you're doing it for him?" His face, straining after hers, registered a sudden sadness inside him so intensely it took him instant after instant to see her expression had changed.

"I used to be the smartest person in my class!" she said, suddenly.

He wondered why his eyes were burning till he saw tears in hers.

"I used . . . to be the smartest person in my class!" She dropped her head.

He dropped his, whispered, "Hey . . ." and put his hand (too gently, he thought) on the back of her neck, touched his forehead to hers.

"Why don't you go away?" she said with sad, ex-hausted anger.

"Okay." He squeezed, snorted the faint laughter of withdrawal, and went back up the steps (his palm cold; her neck had been warm). Halfway up the hall, though, he was frowning.

When he climbed back into the loft, Denny (between Kid's fists) turned over and blinked and grunted.

"Hey, your girl friend's outside all upset."

"Oh, shit!" Denny said and sat up. He ground the heels of his palms against his eyes, then started for the edge of the loft.

Kid grabbed his unchained ankle.

Denny looked back.

"You guys go through this much trauma every time you screw?"

"It's my fault," Denny said.

"Sure," Kid nodded. "Come on back here, will you?"

448

"I better go. I guess I been doing too much talking about you. I guess I ain't talked to her about nothing else for a pretty long time."

"Which reminds me," Kid said. "You're making a lot more out of that lady in the department store with the bee-bee gun than it's really worth, you know?"

Denny grinned. "I been talking about you a hell of a lot longer than that," and went over the side.

Kid lay back, grunted, "Fuck . . ." and rolled over, wishing there was someone else there. Maybe, he thought, very tired, he'll bring her back. Denny, he figured, would return. Should he have actually touched her? (He recognized the beginnings of a welter of paranoid speculation; recognized as well that sleep lay on the other side of it.) Touched her in the street? If they were lovers, he would be able to find out in a day, a week, a month if it was the proper thing to do. Hell, should he have told Denny about it at all? He *was* being used: he didn't like it. That's not the sort of shit you lay on somebody you just dragged into bed. Lovers? He decided he didn't like her at all. (She, among silent others, had once said, "Good-bye.") On the other hand, he shouldn't go prying around in emotional closets like that. (He turned over again, wishing Lanya had not disappeared.) Silly, stupid kids! Why did Denny drag her in in the first place? Righteous indignation, he finally decided, was easier. For the first time in a long while he was aware of the chain around him. Careful, he mulled, that it doesn't come apart—not sure why he should be afraid it might.

2

He woke alone.

Kid sat up, with his eyes closed, for half a minute. The air in the loft was heavy and dry. Would the pulsing at the back of his head become a headache? People moved in other rooms. The bathroom door closed three times. Grinding his knees on the blanket, he turned for his clothes.

Denny's were gone.

In another room a black woman laughed.

His pants were still on. He shrugged up his vest and, with neither buttoned, climbed down. One of the sleeping bags was still occupied. Two others were shed in quilted rings.

He leaned on the wall to pull up his boot. He wished again he had the other, but felt habit dissolve the wish. He went into the hall wondering if he'd encounter Denny or the girl first.

From the door ahead, light slapped across the hall and made him squint.

"Hey, Dragon Lady!"

Kid looked in.

Nightmare, squatting on one of the mattresses, kneaded his thick, scarred shoulder. "Hey, Dragon Lady, you been *down!*"

The gorgeous beast dazzled about the shabby room.

Nightmare let himself thud backward against the wall. A figure under a blanket moved away. Nightmare laughed and rocked and jangled.

"Down and back! Oh, hey, man. And *back!*" Dragon Lady turned, killed her lights. And laughed. Kid watched her stained teeth gape.

A dozen people slept around the room. Nightmare and Dragon Lady talked on raucously:

"I brought you coffee!" She breathed heavily, breasts stretching her vest's rawhide laces. "Adam and Baby are out there now putting it together. Found a whole fucking warehouse full!" Her face was long and dark as bittersweet chocolate. "Brought you back a whole carton."

"Instant?"

"No." She made a fist. *"No!"*—insistant as an economics teacher. "The real thing. My boys are making it in the kitchen."

Nightmare rocked and hugged his shoulders. "Hey, we're gonna do up a little caffeine here! That's really good. Oh, Yeah!"

Copperhead suddenly, knees wide, swung up to sit. Head low between his shoulders, he shook his hair. Freckled hands crossed on his darker genitals, he blinked at the room. His lids were puffy so that you just saw two slashes of gold; which turned toward Kid. Copperhead frowned, cocked his head; his mouth hung open, his lips, marked with a line Kid knew was dried blood (because his own gums bled when he slept), sagged from even, yellow teeth. The girl in the pea jacket moaned and tried to wedge between the cushion and the couch-back.

Nightmare swung his hand at Kid. "That's him."

"Sure looks like him." Dragon Lady's heavy lips pursed.

Nightmare's thin ones grinned.

"What you wearin' that thing around the house for?" Copperhead asked.

Kid looked down at the orchid—on his hand. "It makes shaking my dick after I take a leak a real adventure." He took a breath, tried not to search out the memory, searched and found a blank.

"Not to mention zipping up your fly," Copperhead said. "It's open." He turned to pull his pants out from under the blond girl, who squeaked and tried to roll into the upholstery again.

"That's him?" Dragon Lady asked, mocking.

Kid nodded. "It's me." He leaned back on the door jamb and dropped to a squat. "It's going to stay open for a while, too, I guess. I don't feel like castrating myself."

"He's really funny." Nightmare pushed the end of his braid back over his shoulder. "He's a good kid. He doesn't make a lot of noise. But when he does something, it usually turns out pretty good."

451

That's a good image to live up to, Kid decided; and decided not to say very much more. *When* had he put on the orchid . . . ? When . . . ? Copperhead looked unpleasant, yanked again: "Will you get off my fuckin' clothes? I wanna get dressed!"

"Hey, will you guys bring in that coffee!" Dragon Lady hollered.

Somebody half hidden by the couch raised her head from the crook of her arm, and dropped it. It was not Denny's girl.

"They been talking a lot about you," Dragon Lady said. She frowned at Copperhead. "*He* ain't been saying nothing nice." She laughed.

"I ain't been saying *nothing*." Copperhead fumbled at the snap on his fatigues. One of the thigh pouches was torn. There were holes in both knees. "I don't got nothing to say about the Kid."

Nightmare hunkered a little. "Kid, what you got to say about Copperhead?"

Kid shook his head. They want us to fall out and fight right here, he thought.

Nightmare's laugh started wide, then pulled into gruff, belligerent, good nature.

Somebody else raised his head from a pile of blankets, blinked sleepily, then grinned—"Hey!"—and stood, clumsily, scratching first at the sweaty hair across his forehead, then at the belly of his undershirt. His other arm was bandaged to the shoulder. "Hey, it's the Kid! You come on back here for a while?"

"How you doing, Siam?" Kid hazarded. The brown, agonized face rocking back and forth on the bus floor had been . . . different? No, not that different . . .

"Fine!" Siam ducked his head, grinning hugely. "I'm okay. I'm fine!" His good hand touched the bandage; the finger bounced down dirty cloth (Nightmare still kneaded the multiple-headed bulge of a shoulder that spoke of weightlifting sessions). Siam glanced at the others, got an uneasy look, grinned through the uneasiness, and squatted too, aping Kid.

Dragon Lady called, "I want some God-damned coffee!"

"They ain't got very many cups." The guy had two in each hand and three in his arms. His hair was a jangle of scrap gold; chest, chin and buttocks were all blebs and pustules, his toenails and fingernails filthy, and he

was naked. "I don't think they got enough for everybody."
He looked around.

"Give one to Nightmare, Baby." Dragon Lady took one for herself.

Denny walked in. He sat next to Kid, quietly, and leaned on his crossed legs: the knee of his jeans brushed the shin of Kid's.

Nightmare took a cup and motioned Baby to give one to Denny. "And give the Kid one—"

"—As long as there's one for me." Copperhead got on his second boot and stamped twice. He looked at Kid.

"I guess Adam and me can share one." Baby frowned at the cups clutched to his chest.

Kid took his cup and thought: if there weren't enough, I suppose we would have to fight.

Copperhead got one. So did Siam.

"Adam!" Dragon Lady called. "Baby done passed out the glasses. What you doin' with the brew?"

Adam came in, brown face veiled by steam. Steam rolled down over the chains on his chest. He had lots of thick, dark hair. "Here you go." He poured for Dragon Lady, and went on to Nightmare. His pants were too big, bunched under, or just sagging from the chain he used for a belt.

Kid held his cup with both hands, feeling its heat.

In the middle of the room, Baby was examining the last cup to see if a crack went all the way through.

"A whole warehouse," Dragon Lady reiterated. "You can go down and get it yourself when you run out of what we brought you."

"Shit." Adam squinted through the steam. "We got 'em a whole carton." He rubbed his chest; chains growled.

"I don't make no food runs." Nightmare blew steam down over his hands. "You know I don't make no fuckin' food runs."

"We got so many free loaders," Copperhead said at the coffee cup he held on his right knee, "you just may have to." Head still low, he looked at Kid again. "We get more of 'em every day."

"You got some in there for you?" Dragon Lady finished saying to Adam, who checked the fuming pot and nodded. Then she looked at Copperhead and hooted: "You really down on the Kid, hey? Why you so down on him?"

"Cause Copperhead's big and dumb," Nightmare said.

"Now I like Copperhead. He's big, dumb, and mean. The Kid's small and smart. But I bet he's just as mean as Copperhead."

"When I got shot," Siam said, "the Kid pulled me onto the bus. Kid ain't mean—"

"Aw, fuck you!" Nightmare bellowed, and rolled sharply to his knees.

Siam spilled coffee over his hand.

Nightmare didn't.

Siam put his cup down, shook his fingers, sucked at his knuckles.

Nightmare guffawed, sipped and guffawed again.

Copperhead blinked, rubbed his beard against his freckled wrist, and retreated even farther between his shoulders.

Kid gripped his cup; his palm was uncomfortably hot. "Hey, Copperhead?" He flexed his nubs on burning porcelain. "Hey, Copperhead, why you think they're so anxious to get us after each other?"

The redhead glowered from the couch.

"I'm half Indian," Kid said. "And you're about . . . what? Half nigger?" He glanced at Dragon Lady, who looked back and forth between them, black eyes a glint in her dark face, as though she were holding a snicker. Nightmare, his skin, for all his muscles, translucent white, peered over his cup, and actually looked surprised.

"So I guess they just figure it'll be easy, huh?"

Copperhead's glower turned to puzzlement. Then suddenly it broke out in a laugh.

"Yeah," Copperhead said. "Yeah, only—" He pointed a thumb at Nightmare, at Dragon Lady. "Easy, sure. Only half an Indian's a halfbreed or something, right? Half a nigger, anywhere around this part of the world, is still just plain old nigger." This laugh was a bark that threw back his head. But the building anger was loosed in contempt about the room.

Dragon Lady's laugh got drowned in coffee, which chattered loudly below her lowered eyes.

"Copperhead and me—" Kid jutted his arm forward for balance and rocked to standing—"we're on the same side, aren't we?" He stepped over someone asleep. "We better be, with you bastards around."

"Man, he got your number, white boy," Dragon Lady said to Nightmare, chuckling.

"Aw, shut up," Nightmare said.

"He got both your numbers," Copperhead said, "Jesus Christ—" He began to dig his hand under the girl on the couch, pulled out his vest.

Kid was about to look at Denny; but Denny's girl stepped into the far doorway.

She looked very surprised.

Kid walked across the room. He saw Copperhead shrugging into his vest, watched him. So did Dragon Lady and Nightmare, each with differing smiles.

"You want some coffee?" Kid asked.

The girl took the cup he thrust and looked even more surprised. He pushed past, through the door.

The sink and counter were heaped with dishes. The table was piled with garbage. A garbage bag underneath had broken.

Outside the screen door, the sky heaved and twisted like a thing chained.

Kid stopped on the littered linoleum and raised his hands to his face—

He'd forgotten the blades.

He pressed the heel of his other hand against one eye. Clean metal and dirty flesh—be brought his armed hand closer, till metal tickled his cheek.

Beyond metal and skin and screening, and wooden roofs across the street, the sky ran and blistered and dribbled on itself.

I will play, he thought, this game another hour. One more hour. Then I will go do something else. I'm tired. That's not complicated. I'm just tired.

He ground one eye, till light spots superimposed blades, hand and sky.

They were laughing in the other room.

What do I want here?

The boy? he thought to see it fall. I still like him, don't I? He bores me already (thinking: All that guarantees is that he still likes me).

Lanya, Kid thought angrily, has gone away. Why. Because I'm impossible. And realized, astonished, what he wanted was her.

Double laughter separated into a boy's and a girl's. When they stepped around him, hand in hand, she looked quickly away. Denny didn't.

Kid felt his expression change, not sure to what. But it made Denny stop.

"Get out of here," Denny said to the girl.

455

She looked between them, puzzled and—eager? Then she fled back into the living room.

After a second, Kid said, "Your girl friend doesn't like me very much."

Denny's shoulders made some small, sharp motions. "You been pretty nice to her."

"Like hell." Maybe, Kid thought, I should tell him to go away, like he told her. "Come here."

Denny walked over.

Kid reached in his pocket for Tak's battery. "Put this in for me?"

Denny's face made motions small and strange as his shruggings. I make up rituals, Kid thought. They try to comprehend them; and forced the memory of Lanya's green eyes shut.

Denny fingered the projector. (The chain tickled Kid's chest.) Biting his lower lip, Denny unsnapped the sphere. He pushed the battery between the clips with his thumb.

Kid moved both caged and free fingers on the blades, and let his hand swing against Denny's pants. "You got a hard-on."

"I know." Denny sucked in his lips and thumbed the projector case closed. It clicked. "Okay." Without looking up, he turned for the door.

Kid put his thumb between his own legs and hooked his genitals forward against his pants. "Hey, turn around."

Denny turned.

"And smile."

Denny laughed, and then tried to stop the laughter. Shaking his head, he said, "You're real crazy." Then he went out.

"Jesus Christ!" Thirteen pushed in around the boy. "Hey, it's the Kid!" He turned and repeated to Smokey, like an after-image at his shoulder: "It's the Kid. Hey, Kid, they told me you were around here but I thought you split already. How you doing?"

Kid nodded. The door closed behind them. There isn't room in this kitchen for all these people. Kid thought.

"Glad to see you!" Thirteen nodded back. "Before you cut out. I mean . . ." He held the strap of his tank top from his shoulder. ". . . you cutting out?"

"I don't know."

"I mean, you stay as long as you want. That's fine

456

with me. They got all those God-damn freaks in here, I'm really glad to have somebody like you, you know?"

"Thanks," Kid said and wondered what Thirteen wanted.

"Um . . ." Thirteen said, obviously uncomfortable. "Um . . . somebody told me you been fuckin' around with the kids, huh?"

"Huh?"

"I mean somebody heard you guys going at it in the loft. You know?" Thirteen grinned; and still looked uncomfortable. "I mean, how old are they, fifteen? Sixteen? I mean, I just sort of feel responsible for them, because they're not that old, you know?"

"I wasn't fucking with them. They were fucking with me."

"Yeah," Thirteen said and nodded. "They're too much, huh? I mean, I don't care what you do, man. It's not a moral thing." Suddenly he reached behind him and drew Smokey up under his arm. "I mean, Smokey here is, what are you, honey? Eighteen? And I mean, seventeen, eighteen, there ain't that much difference. I just don't want to see anybody hurt them, that's all."

"I'm not out to hurt anybody."

"Yeah, man. Sure." Thirteen nodded deeply. "I didn't think you were. It's just that, well . . . some people *have*, that's all. Come on inside, hey, and smoke some dope with me, hey? I mean, if you feel like it."

Kid let his caged hand fall to the side.

"I mean, maybe later, then, if you want to." Thirteen grinned again.

"It's good you . . . don't want anybody to get hurt."

Thirteen hesitated. "Thanks." Then he pulled Smokey a little closer, and they walked around Kid into the other room, while somebody outside the door said:

"Hello . . . ?"

She and her shadow on the screening were out of register.

"Kid? That *is* you . . . ?"

The door opened—she and his memory of her were, too.

She watched him with small things happening at her mouth that could have been preparation for either laughter or recrimination; and other small things happening in her green eyes.

"Oh, *hey—!*" he said anyway, because something was

worming in his chest. It rose to heat his face, left him grinning and squinting. "Hey, I'm glad you . . ." His arms went out. She and his memory of her (the screen door clacked) came together between them. Her cheek butted against his, her laughter roared happily at his ear. "Oh, hey, I'm glad you came!" His arms had whipped across her back—one slightly out (and quivering for wanting to close) for the orchid.

She leaned away, "You sure?" and kissed him. "I'm glad too."

He kissed her—harder, longer, losing himself in it (as his hand hung, lost in air and metal; he bunched his fingers, loosened them) till he felt the thing in her shirt pocket, cutting.

He pulled back: Next to her harmonica was his pen.

She said, because she saw him looking, "The bartender at Teddy's told me to give it to you. He said you dropped it there—" and then he kissed her (it still cut) again; but he held on.

She pulled away, once more, wrinkling her nose. "Something smells good." Looking around, she went to the living-room door—he followed—leaned through with one hand on the white frame. "Hey, Nightmare—is there any more of that coffee?"

"You want some, sweetheart?" which was from Dragon Lady. "Help yourself."

Kid watched her cross the room, leaned back on the frame.

She squatted to fill a cup—looked in it first; someone must have used it, but she shrugged—from the enamel pot. Once she glanced back at him, pushed hair from her forehead, grinned. She picked up the cup and returned. The warmth inside him still grew.

On the couch, Denny's girl and Copperhead were going through some sort of toasting game, clicking brims and laughing.

Nightmare was saying, "I can't hang around this place all day! Hey, Dragon Lady, you gonna come with me? I mean I can't hang around—"

A woman stuck two brown arms from under a blanket, with quivering fists, waking.

Dragon Lady and Adam were whispering about something, dark brown and light brown heads together. Adam rubbed his chains.

Suddenly Baby came up. Among the faint fuzz of a new moustache, his nose had run all over his upper lip. Clutched in scrawny, filthy-nailed fingers was a cut-glass bowl, caked at the edges with sugar. "You want some?" He gestured with his chin toward the tablespoon handle.

"No thanks," Lanya said.

Kid shook his head too. Baby said, "Oh," and went away.

Lanya held up the cup for Kid to sip. His hands came up to guide hers. A blade ticked the crock, so he took that one away, felt the ligaments in the back of her hand with the other.

Coffee slapped bitter back across his tongue; he swallowed. Steam tickled his nostrils.

She blew; she sipped; she said, "It's strong!"

"Hey, Baby! Wait—come on back here, Adam!" Dragon Lady bawled, turning, jangling. "Come on, now!"

Through some door, not the kitchen's, a lot of people came into the house.

Lanya frowned, blinked.

A lot of people came into the room. Coffee, chocolate, and tamarindo faces, hands, and shoulders swung by, turning, as chains from long or stocky necks swung under several hairdos of beachball dimensions. Two of the men were arguing, while a third, his arm supple as a blacksnake, waved and shouted to quell them: "Com'on, man! Come on, now, man! Come on—" A minimal half-dozen white faces were occluded or eclipsed before Kid could fix them. Most, blacks and others, Kid recognized from the Emboriky run. A dark mahogany guy in a black vinyl vest stopped by the couch to regale Copperhead, while a diffident white, vestless and a scorpion only from the chains (his belly and chest were scarred with a single, long pucker, still-scabbed and pink), stood by, waiting to speak. In trio, they seemed oddly familiar. The black in the vinyl was the one who'd been friendly to him in Denny's group in the department store.

A hand the color of an old tire suddenly landed on Lanya's shoulder, another on Kid's; the close-cropped head bobbed between them; the long black body, under the swinging vest flaps and hanging chain loops, was sour with sweat, the breath, over small teeth and a heavy, hanging lip, sour with wine. "Shit . . ." drawled in two syllables.

459

"Hey, Ripper," Lanya said, "get *off!*" Kid was surprised she knew his name.

But Ripper—yes, it was Jack the Ripper—got off.

A stocky white girl with a tattooed arm was talking to Nightmare when two more blacks joined the colloquy, loudly. Nightmare, louder, cut over: "Man, I can't hang *around*—"

"Come on," Kid said to Lanya. "I want to talk to you."

Lanya's eyes flicked from the room to Kid's face. "All right."

He gestured with his head for her to follow.

Stepping around one person and over another, they went into the hall.

The noise erupted and trundled and careered.

Looking for the room with Denny's loft, Kid pushed open the second door he saw. But there was too much light—

Siam on a crate by the green sink, said, "Hey!" and put the newspaper over his lap. He looked at Kid with a smile that fell apart into awed confusion. "I was . . . was reading the paper." At the edge of the bandage over his hand, the flesh was scaling. Siam offered his brown smile again, thought better, took it back. "Just reading the paper." He stood; the paper fell on the floor. The boards had once been painted maroon.

There was neither glass nor screening in the wide porch window. The city sloped away down the hill.

"You can see . . . so far," Lanya said at Kid's shoulder. She took another sip of coffee. "I didn't realize you could see so far from here."

But Kid was frowning. "What's that?"

Beyond the last houses, beyond the moiled grey itself, at a place that might have marked the horizon, a low, luminous arc burned.

"It looks like the sun coming up," Lanya said.

"Naw," Siam said. "It's the middle of the afternoon. Maybe it's . . ." He looked at Kid again, stopped.

"Maybe it's a fire," Kid said. "It's too wide for the sun."

Siam squinted. The arc was reddish. Beyond the gash of the park, a few houses were touched here and there with a copper that, in the haze, paled almost to white gold. "Sometimes," Siam said, "when you see the moon

460

real close to the horizon, like that, it looks much bigger. Maybe the same thing happens to the sun, sometimes?"

"But you just said it was the middle of the afternoon." Kid squinted too. "Besides, it's *still* ten times too wide." He looked back at Lanya. "Let's go."

"Okay." Lanya took his hand, the bladed one, slipping her fingers between the metal, to hold two of his.

They went back into the hall.

The room with Denny's loft didn't have a door.

"If there's nobody in here," Kid said, "we can talk."

"Want any more coffee?"

"No."

She finished half the cup (while he thought how hot it must be) and put it down on a cluttered ironing board behind the motorcycle.

"Get up in the loft."

She climbed, looked back. "Nobody's up here."

"Go on."

She crawled over, first one tennis shoe, then the other disappearing.

He came up after her.

"Look," she said, as he got his other knee over, "I came by because I wanted to apologize for being so— well, you know. Running off like that. And acting so angry."

"Oh," he said. "That's okay. You *were* angry. I'm just glad you come." One fist balled on the blankets, he settled to his haunches, watching her silhouette against the windowshade. "How did you know I was here?" He wanted to put his head in her lap; he wanted to nuzzle between her legs. "How did you find me, this time? Who saw me wander up here this morning and came running back to tell you?"

"But this is where they said you'd been for—"

"I know!" He sat back, laughed sharply. "I've been gone another five days! Right?"

Her silhouette frowned.

"Or six. Or ten . . . people have been talking about me again, saying how I've been living it up here, running with the scorpions, making my rep." He wanted to cup her warm cheeks in his rough, ugly hands. He said, and his voice suddenly became rough, ugly: "I've seen you every day since I met you . . ." He dragged his hands, bladed and unbladed, into his lip, where bone and muscle and chain and leather and nerve and metal, all mixed up, lay, heavy and confused and gripping. "I have!" He said, swallowed. "That's what it *feels* like. To me . . ."

She said: "That's one of the things I wanted to talk about. I mean, after I left you asleep, in the church, I thought maybe you'd want to *know* some of what happened while you . . . were away. You told me you went looking for me at the park commune. I thought you'd want to know what happened there after that guy with the gun—"

"I—" fingers and metal and harness moved in his lap—"I don't . . . I mean, I live in one city." He moved but couldn't lift. "Maybe you live in another. In mine, time . . . leaks; sloshes backwards and forwards, turns up and shows what's on its . . . underside. Things shift. Yeah, maybe you could explain. In your city. In your city, you're sane and I'm crazy. But in mine, *you're* the one who's nuts! Because you keep telling me things are happening that don't fit with what I *see!* Maybe that's the only city I can live in. Some guy with a gun? In the park?" He laughed, harshly. "I don't know if I *want* to live in yours!"

She was silent; once he saw her head jerk at some idea; but she decided not to say that one, seconds later decided to say another: "You say you saw me . . . last night, at the church? And then before that, yesterday . . . morning? In the park? All right. I'll accept that's what it looks like to you, if you'll accept that it doesn't seem that way to me. All right." She gestured toward his knee, did not quite touch it. "I'm curious about your . . . city. But some time soon, ask me about what goes on in mine. Maybe something's there that can help you."

"You have my notebook?"

"Yes." She smiled. "I figured you were so out of it, you just might leave it behind on the floor. You've written some strange stuff in there."

"My poems?"

"Those too," she said.

Which made him frown because some of this warmth, still unresolved, was connected with wanting to write.

"I'm glad you have it. And I'm glad you came to see me. Because I—"

Footsteps below.

And Denny's head came up over the loft edge.

462

"Hey, look. This is—oh. You." Denny crawled up over while someone else climbed.

She stopped with her head just visible, and recognized Kid with a frown that faded to resignation, then climbed the rest of the way, breasts swinging in blue jersey.

"Um . . . this loft is theirs," Kid said to Lanya.

"It's his," the girl said. "It isn't mine. All the junk up here is his. We just came to get away from the mob."

"You see," Kid said, "instead of telling me what's been going on while I was there, you should be finding out what's been going on here."

"Sure," Lanya said. "What?"

"I been balling these two, for one thing. *That* seemed like days . . ."

Denny's chin jerked.

The girl sighed a little.

"Denny's a good fuck," Kid said. "She is too. But sometimes it gets a little hectic."

"Denny . . . ?" the girl said.

Denny, sitting back on his heels, darted his eyes from Lanya to Kid.

"Maybe," Kid said, and suddenly his hands came apart, "we all could ball again. I mean the *four* of us. That might work out better—"

The girl said, "Denny, I'm supposed to be going some place with Copperhead and his friends. I *told* you that before. Look I gotta . . ."

"Oh," Denny said. "Well, okay."

"You sure?" Kid asked the girl. "I mean, the whole idea was because I thought maybe it would make *you* feel better if . . ."

The girl poised at the edge of the loft. "Look," she said. "You're probably trying to be very nice. But you just don't understand. It isn't *my* thing. Maybe it's his." She nodded toward Denny. "I don't know . . . is it yours?" That was to Lanya.

"I don't know," Lanya said. "I've never tried."

"I don't mind somebody *watching*," the girl said, "if it's a friend. But what we were doing," she shrugged; "It isn't me." She got down from the platform, paused again, just a head showing. "Denny, I'll see you later. Goodbye," with the same tone Kid remembered from the sixteenth-floor apartment in the Labrys. A second later she

463

tripped on something, gave a startled, stifled, "Shit . . ." and was gone.

Kid looked from Denny to Lanya, back to Denny. "We . . ." he started. "We were just . . . we figured we'd use your loft because, well, there were so many other people around. Like she said; the mob."

"That's okay," Denny said. He crossed his arms. "Is it okay if *I* watch?"

Lanya laughed and sat back against the window edge. A scar of light from beside the shade lay on her hair.

Denny looked at her. "That's what I like to do. Sometimes, I mean, since it's my place. He knows."

"Sure," Lanya said. "That's reasonable." She nodded, laughed again.

"We were just using it to *talk*," Kid said.

"Oh," Denny said. "I just thought because you were saying we should all . . . you know. All of us."

"You *do* live in a strange city," Lanya said. "Maybe I do too." She looked at Denny. "Where do you live?"

"Right here." Denny frowned. "Most of the time."

"Oh." After a moment, Lanya said: "You two've been at it? Why don't you two make it then—" she moved her tennis shoes from beneath her, raised her knees, dropped her meshed fists between—"and *I'll* watch. I've been in the other room when two guys were balling. But I've never been in the same bed. The idea sort of turns me on."

Kid said: "I just meant—"

"*I* know," Lanya said. "You want Denny and me to ball, and *you* want to watch. Well—" she shrugged, tossed her hair and grinned—"I think you're cute—" at Denny. "I wouldn't mind that."

"Gee," Denny said, "I don't know if . . ." and shifted into some other emotional gear: "because you see that's what we were . . ." and into another: "before. It was okay. But . . ." He went forward on his fists, lowered his haunches. "It's just that it wasn't her . . ." He glanced over the edge. "Like she said. And I'd never done it *that* way either."

"Oh." Lanya said, pushing her elbows together.

Kid thought: I *still* don't know her name. "Hey," he said to Lanya. "Come here."

Lanya pursed her lips, hesitated with stiffened arms; then they unstiffened. She came forward.

464

"You too, mother-fucker." Denny practically fell against his side. Kid caught the boy's neck in the crook of his arm. The blades swung beyond Denny's face, dim in half light. Kid pulled his arm tight around Lanya's shoulder, his hand an epaulet over blouse, collar bone, muscle.

"If you don't play, you don't watch."

He had been planning to squeeze them affectionately, maybe say something else funny, and let go. But, for a moment, he was aware they were two entirely different temperatures; and something in his own heat was defined, resolved, released. And Denny (his shoulder hot and still powdery dry) reached across Kid's chest, put two fingers against Lanya's cheek (her neck against Kid's arm cooler and softer, as though it had been recently dried after rain) and said. "You're . . ." and stopped when she reached out and put her palm on Denny's neck. Kid said: "Yeah . . ." She watched, something happening in her face, which became quiet laughter, her eyes going back and forth between Kid's and Denny's, pulling herself closer.

Denny's head suddenly moved. His laugh back was sharp, shrill. Still, whatever tensions were in it eased in it.

"You open your mouth after this morning, cocksucker," Kid said, "and it won't be my dick you get in it—"

"Kid . . ." Lanya's protest was real.

But Denny caught Lanya's forearm, turned his face into her palm.

Something in the machinery between Kid's belly and loin tightened. Denny was trying to climb over him. Kid moved a leg between them—something scraped. Lanya got one elbow under her. Kid's hand dragged her back. It's clumsy, Kid thought. It *is* clumsy! and a despair that he had been trying to hold in suspension for—how long? broke. He thought he was going to cry. What came out was a great, voiceless gasp.

Denny lay his head down on Lanya's hand that was on Kid's chest. Then he said, softly, "Aren't we gonna take our clothes off . . . this time?"

Lanya moved her other hand down Denny's head till she was holding his ear.

"Don't pull," Denny said.

"I'm not pulling," she said. "I'm tickling."

"Oh," Denny said. And then: "That's nice." And then, raising his head, "I think you better take *that* thing off—at least."

(Kid looked at his hand still in the air. It was quieter in the other room.)

Lanya suddenly sat. "Oh wow. Sure." She wore one of her stranger expressions. "I didn't even see!"

Kneeling over him, she took Kid's wrist, got the clasp. Kid was completely astonished when Denny's hands joined hers and, with no clumsiness, the blades opened, fell away: the harness was lifted from his tingling wrist.

Lanya put it on the window ledge by the blind, where it stood, upright, a long, bright crown.

Kid turned his freed hand in the air, looking at the hirsute joints and ruined tips flex, horny palms and knuckles folding, opening, till, tired, it began to waver, fall. Someone tugged at his belt. Someone pulled at his vest shoulder. He laughed, turning, while through some door in another room a lot of people left.

They made love.

It was energetic. It was graceful. It was intense. He was a warmth that moved around and between them. They were warmths that moved around him, between him and each other. Once, eyes closed against the damp blanket, he moved his hand across her rib cage, brushing beneath her breasts with the knuckle of his thumb (she caught her breath . . .) till he reached her arm (. . . then let it out) and followed her arm to where her elbow bent on Denny's belly, and on to where her hand held Denny's penis.

After moments, his hand came away, against the embankment of her hip, crossed it. He pressed his fingertips in the hair over her pubic bone, slid them down to cup, to press in. First one, then the other, he touched their genitals. Finally he pushed himself to his knees, put one knee across them, watched them watch him, blinked. Sweat dribbled his cheek. A drop caught in his eyelash and shook. He bent his head.

Is it *only* an hour, he wondered, that encompassed three people's four orgasms? Now I know why, though foreplay can be delineated in all its fascinating and psychotropic detail, a poet must use / asterisks or blank paper for orgasmic mechanics that satisfying: they open

466

to something so wide you can now understand why, when sex is *that* good, you may say, "The sex is not the most important part," and feel these words analogue some shadow of truth.

Then he remembered, amidst his auto-pontifications, there were *two* other people who would have to agree with him before he could even suspect such maunderings correct. Grinning, he pushed up on his hands, climbed over one of them (stopped to stare at the sleeping face, full up, lips momentarily pressing, nostrils flaring, two fingers coming to scratch the nose and fall away, still in sleep), looked over at the other (this one on the side, lips parted, lower eyelid mashed slightly open revealing an albumen line, breath whispering against curled knuckles) and, after taking the pen from Lanya's pocket and putting it in a bottom hole of his vest, climbed down, dragging his clothes on top of him.

He wondered, if they woke, would they think he had gone to the bathroom.

In the doorway, he pulled on his pants, put on his vest. There was a cold line against his chest . . . The pen. The chain around him was hot. He ran his fingertips along it, concerned and trying to recall why.

In the strangely quiet hall, he went to the porch door, opened it. And squinted. Gold trapezoids lay high up the lapped-plank wall. His moist skin was slathered with bronze. Each hair on his forearm glowed amber.

He heard his own loud breath; he closed his mouth.

Looking down at his chest, before his vision blurred with tears, he saw that one prism had laid out on his skin a tiny chain of color.

The house was perfectly silent behind him.

He rubbed his eyes, shook his head.

The tearing stopped, anyway.

He raised his eyes again, looked out the porch window at the horizon again—

When he'd first moved to New York City to go to Columbia, he had brought with him an absolute panic of the Bomb. It had been October; he had no Thursday morning classes, was still half-asleep in the sweaty sheets of a persistent, Indian summer. Sirens woke him—he remembered no scheduled test. A jet snarled somewhere on the sky. He got chills and immediately tried to logic them away. This is the sort of coincidence, he thought, blinking at the dull window, that can ruin a good day.

Then the window filled with blinding yellow light.

He'd leaped from the bed, taking the sheets with him. His throat cramped and his heart exploded while he watched gold fire spill from window to window in the tenement across the street.

The fireball! he thought, beyond the pain in his terrified body. The light's here now. The shock and the sound will arrive in four seconds, five seconds and I will be dead . . .

Four seconds, five seconds, seven seconds, ten seconds later, he was still standing there, shaking, panting, trying to think of someplace to hide.

The clouds, in coincidence compounded, had pulled away from the sun. The plane was gone. The clock radio in the bookshelf said noon. The siren lowered its pitch, softened its whine, and ceased.

What he'd felt then had been active terror.

What he felt now was its passive equivalent.

It couldn't be a fireball, he thought. That was impossible.

Beyond the mist, it shone through as moon or sun shone through an even veil of clouds. It was the color of the sunrise: perhaps a sixth of the circle had risen, secanted by the horizon. But already it was, what? A hundred? Three hundred? Six hundred times the area of the platinum poker chip he remembered as the sun.

. . . If the sun went nova! he thought. Between his loudening heart he ferreted this information: If that's what it was, then the earth would boil away in seconds! His heart stilled. What a silly fact to base one's confidence on before this light!

The clouds over half the sky were a holocaust of pewter and pale gold.

Was the light warm?

He rubbed his bronzed forearm.

The verdigrised spigot on the wall dropped molten splashes on the muddy drain. Torn paper tacked to the frame of the window filigreed the shadow on the wall beside him.

When he had thought the bomb had fallen, back in New York, he had been left with a tremendous energy, had paced and pondered and searched for something to do with it, had ended up just walking it away.

I may be dead, he thought, in . . . seconds, minutes, hours? He squinted at the brilliant arc, already perhaps

468

thirty houses wide. The thought came with absurd coolness, I'm going to write something.

He sat quickly on the floor (despite callous, he noticed again it was so much easier to distinguish textures
in the gritty boards with the foot he kept bare than the
one he wore booted), pulled the paper Siam had left up
from the top of the crate. (His pants pulled across the
place he'd scraped his knee climbing into the loft.) *The
Times* was often sloppily laid out with frequent white
spaces. Paging through, he saw one, and pulled his pen
out of his vest.

I had a mother, I had a father. Now I don't remember their names. I don't remember mine. In another
room, two people are sleeping who are nearer to me by
how many years and thousands of miles; for whom, in
this terrifying light, I would almost admit love.

He opened the pages back and placed the paper on
the crate. The pages were yellow in the new light.

And it was not blank space.

The bottom quarter was boxed for an advertisement.
Inside, two-inch letters announced:

BRASS
ORCHIDS

In smaller, italic type beside the title, set off in quo-
tation marks, were lines of verse.

He mouthed: ". . . at this incense . . ." and balked.
He threw back his head at the chills on his neck (and
closed his eyes against the light: inside his lids was the
color of orange rind), opened his eyes to look at the
paper. A misreading: ". . . this incidence . . ." He let his
breath out.

Why had they taken *those* lines, he wondered. Without the two before or the one after, they meant . . . nothing? He puzzled on the severed image, clicking his pen
point.

What was the purpose of it?

(What had he wanted to write?)

His forehead moistened; his eye drifted to the column of type down the left of the . . . advertisement; and
snagged on ". . . Newboy . . ." He went to the top, to
shake loose the confusion:

We have lost our poet in residence: To be
precise, at six-thirty, after a farewell breakfast

469

prepared by Mrs Alt—Professor Wellman, Mr and Mrs Green, Thelma Brandt, Colonel Harris, Roxanne and Tobie Fischer were among the guests who rose in time. After a rushed (alas) second cup of coffee, our driver, Nick Pedaikis, arrived from Wells Cottage to drive Ernest Newboy down to Helmsford.

A moving incident at the regretted departure: a young man whom Mr Newboy had been encouraging with his poetry came to wave an admiring farewell at the mouth of Bellona's own Pons Asonorum. So, another celebrity leaves, loved. But Bellona, it would seem, in all its impoverishment, holds myriad fascinations.

We had heard rumors of the coming of our most recent guest; still we had, frankly, entertained some doubts as to whether this visit would, as it were, come off. Communication with the outside world, as all of you know who have tried it, is an exhausting, inaccurate, and frustrating business here at best. How convenient! In the same trip with which our Nick delivered Mr Newboy onto his journey to Pittsfield, he was able to meet, as per tentative arrangements, w. Captain Michael Kamp. They arrived in Bellona shortly after three o'clock. Captain Kamp is indefinite about the length of his stay. We cannot express what a privilege it is to have this illustrious gentleman with us in

Incense had come as a misreading of *incidence;* did illustrious echo illusion? Kid wondered.

He raised his eyes to the bright vista, squinted, and thought: The problem of hallucinating red eyes, even a great red one rising into the sky . . .

The thought came with a load of monstrous comfort: This is impossible. He stopped clicking his pen. Momentarily he wanted to laugh.

Hallucination?

He gazed into the light, tried to open his eyes full to it; they hurt and refused.

He had wanted to write something?

This wasn't even hallucination. I'm probably lying in

bed, somewhere, with my eyes closed . . . is that called dreaming?

After-images deviled the walls.

He turned his head away, and into darkness . . . dreaming?

His cheek was on a blanket. One arm was cramped beneath his side. He was filled with the tingling one has after having laughed a long time. He lay, trying to remember what had just passed, gnawing at his fingers till he tasted blood. And kept gnawing.

Lanya shifted, made some slow, sleepy sound.

Kid took his hand from his mouth, curled his fingertips tight against his palm. "Hey," he said. "Are you asleep . . . ?"

Lanya stretched. "More or less . . ." She lowered her chin and looked down at the blond head between their hips. "*What* was his name?"

Kid laughed.

Denny's hand uncurled on Kid's thigh. Then the blond head came up. ". . . huh?"

"What's your name?" She pushed back cords of his hair.

Denny's lids slid closed. He sighed without answering and lay down again.

Kid held his laughter in this time.

Lanya shook her head; her hand at Kid's forehead pushing at his coarser hair.

"How was he?" he whispered, from somewhere down in his chest.

"Mmmm?"

"I heard you two when I was sort of half-asleep." He cupped her cheek and she turned to lip the ham of his thumb. "How'd he do?"

She turned back. A smile and a frown mixed themselves on her face. "Now which one of you was that—" She laughed when he shook her ear. "Very sweet and very energetic." She glanced down again. "Sort of . . . up and down, you know? He's got quite a sense of humor."

"That's one name for it."

Her eyes came up again; even in the shadow their green was bright between his fingers baring her face.

"Terribly, terribly sweet, mainly."

"And how are you?"

"Mmmmm." She closed her eyes and smiled.

"You know what he did this morning?"

"What?"

"He dragged me in here and said he was going to blow me, and then he got that girl in here."

She opened her eyes; "Oh, is *that* how it happened." He felt her eyebrows raise. "Well, I guess turn about is fair play."

"I dig that scene—"

"So I noticed. You're sweet too."

"—but she was sort of funny about the whole thing. I didn't like it, I mean with her."

"So I gathered. Also he's a little boy, isn't he? Or is he another baby face like you?"

"He's fifteen. She's seventeen. I think."

Lanya sighed. "Then perhaps you just have to give them time to grow into their own perversions. And by the way, how are you?"

"Fine." Kid grinned. "I'm really fine."

And laughing, she pushed her face toward his.

Hands scrabbled on Kid's belly; Denny grunted.

An elbow hit Kid's stomach. A knee hit his knee.

"Hey, watch it," Lanya said.

"I'm sorry," Denny said, and fell on top of them.

The scent of Denny's breath, which was piney, joined Lanya's, which reminded Kid of ferns.

"Oof," Lanya said. "Would you please tell me what your name is?"

"Denny," Denny said loudly in Kid's ear. "What's yours?"

"Lanya Colson."

"You're the Kid's old lady, huh?"

"When he remembers who I am." Her hand on Kid's wrist squeezed.

Kid rubbed the back of Denny's neck with one hand and held Lanya's with the other. Again he felt how chalky Denny's skin was. Lanya's was warm.

"You like this?"

Lanya laughed and moved her arms farther around Denny's back.

"Up here, where I live." Denny suddenly pulled back. "You like this?"

They watched him hunker on the blankets. The side of Kid's thigh on hers was warm. The top, where Denny had been, cooled.

"You can't stand up," Lanya said. "But it must be good for sitting and thinking."

"I stay up here a lot," Denny said. "Cause it never gets that hot. Then sometimes I don't come up here two or three days." Suddenly he sat back and pulled a plastic envelope into his lap. "You like this?"

"What is it?" Lanya asked and leaned forward.

"It's a shirt." Denny said. "It's a real pretty shirt." Kid looked too.

Beneath the plastic cover, and over green satin, gold strings tangled: the fringe was attached to the velveteen yoke. Velveteen cuffs sported gilt and green glass links.

"I found it in a store." Denny reached behind him. "And this one."

Silver thread elaborately embossed the black.

"Those were the two I liked," Denny explained. "Only you can't wear stuff like this around here. Maybe if I go someplace else . . ." He looked between the two quickly.

Kid scratched the hair between his legs and drew away a little.

Lanya had leaned closer. "They are pretty!"

"What is that one made of?" Kid asked.

Lanya pressed the plastic covering with her palm. "It's crepe."

"And I have these." Denny pushed the shirts behind him. "See."

When the lid clicked off the plastic box, the cubes inside bounced.

"It's a game," Denny explained. "I found it in another store. It's too complicated for me to play, and there's nobody here to play it with. But I liked the colors."

Lanya picked up one of the green blocks. On each face was an embossed gold letter: p,q,r,s,o,i . . .

Denny blinked and held the box open for her to replace the playing piece.

She turned it in her fingers a long time, till Kid's awareness of Denny's restrained impatience made him uncomfortable.

"Put it back," Kid said, quietly.

She did, quickly.

"And this." Denny pulled out an oversized paperback book. "You got to look at those close. They're very funny pictures—"

"Escher!" Lanya exclaimed. "They certainly are."

Kid reached over her arm to turn the page.

"Where did you get those?" Lanya asked.

"In another . . . store." (Kid idly wondered at the

473

hesitation but didn't look up.) "In somebody's house," Denny corrected himself. "We broke in. This was there, so I took it. You seen 'em before, ain't you."

"Um-hm." Lanya nodded.

Kid turned another page of etched perspective imploded on itself and put back together inside out. Lanya bent to look now.

"This!" Denny said.

They both looked. And Kid took the book from Lanya and handed it back to Denny. ("That's all right," Denny said. "She can look at it," ignoring Kid's gesture.) He showed them a silver box. "Ain't this a neat radio? It's got AM and FM and it even says Short Wave." It was the size of a box of kitchen matches. "And all sorts of other dials."

"I wonder if they do anything," Lanya said.

"That one says the 'volume'," Denny explained. "The button's there, that one is the AFC thing so it doesn't slide around. But you can't tell around here because radios don't work here any more."

"Like the shirts," she said. "When you go someplace else, you'll have something nice."

"If we go someplace else," Denny considered, "I'll probably leave all this stuff here. You can get lots of nice things anywhere around. You just pick it up."

"I meant somewhere outside the . . ." Kid watched her realize that Denny had not.

Suddenly she touched the radio. "It isn't square!" she announced. The black and metal box was trapezoidal. She flattened her hands to the sides of it. "It *is* beautiful," she said in the voice of someone admitting that a puzzle was still insoluble. (*What* was the name of his roommate in Delaware who had had so much trouble with the paper on mathematical induction? Another thing he couldn't remember . . . and was sad at his ruined memory and happy for Lanya.) "It really is . . . just lovely."

Kid leaned close to her and kneaded the inside of his thighs. He'd laid the Escher against his calf. The corner of the book nicked; he didn't move it.

"You seen these pictures too?" Denny brought out another paper-covered book.

Lanya said: "Let me see."

She turned over the first page and frowned.

". . . Um, did Boucher ever paint religious pictures?" Kid ventured.

"Not," Lanya said, "for three-dimensional, laminated-plastic dioramas."

"I think 3-D pictures are great," Denny said, while Kid felt vaguely embarrassed.

"These are strange." Lanya turned another page.

A crowned woman in blue stood one foot on a crescent moon while below her two naked men cowered in a rowboat. Ghosts of the same picture at other angles haunted the striated plastic.

"What's the next . . ." Lanya asked.

A man who looked like a classical Jesus, in a loincloth, limped on a single crutch, one hand, with stigma, extended.

"Spanish . . . ?" she mused.

"Puerto Rican," Kid suggested.

Lanya glanced at him. "It doesn't have any writing anywhere."

A woman, perhaps the virgin, as likely an empress, rode on a tiger. "The rocks and moss and water in the background, that's lifted from Da Vinci." Lanya turned to the next. "These are really . . ." She closed the book to a white cover on which was a crowned and bleeding heart behind a cross. "You can't tell *me* those are Christian. Did you find this in somebody's house too?"

"In a store," Denny said. He was hunting at the edge of the blanket again. "And these."

In his cupped hands were three glass cubes set with glittering stones.

"Dice?" Kid asked.

"I had four of them," Denny said. "One broke." He rolled them against Lanya's leg.

Three, two, and six: counting the top numbers was difficult because of pips on other faces.

"You're really into collecting pretty things." Lanya picked up a cube.

Denny sat back against the wall and hugged his knees. "Um-hum."

"Me too." She watched him. "Only I leave them where I find them. Like buildings. Or trees. Or paintings in museums."

"You just—" Denny let his knees fall open—"notice where they are; and go back and look at them?"

She nodded.

Denny tangled his fists in the blanket between his feet. "But you don't have to do it that way here. You can

475

just take what you want. Well, maybe not the trees and the buildings. But the paintings, if you find one you like, you just carry it with you. Shit, you can go live in a fuckin' building if you like it! In front of the fuckin' tree!"

"No." Lanya let her thin back bend. "I'm into collecting pretty, useful objects. Yours are just pretty."

"Huh?"

"But if they're supposed to stay useful, I have to leave them where they are."

"You think there's something wrong with taking that stuff?"

"No . . . of course not. As long as you didn't take it *from* somebody."

"Well it must have belonged to somebody once."

"Do *you* think there's something wrong with taking it?"

"Shit." Denny grinned. "Nobody's gonna catch me. You like taking stuff?"

"It's not——"

"Say," Denny came to his knees. "You ever hustle?"

"Huh?" Lanya recovered from her surprise with an unsteady grin. "I beg your pardon."

"I mean take money for going to bed with somebody."

"No, I certainly haven't."

"Denny has, I bet," Kid said.

"Yeah, sure," Denny said. "But I just wanted to know. About you."

Her amusement faltered toward curiosity. "Why?"

"Would you?"

"I don't know . . . perhaps." She laughed again and took his knee in her hands. "Are you planning to set me up in business now? There isn't any business here."

Denny giggled. "That's not what I meant." Suddenly he picked up the plastic box, opened the lid, tossed.

"Hey!" Lanya shrieked, and scrambled back under the cubes of colored wood.

Denny picked up a fallen cube and threw it at her.

"Oh, cut that out——"

He threw another one and laughed.

"Damn it——"

Scowling, she picked up a handful and flung them back, hard. He ducked: they clicked the wall.

She hurled another that hit his head.

476

"Ahh . . . !" He flung one back.

She laughed, and threw two more, one with the left hand and one with the right. Both hit. Denny rolled away in hysterics, and scrambled after more gaming pieces.

"You're gonna lose the . . ." Kid started. Then he stretched across the front edge of the loft to keep the pieces from rolling over. Denny's laughter bobbed between octaves. Kid thought, His voice hasn't even finished changing.

Lanya was laughing too, almost so hard she couldn't throw.

A cube hit Kid's hip. He knocked it back onto the blanket. Another went over his shoulder, clattering to the floor. He watched them turn and duck and toss and wished they would throw pieces at him. After a while they did.

He threw them back, tried to guard the edge, gave up, by now laughing himself, till it hurt beneath his sternum, and couldn't stop laughing, so hurled the bright cubes with gold p's, q's, K's, and r's.

"It's not fair!" Lanya cried against Kid's arm, then laughed again, when they had made him abandon the loft edge.

"Just 'cause you throw so hard!" Cube in hand, Denny ducked first left, then right.

"Come on . . . now . . ." Kid panted, and couldn't laugh any more.

Denny looked over the edge. "There're a lot of them on the floor."

Lanya pulled back, threw another. It deflected from Denny's thigh. She ducked behind Kid.

Denny glanced back. "There goes another one."

Lanya looked out tentatively. "Maybe we better go down and pick them up."

Frowning, Denny turned back for the box. "Yeah . . ." He stopped to place the shirts and books and the glass dice in the corner. Koth regarded the board from his day-glo poster.

A shirt casing had gotten torn.

"Let's go down," Kid said.

Lanya followed him on the ladder.

They picked up cubes. When Denny came down, she threw one at him as he stepped to the floor.

"Hey, don't—" Denny said, because the cube went off into the junk beneath the platform.

"I'm sorry!" Lanya snickered again. "Here, let me

477

help." She followed him into the leaning tools, piled chairs, cartons. She held back an ironing board while Denny dropped down. "Got it . . ."

She came over with the box, and held it for Kid to put in his handful. While he fingered them clumsily into place, she asked, "Have you ever taken money for having sex with somebody?"

"Yes."

"Men and women?"

One cube stuck against another; Kid pressed, and another jumped out of the matrix. "Just men."

"Maybe I should try it," she said after a moment. "Everybody thinks about it."

"Why?" Kid stopped for another cube by his foot.

"And maybe you've just made a good point."

When Kid stood to place the cube, she added:

"But that wouldn't stop me."

She snapped the lid and turned toward Denny.

Kid grinned, watching her backbone like an arrow into her buttocks' heart. I do not know, he thought, what goes inside her. All I'm sure is that it's very different from what it looks like is going on.

"There're still some up top." She started up the ladder.

"I don't see any more here." Kid started behind her.

"Hey—!" Denny said.

Then something locked around Kid's neck, scraped his sides, and hung on.

"Fuck, what the—"

"Carry me!" Denny shouted, clinging. "Go ahead, carry me on up."

"Fuck *you!"* Kid shouted, sagging on his grip. He tried to shake the boy loose. "Don't choke me to death, you stupid . . . bastard!" He hauled up another rung.

Lanya crouched on the ledge. "You'll drop him—!"

Kid hauled up one more. "Get on up there, cocksucker!"

Lanya was tugging at Denny's arm.

Kid tried to heave Denny up.

"Hey—!"

Kid felt Denny slipping. Bare feet pawed his hip. Then something scrambled over his head. "Hey," Denny repeated in a different voice. He tugged at Kid's shoulder. "Are you all right?"

478

Lanya sat behind him, slapping first her thighs and then her stomach, once more helpless with laughter.

"Fuck you." Kid crouched on the loft edge. As he leaned forward, something hissed across his chest.

"Hey, my chain!"

"What?" Denny pushed himself backward, pulling the blankets from the board. He reached, without looking, for his own anklet.

Kid wondered if that was what had scraped so at his side.

Lanya watched, her lips apart.

"My chain." Kid repeated; he turned to sit on the edge of the loft, and looked down. The end, dangling from his foot, swung inches above the floor. He reached down to pull it up. "It broke this morning . . . somebody broke it."

"Who?" Lanya asked.

"Somebody broke it. I tried to fix it, but I knew it probably wouldn't hold."

With two fingers he followed it across his shoulder. The break was at the same link. He pulled the ends together.

"Wait a second," Lanya said. "You don't have any nails. Let me look." She crouched before Kid, so close her hair tickled his chest. How can she see, he wondered. "I just about got it."

She did something with her teeth.

"Hey?" Kid said.

"There," and pushed herself backward.

Behind Lanya, Denny asked now, "Who broke it?" Denny lay his foot on Lanya's knee. He put down the box, and brought his arms around her stomach, pulled her to him, laid an arm along hers.

"Don't those get in your way?" She glanced over Denny's leg at his dog-chained ankle. "Sexy, I suppose."

"Who?" Denny repeated his question.

"I don't know," Kid said. "I really don't."

He fingered for the weak link. Part of it was the dimness, but he doubted he could find that link now even in full light. He tugged, first here, then there. "You really fixed it?"

Lanya, her shoulder under Denny's chin, bit her lip to retain laughter. The words ". . . in time," fell through his head, and he was unsure what they referred to. I've

479

found something, he thought, in time. Who needs monasteries? He laughed out loud for Lanya's caged humor.

She let go Denny, and picked up the box, looking about her legs to see if any more pieces had fallen out.

A cube gnawed the side of Kid's foot. "Here!"

Lanya recovered herself to hold out the box.

Kid tossed the cube in. She put the box on her thigh to fit the cube in place.

"You really think you're a funny little cocksucker, huh?" Kid stood up, crouched, moved forward. His head tapped the ceiling. Not hard, but he staggered. "Yeah?" He crouched again, turning toward Denny and rubbing his groin. "Look at you. You suck a nice dick. You give some good head, what do you think that makes you?" He nudged Lanya with his elbow. The cubes rattled; she looked up. "Yeah, I like his tongue up my ass. But you think that makes you anything more than lukewarm shit— Hey, look at Denny!" Kid pointed between Denny's legs. "See, I do like that and he's got a hard-on already." He sat down and smiled. "Come on, let's get out of here."

"Now?" Lanya asked.

"Yeah, now!"

Denny crawled over to look in the box. "We got all the pieces." He sighed.

"Um-hm," she said quietly, and closed the lid.

Denny put the box in the corner. Kid pulled out his vest and put it on.

Lanya sat cross-legged in the middle of the bed. Kid could not decide if her expression were pensive or absent. "Come on." He tossed her blouse, and did not wait to see what she did with it, but reached for his pants.

"Did *everybody* leave the house?" Lanya asked.

"It sure is quiet." Denny said.

Kid looked back.

Lanya pushed another button through its hole. The blouse tails lay a-tangle in her lap.

Denny stooped listening, his cock, finally, lowering.

"I'm hungry," Kid said. "I haven't done anything but fuck for twenty-four hours: you, him, his girl friend—"

"You're a busy—" Lanya pulled on her jeans—"son of a bitch."

"Huh?"

"Nothing."

"—him, then you again." The two hooks came through the belt. "Jesus!" He looked up.

480

Denny said: "It sure is quiet. Maybe everybody went out."

"That'd be nice," Lanya said.

"Do you guys keep food in the house?" Kid asked.

"Not very long." Denny tossed Kid his projector.

Lanya started down first. She held the laces of her tennis shoes in her teeth. "I can't carry them and climb too," she had to say three times before they understood.

While Denny dropped over the edge, Kid turned to get the orchid.

The light around the window shade was neon orange. As he picked up the clustered blades, red gleamings poured down the edges. Kid frowned and backed to the ladder.

In the hallway, Lanya asked, "Has the smoke cleared up outside?" The window in the hall door was filled with light like bloody sunrise.

"I guess they all *have* gone out." Denny looked in another room.

"Do you think maybe it *is* clearing off?" Lanya asked. "Let's go outside and see."

Kid followed them to the front door.

Lanya opened it and went down the steps. "There're still clouds all over the sky." She reached the sidewalk, turned around, looked up—and screamed.

While Kid and Denny hurried down, the scream lost voice and became just expelled air.

On the sidewalk, they turned to look up in the direction she stared:

From the edge of the sidewalk, three-quarters of the disk was visible above the houses. The clouds dulled it enough to squint at, but it went up, covering the roofs, and up, and up, and up. What they could see of it filled half the visible sky. And, Kid realized, half of the sky is *huge!* But that fell away into impossibility. Or unverifiability, anyway. The rim was a broil of gold. Everything was like burning metal.

Lanya pressed his shoulder, gasping.

Denny was saying, "Huh . . . ?" and taking a step backward, and saying, "Huh . . . ?" again. He backed into Kid. His head snapped around, and the expression (the sockets of his eyes were cups of molten brass spilling down his cheeks) was maniacal. "Hey, that's really . . . something, ain't it?" The question was not rhetorical. "Ain't it something?" He turned to squint again.

481

"What *is* it?" Lanya whispered.

"It's the sun," Kid said. "Don't you see, it's just the sun."

"My God we're falling *into* it . . ." Lanya caught her breath, released it, then began to cry.

"Aw, come on!" Kid said. "Cut it out, will you—"

"My God . . ." she whispered and looked again.

He watched her face, open and glistening and shaking.

"Is it dangerous?" Denny whispered. "I'm scared as a mother-fucker!"

"It's getting bigger!" Lanya shrieked, turned, and crouched with her hands against the side of her face.

"No, it's *not*," Kid said. "At least not fast enough to see! Hey, come on!" He hit at her shoulder.

The orchid swung from the chain on his chest, tickling and glittering. It isn't a dream, Kid thought. I was dreaming already. It isn't a dream; that would make it . . . Bands of muscle made his throat so tight it hurt. "Hey!" He pounded his fist on Denny's back. "Hey, are you okay?"

Eyes wide, and chest all filled up with air, Denny got out, "Yeah!"

Lanya knuckled at her face, pulling creases into it, as she squinted at the great, great, great circle.

"Come on," Kid reiterated. "Let's go, huh?"

Denny followed, too quickly to tell why.

Lanya waited till they had gone three steps (Kid looked back), then ran after them, her face bewildered. She caught Kid's hand. Kid held his other one to Denny who took it tightly. Denny was sweating: "That *is* something." (Kid glanced up again.) "I never seen anything like that before in my life."

Kid looked at Lanya who was watching him oddly, and not where she was going. "We're not falling into the sun or anything like that," Kid said. "Otherwise we'd be burned up already. It isn't even hot." He looked at Denny, who dropped his eyes from the sky and looked back. "Well, Jesus Christ," Kid said. "Don't you think it's pretty fucking funny?" They didn't laugh. "I mean, there's nothing you can do about it." He did, alone. It felt good.

"What in the world *is* it?" Lanya repeated. Her voice was calmer.

"I don't know," Kid said. "I don't know *what* the fuck it is!"

Copperhead, hair like hell-bright rust, sprinted around the corner, and stopped in the middle of the street, boots apart, elbows bent, fists swinging about his hips and belly.

The other scorpions caught up. Among them was Siam and Jack the Ripper and Denny's girl, but neither Dragon Lady nor Nightmare.

Kid let go their hands and pointed to the sky. "Ain't that too fucking much!" He laughed, and the tight things in his throat loosened. He came out of the laughter, which had closed his eyes and jerked the small of his back almost into spasm, to find them watching. "Hey, Copperhead! Where you going? You going to come with me?"

"What . . ." Copperhead began to bellow, then coughed, and there was nothing left in his voice to sustain. "What is that?" His voice was tearfully inane. "Is it some kind of *heat* lightning?"

Someone else said: "Does that look like lightning to *you?*"

Kid blinked and wondered. "You better come on with me," he dared.

"You all right, Kid?" the black in the vinyl vest asked from behind Copperhead, drifting there as Lady of Spain drifted behind him.

"You," Kid spoke carefully, explaining to them as though it were a lesson, "come on with *me!*" He took a breath and started across the street. As he stepped up on the curb, a hand caught his shoulder. He looked back; it was Denny, and behind him, Lanya; black scorpions moved around them, passed in front of them.

And footsteps.

He didn't look back again.

Perhaps, he thought, we are all going to die in moments, obscured by flame and pain. That is why this. And then, perhaps we are not. That is why this in this way.

Scorpions milled and clustered, and he chuckled again.

That was as silly as the blades tickling his chest.

Laughter grasped the back of his tongue to shake it loose. Flesh lay too heavy in his mouth. So it retreated, and heaved itself against the spike of his spine. I am happy, he thought. And heard somebody else, a white girl (not Lanya; the scorpion, who wore a vest and was called Filament), laughing too.

483

So he let his own.

It doubled him up, staggering.

Somebody—that *was* Lanya, and that was, almost, enough to stop him—cried out.

But others laughed.

Somebody else—that was Denny, and when he saw it was, he kept laughing through his puzzlement—ran past, picked up the lid of a garbage can leaning against the curb, and hurled it up the street. It went clattering against a stoop. Denny danced back in the blood-colored light.

Gold nodes ground in the clouds.

Kid reached out, had to lean to catch Lanya's fingers; his fingers, between hers, pummeled the back of her hand. She came up against his side, and watched in wonder as others pushed ahead on the cobbled street.

"Pick a house," he told her.

"Huh—?"

"Just pick a house on the street," he whispered (she bent nearer to hear). "Maybe one you don't like very much."

Copperhead bounded past them, flung his arm: the brick-shard flew across the street, shattered the window; Copperhead, full hair and sparse beard furious, turned back, grinning.

"That one?" Kid asked.

"No!" with an urgency he could not follow. "At the top of the hill. That one. There."

"Okay." Kid wheeled.

The blond girl in the pea jacket was falling back through the loose blacks. She was crying; she looked at the sky, and cried harder. Denny's girl put her arm around her, was talking, was making consoling motions with her head. Once she glanced at the great, burning wheel; her face was webbed with rage.

Kid's hand went up across his cheek. Bristle clawed his palm. "This way!" He waved and turned again. They passed around him as he turned in the light. "Hey, Ripper, Denny, Copperhead!" He caught at the jouncing projector, and thumbed at the bottom pip. "How do you turn this thing on?"

"Huh?" Ripper looked back. "Oh . . . to the *side*. Not in."

The pip slid.

Of course, he thought, I can't see anything from inside. And wondered what he looked like.

Lanya had stepped away and was looking all over him. Kid beat his knees, and swung about. And Denny had disappeared in his own deformed explosion.

"Hey," the espresso-hued Ripper called, "we goin' on!"

Figure passed figure as they milled about the cobbles. Kid looked where Copperhead was laughing; and Copperhead disappeared in his lucent arachnid. The menagerie formed in the terrible light.

Thirteen, whom Kid hadn't seen till now, passed him. "Come on," he whispered to Smokey beneath his arm, "let's get out of here. This ain't gonna be no good—"

"I want to watch!" she insisted. "I want to *watch!*"

Kid reached the porch. Some people were running behind him. He'd broken down three doors in his life: so he expected to bruise his shoulder. (The light that was Denny blinked beside him: the boy was climbing the rail.) Kid crashed into the weathered wood. It flew back so easily he went down on one knee and grabbed at the jamb. (About him, the mystic aspects lurched.) At the same time, glass broke and light filled the hallway as Denny's apparition came through the shattered porch window.

"Oh—Jesus . . ." A girl's black face passed the door opposite.

Then another's: "It's scorpions . . . !"

A skinny black boy ran into the room with a stick. He opened his mouth and his eyes wide.

"Jimmy, you come on—!"

The boy (*was* he twenty? Kid staggered to his feet, a little scared, and not believing he was invisible behind some bright beast) kept on jerking at the stick.

"*Jimmy!*" she shrieked, "come out of there! It's the scorpions, for God's—"

Jimmy (Kid was surprised) suddenly closed his mouth, flung away his stick, and ran back through the doorway. Somewhere else in the house footsteps banged down steps.

Denny beat Kid to the doorway and extinguished. He leaned through, then looked back with a puzzled grin (others had already surged into the room, to fling their shadows in the red light across the wall.) "Hey, you see the way those niggers run?"

Behind Kid somebody overturned a chair.

He frowned, realized no one could see it, stopped frowning, and slid the stud over the bottom of his projector.

"Shit, man," Denny said. "Them was some scared, black mother-fuckers." Shaking his head, he went on through the doorway.

"Don't do that! Don't do that! Don't—"

"What the fuck they got in here?"

"Come on, God damn it, don't do that!"

In the maroon light across the wall in front of Kid, an apish shadow grew smaller, and smaller, and smaller, till the hand, only slightly bigger than Kid's, raised.

The hand clapped Kid's shoulder.

"Hey," Copperhead said. "They got some place here! Carpet on the floor . . ." His other hand gestured down; and up: "And look at all that shit on the ceiling."

Kid looked.

Women in gauze and men in armor careened through woods, by lakes, and over hills above the molding.

Kid looked down to see Copperhead squinting out the door at the reddened street. "Well." He looked back. "I'm gonna go see what they got in here." While somebody screamed in another room, Copperhead's hand fell twice again, in perfect amicability. Then he stepped through. Kid walked back through the room, looking for Lanya.

She was standing just inside the door, and angry.

"What's the matter?"

"There were people living here!" she hissed. "What in the world . . ." She shook her head.

"I didn't know that," Kid said. "You picked the house."

"And I didn't know what you wanted to do with it!" She spoke with intense softness, as though she did not want the disk beyond the roofs to hear. "What the hell did you want to do?"

"Anything." He shrugged. "Let's go see."

She sucked her teeth and gave him her hand. He led her back through the room, only half as crowded, now.

Before neon confetti from the humming television in the other room, figures staggered and swayed.

"Here." Siam thrust out a bottle with his bandaged hand.

486

Kid pushed out onto the narrow balcony, surprised to find it empty, and looked up:

It was wide enough to be cut off both by the roof across the street and his own roof. I remember this, he questioned, from the other side of sleep? Then added, somberly quizzical: Deadly rays!

A weathered pride glared from beneath the chipped rail, with hints of gold paint, inward (shouldn't it be out? Kid thought) toward the wooden doors, at isocephalic attention.

With light (he thought logically as music) from such a source, there could be no shadows.

He put his bare foot on the railing to examine it, to see if this new illumination told him anything. The rail pressed the ball up which stretched the toes down. The concavities at each side of his heel were scaly as the skin at the rim of Siam's bandage. The knuckle of each toe, with its swirl of black hair, pulled the skin on either side of itself, intimating age. I am closer to thirty than twenty, he thought, put that foot down and raised the other.

The suede boot was blotched with what he'd always called salt stains, that came from walking in rain puddles. Only it hadn't rained. Below the wrinkled leather—forty feet below—cobbles stretched off between the houses like a mahogany anaconda.

He examined his left hand. I don't like what they look like, he thought. I don't like them: Like something vegetative, yanked from the ground, all roots and nodules, with dirty, chewed things at the ends, like something self-consumed: And remembered the times, on acid, they had actually terrified him.

He examined the right hand. There were scabs along the places where he'd bitten to blood. He'd always considered his baby face, despite passing inconveniences, as, essentially, a piece of luck. But the hands, of some aged and abused workman, he felt wronged by. They frightened people (they frightened him); still he could not believe, because it was their shape and their texture and their hair and great veins, that breaking, by force, the habit of biting and gnawing and biting would do any good. (Sitting on the sidewalk, once, when he was ten, he had rubbed his palms on the concrete, because he wanted to know what callouses would feel like when he masturbated: had that, that afternoon, triggered some irrevocable pro-

489

cess in the skin which, still, after a few days of labor, left his hands horn-hard and cracking weeks, even months, later?) He liked Lanya to cradle them in her soft ones, kiss them, tickle the inner flesh with her tongue, make love to them like gnomes, while he, voyeuristically, observed and mocked and felt tender.

He looked down at the chains: ran his fingers behind them; lifted up the hanging orchid and watched it turn under the sourceless gold. Then he sat against the shingled wall, with his feet at the feet of the lions, took the pad into his lap, and began to click his pen.

Among other sounds inside, somebody was shrieking and gasping and shrieking again, which meant somebody was doing something terrible. Or somebody thought somebody was.

Actions are interesting to watch. I learn about the actors. Their movements are emblems of the tensions in this internal landscape, which their actions resolve. About-to-act is an interesting state to experience, because I am conscious of just those tensions. Acting itself feels fairly dull; it not only resolves, it obliterates those tensions from my consciousness. Acting is only interesting as it leads to new tensions that, irrelevantly, cause me to act again. But here, beneath this gigantic light, with the cardboard-backed phone pad covering the hole in my jean knee, that isn't what I want to write. I am about to write. I take my thumb from the ballpoint's button. I work the pen up till my fingers (hideous?) grip the point. I begin.

Lanya crashed Kid's ken like a small, silent iguanodon. Kid did not move. Lanya sat sideways on a lion's head and looked across the street for forty-five astounding seconds: Then at Kid: "You're still writing on that . . . ?"

"No." The hypersensitivity left over from working had resolved with Lanya's voice. "No, I've been finished a few minutes now."

Lanya squinted at the immense semi-circle. Then she said, "Hey . . ." she frowned. "It's going down!"

Kid nodded. "You can see it falling almost."

The clouds that moiled the edge had deepened from gold to bronze. Three quarters of the circle had been visible above the roofs when they had first walked in the street. Now it was slightly under half. (And still half was awfully huge.) Lanya hunched her shoulders.

Denny came through the doors, paused, a hand on each, to screw his face in the glare. Then, silently, he sat on the rail beside Lanya, gripped his knees, his arm an inch from hers.

Denny comes: some fantastic object.

She comes: some object more fantastic, and with a history.

Lanya bent forward, picked up the pad, read. After moments, she said "I like that."

But what, Kid went on thinking, if someone were stupid enough to ask me for a choice? He tried an ironic smile; but the ironic part got fumbled in the machinery of his face. So he guessed it was just a smile.

Anyway a smile's what they gave him back.

Denny said, "It's going down," unnecessarily for her.

One hand pressed against her knee, the other went across her face, and she let out all breath.

Terror clanged in him like a spoon against a bent pan. Kid reached forward, touched her shin. Terror? he thought: When what terrifies is neither noisy, nor moves quickly, and lasts hours, then we become very different. I don't know who she is! He gripped harder.

She frowned, moved the toe of her sneaker from his bare foot.

So he dropped his hand.

With her hand on her stomach, she took a breath, and raised her perspiring face, blinking and blinking her green eyes, to watch.

While somebody else came out, Lanya asked, "Why aren't you afraid?" Kid thought about dreaming, could think of nothing to say, so nodded toward the falling light.

She said: "Then I won't be either."

The boy who'd come out was the pimply, stubble-bearded scorpion. He looked around uncomfortably as though he felt he might have interrupted something, seemed about to turn and go (what is he feeling, Kid wondered; what makes him look this conventional part?), when Frank, the poet from the commune, came out.

Then two black girls (thirteen? twelve?) holding hands, stepped out, not blinking, their hair almost shorn, small gold rings in their ears. And there were more people in the doorway. (Will the balcony hold?) He wondered also at how much easier that was to wonder than about what blotted out the sky.

491

"It's going down, see," Denny repeated.

He enjoys, Kid thought, saying that to Lanya: But with nine people here, the equations are different; he can't get the same reactions.

Briefly he pictured Nightmare and Dragon Lady.

Milly pushed by Copperhead. The light stole the brilliance from the different reds of their hair by dealing equal flamboyance to everything. She kneeled at the rail. Light between two lions made a ragged bandage across her calf.

The scabs, Kid thought, are bright as red glass.

There were too many people.

Milly brushed at her cheek.

Why is a given gesture given as it is? Hers? She's guilty making any motions at all in a situation demanding immobility. (He looked at the scratch.) She's guilty . . . ?

There were too many people.

The long-haired youngsters, hands linked, stepped through; one took the hand of the pimply, unshaven scorpion (who was also very drunk): he breathed loudly and swayed into people.

They didn't move.

"What are you going to do with that?" Lanya asked, softly enough to sound soft even in this silence.

The scorpion's breath was thunderous.

"I don't know." That sounded thunderous too.

"Let me take it." She tore off the three pages, corrected, and recorrected. (Does it take this much light to illuminate the material for another poem?) With a head movement (shadow spilled from the green target of her eye down her cheek) she stopped him. "I have your notebook at home. I'll put these with it. I want to go." She turned to Denny. And the shadow had rolled somewhere beneath her chin; in the creases of her eyelid he could see sweat. "You want to walk me home?"

Kid wanted to protest, decided no; offer to come too?

She touched Denny's arm. Her nose and ear were shadowed: the incredible disk had lowered so that what remained was small enough that everyone around them, beneath a folded elbow, behind a heel on reddened tile, under frayed denim where a sleeve had been torn off, or within and behind the curves of flesh in flesh of the ear, had once more grown shadows. She looked afraid.

Lanya stood, and people stepped apart.

Denny, like someone just awakened, clambered from the rail, and, blinking about him (at the others as much as Kid) followed her.

Denny left, and people closed around.

"When it goes down . . ." the pimply scorpion began.

Kid, and the two people who held his hand, looked.

Something white had dried on his mouth. His lashless lids were pink and swollen.

The two looked away.

"When it goes all the way down, there won't be any fuckin' light at all, again . . . ever." He shook his head, scuffed his boots, rocked on the doorsill. "Black as a fucking bitch . . . yeah!"

They've gone, Kid thought. No light at *all?*

Fifteen minutes later, when it *had* set completely, the sky had returned to its ordinary grey.

3

He woke . . . alone?

Someone was climbing to the loft ladder.

He struggled to choose between dreams and . . . the rest. Because they had all left the muraled house, and wandered back to the nest. Milly had talked to him, aimlessly, in the sloped street, mostly all surprised that he was the same Kid everybody had been talking about, and how glad she was to know that she knew him, till he'd decided she was trying to put the make on him and had gotten angry. "Get the fuck out of here, you stupid bitch!" he'd yelled in the street and made to hit her. She'd run away; he'd laughed, loudly, till he was staggering. Copperhead had come up to him and beat him on the shoulder, laughing too. "I didn't like that one either. Shit, you can have one of mine . . ." He'd kept laughing, so he wouldn't have to speak, thinking with perfectly maniacal pride: I have, I have already—

"Kid, are you okay?" Denny's ears were lit from behind and below. His face was dark.

"Yeah . . . ?"

Denny came up over the edge.

"They're making food—" and at the word, Kid smelled it—"inside. Nightmare and Dragon Lady just came back. You sleepin'?"

"Come—" and at the word, Denny, all shoulders and chin and elbows, wedged against him—"here. Yeah." He held the warm knobby shapes and lay there smelling grease and a hot, vegetative stench that defined no food he recognized; but he liked it anyway.

"Lanya's got a nice place," Denny said.

"Yeah?" Kid thought: he's so light; but his edges are sharp. "You ball her again?"

". . . Yeah." Denny said. "In her room, at her house. I guess that was all right."

494

Surprised, Kid opened his eyes. Cracks cross the dim ceiling. "Oh." He shifted Denny to the side. "You got more energy than I do. I was tired when I got back here."

"She's got a nice place," Denny repeated. "Real nice."

"Why'd she want to go?" He nubbed his rough chin for the itching.

Denny squirmed to get comfortable. "To see about her class, she said." Denny squirmed again.

"Class?"

The L about the window shade had finally taken on the deep color of evening.

"Her kids. She's been looking out for this group of kids, you know? About eight and nine years old. Black kids mostly."

"No, I didn't know." He let his lips purse to a tent where, with the help of air, they were off his teeth. Well, he *hadn't* seen her much. *How* many days gone? She'd said she had a place, yes; "No, I didn't know."

He frowned at the top of Denny's head.

"I like her," Denny said. "I like her a lot." Denny's face came up from under the hair. "You know, I think she likes me too?"

"Guess she does," Kid said. "Did she check . . . her class?"

"No," Denny said. "Not while I was there. She was going to. But we got to fuckin' around again. Screwin', you know. She said she was going to, after I left. If she didn't go to sleep first. I think she was pretty tired."

Kid looked at the ceiling again. "How long she had the kids?"

"A couple of weeks," Denny said. "That's what she told me. She said she likes it. They meet a little way from her place. That's real nice."

"What's it like?" A couple of weeks? He was too exhausted to be upset.

"*Real* nice." Some of Denny's hair brushed and caught on Kid's chin.

"Well, you're good for something, cocksucker. Hey!" Kid bunched the muscles of his leg under Denny's stiffening groin. "No, man. Fuck off. I don't want to now."

Denny pulled himself back on all fours. "You better go eat something, then. They don't got that much. They'll eat it all."

Kid sat, nodding. "Yeah, come on." He climbed groggily down, and stood in the doorway.

Why (watching Denny climb) did she tell him all that about her new place, and her class, and not me? Why didn't I ask? he answered. He could smile at that, finally.

"Come on." Denny took Kid's elbow and led him down.

Halfway up the hall, Kid sucked his teeth and pulled free. It was a gentle pull; but Denny's head leapt away at the motion, frightened and anticipatory, despairing and wild. Without looking at him particularly, Denny stepped back to let him through.

"Jesus Christ!" Nightmare exclaimed, turning with a full plate in his hand, gesturing first, then scooping with his fork. "Wasn't that something this afternoon? I mean, wasn't that too much!" He filled his mouth and spoke on, scattering little pieces. "We heard about you chasing out the niggers! Hey—" he gestured to Dragon Lady who sat against the wall—"we heard about what he did to those niggers."

"Shit," Dragon Lady said dryly, and looked at Kid only from the corner of her eye. "I don't care what he do to any God-damn niggers."

"I didn't even know they were in the house," Kid said.

Dragon Lady took another mouthful. "Shit," she repeated, and pried with her spoon tip through what was on her plate.

"Give 'em something to eat," Nightmare yelled toward the kitchen.

"*Baby!*" Dragon Lady bellowed; her shoulders shook; nobody stopped doing anything. "*Adam!*" She flung the words up like grenades. "Bring some more *food* out for 'em!"

"Here you go!" Baby, *still* naked, pushed between the people at the door, leading (dangerously) with steaming plates.

"This is yours."

Kid ignored the dirty thumb denting what must have been a hash of canned vegetables (he pulled the fork out from where it had been buried: corn, peas, okra, fell off) and (he tasted the first mouthful) meat. (Spam?) Baby gave the other plate to Denny. He returned to serve Cathedral, Jack the Ripper, Devastation, all sitting about silently.

Copperhead, not served yet, watched from the couch, and grinned and nodded when Kid looked at him.

"Here you go." Adam shoved a plate at Copperhead. He took it, saluted Kid with a fork with twisted tines, then dropped his shoulders and shoveled.

Denny's girl friend (should I find out her name?) with a coffee cup of the hash, came out of the kitchen, crossed to sit right by Denny on the floor and made a big thing of not looking at Kid. The girl in the pea jacket, next to Copperhead on the couch, occasionally picked food from Copperhead's plate with a spoon: Copperhead more or less ignored her.

"You had a party?" Nightmare exclaimed in answer to a question Kid hadn't heard asked. "We *ran!* Adam, Baby, the Lady, and me! I was so scared I didn't think I was gonna make it. Shit, I'm still scared."

The last laughter to trail away was Dragon Lady's gusty chuckle.

"We were in the park." Nightmare waved his fork above his head; more people sat down. "Baby, Adam, Dragon Lady, and me. You know the old weather tower in the park?"

(What, Kid wondered, had George been doing in the brazen light of the noon? What had June?)

"When it began, I mean after it began—first we thought that whole side of the city was on fire—after we could see what it was—" he shook his head at somebody who started a comment—"no, no, I don't *know* what the fuck it was. Don't ask me. After we could *see* it, we went up the steps to watch. Didn't we?"

Dragon Lady sat, smiling and shaking her head, which, when she noticed the shift of attention, changed to nodding: the smile stayed.

"We just climbed up there and watched the whole thing. Go up. And go down." Nightmare whistled. "Jesus Christ!"

We live, Kid thought; and die in different cities.

"You were out there in it," the scorpion in vinyl asked, watching, "until it was all over?"

Copperhead protested: "We watched it going down—"

"All over?" But Nightmare's mouth hung open, mocking his interlocutor. "What's all over?"

Adam rubbed the chains on his chest: the rest were still.

"You think it's all over?" Nightmare demanded.

The blond girl in the pea jacket held her spoon in

both hands tightly between her knees. "When it went down," she said, "it was just like regular day again . . . here. And then it was light for four or five hours till it was time to get dark." She looked back over her shoulder at the black glass; the brass lion on the windowsill watched the night from beneath his bulbless stalk.

Dragon Lady's laughter built in the silence.

"Shit." Nightmare filled his mouth again and yelled at his plate: "You don't know if the sun is ever gonna come *up* again! We could all be burned up to death by tomorrow. Or frozen. What were you saying, Baby, about maybe the earth got pushed off its orbit or something like that, maybe into the sun, or out past it—"

"I didn't say that." Baby looked down at himself, pimply chest, uncircumcised genitals, bowed knees, dirty feet; his nakedness for the first time was out of place. "I wasn't sayin' it that serious—"

"There'd be an earthquake if that happened." Brown Adam, with his Philadelphia accent, held his chains in his fist. "I told you that. A big earthquake, or a tidal wave; both maybe. Nothing like that's happened. And there'd have to be if the earth got pushed somewhere—"

"So maybe—" Nightmare looked up—"in ten minutes there's gonna be a big fuckin' earthquake!"

Then the lightbulb hanging from the ceiling dropped to quarter dimness.

Kid tried to swallow his heart; it threatened to burst and fill his mouth with blood.

Someone was crying again.

Kid looked to see if it was Denny. But it was another scorpion (Spider?) on the other side of Nightmare. Denny's face, even in the yellowish half-dark, was cut with blades of shadow from his hair.

"Oh, come on!" Smokey edged from behind Thirteen's shoulder. "Look, it used to do that four or five times a day when we stayed here."

In the kitchen something hummed: the light returned to full brightness.

Nightmare ate doggedly.

No one else did.

"You guys make up any more of this shit?" Nightmare nodded toward Adam and Baby. "It's good." Then looked around. "You don't know if it's over or not."

"I could use some more," Dragon Lady said.

498

Baby came forward with his hands out for their plates.

"The mistake—" Kid surprised himself by speaking, took a mouthful to stop, but went on anyway—"isn't thinking that it's finished." I'm imitating Nightmare, he thought, then realized, no, I'm doing what Nightmare did for the same reason. "The mistake is thinking it began this afternoon."

"Right on, mother-fucker!" Nightmare shook his fork for emphasis.

Kid took another mouthful, and thought: I may throw up. And then thought: No, I'm too hungry.

"We got some more out there in the big pot," Adam was saying. "Why don't you guys go out and get it till it's all gone."

A shadow made Kid look up from the last of his eating.

Adam stood there, hand out for Kid's plate, about (Kid realized) to burst out crying too. Kid gave it to him.

Nightmare, Dragon Lady, and me get served first, Kid reflected as Baby brought his seconds. Well, Copperhead seemed at ease.

Finished, Kid put his fork on the floor and stood up.

"Hey, where're you going?" Copperhead asked, no belligerence, all bewilderment.

"Taking a walk."

On the bottom step of the house, he noted two streetlights in the distance. Burn up at any minute? Or freeze at the advent of an ice age, twenty minutes to completion? The air was the same excruciatingly bland temperature it had been night after night after night. The door opened behind him: Denny looked out.

"I want to go over and see Lanya's place," Kid said, turning. "You want to show me the way?"

"I . . . I can't," Denny said. "She's upset. And she wants to talk . . . to me."

"Fuck you, cocksucker." Kid started down the block. "See you later." (He wasn't angry at all.) That was pretty good. Halfway to the corner, however, he realized Denny would be the only way to find Lanya's new place. (Then he was.)

He could try the bar. But if she had a house now, what was the chance she'd be at *Teddy's* tonight?

He looked back, ready to yell to Denny to get the fuck on down here.

The door was closed.

And I *still* don't know her name!

He took a breath between his teeth. Maybe he'd find Lanya at the bar.

At the corner of the hill; surprised at how many street lamps—perhaps one out of five—worked in this neighborhood. The one diagonally across the street gave enough light to make out the charred walls of the big house. (The stronger burned smell had made him stop.) The columns supporting the balcony over the door had charred through, so that the platform, with its rail of lions, hung askew. Even so it took Kid a whole minute to be sure what house it was. Only houses he could see around confirmed it.

Four, five, six hours since they had screamed and laughed and yelled inside it?

Chilled to gooseflesh in the neutral air, he hurried away.

". . . definitely *saw* it?"

"Oh, yes."

"You were already in the city?"

"That's right."

"You said earlier you didn't see the whole thing though."

"I caught, I guess, now it must have been, the last ten or fifteen minutes. Roger came and woke me up to see."

"You saw it from *inside* the house then?"

"Well, first out my window. Then we went down to the gardens. I tell you, now, it was pretty strange."

The others laughed. "Hey," Paul Fenster said, half standing to look at the others seated. "We've just about got the Captain boxed in here. Why doesn't somebody move back, there?"

"That's all right. If I want to get out, I'll just bust on through."

"I imagine—" Madame Brown reached down to play with Muriel's muzzle—"you aren't any closer to an explanation than we are."

"I think that was about the strangest thing I ever saw, I'll be honest now."

"As strange as anything you ever saw in space?" from the man in purple angora.

"Well, I tell you, this afternoon was pretty . . . I guess you'd say, spaced out."

They laughed again.

The heavy blond Mexican with the blanket shirt rose from beside Tak and walked to the door, passing within a foot of Kid, and left. Tak saw Kid. With tilting head, he beckoned.

Kid, curious, went to sit in the vacated seat.

Tak leaned to whisper, "Captain Kamp . . ." A dozen

others had pulled chairs up to listen to the crew-cut man in the green, short-sleeved shirt who sat in the corner booth.

Tak sat and folded his hands across the bottom of his leather jacket so that the top pushed out from his blond chest.

"What I want to know," purple angora announced, ". . . down, sweetheart, down——" Muriel had momentarily switched allegiances—"I want to know is, if it could possibly have been some kind of trick. I mean, is there any way somebody could have made that seem to happen? I mean . . . well, you know: in a man-made way."

"Well . . ." The Captain looked among his listeners. "He's your engineer, isn't he?" His look settled on Tak—who reared back with a high laugh.

That must be as self-conscious as I've ever seen him, Kid thought. He'd never heard Tak make that sound before.

"No," Tak said. "No, I'm afraid that doesn't have anything to do with any engineering I'd know anything about."

"What I want to know—now what *I* want to know," Fenster said. "You've been in space. You've been on the moon . . ." He paused, then added in a different voice: "You're one of the ones that was actually on the moon."

Captain Kamp was only attentive.

"We've had here some sort of . . . astrological happening, and it's got us all pretty shook. I want to know if you . . . well, from being up on the moon, or like that, you might know something more about it."

Kamp's face ghosted a smile. Kid searched for the names of the astronauts from the four moonshots he'd followed closely, tried to recall what he could about the fifth. Captain Kamp crossed his arms on the booth-table. He wasn't very tall.

"Now it's certainly possible——" Kamp punctuated his southwestern speech with small nods—"that there's an astronomical, or better, cosmological explanation. But I'll be frank: I don't know what it is."

"Do you think we should worry?" Madame Brown asked in a voice with no worry in it at all.

Kamp, whose crew mixed grey and gold, nodded. "Worry? Well, we're all here. And alive. That's certainly no reason *not* to worry. But worry isn't going to do us much good, now, is it? Now yesterday—about this time yesterday—I was in Dallas. And if that thing was as big as it looked and really some sort of body in the sky, a comet or a sun, I suspect it would have been seen a long way off coming, with telescopes. And nobody told *me* about it."

"It sounds, Captain, as though you don't believe it's serious."

Kamp's smile said as much. Kamp said, "I *saw* it—some of it, anyway."

"Then," Kid said, and others turned, "you don't know how big it really was."

"Now that," the Captain answered, "I'm afraid, is it." His jaw was wider than his forehead. "Now you all, Roger too, described something which practically filled up half the sky. So obviously what I saw was only a little bit. And then there was the story about—George, was it?"

Tak looked around the room, frowned, and again whispered to Kid: "George was here a few minutes ago. He must have gone out just before you came—"

"Now I'm afraid nobody outside . . . of Bellona, saw that one. And Roger tells me he didn't either."

"I certainly did," Tak whispered.

"I certainly did!" someone cried.

"Well." Kamp smiled. "Not too many other people did, and certainly nobody outside Bellona."

"You saw what happened today." Teddy, arms folded, leaned against the back of the next booth.

"Yes, I guess I did."

"You mean," Fenster jovially announced, "you went from here to the moon and back, and you didn't see anything on the way that would tell us something about all this thing this afternoon?"

Kamp said, "Nope."

"Then what use was it, I ask you?" Fenster looked around for somebody's back to slap. "I mean now what was the use of it?"

Someone said, "You haven't been with the space program a while?"

"Now you don't really leave it. Just last week I was down for medical testing for long-range results. That I don't ever expect to stop. But I'm much less involved with it now than some of the others."

"Why did you leave?" the purple angora asked. "Was it your idea or theirs—if you can answer a question like that?"

"Well." This, a considered sentence. "I suspect they thought it was a touchier question than I did at the time. But I doubt they wanted me that much if I didn't want them. My interest in the space program just about ended with splashdown. The tests, the research work afterward, that was important. The parades, the celebrations, the panels, the publicity—I think the fun in that was exhausted a month after I came out of the isolation chamber. The rest—probably more so for me than for the others, because that's the kind of person I am—was just a nuisance. Also," and he smiled, "I've occasionally been known to pick up a guitar at a party and a sing a folk song or two. Nothing political, mind you. But they still frown on that sort of thing."

Everyone laughed. Kid thought: Is he for real?

And a second thought, like a stutter: My reaction is as fixed as his action. And Kid laughed, though later than the others. Two or three glanced at him.

"No," Kamp went on, "I suppose I saw myself as something of an adventurer . . . as much as a navy test pilot can be. *Apollo* for me was an adventure—practically an eight-year adventure, with all the preparation. But when it was over, I was ready to go on to something else."

"So you've come to Bellona," Madame Brown said, as Fenster said: "After the moon, where else *is* there?"

"Now, you're right . . ."

Kid wondered which question Kamp was answering.

". . . but I'm just beginning to see that myself."

"Are you here in any official connection?" asked another woman.

"I'd imagine," Fenster said, "you're never officially disconnected."

"No. I'm here unofficially."

"What does that mean?" someone challenged.

Fenster scowled, offended for Kamp, who merely said, "They know I'm here. But they gave me no instructions before I came. They won't ask me anything about what I did or saw after I come back."

"Why don't we break up this Star Chamber?" Fenster stood. "Come on, the Captain is nice enough to talk to us all at once, but we've got to give the man a chance to circulate."

"Now this is quite informal," Kamp countered,

"compared to what I'm used to. I would like a chance to walk around though."

"Come on, come on." Fenster made shooing motions.

Some rose.

The bartender rolled his cuffs above the blurry blue beasts and strolled to the counter.

Tak's chair scraped.

"Come on, now, let's let the Captain get himself a drink. Madame Brown, you look like you could use one too."

Kid shook his hands below the chair edge to stop the tingling.

Tak stood, stretched to tiptoe, looked around. "Wonder where George got off to. He was all curious when he discovered we had a genuine man in the moon with us."

They walked to the bar.

Teddy was returning chairs.

Once the dozen clustered at the Captain's booth dispersed, the place looked empty.

"I thought Lanya was here, maybe."

Tak's hands locked. "I haven't seen her. Madame B. might know where she is." And unlocked. "Hey, I saw the big advertisement in the *Times,* all over page three. Congratulations." Tak frowned. "By the way, what did *you* do at the coming of the great white light? Orange, I guess it was, really. You got any opinions to pass the time with while we wait to see if there's going to be a tomorrow?"

Kid leaned on meshed fingers. "I don't know. I didn't do anything much. I had some people with me. I think they were more upset than I was. You know, Tak, for a while I thought . . ." The bartender set down a beer bottle. ". . . no, that's silly." Kid pulled the bottle to him, leaving a sweat ribbon. "Isn't it?" The candles glittered in it.

"What?"

"I was going to say, for a while I thought it was a dream."

"If I woke up right now, I'd feel a lot better."

"No. Not that." Kid lifted his bottle once, twice, a third, a fourth, a fifth time from lapping rings. "When it was rising, I remember I went out to take a look from the back porch; and thinking maybe I was dreaming. Suddenly I woke up. In bed. Only, when I got up, later, it

505

was still there. Finally, after it went down, I went to sleep again. You know, right now—" he smiled, to himself till it overcame the strictures of his facial muscles and burst stupidly onto his face—"I still don't know what I dreamed and what I didn't. Maybe I didn't really see any more than the Captain."

"You went to *sleep?*"

"I was tired." Saying that annoyed Kid. "What about you?"

"Christ, I—" The bartender brought Tak's bottle. "What did I do?" Tak snorted. "I saw the light coming through those bamboo blinds I have, and I went out on the roof to take a look. I watched it rising for about three minutes. Then I freaked."

"What'd you do?"

"I went down into the stairwell and sat in the dark for about an hour or so . . . I guess. I'd got this whole paranoid thing about radiation—no, don't laugh. We might all start losing our hair in the next six hours while our capillaries fall apart. Finally I got scared of just sitting in the dark and went up to look again . . ." He stopped moving his bottle around the wet circle. "I'm just glad I don't have a heart condition. It stretched over so much of the horizon I couldn't look at one edge and see the other. I couldn't look at where the bottom was cut off by the roofs and see the top." Tak's bottle rumbled about. "I went back down into the stairwell, closed the door, and just cried. For a couple of hours. I couldn't stop. While I was crying, I thought about lots of things. One of them, by the way, was you."

"What?"

"I remember sitting there and asking myself if this was what the inside of insanity felt like— Ah, there: you've taken offense."

He hadn't. But now wondered if he should.

"Well, I'm sorry. That's what I thought, anyway."

"You were really that scared?"

"*You* weren't?"

"I guess a lot of people around me were. I thought about all the terrible things it could have been—like everybody else. But if it was any of them, there wasn't anything I could do."

"You really are almost as weird as people keep trying to make us think you are. Look, when you come up short against the edge like that, when you discover the

506

earth really *is* round, when you find out you've killed your father and married your mother after all, or when you look at the horizon and see something, like that, rising—man, you have to have *some* sort of human reaction: laugh, cry, sing, something! You can't just lie down and take a nap."

Kid lingered in the ruins of his confusion. "I . . . did a lot of laughing."

Tak snorted again. "Okay, so you're *not* that flippy. I'd just hate to think you were as brave as everybody keeps going on you are."

"Me?" This couldn't, Kid thought, be what the inside of courage felt like.

"Excuse me," the southwestern voice said from Kid's other side. "You were pointed out to me as . . . the Kid?"

Kid turned, with his confusion. "Yeah . . . ?"

Kamp looked at it, and laughed. Kid decided he liked him. Kamp said, "I'm supposed to deliver a message to you, from Roger."

"Huh?"

"He told me if I came here I would probably meet you. He'd like—if it's all right with you—if you'd come up to the house three Sundays from now. He says that he'll be squeezing more time together, so it will be in slightly less than two weeks—now I don't know how you guys put up with that—" He laughed again. "Roger wants to have a party for you. For your book." The Captain paused with a considered nod. "Saw it. Looks good. Good luck on it, now."

Kid wondered what to say. He tried: "Thank you."

"Roger said to come in the evening. And bring twenty or thirty friends, if you want. He says it's your party. It starts at sunset; in three Sundays."

"Presumptuous bastard," Tak said. "Sunset? He might at least wait and see if there's a tomorrow morning." With his forefinger he hooked down his cap visor and walked off.

Kid was pondering statements to place into the silence, when Kamp apparently decided he'd try: "I'm afraid I don't know much about poetry."

Liked him, Kid felt. But for the life of him he didn't know why.

"I read some of Roger's copy, though. But if I started asking questions about it, now, I'd probably just end up looking worse than I already do."

"Mmmm." Kid nodded and pondered. "You get tired of people asking you all those questions?"

"Yes. But it wasn't too bad this evening. At least we were talking about something real. I mean something that happened, today. It's better than all those discussions where they ask you whether, as an astronaut, you believe in long hair, abortions, race relations, or the pill."

"You're a very public man, aren't you? You say you're not really into the space program any more. But you're doing public relations work for them right now."

"Exactly what I'm doing. I don't claim to be doing anything else. Except enjoying myself. They're beginning to accept the idea of having a non-conformist doing front work for them." Kamp glanced around. "Though I suspect compared to most of you guys here, even some of the ducks up at Rogers, I'm more or less the image of the establishment, folk songs or not, hey? Well, that makes me Bellona's biggest nonconformist. I don't mind."

"Questions like, did you leave, or were you kicked out—what do you do when people ask you the same questions over and over? Especially the embarrassing ones."

"If you're a public man, as soon as you get a question more than three times, you figure out the most honest public answer you can give. *Especially* to the embarrassing ones."

"Is *that* a question you get asked a lot?"

"Well," Kamp mulled, "more times than three."

"Then I guess it would be okay to ask you questions about the moon." Kid grinned.

Kamp nodded. "Sounds like a pretty safe topic."

"Can you tell me something about the moon you've never told anybody else before?"

After a second, Kamp laughed. "Now that *is* a new one. I'm not sure I know what you mean."

"You were there. I'd like to know something about the moon that someone could only know what was actually on it. I don't mean anything big. But just *something*."

"The whole flight was broadcast. And we were pretty thorough in our report. We tried to take pictures of just about everything. Also, that's a few years ago; and we were only out walking around for six and a half hours."

"Yeah, I know. I watched it."

"Then I still don't get you."

"Well: I could bring a couple of television cameras

in *here*, say, and take a lot of pictures, and report on all the people, tell how many were here or what have you. But afterward, if somebody asked me to tell them something that wasn't in the coverage, I'd close my eyes and sort of picture the place. Then I might say, well, on the back of the counter with the bottles, the bottle second from the left—I don't remember what the label was—but the little cone of glass at the bottom was just above the top of the liquor." Kid opened his eyes. "See?"

Kamp ran his knuckles under his chin. "I'm not used to thinking like that. But it's interesting."

"Try. Just mention some rock, or collection of rocks, or shape on the horizon that you didn't mention to anyone else."

"We took photographs of all three hundred and sixty degrees of the horizon—"

"Then something else."

"It would be easier to tell you something like that about the module. I remember . . ." Then he cocked his head.

"I guess that would do," Kid said. "But I'd prefer it was about the moon."

"Hey, here's something." Kamp leaned forward. "When I got down the ladder—do you remember the foil-covered footpaths that the modules rested on? You say you watched it."

Kid nodded.

"Well, now, when I was getting some of the equipment out of the auxiliary compartments—I'd been actually on surface maybe a minute, maybe not quite: A lot of people, back before the probe shots, had the idea the moon was covered with dust. But it was purplish brown dirt and rock and gravel. The feet didn't sink at all."

Kid thought: Translation.

Kid thought: Transition.

"The module's feet were on universal joints, you know? Anyway. The one to the left of the entrance was tilted on a small rock, maybe two inches through. The shadows were pretty sharp. I guess when I was passing by it, my shadow passed over the module foot. And the shadow from the pad, made by the rock it was sitting on, and my shadow, joining it, for just a second made it look like something moved under there. You know? I was excited, see, because I was on the moon. And it just isn't like anything in the training sessions at all. But I do remember for maybe three seconds, while I was going on doing all the things I had to do, thinking, 'There's a moon-mouse, or a moon-beetle under there.' And feeling silly that I couldn't say anything—I was broadcasting all the time, describing what I saw—because there *couldn't* be anything alive on the moon, right? Like I said, it just took me a couple of seconds to figure out what it really was. But for a moment it was pretty funny. Now there. That's something I never told anybody . . . no, I think I did mention it once to Neil, when I got back. But I don't think he was listening. And I told it just like a joke."

Formation. Kid thought: Transformation.

"Is that the sort of thing you mean?"

Kid had expected Kamp to be smiling at the end of his story. But each feature rested just within the limit of sobriety.

"Yes. What are you thinking now?"

"I'm wondering why I told you. But I guess Bellona is the kind of place you come to do something new, right? See new things. Do new things."

"What do people say about this place, outside? Do people who come back from here tell you all about life under the fog? Who did you talk to that made you want to come?"

"I don't think I've ever met anyone who's actually gone and come back from here—except Ernest Newboy, that morning. We just shook hands in passing and didn't get a chance to talk. I've met some people who were evacuated back at the beginning. Once they stopped trying to cover it on TV, people stopped talking, I guess—people don't talk about it now."

Kid let his head lean.

"They refer to it," Kamp said. "You can be sitting around somebody's living room, in Los Angeles or Salt Lake, talking about this, that, or the other, and somebody might mention somebody he used to know here. A friend of mine in physics, driving down from the University of Montana, said he gave two girl hitch-hikers a lift who told him they were going here. He thought that was very strange, because, the last the paper reported, there was supposed to be some national guards around."

"That's what I heard too," Kid said. "But that was a while before I came. I haven't seen any."

"How long have you been here?"

"I don't know. It feels like a pretty fair time. But I really couldn't tell you." Kid shrugged. "I wish I did know more than that . . . sometimes."

Kamp was trying not to frown. "Roger said you would be an interesting person. You are."

"I've never met him."

"So he told me."

"I guess you don't know how long you're going to stay either?"

"Well now, I haven't really made up my mind. When I came here, I wasn't thinking of the trip exactly as a vacation. But I've been here a few days, and I'll tell you, especially with the business this afternoon, I don't quite know what to make of it."

"You're interesting too," Kid said after a moment. "But I don't know whether it's because you've been to the moon; or just because you're interesting. I like you."

Kamp laughed, and picked up his beer. "Come on, since we're trying so hard to be honest: What reason could you possibly have for liking me?"

"Because even though you're a public person—and public people are great if you happen to be the public— some of the private 'you' gets through. I think you're very proud of the things you've done, and you're modest about them, and don't want to talk about them unless it's serious—even joking serious. To protect that modesty, I think you've had to do some things that haven't made you all that happy."

Measuredly, Kamp said, "Yes. But what do you get by telling me that?"

"Because I like you, I want you to trust me a little. If I can show you I understand something about you, perhaps you will."

"Ah, ha!" Kamp drew back, ineptly mocking something theatrical. "Just for argument now: Supposing you do know something about me, how do I know you won't use it against me?"

Kid looked down at the optical jewels on his wrist, turned his wrist: two veins joined beneath the ham of his thumb to run under the chain. "That's the third time somebody's asked me that. I guess I'll have to think of a public answer."

Tak was talking with someone by the door: Unshaven, and a little wild looking, Jack stepped in. Tak turned

511

to the young deserter, who looked around, looked at Captain Kamp. Tak nodded in corroboration to something. Jack turned, picked up something that could have been a gun leaning against the wall, and practically ran out of the bar.

"I think I've figured out an answer already." Kid said.

Captain Kamp said, ". . . mmmm," and then, "so did I."

Kid grinned. "Good."

"You know—" Kamp looked down at the counter— "there *are* some things I'm not happy about. But now, they're just the things a guy would be reluctant to tell, ordinarily, to . . . well, one of you fellows with the shaggy hair, the funny clothes, and the beads and things. Or chains '. . ." He looked up. "I am dissatisfied with my life and my work. It's a very subtle dissatisfaction, and I don't want to be told to take dope and let my hair grow. I mean that's just the last thing I want to hear."

"Why don't you take dope and let your hair grow? See, it wasn't that bad. Now that the worst has happened, maybe you can go on and talk about it. I'll just listen."

Kamp laughed. "I'm dissatisfied with my life on earth. How's that? Not clear, I guess. Look—I'm not the same person I was before I went to the moon—maybe this is the sort of thing you were asking about. Perhaps it's the sort of thing that should only be told to one person. But I've told a couple of dozen: *You* know the world is round, and that the moon is a small world circling it. But you live in a world of up and down, where the land is a surface. But for me, just the visual continuity from that flat surface to a height where the edge of the earth develops a curve, to where that curve is a complete circle, to where the little soap-colored circle hanging in front of you enlarges to the size the Earth was, and then you come down. And suddenly that circle is a surface—but up and down is already not quite the same thing. We danced when we got out on the moon. What else could we do with that lightness? You know, seeing a film backward isn't the same experience as seeing it forward in reverse. It's a new experience, still happening forward in time. What falls out is all its own. Returning from the moon was not the same as going, played backward. We

512

arrived at a place where no one had walked; we left a place where *we* had danced. The earth we left was peopled by a race that had never sent emissaries to another cosmological body. We returned to a people who had. I really feel that what we did was important—folks starving in India not withstanding; and if there's a real threat of world starvation, technology will have to be used to avoid it; and I can't think of a better way to let people know just how far technology can take us. I was at a point of focus, for six and a half hours. I'm happy with that focus. But I'm not too terribly satisfied with the life on either side. The things that are off are like the things off about the way Bellona looked when we were driving through the first day I got here: there aren't many people, but there's no overt signs of major destruction—at least I didn't see any. It's grey, and some windows are broken, and here and there are marks of fire. But, frankly, I can't tell what's wrong. I still haven't been able to figure out what's happened here."

"I'd like to go to the moon."

"Cut your hair and stop taking dope." Kamp's tongue bulged his upper lip. "You don't even have to join the services. We have civilians in the program. Worst thing I could say, huh? But it really is the basic requirement. I mean all the rest comes after that. Really."

He thinks, Kid thought, he may have offended me. Kid tried not to smile.

"You're frowning," Kamp said, "Come on, now. Turnabout's fair play . . . well, all right. Tell me this. Are you all that happy? Be honest now."

Tak was ambling, slow and aimless, across the room.

"I think," and Kid felt his feelings change to fit the frown, "there's something wrong with your question, you know? I spend a lot of time happy; I spend a lot of time unhappy; I spend a lot of time just bored. Maybe if I worked real hard at it, I could avoid some of the happiness, but I doubt it. The other two I know I'm stuck with . . ."

Kamp was brightly attentive to something not more than a degree or so outside of Kid's face. Well, Kid reflected, I said I'd listen. When Kid had been silent five seconds, Kamp said:

"I'm not the same person I was before I went to the moon. Several people have explained to me that nobody

513

else on Earth is either. Someone told me once that I have begun to heal the great wound inflicted on the human soul by Galileo when he let slip the Earth was not the center of the Universe. No, I am not really satisfied now. I wonder at that light in the sky, this afternoon. I wonder at the stories I've heard about two moons when I know, first hand, what I do about the one. But I observe it from a very different position than you. We could sit and discuss and have conferences and seminars until a much more reassuring sun came up, and I still doubt if I could say anything meaningful to you, or you could say anything meaningful to me. At least about that."

"Hey, there." Tak put his hand on Kid's shoulder—but was talking to Kamp: "That was my friend Jack. You know, we have a good number of army deserters with us. I told him we had a full-fledged Captain with us this evening. He wanted to know whether you were a deserter too. I told him that as far as I knew you were still a member in good standing. I'm afraid he just turned around and ran without even waiting to find out you were in the Navy. Are you on your way, Captain?"

Kamp nodded, raised his bottle. "Glad I got a chance to meet you, Kid. If I don't see you before, I'll catch you at Roger's." Again he nodded at Tak, and turned.

"I hope I make him as uncomfortable as he keeps pretending I do." Tak sucked his teeth. "Wish he'd come in uniform. Before I went on to more complicated pleasures, I used to have a real passion for sea-food."

"You're flattering yourself."

Tak gave a few small nods. "Possibly, very possibly. Hey, I'm sorry I kicked you out last night. Come home with me. Fuck me."

"Naw. I'm looking for Lanya."

Tak enfolded his beer with his big, pale hands and looked down the bottle mouth. "Oh." Then he said: "Then come with me somewhere else. I want to show you something. You probably want to see it, too."

"What is it?"

"On the other hand, maybe you have seen it already and you're not interested."

"But you're not going to tell me what it is?"

"Nope."

"Come on," Kid said. "Show me."

Tak clapped Kid's shoulder, then pushed away from the bar. "Let's go."

Between the buildings black bulged down like a tarpaulin filled with rain.

"This is the sort of night I'd give anything for a star. When I was younger I used to try to learn the constellations, but I never really got them down. I can find the Big Dipper." Tak opened his zipper. "Can you do that?"

"I know them pretty well now. But I learned them a few years ago, back when I was traveling, and on boats and stuff. There're the only things that stay the same when you're really moving around a lot. I picked up this pocket book for fifty cents, when I was in Japan—it was an American book though. In about two weeks I could pick out just about anything."

"Mmmmm." Tak glanced up as they neared the corner lamp. "Just as well we can't see them, then. I mean, are you ready to have to learn a whole new set?" The shadow drew over his face like a shade. "This way."

The street sloped. At the next corner they turned again. Half a block later Kid asked, "Can you see anything at all?"

"No."

"But you know where we're going . . . ?"

"Yes."

The smell of burning had again become distinct. The air was cooler, much cooler: he felt a crack in the pavement beneath his bare foot. Something with edges rolled away from his boot. The woody odors sifted. For one instant they passed through a smell that brought back—it hit with the force of hallucination: a cave in the wooded mountains where something had crackled in a large, brass dish on the wet stone, while above he had seen, glittering . . .

The chain around him tingled and tickled as though the memory had sent current through it. But the particular odor (wet leaves over dry, and a fire, and something decayed . . .) was gone. And cool as the darkness was, it was dry, dry . . .

Edged by a vertical wall, light a long way away diffused in smoke.

At the corner, Tak looked back. "Checking to make sure you were still with me. You don't make much noise. We're going across there." Tak nodded forward and they crossed the street, shoulder bumping shoulder.

Beyond plate glass, an amber light silhouetted black wire forms.

"What sort of store was this?" Kid asked, behind Tak who was opening the door.

It sounded like a machine was running in the basement. Empty shelves lined the walls, and the wire frames were display racks. The light came from no more than a single bulb somewhere on the stairwell. Tak went to the cash register. "First time I came in here, would you believe there was still eighty dollars in the drawer?"

Tak rang.

The drawer trundled out.

"Still there."

He closed it.

In the cellar the sound stopped, then started again: only now it didn't sound like a machine at all, but someone moaning.

"We want to go downstairs," Tak said.

Someone had scattered pamphlets on the steps. They whispered under Kid's bare foot. "What was this place?" Kid asked again. "A bookstore?"

"Still is." Tak peered out where the single hanging bulb lit empty shelves. "Paperback department down here."

Tacked to an edge was a hand-lettered sign: ITALIAN LITERATURE.

A youngster with very long hair sat cross-legged on the floor. He glanced up, then closed his eyes, faced forward, and intoned: *"Om . . ."* drawing the last sound until it became the mechanical growl Kid had heard when they'd entered.

"Occupied tonight," Tak said, softly. "Usually there's no one here."

Between the checked flannel lapels, the boy's chest ran with sweat. Cheek bones glistened above his beard. He'd only glanced at them, before closing his eyes again.

It's cool, Kid thought. It's so much cooler.

Beside ITALIAN LITERATURE was POLITICAL SCIENCE. There were no books on that one either.

Kid stepped around the boy's knees and looked up at PHILOSOPHY OF SCIENCE (equally empty) and walked on to PHILOSOPHY. All the shelves, it seemed, were bare.

"Ommmmmmmmmmmmmmmmmm. . . . . ."

Tak touched Kid's shoulder. "Here, this is what I wanted to show you." He nodded across the room.

Kid followed Tak around AMERICAN LITERA-

TURE which was a dusty wooden rack in the middle of the floor.

The unfrosted bulb pivoted shadows about them.

"I used to come down here for all my science fiction," Tak said, "until there wasn't anything on the shelves any more. In there. Go ahead."

Kid stepped into the alcove and stubbed his booted toe (thinking: Fortunately), hopped back, looked up: The ivory covers recalled lapped bathroom tiles.

All but the top shelf was filled with face-out display. He looked again at the carton he had kicked. The cover wagged. As he stared into the box, something focused: a shadow, first fallen across his mind at something Lanya had said at the nest, almost blurred out by the afternoon's megalight, now, under the one, unfrosted bulb, lay outlined and irrefutable: As manuscripts did not become galleys overnight, neither did galleys become distributed books. Many more than twenty-four hours had passed since he had corrected proofs with Newboy in the church basement.

Frowning, he bent to pick out a copy, paused, reached for one on the shelf, paused again, looked back at Tak, who had his fists in his jacket pockets.

Kid's lips whispered at some interrogative. He looked at the books again, reached again. His thumb stubbed the polished cover-stock.

He took one.

Three fell; one slid against his foot.

Tak said: "I think it's very quaint of them to put it in POETRY," which is what the sign above said. "I mean they could have filled up every shelf in the God-damn store. There're a dozen cartons in the back."

Thumb on top, three fingers beneath, Kid tried to feel the weight; he had to jog his hand. There was a sense of absence which was easiest to fill with

BRASS
ORCHIDS

lettered in clean shapes with edges and serifs his own fingers could not have drawn, even with French curve and straightedge. He reread the title.

"Ommmmmmmmmmmmmmmm . . ." The light blacked and went on again; the ". . . mmmmmm-mmmm . . ." halted on a cough.

517

Kid looked over the six, seven, eight filled shelves. "That's really funny," he said, and wished the smile he felt should be on his face would muster his inner features to the right emotions. "That's really . . ." Suddenly he took two more copies, and pushed past Tak for the stair. "Hey," he said to the boy. "Are you all right?"

The sweating face lifted. "Huh?"

"What's the matter with you?"

"Oh, man!" The boy laughed weakly. "I'm sick as a dog. I'm really sick as a fucking dog."

"What's wrong?"

"It's my gut. I got a spastic duodenum. That's like an ulcer. I mean I'm pretty sure that's what it is. I've had it before, so I know what it feels like."

"What are you doing here, then?"

The boy laughed again. "I was trying yoga exercises. For the pain. You know you can control things like that, with yoga."

Tak came up behind Kid. "Does it work?"

"Sometimes." The boy took a breath. "A little."

Kid hurried on up the steps.

Tak followed.

From the top step Kid looked around at the shelves, and turned to Tak, who said:

"I was just thinking, I really was, about asking you to autograph this for me." He held up the copy and snorted rough laughter. "I really was."

Kid decided not to examine the shape this thought made, but caught the mica edge: It's not not having: It's having no memory of having. "I don't like that sort of shit anyway . . ." he said, awed at his lie, and looked at Tak's face, all shadowed and flared with backlight. He searched the black oval for movement. It's there anyway, he thought; he said: "Here. Gimme," and got the pen from the vest's buttonhole.

"What are you going to do?" Tak handed it over.

Kid opened it on the counter by the register, and wrote: "This copy of my book is for my friend, Tak Loufer." He frowned a moment, then added, "All best." The page looked yellow. And he couldn't read what he'd written at all, which made him realize how dim the light was. "Here." He handed it back. "Let's go, huh?"

"Ommmmmmmmmmmmmmmmmmmm . . ."

"Yeah." Tak glanced down stairs and sucked his teeth. "You know?" They walked to the door. "When you took it from me, I thought you were going to tear it up."

Kid laughed. Perhaps, he thought, I should have. And thinking it, decided what he had put was best. "You know—" as they stepped into the night, Kid felt his fingers dampen on the cover: fingerprints?—"people talk about sexual inadequacy? That doesn't have anything to do with whether you can get a hard-on or not. A guy goes out looking for his girl friend and doesn't even know where she lives, and doesn't seem to have bothered to find out . . . You said Madame Brown might know?"

"I think so," Tak said. "Hey, you're always talking about your girl friend. Right now, do you have a boy friend?"

Kid figured they had reached the corner. On the next step he felt the ball of his bare foot hung over the curb. "Yeah, I guess I do." They stepped down.

"Oh," Tak said. "Somebody told me you're supposed to be making it with some kid in the scorpions."

"I could get to hate this city—"

"Ah, ah, ah!" Tak's voice aped reproval. "Rumor is the messenger of the gods. I'm sort of curious to find out what you wrote in my book."

At which Kid started to balk, found his own balking funny, and smiled. "Yeah."

"And of course, the poems too. Well . . ."

Kid heard Tak's footsteps stop.

". . . I go this way. Sure I can't convince you . . . ?"

"No." He added: "But thanks. I'll see you." Kid walked forward thinking, That's nuts. How does anybody know where anything is in this, and thought that thought seven or eight times through, till, without breaking stride, he realized: I cannot see a thing and I am alone. He pictured great maps of darkness torn down before more. After today, he thought idly, there is no more reason for the sun to rise. Insanity? To live in any state other than terror! He held the books tightly. Are these poems mine? Or will I discover that they are improper descriptions by someone else of things I might have once been near: the map erased, aliases substituted for each location?

Someone, then others, were laughing.

Kid walked, registering first the full wildness of it, the spreading edges; but only at the working street lamp at the far corner, realizing it was humor's raddle and play.

Two black men, in the trapezoid of light from a doorway, were talking. One was drinking a can of beer or Coke. From across the street, a third figure (Kid could see the dark arms were bare from here, that the vest was shiny) ambled up.

The street lamp pulsed and died, pulsed and died. Black letters on a yellow field announced, and announced, and announced:

JACKSON AVENUE

Kid walked toward them, curious.

"She run up here . . ." the tall one explained, then laughed once more. "Pretty little blond-headed thing, all scared to death; you know, she stopped first, like she gonna turn around and run away, with her han' up in front of her mouth. Then she a'ks me—" The man lowered his head and raised his voice: "'Is George Harrison in there? You know, George Harrison, the big colored man?'" The raconteur threw up his head and laughed again. "Man, if I had 'em like George had 'em . . ." In his fist was a rifle barrel (butt on the ground) that swung with his laughter.

"What you tell her?" the heavier one asked, and drank again.

"'Sure he's inside,' I told her. 'He better be inside. I just come out of there and I sure as hell seen him inside. So if he ain't inside, then I just don't know where else he might be.'" The rifle leaned and recovered. "She run. She just turned around and run off down the block. Run just like that!"

The third was a black scorpion with the black vinyl vest, his orchid on a neck chain. It's like, Kid thought, meeting friends the afternoon the TV had been covering the assassination of another politician, the suicide of another superstar; and for a moment you are complicit strangers celebrating by articulate obliteration some national, neutral catastrophe.

Remembering the noon's light, Kid squinted in the dark. And wished he were holding anything else: notebook or flower or shard of glass. Awkwardly, he reached back to shove the books under his belt.

The three turned to look.

Kid's skin moistened with embarrassment.

". . . She just run off," the black man with the gun

520

finally repeated, and his face relaxed like a musician's at a completed cadence.

The one with the beer can, looking left and right, said, "You scorpions. So you come down here a little, huh?"

"This is the Kid," the black scorpion explained. "I'm Glass."

His name, Kid thought (he remembered Spider helping with Siam's arm on the rocking bus floor . . .): It. isn't any easier to think of them once their names surface. They might as well be me. Surfaced with it was a delight at his own lack. But that joy still seemed as dull and expected as a banally Oedipal dream he'd had the first night he'd been assigned a psychiatrist at the hospital.

"You the Kid?" The man hooked the can's bottom on the top of his belt buckle. "You fellows gonna come down here and give *us* protection?"

"Yeah, they all shootin' up black people now, you come on down to Jackson."

Far inside, other blacks were talking and laughing.

"What happened?" Kid asked.

Glass stepped over closer to Kid. (Kid thought: I feel more comfortable. He probably does too.) The others moved to accomodate the shift.

"Someone been shooting up down here?" Glass asked. "That was this afternoon?"

"Sure was." The barrel went into the other hand. "Like a sniper, you know? Ain't that something. I mean, this afternoon, with that thing hanging up there."

"What happened?"

"Somebody climbed up on the roof of the Second City Bank building down on the corner, and started shooting people with a gun. Just like that."

"Did he kill anybody?" Kid asked.

The man with the can pursed his lips to a prune.

The man with the gun said: "About seven."

"Shit!" Kid said.

"Like he got four people together, you know—bip, bip, bip, bip. The woman wasn't dead yet, but she couldn't move very far. A little later some people came out to help them, 'cause they thought he'd gone. But he stood up again and picked off three of them. Then he run."

"It was a white boy, too." The other gestured with his can. "And he gonna come all the way down here to shoot niggers."

"The woman died, hey . . . when?" Glass asked.

"A little later. She didn't say nothing about the guy did the shooting though. Some others saw. That's how they know he was white." He grinned, finished the can, tossed it. "You scorpions gonna—" it clunked and bounced—"gonna come down to Jackson and give us some protection? Keep them crazy white mother-fuckers from shooting up people in the street?"

The gun came up. "We don't need no scorpion protection," and a deprecating: "Shit."

"That's good," Kid said. "Because we don't protect anybody." This all sounds sort of familiar. Didn't somebody get shot from a roof . . .

The two men looked at each other, looked uncomfortable.

Glass repeated, finally, "That's not what we do."

The man with the gun slid the barrel up to his shoulder. "Naw, we don't need no protection."

"We don't need no mother-fuckers standing on the roof of the Second City Bank building shooting people, either." The other man's hands moved on his belt to finger the buckle, as though he wished the can back. "You know, without having no doctors. Or undertakers."

"What'd they do with them?" Glass asked.

"Put them in a house way down there. And after about three or four days, people gonna start crossing the street when they was going past that stretch."

The man with the gun didn't laugh. "What you scorpions doing over here? Cause that sun comes up—" the butt clacked down on the concrete—"you gonna come on down here?"

"George told me to come down and see him," Kid said. "I saw him over at Reverend Amy's church and he told me to come down and visit."

"Yeah," Glass said. "We comin' to see George."

After a while one said, "Oh."

"Well, go on in," the other said. "Sure, go on inside. He's in there."

"Come on," Kid said to Glass.

Halfway down the hall, Glass said, "You think he ever had a gun before? The way he was banging it around, he gonna shoot off his ear or his nose or his head or something."

"Or my head," Kid said. "Yeah, I was thinking that too."

Three lanterns hung together. Their magnesium-white light harshened the battleship linoleum, the institutional yellow walls. Through an iron elevator gate, Kid could see a web of shadow on the cinder block.

He knew he reacted, but could not tell by what it showed. "Where to put the bodies? I'm not going to like it when I run into that a third time."

Glass was watching him.

"Why're you wearing your orchid around your neck? When I first saw you the day we broke into the department store, you had it in a piece of leather."

"I know," Glass said. "But you were wearing yours that way."

"Oh. That's what I thought."

Beyond the turn they could hear people.

"Hey."

Glass turned. Slabs of light slid across his black vinyl. "Huh?"

"What did you guys think when I showed up, I mean back at the department store?"

Glass laughed through his nose. He looked embarrassed. He pulled his pants across his stomach, scratched the twice-crossed T of an appendectomy scar showing above his belt. His knuckles were much darker than the rest of his skin; the places between his fingers looked like they had been brushed with ash.

"What did you think? Tell me."

Glass shrugged and shook his head to settle the smile about the yellow corners of his eyes. "We . . . well, we knew you were coming. Only we didn't know you were coming then. I mean, you remember the morning we woke you up in the park?"

Kid nodded.

Glass nodded too as though the reference explained something, then looked up the hall.

Kid walked on.

At a party, I hand out a hundred and fifty copies of my book, and they all turn down the music and sit around cross-legged on the floor, reading so intently I can walk among them, lean down, and examine each expression flickering from humor through compassion to the visage of the deeply moved.

He sweated under the books in his belt. A drop rolled, tickling his buttock.

Kid and Glass stepped inside the wide-swung doors.

He'd thought there was music.

". . . wants more of it, can't get enough of it, how to get out of it: Time—" a woman cried over the loose crowd—"is the hero!" She swayed in dark robes on some platform—or maybe just a table—that brought her knees high as the highest, close-cropped, black (with a brown bald spot vague in the middle) head. "Time is the villain!" Reverend Amy Tayler, thirty yards across the balconied hall, shook her head and her fist, glared around at craning women and men with faces of humus, sand, and all in-between colors earth can have. "Where is this city? Struck out of time! Where is it builded? On the brink of truths and lies. Not truth and falsity— Oh, no. No. Nothing so grand. Here we are sunk on the abyss of discrete fibs, innocent misobservations, brilliant speculations that turn out wrong and kill— Oh, there is so much less truth in the universe than anything else. Yes, even here we founder on the fill of language, the quick ash of desire." Glass touched Kid's arm. His expression looked stranger than Kid's felt. Lanterns hung on the walls. Shadows were multiple and dim on blood-colored linoleum. Near them, strung crepe-paper had fallen behind the potted . . . not palms. Cactuses! "So you have seen the moon! So you have seen George—the right and left testicles of God, so heavy with tomorrow they tore through the veil to dangle naked above us all? Then *what* was that in the sky today? God's womb punched inside out and blazing with Her blood, looking like a moment ago She had passed the egg of the earth and its polar body we've so cavalierly dismissed from singularity? Is God a sow who devours Her young and gets heartburn? Is God the garter-snake Ouroborus, gagging on the tip of His own tail? Or is God just a category-concept mistake, like Ryle's *mind*, a process the materia of the universe preforms, indulges in, or inflicts on itself, through necessity or chance, for arcane reasons you and I will never discover? Being is a function of time, ey, Martin? Well, now, where does that get us? Now seems pretty specious to me . . . for it's just a hole, a little hole on whose rim we've been allowed, for an eye's blink, to perch, watching that flow, terrible for all of us, tragic for some of us, in which the future hisses through to heap the potter's field of the past. Very deep, indeed; and dried up. And dusty. And spiked with bone like pongee pits. Was it a heart of fire, up there today? Or just a dollop of what burns, squeezed out of the cosmic gut—to its great relief! Maybe it *was* our sun, hurtling by, on its way somewhere else; and all that's left to us now is to grow colder and older, every day in every way, gracefully as possible. How long did this light last? Oh, my poor, sick, doomed, and soon to be obliterated children, ask instead how long is the darkness that follows it!"

It was not, Kid had noticed, a particularly quiet nor attentive crowd—save the thirty or forty actually clustered at the Reverend's podium. People wandered, talked; and now laughter began somewhere, obscuring her words. Up in the dark balcony, a few people, widely distant, slept like darker blotches among the brown wood seats. Somebody moved along the railing, checking spotlights; none seemed to work. Fat, bald, the color of terra cotta and wearing just some bib-coveralls, he stood up, wiped at his forehead with the back of his arm, and moved to the next dead light.

On the walls, were high barred windows. As Kid's eyes came down the gates, a group of six middle-aged men and women ran across the floor: one woman knocked over a statue that one man caught and struggled to right, till a plaster wing fell. Plaster shattered over the floor. Others clustered to laugh, to shout advice.

Beyond them, Reverend Tayler waved her arms, ducked her head and tossed it back, haranguing the powdered floor, the shadowed ceiling; but only a word or two could tear clear now of talk and laughter.

The group fell apart from a sunburst of white footprints: George Harrison stalked through.

One arm was around the neck of a yellow-haired, plump, pink woman, the other around the waist of a gaunt, tan girl with a brick-colored natural and freckles. (He'd seen her, at the church, with the blond Mexican, who had stopped him on the street, how many mornings later, how many mornings ago?) George saw Kid, veered over, and called: "Hey, so you gonna come here, now? Shit!" His sleaves were rolled high on biceps like French-roast coffee. "You sure pick a hell of a time to come. Right in the middle of super-night. This is super-night, ain't it?" and nodded and hallooed people passing ten yards away. "Today sure as hell was super-day, when that super-sun come up in the super-sky! Hey—?" He released the gaunt girl's waist. Between the lapels of her jump suit hung a glittering catenary. "What you got there? Lemme see." His black fingers (pink nails, scimitared with yellow) clawed up the optical chain. "I see all the people running around wearing these things. Him . . ." He nodded at Kid. "You see all of them walking around with them. Come on, gimme that one. I'm gonna be a hippie too and wear them little glass beads."

"Ohh!" She complained, "George!"

"You give me those, and you can get some more, right?"

"No honey." She lifted them from his fingers. "You can't have these."

"Why not?"

"'Cause you can't, that's all."

"You know where to get them. You just give me these, and you go get yourself—"

"Not these, honey." She shouldered back into the bend of his arm. "You tell me what else you want and I'll give you that, okay?"

"Well, *that's* what I want!"

"Oh, George." She snuggled, closer—and out of his line of sight.

"All right, you just watch it. I may not get them now, but I'm sure gonna get them later." Harrison guffawed.

The gaunt girl smiled, but raised her hand where ribs and sternum ridged her skin, and covered the chain with her small, brittle-looking palm.

"What is all this?" Kid asked. The books pressed one of the prisms into the top of his left buttock. Uncomfortable, he shifted. The prism dragged. "I mean, what's everybody *doing* here? And the preacher—?"

"Got to give the preacher lady a place to preach!"

"She sure been going on," the gaunt girl said. "She just don't stop."

"This here is my house," George said, with a grave nod. "Got a lot my friends in here, you know? And you welcome, too. Any time. Got me an apartment downstairs. Some of the rooms upstairs people done fixed, you know? This is the big meeting room, like. The preacher lady, see, she figure after this afternoon, she wouldn't be able to fit 'em all in the church. So we say, come on and we gonna open up the big meeting room. And you just put a sign out say everybody come on over."

"I think that's real nice," Plump Pink said in an accent that, during three weeks at the Georgia border loading melons, Kid had learned to identify as South

Alabama Flats. "She always preaching about George and telling everybody about George. So I think it was very nice of George to say why not come on and do it here."

"Don't look to me like there any more people than she could fit in the chapel," the girl said.

"We got a bar over there—" the blond woman turned up her hand to point—"where you fellas can go get a drink. Then you can go listen to the preacher lady. George just wants everybody to make themselves at home."

"Shit," George said. Then he laughed.

Glass laughed too; the blond woman looked satisfied, did something with two fingers under the flowered cotton of her bodice, smiled.

"Gotta give the preacher lady a place to preach," George repeated. He nodded, dropped the gaunt girl's waist.

"Who lives in this city?" Reverend Amy's voice came on through a lull. "Logicians love it here!" George turned to listen. So did the gaunt girl and Glass. "Here you can cleave space with a distinction, mark, or token, and not have it bleed all over you. What we need is not a calculus of form but an analytics of attention, which renders form on the indifferent and undifferentiated plurima. No, Che, no Fanon, you are not niggers enough! Look—" Once more she waved her fist high. Her black sleeve flung out below it. "I have a handful of monads here. Listen— They're chattering and gossiping away like eight-opera-tion logic-cells calling up order from a random net . . ." At the mention of Che an (unrelated? Kid wondered) wave of noise had started in one corner of the hall. Now another, which had at its center crashing bottle glass, rose over her voice. On the brown scape of the Rev-erend's face, a constellation of droplets gleamed on each temple. Her mouth moved, her head bent, her head rose; her eyes sealed, snapped open, stared intently; and again Kid could hear none of her dithyramb.

He did hear George chuckle. Harrison stood with his hands in the pockets of his dirty khaki slacks.

Glass, a few steps away, was craning to see something over somebody's head. The blond woman was shoul-dering her way forward with smiles and "excuse-me's," right and left; the gaunt girl stood, pensive, still watching the preacher, her left hand on her right shoulder, looking pained and picturesque.

"You know your girl friend was outside looking for you again," Kid said.

"Yeah?" George said. "Which one?"

"A little blond seventeen-year-old white girl." The sweat, Kid realized, was not just under the books. The shoulders of his vest slid on it. The backs of his knees and the skin under his jaw were wet. "She was outside, asking . . . asking for you: 'Is George Harrison in there? Is George inside?' "

George's nose and cheeks like sanded teak, his heavy lips wrinkled as hemlock bark, the planes around his off-ivory teeth and eyes, moved into an expression fixed loosely among irony, amusement, and contempt: It was the expression on Tak's first poster. "Lots of little white girls come around here looking for me."

"Her name rhymes with moon, and she—" Kid's right fist clamped, fingertips and knuckles scraping his jeans—"she killed her brother for you: George? She had your poster, all big and black and naked and he saw it, her little brother. He saw it and was teasing her—you know how little brothers are, George? He was teasing her and he was gonna tell on her, you see? He was gonna tell her mother, tell her father: only she was afraid if he did, they'd know—know that it wasn't just a picture; know that she'd found you once; know that she was trying to find you again! See, they'd already threatened to kill her older brother. Already. And he'd run away. So she pushed him, her little brother, down the elevator shaft—sixteen, seventeen, eighteen stories down . . . ! I don't quite . . . remember!" Kid shook his head. Something that was not pain pulsed in it, pulsed in it again. "Oh, Christ, there was . . . blood! I had blood all over me. I had to pull him up out of the basement, by the armful! And carry him back upstairs. After he was dead. But . . . it was for *you!* That's why she . . . that's why she did it! That's why I . . ." What pulsed became pain. "She told me herself. She told me that she was afraid he was going to tell. And that she . . ." Kid stepped away, stepped again, because the first step was unsteady and he had to catch himself on the second. He looked back.

George watched, as if from a long hall whose walls moved with indifferent faces, black and brown.

His eyes will explode like blooming poppies, Kid thought. His teeth will erupt like diamonds spat by the mouthful. His tongue will snake the yards between us, nearly touch my mouth before it becomes pink smoke. Steam in two columns will hiss down from his nostrils . . .

George stared with—and recognizing it, Kid suddenly turned away and lurched away—the indulgence reserved for the mad.

Is this, Kid thought (saying, "Hey, I'm sorry, man . . ." and patting someone's shoulder he'd just bumped), one of those moments that, momentarily, will slip out of mind to join my purpose, age, and name? He made it between those two; then somebody, laughing, steadied his arm and handed him on. He came up against the thin metal bars with his cheek and both hands, clutched them, leaned back, looked up:

Someone was coming down the spiral stairway. The fat, bald man (whose skin looked now more like oiled wrapping-paper) in the bib-overalls, descended, by Kid, stepped from ringing, black, triangular steps that circled the central pole, up, around, and up through the open square in the balcony floor—

When Kid looked down again, the man was working sideways through the people wandering about the center of the room.

"You all right?"

"Yeah, I . . ." Kid looked around.

"Good." Glass, with a bobbing walk, almost slow motion, came toward him. "I was just wondering. You know . . . ?"

"I'm all right . . ." But he was cold; the sweat was drying on his neck, his forearms, his ankles. "Yeah."

Glass ran his thumb along his belt. Vinyl flapped back from the appendectomy scar in his dark, matte skin, swung over it again.

Multiple caucasian laughter fell down through the spiral railing.

Glass and Kid looked up together, looked down together.

A lantern high on the wall brushed soft highlights on Glass's arms, slapped harsh ones on his vest, and slipped a line of light along an orchid petal against his chained and chain-lapped chest so bright Kid squinted.

"You wanna go see?" Glass said.

"Sounds like the kids from the park." Kid pressed his lips, glanced up again; suddenly he swung around the rail, started up the steps, one hand on the gritty pole, one trailing on the banister. Glass, behind him, kept bumping Kid's fist with his fist on the rail. The toe of his boot caught Kid's bare heel one step before the top.

From the shadowed kiosk at the head of the aisle, Kid looked down the balcony's raked seats. He heard Glass breathing inches behind his ear.

They sat—six, no seven of them—just back from the balcony rail: The blond woman in the third row, leaning forward to see between the shoulders of the two men in front, was Lynn, the woman he had sat next to at the Richards, the woman from whom he had wrested the gun in the Emboriky.

A tall, curly-haired man sat beside her, his hands locked around the barrel of a gun. He leaned forward, the barrel tip higher than his head; he looked almost asleep.

Another man was still laughing.

Another was saying, "Where is that damn woman's dog? Hey—" He half rose, looked over the empty seats: "Muriel! Muriel—"

"Oh, for God's sakes, Mark, sit down!" Lynn, in her green dress, said.

Another man, in a worn suede jacket, said: "I want to know where that damn *woman* is. She was supposed to be back by . . ." The last of his sentence was lost in laughter and applause from below, that must have had something to do with the Reverend; but Kid could not see her from here.

And one man had cuffed the man next to him. The other woman, in an off-the-shoulder peasant blouse, was trying to separate them, laughing.

A seat away, scuffed shoes on the back of the seat ahead, knees jackknifed in shiny slacks, and a rifle across his chair arms like a guard bar on the seat of a carnival ride, sat Jack. While the others joked and laughed, Kid could see his hollow, unshaven cheek pulse with swallowing as he balanced his chin on his joined fists and brooded down on the milling blacks.

"Ain't some of those guys look awfully familiar?" Glass whispered, too loudly, it seemed, near Kid's ear. But none of them turned.

Kid glanced back—"The department store . . ."—and saw Glass nod before he looked away.

Widely scattered in the dark balcony (there were only two lanterns that someone had set up about twenty

530

yards down the balcony rail; all the other light came from
below), perhaps a dozen people lounged in the ply-backed
seats. The bolts in the wrought metal braces holding the
seat, in front of Kid's knee, to the dusty floor were half
out—

"What's she saying? Can you hear what the preacher
lady's saying down there?"

"On, come on! You can't hear anything up here except noise! I want to go downstairs and wander around
the party!"

"You want to go down there, with all of them? Go
on, then!"

"That guy down there looks all right . . . Who is he,
anyway?"

"The white guy over there?"

"That's who I was *pointing* at, wasn't I?"

"Man—" The curly-haired one dragged the barrel
back against his chest. "We could really just pick them
off from up here. Just like—" He suddenly raised his rifle
to his eye. "Pow!" he said, then glanced over and laughed.
"Just like that, right? Wish I knew which one was George
Harrison." He sighted down the gun again. "Pow . . ."
he whispered.

"Cut it out," the man who was Mark said. "We just
snuck in here to see what was going on."

The curly-headed man leaned forward and called,
"Hey, Reb? Don't you think we could stir up a little
excitement down there with a few well-aimed ones—just
for target practice, mind you? What you think of that
idea, Reb?"

Jack said, soberly and not looking over: "*All* you
folks got some strange ideas. Everybody I met since I
come here got strange ideas." *Not* soberly, came to Kid
as a second thought: Jack's voice had the slurred gravity
of a very grave drunk.

"Why do you two want to bring guns to a place like
this for anyway?" Mark said.

"*They* had guns," the curly-headed man said, putting his rifle butt back on the floor. "You see the way
them niggers tried to kick us out, because we had guns?
Now that's not right. They had guns, we had guns—all
men are created equal. Didn't you know that?— Hey, get
your hand off!"

"I just wanted to see it," the woman in the peasant

531

blouse said. "Besides, I'm a better shot than you, anyway."

"Yeah?" the man said. "Sure you are." He hung his curly head back against the barrel.

"Well, I *am!*"

"Which one *is* Harrison?" one of the other men said. "You know, they all *do* look alike." He laughed. "At least from up here."

Jack put one shoe down. Other than that—elbows on the chair arms across his rifle, chin on his fists, and one shiny knee angling wide—he did not move.

"What *is* that woman shouting about down there? Jesus . . ."

Kid looked at Glass, who had stepped up beside him now. Glass, frowning, glanced back at the small group, with a small, disgusted head shake.

Kid gestured down the spiral steps with his chin, turned, and started.

The hall of milling men and women revolved and received him.

"Too *much!*" Glass said at the bottom, stopping Kid with a warm hand on the shoulder. "I mean, Christ, man . . ."

"Let's find George." Kid took a breath. "We'll tell him they're up there and see what he wants to do."

"They probably ain't really gonna *do* nothing . . ." Glass said, warily.

"Then we find George, tell him there's a bunch of white people up in the balcony, two of them with guns, who *probably* ain't gonna do anything." Kid wondered which way to go, saw an opening in the crowd, and loped into it.

Behind him, Glass suggested on the run: "Maybe George already knows they're there?"

"Fine," Kid said, back over his shoulder. "Then he can tell us that too."

Three tubs near the wall held the four- and five-foot cactuses—the sort Kid had always heard sent roots thirty and forty feet down into the desert for water.

On the nearest, among browned and crisscrossed needles, hung what looked like a pink tissue. Two steps nearer, and Kid saw it was the rag of a flower, wide as his hand, limp on the succulent's flesh.

Before the furthest, George joked among a loud and jocular group. One woman with arms like brown sacks, wrinkled at elbows, wrists, and knuckles, waved a bottle, offering it here and there, with kisses and explosive shrieks.

Kid glanced at the balcony. No, they were not visible from where he stood.

Kid edged forward into the group. An arm pressed his arm, a hand steadied against his back to steady someone unsteady: He was sweating again. "George—! Hey, George?" He wondered why, and for answer found all the memories of ten minutes ago's encounter: the compulsive tale of June, his own terror, returning now. "George, I got to—" He took the bottle passed him, drank, passed it on. "George, I got to see you for a minute, man!" Am I afraid of him? Kid wondered. If that's all it is, then all I know to do is not be afraid of the fear. "George . . . !"

Harrison had the bottle now. His arm rose, his laughter fell—"Hey now, how you doing, Kid? This here is the Kid. The Kid wants to speak to me for a second—" then the arm fell around Kid's shoulder—"so I'll be with you in a second." The dark head lowered next to Kid's with an anticipatory swig, fixing attention.

"Look," Kid said. "Outside, there was some guy talking about some people getting killed in the street by snipers from the roof this afternoon? Well, up in the balcony, you got about half a dozen white guys—two of them with guns. They're sitting there joking about picking people off. And they're particularly interested in which one is you. Now they probably aren't gonna pull anything, but I thought you ought to—"

"Shit!" George hissed. He raised his eyes, but not his head. "They got three women and a dog with them—?"

"Two . . ." Kid began. "No, three and a dog."

"God-damn thick-headed niggers!" George's breath lurched in sharply. "I *told* them not to let them crazy people in here with no guns! What the hell they think I put them out there for . . . unless they done snuck in some other way—"

"That's what they were saying," Kid said. "They must of snuck in. And—"

George started to stand.

Kid caught his shoulder and pulled him back down, his mind gone bright with recognition of what was inside of it: "—and George! What I told you—" the sweat started to dry, and as his back cooled under his vest, he knew why it had come—"about June, killing her brother . . . ?"

533

George's eyes, the corners blood-heavy; the pupils fading almost evenly into the stained-ivory whites, came close to Kid's.

". . . it wasn't true. I mean, she *did* it. But you see, I don't know whether she did it *because* of you or not. After he was killed, that's when she told me he was going to tell, about the poster of you I gave her. *She* said it was an accident. She said he was going to tell, and then, just by accident . . . So I don't *know*. You see . . . ?"

"You real worried about that, ain't you?" George straightened. His arm still hung on Kid's shoulder, the glass bottle moving, as George breathed, against Kid's chains. "Well that's why she looking for me, not you. 'Cause I don't care about that one way or the other. You so busy blamin' or forgivin', you gonna drive her crazy. Me, see, I don't care if she innocent as a little white bunny rabbit in a brand new hutch, or if she done killed her brother, her mother, her daddy, and the President of the United States, cut up the bodies, and danced naked in the blood. What's it to me? What's it to her—? Another white man out of the way, that's all. She might worry about it a bit more than I do, but not much. And, finally, it's just gonna make both our lives easier—maybe even yours. When she come to me, I do her just the same, both ways. You say she looking? Well, I'm here, man, I'm still here. Hey—!" which was called out across the crowd. George waved the bottle high. "We all getting tired out, now. I think we got to all think about going home."

The blades clicked on Kid's chest, turned. Kid said: "You want us to go up and get 'em down for you, George? We'll take them out of the balcony."

George looked back at Kid, hesitated with narrowed eyes. "We get my boys up there to cover them. Then we get some people to take them away. My boys let them get in. So they can get them out. I know you guys is pretty handy with them bunch of thorns hanging around your necks, but they got equalizers, and if all men is created equal, we might as well keep it that way. Party's been going on too long, anyway. We all gonna go home now, So you can oblige me by moving out too, okay?"

Kid grinned, aped an over-polite bow—

"Much obliged to you, there," George said. "For *all* your trouble" —and laughed. Kid looked at the cactus in its wooden tub: for a moment he considered throwing

534

himself against it to embrace the spiked, fleshy trunk; which was so ridiculous he merely turned and walked away. They will meet, he thought, by sun, by moons, by laughter or lightning. Why I sweat is because I do not know what will happen to me, then. What will happen to me . . .

Glass fell in beside him. After about six steps, Glass said: "What would you have done if he'd said, 'Why, sure, man! Go on up there and bring the mother-fuckers down'?"

"Probably—" Kid dodged a drunk who was going to fall three steps beyond them—"pissed all over myself."

"Maybe." Glass laughed. "But then, you'd probably of tried to go up there and get 'em down, too."

"I don't think they'd have been much trouble." Kid said. "I hope."

The white man coming toward them, shouldering through the blacks and smiling, was Captain Michael Kamp. "Well, hello, there. Now I didn't think I was going to see you again. I mean, not this evening." His smile took in Glass.

"Hello, sir," Kid said. "Good to see you again. But I think the party's breaking up. They got some problem upstairs. Nothing serious. But there just *might* be some shooting. And it's awfully easy pickings from up there." Kamp's eyes followed Kid's up to the balcony and came back, confused and half again as wide. Kid said, "Oh. This is my friend Glass. Glass, this is Captain Kamp."

"Hello, sir." Glass put out his hand. "Glad to meet you."

Kamp had to remember to shake. "What is . . . I mean?"

"Come on," Kid said. "Let's move over this way."

"What's going on now?" Kamp followed them. "Now, well . . . Roger gave me a list of places to hit this evening. I'm afraid I'm one of those guys who likes to drink booze and chase women—the Navy's favorite kind. While that bar is all very interesting—a very interesting bunch—" he nodded—"really, I thought I might do better, at least on the second part of that, some place else. Like here." He looked up at the balcony again, while a sudden mass of people moved noisily toward the door and out. "They got some pretty women, too . . ." Another bunch followed them. "What is it?" Kamp asked.

"Some crazy white folks with guns," Kid said. "They aren't doing anything but making people nervous. But they shouldn't be up there, anyway."

"Didn't I hear somebody saying something about people getting shot in the street this afternoon?"

"Yeah," Glass said, and grimaced.

"Oh," Kamp said, because he could apparently think of nothing else. "Roger said they didn't even let white people *in* this place. What are they doing here?"

Kid frowned a moment at Kamp. "Well, some of us get by."

"Oh," Kamp said again. "Well, sure. I mean . . ."

"You from the moon, ain't you," Glass said. "That's pretty interesting."

Kamp started to say something, but a voice—it was the Reverend's, coming through the half-silence that followed the exodus:

". . . of the crossing taken again is not the value of the crossing? Oh, my poor, inaccurate hands and eyes! Don't you know that once you have transgressed that boundary, every atom, the interior of every point of reality, has shifted its relation to every other you've left behind, shaken and jangled within the field of time, so that if you cross back, you return to a very different space than the one you left? You have crossed the river to come to this city? Do you really think you can cross back to a world where a blue sky goes violet in the evening, buttered over with the light of a single, silver moon? Or that after a breath of dark, presaged by a false, familiar dawn, a little disk of fire will spurt, spitting light, over trees and sparse clouds, women, men, and works of hand? But you *do!* Of *course* you do! How else are we to retain the inflationary coinage and cheap paper money of sanity and solipsism? Oh, it is common knowledge, the name of that so secondary moon that intruded itself upon our so ordinary night. But the arcane and unspoken name of what rose on this so extraordinary day, for which George is only consort, *that* alone will free you of this city! Pray with me! *Pray!* Pray that this city is the one, pure, logical space from which, without being a poet or a god, we can all actually leave if—what?" Someone reached up to her: the Reverend looked down. "What did . . . ?" It was George. The Reverend bent. For a moment she started to look up, did not, and hastily

536

climbed from her platform. Her small head was lost among the heads around her.

"Well, I guess it's about time for me to be getting up to Roger's then." Kamp looked around. "Though they have some pretty nice-looking ladies around, I must admit."

"Guess it's time for us all to get going," Kid said, and noticed Kamp did not move. He tried to glance in the direction Kamp looked, wondering which lady his eyes had come to rest on, found only the blank, barred window.

Kamp said: "Um . . . Getting up to Roger's in the dark . . ." He shifted his weight, put his one hand in his slacks pocket. "I don't really enjoy the idea." He shifted back. "Say, you guys want a job?"

"Huh?"

"Give you five bucks if you walk me up to the house—you know where it is?"

Kid nodded.

"I mean, you guys are in the protection business, aren't you? I'd just as soon have some, walking around this town at night."

"Yeah?"

"Walking around the streets in the dark, in a city with no police, you don't know what you're going to find . . . both of you: I'll give you five apiece."

"I'll go with you," Glass said.

"We'll go," Kid said.

"I really appreciate that, now, I really do. I don't want to rush you out. If you want to stay around and have a couple more drinks, fine. Just let me know when you're ready—"

Glass looked at Kid with a sort of Is-he-crazy? look.

So Kid said, "We'll go now," and thought: Is he that much more terrified of the dark than known danger?

"Good," Kamp said. "Okay. Fine, now." He grinned and started for the crowded door.

Glass's expression was still puzzled.

"Yeah," Kid said. "He's for real. He's been to the moon."

Glass laughed without opening his lips. "I'm for real too, man." And then he clapped his hands.

Kamp looked back at them.

Kid, followed by Glass, shouldered through the bunch milling loudly at the exit.

In the hallway, Kamp asked, "Do you fellows— you're scorpions, now, right?—do you fellows have *much* trouble around here?"

"Our share," Glass said.

Kid thought: Glass always waits before he speaks as if it were my place to speak first.

"I'm not the sort of man who usually runs from a fight," Kamp said; "But, now, you don't set yourself up. I'm not carrying a lot of money, but I want to get home with what I've got." (People before the door listened to a woman who, in the midst of her story, stopped to laugh torrentially.) "If I'm going to stay in Bellona for a while, maybe it would be a good idea to hire a bunch of you guys to hang around with me. Then again, maybe that would just be attracting attention. Now, I really do appreciate you coming with me."

"We won't let anything happen to you," Kid said and wondered why.

He contemplated telling Kamp his fear was silly; and realized his own nether consciousness had grown fearful.

Glass settled his shoulders, and his chin, and his thumbs in his frayed pockets, like a black, drugstore cowboy.

"You'll be okay," Kid reiterated.

The woman recovered enough for the story's punch-line, which was ". . . the sun! He said it was the God-damn *sun!*" Black men and women rocked and howled.

Kid laughed too; they circuited the group, into the dark.

"Did you talk to George when you were inside?" Glass asked.

"We sort of talked. He offered me one of his girl friends. But she just wasn't my type, now. Now if he'd offered me the other one . . ." Kamp chuckled.

"What'd you think of him?" Kid asked.

"He isn't so much. I mean, I don't know why everybody is so scared of him."

"Scared?"

"Roger's terrified," Kamp said. "Roger was the one who told me about him, of course. It's an interesting story, but it's strange. What do you think?"

Kid shrugged. "What's there to say?"

"A great deal, from what you hear."

538

On the brick wall, beneath the pulsing streetlamp, George's posters, as shiny as if they had been varnished, overlapped like the immense and painted scales of a dragon, flank fading off and up into night. Glass looked at them as they passed. Kid and Kamp glanced at Glass.

"From what I've gathered, now, everybody spends a great deal of time talking about him."

"What did you two talk about, beside swapping pussy?" Kid asked.

"He mentioned you, among other things."

"Yeah? What did he say?"

"He wanted to know if I'd met you. When I said I had, he wanted to know my opinion of you. Seems people are almost as interested in you as they are in him."

That seemed like something to laugh at. Kid was surprised at Kamp's silence.

Dark pulled over Kamp's face. "You know, there's something—well, I'm not a strictly religious man. But I mean, for instance, when we were up there and we read the bible to everybody on television, we meant it. There's something about naming a new moon, for somebody—somebody like that, and all that sort of stuff, now, it's against religion. I don't like it."

Glass chuckled. "They ain't named the sun yet."

Kamp, baffled by Glass's accent (by now Kid had set it somewhere near Shreveport), made him say that again.

"Oh," Kamp said when he understood. "Oh, you mean this afternoon."

"Yeah," Glass said. "I hope you don't think they gonna name it after *you?*" and chuckled on.

"You think you could live up to that?" Kid asked.

Kamp gestured in the dark. But they could not tell the curve of his arm, whether it were closed or open-handed, so lost the meaning. "You fellows know where we're going, now?"

"We're going right," Glass said.

Kid felt distinctly they were going wrong. But distrust of his distinct feelings had become second nature. He walked, waiting, beside them.

"See," Glass said, surprising Kid from his reverie, maybe twenty minutes later, "This is that place between Brisbain North and Brisbain South. Told you we're going right."

Two canyon walls collapsed inward upon one another, obliterating the time between.

"What?" asked Kamp.

"We're going right," Glass said. "Up to Mr Calkins'."

Lamps on three consecutive corners worked.

They squinted and blinked at one another after blocks of darkness.

"I guess," Kamp said, jocularly, "it must be pretty hard for *any*body to navigate after dark in the city."

"You learn," Kid said.

"What?"

What sort of accent do *I* have? "I said 'You learn.'"

"Oh."

Ahead, black was punctured by a streetlamp at least five blocks off, flickering through branches of some otherwise invisible tree.

"You fellows ever have any trouble on the street?"

"Yeah," Kid said.

"What part of the city," Kamp asked. "You know, I want to know what neighborhoods to stay out of. Was it over where we were? The colored area, Jackson?"

"Right outside of Calkins'," Kid said.

"Did you get robbed?"

"No. I was just minding my own business. Then this bunch of guys jumped out and beat shit out of me. They didn't have anything better to do, I guess."

"Did you ever find out who it was?"

"Scorpions," Kid said. (Glass chuckled again.) "But that was before I started running."

"Scorpions are about the only thing in Bellona you got to worry about," Glass said. "Unless it's some nut with a rifle in an upstairs window or on the roof who decides to pick you off."

"—because he don't have anything better to do," Kid finished.

Kamp took a breath in the dark. "You say the neighborhood up here, around Roger's, is really bad?"

"About as bad as anyplace else," Kid said.

"Well," Kamp reflected, "I guess it was a pretty good idea to get you guys to come up with me, now."

He is using his fear to use me, Kid reflected, and said nothing. Ten dollars for the walk? Kid wondered how much this parallelled the genesis of the protection racket in the park commune. He put his fingertips in his

540

pockets, hunched his shoulders, grinned at the night and thought: Is this how a dangerous scorpion walks? He swung his steps a bit wider.

Kamp coughed, and said very little for the next quarter-hour.

. . . am a marauder in the internal city, tenuous as the dark shaken on itself with a footstep, eyeblink, heartbeat. Intrigued by the way his fear has given me purpose, I swagger down the labyrinth of least resistance. Where is the sound? There is a sound like glass and sand, or a finger turning in the channels of the ear. I acknowledge my own death with an electrified tongue, wanting to cry. These breaths I leave here disperse like apparitions of laughter I am too terrified to release.

Which was the conclusion of the reverie he'd begun before: but could not remember its beginning.

"Do you know how far along the wall here the gate is?" Kamp asked.

"The wall makes your voice sound funny in the dark, don't it?" Glass said.

"Won't we be able to see some light from the house?" Kamp asked.

Kid asked, "They still got light?"

They walked.

"There," Kid said. "I see something—" stumbling at the curb edge. ". . . hey, *watch*—!" but did not fall. He recovered to Kamp's nervous laugh. He thinks, Kid thought, something almost jumped out at us. Only my eyes are bandaged in darkness. The rest of my body swerves in light.

"Yes," Kamp said. "We're here."

Between the newels, through the brass bars and shaggy pine, light slid into the crevices of Glass's face (sweating; Kid was surprised) and dusted Kamp's that was simply very pale.

I thought I was the only one scared to death, Kid thought. My luck, on my dumb face it doesn't show.

"José," Kamp called. "José, it's Mike Kamp. I'm back for the night." "José," Kamp explained somewhat inanely, "is the man Roger has on the gate."

K-k-klank: the lock (remotely controlled?) opened and bars swung inches in.

"Well," Kamp put his hands in his pockets. "I certainly want to thank you guys for—oh." His hands came out. "Here you go." He rifled through his wallet, held it up to his eyes. "Got to see what I have here, now . . ." He took out two bills.

Glass said, "Thanks," when he got his.

"Well," Kamp said again. "Thanks again. Well now. If I don't see you before, Kid, I'll see you in three Sundays." He pushed the gate. "Do you fellows want to come—"

"No," Kid said, and realized Glass had gotten himself ready to say yes.

"All right." *K-k-klank.* "Good night, now."

Glass shifted from one foot to the other. "Night." Then he said: "Those curbs are too much in all this dark shit. Let's go down the middle of the street."

"Sure."

They stepped off the sidewalk and started back.

You'll get to see what it looks like inside in a couple of weeks, Kid thought of saying and didn't. He also thought of asking why Glass was a scorpion, how long he'd been, and what he'd done before.

They did not talk.

Kid constructed the stumps of a dozen conversations, and heard each veer into some mutually embarrassing area, and so abandoned it. Once it occurred to him Glass was probably indulging in the same process: for a while he pondered what Glass might want to know about him: that too became fantasized converse, and like the others, embarrassing. So their silent intercourse moved to another subject.

"All this walking ain't worth five bucks," Glass said at the North-South connection.

"Here." Kid held out his bill, crumpled by the hour in his fist (the crisp points had blunted with perspiration). "It probably ain't worth ten either. But I don't need it."

"Thanks," Glass said. "Hey, thanks, man."

He was both surprised and amused that the interchange released him from his preoccupation with who Glass was.

They ambled the black street into the city, neither moving to illuminate his projector, in memoriam—Kid realized—to the sun.

How long had they been? Three hours? More? The distance between then and now was packed full of time during which his furious mind had prodded the outsides of

542

a myriad fantasies and (if he were asked he would have said) nothing had happened. Thoughts of madness: Perhaps those moments of miscast reality or lost time were the points (during times when nothing happened) when the prodding broke through. The language that happened on other muscles than the tongue was better for grasping these. Things he could not say wobbled in his mouth, and brought back, vividly in the black, how at age four he had sat in the cellar, putting into his mouth, one after the other, blue, orange, and pink marbles, to see if he could taste the colors.

They passed another lamp.

Glass's face was dry.

The way anywhere in this city was obviously to drift; Kid drifted, on kinesthetic memory. To try consciously for destination was to come upon street signs illegible through smoke, darkness, or vandalism, wrongly placed, or missing.

When they crossed Jackson, Kid asked, "I want to go back to the party."

"Sure, mother-fucker." Glass grinned. "Why not? You really want to?"

"Just to see what happened."

Glass sighed.

Across the pavement, at the other end of the block, Kid saw the dim trapezoid. "Light's still on."

Of the cluster of three lanterns inside the door, one still burned. Inside, the doors to the hall were closed.

"Don't sound like nobody's there."

"Open the door," Kid said because Glass was ahead of him.

Glass pushed, stepped in; Kid stepped after.

Only two lanterns were working: a third, in the corner, guttered. The meeting room was empty; the party's detritus lay in ruin and shadow.

Near the one-winged statue, fallen among the prickly plants, the tip of the barrel on his belly, the butt on the linoleum, the black guard whom they had talked to outside lay on his back and snored. The tracked plaster, overturned chairs, and scattered bottles momentarily brought Kid an image of a drunken shooting, the barrel swinging around the room moments before he'd passed out—but he saw no bullet holes.

He could see no one in the balcony.

On a chair by the far wall, muffled in an absurd

543

overcoat, the only other person in the room swayed to one side, froze, recovered, swayed once more, once more froze at an angle that challenged gravity.

"What does he have inside him, a gyroscope?" Glass asked.

"More like half a spoon of skag."

Glass laughed.

In the hallway, a door that had been closed before now stood ajar on a stairwell.

"You wanna go exploring?" Glass asked.

"Sure," Kid said.

Glass pinched at his broad nose, twice, sucked in both lips, cleared his throat, and started down.

Kid followed.

A door at the bottom was open. Kid's foot crushed a *Times,* which caught some low draft (the dirty stair was cold; the banister pipe warm) and doffed down. It rasped again beneath his boot on the last step.

Kid came up behind Glass in the doorway:

The couch had been opened into a bed. The gaunt, brick-haired girl who had been with George, her neck looped with the optical chain, slept beneath a rumpled blanket, bearing small, light-coffee breasts, dollopped with dark nipples.

A lamp by the bed had a shade of glass from which a triangle was broken away. The wedge of light, molding to body and bedding, just touched one aureole at the height of her blowy breath.

"Hey, man!" Glass whispered, and grinned.

Kid breathed with her, swaying on the bottom step, and had to move his feet apart.

"How'd you like some of that?"

"I think I could eat about three helpings," Kid said. "Where's George?"

"Man, he probably gone off with the *other* one—" Glass's emphatic whispers broke into and returned from falsetto.

Then: "What the fuck are you doing!" She sat up, sharply, face going from sleep to anger like two frames of film.

"Jesus Christ, lady," Kid said, "we were just looking."

"Well stop looking! Go on, get the fuck out of here! Where the hell is everybody? You, both of you, get out!"

"Sweetheart, don't go on like that." Glass said. "Now you got your door wide open—"

"Did that nut leave the damn *door* unlocked—" She pulled up the sheet, reached down by the bed, and whipped up some article of clothing. "Come on. Out! Out! Out! I'm not kidding. Out!"

"Look—" Kid glumly contemplated the difficulties of rape (a surprising memory of his arms filled with the bloody boy; he moved his feet back together) and wondered what Glass was contemplating—"if you just stop yelling, maybe we can discuss this a little; you might change your mind—?"

"Not on your fucking life!" She shook out the wrinkled jump suit, swung her legs off the bed, and stuck her feet in. "I don't know what you got on your mind to do. But if you try it, you gonna get your ass hurt!"

"Nobody wants to hurt anybody—" Kid stopped because Glass was looking up at the small, high window. Kid felt his cheeks wrinkling and the pressure of surprise on his forehead.

She started to say something, and then said, "Huh?"

The foggy air outside had lightened to blue.

Then Glass turned and ran up the stairs.

"Hey!" Kid followed him.

Behind, he could hear her fighting with shoes.

Kid ran down the hall, swung outside.

Glass, a dozen feet from the sidewalk, stared along the street.

Kid joined him, stopping to look back, at the sound of footsteps: She stopped at the edge of the door, leaned out, her face contorted. "Jesus God," she said softly, stepped out and raised her head. ". . . it's getting . . . light!"

Kid's first thought was: It's happening too fast. The uneven roofs descended in a paling V, vortex blurred with smoke. He stared, waiting for an eruption of bronze fires. But no; the arch of visible sky, though modeled and mottled with billows, was deep blue, except the lowest quarter, gone grey.

"Oh, man!" Glass looked at Kid. "I'm so tired." Below one eye, water tracked his dark cheek. Blinking, Glass turned back to the morning.

Kid got chills. And kept getting them. I don't trust this reaction, he thought, remembering the last late-night TV drama where the frail heroine's tearful realizations

545

of burgeoning love had caused him the same one. I'm going on like this because there's a nigger next to me about to bawl, and another in the doorway who looks so scared and confused I'm about to . . . No, it's not the light. No.

But the chills came on, frazzling his flesh, till even his thoughts stuttered. Chills sandpapered his spine. His palms hummed. He opened his mouth and his eyes and his fingers wide to the raddled and streaming dawn.

5

Sunday, April 1, 1776—There is reason to speak of this on page two rather than lend the phenomenon the leading headline it could so easily claim. We, for one, are just not ready to grant the hysteria prevailing beneath this miasmal pollution the reinforcement of our shock.

We saw *this* one ourselves.

But in the city where *we* live, one doubts even the validity of that credential.

We went so far as to entertain a while the idea of devoting *this* issue to accounts only by those who had slept through, who were busy in the cellar or windowless-back room when, or—hope on hope—could claim to have been strolling about yesterday afternoon and observed during, nothing extraordinary in the sky.

But if the advent in our nights of George is anything to go by, we should have to look outside our misty and deliquescent city limits to find a negative witness. At least we hope so.

Please, return to page one. The plight of Jackson's Lower Cumberland area, where apparently *all* power has gone out with the breaking of the water main on my last Thursday (how dangerous that is for the rest of us nobody can say because nobody can estimate the losses from the fractured dam in terms of our decreased population) is a real dilemma. More real we would like to feel, than yesterday's portent.

We are not anxious either to describe or even name what passed. Presumably some copy of this will get beyond our border; we should like to keep *our* good name. We would much prefer to give our opinions on Lower Cumberland Park. But another writer (page one, continued page seven) has already rehearsed his eyewitness, first-hand account. And, anyway, in his words, ". . . chances are, no one lives there any more."

Dubious to time, the arc became visible in the late afternoon of the overcast day. In a spectrum ranging only through grey, black, and blue, you would have to see to judge the effects of those golds and bronzes, those reds and purplish browns! Minutes later, most of us here had gathered in the August Garden. The view was awesome. Speculation, before awe silenced it, was rampant. When, after fifteen minutes, perhaps a fourth of the disk had emerged, we had our first case of hysteria . . . But rather than dwell on those understandable breakdowns, let us commend Professor Wellman on his level-headedness throughout, and Budgie Goldstein on her indomitable high spirits.

More than an hour in the rising, the monumental . . . disk? sphere? whatever? eventually cleared the visible buildings. There is some question, even among those gathered in August, as to whether the orb actually hovered, or whether it immediately changed direction and began to set again, slightly (by no more than a fifth of its diameter) to the left—this last, the estimate of Wallace Guardowsky.

The lower rim, at any rate, was above the horizon for fifteen or twenty minutes. Even at full height, it could be stared at for minutes because of the veiling clouds. Colonel Harris advised, however, that we curtail prolonged gazing. The setting, almost all are agreed, took substantially less time than the rising, and has been estimated between fifteen minutes and a half an hour. We have heard several attempts now, to estimate size, composition, and trajectory. We doubt recording even the ones we could understand would be much use—the merest indulgence in cleverness before something so . . . awful! Do we hear objections from you eager for meaningful cosmologic distractions? May we simply ask your trust: of the explanations heard, none, frankly, were *that* clever. And we do not choose to insult our readers.

We recall, with distrust and wheedling astonishment, the speed at which the last such celestial apparition acquired, by common consent of the common, its cognomen. How heartening, then, that this vision should prove too monstrous for facile appellation. (One has been suggested from a number of quarters, but all common decency and decorum forbids us to mention it; we have defamed the young woman, many feel, enough in these pages already.) Indeed, though a label might cling to such

when we review it with a smile, certain images lose their freedom and resonance if, when we regard them with a straight face, we do so through the diffraction of a name.

"What do you think of that?" Faust asked, coming a little ways across the street.

Kid laughed. "Calkins is pretty quick to call a spade a spade. But when it comes to naming anything else, he's still chicken-shit!"

"No, no. Not that." Faust had to toss the rolled paper three times before getting it into the second story window. "I mean on page one."

Kid, sitting on the stoop, leaned down to scratch his foot. "What—?" He turned back to the front of the tabloid. "Where is Cumberland Park, anyway?"

"Lower Cumberland Park?" Faust craned his ropy neck and, beneath his corduroy jacket, scratched his undershirt. "That's down at the *other* end of Jackson. That's where they got some really bad niggers. It's where the great god Harrison lives."

"Oh," Kid said. "Where I was last night. It says here something about nobody living there any more."

Faust hefted the bundle on his hip. "Then all I know is that I leave a God-damn lot of papers in front of a God-damn lot of doors, and they ain't there the next day when I come back. Damn, splashing around in all that water in the street yesterday morning!" He squinted back at the window. "It was better this morning though. Hey, I see you again tomorrow. That your book the office is full up with?"

"I don't know," Kid said. "Is it?"

Faust frowned. "You should come up to the office sometime and take a look where they print the paper and things. Come up with me, some day. I'll show it all to you. Your book went in the day before yesterday—" Faust snapped his fingers. "And I put cartons of it in the bookstores last night. Soon as it . . . well, you know, got dark."

Kid grunted and opened the *Times* again, to look at something not Faust.

"Get your morning paper!" The old man loped down the block, hollering into the smoke: "Right here, get your morning paper!"

What he'd opened to was another quarter-page advertisement for *Brass Orchids*. He left it on the stoop, and walked toward the corner, when a sound he'd been dimly aware of broke over the sky: Roaring. And nestled in the roar, the whine a jet makes three blocks from the airport. Kid looked as the sound gathered above him. Nothing was visible; he looked down the block. Faust, a figurine off in a milky aquarium, had stopped too. The sound rolled away, lowering.

Faust moved on to disappear.

Kid turned the corner.

It's different inside the nest, he thought, trying to figure what should be the same:

The crayoning on the dirty wall—

The loose ceiling fixture—

In his hand, the knobs squared and toothy shaft rasped out another inch—

A black face came from the middle room, looked back inside; shook his head, and went down to the bathroom. Among voices, Nightmare's laugh, and:

"Okay. I mean, okay." That was Dragon Lady. "You said your thing, now what you want us to do?"

While someone else in the hubbub, shouted, "Hey, hey, hey come on now. Hey!"

"I mean now . . . yeah!" Nightmare's voice separated. "What do you want?"

Kid went to the door.

Across the room, Siam and Glass noticed him with small, different nods. Kid leaned on the jam. The people in the center, their backs to him, were not scorpions.

"I *mean*—" Nightmare, circling, bent to hit his knees —"what do you want?"

"Look." John turned to follow him, holding the lapels of his Peruvian vest. "Look, this is very serious!" His blue work shirt was rolled up his forearms; the sleeves were stained, dirty, and frayed at one elbow. His thumbnails, the only ones visible, were very clean. "I méan you guys have got to . . ." He gestured.

Milly stepped out of the way of his arm.

"Gotta what?" Nightmare rubbed his shoulder. "Look, man I wasn't there. I didn't know nothing about it."

"We were someplace else." Dragon Lady turned a white cup in her dark hands, shoulders hunched, sipping watching. "We weren't even anywhere around, you know?" She alone in the room drank; and drank loudly.

Mildred brushed away threads of red hair and looked much older than Dragon Lady. (He remembered once thinking when neither were present that, for all their differences, they were about the same age.) Dragon Lady's lips kept changing thickness.

"This is shit!" Nightmare kneaded his arm. "I mean this is real shit, man! Don't load this shit on me. You want to talk to somebody—" His eyes came up beneath his brows and caught Kid—"talk to him. He was there, I wasn't. It was his thing."

Kid unfolded his arms. "What'd I do?"

"You—" Mildred turned—"*killed* somebody!"

He felt, after moments, his forehead wrinkle. "Oh, yeah?" What cleared inside was distressingly close to relief. "When?" he asked with the calm and contrapuntal thought: No. No, that's *not* possible, is it? No.

"Look," John said, and looked between Nightmare and Kid. "Look, we could always talk to you guys, right? I mean you're pretty together, you know? Nightmare, we've always done right by you, hey? And you've done right by us. Kid, you used to eat with us all the time, right? You were almost part of our family. We were gonna put you up the first night you got here, weren't we? But you guys can't go around and murder people. And expect us to just sit around. I mean we have to do something."

"Who'd we kill?" he asked, realizing, they *don't* mean *me!* They mean *us.* The feeling came cold and with loss.

"Wally!" Milly said from the edge of hysteria. "Wally Efrin!"

The name rang absolutely hollow in his mind. Kid searched the company squatting in memory before the communal cinderblock fire over beans and vegetable hash with spam; Wally Efrin? (The short-hair he'd once asked to help him get wood who'd said no because he was too frightened to leave the others? The one who had sat between him and Lanya and talked non-stop of Hawaii? The heavy one with the black hair long enough to sit on who kept asking people whether or not we'd seen his girl friend? One he'd seen but never noticed? One he'd never seen? He remembered Jommy and a half dozen others.)

"Where?" he asked, at her silence. "What'd we kill him for?"

"Oh, for Christ's sake . . . !" Milly shook her head.

"Yesterday," John said. "Yesterday afternoon. When you were all at that house, with the . . . sun. Mildred was there—"

"I didn't know about it till after I got home," she said, in the voice one used to make excuses.

"Me neither," Kid said. "So do you want to tell me?"

"No, I don't want to . . ." Milly exclaimed. "This is really just terrible! This is animal . . . !"

"You were in charge there, Kid, weren't you?" John asked.

"So everybody tells me."

"Well, it seems that—now I wasn't there, but this is what I've been told . . ."

Kid nodded.

". . . It seems like some of the guys started a fight. And . . . what? Wally tried to break it up?"

"He may have started the fight," Milly said to the floor, "with them."

"I guess most of the people were upstairs. This was downstairs in the kitchen. He got beat up pretty bad, I guess. Someone hit him a couple of times. In the head. With the bar of a police lock. Then everybody left I guess. Apparently lots of people there didn't even know about it. It was downstairs." John repeated: "In the kitchen. I mean, Mildred didn't know until after she got back and Jommy told her." A movement of John's tanned chin indicated that Jommy was the emaciated boy with a lot of brown hair, and small, pale eyes. (He *had* remembered Jommy; but he had not recognized him . . .)

"Everybody left him, because they thought he was just knocked out or something. Or they were scared. Then we went back for him. He was dead."

"Who did it?" Kid shifted his bare foot, which was tingling.

Copperhead stood in the kitchen door, one fist on the jamb.

John looked at Jommy who pointed immediately to the scorpion on the couch, the unshaven, pimpley, white youngster: "Him!" who grunted at the accusation and raised his head a little. He was also the scorpion whom the long-haired youngsters had held, crying, on the balcony as the great circle set.

"You kill somebody yesterday afternoon?" Kid asked.

"No!" He said it thickly and loudly and questioningly, trying the answer for effect.

Nightmare sat, now, at Dragon Lady's feet. Head against the wall, he looked from speaker to speaker, with the smile of an enthusiast at a tennis match.

"You beat anybody up?" Kid asked.

"Beat the *fuck* out of 'im!" The scorpion's fists bounced on the couch's rim. "Yeah! With a fuckin piece of pipe. But I didn't know what kind of pipe it was! . . . or if he was dead!"

"Shit, *I* sure did!" Glass chuckled. "I knew it when you hit the mother-fucker the first time. The second, third . . . all those other times you were banging on him, man, that was just extra."

"You shut the fuck up!" (It was, Kid remembered, the scorpion for whom he had rescued the bronze lion.) "I didn't kill nobody."

"But you *did* beat somebody over the head with a piece of pipe yesterday?"

"Look, I didn't . . ." He stalled on the word, and stood, fists flailing about his shoulders to beat away the barrier to speech, then yelled, ". . . didn't kill any God-damn body with no—"

"SIT DOWN, GOD DAMN IT . . . !" Kid bellowed, coming away from the door by three steps. That, he thought in the silence, was pretty theatrical. But he was astonished by its efficacy. Twitching behind his face, he felt an embryonic giggle. Both feet and hands were tingling. Shall I *say* the next thing, or shall I *yell* it? (The scorpion was leaning back on the couch, balanced on his fists, his seat not quite on the cushion, an expression not quite on his face.) "DID YOU BEAT ON SOME KID'S HEAD WITH A PIPE . . . ?" He'd made the choice to avoid laughing.

The scorpion sank to the cushion. The expression was terror. "I guess so?" the scorpion asked quietly. "I don't know . . . ?"

Kid shook both hands hard, by the hips, to return the feeling. He heard one of the people beside him creak a floor board and catch breath.

"Look," he said to John. Milly, behind him, seemed more frightened than the scorpion on the couch. Little Jommy had an intent expression of cold interest. "Why don't you people just get the fuck out of here, all right?"

"Um . . ." John's thumbs had gone beneath the lapels with the rest of his fingers. "You know we haven't

553

had a . . . trial or anything." He glanced at the scorpion. "Mildred said maybe Wally started it, you know—"

"I didn't see it," Milly reiterated. "Somebody just told—"

Kid breathed in, and was still surprised that it cut the ribbon of her whisper like scissors. "You all get out."

"Now we're not trying to . . ." John began; Milly, Jommy, and the others had all started for the door. He let go his lapels and followed.

"What'd you do with Wally, huh?" Kid called.

"Huh?" John stopped a moment. "We just left—"

"No," Kid interrupted. "No, don't tell me about it!" He kneaded one fist in the other. Feeling was beginning to return. The gesture sent John pushing against the people in front of him to get out of the room, beating nervously against his leg.

The scorpion on the couch looked very miserable. Clutching his lamp, or on the balcony crying; Kid thought: He's looked miserable every time I've ever noticed him.

"Shit!" Kid said. (Outside, he heard the door close behind the commune deputation.)

The scorpion bounced a little and blinked.

"Aw, shit!" Kid turned and walked out of the room.

Three steps down the hall, Kid heard a noise behind him, and turned.

Nightmare swung around the door jamb, an incongruous grin on his face. "Man, you're too fuckin much!" Nightmare pranced, jingling, in the hall, slapped the wall. "Really! You're too much."

Right behind him, Copperhead came out and asked, "Hey, what you want to do with Dollar in there?" He thumbed back in the room.

So that's his name, Kid thought (Dollar?), while asking, "Huh?"

"You want me to rough him up a little for you?" Copperhead asked. "Yeah, I'll do it. I don't mind doing shit like that. I mean if he goes around hitting people over the head, he's gonna get us in trouble, you know? You want me to work him over?"

Kid made a disgusted face. "No! You don't have to do anything like—"

"If you *want* me to," Copperhead announced over Nightmare's shoulder, "I'll kill the little white bastard. Or I could just work him over to scare him, you know . . ."

554

"No," Kid repeated. "No, I don't want you to do that."

"Maybe later . . . ?" Copperhead said. "When you thought about it?"

"Well, not now," Kid said. "Just leave him alone now."

Nightmare laughed as Copperhead went back into the room. "What were you trying to *do*, huh? Man, you *are* too much!"

"Just find out if he did it. That's all."

Nightmare held his laughter in his mouth; it bellied his cheeks till he swallowed it. "Did you find out?"

From inside, there was a sudden crack and a cry. Voices silenced around the sound of loud sipping:

"Now the Kid told me I'm supposed to wait till later to work you over, cocksucker. But don't give me any shit, you hear? You go around breaking people's heads, I think I'm gonna have some fun breaking yours. Now get out of here."

"I . . . guess so," Kid said.

"I mean," Nightmare shook his open palms in front of Kid's hips, "I was just wondering if you found *out*. I wasn't there. You was, right? So you should know if he done it or not." He backed away, grinning.

"Hey!"

"What?"

"Come here. I want to talk to you."

Nightmare's arm folded low on his stomach, then raised up his broad chest so that the chains looped across his forearms. "Sure." He tilted his head, warily. "What you want to talk about?"

"I just want to know what—hey, you come on with me."

"Sure," Nightmare said; then his tongue went into the side of his jaw, licking for something among back teeth.

They went up the hall and onto the service porch. Nightmare, arms still folded, stood in the doorway squinting. Dulling smoke hung only yards beyond the screening. Kid asked: "What are *you* trying to do, huh?"

"What do you mean?" Nightmare's forearms slid across one another to tighten toward a knot.

"I mean you. And Dragon Lady and all. How come I suddenly get to be the boss about everything?"

"You do it pretty well."

"But I want to know why."

"Well." Nightmare looked at the floor and let himself fall against the jamb. "It's gotta be somebody, right?" Boards around them creaked.

"But what about you?"

"What about me?" The boards creaked again, though Nightmare hadn't moved. "What you want to know about me?"

"Just why, that's all. You want a new boss—why not one of the spades, or something. I mean what's *with* you?"

Nightmare rolled his wet, red underlip back into his mouth, and nodded. His left eye, Kid noticed again, had the slightest cast.

The water puddling in the sink shook beneath the crusty faucet.

"I thought it would be sort of interesting to see what would happen if one of you brainy, crazed types was running things for a while. All the brainy niggers in Bellona had sense enough to get out. We don't got too much to choose from so we might as well make it interesting, right? I ain't gonna stay in this fucking fog hole the rest of my life. It's a real gas being Nightmare, you know? But I'm gonna get back to St. Louis, get me a little foreign car, do some work in the gym, and put two or three ladies back to work for me, and I'm gonna be Larry H. Jonas all over again. And I hope I don't ever hear about no Nightmare no more. If somebody shouts it out on Sixth Street, I'm gonna walk down Olive. I've done too many things here I'd just as soon leave here." He stood up. "You strip off the Nightmare, and I *got* me a name. I know people. In St. Louis." His hand slid up to his shoulder, big fingers working. "So I figured I'd leave you here. Besides, Denny likes you. That little cocksucker's got a head on his shoulders. Not like some of these dumb nuts. You don't look like you mind." Among the links sagging on his chest, bright beads caught more light than there was to catch, winking and dying and winking.

"Hey, that scar on your shoulder?" Kid asked. "You and Dragon Lady getting on pretty good?"

"Like a bitch. Sometimes." Nightmare's face twisted a moment about his broken tooth. "And then sometimes—" he frowned—"well, you know." After the faucet dripped three more times, he turned to leave, but paused to look over his shoulder. "You want to talk about anything else?"

"No." Kid said. "That's all."

Nightmare left.

Across the hall was a room Kid had never been in. He opened the door.

Dollar, silhouetted before the torn window shade, turned. The lion peered by his hip from the sill. The taste of burning at the back of Kid's throat flooded forward, into an amazing stench: on one of the overlapping mattresses was a charred halo around a crater two feet across of ashes and burned cotton. Newspaper and magazine pictures had been pasted over one wall; many had been ripped off again.

One of the three blacks sitting on the floor glanced at him. The little blond girl shrugged her pea jacket back up her shoulders and pulled it across her breasts.

"What are you . . . I mean, hey, man . . . ?" Dollar stepped up unsteadily. "Kid, look, you're supposed to be an all-right guy, huh? You don't gotta hurt me. Please? Man, I ain't never done nothing like that before in my life, you know? . . . You want me to . . . ?" He took another step. "Hey . . . what are you trying to do? Huh?" His hand strayed in the chains around his neck, twisted in them.

"Whatever it is," Kid said, "it looks like I'm doing it." All the muscles in his face felt tight: he went back into the hall.

Noise was coming from the front room. Nightmare's laughter rose. Dragon Lady's cut across it.

As if they'd suddenly heated, Kid pawed beneath the back of his vest and, from his belt, pulled loose the books. Both were creased. The face of one was rubbed and dirty. So was the back of the other.

"Hey, come on, come on, sweetheart!" Nightmare hollered. "What are you trying to do to me, huh? What are you trying to . . ." and exploded in laughter.

"I just asked," Dragon Lady announced with hysterical deliberation, "if you wanted some more God-damned coffee . . ." The last syllable became a shriek, tumbling in counterpoint to Nightmare's laugh, till both splashed into the cistern of mirth.

Kid took refuge in the bathroom.

Pants about his knees, he sat. A fugitive bubble in the gut cramped his abdomen; the cramp faded. He broke wind and knew he was empty.

He turned the books over, flipped through one, then

557

the other. He wanted to read one poem, at least, through. A minute later, he realized he'd actually been deliberating not which poem, but in which book to read it. Was the discomfort in his belly a ghost of the gas? No.

A book in either hand, he joggled them. *Time* had been spent writing these. The time was mornings with his forehead wrinkled and the grass obligingly silent beyond the blanket's edge; was evenings at the bar with candlelight scoring bottles with their different contents at different heights like pistons in an engine; was a broken curb on either side while he sat with the ballpoint burning his middle finger. Writing, he had not thought to retrieve any of it. But the prospect of publication had somehow convinced him magic was in process that would return to him, in *tacto* (not *memorium*), some of what the city had squandered. The conviction was now identified by its fraudulence, before the inadequate objects. But as it died, kicking in his gut, spastic and stuttering, he knew it had been as real and unquestioned as any surround: air to a bird, water to a fish, earth to a worm.

He was exhausted, with an exhaustion that annihilated want. And all he could conceive of wanting was to try again; to make more poems, to put them in a book, to have that book made real by reproduction, and give that hallucination another chance!

He had nothing to write. He could not imagine what another poem of his would be, how it might lilt, or even look. Is that, he wondered, why they call it "creation?" The texture on the eye, the corrugation on the air around him had absorbed all. There was nothing left (. . . about what you see about you, what's happening to you, what you feel. No.) No. Something had to be . . . created. As these had been.

A muscle in his shoulder tensed.

He'd once been scared of things like that: (. . . a blood-clot breaking loose from the vein wall to race toward the heart, jamming a valve!) Habit commenced a shiver.

He caught up his breath, and his pants, and the books from where he'd dropped them. The leering mannequin, chained and bloody, leaned against the tank and smiled benignly up at Kid's left nipple. Kid scratched it, put the books back under his belt, and went out.

In Denny's room he took two rungs of the ladder at once. His chin gained the loft. "Hey, wake up!" Denny didn't, so he climbed up the rest of the way, kneeled astraddle, and took hold of the boy's head. "Hey!"

"God damn—!" Denny tried to roll to his back. One arm shot out and waved. "What the fuck are you . . ."

"Come on, get up!" Kid's hands clamped, and Denny's came back to grasp his wrist.

"*Okay!*" Denny said, his cheeks pushed together, distorting his voice. "Shit, man. I'm getting up, all right . . . ?"

"You got to take me to Lanya's place." Kid raised his leg and sat back. "You know where it is, huh? You took her there. You know!"

Denny grunted and pushed himself up on his elbows. Boots and chains by his head lay on a crumple of green. His vest's leather edge fell back from a pinkened line across one waxy pectoral. "Yeah, I guess so."

"Get the fuck up, cocksucker." Kid gestured. "I want to go see her."

"Okay, okay." Denny reached back for his boots and started to put them on. Once he glanced up and said, "Shit!"

Kid grinned at him. "Move your ass."

"Fuck you," Denny said dryly and ducked his head through rattling links. "Come on." He swung his feet over the edge and jumped.

Kid swung over the ladder while Denny bobbed erect in the doorway.

"What's all the rush for?" Denny asked. "Hey, stop pushing me, will you?" as Kid shoved him into the hall.

"I'm not hurting you," Kid said. "Did you know Dollar beat some kid to death with a pipe?"

"Huh? When?"

"Yesterday."

Denny tried to whistle. It squeaked at the beginning and was all air. "Dollar's a crazy mother-fucker, you know that? I mean he always was crazy. Hell, all the white guys in the nest are nuts."

"Sure." Kid herded Denny toward the hall door. "Why'd he do it?"

Kid shrugged. "I dunno."

The hall door opened. Thirteen (Smokey behind) stepped inside, looking around as though he expected something . . . different. "Hey, Kid! Oh, hey man, I got to talk to you! You know Dollar? Well, we just got here, but . . . somebody told me yesterday he got a bar, from a police lock, and beat some kid to—"

"GET OFF MY ASS!" Kid said very loudly in Thirteen's face, hefting his fist. If I keep this up, he thought, I'm going to hit somebody. "Now just get off my ass, will you?"

Thirteen, one hand against his green tank top (the "13" tattoo stretched wide), had backed against one wall, and Smokey, wide-eyed, against the other.

Kid put his hand on Denny's shoulder. "Come on. Let's go!"

They stalked between them and out the door; it swung to behind.

VI

". . . just watch out. Oh, yeah, you just better watch out. I know. I know." He wagged his finger, backed away, talked Spanish. Then: "They gonna *get* you—"

"Look, man," Kid said. "Will you—"

"It's all right. It's all right. You just watch out, now. Please? I'm sorry. I'm sorry." His thick neck sweated. He tugged at the wool. "I'm sorry. You just lemme 'lone, huh? They gonna . . ." Suddenly he looked around, turned, and lumbered into the alley.

"Jesus Christ." A smile hovered about Denny's face. "What . . . was that about?"

"I don't know." One book had fallen on the sidewalk. The other leaned against the curb.

"I mean this guy just comes up and starts to push you like that. I thought you were gonna hit him." Denny nodded heavily. "You should've hit him. Why'd he just want to come up and start messing on us like that?"

"He didn't mess on you any." Kid picked up the books and put them back under his belt.

"He's just crazy or something, huh?"

"Come on," Kid said. "Yeah, he's . . . crazy."

"Jesus Christ. That's really funny. You ever see him before?"

"Yeah."

They walked.

"What was he doing then?"

"Just about the same thing . . . one time. The others? He was pretty normal."

"A nut," Denny pronounced, and scratched his groin

561

inside both pants pockets. "She lives over there. I thought you knew already. She didn't tell you?"

"No."

Denny wrinkled his nose. "All this shit in the air. I don't think it's very healthy, you know? What's the matter?"

Kid had stopped, to hook up a section of the chain across his stomach. A glass circle distorted the pad of his thumb into a zebra's flank: dirty troughs whorled the flesh.

"She lives right over there," Denny reiterated, warily.

"All right."

In step, they angled into the street.

"She got a nice place."

A tension held, suspended: Kid wished he could examine it more closely: defract, reflect, magnify . . .

They turned the corner and went down the empty street. "Looks like rain, doesn't it?" Denny said.

"It always looks like rain."

"It doesn't feel like rain."

"It never feels like rain."

"Yeah, you know, that's right?" Denny hopped up the concrete steps, holding the aluminum rail. "It never does!"

Kid followed, surveying the three-story facade. Denny thumbed the bell.

"They live on the top floor. The first two floors are empty so people won't think anyone's in the building."

"It's a good idea not to attract attention, I guess." Kid contemplated asking who was the rest of "they" when footsteps clacked on a stairway.

"Who is it?" asked a woman. Voice familiar? He wondered from where.

"I'm a friend of Lanya's. I'd like to see her."

The peephole darkened. "Just a second."

The door opened. "You know, I didn't recognize your voice at first," Madame Brown said. "How have you been, Kid?" She took in Denny: "Hello. It's nice to see you again . . . Denny, isn't it?" Her neck glittered.

"Lanya's living with you?" Kid, shocked, was unsure why.

"Um-hm. Why don't you come inside?"

Somewhere above the first landing, Muriel barked.

562

"Hush!" Madame Brown commanded the air. "Hush, I say!"

The dog barked three times more.

"Come in, come in. Pull the door behind you. It locks itself."

They followed her up the steps.

"I think," she let fall behind, "Lanya's asleep. Even with her school we've both been having an incredible time keeping to any sort of schedule. I don't know when she went to bed. I suspect it was rather late."

"She'll want to see me," Kid said. He frowned at the back of Madame Brown's red rough hair.

"Oh, I'm sure she will."

They rounded the first landing.

Muriel, visible now, barked again.

"Hush! Now hush up! These are people you know, dear. It's Kid. And Denny. You played with Denny for hours the last time he was here. Don't carry on like that." She reached for the dog's muzzle; Muriel quietened. "Did I say Lanya was asleep? I doubt it after all that. *Naughty!* Naughty!"

Denny was looking up and down and sideways—not like somebody who'd played there for hours. Candlesticks were everywhere: three on a small table beneath a framed portrait, an iron brace full in the corner, two more on the windowsill between white curtains dulled by the sky behind.

"You got electricity here?" Kid asked.

"In two rooms," Madame Brown explained. "Oh, the candles? Well, we're so near Jackson, we thought we better have them around, just in case."

Two rooms away, unlit: a wall of books, a desk, an easy chair.

"That's my office in there," Madame Brown commented on Kid's stare.

Which brought his eyes to more candleholders in the next room. "Um . . . this is really a nice place."

"There're some marvelous houses all through this area, if you just look. They're not hard to find at all. Though I suppose we were lucky with this one. Most of the furniture was already here."

"The rent must be a steal," Kid said, "if you don't mind the neighborhood."

"Oh, we don't pay any—" After an emotionless mo-

563

ment (Kid stopped and Denny bumped into him) she laughed, loudly, shrilly. "By the way, congratulations on your book! Mary Richards showed me a copy the other day. She just tells everybody about how she knows you now."

"Yeah?" He'd intended the smile to be cynical; but pleasure pushed him into joyous, goofy sincerity. "She does?"

"She reads people passages out loud after dinner. I'm sure if you came by, you'd get a positively ebullient welcome." She raised an eyebrow. "You really would."

"Maybe from her," Kid said. "Not from him. Don't you think those people are . . . ?" and, watching her, decided to let it drop.

But she took it on:

"What is it that writer all you youngsters were reading here a few years ago was saying: 'The problem isn't to learn to love humanity, but to learn to love those members of it who happen to be at hand.'

Collected Poems 1930–1950, Stones, Pilgrimage, Rictus, The Dynamic Moment, A Sense of Commencement and *The Charterhouse of Ballarat*, all by Ernest Newboy, were book-ended at the back of the desk with two African statuettes. The last three volumes together were twice as thick as the first four.

"Well, they're not at my hand. I mean, I don't hold your friends against *you*. I got some pretty strange ones myself."

"I didn't think you did, which is one of the reasons I like you. And they haven't done anything to me . . . yet."

The "yet" challenged him to possibilities. It also tested his reticence. So he asked, "How'd you and Lanya get . . . together here?"

"Oh, she's a fine roommate! Energetic, lively . . . It's nice to have someone so sharp around. When I had to leave my other place—but you weren't here for that. You could have helped us move. I was being terrorized to death. Nothing had happened, definitively, but I had to move. Lanya helped me find this place. I've always liked her and . . . well, I suggested that we share. It's worked out very nicely, I think. The school is only a couple of blocks from here. The few patients I've taken on—"

The bell rang.

"One now. You know—" as she moved around them toward the hall—"I really thought that's what you were. When I came down to let you in." She waved toward another hallway. "Lanya's room is down there. Go in and wake her up. I know she wants to see you." They heard her gait go from the hallway's measured rush to the stairwell's hurried canter.

Denny said, "Nice, huh?" softly, then sucked at his upper lip where pale hairs stabbed about in reddened flesh. "You want to . . . go to her room?"

"Yeah."

"Okay." Denny went into the corridor.

There were no bulbs in the elaborate ceiling fixture. An immense painting (Denny-tall by Kid-long), bordered in gilt, looked, as they passed in shadow, completely black.

"That door," Denny said.

It was ajar.

"Go in, go on in," Kid said. Denny didn't; so Kid did.

Warm air puffed at his face. The burning here had a hint of gas—in front of a tile fireplace a heater flickered and hissed through its lower grille.

She slept on a daybed, under a pink blanket. Before a huge canvas with violent colors and no frame, arms of vegetation, white and purple, bent over her from a dozen pots, spidered in the bay window, or hung from the mantle.

"Christ, it's hot!" Denny said. "How she sleep in here?"

"Go on," Kid said. "Wake her up."

Denny frowned at him.

"I want to watch," Kid said.

Denny's tongue pushed out his lower lip a moment. He stepped forward—

Her cheek was flat on the pillow, and both bare shoulders touched the sheet. Her hand near her face bent sharply at the wrist. One heel, greyed at the rim, stuck out, toes turned in.

—put one knee on the mattress (she went *Uhhhh*, turned her face down, and her heel pulled under the cover), swung the other over to straddle her and grabbed her head.

"Hey . . ." One arm shot out and waved. "God damn, let go of my . . ." She got over on her back. "What are

565

you doing, huh . . . Oh, hey . . ." The arm came back and locked around Denny's thigh. "Look, babes, I'm sound asleep, huh? . . ."

Denny shook her head again—

"Oh, come *on* . . ."

—and laughed. "Kid said I should wake you up."

"Huh?"

"He wanted to watch."

"With binoculars from the roof across the street?"

"He's right here."

"Where?" She pushed herself up and looked around Denny's leg. "Hey!" Then a smile poured into her face, mixing with the sleep like milk poured into water, while her eyes cleared like jade.

"I brought you something," Kid said.

"Him?" She laid her head on Denny's hip. "I like him. He's great and it's very sweet of you. But I'm awfully sleepy."

"Not that." Kid pulled out the books. "These." He sat down on the bed.

Her T-shirt was torn at the side and he could see the place her breast started, and then the nipple under cloth. (He contemplated the difference in the two colors for which even he could only think of the word white.)

"What are—?" Then she let go of Denny who sat down, shaking the bed. "Oh!" She took them from him, grinning.

"What are those, anyway?" Denny asked.

"Kid's poems!" Lanya said.

"I guess one of those can be for you."

"Yeah?" Denny asked. "Why didn't you give it to me before, then?"

Lanya gave Denny his book and opened hers. "It really looks nice . . . I think you sat on this one a while, though."

"You're not mad at me now?" Kid asked.

"Was I ever?"

"Sometimes I think you're stranger than I am."

"Women's Liberation has really lost us the prerogative of changing our minds, huh?" She sighed. "Enough people will be glad to see it go."

"Hey," Kid asked, "are you balling Madame Brown?"

"No!" Lanya looked up from the book, surprised. "What gave you that idea?"

"I don't know." Kid shrugged. "She likes chicks, and, well, you're here—"

Lanya frowned. The book slapped the blanket. "Can't two people just be friends in this city?"

"You should be balling her." Denny didn't look up from his.

"Why?" Lanya demanded.

" 'Cause she's your friend." Denny said.

Lanya's frown lingered a moment. Then she laughed. "What are you, the Counter-Culture Dale Carnegie? Hey, move off my foot, huh?"

Denny moved. "You write all this stuff?" He turned another page, turned back to the cover, opened it again. He turned another page, closed it, opened it. "Hey, *this* is the thing they keep on advertising in the God-damn newspaper, huh?"

"Sure is." Lanya turned another page too. "Oh, you're a doll to bring me this." She glanced at him, looked back. "I . . . I'm afraid I have a confession, though."

"What . . . ?"

"I've already given away about twelve copies each to practically everybody I know. And I think I have about half the poems down by heart—I knew them before they were published, really."

"That's all right." Kid tried to discover whether that made him feel bad or good.

"I was going to ask you to write something in the copy I've been holding onto for myself. But this one's mine now." She held it up to her nose. "It smells like you. That's much better than an autograph, I think."

Denny closed his book for the sixth time and sniffed it. "You like the way Kid smells?"

"Mmmmmm." Lanya put her arm around Kid's chest and tugged him backward. "Don't you?"

"It gives me a hard-on," Denny said, "sometimes. But I don't know whether I *like* it."

Kid lay back. "I guess that's nice you've been giving them out. I didn't know you could get hold of it that long. No, you're going to tell me about some more days I missed. How do you get this jungle to grow in here?"

"It's all coleus," she said. "They'll grow any place."

"Creepy." Kid said. "You've got it like a fucking jungle."

"Plants are relaxing."

567

"Long as they don't take a bite out your hand when you're trying to water them." Through the variegated purple, he focused on the plaster ceiling (another white than either cloth or flesh). "Do I know Wally Efrin?"

"Wally? Of course you do. He was in the park commune. Why?"

"We murdered him yesterday."

He thought she might move suddenly; she didn't. "What?"

"Yesterday, one of our more retarded honkeys beat in his head with a pipe: to death. You were there. It was happening downstairs in the kitchen while we were out on the balcony."

"It was Dollar." Denny said.

"Lord . . ." she whispered, grave with shock.

"Dollar was the one you were talking to who was so—" Denny went on.

Till she interrupted: "—I remember Dollar. Wally?"

"Which one was Wally?" Kid closed his eyes.

"He was the boy who was always talking about Hawaii."

"Oh." Kid opened his eyes again. "Yeah. I remember."

"He's . . . dead?"

"Some stupid fight. I don't know what happened. We were all there, and nobody—"

"I know what happened," Denny said. "Dollar's a fuckin' nut! Somebody probably said something he shouldn't've and Dollar didn't know when to stop."

Lanya sucked her teeth. "That's Wally. Kid, that's terrible! What's going to happen?"

He shrugged. "Like what?"

At which point Denny drew in his breath and said, "Shit, man! You write some God-damn bloodthirsty poems. This one about the kid who fell down the elevator. Wow . . . !"

Kid looked up at Denny.

". . . 'Both legs . . . broken,'" Denny puzzled out, "'pulp-skulled, jelly-hipped—'"

Kid suddenly rolled over, grabbed the book edge, and pulled it down (". . . Hey, what the . . . !" Denny said), craning over Lanya's lap to see the print.

But Denny *had* misread the line.

Kid lay his cheek on Lanya's and Denny's legs.

"You all right?" Lanya asked, and Denny touched his face.

"Yeah," Kid said. "Sure, I'm fine." He raised his head again. "How'd you know what it was about? It doesn't say anything about an elevator shaft in the poem."

"I . . . well, I figured that's what it . . . ?" Denny looked surprised. ". . . had to be about. I mean I was there, remember?"

"Oh." Kid put his cheek down. "Yeah."

"Is Dollar still over with the scorpions?"

"Yeah."

"Is he all right?"

"If Copperhead doesn't decide to kill him. John and Milly came over with a delegation this morning. To protest. I started to yell at Dollar. Just yell, that's all. Just to find out what had happened. He's not really all there, and you have to talk loud to get through, you know? And they started to get squeamish."

Lanya said: "I've never believed in capital punishment either. And Wally wasn't the most popular person around. Rap, rap-rap-rap-rap: He *could* be annoying—"

"That's *not* the point—"

"I *know!* I know, believe me. I know." She rocked him, bending above. "I mean I just . . ."

"You don't believe in capital punishment as long as there're mental hospitals, right? With violent wards. Well, we don't have any violent wards. We don't have any jails either."

"But you have to—"

"Look." Kid pushed himself up and twisted around. "*I* don't believe in capital punishment period! I think if one person kills somebody else because he gets his rocks off, or he just wants to, that's . . . well, maybe not right. But a bunch of people getting together and deciding to kill somebody else because it's anything from right to expedient, is *wrong!*"

"Lord," Lanya said again. "Donatien Alphonse François de—"

"What?" Denny said.

"Never mind." She pushed the covers down. "Let's go for a walk or something. I'm not sleepy any more."

Kid suddenly reached across to yank Denny's hair.

"Hey—!"

Kid pulled the boy down. Denny dropped the book and grabbed at Lanya's arm. "What the fuck—"

569

"You like my smell?"

Lanya said, "Hey, what are you—" and backed away, frowning.

Denny's arm flapped. Kid caught it with his other hand and forced the head into his lap. "Come on, you like it?"

"Shit!" Lanya tugged Kid's wrist. "Let *go* of him!"

"Hey . . . !" Denny laughed loudly, nervously, and pulled; couldn't get loose, and yelled a little. "Come on, lemme—"

"You like it, you little bastard!"

Denny held onto Kid's hip and twisted his face.

"Yeah . . . !"

"Kid, will you stop that, for God's—"

Kid suddenly let go, held both his hands in the air. "See?"

Denny put his other arm around Kid's other hip. His face against Kid's jeans, he took a breath.

"It's okay when I do him like that," Kid said to Lanya. "He likes it. You like it, don't you?"

"Fuck you," Denny said. "Yeah, I like it."

"*You* like *my* smell?" Lanya suddenly swung up on her knees. One knee went above Kid. She grabbed him by the ears. He started to say, "Hey . . ." but let it turn into a roar, and raised his head to muffle it between her legs. She bent and locked her arms behind his head. "You like my fucking smell? Yeah, you like it . . ." and then she laughed and fell over on her side. The bed's feet bounced.

He said, "Yum yumyumyumyum," as fast as he could. Her legs were warm and blocked his ears. A ligament defined itself across his jaw.

Still laughing, she said, "I don't think I can keep the rough act up as long as you can, though."

He got his mouth free. "I like it anyway. For break-fast, for lunch, for dinner . . ."

"Hey." Denny's face appeared above Lanya's thigh. "Ain't we making a lot of fucking noise? What sort of patient she got in there anyway?"

"Jesus . . ." Lanya laughed.

"She's a shrink," Kid said. "She's a God-damn fucking head-shrinker. She takes crazy people like us and makes us all better."

"I want to go for a walk," Lanya said. "Will you two please get up and let me put my pants on?"

570

"She's really a head-shrinker?" Denny asked. "She got some crazy man in there?"

"Yes," Lanya said. "Now will you please move your ass off my foot?"

"You just don't want to ball," Kid said.

"Not true. I just *do* want to get some air."

Kid rocked up, stood. "Okay. Fine. Who can ball with all these venus fly traps leering at you anyway?" And realized they made him feel far more uncomfortable than he could, comfortably, admit. On the desk in the bay window lay his notebook.

"Fine reason to get out of here," Lanya said.

"I dropped my book behind the bed," Denny said. "Just a . . . eh . . . there, I got it."

Kid went to the desk and opened the grimy cover. Folded inside was the sheet from the telephone pad, grilled with his handwriting.

"And the galleys with your corrections are in the top drawer on the right." The last of her sentence was muffled by the T-shirt coming off. "Mr Newboy gave me everything just before he left, when we didn't know where you were."

Kid sat down on the chair's torn caning.

Quickly he flipped through till he found a three-quarter-blank page. He pulled loose his pen. The raddled pages chattered at the pressure of his ballpoint. He wrote very quickly, with his face screwed; his lips parted across his teeth, then pressed together again. Where his spine settled in the sacrum's socket, a suspended tension began to release. Neither he nor it had finished when Denny, behind him, said: "Kid?"

But he closed the notebook cover over the page. Then he turned around. Lanya, sitting on the bed in her jeans and sneakers, but no shirt, looked up from the book of poems.

Denny stood in the middle of the room, one hand flat on his thigh. "I . . . mmm . . . you said . . . I wanted to tell you, Kid, that, well, when you go on like that with me and call me names and stuff and push me around, I guess I don't mind it." He looked down and swallowed. "But I don't like it *that* much." The inflection of the sentence didn't resolve, so he added . . . "you know?"

Kid nodded. "Okay."

Denny swayed a little, uncomfortably. Lanya suddenly put the book on the floor, and walked up behind him. She put her chin on his shoulder, her arms around his stomach. Denny put his forearm along hers, rubbed the back of her wrist, and waited.

Kid went and put his arms around both of them; Lanya's bare back under his hands was very warm. One of them held on to his waist. After a moment Denny said: "You're both in the wrong position. Him in front and you on my ass, I don't get a chance at nothing— Hey . . ." And pulled Kid close again when he started to back off. Lanya, head bent, hair brushing Kid's nose over Denny's shoulder, looked up with wide, wide eyes— brighter than any leaf about them. Kid blew at her nose. Denny wriggled. "I don't think three people can kiss each other at the same time . . ." he said.

"Yes we can," Lanya said. "Here, see . . ."

A minute later, heads together, arms locked around one another's backs, Kid said, "This is comfortable."

"I think," Denny said, moving his head down between their chins, "I smell more than either of you."

"Mmm . . ." Lanya nodded.

"Didn't you say something about wanting to go out?" Kid asked.

She nodded again. "Mmmm? Let's go."

First cold air under his left arm, then his right. Her fingers on his chest were the last to leave him.

He looked at the desk and wondered whether he should take the notebook.

"You sure keep it hot in here," Denny said.

"Oh, would you turn that off for me?"

"How?"

"Never mind. I'll do it."

Kid looked up: Lanya squatted before the heater, grunting and twisting at something inside.

"There." She stood. "Let's go."

"You ain't gonna put no shirt on or nothing?" Denny asked.

The sides of the heater, cooling, clanged.

"Be a doll and let me wear your vest?"

"Sure," Denny shrugged out of his. "But it won't cover your tits."

"If I wanted them covered, I'd put on a shirt." She took the vest from him. "There're some advantages to living in this city."

"You're a funny lady."

"You're a funny boy."

Denny bit on his lip a moment, then nodded deeply. "I guess I sure as fuck am."

"What are you grinning about?" Lanya asked Kid.

"Nothing," and ended up grinning harder. "You gonna take up chains too and be a member . . ."

She considered a moment, sucking her underlip. "Nope." One nipple was just visible inside the leather lapel. The other was covered. "Just curious." And picked up her harmonica from the floor by the bed.

They play me into violent postures. Adrift in the violent city, I do not know what stickum tacks words and tongue. Hold them there, cradled on the muscular floor. Nothing will happen. What is the simplest way to say to someone like Kamp or Denny or Lanya that all their days have rendered ludicrous their judgment of the night? I can write at it. Why loose it on the half-day? Holding it in the mouth distills an anger dribbling bitter back of the throat, a substance for the hand. This is not what I am thinking. This is merely (he thought) what thinking feels like.

They were quiet through the living room. At the head of the steps Denny began giggling. Lanya hurried them down. They reached the porch, hysterical.

"What's so funny?" she asked three times; three times her face recovered from the contortions of mirth.

Kid thought: There's a moment in her laughter when she's *very* ugly. He watched for it, saw it pass again, and found himself laughing the harder. She took his hand, and he was very glad she did. The stridence smoothed in his own voice.

Denny's leveled, too, from some relief Kid did not understand.

"Where's your school?" Kid asked.

"Huh?"

"Denny told me you were teaching in a school. And Madame Brown said something about classes."

"*You* told me about the school," Denny said.

"It's right down there. That's where we're going now."

"Fine."

She bit both lips and nodded; then slid her arm up to link Kid's elbow, held out her other hand to Denny . . . who pretended not to see and tightroped along the curb. So she dropped Kid's hand too.

573

The green jacket was new. The shirt between the brass zippers looked old. He came from the corner, unsteadily, head slightly down. His varying steps took him indiscriminately left or right. Twenty-five? Thirty? His black hair was almost shoulder length. In the bony face there was nothing like eyes. He . . . staggered closer. Tiny lids were pursed at the back of fleshed-over sockets otherwise smooth as the insides of teacups. One leaked a thread of mucus down his nose. He came on, missing the lamppost by a lucky detour. On twine around his neck hung a cardboard sign, lettered in ballpoint:

"Please help me. I am deaf and dumb."

Denny stepped closer to Lanya and took her arm. The blind-mute passed. "Wow—" Denny started, softly. Then breath stopped.

The heavy blond Mexican in the collarless blanket-shirt hurried from a doorway. The irregular tap of the blind-mute's cowboy boots stopped when the Mexican seized his shoulder; his head came way up and swung in the air like sniffing as the Mexican took the blind-mute's hand. He pressed his fist against the mute's palm, and pressed again, and pressed again, making different shapes. The blind-mute nodded. Then they hurried to the corner, holding one another's arm.

"Shit . . ." Denny said, wonderingly and lingeringly. He looked at Lanya. "We seen him before, you know? The big spic. He pushed Kid, you know? Just came up to him in the street and pushed him."

"Why?" Lanya asked. She reached across to hold the right lapel of Denny's vest with her left hand.

"Don't tell me everything in this fucking city happens for a reason," Kid said. "I don't know."

"Well," Lanya said, "usually, in Bellona, everything happens for . . ." Then she sucked her teeth. "Deaf and blind? That's heavy. I was in San Francisco once. You know the welfare office on Mission Street?"

"Yeah," Kid said. "I tried to get on welfare out there, but they wouldn't let me."

She raised an eyebrow. "I was walking by it once . . . reading the signs on the Page Glass Company? When I looked down, I saw a dumpy woman in a flowered house dress leading this old man who was tapping a cane. But when she got to the steps, she stooped down to feel around. And she was saying, 'Now I know . . . I know

574

where it is.' Three more steps, and I realized she was blind, too. I watched them till she finally got them through the door. It was fascinating, and a little horrifying. But when I went on, I began to think: What a marvelous image for most of human history, not to mention current politics. Practically every relationship I know has something in it of—and then of course it struck me, and I began to laugh right there on the street. But the point is, it really hadn't occurred to me all the time I'd watched them. And all I could do was think how lucky I was and I had decided not to be an artist, or a writer or a poet. Because how could you use a perfectly real experience like that in a work of art today, you know?"

"I don't get it," Denny said. "What do you mean?" (Without Denny's vest, Kid noticed one of the five chains Denny wore was copper. His back and shoulders, here and there pricked with pink, looked white as stone.)

"It's just that . . ." Lanya frowned. "Well, look, Denny—you've heard the expression . . ."

He hadn't.

When they'd tried to explain for a block and a half, Kid realized that Denny was now between them once more ("But *why* can't you use something anyway that somebody already said?" Denny demanded once more. "I mean if you say where you got it from, maybe . . ."), but Kid could not remember switching positions: gruffly he switched back.

"That's the school." Lanya squeezed Kid's arm. "It doesn't look like one, I know. But I guess that's the point."

"It looks like a drug store," Denny said. "I wouldn't want to put a school in no place that looked like a drug store. I mean not around here."

"It was a clothing store," Lanya said.

"Oh." Denny's tongue made a hillock on his cheek. "It sure looks like a drug store."

"I hope not." Lanya actually sounded worried.

"I don't think it should look like any sort of store at all," Kid said. "I mean if you don't want people busting in."

"That was the idea," Lanya said. "I didn't think it looked like a store at all. At least since we took the sign off. Just a house with a large front window. There isn't any writing on it."

"I seen drug stores like that." Denny nodded in self-corroboration. "People around here are always busting in-to drug stores and doctors' offices 'cause they think they can find shit. And they find some, too."

Lanya jiggled the handle. "I thought it looked like a coffee shop." The door swung in.

Turning inside, Kid saw curtains in front of the window. Light prickled the weave. "I didn't notice those from the outside."

"That's because the window's so dirty it really doesn't matter."

"It sure is dark," Denny muttered. "You got elec-tricity here, don't you?"

"There're lanterns," Lanya said. "But I don't think we'd better use them now."

"Put your lights on," Kid told Denny. Denny's hand rattled in chains.

Lanya's hand leapt to shadow her face. ". . . that surprised me!" She laughed.

Shadows from the chairs swung on the linoleum as what had been Denny moved toward a blackboard stand. "It sure looks like a school *in*side."

"Actually started out just as a day-care center. You have no idea how many children there are in Bellona! We don't either. They don't all come here."

"You take care of them while their parents go to work?" Kid asked.

"I really don't know what their—" she glanced at him, closed her lips, moved them across her teeth—"what their parents do. But the kids are better having each other to play with some place where it's safe. And we can teach things here. Things like reading; and arithme-tic. Paul Fenster got the thing started. Most of the kids in my section, in all the sections really, are black. But we've got three white children who're holed up with their parents over in the Emboriky department store."

"Shit," Denny said. "You take those bastards?"

"Somebody has to."

"I don't think *I'd* fall in love with any of them."

"Yes, you would. They're all cute as the devil." She picked up a lantern that had dropped from its nail and hung it back. "When Paul suggested that I take over a section, at first I really wondered. I'm not a social crusader. But you wouldn't believe how good these kids are. And quiet? With a bunch of seven, eight, and nine

576

year olds, it's a little unnerving just how quiet they can be. They do practically anything I say."

"They're all probably scared to death."

Lanya made a face. "I'm afraid, really, that's what it is."

"Of you?" Denny's great light bobbed.

"No." Lanya frowned. "Just scared. It was my idea to try actually *teaching* something . . . just to pass the time. It works out a lot better than letting them run loose—mainly because they don't run." She blinked. "They just sat around and fidgeted and looked unhappy." She turned to the table. "Well, anyway, here—"

The aluminum face of a four-spool tape recorder, interrupted with a quorum of dials, twin rows of knobs, tabs, and multiple ranks of jack-sockets, gleamed above coiled wire, on which lay three stand-mikes and several earphones.

". . . since you're here—" Lanya sat one rod-mike upright—"you might as well help. I was going to try something out that I've been working on—Denny, if you're going to keep that thing on, please be still! It's distracting!"

"Okay." A chair rasped back. Denny's light, quivering, lowered about it; and consumed it. "Okay. What do we do?"

"You can start off by keeping quiet." She pressed a switch; two spools spun. "Then it gets more complicated. This is a great machine. It's two free and reversible four-track recorders on one chassis, with built in cell-sink." She pressed another tab; the spools slowed. She blew a run on the harmonica toward the mike, pressed the *off* button. Another finger went down on a black tab. The spools halted, reversed; another finger went down.

The spools slowed, stopped.

Another finger.

They reversed.

From under the table—Kid's eyes jerked down to the metallic-shot speaker cloth—the harmonica, twice as loud and with echo, rang like a mellophone.

Lanya turned a knob. "Level's a little high. But that's the effect I want for the third track."

The tape ran back (more tabs: *chud-chuk*), reversed. Lanya blew another run, and replayed it.

"Gee," Denny said. "On the tape, it sounds just like you playing."

No, Kid thought. It sounds entirely different. He said: "It sounds pretty good." But different.

Lanya said: "It's about okay." She turned one knob a lot, and another only a little. "That should do it." She pressed another tab. "Here goes nothing. Be quiet now. I'm recording."

Denny's chair leg squeaked on the floor.

Lanya scowled back over her shoulder, and positioned herself at the mike. Without lifting her sneaker heel, she began swinging her knee to keep time. Her shoulders rounded from the armholes of Denny's vest. She blew a long, bending note. And another. A third seemed to slide from between them, bent back, hung in the half-dark room—light glowed in three of the dials; red hairlines shook—and turned over, became another note, did something to Kid's eyebrows so they wrinkled. And Denny had turned off his shield.

She played.

Kid listened, and remembered crouching in dim leaves, leaves tickling his jaw, while she walked beyond him, making bright music. Then something in the playing brought him to the here and now of the room, the plastic reels winding, the tension-arm bouncing inside its tape loop, the needles swinging, three (of the four) signal lights glowing like cigarettes. The music was more intense than memory; emotional fragments, without referent scenes, resolved through the brittle, slow notes. She moved her mouth and her forehead; her two forefingers rose vertical over the silver (her nails were slightly dirty; the music was wholly beautiful), then clamped. Silver slid between her lips. She played, played more, played some phrase she'd played before, then turned the tune to its final cadences, taking it to some unexpected key, and held and harped on the resolving chord sequence; a little trill of notes kept falling into it, every two beats; and falling; and falling.

She dropped the harp, clutching it in both hands, against her bare breasts, and grinned.

After maybe ten seconds, Denny applauded. He stuck out his legs from the chair, bounced his heels, and laughed. "That's pretty good! Wow! That's pretty nice!"

Kid smiled, pulled his bare toes back on top of his

578

boot, pushed his shoulders forward; in his lap his hands knotted. "Yeah . . ."

Lanya grinned at them both, stopped the tapes. "I'm not finished yet. You guys have to help on the next part." She plugged in one earphone set, tossed it to Denny: "Don't drop—"

He almost did.

She started to toss another set to Kid; but he got up and took it. Tangled cords swung to the floor. "I'm going to lay in another track on top of it. Remember that little part just before the end? Well, this time you have to clap there, five times, each time a little louder. And sort of shout or hoot or something on the last clap." She played the section over.

Denny started to beat his hands together.

"*Just* five times," she said. "Then shout. I'll bring you in. Let's try it." They did. Denny hooted like a choo-choo train, which broke Kid up laughing.

"Come *on*," Lanya said. "You guys don't have to over-do it!"

They tried again.

"That's it. Put your earphones on, and we'll lay it in."

The rubber rims clasped Kid's ears and damped the room's silence down a level.

"I'm going to be playing something entirely different." Lanya's voice was crisp and distant through the phones. "But I'll signal you two in with my elbows." She flapped one at them and put on her own phones. The vest swung from her sides. "There we—" she turned on the tape. Momentarily the silence in Kid's phones crackled—"go."

Kid heard Denny's chair leg squeak; but it was on the tape.

Then, a long note bent.

Over it, Lanya began, as the beat cleared, to rattle out, like insects, high triplets, first here, then up half a step, then down a whole one. Her mouth jerked across the organ and she dragged a growl up from the windy lower holes. Then jerk: bright triplets rattled. The old melody wound, beneath them and decorated by them: each time the third batch arrived, they thrust it into a new harmony, and toward Kid's and Denny's cadenced entrance:

579

Denny leaned forward, eyes wide, hands out and up, cradling an invisible globe. Kid's fingertips tickled his palm . . . His head was down, to feel the rhythm; his eyes were wedged at the top of his sockets, to watch her.

Lanya swung her whole body back and brought both elbows in to her sides.

Denny's globe collapsed.

Kid's palm stung. And stung again. And again. And again—the sound, and his head, rose—and again: his face burst with noise and sudden joy.

Through the phones, from under his own cry, the rough fabric of the ending, with the little trill falling into it again and again, secured in its foreign key, brought all to its proper close.

Denny, still seated, looked about to explode. And, after five seconds shouted: "Whoop-eee!" and bounced in his chair.

"You like that, huh?" Lanya grinned over her shoulder, ran the tape back. "I want to lay in one more track. You guys have to do the same thing again." To Denny's frown, she explained: "Because I want it to sound like a whole *room* full of people clapping, not just you two. See if you can shout on a different note. I mean, if you hooted high before, hoot low. And vice versa."

"Sure," Denny said. "Where'd you learn to do this?"

"Shhh," Lanya said. "Let's just do it. I don't have too much to play on the harmonica this track. But don't let what I do throw you off."

Kid nodded, pulled apart the phones at his ears—two rings of perspiration cooled—then let them clamp back.

"Here we go." She glanced back. "Ready?"

The crackle . . .

The chair squeak . . .

Then the long note, bending . . .

Lanya reinforced the first phrase with middle notes, dropped the harp from her mouth, took a step back, and whistled a phrase over the quiet beginning. One of the harmonicas, already recorded, took it up. Kid suddenly understood the movement between soft and loud built into the two tracks already down; Lanya whistled again. Again the harmonicas carried the whistling into their organ-like development. She put the harp to her mouth, gave some bass strength to another section, waited, glanced at Kid, at Denny. Another thirty seconds of music

580

gathered itself together: suddenly she whistled shrilly, and her elbows came down.

Kid and Denny clapped.

So did Lanya, taking a large step back from the mike, bobbing her head and whacking the back of her harmonica hand against her palm. They clapped through the ringing five, and all shouted together with the voices already taped. Once more Lanya was at the mike, harp at her mouth, weaving high shatter-notes through the ending tapestry.

Then silence.

She said, softly, breathing hard: "There . . ." and pressed a button. The tapes halted.

"Jesus . . . !" Denny stood. "That's wild! Where'd you get the tape recorder? I mean, how'd you learn—"

"Paul borrowed it from Reverend Tayler for me."

"You do a lot of that stuff before?" Denny asked.

"Nope." Lanya took off her own earphones, hung them over the mike's jutting bar. "It's just something I wanted to try out. I've worked with tapes before but—"

Kid said: "Let's hear the whole thing!" Taking off his earphones, he came up beside her.

"What are you gonna call it?" Denny clacked his earphones down on the table.

"—Watch it," Lanya said. "Those are delicate."

"Sorry— What's its name?"

"For a while—" she ran her thumb across Kid's chest—"I was thinking of calling it *Prism, Mirror, Lens.* But then—" Denny disappeared in his ball of light; Lanya squinted, stepped back—"what with that big thing we saw up in the sky . . . I don't know. Maybe I'll just call it *Diffraction.* I like that."

Holding his lips between his teeth, Kid nodded. "Go on." His lips came loose and tingled. "Play it."

Denny turned on like a frozen node of incandescent gas, moved center floor.

Tapes turned.

"Here we go . . ."

Denny stilled.

". . . I want you to note—" Lanya lay her harmonica on the table, then raised one finger—"that something like that usually takes six or eight hours to do; we have been at this no more than two hours."

From the speakers beneath the table, Denny's chair leg squeaked.

581

Kid put his own phones down softly and listened (thinking: Temporal diffraction? Two hours? It had seemed perhaps twenty minutes!):

The long note bent.

Somehow, lost in a machine, I have been able to grasp and strip from the body of experience three layers of living theme: she inscribed them with her music, laid them over one another so that, thinned by tape and transistors, their transparent silences and aural aggregates, as she, the inventor, conceived them, clear for me, the invented one, at last. (On the tape Lanya whistled and played with her own whistling, the harmonica cradling its brittle, upper notes with low, breathy ones.) Is that where it goes (thinking:) when it goes? This is melody and there—the shrill whistle which Kid realized now was the real, musical signal for the clapping to begin—which began! He listened to a room full of people clap in time. One of the tracks was heavily echoed and made the clapping seem to come from dozens. The claps mounted; a final clap, and the dozens shouted—among them he recognized his own voice, and Denny's, and Lanya's; but there were many others. Their shouts died over a discord no single harmonica could make.

But probably any three could.

The finale cleared in its higher, supporting key; trills of notes fell into, and trills of notes rose out of, the moaning chord. The sound clutched at him, tightened his stomach.

Lanya listened, arms at her sides, head down, frowning with concentration. The white pips of her upper teeth dented one side of her lip.

The piece ended.

She still listened.

Then Denny applauded and laughed. Another Denny, on top of him, shouted, "Whoop-eee!" And Denny across the room, encased in light, said: "Hey, you know we got company in here? Look back there . . ."

Lanya's head came up suddenly. She turned off the tape.

Denny's light was over near the darkened corner. "Back behind the blackboard there."

"Huh?" Kid stepped forward.

"There's a big old nigger bitch in here, and, man, she's about to shit!"

582

"Denny!" Lanya exclaimed, and ran through the edge of his light, which turned, laughing, after her.

Kid pushed away the blackboard, looked down.

The board-stand's wheels stopped creaking.

The woman wore a black hat and a black coat, the hem rumpled on the floor around her. She blinked up at them, feeling for the string handles of the shopping bag beside her. Catching the bag up, she breathed a word all wind.

"What do you want?" Lanya asked. "Are you . . . all right?"

The woman's eyes narrowed at the light that was Denny, came to Kid's and widened. She blinked again. "You got juice and cookies . . ."

"What?"

"This is the school?" Her voice was still breathy. "You got the juice and the cookies for the children? Oh, I'm sorry!" Her knuckle rose to dent her double chin, a gesture recalling June. "I thought I could get some from here, you know? I live in Cumberland Park? And the store where I go all the time ain't got none no more. I go in there every day and I get some every day, but I go in there yesterday and there just ain't nothing. Nothing at all. Oh, God . . . from the children! I'm so sorry!"

"Then," Lanya said, "why don't you go to another store?"

"Oh, I'm sorry! I really am . . ."

"You got juice and cookies?" Denny asked. "Whyn't you give her some?"

"Because this is . . ." Lanya's lips worried the teeth behind them. "You wait here." She walked from the circle of Denny's illumination; Kid heard a door.

The woman transferred her bag to the other hand. "Taking from the children. That's just so awful!" Her voice was weak and low as some man's.

Lanya stepped back into the light. In one arm were two number ten cans of grapefruit juice. In the other were two boxes of Tollhouse cookies, glistening in cellophane. "You take these. But don't come back here. Don't break in here and try and take stuff out. Find another store. There's one four blocks up from here that still has things in it. And there's another one a block and a half down, right by the burned-out dry cleaners."

The woman, her tongue tip pink between her lips, blinking, opened her bag.

The can and the boxes went chattering in.

Lanya walked to the front door and held it open.

The woman glanced at Kid, at Denny's light, quite distressed, and stepped unsteadily forward. At the door she hesitated, suddenly turned to Lanya: "You teach little children dressed like that, half naked with your breasts all hanging out like that? Why, that's *terrible!* It's a disgrace to God!" Then she fled, coat hem swinging above her splayed heels.

"Get that!" Denny (lights doused) ran forward. "You want us to take back our God-damn juice and—!"

"Denny!" Lanya blocked him at the door.

"I mean will you get that shit!" He turned in her restraining arms, shaking his head. "Why'd you give her the damn stuff?"

"Oh, come on. Let's go!"

"I mean, God damn, she didn't even say whether or not she liked your music!"

Lanya held on to Denny's shoulder. "Well, maybe if she was hungry she didn't really care about the music. Hiding back there for a couple of hours—"

"Then what's she care that much about your tits for?" Denny shrugged her hand away. "She could've come out. We wouldn't've done nothing. Shit!"

"Well, I'm not going to let it bother me," she said. "So don't let it bother you."

Kid thought: How did she get in here in the first place? Then thought: What was I just thinking . . . it was something I wanted to ask. "Yeah, let's go, huh?" He laughed, and thought: What was the thought that just slid off the tables of my mind?

Kid followed them outside. And thought: She is bothered.

"Close the door, will you?" Lanya said.

"By the way," Kid began, "how did she . . . ?"

Denny glanced back at him.

Lanya didn't.

"You know?" Kid caught up to her. "I wonder if there're really any children ever in there? I mean I'm having a harder and harder time believing in anything I don't—"

"Huh?" Lanya looked up.

Deep in thought, she hadn't heard.

He grinned at her and rubbed the back of her neck. *"Diffraction,"* he said. "I like it."

"Mmmm." She leaned her head back and shook it. Hair brushed his hand and wrist.

"What are you going to do with it?" he asked.

She shrugged: "I don't know. What are you going to do with your poems?"

He shrugged. "Maybe write . . . some more."

She slipped her shoulder under his arm. "Maybe I'll compose some more . . . maybe." Suddenly she said: "A disgrace to *God?*—really!"

Denny, who walked along the curb, picking at his chest, glanced back. And grinned.

What she's thinking, Kid thought, is seldom what it looks like she's thinking. Sometimes (as he walked, he catalogued incidents) he'd found her thoughts far simpler than her complicated expression of them. Other times (this catalogue was longer) more complex.

Denny, holding his chains with both hands and walking with his head down, to examine what was beside his feet, was easier, nastier, duller and (the attraction beyond the body) predictable.

Lanya lifted her harmonica (when, Kid tried to remember, had she snatched it up from the table inside? But that was lost too, with the others) toward her mouth. Her hair pulled from his forearm as she stepped ahead of him; his arm slid down the vest, fell.

She bent over the silver organ. Then she lowered it. Then turned it in her hands. Then she raised it. Then she lowered it again.

2

At the head of the stairs, Kid bent to scratch Muriel, who licked furiously at the ham of his thumb.

Madame Brown came into the hall and said, "Now I didn't even know you'd gone outside! I could have sworn I'd heard you back in Lanya's room just now. Would you like wine, or coffee?"

"Could I have both?" Denny asked.

"Certainly."

"Just wine for me," Lanya said. "That's probably what you want, too, right?"

"Yeah," Kid said. "Thanks."

They followed Madame Brown into the kitchen.

"You want to come to my party?" Kid asked. "Up at Mr Calkins'."

"The one he's giving for your book, that everybody's been talking about?" Madame Brown smiled. Her necklace glittered.

"Huh? Yeah. I guess that's it."

"I'd be delighted."

Lanya, legs crossed, raised the front feet of her chair. "He hasn't invited me, yet." Above her, in the grey window, an asparagus fern turned on a string.

"Oh, you know you two are invited." Kid sat on the kitchen stool.

"You got a party? Up at Calkins'?" Denny, hands in his pockets, leaned on the stove. He moved to let Madame Brown get the enameled coffee pot.

She said: "That should be quite something."

"He said bring about twenty or thirty friends. I'm going to bring the whole nest up."

"Marvelous!" Lanya clapped her hands. "I'm sure that's what he wants."

"Yeah? You think so?"

Madame Brown, dubious, set out glasses and picked

the gallon jug up from the floor. "Well, it will be interesting." She twisted at the cap, her face lining with effort. "It's in three Sundays, isn't it?" The cap seemed stuck. "Mary will never forgive me if I go. She's invited me for dinner. But I wouldn't miss it for the world."

"Here. I'll do it." Kid opened the bottle and poured out yellow wine. "You got lots of patients here?"

Madame Brown, seated in what looked like a lawn chair, observed her glass. "A few. Would *you* like to come and have a session with me some afternoon?"

Kid looked up. And thought: I'm embarrassed. Why?

"Lanya's told me about some of the things you were feeling, and how upset you'd been. And about your memory problems. If you'd like to talk about them with someone, I'd be very happy to."

"Now?"

Lanya rocked in her chair.

Denny, sitting at the table now, looked back and forth between his wine glass and coffee cup.

"Goodness, no. Perhaps some afternoon next week. That would be best for me. I'm terminating sessions with two patients then, and if we want to work out something further, it would be a little easier to make arrangements."

"Oh," Kid said. "Yeah. You give therapy to people now?"

"Yes, I have been for quite a while now."

Lanya said, "I told Madame Brown you'd been in therapy before."

"You told her I'd been in a mental hospital?"

"You mentioned that to me once yourself," Madame Brown said.

Kid drank some wine. "Yeah. I'd like to come and talk to you. Thanks. That's nice of you."

"You think he's crazy?" Denny asked. He'd only drunk from the coffee. "He acts pretty funny sometimes. But I don't think he's crazy. Not like Dollar." He looked over his cup at Madame Brown and explained: "Dollar's killed somebody already. Beat his head in with a pipe. Now Dollar's a *real* nut. You wanna talk to him?"

"You shut up, huh?" Kid said.

Madame Brown said: "I'm afraid I don't have facilities for handling . . . real nuts. 'Crazy' and 'nuts' are terms doctors don't use—or shouldn't. But, no, I don't think Kid's crazy at all."

Denny's head had gone to the side and his tongue

587

into his cheek, listening for patronization. His mouth changed shape over the cup. He'd apparently found it.

"I don't want to start any long-term thing," Kid said, "where I come back and back—yeah, I know that's how it works. But I just don't want to get into that."

"Whether or not you needed something long term would more or less depend on what we found out in the first sessions, wouldn't it? So we'll do first things first."

"Okay . . ." Kid felt wary.

"You know—" Lanya's chair legs came down— "that whole thing about Dollar killing Wally has really got me upset."

"What is this," Madame Brown asked, "about someone killing somebody?"

So they told her.

"Now *he* sounds nuts." Madame Brown nodded.

"Oh, he ain't *that* nuts," Denny answered.

Madame Brown sighed: "Well, I suppose that afternoon did provide some extenuating circumstances." But she sounded more worried than convinced.

The bell rang.

"My patient. Well, my break is over." Madame Brown left the room.

As soon as she'd gone, Denny said: "Did you know that while you was asleep last night, the guys had two girls in the back they were shagging? Man, them niggers really went to town! I used to watch a lot, but I never took no turn before. One of them, the little white one, she was freaky, man! Really. Freaky. Glass said I could take a turn, if I wanted." He revolved the cup to align the handle with a crack between the table boards. "So I did. To come, though I had to pretend—" Denny glanced at Kid—"stuff with you."

"You been *busy*, huh?" Kid hadn't known; he was surprised.

Denny looked at Lanya. "I pretended about you too."

"I don't know whether I should be flattered or not." She rocked her chair again. "I've always pictured myself as a pretty worldly young lady, but you guys have a way of making me feel like I just got out of a convent. Not—" she let the chair legs down—"that I'm trying to keep up . . . well, maybe I am, just a little." She stood, stepped around the table corner, and put a hand on either side of Denny's face, which rotated between her palms, mouth opened. She dropped her mouth on his. He held the edge

588

of the table and strained his neck to kiss her. Finally, he let go with one hand and put it around her waist. "Hey—" he pulled his face away from hers—"that's nice," giggled, and kissed her again.

Kid's laughter made them look.

"What would you do," Kid said, "if I brought the whole nest around and had them *all* lined up, taking turns?"

Leaning against Denny's shoulder, Lanya frowned. "I wouldn't put it past you, you bastard . . . Naw, that's not true. You wouldn't." She glanced down and sat on Denny's knee. Denny immediately settled one hand over her breast and frowned at her. "Gang bangs, chains, leather—it isn't my scene."

"I've got a hard-on," Denny said.

"You've had a hard-on ever since I met you," Lanya told him. "Look, you two: two guys making it together turns me on. That's all. Most of my friends have always been gay. That's what I dig."

"I know a lot of guys who dig dikes," Denny said.

Lanya bit his ear.

"Owww . . . !"

"Anyway," she said, "that's the turn-on for me. *Not* getting gang-shagged."

"Glib." Kid rocked his stool legs now. "But logical."

"I think you look cute in my vest," Denny said. "You think I look cute without it?"

"As a bug, babes," Lanya told him.

"Hey," Denny said. "Are you mad at me?"

"No," she said. "Just a little confused." She looked at Kid. "I can never figure out if you're the person I keep thinking you are."

Kid stood up, walked over, and stopped with his hands on Lanya's shoulders, his legs astraddle Denny's knee. "If I talk about you screwing Denny or me, it's for real. If I talk about you screwing anybody else, I'm joking. See? And you can do or talk about whatever you want."

"And I think you misunderstand me entirely—" she nodded with a look both wary and wry—"sometimes."

He kissed her (face turning between his palms) and had to bend his legs. She turned her head gently back and forth, rubbing his tongue with hers, and meshed her fingers behind his neck, pulling his down, harder. Finally he had to settle his weight on Denny's thigh. Denny took

Kid's shoulder with one hand. The knuckles of the other moved against Kid's breast, fondling hers. Kid's hands slid between Lanya's back and Denny's belly.

"Both of you," Denny said, "weigh more than I do. Either me or the chair is gonna go, one."

Lanya laughed into Kid's mouth.

"Let's go back into your room and ball." Kid said.

He had actually thought one or the other of them would protest.

Geoff Rivers	Arthur Pearson
Kit Darkfeather	Earl Rudolph
David Wise	Phillip Edwards
Michael Roberts	Virginia Colson
Jerry Shank	Hank Kaiser
Frank Yoshikami	Gary Disch
Harold Redwing	Alvin Fischer
Madeleine Terry	Susan Morgan
Priscilla Meyer	William Dhalgren
George Newman	Peter Weldon
Ann Harrison	Linda Evers
Thomas Sask	Preston Smith

At her desk, he read the list for the sixth time. The sky beyond the bay window, dense and low, darkened toward evening. Roberts or Rudolph, Rivers or Evers: Fantasize a persona for any. Which, he pondered, would I pick myself? Some permutation . . . Gary Morgan, Terry Rivers, Thomas Weldon? None was his. Was one perhaps nearer than the other? No . . . if they are all real people, he reflected, then each is just as important. Hey, Kamp, isn't this what that democracy's about that put you up on . . . a moon? (But I don't *want* one. I need one about as much as I need a handful of dollars.) Lips tight, he picked up the papers: Three sheets from the phone pad, two pieces of newsprint, the back, blank pages of a paperback, some sheets of Lanya's paper—all he had written since *Brass Orchids*. I promised not to write any more; Newboy promised I would. Kid smiled, putting one paper behind the other. He slipped *Brass Orchids* from beneath the notebook, opened it, closed it, opened it again. Holding it on his palm too long made his stomach ache. Such a strange, marvelous, and marvelously inadequate object! He was still unable to read it

590

through. He still tried. And tried again, and tried till his throat was constricted, his forearms wet, and his heart hammered down where he'd always thought his liver was. Neither dislike nor discomfort with the work explained that. Rather the book itself was lodged in some equation where it did not belong, setting off hyperradicals and differentials through all the chambers of his consciousness. He looked over at the notebook, read what was on the page behind the list:

> Lingual synthesis: Wittgenstein, Lévi-Straus, Chomsky—I suspect it is what they were getting at: Attempts to reduce vast fields of Philosophy, Anthropology, and Linguistics to sets of parameters that not so much define as mirror the way in which philosophical, anthropological, and linguistic information respectively fit into, upon, and around the mind itself. Those particularly parametric works (the Tractatus. La Geste d'Asdiwal, Syntatic Structures—though all three men have written much longer works, work of this type must be very short; none of these is above 30 thousand words) do not discuss fields of study; they drop careful, crystalline catalysts, which, on any logical mind (as opposed to trained minds familiar with galleries of evidence and evaluations) perforce generate complicated and logical discussions of the subject using whatever evidence is at hand, limited only by the desire or ability to retain interest in the dialogue propagating in the inner ear.
>
> In an age glutted with information, this "storage method" is, necessarily, popular. But these primitive

was the end of the page. He did not turn to the next. Wittgenstein, Lévi-Straus, Chomsky: He mulled their sounds. A year, a year and a half ago, he had read everything he could find by one.

He had never heard of the other two.

"Lingual synthesis . . ." That was nice on the tongue. ". . . particularly parametric works . . ." He picked up *Brass Orchids,* balanced it on blunt fingers. ". . . careful, crystalline catalysts . . ." He nodded. A

591

particularly parametric work of careful, crystalline catalysts in lingual synthesis. That, at any rate, was the type
of object it ought to be. Well, it *was* short.

One of them turned in the bed.

One of them turned again.

He looked across the room:

The tent of a knee. An arm over an arm.

The chair back was cool against his. Caning prickled
the bottom of one thigh. The plants leaned from their
pots.

He pinched the bright chain across his belly.

Dark ones coiled the clothing on the floor.

Suppose, he thought, she wants me to stay and him
to go. Well, I get rid of the bastard. Suppose she wants
me to go? I get rid of *all* the bastards.

But she won't. She likes privacy too much. Why else
would she go along with this? Along? Something in me
would like to have it that she is doing this *for* me. But
all joy in it comes from those moments when it is obviously real as her music, and personally otherwise.

I am restless.

She turns restlessly.

His arm, limp, moves with her moving shoulder.

Lanya blinked, raised her head. Kid watched her
eyes close and her head lay down. He was smiling. He
turned *Brass Orchids* in his hands, turned the loose pages,
as though he might heft, through some quality other than
weight, the difference.

The notebook was open again at the list. Puzzling,
he read the names once more (it was almost too dark),
this time right to left, bottom to top:

Preston Smith	*Thomas Sask*
Linda Evers	*Ann Harrison*
Peter Weldon	*George Newman*
William Dhalgren	*Priscilla Meyer*
Susan Morgan . . .	*Madeleine Terry . . .*

3

"Why'd she kick us out?"

"She didn't kick us out. She had things to do. She'll be down to see us. Don't worry."

"I ain't worrying." Denny balanced along the curb edge. "Shit, I could have stayed up there for the rest of my life and been happy. You on one end and her on the other."

"How'd you manage to eat?"

"Present company excepted—" Denny tugged at his vest—"I'd just send out for it. You sure she wasn't mad at us?"

"Yeah."

"Okay . . . you really think she's gonna come down and visit the nest?"

"If she doesn't, we'll go up and see her. She'll come."

"She's a nice person!" Denny emphasized each stress with a beat of his chin. "And I really like that song. *Diffraction*, huh?"

Kid nodded.

"I hope she comes down. I mean I know she likes you, 'cause you wrote a book and everything, and you known her a long time. But I'm just a fuck-up. She ain't got no reason to like me."

"She does anyway."

Denny frowned. "Sure acts like it, don't she?"

The street light above them pulsed . . . at half strength; then died. The sky sheeted over with one more film of darkness. The only other light to come on was two blocks away; it pulsed, pulsed, pulsed again.

Someone moved into it and shouted, "Hey! Hey, Kid! Denny!" Others trooped into the wavering circle.

"What the hell are they doing here?"

Denny shrugged.

In the middle of the next block, Dollar, lugging the brass lion on its broken base, pushed between Copperhead and Jack the Ripper. "Hey, we gotta move, you know? We're movin' again!" Dollar was grinning.

Copperhead was not. "The fuckin' house burnt up on us! How you like that? The fuckin' house burnt up!" A knapsack, one green with his fatigues, swung about his shins. He hefted the strap to the other hand.

"Jesus," Denny said. "All my shit . . . ?"

"What happened?"

"Nothin'," Copperhead shrugged. "You know . . . it just, well. . . ."

"The whole damn block," Siam said. "About an hour ago. Shit, it was something!"

Kid felt his heart thump once (like it always did when he found out somebody he knew had died) and in the hollow remains, he thought: That isn't so much a reaction as it is a fear of what the reaction might be. The house burnt down? The . . . house burnt down? But that seems so easy. The house . . .

He asked: "Was Nightmare there?"

"Fuck," Copperhead said. "Fuck. He and the Lady was off somewhere. Thirteen was gone somewhere too. Fuck."

Glass chuckled. "I could smell Thirteen's stash burning right up. Sure wished I knew where he kept it, and I would have got it out for him. But when it was burning—" he swung a pillowcase down from his shoulder into his arms—"you sure could smell it. You know I been in seven God-damn fires. Seven times I had my house burn out from under me. Lost my mother in a God-damn fire."

"In Bellona?" Siam asked.

Glass looked at Siam, realization in his face that he had been misunderstood. "No . . ." He hugged up the pillowcase. "I ain't been in no fire in Bellona, except this one."

"Where are we going to move?"

Denny said, "You want to go back to Lanya's and see if she'll put us—"

"Not on your fucking life," Kid said.

"I mean," Denny questioned, "you said she wasn't mad at us none."

"You got some place for us to move?" Copperhead asked.

594

"Nope," Kid said. "Come on. We'll find one."

"Now we don't want no place that's gonna burn up again before we get in it," Copperhead said. "Do we?"

Scorpions mumbled outside the circle of the lamp. Some carried mattresses, some cartons, some shovels and tools.

"Come on down this street," and the cavalcade practically filled the alley. Trees had been planted and ringed with ornamental fences. But each trunk was charred to a black fork with twisted tines. "That wooden house must have gone up like a matchbook."

"Naw," Copperhead told him. "Nobody got hurt. Nobody didn't really lose nothing they didn't want to lose. We all got out in time."

"I got the lion!"

Kid turned on Dollar's pocked and stubbled grin.

"Man, I wouldn't've left my lion behind for nothing. It's the only fuckin' thing I own. You got that for me, Kid, remember? You got that for me and I wouldn't leave behind nothing like that for anything in the world, you know?"

"Denny . . . ?"

Behind Dollar, she pushed her way forward. Her arms were full, her hair was tangled, and one heavy cheek was smudged.

"Denny, I got your stuff out!"

Her eyes, sweeping among them, caught Kid's and swept away.

"Denny? I *think* I got it all . . ."

"Oh, wow!" Denny said. "Oh, hey, you did? Wow, that's great!"

"Here: I got your shirts." She caught up with them. "And—" she glanced up blankly at Kid; the heavy breasts in her blue sweatshirt pressed out against bags and packages. Her small, full fingers had left the brown paper sweaty so that it bellied between them—"and the posters down from your wall. And the picture books. I didn't bring the blankets . . . I didn't bring the blankets because I thought it wouldn't be too hard to get some more blankets—"

"You got my radio?"

"Of course I got your radio. I *think* I got everything—there wasn't very much—except the blankets."

"I don't care about the God-damn blankets," Denny said. "You okay? I mean the house was burning down,

595

and you were back up in there getting my stuff?" He took a paper bag from her—

"Oh, watch out . . . !"

—pulled *Brass Orchids* from his back pocket and dropped it inside.

"What's that?"

"Nothin'. What you so curious about? Oh, hey! You got my game in there."

"Un-huh. Denny?"

"Why don't you let me carry the rest of those?"

"That's all right. Denny?"

"What?"

"I don't think me and my friend—"

She glanced back.

Kid did too.

The blond girl in the pea jacket was just behind them.

"—are going to stay with you guys any more. I just wanted to bring you your stuff."

"Hey," Denny said. "Why not?"

"I don't know." She adjusted the other bags. "We just want to go somewhere else. We don't want to be members. And we know some nice people who have a house where we thought we could stay. It's just girls there."

"Just girls?" Denny said. "You ain't gonna have no fun there."

"Boys can visit and stuff like that. Boys just don't *live* there. I just don't think I want to live with you guys any more. I mean after the fire—" once more she glanced at Kid—"and everything. You know."

"Jesus," Denny said. "Jesus Christ. Well, I mean, I guess so, if you don't want to any more."

"You can come visit me, too. If you want."

"Shit," Denny said. "God damn."

"I just think it would be better. I mean if I live someplace else. It's a very nice place. They're very nice girls."

Denny was looking into the bag.

She said: "I'm pretty sure I got everything. What are you looking for? If it's not in there, it's probably in here."

"I'm not looking for anything."

"Oh."

The mask of Kid's face tingled. Suddenly he turned to Copperhead. "You ever been in any of these houses?"

"No."

"Let's try that one."

"Sure."

Kid turned to the others. "Hey! Hold up there, will you?" He walked up the unpainted steps. Halfway, he glanced back:

She shifted paper bags in her arms, biting at her lip while trying to get them comfortable. Denny looked at her, then at Kid, then back at her. The others shuffled and talked.

In his hand, the knob's squared and toothy shaft slid out another inch—

Kid pushed the door in.

The loose ceiling fixture—

He ran his eyes over the hall, waiting for sounds of occupancy.

The crayoning on the dirty wall—

He had the oddest feeling. "Anybody home?"

"Well, if they are," Copperhead said, "they can damn well get ready to move the fuck out. 'Cause we come to pay a long visit, right?" Others laughed. Copperhead called up: "Does it look okay?"

"Yeah. It looks pretty . . ."

"Should we come on up?"

"Yeah, come on."

At the end of the hall the bathroom door was open. Footsteps behind him passed around him; and somebody carrying the chained mannequin pushed by.

The house came alive with scorpions.

With a feeling of suspended confusion, he wandered through the front room into the kitchen.

Copperhead was looking in the cabinets above the sink. "Whole lot of canned stuff. That's pretty good. Too bad they left all their garbage though." A bag had broken under the table. The table was piled with garbage. The sink and the counter were heaped with dishes.

Kid decided he didn't like it here.

Outside the screen door, the sky heaved and twisted like a chained thing.

He turned abruptly into the living room.

The blond girl in the pea jacket sat on the couch, fists between her knees, watching two scorpions lay out a mattress on the floor. She looked at Kid, hunched her shoulders, and looked back at the scorpions. She seemed very tired.

"Hey, man," Dollar said behind his shoulder, "this is a really fine place." Clutching his lion, he shouldered open a door across the hall. Several guys were inside, straightening out mattresses and sleeping bags. Dollar pushed his way among them to set the lion in the window. He turned, silhouetted before the torn window shade. The brass beast peered by his hip from the sill. "Hey, man. You shouldn't have brought that old burned-up mattress with us. It's gonna smell up the whole fuckin' place." On the ticking was a charred halo around a crater two feet across of ashes and burned cotton.

"It's the only one I had," the scorpion (another white guy named California) said, and yanked it across the floor. He dropped the corner to overlap another.

Newspaper and magazine pictures had been at one time pasted over the wall; then some of them ripped off.

A black scorpion Kid didn't know stood up and grinned. "This sure beats the place were we staying, hey, Kid?" Squinting, he looked around. "Yeah, this is pretty nice."

I prefer, Kid thought, the red eyes, God damn it!

Across the hall, the door to the service porch was open. He started in, and stopped, one hand on the jamb. There was neither glass nor screening in the windows. Siam sat on a crate. "Hey . . ." He pulled the newspaper into his lap, and looked at Kid with growing confusion. "I was . . . was reading the paper." Siam offered a smile, thought better, and took it back. "Just reading the paper." He stood; the paper fell on the floor. The boards had once been painted maroon. "Is there something you want me to do . . . ? I was gonna help out with the moving, but my hand . . ." He gestured with his bandaged arm. At the place where the bandage wrapped his hand, the flesh was scaling. "I guess I can help set up some stuff," Siam said, looking at his grimy fingers. "If you want . . . ?"

"Naw," Kid said. "Naw, that's all right."

The verdigrised spigot on the wall splashed on the muddy drain.

Something clanked and ground behind him.

Kid turned.

The Ripper and Devastation wheeled the Harley up the hall:

"I don't see why you wanted to bring this piece of junk along. You can't get no gas for it, and you say the motor's all shot any way."

"Well, it's a good bike, if I could get it fixed."

"You want to put it in the bathroom like last time?"

"Shit, these cocksuckers get drunk and don't aim at all. And you know one of 'em's gonna piss on it just to see it rust."

"Aw, come on, mother-fucker—"

"No, man! Hey, Denny, can I put it in there?"

"I guess so." Denny stood by a doorway, both arms full of paper bags.

Kid walked up to him, took his shoulder. "She go?"

Lips pursed, Denny nodded, looking from one bag to the other.

Inside, someone leaned the shovels against the wall beside an ironing board.

They backed up the Harley to wheel it in.

"Hey, is this gonna be your room, Kid?"

Kid said, "Probably."

"It ain't gonna take up too much space. Later I can maybe find some place else for it, you know?"

"If it's in the Kid's room, nobody's gonna bother it."

"That's okay."

Kid squeezed Denny's shoulder. They stepped inside.

"Hey," Denny said. "It's got a loft!"

Kid's spine chilled. He stood very still. "Denny?"

"What?"

"Did the place where we came from have a loft?"

Denny looked puzzled. "Sure it did. But it wasn't as nice as this one."

"It wasn't?"

"This one's a lot bigger," Denny said. "And it's got a mattress on it."

"What was the place like we were living before?"

"Huh?"

"Describe it to me. I can't remember it. I can't . . . remember anything about it."

"What do you mean?"

"What color were the walls painted?"

"White weren't they?"

Frowning, Kid nodded. The walls about them were green.

"You really don't remember where we lived before?"

Kid shook his head.

"We had," Denny began, prompting, "a bunch of spades across the street from us? It was down about eight or nine streets from here. And over a little."

"How did it compare to here?"

"What . . . do you mean?" Denny asked again.

"How is this place different?"

"Shit," Denny said. "This place is about twice as big! Don't you remember how cracked the walls and everything were? This place is in pretty good condition." After a moment, Denny asked: "Is this gonna be your place?"

"I guess so," Kid said.

"Can I put some of my shit up there? These cocksuckers will walk off with anything you just leave around."

"Sure. Go ahead."

Denny flung up one of the bags, then the other. "I sure wish this one had a ladder. You're supposed to really climb up and down this thing?" The supporting beam had triangular notches cut into the side. Denny climbed up two, and looked back. "Hey, it ain't that hard . . . you really don't remember where we were before?"

"I guess . . . no."

"Wow," Denny said and pulled himself up onto the mattress. "You lived there an awful fucking long time." He looked at Kid again, frowned, responding to something Kid could feel moving in his face but could not identify. ". . . maybe not *that* long," Denny recanted, dubiously. He disappeared.

More people moved in the hall behind him.

"Hey, Kid," somebody said, but was gone when he looked.

He went to the post and climbed up after Denny. In the corner, he sat back and watched the boy thumbtack Koth the Dark Angel next to the day-glo Scorpio. Now Denny emptied the other bags between his knees. "I guess," he said after a moment, "she really got it all. That was pretty nice of her, huh?"

Kid nodded.

Denny crawled over the mattress, hesitated, then put his head in Kid's lap. Kid rubbed Denny's neck, looked down, surprised. Denny took two deep breaths.

He's gonna cry? Kid wondered.

"You all right?" Denny asked in a perfectly controlled voice.

"Yeah," Kid said. "What about you?"

"I'm fine," Denny said, listlessly. After a while, he said, "I'm gonna go down and check things out, huh?"

"Okay."

He sat alone, listening to the sounds of the house. Once he picked up Denny's radio and turned it on. There was not even static. No battery?

He turned the glass dice, watching reflected ghosts of his face. He turned up a mirror on his chain; comparison of the two images told him nothing. But he looked back and forth.

Someone banged on the boards beneath him.

"Hey, you up there? Kid?"

He opened his eyes; the dice rolled from his lap as he crawled to loft's edge.

Black eyes, broken tooth, hair with a braid undone: Between huge shoulders, the smooth and the scarred, Nightmare grinned. "Hey, you got yourself a real nice nest set up for you here, huh?"

"How you doin', man!" Kid swung his legs over, dropped to the floor. His body tingled, heels, chin, knuckles and knees.

Nightmare took a stiff step back, another to the side, and bobbed his head. "Yeah, you really got yourself set up. Really nice." He looked into the hall, nodded at someone who hailed him. "Stealin' all my folk away from me?" He glanced back, brows high and forehead furrowed. "You're welcome to the scroungy mother-fuckers! The niggers are okay. But the white ones, man. Shit . . . !"

Dollar said, "Hey, Nightmare—"

Shoulders raised; head lowered, Nightmare spat on the floor.

Dollar swallowed, and disappeared at a gesture of Nightmare's fist.

Nightmare turned, annoyance and concern weighting the ends of his eyebrows, the corners of his mouth. "Fuckin' psycho! You gotta treat these bastards like horse turds, man! Like fuckin' monkey puke! They all like you now. But you're gonna have to show 'em soon." He turned his boot on the gobbet. "And watch out for the ladies, they are particularly bad."

"Nightmare," Kid said, "most of the time, I can't even tell which ones the ladies are!"

"Got a point there." Nightmare nodded. "Altogether, how many you got here?"

"Don't know."

"I never did neither." In the hall, Nightmare squinted at the ceiling. "Yeah, this is going to be interesting."

Kid followed him.

"Somebody told me you fool around with boys, huh?" Nightmare nodded again, considering. "I was in reform school four years. Yeah, I know about that shit." He leaned out on the service porch (where two blacks man-handled a chipped washing machine), and pulled back, still nodding. "So you got Copperhead, Glass, and Spitt all here in the nest with you. That's pretty cool, I guess. I wouldn't have the balls for that. I tell you that now."

"Which one is Spitt?"

Nightmare's face swung back, ruptured with dis-belief. "Which one is Spitt?" Disbelief erupted into mockery. "You wanna know which one is Spitt?" Mockery erupted into laughter. "Hey, Spitt! Come here." He turned in the hall.

"Yeah?" The white youth came from the room. A matted belly, massing toward the pubic, disappeared under a turquoise and silver buckle. A scar careened across the tight, bald pectorals, and turned down toward his navel. He wore no vest. His only chain was his pro-jector. Wrists and forearms were furry, his biceps veined and bald. His cheeks wore the few hairs of someone who could never have a beard. "What you want?"

"The Kid here thought he'd like a formal introduc-tion. Kid, this is Spitt. Spitt, this is the Kid."

"Huh?" Spitt said. "Eh . . . Hi." He wiped a wet hand on his black jeans and held it out.

"Hi," Kid said, but didn't shake.

Spitt put down his hand and looked uncomfortable. "I was in the kitchen, trying to wash up some of the God-damn dishes. They ain't gonna stay clean very long, but I thought for the first day, maybe. Did you want something?"

"You go on back," Kid said. "Nightmare's a clown, you know? Yeah, and throw out some of that garbage, huh?"

"I was gonna." Spitt's eyes flicked, questioning, be-tween them. He looked down, moved his feet a couple of times, grunted, then went into the other room.

"Now you mean to tell me you don't know who put the split in Spitt's tit?" Nightmare demanded; with his finger, he flicked the orchid hanging at Kid's neck. It ticked and chattered in the chains.

After silent seconds Nightmare, aping frustration, shook his head and assumed a theatrical whisper. "He's the guy you cut, man, when him and Glass and Copperhead first beat the shit out of you up at Calkins'! You mean you didn't know that?" Nightmare's expelled "Ha!" of laughter made at least two of the scorpions in the front hall turn around. They turned back. One, a black woman, was hammering a nail into the wall, using a piece of plank to hit with. "They been tellin' me you're a little punchy sometimes, too. Like you're not always there, you know? Well, I tell 'em just to watch out for you, huh? The Kid knows what he's doing better than any of you mother-fuckers, I tell 'em."

"Glad you think so," Kid said. "You going to stay here?"

"Me?" Nightmare buried a thumb in the links looping his chest. "Am *I* gonna stay here, with these scroungy mother-fuckers?" The thumb wagged. The links rattled. "Shit!"

"What about you and Dragon Lady?"

"We're around, you know. Dragon Lady used to have this all-suede gang, man, over on the edge of Jackson. You know where Cumberland Park is?"

Kid nodded.

"Man, they were some mean mother-fuckers. I mean, *man* . . ." Nightmare looked in the living room again, stepped inside.

Kid followed.

On the table in the corner were stacked a dozen copies of *Brass Orchids*.

"You got to watch out, down there," Nightmare said. "I mean it's getting pretty hungry, down there. Since the water main broke, it's just been sort of terrible. Two guys I know already got killed, down there. Yesterday. And somebody else two days before that."

"I heard most of the people moved."

"And the one's that are *left*, man, are pretty God-damn strange, you better believe it. Dragon Lady got her nest down there. She's pretty cool, you know?"

"And you're really going to leave all this for me?"

"I don't want it." Nightmare frowned at the table.

"Why?"

"You asked me that already."

"And I may God-damn well ask you ten times more, too! Until I find out."

603

"I told you I was just curious—"

"Me! Why *me!*" The three scorpions who came through the room now and didn't look were making a noticeable effort. "Come on, Nightmare. Talk to me."

"Well; you come." Nightmare turned around and leaned his butt on the table edge. "You go. You got a certain style." He shook back his hair. "You're crazy. People say you don't even know who you are. That's okay by me. I don't want nobody asking about Larry H. Jonas before he come here, either— Then, every once in a while, you do something really crazy-ass brave." Nightmare gripped the edges of the table. "Now I ain't brave. I think anybody who is, is stupid. I'm just not so spaced out today I can't remember what I did yesterday—which is more than I can say for you. I think that's the only reason I ended up the boss." He shrugged. "Now you got it. You don't want it, you just take off all them chains, ball 'em up in a little ball, throw 'em in Holland Lake and go on do something else. Somebody else'll pick it up—Copperhead, Raven, Lady of Spain . . . maybe some nigger you don't even know their name yet." Nightmare's face twisted. "But I don't see you doing that, you know?" He pawed something from his back pocket, brought it up between them. "And this shit—" A copy of Brass Orchids, folded. "You know I been actually trying to *read* this? I don't understand shit like this, man! But every day for a fuckin' week you got a fuckin' page or half-page in the fuckin' newspaper. Like it was a fuckin' movie, or something." Nightmare turned, and with his book knocked the stack. Copies spread the table. Three fell on the floor. "You don't ever talk about it; least I never heard you." Nightmare turned the folded book. "It ain't got no name on it. I mean I don't even know if it was really you wrote the stuff. I mean that's what some people are saying. But I'm gonna look at it anyway, see? Amd I'm looking. Then I find that part about *me!*"

Kid frowned.

Nightmare conducted the next sentence with the folded book. "Yeah, you know; don't tell me you didn't put nothing about me in there." He opened the cover, brushed over the pages.

Kid stepped around to see.

"Here!" Nightmare thumped the page with bunched fingers, leaving four prints. "That ain't me you talkin' about?" The whole page was grey with finger marks, the corners limp.

Kid took the book. The next page was clean. So was the page before. "Yeah . . ." Kid said. "I guess I had you in mind when I was writing that."

"You did?" The question's falling inflection rang with mistrust.

Kid nodded, closed the book and thought how inaccurate a truth he was perpetrating.

"Oh." Nightmare pulled the book from him. The pages parted automatically at the questioned passage. "Well, reading a fuckin' book and finding somebody talkin' about *you* is some pretty weird shit, you know? I mean I haven't made up my mind whether I like it . . . course, you didn't say anything bad about me." Once more he nodded, pursed his lips, parted them in a silent shape: "You don't say anything good, either." Again he stared at Kid. "That is pretty weird. I just wish I understood shit like this better, you know?" Suddenly, a grin opened around Nightmare's broken tooth. "That really is me, huh? And you weren't puttin' me down or nothing? I told Dragon Lady that was me, and she tried to tell me I was full of shit. You just wait till I tell *her*." He folded the book, tapped Kid's arm with it, and stabbed at his back pocket a couple of times, till it went in. "You are a very strange person. And you do some very strange things." Nightmare stood up and walked out of the room.

Kid saw Spitt and Glass, who had been standing just inside the kitchen door, going toward the table.

Nightmare mumbled very loudly:

"Too much."

"You want to come to a party?" Kid called after Nightmare in the hall.

"Here?"

"At Roger Calkins'."

Nightmare's head went to the side. "What am I gonna do at a party up there?"

"It's my party. Calkins is giving it for me at his place. Bring Dragon Lady along."

"Just your friends? In his place?"

"His friends, too."

"Oh," Nightmare said. "She ain't gonna come without her sidelights."

"Adam and Baby?"

605

"Yeah."

"That's all right. All of you come on up. It's in three Sundays, by the paper date. Soon as it gets dark."

"Calkins' friends, them people you read about in the paper?"

"Probably."

"That astronaut guy gonna be there?"

"I guess so."

"Mother-fucker," Nightmare said. "You know, Baby don't put no clothes on. I mean he's funny and he just refuses, flat out, you know? And Dragon Lady ain't gonna come if he don't."

"He can come. If he wants to come buck naked, that's all right with me."

"Yeah?"

"You guys come any way you want. Bring your lights. That's all they probably care about."

"I don't got nothing to dress up in," Nightmare said. "This ain't a party you have to dress up for?"

"I'm coming like this."

"You know I'm gonna tell Baby you said to come on up to that party buck naked." Nightmare frowned. "He probably gonna do it, too. Cause he's a real funny mother-fucker. I mean he walks around in the street like that, all the God-damn time." The frown broke before laughter. "I gotta see that. Yeah, I gotta go see that shit."

"Three Sundays," Kid said.

"Maybe we all come over here first?" Nightmare offered.

"Okay. I'll see you then, if I don't before."

From the nail hung the framed photograph with the broken coverglass. Father, Mother, the two brothers and the sister gazed reprovingly in their dated dress. With black marker, on the glass, someone had drawn, across the boy's and the woman's mouth, outsized moustaches.

"Hey, there, pops!" Nightmare saluted the bearded gentleman in the photo. "Kid, I'm gonna split. Thanks for the invitation. I'll tell the Lady. We're all waiting to hear about your next run."

Nightmare opened the door.

Their shadows spilled the steps into night.

"So long." Nightmare trampled his own down to the sidewalk, waved, and stalked away.

Kid looked back down the hall. All three light bulbs were working, as well as the one in the bathroom. I guess, he thought, I picked a good nest. The films of his thought hanging beyond words curled and withered, made all the motions of the thinnest tissue caught in blasting flame. I guess . . .

Spitt stepped out of the living room. "We gonna eat out back, hey, Nightmare still here?" His hand, straying on his chest, concentrated its motions around the scar.

"Nope."

"Oh."

Behind Kid, the closing door clicked.

"He could'a stayed," Spitt said. "We got plenty of food for tonight—"

Kid wandered down the hall.

I am a parasite. I have never made a home. Even here, I have not instructed a home to be made. In my whole stay, though I cannot recall looking for food, among these twenty, twenty-five faces, some among them must take that care. I crawl from place to place, watching homes created or crumbling around me.

He wondered what kind of party Calkins expected.

Breath bucked from his nose; that was laughter.

On the service porch, Kid looked down into the yard (fire light on the ceiling beams), grabbed the sill of the window, reared back, vaulted: "Whooop-*peee!*"

Others laughed.

"Jesus Christ," Raven said. "You'll break your fuckin' neck!"

Kid staggered, agonized.

Three hands came to steady him.

And three voices:

"Man, that must be fifteen feet!"

"It ain't fifteen feet—ten? Twelve? Here, Kid, have a drink. You know there's a God-damn liquor store just around the corner and ain't nobody even broken in the window?"

"It's broken now. Shit. We're gonna have to work a week to drink up all that booze."

Kid took another step, grinning, between the scorpions who flanked him. Pain shot again from calf to thigh. Did I break my knee, he thought. No. It'll be all right in a minute . . .

"You all right, Kid?" That was one of the black girls with bare breasts joggling jingling links. "Man, you scared me good when you come leaping out like that!"

Kid took another breath and grinned. "I'm okay." He

leaned on the black shoulder, while she pulled away from another girl to support him. She laughed, shifted, steadied; and Kid pulled away, took another step, another breath. "Yeah, I'm okay. What we got to eat?"

The Ripper, with a can opener, kneeled over a big, odd-shaped can. "One of them canned hams." The tin wept gelatin down its red and blue label. "We found three of them."

The fire crackled on the bottom of a kettle hung on a pipe propped on cinderblocks. "The gas isn't working in the stove?"

"Yeah," Denny said, across the fire, "but we thought we'd cook out."

The first bubble on the . . . soup? stew? grey at the kettle edge, shook its reflection of the porch window frame, and burst. Another bubble grew.

Kid took his weight off his throbbing leg. Better. He flexed, feeling the tender machinery of knee and ankle jarred from place. It was his booted leg. Perhaps the soft sole had hit a rock?

"Don't throw your God-damn bottle in the yard, man. Don't you know about pollution? We gotta live here."

"You shut up, or I'll pollute you!" a short-haired white woman said.

"Throw your fuckin' bottle over in the *next* yard, will you?"

"Okay, okay . . ."

Light snarled in the loops of chain, laid out dull splashes on dark leather, lit the trough beneath a black lip, put wires of light in greasy brass hair, glistened on the puffed rim of a lashless eye, sank in the graphite nap bushing an ovoid skull.

The Ripper laughed and bent and wiped at his mouth with his wrist. The orchid, from the chain at his neck, spun bright petals.

"Here . . . !" A bottle neck hit Kid's mouth, clicked his teeth, hurting his gum.

"Christ, man!" Kid beat it away. "I don't want no God-damn wine," which was the taste he licked from his lower lip; he rubbed his mouth. "Somebody get me something real."

"You want this?" Denny asked.

"Yeah. What is it?" Kid drank, and cleared his burning throat. "You know when I was your age I use to be a fuckin' booze hound? I don't even like the stuff now." He took another, smaller drink, and handed the bottle back to Denny; "But I was a fuckin' hound." Guys argued:

"*Now* what you gonna do with that?"

"Cut it up, cook it over the fire."

"You can eat it right out of the can like that."

"Hell, no. That's ham, man. You'll get trichinosis!"

"Man, you can't get trichinosis from no canned ham!"

"Well, you're gonna cook mine before I eat any."

Somebody passed out long-handled kitchen forks. ("That's all right. I got my huntin' knife.") Bubbling soup dribbled the kettle's side. Kid's leg felt about okay. He turned, smiling at the dark, as scorpions joggled him to get at the meat. ("Hey, somebody start opening up the other one, will you?") Soup hissed and chattered in the flame. The edges of the evening softened with the liquor. He looked for Denny and Denny's bottle.

"*Hey*, Kid!" The smile was a pit of flickering rot and silver. "You really doing nice here, huh? Beautiful, yeah. Beautiful."

"Well, I'll be a mother-fucker!" Kid announced. "I didn't even think you were gonna *live* another twenty-four hours, much less show up here."

Pepper gaped wider. "Sort of . . . *hun*gry!" His chin jutted on the syllable. He joggled a wine bottle in his spiky hand. "You got a really nice nest here; and I'm all ready for a run."

"Help yourself." Kid gestured over the heads around him. "You just go right on and help yourself."

A very blond and square-jawed scorpion pushed from the center of a bunch of blacks (Raven, Jack the Ripper, Thruppence, D-t, Spider) stepped up behind Pepper, and said, "Jesus Christ . . . Shit!" He seized Pepper's scrawny shoulder. "What are you doing back here, you sad-assed mother-fucker? Why don't you get your ass out of here before I—"

"Hey, now . . ." Pepper said. "Hey . . . !"

Others, looking, moved aside. The short-haired woman stepped forward. Copperhead stopped her with a freckled hand on her chained and vested shoulder.

"Come on and get the fuck out of here," the square-jawed blond said. "Nobody wants you around stinking up the place now. You been run out twice. Somebody gotta run you out again?"

"Man, I'm *hun*gry!" Pepper complained. "Kid said I

could—" And under the thrusting hand, stumbled into Kid.

Kid stepped back, thought, no, with no word on top of it. He swung his hand, and caught the back of the blond head so hard his palm stung.

"Owee . . . !" came unaccountably from Pepper, who scurried to the side.

The scorpion Kid had hit turned, his face screwed up.

No, Kid thought, this time *with* the word. I got a bum leg, I'm half drunk, and I'm beating on people? No. This is going to get me in trouble. "Leave him *alone!*" Kid said loudly.

Scorpions shuffled in the silence.

Priest kneeling over the ham squinted. He was so close to the fire his dark shoulders sweated.

Kid walked toward the scowling blond and took his shoulder. "Now you just go *on* and get yourself something to *eat!*" He shook the scorpion's shoulder in large motions. "There's enough for everybody, see?" Am I really getting away with this? Kid began to laugh. "Come on, give him a piece of ham." He pushed the scorpion toward the fire. And I'll just turn, walk away, and wait for a fork in my shoulder.

Kid turned.

Copperhead stood before the others, arms crossed, Glass to one side of him, Spitt to the other. The short-haired woman, shaking her head, was walking away.

Kid moved toward them thinking; I can't tell whether they're about to back me or jump me. Do the others know? "Whyn't you get yourself something to eat, too?" He walked by.

Some tension had broken with his laughter.

Thruppence said, "You got a ladle or a cup or something?"

Jack the Ripper said, "We got bowls and cups and things. Somebody washed all the fuckin' dishes."

Half a dozen crouched together behind the fire, shoulders smooth as great plums, hair wrinkled as prunes, holding forks over the coals, shifting hands suddenly sucking their knuckles.

He looked at a bottle.

"You want some of—?"

"Yeah." He took the bottle and another drink,

"Thanks," and kept circling. Two were necking under a tree. Momentarily he thought they were both boys.

Dollar lifted his face from the girl's disarrayed hair. "Hey, Kid . . ." He blinked in the firelight, his stubbly jaw blebbed here and there.

Kid stepped over Dollar's boots.

"You got something to eat yet?" Denny asked.

Kid shook his head.

"You take this. I'll get another one."

The cup was hot and soup had run down the sides. "Thanks."

"You won't get trichinosis from that ham if it isn't cooked through, will you?" Denny asked.

"If it comes out of a can," Kid said, "it's cooked."

"That's what I thought," Denny said.

He sipped, stinging the roof of his mouth. The sensation took seconds to subside to simple heat. He was looking, desultorily, for either Pepper or the scorpion who'd harassed him. He could spot neither around the fire. And people were going in and out of the house again.

Glass, Spitt, and Copperhead, less formally posed, but still together, stood to the side of the yard eating ham and soup. Kid doffed his cup.

"Can you hear that?" Glass asked.

"Hear what?"

"Listen," Spitt said.

Kid bent over the soup while it steamed his chin. The yard was filled with voices. "What?"

"There," Spitt said.

Perhaps two blocks away, a man screamed. The sound went on and on, died at the length of a long breath, and began again, this time shaking and breaking.

"You wanna go check it out?" Copperhead took another bite of ham. A line of grease glistened from the corner of his mouth into his beard.

"Naw," Kid said.

"You're the big hero, man," Copperhead said. "Don't you wanna go help a gentleman in distress?" Copperhead laughed.

"No, I . . ."

The man screamed again.

Momentarily Kid pictured the four of them foraging beyond the firelight, through darkened streets, the ululation filling the night about them.

611

"No, I don't wanna. I got Pepper fed. That's my heroics for the night." He sipped loudly and walked back among the scorpions around the fire. *When the neighbors are shrieking . . .* went through his mind but could not remember who'd said it.

"Here, Kid. You wanna use my fork?"

It was the blond scorpion who had tried to eject Pepper.

"Thanks." It was a long-handled, three-pronged laundry fork. Kid took a chunk of ham and squatted beside the fire. He squinted before flame. Trying to drink his soup, he spilled more over his hand. And even with the long fork, his knuckles were painfully hot. The blond scorpion, squatting beside Kid, watched the meat bubble and char. "Thanks for the fork," Kid said again after a few minutes and sipped from the cup once more.

The screaming had stopped.

Or there was too much noise to hear.

4

"Hey, Tak!"

"Kid?"

"What are you doing?"

"What are *you* doing? Can you get down from there? You better watch out . . ."

Kid let go of the beam and crabbed down the rubble, raising dust banks behind and an avalanche before.

"That was impressive," Tak said. "You're still going around with one shoe? You must have a sole on that foot like an oak board."

"Naw." Kid beat his foot again his black jeans, both legs grey to the knee. "Not really."

"You exploring in there?" Tak pushed up his cap to watch the smoke curl back through the girders. "How come you don't have the rest of the nest? I didn't think scorpions ever traveled alone."

"I come," Kid shrugged. "I go. I take them on runs. Where you going?"

"I'm on a mission of mercy for your girl friend."

"Lanya?"

"I volunteered to help her with her dress for your party."

Kid tried to hold back his laughter. It burst his lips' seal and lights shot either in his eyes or in the windows of the warehouse across from them.

"What's so funny?"

"She's got you turned into a seamstress?"

"She does not. Come on and I'll show you something interesting."

They walked the littered streets.

"You're going to come to the party, aren't you?"

"Not," Tak said, "on your fucking life."

"Huh? oh, man, come on. Calkins wants me to bring my friends. I'm going to take the whole nest along. Don't you want to see what happens when all us freaks get turned loose in there?"

"Not terribly. But I suspect Calkins does—though I've never met the man."

"Aw, come *on*, Tak—"

"No. Somebody's got to be around to read about it in the next day's gossip column. That's *my* job. You just have a good time and drink a glass of brandy for me. Swipe a bottle if they've got any good stuff and bring it back. I'm down to *Gold Leaf*. Somebody got into my liquor connection and made off with just about everything worth drinking."

"We got a liquor store right around our corner. What do you drink? It's got everything. Anything you want. You just tell me, and I'll get it for you."

"Five Star Courvoisier." Tak laughed his whisky growl and hooked his cap down. "Come on." As they left the corner, he asked, "How long you been up?"

"A few hours."

"Oh," Tak said. "Because I got up very early, when it was still getting light. I came over here, and you could see flames . . ." He nodded down the side street where turbulent smoke blocked vision less than two blocks away.

"You could?"

"Now it's just . . ." Tak nodded again.

Smoke bellied and heaved about the upper stories. The sky was thick as cheese and eveninged without shadows. I don't (Kid thought) get thirsty any more, but I'm always hoarse. Three boots and one foot ground the gritty street.

"Tak, where's the monastery from here? I don't mean Reverend Amy's church. I mean the monastery."

"Now this is . . ." Tak stopped. "This goes up into the city and turns into Broadway. You just go straight on to the other end of Broadway and you run right into it."

"Yeah? . . . Just like that?"

"It's a long walk. I don't know if that bus is still running. Over here." Tak stepped into the street.

The freight ramp sloped to a wooden door studded with rivet heads the size of fifty-cent pieces. Above, on rust-ringed iron, aluminum letters, forward on bolts, announced cleanly: *MSE warehouse space*. By the door a black plaque reflected Kid's face askew. White letters obscured his eyes and lips: *Mateland Systems Engineering Warehouse*. Kid struggled momentarily with a memory of

614

Author Richards while Tak took the hasp in both hands, grunted. The door rumbled back from a plank of blackness. Tak looked at his hands, their cleanness emphasized by swipes of rusty grease.

"Go on in." Tak held his hands from his hips to keep them from his pants.

Kid stepped in and heard his breath's timbre change. Iron steps rose to a concrete porch.

"Go on up."

Kid did and stepped sideways through the door at their head.

The skylight, three stories above, mapped continents in dirt and light, among longitudinal and latitudinal tessellations.

"What's in—" the reverberation halted him—"what's in here?"

"Go on," and Tak was without face. He passed ahead of Kid. Each boot heel on the concrete cast back stuttering echoes.

It was very cool.

Blocked by eight-foot plank X's, spools big enough for underground electrical cable sat about the floor among twenty- and thirty-foot stacks of cartons. Kid passed two before he recognized what was wound on them.

Later he tried to figure out what the process of recognition had been. At the moment of seeing there was a period in which all emotions were dead, during which he had gone up to one—yes, he had put out his hand, pulled it back, and just stood there a long while.

In hanks, in dripping loops from the drum (hundreds of feet? Hundreds of thousands? And how many drums were there in the block-square warehouse?) the brass chain, set with prisms, mirrors, lenses, looped.

He stood before the ranked glitter, waiting for it to strike up some explanatory thought.

The end of the chain hung to the floor, where a few feet formed a full (c.300 stars?) Pleiades.

There was an open cardboard carton beside the spool. Kid bent down, pushed back the flap. They looked like copper beetles. He pushed his hand into the metal tabs, picked out one—there was a hole at one end—and tried to read what was embossed on it. The light was too dim, and the corners of his eyes were stinging.

On the carton, however, stenciled in white, was: PRODUCTO DO BRAZIL.

Kid stood.

Tak had wandered some forty feet down an avenue of cartons.

Kid's eyes had cleared to the dim light enough to make out the stenciling on the boxes piled around him.

FABRIQUE FRANÇAISE

MADE IN JAPAN—the initial smudge must have been an 'M.'

ΠΡΑΡΜΑΤΑ ΕΛΛΕΝΙΚΑΙ.

Kid turned back to the chain. He had begun his observations in curiosity, but what generated had so little to do with answers that even curiosity blanked.

"Tak!"

"What? Hey, come over here. You seen these?"

Kid sprinted up the aisle between the piled cartons.

Tak kicked back a board cover. Nails squeaked, and the echo rolled among pyramided crates. "This is where you come to get 'em if you need any more."

The holders inside the slats reminded Kid of the square cardboards on which eggs were racked.

Some dozen had been removed.

The ones remaining, the size of golf balls and the color of gun metal, were blistered with lenses. The switch-pips all pointed to the left side of the crate. To the right were the metal loops to link them.

Kid picked up his own projector, watched it swing on its chain.

"They don't have any batteries inside them," Tak said. "You have to get those from stores in the city."

Stenciled across the inside of the crate top it said, "SPIDER."

On the crates piled around, Kid read:

DRAGON
LIZARD
FROG
BIRD OF PARADISE
SCORPION
MANTIS
MANTICHORE
GRIPHON

Kid lifted the corner of the holder. The layer beneath was full. "There must be—" he frowned at Tak—"*thousands* of them here?"

"I gotta get some stuff from upstairs," Tak said. "Come on."

"Tak." He looked at the myriad crates labyrinthed around. "There must be thousands of these things here! Millions, maybe!"

Dust filled a slant column from the skylight's marbled panes.

Tak went to the metal steps against the wall. "There's a whole lot of weird stuff in here." He leaned over the banister, grinned at Kid, and started up.

"Hey." Kid swung around the metal newel and followed him. "What did you come here to get?"

"It's upstairs."

The cardboard cartons piled by the wall were water stained. Plumbing rose beside them; the asbestos covering the pipes was mottled too.

"Here you go."

They walked down the balcony. Kid ran his hand along the rail, looking out across the warehouse.

"This place always remind me of the last scene in *Citizen Kane*," Tak said. "This is what I want."

Two bolts of . . . cloth (it was some sort of lamé. Kid couldn't tell, in this light, whether it was gold or silver) leaned against the wall.

"For the dress?" Kid asked.

"She was talking about it, and I told her I remembered seeing some stuff lying around." He picked up the bolt and unwrapped it. "I don't know if this is what she wants. It's pretty special. Go on and explore, if you want. I'll give a yell when I'm leaving."

Kid walked a dozen steps further, glanced back— Tak was still stretching out yards of cloth—then walked on.

The cartons near him—smaller and piled haphazardly—were stenciled with clumsy representations of zodiacal signs. He stepped around them. Another, opened like the box of tags downstairs, had been left in the middle of the plated walkway.

His own steps, even his bare foot, set off a metallic ring. The open top joggled with the shaking of the floor.

Diagonally across the cardboard was stenciled:

RED EYE–CAPS

He did not frown. All the muscles of his face urged him toward the expression. But something else was paralyzed. He squatted, pushed back the top.

They had probably all been stacked neatly together once. But movement had jumbled most of them. He picked up one. It was like a concave disk the size of a quarter, cut from a pingpong ball.

It was red.

He turned it in horny fingers. But it doesn't *explain* it, he thought. Then blinked, because his eyes were filled with water. It doesn't! Gooseflesh settled over his shoulders, his back, his buttocks, like gauze. What could anybody want with . . .

He blinked again.

The tear fell on the cap's matte surface. Where it spread, the color deepened to the luster of scarlet glass.

No: That was a double thought, with and without word, and hardly an overlap.

The cap cracked in his fingers.

He dropped it in the box, stood in a motion. He let out all his breath, took in some more, and swallowed in surprise at the echo.

He stepped back.

When do they put them on? When do they take them off?? *Where* do they put them . . . I would rather think (the thought kaleidoscoped and went lucid) that these have nothing to do, nothing to do with . . .

Kid stepped back again, turned, hurried up the balcony.

Tak, the lamé folded over his arm, squatted by another box. "I got everything I need. Find anything interesting?"

From where Kid stood, looking down, the visor masked the engineer's eyes.

The terrible thing, Kid realized, is that I'm too scared to ask!

"Hey, are you all right?" Tak raised his head. The shadow bobbed on the top half of his face. "You're not going to go into another one of your flip-outs, are you?"

Kid tried to say, I'm all right. All he did was expel another breath.

From the carton Tak removed some square piece of metallic equipment and stood. "Let's go." He sighed.

Halfway down the stairs Kid managed to say, "I'm all right." It hung detached in dusty light, blunted by echoes. Tak gave him a sarcastic glance.

Is this, Kid thought, one of the things that, a minute

hence, will slip from the register of memory to take some inaccessible address beside my name? (He closed his mouth, and the roar he had moved through for the last minutes ceased.) More likely it is one of those things that I will never be able to speak of, and never forget.

They were halfway to the door before the first voice proportioned with amusement yawned somewhere and inquired, *Never?* then giggled, turned over, and went to sleep.

Well not for a hell of a long time.

But he felt a little bit better.

"Did you see those?" Tak nodded down another aisle of crates.

"What?" Kid's heart still beat very fast. He felt light-headed.

"Come on." Tak led him along.

The orchids hung on wooden racks pegged over with dowels.

Kid walked to one stand. "This is . . . the fancy kind." He looked back. "Like you have, isn't it?"

"Plain ones are over there." Tak stepped beside him. "I really thought you'd probably been in here before."

To Kid's questioning glance, Tak took down the nearest. Beneath it was lettered:

BRASS ORCHIDS

Kid laughed. It made a weak sound in his throat, but echo lent it body. "Here, let me see that?" Kid took the scrolled contrivance and turned it around and around. "I guess it would be okay if I took this one . . . wouldn't it?"

Tak shrugged. "Why not?"

Kid folded his fingers together and pushed them through the wrist band. "I left my other one back at the nest. Might as well have two—one for special occasions." He made a sudden feint at Tak. "You like that?" He laughed again.

"Come on." Tak had not moved at all. "Let's go."

They were in sight of the door when Kid got another attack of gooseflesh. But this one just made him grin. He looked up at the skylight, hunched his shoulders, and hurried after Tak. I'll probably never be able to find this place again, he thought. To steal a souvenir (he looked down at the yellow blades about his hand) seemed suddenly the ultimate cunning.

Outside, Tak smoothed the folded material across his arm. "Since this is going to be your girl friend's ball gown, I shouldn't show you how it works. But it's sort of neat. Just a second." He took out of his pocket the piece of equipment—a metal box the size of a cigarette pack with three dials, two knobs, and a small light on one corner. "Give me a loan of the battery in your shield."

"Oh, sure." Kid fumbled the sphere through the blades. The projector clicked open. "I only got one hand. You take it out."

"Right."

Tak opened the back of the box and put the battery in.

"Now watch."

He turned a knob.

The light on the box's corner flickered argon-orange. "Here we go." '

He turned another.

The cloth over Tak's arm—at first Kid thought Tak was shaking it—turned purple.

"Huh?" Kid said.

The metallic scales from which the cloth was made all seemed to have reversed. Some reversed again, and a blot of scarlet grew in one corner, occluded the purple, till it in turn was swept by glittering green.

"Oh, hey . . . !" Kid stepped back. "That's going to be a dress?"

"Pretty, isn't it?"

The parti-colored flicker, like insect wings, resolved to blue that deepened, and deepened more, to black.

Tak turned off the box. Most of the cloth fell into dull silver. He shook it; and it was all one metallic grey.

"You know how it works?"

"Um-hm." Tak put the box back in his pocket. "It's simple, really. Hey, don't tell Lanya I showed you this. She wanted it to be a surprise."

"Oh, sure," Kid said. "Sure." He looked back at the warehouse. "Hey, Tak, who . . . ?"

"Now *that* question," Tak said at his shoulder, "if I knew the answer to, I would have already told you."

"Oh," and Kid began to list those to which that could have been an adequate response.

"You want to come up and have a drink?"

Kid said, "Hey, let me see how that stuff works again. That's what I want to see."

Tak sighed. "Sure."

". . . gonna kill you, mother-fucker!" shrieking like a baby in pain. Kid leaped from the loft, pivoted around the door jamb. Dollar danced in the hall, swinging the plank above his head.

"Hey . . . !" Copperhead stepped back, his arm before his face.

"—*Kill* you if you don't leave me *alone!*"

Copperhead ducked. The plank hit the wall.

Three scorpions (two black, one white) crowded the living room doorway. Two (one man, one woman) stepped in, staring, from the service porch.

Dollar's head went back.

Kid lunged and grabbed; his hand tangled Dollar's hair. He grasped the scorpion's shoulder and spun him back against the wall. Dollar crashed, and clicked his long teeth. The plank corner hit Kid's shoulder and clattered to the floor, while Dollar opened his mouth again. His lips strung out gummy saliva. Dollar tried to shove forward, gasping, Copperhead was trying to pull Kid away.

Kid jammed his elbow back. "Get off!"

"I'm gonna kill 'im!" Dollar shrieked in Kid's face. "He won't leave me alone. I'm gonna kill 'im! He knows I'm gonna kill 'im! I'm gonna kill 'im! I'm gonna kill—"

Kid flung himself against Dollar, spread-eagled them both on the wall. Then his shoulder, still stinging from the plank, exploded in pain, so surprising he couldn't cry out. He just grunted and clawed at Dollar's head. Dollar's teeth came open with a rush of air. He heard Dollar's skull hit the wall twice, and realized he was pounding it. He felt blood dribbling his arm. Dollar's eyes were unfocused. He was trying to shake his head. His upper teeth were filmed with blood, his lower lip flecked with it.

"You gonna let me take care of him?" Copperhead's voice came out a fifth too low; his words wobbled. "This fuckin' loony is gonna hurt somebody! And then there ain't gonna be no telling. You gonna let us take care of him?"

Kid looked back. Copperhead's bearded chin was

buried back in his neck. His freckled fists opened and closed, and he swayed and panted.

"You gonna let us take care of him?"

Dollar rocked his head over the wall. "You tell him to leave me alone!" Tears made the lashes of his left eye glisten. "I'm gonna kill 'im! He knows it!" Dollar blinked. Tears rolled into the stubble that grew high up his pustuled cheek.

In the stillness, Kid's panic died. What surged in its place was rage. But he could find no words to bellow. He raised his hands and let a roaring breath.

Copperhead blinked and stepped back.

Dollar's eyes stopped rolling.

Kid felt some muscle leaping in his jaw and flexed his mouth to control it. He rubbed his sticky shoulder.

Glass stood in the bathroom door, Spitt, a few steps behind of him. In the open front door, Denny had one hand on the knob and the other on the molding.

Waiting for words to come to him, Kid heard talking.

". . . You see that? You see that, the way he did? . . ." Pepper crowded in the living room door, whispered intently the D-t, who wasn't listening. ". . . You see the way Dollar went after that nigger, with a damn board? I bet he would've really messed him up, I bet. He better watch out for Copperhead, now, 'cause Copperhead gonna get him. You think he could beat up Copperhead? Huh? If Kid ain't come in to stop it, who do you bet would've got the other one first, huh? If Kid ain't come in . . ."

Between thin shoulders, heavy with chain, Pepper's face bore its ecstatic, rotted grin.

"You wait, Copperhead," Kid said, "till I tell you to."

Copperhead closed his lips and, more just to move his head than to agree, nodded.

"Go on," Kid said. "Just don't bother with him."

". . . Yeah," Copperhead said. His fists opened, ". . . only 'cause that's what you sayin' . . ." He turned and walked up the hall; Glass and Spitt shifted their weight.

"I'm gonna *kill* 'im! He knows I'm gonna—"

Copperhead turned and barreled back.

Kid hit Dollar on the side of his face with both fists meshed. It was a weak and awkward blow (and his shoulder stung and throbbed beneath the sting) but Dollar crumpled with his hands over his ears.

Copperhead grabbed Kid's shoulders (the pain in the left one went up another level) and got two kicks in around Kid's legs.

"Owe . . . ! Naw . . . !"

Kid shoved Copperhead back. "Someone get him *out* of here!"

No one moved.

"You two! Get this bastard out of this God-damn nest before somebody kills him!" He turned and put both hands on Copperhead's chest. Copperhead's vest hung down one arm. A chain had fallen over the other. "You leave him alone . . . otherwise I'm gonna have to bust you too, and then we'll *both* get hurt!"

Behind him there was a scraping and jangling.

He looked over his shoulder. Denny and another scorpion (neither were the two he had yelled at) supported Dollar, who panted, lurched, and couldn't get his feet under him at all. Kid thought: He must be faking. Damn it, nobody hit him that hard.

Copperhead took another breath, swallowed, shook his head, took another.

". . . Dollar would have really busted up Copperhead if Kid didn't stop him, I bet? You think he would've killed him? I bet he would've, I mean you see the way he went after Copperhead with that board? Then Kid just runnin' in like that . . ."

The front door opened; Dollar's feet struggled with the steps.

Kid breathed hard, clapped Copperhead's shoulder and walked past. He tried to atomize the fragments of the action. He felt terribly clear-headed. But for all his clarity, he could trace no motivations through the memories of blows and pain.

He stood on the service porch kneading his shoulder, listening to people moving again in other rooms.

"Kid . . . ?"

The girl Dollar had been necking with last night (from her clothes, Kid saw, she wasn't a scorpion) tucked under one arm, Copperhead, still breathing hard, stepped onto the porch. Spitt and Glass were wedged behind him.

"What?" Kid squeezed his shoulder again. "What do you want?" The scrape from the plank had done more harm than Dollar's bite. Rabies, he thought; I'm gonna get rabies from the bastard.

"You let us go out and take care of him, okay? He's

623

hanging around the house. He's just gonna try and make trouble. We work him over, and he'll be all quiet and nice again, once he gets better. I don't know what you're trying to do," Copperhead said. "But it won't work no other way."

"I don't care," Kid said, mainly because his shoulder hurt, "what you do with him as long as you do it outside."

Copperhead looked back at the other two scorpions. "Okay," he said thickly. "Come on."

The girl stood in the doorway alone, fingering the waist of her maroon jeans. "They shouldn't do that," she said, with an accent out of Florida and an expression of concern.

As clear as he had felt moments back, Kid felt that dull now. Mouth opened, he nodded at her.

Later he stalked through the house, ignoring the people who moved around him. He stood at the front door, then suddenly turned and went to the porch, and stood before the door there, not really looking at the yard outside; when he became aware of it, he went into the kitchen.

Outside the screening a girl was asking: ". . . inside? Do you know if he's in there? The big . . ."

Kid opened the door.

Her knuckle leaped to her chin. Her blonde hair, caught in a barrette with plastic flowers, slipped off her shoulder as she turned her head.

"You're about eight blocks off Jackson," Kid said.

June shook her head. "I wasn't looking for . . ."

Raven (one of the scorpions who owned the Harley) rubbed his dirty hands on his vest, squeezed his long, rough hair together, took the thong from between his teeth, and tied a top-knot large as his head. "I don't know what she wants."

"You . . . *you* live here?" June asked.

Kid nodded. "What do you want? If you're not looking for George, who are you looking for?"

Her hand fell from button to button on her blouse. "My brother."

Kid frowned.

"My big brother, Edward."

"Oh . . ." Kid frowned harder. "What makes you think you'll find him here?"

"Somebody saw . . . said they saw . . . you just . . ." She looked at Raven.

624

He had settled his thumb in his belt and stared back.

Kid beckoned her inside with a nod. She came side-ways through the door. Because the sink had filled up once more, somebody had put the kettle, sides streaked with hardened soup, in the middle of the floor.

June looked at it.

Kid tried to remember how long he'd been stepping around it.

"Somebody told my · mother that they'd . . . they thought they'd seen somebody who . . ."

They went into the next room.

"My parents don't know I came," she said. "They wouldn't have wanted me to . . . come here."

Two black girls turned to watch her. A blond boy came up behind them, leaned on their shoulders, sucked in his lower lip and drawled. "Shit . . ." The three laughed.

"He isn't one of them?" Kid asked. "Is he?"

She looked at the toes of her black shoes; spots of red spread her cheek.

"You want to hunt around?"

She nodded and hurried ahead to interpose him be-tween the leering scorpions and herself. Two more pass-ing the doorway, the short-haired white woman (with a tattoo on her arm) and D-t, caught her eyes, till she sud-denly jerked her head away and closed her mouth.

"Come on, I'll show you around."

In the hallway the girl in maroon levis was talking to Siam. June looked at the photograph with its cracked glass at the same time Siam and the girl looked at her.

It's because, he realized, she stands so far away from me, so nervously, that makes them stare like that. She circles, she still circles, she circles in. Yet she's so far away! It's not even (the realization went on) that she's a pretty girl, but rather that there are over two dozen peo-ple living in here and the isolation she demands about her destroys our concept of human space. That their hos-tility comes out in sexual leers and sexual jibes ("You see that pussy walk through here?" somebody, male or fe-male, he wasn't sure, said in the next room. "Where's my knife and fork?") is a generic response to something far more personal than her gender—though she may not un-derstand that for years. Some people *are* very young at seventeen.

"You don't live in the park any more?" June asked.

"Nope." He looked out on the porch and into the yard. "He's not one of those?"

She shook her head without, he thought, looking.

"Maybe in here." They crossed the hall; Kid opened the door.

It was hot and even Kid sometimes wondered how they slept in the charred half-dark. Four, a girl among them, naked on the big mattress in the corner, sweated inertly, breaths hissing in different rhythms. Cathedral with his back against the wall reading a book whose cover had come off (—*Brass Orchids:* Kid recognized the title page). In deference to the sleepers, he had not raised the shade. The lion, crouched on the sill, read over his shoulder.

Kid stepped forward.

June, her hand loose before her face once more, followed.

The closet door had been taken down and propped up on boxes. An open sleeping bag hung off it onto the floor. A boy and girl, both with long hair, slept there together. Neither were scorpions and the boy (his hand curled against her neck) looked as though he would have slept easier in the commune.

Someone (Angel?) rummaged inside the closet. Things rumbled and fell and growled, punctuated by, ". . . shit . . ." and ". . . God damn . . ." and ". . . shit! . . ." and ". . . shit . . ."

Since Kid had last been in the room, someone had hung up a poster of George as the Moon. Around it were a half dozen *Playboy* centerfolds, two covers from Black Garters, and lots of naked women playing tennis at some nudist camp.

June closed her fists so tightly in the skirt of her green jumper, they shook.

This is an act, Kid thought. But then, so is this.

"Eddy?" Her voice was firm for all her quivering arms.

"Huh? . . . Oh, hey . . ." It was the square-jawed blond scorpion who'd harassed Pepper. "What are you . . . just a second." He pushed the blanket off his feet and began to lace his sneakers. He snapped his jeans together and searched for his vest. Hair, light as his sister's, made a crushed and sprung helmet of gold foil too big for his head.

"I've . . . I've *never* seen anything like this in my life!" June accused, softly. Her face looked as though, expecting milk, she had swallowed orange juice. She actually said: "Eddy . . . is it really you?"

"Just a second," the blond repeated, got his vest on, and stood, unsteadily on the mattress. He looked too old for Kid's picture of June's other brother. His forehead was creased. His temples were high. Like I'm a baby face, Kid thought, maybe you'd just think he was over twenty-five; but there was a certain youthful unsurety of movement. Like his sister's. Their eyes and upper lips were identical. His lower one was fuller than hers—more like Mrs Richards'. He came toward them. "What'd you come here for?"

"We thought you'd gone to another city, Eddy!" She looked past his shoulder and back. "Oh . . . if Daddy and Mommy could see you here, in this, like this, they'd just . . . die . . . they'd die . . ."

"What do you want?"

"To talk to you. To see you. To see if you were really . . . Somebody said they'd seen somebody who looked like—"

"Just a second," Eddy said. "I gotta go to the—I mean I just woke up." He touched his sister's shoulders, then stepped past Kid into the hall. "I'll be right back . . ."

California turned over on the mattress.

Cathedral looked up from the book.

June's eyes flicked about the shadowed room, caught once on the poster, dodged it. "I liked your book very . . . I thought it was nice . . . the part you wrote about us when . . . no, no!" She said after a moment: "Eddy lives here with you . . . I mean how long has he . . ."

Kid shrugged.

"My mother likes your book too," she said after another moment. "She gave it to a few of . . ."

When she didn't finish, he said: "Say hello for me."

"I wouldn't *dare!*" After a second, she closed her mouth. "Oh, I *couldn't* . . ."

It isn't worth getting angry, Kid thought. He leaned against the doorway edge. Angel, in the closet, looked out, said, "What . . . ?" got no answer, shrugged, and went back in. I don't answer because there is nothing to say. She turns and stares fixedly at some pile of bedding on the floor she does not really see, sure an answer is demanded of her.

He could walk away and leave her to wait alone.

"Watch it," Glass said behind him.

Kid turned.

"Got it." Spitt hefted Dollar's ankles up under his arms.

"You just put him in there," Copperhead said. "He'll be all right."

June had turned too. Kid was impressed how well, for her nervousness, she looked interested but not hysterical.

Dollar's shoulder hit the door.

"Back him up there, huh?" Glass lifted Dollar roughly by the arm, stepped over, and walked him through.

". . . you see that? You see how they done him? He was just hanging around outside, he didn't even run or nothing, when they came after him. Shit, they didn't do that much. Soon as Copperhead hit him the third time he crumpled right up like that. He ain't even got a bloody nose. His eye looks pretty bad, though . . ."

Below the eye the puffy cheek was scraped. Dollar's arms flopped out on either side. His belt was opened.

"I think he fakin'," Copperhead told Kid, scratching his head. "I think he just didn't want to get hit no more, and he's just fakin'. But he's fakin' pretty good."

"He didn't run when he saw you coming?" Kid asked.

"Where was he gonna run?" Copperhead held his right fist in his left hand. The freckled knuckles were bleeding. "Put him down on that one."

Kid looked, but couldn't see Glass's hands.

Angel came out of the closet again, looked around, said, "Aw, Jesus Christ . . ." shook his head, and again went back inside.

By the window, Cathedral, who had closed his book, opened it again.

"They put him on Eddy's . . . ?" June began.

The couple on the door shifted. The counterpoint of the naked scorpions' snoring went on without change.

"Excuse me, huh?" With a glare Eddy stepped around Pepper. He walked to his mattress, squatted, and pulled a hank of chains out from under Dollar's shoulder. He looked up at Kid. "They got him?" He shook his head, picked up the blanket and pulled it up over Dollar's shoulders.

That, Kid thought, is for her. The room was too hot for blankets.

Putting on his chains, Eddy came back to the door. "What did you come here for?"

"I don't know . . . I just don't know—I just don't understand how you can . . ."

Spitt and Glass had gone. Copperhead looked at June, frowned at Kid, and left.

"Come on," Kid said. "You people want to talk? Let's go out on the porch, huh? People are sleeping here, right?"

Kid let them go first, and took up Eddy's rear.

In the hall, the bathroom door was open; Filament —yes, that was the short-haired white woman's name, he suddenly remembered—was taking her morning crap, jeans around her shins, the *Times* folded across her knees.

"In there," Eddy pointed over June's shoulder.

June turned through the service porch door, and said, "Oh, I'm sor—"

"Huh?" Raven's stream halted. "There's somebody using the bathroom," he explained, bewildered, to June's bewildered stare; and his urine chattered in the sink again.

"Come on, come on," Kid herded them in. "He'll be finished in a minute."

Raven shook himself, pushed himself back into his pants. "Yeah, I'm finished."

This has been planned, Kid thought smugly. This couldn't just be happening.

Raven left—

"I'll shoo anybody else out," Kid said.

—then ducked back in the door. "Hey, I meant to run some water in the sink, you know . . . ?"

"Later," Kid said.

"Okay." He left again.

June was looking out the window. Eddy was watching her and pulling the hair at the back of his neck. "What did you want, huh?"

June turned.

"I figured," Eddy said, "you would all get out. I mean I thought Mom and Daddy would take you and Bobby to another . . . city . . ."

"You didn't tell him," June asked, "about Bobby?"

"I didn't know he was your brother until three minutes ago." Kid said. "June pushed Bobby down an elevator shaft and broke his neck, accidentally. He's dead." And immediately George's face filled his mind, obliterating all other reactions.

629

"Mother's very sick," June said. "She really isn't well at all. And I'm worried about Daddy. He goes out to work every day, you know; in spite of it all. But sometimes now he doesn't come home for three, or four days . . ."

"Huh?" Eddy leaned back against the washing machine. "What . . . ?" which was not a reaction to what June was saying at all.

"I'm so worried I don't . . . know what to do. I swear . . . !" Though her sentences were as halting as before, she spoke each fragment more firmly. "Since you've gone, it's all . . . everything has just fallen apart. Everything, Eddy. Since you went, it's like . . . like the plug was pulled out and everything ran out. All of it."

"Jesus Christ . . ." Eddy looked at the floor and shook his head. "Bobby . . . ?"

She circles, Kid thought, she circles, magnificently banal, denying guilt or innocence: if only in her single-mindedness, she is heroic!

Biting both lips, June shook her head. "Are you going to come home?"

And, like an afterthought; She is only a seventeen-year-old, overprotected god. (Somewhere, George leered.)

"Well," Eddy said, "what for . . . ?" Then he said, "Bobby's dead? And Dad doesn't come there any more?"

"Some," she said. "Oh, he comes back . . ."

Eddy looked up. "What would I come back for?"

"Oh, if you got some nice clothes, and a haircut and stuff, and told them you were sorry. . . ."

"Sorry for what! He said he was going to *kill* me if I came back!"

"But that's just because—"

"They start it," Eddy said. "They start it every time I go back there and I can't stop it. I don't know how. That's why I went *away* . . ."

"But if you said you were sorry for the way you acted—"

"Sorry for what? Yeah, I'm sorry that every time I go back there they start needling me until I blow up and then they blow up right back! I'm sorry Momma's sick, I'm sorry Dad's all upset. I'm sorry Bobby's dead." Eddy frowned, and after a second, he asked, "You killed him . . . ?"

June began to cry, silently, eyes streaming.

"Oh, hey, I'm . . . look, I didn't mean . . ." By his
630

hips his hands closed and opened and closed with the motion Kid recognized as the one that had proceeded Copperhead's fury.

"You could take us away . . . !" Her crying burst full. What Kid *thought* she said through it was ". . . from this horrible place!" But with her sobs she was as difficult to understand as some Jackson black. Finally she clamped her mouth, rubbed her eyes, sniffed. "I just wish someone would . . . take me away!"

"Why doesn't Dad go?"

"He doesn't think Mother will. And . . . I don't even think *he* wants to."

"You take them."

"I'm just a girl," June said. "I can't do anything. I can't do anything at all!" She rubbed her forehead on the heels of her hands.

(Eddy's hands turned over on his knees.) "They wouldn't go before?" Eddy said. "*I* couldn't make them go!"

June lifted her face from her palms. "What are you *doing* here?" she demanded, softly. "Oh, Eddy, please come home! What are you doing in a place like this? This is just . . . here . . . awful!"

"What?"

"I mean," she said, "what do you do here?"

"Mm," Eddy shrugged, "we don't do too much. We all just live here, the scorpions. You know? We're all to-gether. Here. That's all."

"You don't," she began tentatively, "rob people on the street, and beat up people and take their money, and things like that . . . do you?"

"Naw," Eddy said, indignation. "Naw, we don't do things like that. Why do you think we do things like that?"

"That's what people say," June said. "Sometimes in the newspaper, it says things like that."

"The newspaper says a lot of things that aren't true, you know? You know that. Besides, now the Kid's a friend of the guy who runs the paper, he's having a party for the Kid, and we're all going up there. So the paper will probably do a little better by us, huh?" —this last to Kid.

Kid, by the door, with folded arms, shrugged.

"What *do* you do, then?"

"I don't know," Eddy said. "We make runs."

631

"What's that?"

"You know . . ." Eddy looked at Kid. "Kid is the boss here; he takes us out on runs."

"What do you do on a . . . run?"

"The guys all get together and we . . . go some place, check it out; get stuff, stuff we want, stuff we'd like to have."

"Like food?"

"Not food! You don't make food runs if you're a scorpion, unless things have really gotten up tight. You go for other things . . ."

"Like what?"

"Stuff."

"And bring it back here?"

"If it's something we want."

"You don't look like you have very much here?" June said.

"We don't need much."

"Then what do you do on these runs?"

"Well, we . . ." Eddy shrugged.

"We break things," Kid said. "Mainly. And if there're people around who don't like it, we rough them up."

"Is *that* what you do?" June asked Eddy.

"Sometimes. Yeah, sometimes we do that. But most of the places we go, there isn't anybody there. The people you do find, they're so scared they usually split." He looked as though he was trying to remember something. "Oh, yeah. We keep things quiet if somebody has a problem and comes to us. That doesn't happen too much. People are scared of us. So they don't act up."

"That's what other people call our protection business," Kid explained. "Only we don't protect anybody."

"Yeah," Eddy attested.

"But why . . . ?"

"We'd do something else," Kid said, "if there was something else to do—"

"—Cause it's . . ." Eddy began. "Look, I'm a scorpion and I like being a scorpion. It's better than anything else I've done. It's a tough, dangerous world out there, and we gotta survive . . . you know? People are scared of us, and maybe they shouldn't be. But it makes it easier. To survive. The reason I'm a scorpion is because when a bunch of us walk down a street, and somebody sees us, they think—" Eddy snapped his fingers—"yeah. We come along and we get the first pick of whatever is

632

there; and if anybody tries to keep it from us, they better watch out. We're together, you see? For one another. If one scorpion gets in trouble, then the nest comes down and *swarm!* If something comes at the nest, then you'll have scorpions from all over. The guys here don't care who you are, where you come from, or what you do; they're for you . . . like a family. When you're a scorpion, you know you're part of something that's important, that means something, that makes people stop, and then think . . . You know . . . ?"

In the silence, June looked confused.

"Is *that* why you're a scorpion?" Kid stood in the doorway and shook his head. "Shit . . . Hey!"

Her eyes snapped at him—

"You haven't found George yet?"

—and widened; her head vibrated, rather than shook in negation.

"Keep looking." Kid tried to smile, succeeded, and found the effort honest. "You will."

Walking down the hall, Kid pondered the probability that Eddy would leave with June. That would be pretty good. He looked in the back room to check Dollar. He was in the same position (as was everyone else) breathing roughly and evenly.

In the loft room, Kid, with his bare toes, nudged Raven's knee. Raven was sitting crosslegged before a pile of bolts and screws. "You can go run the water in the sink now."

"Huh?" Raven looked up. "Oh yeah, in a second."

Kid kicked the knee again with his boot toe. "Will you go wash out the fuckin' sink!"

"Okay, okay. It ain't gonna smell no more in another minute—!"

"I'm not worried about the fuckin' smell. Just go on." Which was true.

"Okay!" Raven got up and left the room.

In sudden fury at the brother and sister, Kid wanted their talk interrupted and both of them out.

He climbed up the notched beam into the loft. Denny, his feet up on the wall, glanced from the Escher propped on his chest, then turned another page. Kid sat with his back against the wall. "Hey?"

"What?"

"Have I taken you guys on any runs, yet?"

"You forgetting things again?"

"You tell me if I have or not and I'll tell you."

"Just that one."

"When?"

"You don't remember?"

"Tell me, cocksucker!"

"When the . . . sun came up, and you ran everybody over to that house. Where Dollar killed Wally. That's the only run you made, so far. I mean you didn't plan it out like a run or anything. But that's all."

"Oh."

"You remember that?"

"I remember."

"Mmm." Denny nodded and went back to his book.

"I guess I'm going to have to make another one soon."

"Mmm," Denny said again, but did not look up.

Why do we make runs? Kid thought: Because if we didn't, we'd be a little more crazy than we are now.

Eddy passed the door.

"Hey, Eddy?"

Eddy stopped. "What?"

"She gone?"

Eddy let out a breath. "Yeah."

"And you're gonna stay here?"

"Man," Eddy said, "I can't do anything for them. And she's . . . Well—"

"I know," Kid said. "Hey, Eddy . . . don't make any more speeches. You're a really bad press agent."

"Huh?" Eddy stepped into the room. "Oh . . . yeah. Uh . . . Kid?"

Kid heard bolts roll across the floor. "Yeah?"

"Well . . . 'Eddy', see, that's what my sister and family call me. But the guys around here, they all call me Tarzan."

"Tarzan?" It was a question, but with a lowering, not a rising inflection.

"Yeah."

"Okay."

Eddy turned to leave.

"Hey, Tarzan?"

"What?"

"Sorry about your family."

Eddy smiled, briefly and weakly. "Thanks." He left.

Raven came in and said, "Aw, shit! Somebody kicked

my fuckin' screws all over the God-damn floor!" He sucked his teeth, squatted, and, out of sight from the edge of the loft, began to roll them back together.

I come. I go. Rather than going, though, I'll stay. This cage seems too easy to flee. Is that what keeps us here? To leave the city: That is the thought that makes me weak in the small of the back and watery in the mind, so much so that it is easier not to remember it once the thought is past. Waiting for a word to push on these walls, with its bass hiss, there is no way to begin. Adjusting the frame to accommodate the day, I am swollen with terror at my inability to distinguish, at any action, what differentiates time after from time before.

"Hi, what are you putting together?" she asked.

"Just a piece of junk—" Raven said.

Denny clapped Escher closed, and rolled to lean over the edge. "Hey! Lanya!"

"Hi, babes. Is Kid up there?"

"Yeah, he's right here."

"Room for me?" Then her head came over the loft's edge, and frowned. ". . . This one is harder to climb than the ladder on the other one."

Kid pushed up to his knees to grab her shoulder. Denny was already at the edge to help.

"Hey, I think I can do it more easily myself. Let's see . . ." She scrunched her features. "Um . . . . No, please. I'll get it." She pushed over the edge, almost slipping once. "There." She took a breath. "Now all I have to worry about is getting down."

"You came down to see us!"

"Sure," she told Denny, who now put both hands on her knee. "I told you I would, didn't I?" She took Kid's hand, and one of Denny's. "Tak told me you saw what's going to be my dress." She was wearing jeans and a tan blouse. "Just as well if it isn't too much of a surprise. Have you decided which shirt you're going to wear, Denny?"

"I thought," Denny said, "I could bring all three and sort of change every once in a while."

"What are *you* wearing?"

"What I have on," Kid said.

Lanya thought a minute. "Wash the pants first. Give them to me and I'll run them through the machine. We have one that works in the basement of our building."

"I only have one pair," Kid said.

Lanya laughed, let go of their hands, and crawled to the back of the bed.

"I'll shave, though."

"I thought you decided to grow a beard."

Raven, from the floor called up, "I got a razor if you want to use it. Everybody else does."

"I probably already have," Kid said. "Thanks."

"I taught all morning and afternoon," Lanya said. "What did you do?"

Denny shrugged. "Nothin'. We haven't been doin' too much of anything. We don't ever do nothin' around here." Denny got his boot out from under him and sat back very close to the edge. "Dollar tried to break open Copperhead's skull with a plank, and Kid jumped in and broke it up—"

"—little bastard—" Kid flexed his shoulder, which still hurt—"tried to chew my arm off—"

"—and so we put him out, but Copperhead and Glass and Spitt went out and got him anyway. He's inside, pretty beat up."

"We don't do too much here," Kid said. "Never guess who came to visit. She left just before you got here."

"Who?"

"June Richards."

"What on earth for?"

"Her brother's here."

"I thought he fell down an elevator shaft and broke his neck."

Denny said, "Was that *her* brother?"

"Her *other* brother," Kid said. Then to Denny. "This brother's Tarzan."

"Yeah, I was just here. Remember?"

"Oh."

"What did she want?"

"Family problems."

"I thought you'd had enough of that family's problems."

"So did I." Kid leaned forward and put his head in Lanya's lap. "What did you think of our new nest here?"

"Shall I be brutal?"

"You don't like it, huh?" Denny moved over to sit next to her. "I think it's pretty neat. It's a lot better than the other one."

"On my way from the front door, to the bathroom, and then back to here, I must have wondered seven distinct times how you could *stand* it!"

"God damn," Kid said, *"we* roughed it for how long—?"

"That was outdoors, in the open air! And we spent most of our time by ourselves, away from other people anyway."

"I don't think she likes it here," Denny said, letting his shoulders drop. "Don't you think it's nicer than the other place? We got a mattress . . ."

"You have fifty people in a space that won't hold—"

"Twenty," Kid said. "Maybe twenty-five."

"—twenty-eight that I counted just now between the front steps, the kitchen, the living room, the service porch, the two back rooms—in a space that would be crowded with five or six! There is a pile of shit—human, I assume—by the side of the back steps, which is understandable considering you only have one bathroom. Which I was in, by the way, and *that's* pretty unbelievable. How do you get these people fed? I mean, I was in the kitchen!"

"We eat pretty well," Denny said. "I think we eat pretty well."

"The lack of privacy would drive me up the wall!"

"You know," Kid said, "that's a funny thing about privacy. If there're two or three people in a room, it's really hard to be by yourself. If there're nine or ten, especially if you're all living together, if you want to be alone, all you have to do is think I want to be alone and everybody else has somebody to pay attention to, and you're alone. I had two roommates in an apartment my first year at Columbia; we had four rooms and it was really impossible. A couple of years later I spent December, January, February and March in three rooms on East Second Street in New York with about ten guys and ten chicks. Cold as a mother-fucker, and we were in there *all* day. All we did is eat, ball, and deal dope: Nicest time of my life."

"Really?" Then she said, "If it was, how did it compare to this?"

"This is *not* the nicest time in my life. But there've been others a hell of a lot worse."

"We got all sorts of good stuff to eat," Denny said. "You hungry? I bet I can fix some stuff up for you?"

637

"Thanks, babes. But I just finished lunch.

"We were a lot cleaner there," Kid said, "maybe because there were a few more girls around."

"Male chauvinist pig," Lanya said dryly. "Import a lot of slave labor to wash the dishes and—"

"I'm not a male chauvinist pig," Kid said. "I'm a commie faggot pervert."

"There's nothing to stop you from being both."

"*Every*body cleaned. Just like here. We made people take their shoes off when they came in the door. New York slush. It's just nicer with more girls."

"You're preaching. That all may be, but it's not here. I can just manage to resist inviting you to come live with me and be my loves."

"I guess with the place you got, you wouldn't want to come live here," Denny said. "But you could stay for a while."

Raven suddenly stuck his bushy top-knot over the edge. "Hey, Lady, if they don't want to come live with you, I'd be glad to. I'm clean, I'm friendly. I do a lot of the cooking around here, too; I'm a pretty good lay—"

"Get the fuck out of here, cocksucker!" Kid said loudly, leaning forward.

"Sure." The top-knot disappeared. "Thought I'd make the offer."

"And don't let anybody else up here. We're busy, huh?"

"Okay," from below. Bolts and nuts rattled.

"Oh, there're other reasons I don't move you in."

"I guess Madame Brown wouldn't like it," Denny said.

"She might not," Lanya said. "But I wasn't thinking of that. I just feel I need a place to retreat. Where I can go lick my wounds; when I get wounded."

"Cool," Kid said.

"Are you afraid of us?" Denny took his hand, which had been between her thighs, away.

"Yes." She took his hand and put it back. "But you keep things interesting. I don't know why I should be . . . oh, nonsense! I can think of four hundred reasons why I should be—or reasons why other people would say I should be. My own? I suppose I'm doing it to find out what they are. Pretty defeatist, huh? Okay, I'm just doing it to find out."

"I guess," Denny said, "it's pretty—"

". . . he up there?" someone said.

"He's busy. You can't go up there."

"I only want to talk with him a *minute!*"

"I said he's busy, man. You can't—"

"Look, lover, I can see the tops of their heads from here so he can't be doing anything *that* complicated."

Kid went over to the loft edge. "Bunny?"

"Now, you see—" Bunny came forward—"he hasn't even taken off his clothes. Hi there! It's—ta-ta-ta, ta-ta-ta, *ta!*—me." Bunny's arms extended straight up, fell; with them fell Bunny's smile. "You're supposed to be in charge here, Kid. Have you seen Pepper?"

"Yeah, he's been around."

"Hi, Bunny." Lanya leaned over the edge. So did Denny.

"Ah-ah-ah!" Bunny shook a finger at her. "You know what they say, dear; one at a time, and slowly. Hello." That was to Denny, who was grinning. "What a charming overbite you have," and looked back at Kid: "I approve. You all *can't* be about to do what I *thought* you were. Can I come up and sit a spell?"

"We probably were," Lanya said. "But come on."

Bunny raised a platinum brow, forehead wrinkling— or crumpling. "I don't understand these modern relationships. Beneath my glittering exterior, I'm just a sweet, old-fashioned girl. No offense, dear," and nodded at Lanya. "Now— How am I supposed to negotiate this?" Bunny grasped the supporting beam, "Oh, it isn't that hard." Head and scrawny throat (in a black jersey turtleneck gone limp), cleared the mattress. "Now how do I get the rest of the way?"

"Here." Denny kneeled up and grabbed Bunny's shoulders.

"Oh, watch it, oh watch it, watch it now, I . . . Oh!" Bunny settled on the loft edge, black jeans bunched a little at the waist. ". . . *Thank* you! Well, I must say this is rather cozy. You said Pepper was *around?* I can't tell you what a load that lifts from my frazzled and distorted little brain. You know, he was staying at my place; a few days ago he disappeared. Again. Well, you *know* I worried. He's managed to take care of himself one way or the other these past twenty-nine years without spending *too* much of that time in jail—did you know he told me he was once arrested for *displaying* himself in public? Isn't that too quaint? But I heard you were running a nest and

639

so I thought I'd take a look-see before I made up my mind whether or not to go frantic with grief."

"He's around," Kid said. "But I don't know if he's here just now. You want to take him back with you? That's fine with me."

Bunny's pupils rolled up. "Oh, I'd give my eye teeth to have him back." Bunny's nails, their pearl polish chipped, strayed on the bright beads that circled the small, dark shoulders. "But then, I'm not going to try and make the poor baby do anything he doesn't want. It isn't good for him. He's got to learn to do what *he* thinks best. If I go directing his whole life—and you wouldn't believe how much he wants me to; he practically demands I make everything *resembling* a decision for him—he'll never grow up. One has to be responsible to the people one loves, whichever way they let one." Bunny, hands folded, pale and knobbly, frowned from one to the other. *"Three* of you? Darlings, that's going to be so much *work!* Well, you'll have each other to lean on in times of *crisis."* The frown changed; the hands broke. "You say I can take him away? He hasn't gotten into any trouble around here, has he?"

"Naw," Kid said. "But I had to make loud noises at someone trying to give him a rough time."

"You did?" Bunny pulled back. "Not only do you write beautiful poems, you have a poetic soul! I knew it, I knew it when Pepper first introduced us. That's why I came; because you had a poetic soul." Bunny pulled back further. "Tell me. In that fifth poem. On page seventeen. *Mab;* now I don't understand the title, and I don't know if I want to, but did I detect a fleeting reference to . . . *me* by any chance?"

"Yeah." Kid said. "Probably. I was sitting in the john at Teddy's when I wrote it. You were outside dancing."

"Ahhhh!" Bunny exclaimed with clasped hands and lowered eyes. "That's just the most exciting . . . Oh!" Suddenly Bunny's hand swirled up and overhead. "Of course, that's nothing to you, dear!" It landed on Lanya's knee. "I mean you're practically the Dark Lady of the Sonnets." Now Bunny leaned forward: "Darling, *don't* make him miserable." Bunny's hand moved on to brush Denny's shoulder. Denny frowned at it. "You too. Be kind to him." Bunny turned once more to Kid. "You're doomed to tragedy, you know. The ones of us, like you and I, with

640

the Ipana smile, we always are. I mean who could possibly love us? And just because our half of the class brushed with Crest; tragedy begins from such tiny things. But that's why all of us with the ultra-bright grimaces have to be content to end up in Hollywood, as movie stars, hideously famous, fabulously rich, trailing behind us all the heartaches, the broken romances, divorce after divorce— Look at *you!* Fame and fortune are already glittering up there on South Brisbain. You see? It's begun, already, you poor thing!"

"Far," Denny said with gravity, "fucking out."

Lanya said: "If Bunny's in your book, you should invite him to the party."

"Yeah," Kid said. "You want to come? Most of the guys in the nest are going up. So Pepper'll probably be along."

"Oh, I couldn't!" Bunny's head dropped, with a small shake. "I couldn't possibly," then looked up. "I'd just love to, I really would. But I can't."

"Why not?"

"Principles."

"How do you mean?"

"Well." The space between Bunny's nose and upper lip got longer. "That astronaut person, Captain Kamp, is going to be there, isn't he?"

"He's Calkins' guest. I guess he will."

"That's" why."

Denny said, "Is that the guy you met who's been on the moon?"

"Um-hm." Kid nodded.

Lanya said: "I don't understand, Bunny."

"Were you there the night the Captain came to the bar?"

"I was," Kid said.

"Then *you* know what happened. To me and George."

"No," Kid said, "I don't."

Bunny took a preparatory breath. "As soon as Teddy realized who that glorified fish-bait was—and don't you know, someone had to *tell* her?—she came over to me and suggested that, considering the clientele that evening, it might be better if I didn't dance!"

"No," Lanya said. "You're not serious, are you? Why?"

"He didn't want to offend the tender sensibilities of

641

our scotch-and-water-sipping national hero. They do not, presumably, have go-go boys on the moon. Teddy figured the shock might be too much."

"When I came in," Kid said, "everybody was sitting around having a chamber of commerce meeting."

"That," Bunny said, "had not begun when Teddy made his pronouncement to me. And when it did, George happened to be there. They were all sitting around asking questions, and George was very interested. So George asked some. One of them—I was watching from my cage —was whether or not Captain Kamp had ever been to *George's* moon. Some people snickered. But George was serious. And I'll say this for the Captain, he answered it perfectly seriously. I mean, considering the afternoon, it was pretty presumptuous to think *any* question was that silly. But after a couple more from George, Teddy went over and said something to him. A minute later, George shoved back his chair and walked out."

"What did he say?" Denny asked.

"I couldn't hear," Bunny said. "But I certainly could see the effect. And I know what he said to me."

"George had just left when I came in," Kid said. "Tak told me."

"That sounds so silly," Lanya exclaimed. "Teddy was always a little—formal, but you make him sound like a member of the Rotary Club."

"Daughter of the American Revolution! That naugahide rimmer of rusty Chevrolet nineteen-fifty-two exhaust pipes! I hope the next time she sucks off a number she rips his foreskin in her bridgework!" —which collapsed Denny on his back with hysterics. "There are two reasons —beside the free hooch—that anyone comes into that roach-infested, crab-breeding collapsed douche bag. One is George. The other is me . . . Oh, yes! A few have wandered by, hoping they might be lucky enough to get a look at the Kid. But don't worry, just give that neo-Nazi time and he'll start asking you to wear a tie next time you come. Mark mother's wise, wise words."

"That's too silly," Lanya said and made an ugly face.

"If I saw George," Kid said, "I was going to invite him. I guess he won't want to go now either?"

"Well," Bunny said, "George is a slightly larger luminary in our local skies; he can, perhaps, afford to be more generous than I. I, I'm afraid, must guard my honor more jealously. After all, dear, it's all I have."

"Next time I saw Kamp," Kid said, "he was down at the blowout George gave for the Reverend Tayler in Jackson."

"Bunny," Lanya said, "you *are* being silly! About the party, I mean. Kid didn't invite Teddy, he invited you. And for all you know, Kamp came down precisely to see you do your act; Teddy was being stupid and presumptuous. That shouldn't stop *you* from having a good time."

"I will not," Bunny said, "go up there and perform for those people."

"Nobody's going to ask you to dance—"

"You don't understand, dear heart." Once more Bunny touched Kid's knee. "As far as Calkins is concerned, or any of them up there: you, me, or anybody you know just going up to make an appearance, is putting on a performance. Calkins set up that bar, put Teddy in charge of it. The whole place exists only for his amusement or the amusement of his guests the once a month they should feel like coming down to slum. And while I don't believe for an instant he gave Teddy orders that I wasn't to be exhibited to his new young man from Mars or whatever, it's an attitude inevitable in such a chain, whether there's money involved or not. I simply cannot be a part of it. Negroes and homosexuals, dear! Negroes and homosexuals! Having been lumped together in so many cliches for so long, we are *beginning* to learn. With women and children—" Bunny nodded toward Lanya and Denny— "it's taking a little longer. Well, *you* have a few more cliches to overcome. You mustn't think I'm trying to throw a wet afghan over the festivities. You've written a beautiful book—though I didn't understand a *line*—and you should go up there and have your party, and *I* hope it's perfectly too fabulous. I really do. I shall just drool over the accounts in the society page next day. But I have to live with myself. You're a dear, dear boy to ask me. And I'm just too crushed that I can not accept."

"You're not going to dance at Teddy's no more?" Denny asked.

"That—" Bunny's hands refolded—"is another thing, No, I still dance there. Every night, three shows. Matinees on Saturdays and Sundays, as soon as brunch is cleared. Oh, we creative types must put up with so much just to do, as it were, our thing. Misery. Pure misery. Shame and humiliation." Bunny regarded Kid. "Oh, you're going

643

to suffer so much it makes me want to weep. But that's the price of having a poetic soul."

"If Teddy is that big a bastard," Denny asked, "why don't you just stop dancing for him?"

Bunny raised an upturned palm. "If I don't dance there, where else can I? I mean here, in Bellona? But we must stop all this. All I'm doing is making me feel sorry for myself. And you're snickering. You said that Pepper was here . . . where—" Bunny's voice dropped—"do you think I should look?"

"Come on," Kid said. "I'll give you the grand tour."

"Oh, now, you don't have to do—"

Kid pushed himself out between Lanya and Denny and dropped to the floor.

"—let me see, how do I get down from here? My, this is complicated; don't you think a—oh dear!—ladder would be much easier than—there!"

"I'll be back in a second," Kid said to the two faces regarding him over the edge. He stepped around Raven, who glanced up from tinkering on the floor, and, followed by Bunny, went into the hall.

"You know," Bunny came abreast of Kid. "I can't tell you how relieved you've made me feel. Just to know he's here and all right. What I see in him I'm sure I'll never know. But sometimes he smiles, and I go all cream custard inside. Or calves-foot aspic. Yes, much more like calves-foot aspic. I mean it's all clear and quivery and cool!"

"Not like an eclair?" Kid felt quieted and pensive from Bunny's tale.

"*Exactly* not like an eclair!" Bunny smiled a white, white smile. "You *do* know!"

"He isn't in the yard," Kid leaned out onto the porch, then pulled back.

"I didn't see him with any of those boys on the front steps," Bunny said. "And he wasn't in the kitchen or the front room."

"Let's try in here." Kid pushed open the door.

Among the sleeping scorpions (Dollar had turned over on his stomach) Pepper, curled on his side in a pile of blankets, hanks of chain over his bony shoulders, fists thrust into the groin of his jeans, slept and hissed through the limp hair across his face.

"He always sleeps like that," Bunny said quietly.

"You want to wake him up and—?"

"No!" Bunny whispered, and raised a wrist before pursed lips. "No . . . I just wanted to, well . . . you know." Bunny's smile was worked through with concern. "That's fine. Really. Just to know he's all right. That's all I wanted. One has to be responsible for them, but in ways . . . in ways they can understand." Bunny's head shook. "And understanding, as I'm sure you know, is not Pepper's strong point. Come, come. There's no need to wake anyone." Black Spider had rolled over and raised his head.

At Bunny's gesture, Kid closed the door.

"Thank you, thank you. A million times, thank you. I've got to run along to greet my audience with—" Bunny thrust out a hip and closed an eye—"the *real* thing. You're a perfect love. Ta-ta!" Halfway up the hall Bunny turned back and flung out one hand while the other wound among the optic beads. "And have a fabulous time at your party. You were too good to ask me. Thank you, thank you. You really are too good. Drink a glass of champagne for old Bun-buns, and remember, whatever happens, give 'em *hell!*"

California and Revelation had stopped to stare. Lady of Spain came out of the front room behind them, leaned on their shoulders, and grinned.

Bunny blew all three kisses, fled to the front door, opened it, turned, sang out, with flourishing arms: " 'The shadow of your smile . . .' " in an astonishing bass; then shrilled, "Bye-bye!" and was gone.

Pondering, Kid went back to the loft.

Seated Raven had a loop of wire and two screws in his mouth. "Who was that?" he asked, voice mangled by metal.

Kid just laughed and climbed up the post. "God damn," he said. "Couldn't you wait for five minutes to get started?"

Denny, naked, lay on top. Lanya still wore her blouse.

"We haven't started very seriously," Lanya said around Denny's forearm.

"Yeah?" Kid climbed up and pushed his hand between their hips (Denny rocked up, Lanya pulled down). "Oh; yeah." He took off his vest.

They made love, breathing softly with wide mouths. For a while, with his belt and pants open, Kid refused to take his pants off—

("I'm sorry, Lady, you can't go up there. Kid's busy."

645

("He ballin'?"

("Yeah. Come back later.")

—but after a while they tickled him and, while he lay laughing, pulled them down. Huddled with their heads together, Denny whispered, "That was nice, huh? Lemme fuck you in the pussy and you can fuck me in the ass again while I'm doing it."

"Marvelous," Lanya said and buried her laughter on Kid's shoulder.

"Sure," Kid said. "If you want. Sure."

But, with knees uncomfortably wide, elbows bent, and the boy's dry back brushing his belly, Kid's penis, pulling along the flexing crevice, lay limp. He started to say something, thought better, and kissed Denny's shoulder, kissed him again.

Lanya opened her eyes and, through her catching and catching breath, frowned. She worked one hand free, and licked and licked her fingers. Then she reached around Denny's back. First just the side of her thumb touched his cock. Then his movement in her fist's tunnel made the thing that was not a muscle tighten (and whole webs above and around his pubis that were, relax). His penis filled through her grip.

"I like that . . ." Denny panted when Kid was inside him.

"It's pretty good . . ." Kid got out, shifted his weight, and decided that Lanya had the right idea: Talking was silly. He didn't come in Denny's ass, but in hers.

They lay on their sides, Lanya sandwiched between.

"I can feel him," Denny whispered, "Moving. Inside your cunt, on my dick, I can feel him."

"So," she whispered, "can I," and *Shhhhhed* him. Both Kid's hands were around her chest. Someone held his thumb. He thought it was her because she always used to, but it was Denny. Once he rose from a half sleep to hear them giggling together. He shifted his fingers on the live warmth of her breast. Someone squeezed his thumb again.

He woke, suddenly and fully. They were both still. His cock was erect; but as he raised his head to look down at himself, he felt it soften. He had rolled slightly to the side. His penis lowered toward Lanya's thigh.

It is not touching her, he thought.

Then, the slightest warmth. And pressure.

It is touching her.

646

Eyes wide, he rolled back, trying to understand by blunt reason that terrifying and marvelous transition.

I am limited, finite, and fixed. I am in terror of the infinity before me, having come through the one behind bringing no knowledge I can take on. I commend myself up to what is greater than I, and try to be good. That is wrestling with what I have been given. Do I rage at what I have not? (Is infinity some illusion generated by the way in which time is perceived?) I try to end this pride and rage and commend myself to what is there, instead of illusion. But the veil is the juncture of the perceived and perception. And what in life can rip that? Is the only prayer, then, to live steadily and dully, doing and doubting what the mind demands? I am limited, finite, and fixed. I rage for reasons, cry for pity. Do with me what way you will.

5

He woke . . .

As Kid sat, Denny's hand fell from his. Lanya rolled back a little to press against him again.

Kid's side cooled.

He thought of her side cooling.

He watched Denny, in sleep, rub his stomach where she had just lain. Kid's pants were wedged against the wall. Hanging his feet over the edge, he shook out the rumpled legs. He lifted one knee and set his heel on the board (his ankle was very dirty) to stare at the circling chain. What circled his mind, what had been running there since sleep, was: ". . . Susan Morgan, William Dhalgren, Peter Weldon . . . Susan Morgan, William Dhalgren, Peter Weldon . . ." Pondering, he shook it out.

He pushed his feet out the cuff, got his boot, his vest, his chains, and swung around to the post and climbed down. Raven was gone.

He noticed the silence just as it ended with voices in the other rooms. He could not decide whether it had been a few coincident seconds, or a protracted hush, begun before his waking, ending. Restless, he walked into the hall.

And recognized her blue sweatshirt as she turned into the service porch. When he reached the door, she was going down the steps into the yard. He followed.

Halfway into evening, the sky above the littered and trampled dirt was without feature.

Angel, Filament, and Thruppence, under Copperhead's supervision, were trying to start a fire.

Raven, Spider, D-t, and Jack the Ripper, with Tarzan the one white among them, sat on crates or stood at the back of the yard, passing two gallon jugs, both half empty, and arguing.

She looked up, saw him at the head of the steps, and (he thought) started. "Hi," she said with a very puzzled look and brushed a feathering of hair back from her face.

"Hey." He came down the steps.

She looked at his foot.

It had been a long time since he had even been around anyone who noticed his half-shod eccentricity. He thought about the coming party, found his mind rummaging again through Bunny's tale of the afternoon, and pushed away the discomfort with laughter.

She looked more uncomfortable. "I just wanted to come over and say hello to some of the guys," she explained. "I'm living over there, now," indicated only with a turned head that turned right back. "You know that commune you guys used to hit up in the park? Well, some of the ones from there come over to our place a lot—our house is just girls—but anybody can come and visit."

Kid nodded.

She folded her arms across the full, faded sweatshirt. "This place is—" she looked around the rubble—"is sort of nice."

"You come over here to see Denny?"

She looked down at her baggy elbow. "What do you want with him? I mean what are you—" she tightened her arms—"going to do with him? I want him back."

Jack the Ripper glanced across the fireplace, glanced away. Kid thought: She has learned, when she lived like this, to hold such converse in a space full of people.

"I want him. What do you need him for?"

He thought she was going to cry, but she just coughed.

"He just isn't that smart. Those poems you wrote? I read them, all of them. When I was in school, we read poetry and stuff and I liked it. I was the smartest person in my class—one of them, anyway. Denny won't read them because he can't even say the words. You ever hear him try to read the newspaper? But I read them. The part about me bringing you the whisky when you were in the bathtub washing off the blood, and saying good-bye? I read about that and I understood it. But the stuff in there about him, if he read it, he wouldn't even get it I bet. What do you want him for, huh? Why don't you give him back?" She began to look to either side. "I'm sorry."

"I don't keep him from seeing you."

649

"I know," she said. "I'm sorry. I'm gonna go."

She dropped her arms and went around him to go up the stairs.

Lanya, in jeans and blouse, stood in the doorway. The two girls looked at one another. Then the one in the blue sweatshirt sighed. Lanya glanced after her, then looked back at Kid.

Kid frowned.

Jack the Ripper, by the fire now, looked over, his smile between sympathy and complicity, and shook his head.

Kid walked up the steps. "You just get up?"

"Only seconds, I'm sure, after you did. I heard you talking to her when we came out of the porch; so I decided I'd come out and listen. She seems like a nice kid."

He shrugged. "Denny still asleep?"

"Nope."

Kid sat on the step below her. They both had to move legs when Devastation came down to wander over to the fire, to stand with his hands in his back pockets.

"He got up with me," Lanya explained. "We were going to come out and surprise you while you were wandering around looking preoccupied. I told him we couldn't do it if you were anywhere near a pencil and paper. But then, when we got to the porch, we saw you talking to her."

"Where's Denny?"

"He saw her, covered his mouth with *both* hands—I thought he was going to blurt out something, God knows what—ducked behind me, and ran. I'm not sure if he's locked himself in the bathroom, or just split. No, the bathroom doesn't have a lock, does it? She didn't see him— he made enough noise!" She rested her chin on her fist. "The poor girl. I feel sorry for her."

"Mean little bastard, isn't he?"

"You think so?"

"He is to her. He is to you. To me. I can take it." Kid shrugged. "What are you going to do when he decides one day when you come to see him he doesn't want to see you?"

"Take it, I suppose." She sighed. "He really should have talked to her. *How* old is he?"

"Fifteen. And she's seventeen."

"You should tell him to talk to her. If they were really all that close."

650

"Shit," Kid said. "I never argue with people I screw. She seems to think there isn't anything to say. I don't blame her for wishing there was."

"Maybe." Lanya sounded doubtful. "I sort of took a liking to her, just listening. She lives in the girls' house? Now that *is* a strange bunch. I've been there a few times."

"Dikes?"

"No more than here. Do you think she'd be interested in helping with the school?"

"You're just going to get yourself in trouble."

Lanya laughed. "It's so nice to know there're one or two things about which I am more worldly than you are! I think it's fine to have an occasional knock-down, drag-out . . . discussion with people you're screwing. *I* never quarrel with the people the people I'm screwing are screwing. Or were screwing. I make a point of being on the best terms possible. Even if you have a knack for it, sometimes it takes a lot of work. But the trouble you avoid—" she turned down her mouth and tapped her knee three times—"is *not* to *be* be*lieved!*" Then she tugged his hair. "Let's go look for him."

But Denny had left the house.

Back in the yard the fire had been completed. Lanya volunteered to go with Priest, Thruppence and Angel to the liquor store. When they came back, Kid had taken the door out of the back room and set it up on some boxes for a table in the yard. Others had begun food.

"Come on. I want to go back up in the loft."

"Sure." She squeezed his hand and followed.

When they had lain together, when they had talked quietly a while, when they had begun to make love, he was surprised to find her somewhat listless and distracted; small movements she made silently angered him. Till she said, "Hey, what's the matter? You seem so far away. Come on back," which returned the whole thing to the realm of the humorous.

After that it was very good.

After coming, while he lay there and held her, the smell woke him. His waking woke her. He lifted his head at the sound. A third plate, in raised hands, was pushed over the loft edge. Then Denny climbed up, crawled across them, and began to take off his clothes. "We can eat up here," he whispered, as though they might still be sleeping with opened eyes.

There were lots of frankfurters on the plates.

And vegetable hash.

"Where'd you get off to?"

Denny shrugged. "Just wandering around. Thirteen's got a place right down the block and across the street. Pretty nice." He picked up a frank in his fingers and bit. Juice ran down his forearm and dripped from his elbow to his knee.

Kid licked it off. "You're gonna gimme a hard-on," Denny said and pushed one of the plates to Lanya. "Here. You wanna eat?"

"Sure." She rubbed her eyes and pulled out of Kid's arms. "Where . . . oh, hey. Thanks!" to the bite of Denny's he offered from his hand.

Remembering not a moment of grace, but a moment laced with it, I am thrown back on a present where only the intensity of the senses can justify this warmth, the look of shadow on her shoulder, light on her hip, a reflection on the blackened glass, light up from below. That is not as good. What have I fallen from, perfected by memory into something only possible, I do not want to falsify any more than that. Now there are only the eyes and the hands to fill out.

They drank some of the brandy he'd had her get for Tak. ("You won't believe my dress, either of you. I know you've seen it, Kid. You still won't believe it.") She said she was going to go home soon, but fell asleep. Somebody yelling in the kitchen once woke them hours later and they all made love again in the dark.

For the second time, from an urge that crossed experimentation with duty, he sucked Denny off; it took twice as long as before. "Don't you think you ought to rest?" Lanya finally suggested.

"Yeah," Denny said. "You rest some."

So he closed his eyes and racked it up to foibles. Still, it was the best time he remembered. He drifted toward sleep, only sad he remembered so little, and closed his eyes.

When the window had gone indigo, Kid opened them. Lanya was kneeling up. "I'm going now," she whispered. So they crawled over Denny, to find their clothes. "But I want some coffee," she mouthed.

"There should be boxes around," Kid said. "We just don't have any pot."

"That's all right. Come on."

In the kitchen, Thirteen and Smokey, with three

652

black scorpions, Raven, Thruppence, and D-t, up the night, sat talking. Kid was surprised when, from the banter, he realized Lanya knew all their names: Even Thruppence's. (He'd had to ask that one several times: "Thruppence, man. Thruppence. That's English for *three cents*.") And "D-t", he found out, stood not for Delirium tremens but Double-time. A bucket was the only thing really clean so Lanya filled it to make boiled coffee.

"You gonna *drink* that?" D-t asked her.

"Sure. Bring it to a boil three times, then throw in a glass of cold water. The egg white will make it settle. Then you just pour it off into a pot and keep it hot," for which purpose Smokey volunteered to clean the kettle.

"You just don't let the Spider know you used up two of his good eggs to make that mess."

"Shit," Raven said, "everybody else use 'em."

Kid and Lanya drank theirs black while the rest went through a confusion of powdered milk (someone remembered the box under the table), cup rinsing, and sugar.

"Now that's nice coffee," Raven (his top-knot, now, undone) admitted, gazing into the cup on the table. "It's just as clear! I gotta remember me that." He pouted heavy lips at the steam and shook his head. The hairy beachball swung side to side.

"Yeah," Thirteen said back over his shoulder. "You gonna remember that, Smokey?" who nodded.

Cathedral and Filament had come in sleepily from the other room. Nine people stood drinking coffee in a space that was crowded with four.

"Now I'm just across the street and down the block," Thirteen was saying. "On the top floor. Any of you guys come over who want to. Kid'll tell you, he stayed in my place. I got so many scorpions around, you'd think I was running a nest. But I ain't. I just like to be friendly, you know?"

"You want to stay," Kid told Lanya as they left, "you just go back up in the loft. Nobody's going to bother you."

She rubbed the back of his neck. "There're just some things I have to get done before school. Give Little Brother a hug for me."

Nevertheless, as he walked her home, he was pretty sure what she wanted was another two hours sleep. He asked, "You coming back tonight?"

653

She squeezed his hand. "Nope. You two can come up and see me if you've got time. For a little while." She squeezed his hand once more.

The gesture became an emblem of her nervous charm.

The paper that day said:

Sunday—July 14th, 1776.

They spent the night at Lanya's.

The next day:

Sunday—June 16th, 2001.

That afternoon tire-colored Jack the Ripper, crouching before the open icebox whose light had just blown, whose insides were crammed, and whose enamel was streaked and stained, looked up and asked, "Say, when you gonna run?"

"Right now!" Inception, impulse, and decision had all fixed between Kid's first word and his second. Kid grabbed the doorway, leaned into the next room and shouted, "WE'RE GONNA RUN . . . !"

D-t, Spider, Angel, Priest crowded in from the hallway.

California shucked quickly from the sleeping bag beside the couch.

Raven and Glass and Lady of Spain came into the kitchen.

Spitt pushed in through the scorpions crowding the doorway.

They swayed and moved their feet and looked uncomfortably serious.

"Come on," Denny was saying as the others clattered down the front steps. "Hey, you! You gonna come? Get on out here."

Within the house they had almost been able to imagine a lucid city. Now catatonic windows watched them stalk. Their boots crunched and thudded on the pavement. They hurried with lowered brows, staring out from under, looking left and right on the neutral avenues.

Kid remembered, later, breaking the plate window of the Second City Bank building.

Jack the Ripper danced on broken glass and cackled: "Man, we gonna bust up nigger-town, now!"

They didn't.

They shuffled and poked in papers and files and adding machines. Copperhead turned over a desk and stood looking at it, breathing hard, a full minute.

They found neither money nor locked boxes; the only things in the money drawers were paperclips, gummed reinforcements, rubberbands.

Kid climbed back over the brass bars of a teller's cage (the top was a strip of greasy filth; a lot was on his hands now,) dropped to echoing marble, and walked to a group with their backs to him. He shouldered between Tarzan and Thruppence.

Knee on the cushion (he took sharp, shallow breaths), Dollar jabbed an orchid-blade into the leather chair and ripped with caged and quivering fist. More stuffing pushed out. Catching his tongue tip in his teeth, he jabbed and ripped again.

Priest sniffed and took his hands from his pocket.

Filament tried not to clear her throat.

As they walked home, Kid searched his memory of what had occurred on Nightmare's run to the Emboriky. Among the black group strolling at his side Kid noticed blond Tarzan at their center. Raven, his arm around Tarzan's shoulder, was saying, ". . . your *sister?* Man, you got you a pretty sister. Tarzan, you got about the prettiest sister I ever *seen.* You gonna have to get me and that sister of yours together! *Ooooooo*—whee!" On *Whee!* he yanked at the crotch of his jeans with his free hand and nearly tugged Tarzan over.

"Now what you gonna talk about his sister for?" Lady of Spain asked.

"Aw, shit," Raven shouted over his shoulder, all his hair swaying. "Tarzan and me are friends. That right, Tarzan?" who grinned across the forearm beneath his chin.

"Tarzan," Glass grunted at Kid, "and the fuckin' apes!"

"Hey!" Jack the Ripper punched at Glass' shoulder. "Who's a fuckin' ape, nigger?"

But when Kid and Glass looked back, the Ripper let both legs go bandy, wheeled his arms about his shoulders, and began to bound about and grunt. Chains flew around his head. Now and then he paused to scratch his sides with underhanded flaps.

Copperhead's laugh was louder and harsher than the other's, rising and dying, as though responding to nuances of the performance no one else could catch.

Raven still draped around Tarzan, they staggered on. Raven's expression was now haunted and grim. Tarzan, hands hanging from his pockets and elbows swinging, smiled at the pavement over which they lurched, happily centered in so much attention.

The next day was:

Sunday—January 1st, 1979

(Headline:)

HAPPY NEW YEAR!

"You sure you don't want to come?" Kid asked Pepper. Kid's face still stung from shaving.

"Naw." Pepper shuffled nervously before the bathroom door. "Naw, I don't like stuff like that. All them people I don't know. You just go on, tell me about it when you come back. I got some wine, from the liquor store."

"Okay," Kid took his hand from Pepper's shoulder.

Copperhead came out of the bathroom. "Hey, you sure we don't got to dress up?"

"You wear your chains," Kid said, "your lights, and your vest, and you're dressed."

"Okay," Copperhead said. "If you say so. Man, Nightmare sure looks something out there in them red velvet pants. Like a God-damn spade!"

Kid's concession to festive dress, beside washing and shaving, had been to hang his brass orchid from a neck chain. As he walked up the hall—a water drop ran his bare ankle—the Ripper stopped him to whisper: "You really gonna let that boy go up there like that?" which was the third time someone had said something about Baby, who had arrived ten minutes ago, naked as promised (and dirty as ever), with Nightmare, Dragon Lady, and Adam.

"Sure am."

"Oh, man, I gotta see this. I was gonna stay home, you know? But I got to go to this one just to watch."

"He doesn't have anything you don't except a foreskin," Kid said. "Can't you be cool, huh?"

"Oh, sure!" The Ripper beat down the doubt with his wide, black hand. "Sure." He laughed and went on.

In the front room, Nightmare turned around and said something to Kid, mauled beyond comprehensibility by laughter. The others laughed too. His thick braid glistened with dressing. To his leather vest, neck chains, chained cycle boots, and garrison, the velvet loaned a scarlet panache.

"Nightmare," Siam (who only wore a small bandage now) was saying, "you're wearing those pants so low your ass has got *cleavage*, man!"

"Shit!" Nightmare caressed his great shoulder, "they *like* to see my muscles!" There was only a trace of the shoulder scar.

Kid glanced down at his own, listening to the laughter.

Dragon Lady, legs crossed, sat on the couch: White levi's, white boots, a silver lamé turtleneck, and over it a white levi jacket, sleeves torn off. Her usual chains (a trip to the hardware store?) had been replaced by silver—or at any rate, stainless steel. Her nails were painted platinum. When she threw her head back to laugh, on her big, stained teeth, sweat glistened just below her rough hair. She looked easy, elegant, and terrifying.

Adam, brown and glum looking, sat on the couch arm in his baggy pants and sneakers.

Baby sat on the floor in front of him, one dirty foot on top of the other, arms wrapped around his knobbly knees, a grubby hand on each grubby elbow, smiling like a happy, blond rat.

"Hey! Hey, come on! Now listen to this!" Blonder than Tarzan (who stood, oddly sullen, by the kitchen door), blond as Bunny, Revelation, perched on the back of the chair, turned over the *Times* and pulled aside his chains. He wore twice as many as anyone else, all brass and copper: "'. . . late in the afternoon yesterday, stalked through the streets of Jackson, terrorizing residents.' How you like that? So you guys were out terrorizing the spades yesterday? Huh?" His skin was the luminous pink some pale flesh becomes either in great cold or great heat. "'. . . committing acts of vandalism, the damage for which there is no way to assess, the rowdy band of black and white youths, necks hung with the chains that we have come to associate with the scorpions—'"

"We didn't terrorize nobody!" Denny (black shirt, silver fringe, beneath his vests and chains) sat with his back against the wall. "There wasn't nobody on the God-damn street!"

"That's cause they were all terrorized," Revelation explained. "Don't you see?"

". . . 'breaking into the Second City Bank—?'"

"Shit," Thruppence said (who had borrowed one of Denny's shirts) "we didn't do nothing yesterday."

657

"We robbed a fuckin' bank!" Filament (who had commandeered another) countered. "What do you mean we didn't do nothing? We robbed a whole God-damn bank!" She clasped her hands before her chin and looked delighted.

"A fuckin' bank?" Nightmare said. "Man, you're into some heavy stuff."

Spider, the youngest, blackest, and tallest scorpion in Kid's nest, leaned against the wall, rubbing the chains on his stomach, echoing Adam.

" '. . . It is nearly impossible, given our situation in Bellona, to identify any individuals in such an incident. Our reports are all from people behind locked doors and closed shutters . . .' "

"I can see all them mother-fuckers now," Dollar said, too loud even for this merriment, "starin' at us out the peepholes. Just a-starin'. God *damn!*"

" '. . . Their number has been estimated anywhere from forty to preposterous figures in the high hundreds . . .' "

"You mean," Copperhead demanded with lip-thinning satisfaction, "twenty of us made enough noise so that they thought we was in the high hundreds?" He stood, triumvirate with Spitt and Glass; all three, staunch to dictum, had made no change in dress.

Glass wore his black vinyl vest.

Spitt wore his projector and his scar and his turquoise buckle.

Between Spitt and Copperhead, Kid saw the little girl in the maroon jeans. Her blue blouse was very clean but unironed. She kept raising her hand to flatten the collar, glancing down at herself, and rubbing her collar again. For the first time she seemed pretty. Kid tried to remember what his reaction had been to her before and what had changed it.

" '. . . in the high hundreds,' " Revelation repeated, " 'which we would like to think—' "

"Maybe they ain't talking about you?" Dragon Lady suggested.

"Sure they're talking about us!" Priest insisted.

"We're the only ones who robbed a bank yesterday, I God-damn guess!"

" '—to think preposterous!' " which made Revelation laugh so hard he crumpled the paper.

"We gonna go to this fuckin' party tonight?" Cathedral demanded, catching both door jambs and swinging his bulk into the room. He swung back. The optic strand glittered around his brown neck, creased twice with fat. "What we waiting for?"

Kid grinned, nodded—was astonished at the silence. "Come *on!*"

They poured after him, laughing and shouting once more, out the front door and down the steps.

Pepper moved aside quickly.

"Change your mind yet?" Kid asked.

Pepper grinned his ruined grin. "Naw, I just don't feel like it, you know? I don't go for that stuff." His eyes flicked from Kid's.

Kid looked too.

From the bottom of the steps, among the milling scorpions, Tarzan watched; with a look of disgust he shook his head, turned away.

"Hey, don't let Tarzan stop you from coming," Kid said, suddenly angry. "I'll put the horsemen—" he nodded toward Copperhead and company—"on him so fast he won't be able to remember—" he started to say: *His name*—"what he thought it was he didn't like about you."

"Naw," Pepper said. "Naw, that ain't it. I'd just be all . . . Look, I thought I'd get me some wine, see. And maybe go over and say hello to Bunny. I ain't seen Bunny in a God-damn long time. She crazy, you know? She really a nut. But she's a good guy."

"Okay." Kid grinned back. "You do that."

"Uh . . ." Pepper said after him, "you have a nice time at the party . . ."

"Oh, hey . . . ! Hey . . . ! Come on, hey!" somebody shouted as Kid descended among them.

They started up the alley.

"Which way?" Nightmare called over a cluster of black heads in which, like, respectively, a lemon, a cumquat, and a dandelion among plums, were Tarzan's, and Copperhead's and Revelation's.

"Up this way. We have to pick up somebody."

Smoke encysted the corner street lamp in a giant pearl.

"God damn!" Somebody coughed. "How do you guys stand all this!"

(Kid couldn't see her because they had left the doorway's light.)

659

"You just ain't been here long enough, man! You'll get so you can't breathe without it after a while!"

"Somebody turn on some God-damn lights!" Kid called out, feeling across his chest for his projector. "Come on, huh?"

Dragon Lady's dragon raised, luminous jade, ahead. The mantis and the griffin flared, swaying, with misty penumbras.

An indigo spider flickered, mandibles higher than Kid's head—flickered out once around Copperhead, then gained full brightness like tardy neon.

Glass disappeared inside his newt.

Spitt's beetle glistened up like bottle glass.

Nightmare turned to Kid and grinned. "You got it pretty bright tonight, Kid," and flashed out beneath raised pincers.

The plastic colors opaled in the smoke.

Peacock (that was the Ripper), mantichor, and iguanadon, the spectral menagerie turned up the avenue.

6

"Are you sure this is where Lanya lives?" Kid asked Denny. The others milled about the stoop.

"Yeah," Denny said. "Yeah! Sure, ring the bell."

Kid did. Moments later, after footsteps (and he heard someone say, "Oh, dear . . ." behind the peephole), she opened the door and stepped out, all silver, into the smokey light.

"God *damn!*" Raven said appreciatively behind him.

Lanya shaded her eyes, looked about, said, "My God!" and burst out laughing.

Madame Brown, in something blue and tailored, stepped out behind her, looking tentative. The diffused light gave back to her heavy face the lines and over-madeup quality Kid had first seen by candle light. Once more her hair was harsh henna. And her neck, bound and bound around again with the optical beads, looked far too heavily decorated—yet it was the same way she wore them with her daytime browns and beiges.

Muriel barked once, leaped forward, and came up on the end of the leash.

"Oh, why don't you leave her home?" Lanya coaxed. "Look at our escort. We'll be—"

"Kid doesn't mind Muriel coming along; do you Kid? You said Roger had all those grounds. She'll be a perfect dear."

"Naw," Kid said, and discovered, saying it, he did. "Bring her along!"

"She just gets so lonely if I don't take her with me." Madame Brown surveyed the arrayed scorpions.

Muriel tried to run down the porch steps, couldn't and barked again.

"Hush, now!" Madame Brown said. "Hush!"

"Here, I'm giving this to you." Lanya handed Denny

661

the piece of equipment Tak had taken from the warehouse with the cloth. "Put it in your shirt pocket for me?"

The silver fringe on Denny's sleeve shook in curtains of light as he put the control box away.

Lanya took Kid's hand. Her dress was sleeveless, scoop-necked, and reached the ground. She leaned to whisper: "I've got something for you too," and handed him her harmonica. "Put this in your pants pocket for me?"

"Sure."

Feeling the metal on his thigh through the dime-sized tear, Kid stepped down among the others. Lanya, Muriel, and Madame Brown came behind.

As they started, he heard Madame Brown: "Your arm looks a lot better. It hasn't been giving you any trouble?"

"No ma'am," Siam answered. "Not much. Any more. But I thought I was gonna die when you just poured all that iodine in there." He laughed.

They crossed the street.

"That was the only way I could think to keep it from getting infected. You were very, very brave."

"Shit." Siam said. "I hollered like a mother-fucker—pardon, ma'am. But you remember how they were holding me down."

"Yes. And I still think you were brave."

"It's nice of you to say so. But if one of them niggers had let go of me, I'd a' probably killed you." He laughed again.

They spread the sidewalk, the street, each beast sailing on a pool of light.

Windows dripped with molten reflections—those with panes.

Perhaps half had their shields lit any one time. A boisterous black in silhouette would turn on a bright hippogryph, a mantichore; some gorgeous parrot or lizard would collapse around an ambling, side-lit figure— Kid tried to recall what *that* one had been, but her apparition, among so many, attracted his attention only by vanishing.

Dragon Lady, lights out, looked skeptically at Lanya, said to Kid, "I thought you said this weren't no dress-up party."

"Then you and I," Lanya told her, "will look that much better!"

Dragon Lady laughed. "You and me? Oh, honey, we sure will!" She dropped back and linked her silver arm in Lanya's bare one. "We gonna strut out fine, honey, and make them sons of bitches suffer!" Which made Lanya laugh. For a block the three of them walked arm in arm in arm.

But at some altercation ahead, Dragon Lady flared in jade and hastened forward to quell it:

Revelation (a frog) had started quarelling with Cathedral (some large bird that could, Kid realized on closer view, have been intended as an American Eagle): The Dragon moved between them, making more noise than both; they quieted.

Behind and to the side, Tarzan fingered, but hesitated to ignite, his parti-colored gila monster.

"That one . . . ?" Madame Brown nodded ahead with a deep frown and theatrical restraint. "Have you noticed, but every time his griphon flickers—" which it just did, revealing stringy yellow hair, knobbly spine, pockmarked buttocks, and grime-rimmed heels—"but doesn't it look just like he doesn't have any clothes on at all?"

"He doesn't." Kid said.

"Is there anything wrong with him?" Madame Brown demanded. "Is he all right?"

Her tone had changed from smutty complicity to puritan distress. Kid recognized each but could not follow the mechanics of transition; he grew fearful of the lightheadedness in which his mind bobbed. "No. He just doesn't have any," he explained, wondering if he were losing again his ability to follow logical connections.

Madame Brown said, "Oh . . ." in a tone at total odds with either previous.

They swarmed across the little park between Brisbains.

"I hope we get a ride back," Lanya said. "This is a long enough walk sober."

"Don't count on it."

"Roger is always talking in the paper about driving people in and out of town. Maybe he could have one of his drivers run us home afterward."

"I've seen his car. It's something from the thirties. Besides, how'd we fit all these people in?"

"You're just too democratic for words." She kissed his cheek. "Do you think I look nice?"

"Didn't I say so?"

663

"You did not. Nor did you say, 'You really made that dress yourself?' Or any of those things for which I'd prepared such very clever answers."

"Did you really make that dress yourself?" Kid slipped his hand around the tickling material on her waist. "It looks nice."

"Don't press too hard," she said. "I don't want to injure the material. No, no . . . I'm not driving you away!"

"*I* think you look nice," Denny said. "I think . . ." He whispered in her ear.

"*Young* man!" Lanya said. "I don't believe I know you—"

"Aw," Denny said, "go suck on my dick . . ." and started away.

"Hey, I was kidding . . ." Lanya called, amused puzzlement at Denny in her voice. Her waist tugged in Kid's arm.

Denny turned, his face flickering in the passing lights. As they caught up to him, he grinned. "I wasn't." He put his arm around her too.

They stepped up on the next corner, watching the jogging luminosities, delicate or bulbous, pass beneath charred branches, under lamp posts suspending inverted crowns of broken glass, by houses with columned porches, entrances gaping on blackness, as if the occupants had rushed out to see, then fled back in too distracted a state to close the doors behind.

Blocks later that image, still working in Kid's mind, finally loosened a chuckle which rolled around in his mouth.

Lanya and Denny were looking at him, she with a smile anticipating explanation, he merely without comprehension. Kid pulled her tighter. Denny's fringe brushed his arm, then crushed against him as he lowered his own arm down her back. Her far hip, moving under Kid's fingers, did not change its rhythm.

"This is all very colorful." Madame Brown strained back on the leash. "But it's quite a walk. Muriel, heel!"

"Roger's friends are pretty colorful too," Lanya said. "He'll rise to the occasion."

Vines climbed the wall. Willow boughs hung over it, sawtooth shadows growing and shrinking as the red, orange, and green lights passed.

"We're just about there, ain't we?" Nightmare called

from the middle of the street. Insects and arthropods floated around him, laughing gigantically.

"Yeah!" Kid called. "The gate's up there."

Denny was fingering in his shirt pocket. "Now what am I supposed to do with this thing?"

"Once we get inside," Lanya explained, "just turn me on. Every once in a while, give a look and if what you see is *too* dull, fiddle with those knobs till something interesting happens. Tak says its range is fifty yards, so don't get too far away. Otherwise I go out."

Suddenly Kid pulled away to shoulder through the bright, boisterous crowd. On a whim's stutter, he thumbed his shield's pip: it clicked.

From the inside, he remembered, your shield is invisible. But people had cleared around him. (I don't know what I am.) He looked down at the cracked pavement. (But whatever it is, it's blue.) The halo moved with him across the concrete.

Three beside him turned off their lights, growing shadows before them from the lights behind.

It's like a game (there were the stone newels), not knowing who, or what, you are. He wondered how long before he would finally get someone aside and ask. And flipped his pip to kill the temptation.

Stepping ahead of the crowd, he grabbed the bars. The others massed loudly around. He wondered, as he stared in at the pines, lit clumsily and shiftingly by his bright entourage, what to call out.

"Hello!" A young—Filipino? (probably)—in a green turtleneck and sports jacket stepped up. "You're the Kid? I thought so. I'm Barry Lansang. I'm on the gate tonight. Just a second, I'll let you all in."

"Hey, we're here!"

"How we gonna get in?"

"Shet up! He's lettin' us in now."

"This here's where we going?"

Lansang stepped aside. The gate went *Clang,* and the noise level around Kid cut by two-thirds.

Lansang swung back the bars.

Kid stepped forward, aware that the others had not.

"Go on up," Lansang smiled. "They're all expecting you. Is this your whole party?"

"Yeah. I think so."

"If you expect anybody else to come by later, just leave their names with me and I'll make a note."

"Naw. This is it."

Lansang smiled again. "Well, if stragglers come along later and we do have an identification problem, I can always go up and find you. Come on in," this last over Kid's shoulder, accompanied by a gesture.

Kid looked back.

The gateway crowded with silent, familiar faces.

"Come on," Kid said.

Then they came.

Dragon Lady was among the first. "This is something, huh?"

"Yeah." Kid said. "And this is just the trees."

"Follow the driveway up," Lansang instructed. He was, Kid saw, enjoying himself.

Lanya joined Kid; her gown blushed pink. As they walked together, robins-egg droplets grew into puddles which swelled to oceans.

"Am I doing this right?" Denny reached under his vest into his shirt pocket with a black and glittering arm.

Lanya looked down at herself. "I think the other knob—the one on the front—is for color intensity. Leave it like this for now. We don't want to shoot it all on the entrance."

Floodlights between the huge pines lit the gravel and, after the night journey, made them squint.

"Here we are," Madame Brown said, looking off between two trees where one light was not working. "All safe and sound."

Muriel walked close to her.

"Where's everybody likely to be?" Kid asked Lanya, whose dress dribbled a metallic green across her left breast.

"Out on the terrace gardens. Where we were that afternoon with Mr Newboy."

Kid did not remember the driveway as this long. "How come they have all this electricity?"

"When it's *all* working, they can get this whole grounds practically bright as day," Lanya said.

They passed the last trees:

The house was bright as day against the night.

"Newboy said something about lanterns . . ."

"It doesn't all work inside," Lanya said. "There was one whole wing where there wasn't a socket functioning." (Some dozens of men and women along the stone terrace turned to look.) "But whenever Roger lights the whole place up like this, I get the feeling I'm watching some really banal *Son et lumiere."*

The scorpions quieted as they saw the other guests.

Suit, shirt, and tie of different blues, one pushed from among them. Short blond hair, a serious expression, he was followed by two women—the older also in blue, hair rinsed the same shade as his shirt. The younger, in a floor-length brocade, looked unhappy.

Calkins, Kid thought starting forward. But anticipation had betrayed him: It was Captain Kamp.

"Kid—!" called out affably enough—"you got here. And these are your friends . . . I . . . um. Well, we've had a little . . ." Initial affability spent, Kamp looked confused. "Now, Roger hasn't gotten back yet. He told us he might be late, and to tell you how sorry he was . . . He asked me and Thelma—" he nodded at the woman in brocade—"and Ernestine—" and at the woman in blue— "to say hello for him when you got here . . . um, since I'd met you—" his eyes kept moving to the people behind Kid—"to introduce you around and things. Now, Ernestine, this is the Kid. And this is Thelma . . ."

Ernestine, who seemed much less nervous than Kamp, said, "I'm Ernestine Throckmorton. How wonderful to have all you young people here. Hi, love," which was a special nod to Lanya, who grinned back. "Now I think the only thing to do is plunge in and go over how everything is laid out. Why don't you all come with us and we'll show you where to get something to eat and drink? Come on, now." She turned and motioned them up the steps onto the terrace.

As the other guests stepped back, staring, she went for the two nearest and brightest scorpions. "And what are your names?"

"Nightmare," Nightmare said rather like a question.

"And your friend?"

"Oh, yeah. I'm sorry. This here is Dragon Lady."

"Very pleased to meet you both. You know, I've heard your names before; well, read them actually, in the paper. Really, I'm quite terrified."

Kid glanced over.

Ernestine, who did not look terrified one bit, strolled by the staring (some smiled) guests, Nightmare on one arm, Dragon Lady on the other.

"Bill!" she cried out. (Bill was smiling.) "Come here, dear."

Bill, a tall, handsome man, perhaps thirty-eight, in a black turtleneck, a can of beer in one hand (the only guest there already, without a jacket), fell in beside them. "Bill, this is Nightmare and Dragon Lady. You mentioned them in that article you did for Roger a little while ago. Now, have you ever met them?"

"I'm afraid I haven't."

"Well, here they are."

"Hello," and "Hello," Nightmare and Dragon Lady said, just out of sync.

"I'm glad to meet you, but I'm not sure that you're glad to meet me after some of the things I said."

"You wrote an article?" Nightmare asked. "In the paper?"

"I didn't read no article," Dragon Lady said.

"Probably all just as well, considering some of what I put down—here, we're all heading for the beer wagon down at the end—" Bill gestured with his can. "I'm really surprised to meet you here with the Kid. I was under the impression that the various gangs—nests—kept at each other's throats."

"Naw," Nightmare said. "Naw, it ain't like that . . ."

While Nightmare explained how it was, Kid looked over again. Bill had replaced Ernestine, who had drifted back to other scorpions: "I'm Ernestine Throckmorton. And you're . . . ?"

Lanya smiled and whispered: "This is going to be work." Concern underlay the smile.

"Huh?"

"Since Roger's not here. To get people mixing. I mean if he's got one, that's his single overwhelming talent. Ernestine's competent. I've seen her work before—"

"I guess you know her."

"I recognize about five people here, I think. Thank God. Roger usually keeps a pretty inspired group. Ernestine can even be brilliant. Roger, however, has genius. And I'm afraid I was sort of counting on it this evening. Don't be mad if I abandon you for a little while. You can take care of yourself. Why don't you start by introducing me to the Captain?"

"Oh," Kid said. "Sure. I know him. Glass and I walked him up here one night."

"Glass . . ." she considered, and her consideration made him pause till she nodded:

668

"Captain Kamp?" he had to say three times before the Captain turned. "This is my friend, Lanya Colson."

"Since everyone's talking to people they've read about in the papers," Lanya said, "I guess I can tell you that I've read about you."

"Um . . ." The Captain smiled uncertainly.

"I spent some time here with Roger a little while ago," Lanya said, which to Kid sounded pretty phony.

But the Captain's "Oh?" was filled with relief.

She seemed to know what she was doing.

"Where has Roger gone? It's not like him to arrange something like this and then not be here."

"Now I'm sure he'll be back," the Captain said. "I'm just sure. He had it all arranged with the lady in the kitchen—"

"Mrs Alt?"

"—yes. And she's really laid out a nice spread. I don't know where he went off to. I was sort of hoping he'd be back in time. Partying isn't really my strong point. And I didn't realize all of you people were going to come. Of course, Roger did say bring twenty or thirty friends, didn't he? But. Now. Well . . ."

The long terrace ended at a patio.

Two tables were set up on the stone flags.

Flame blued the copper bottoms of a half-dozen chafing dishes.

There were paper plates. There were plastic forks. The napkins were linen.

Most of the guests, before on the terrace, had now drifted with them to the patio.

"You just help yourselves to anything you'd like to eat." Ernestine's arms rose like a conductor's. "That's the bar over there. Either of these gentlemen—" one young black bartender, one elderly white one, both in double-breasted blue—"will get you a drink. Those two kegs over there are beer. If you want it in the can, the cooler, here—" she thumbed at it; two people laughed—"is chock-full." In more modulated tones to whoever happened to be beside her: "Would you like something to eat?"

"Sure." Revelation said.

"Yes, ma'am," from Spider.

No full meal had been cooked in the nest that day.

"Captain Kamp," Lanya was saying, "this is Glass. Glass, this is Captain Kamp."

"Oh, yes. We've met, now."

"You have?" Lanya's surprise sounded perfectly delighted and perfectly sincere. (If I wrote her words down, Kid thought, what she's saying would vanish into something meaningless as the literal record of the sounds June or George makes.) "Then I can leave the two of you alone and get something to eat," and turned away.

("Now," Kamp said. "Well. What have you been doing since I saw you last?"

(Glass said: "Nothing. You been doing anything?"

(Kamp said: "No, not really.")

Lanya shouldered through Tarzan-and-the apes. "Hey, come on with me, I want you to meet someone. No, really, come on," and emerged with Jack the Ripper and Raven, herding before them the diminutive black Angel. "Dr Wellman, *you're* from Chicago! I'd like you to meet Angel, the Ripper, and Raven." She stayed a little longer with them. Kid listened to the conversation start, halt, and finally settle into even exchanges (between Angel and Dr Wellman at any rate) about community centers in Chicago, which Angel seemed to think were "all right, man. Yeah I really liked that," while Dr Wellman held out, affably, that "they weren't very well organized. At least not the ones we did our reports on."

"Hey, Kid."

Kid turned.

Paul Fenster doffed a paper plate at him.

"Oh, hi . . . !" Kid grinned, astonished how happy he was to see someone he knew.

"Get yourself something to eat, why don't you?" Fenster said and stepped away between two others, while Kid held the words he'd been about to say clumsily in his mouth.

He wished that Tak had come. And that Fenster had not.

Lanya passed close enough to smile at him. And he was close enough to hear her coax Madame Brown: "Work, work, work!" in a whisper.

Wrapping herself in her leash, Madame Brown turned and said: "Siam, this is a terribly good friend of mine, Everett Forest. Siam was my patient, Everett."

Everett was the man Kid usually saw at Teddy's in purple angora. He now wore a navy blazer and grey knitted pants.

Somewhere across the patio, Lanya was holding paper

670

plates in both hands, about to give them away. Turquoise billowed about her silver hem, trying and failing to rise like a lazy lava lamp. He started to go take a plate, but suddenly thought of Denny, looked around for him—

"I asked Roger if I could be on—"

Kid turned.

"—on your welcoming committee—" (unhappy Thelma of the floor-length brocade) —"because I didn't think I could possibly get to speak to you otherwise. I wanted to tell you how much pleasure *Brass Orchids* gave me. Only now I—find that it's—" her dark eyes, still unhappy, fell and rose—"just very difficult to do."

"Um . . . thank you," Kid offered.

"It's hard to compliment a poet. If you say his work seems skillful, he turns around and explains that all he's interested in is vigor and spontaneity. If you say the work has life and immediacy, it turns out he was basically concerned with overcoming some technical problem." She sighed. "I really enjoyed them. And outside a few polite phrases, there just isn't the vocabulary to describe that sort of enjoyment in a way that sounds real." She paused. "And your poems are one of the realest things that's happened to me in a long time."

"Damn!" Kid said. "Thank you!"

"Would you like something to drink?" she suggested in the silence.

"Yeah. Sure. Let's get something to drink."

They walked to the table.

"I've written—and published—two novels." Thelma went on. "Nothing you're likely to have heard of. But the effect of your poems on me, especially the first four, the Elegy, and the last two before the long conversational one in meter, is rather the effect I'd always hoped my books would have on people." She actually laughed. "In a way, your book was discouraging, because watching your poems gain that effect showed me some of the reasons why my prose often doesn't. That condensed and clear descriptive insight is something I envy you. And you wield it as naturally as speech, turning it on this and that and the other . . ." She shook her head, she smiled. "All I can do is find a lot of adjectives that you've got to fill up with meaning for yourself: Beautiful, perhaps marvelous, or wonderful . . ."

Kid decided they all applied, to her anyway; His delight was awesome. But holding it (the black bartender

671

poured him a bourbon) was an entrancing irritation as pleasurable in building as a sneeze in relief.

Denny stepped up to the table, fingering inside his shirt pocket. "Hey, you wanna see something?"

Kid and Thelma watched.

And across the patio, Lanya's dress splashed around with orange and gold. The people she was talking with stepped back in surprise. She looked down at herself, laughed, searched about till she saw Kid and Denny, and blew them a kiss.

Thelma smiled and did not seem to understand.

Kid introduced Thelma to Denny. She introduced them to someone else. Bill, the reporter, joined them. Thelma left. Kid watched laddering relational torques and tensions, already interpreting them as likes, dislikes, ease and unease. Lanya brought Budgie Goldstein to meet him. Budgie, immense in green chiffon, explained how frightened she'd always been of scorpions but now how nice they all seemed, punctuating her explanation with sharp, short laughs. They had wandered from the terrace onto the—

"These? I believe there are . . . Toby, what *are* these?"

"The September Gardens, Roxanne. September, remember . . . And who is this young man? You wouldn't be the Kid?"

And he was handed on.

He liked it.

It took half an hour to realize he had been kept entirely away from the other scorpions.

Besides what he estimated at two dozen house guests, there were another thirty-odd invited from town, including Paul Fenster, Everett (Angora) Forest, and (Kid was surprised to see him leaning over against the stone wall, talking with Revelation) Frank.

There was a bridge between January and June.

Kid looked over the rail at wet rock; floodlights glistened on a vein of clotted leaves—there was no clear water, Lanya and Ernestine passed on the little path underneath.

Ernestine said into her drink: "The only thing I could think of to do was to physically *push* them at one another . . ."

Kid thought Lanya had not seen him, but a moment after she vanished she said, "Hello," behind him.

672

He turned from the rail. "You've been very busy."

Wrist against forehead, she mimed distress. "Phase one, at any rate, is over. Just about everyone knows now it's *possible* to talk to everyone else. Are you having a good time?"

"Yeah. They're all here for me." Then he grinned. "But they're all talking about you."

"Huh?"

"Three people have told me how great your dress is," which was true. "Denny's doing a good job."

"You're a doll!" She clapped his cheeks between her palms and kissed him on the nose.

Cathedral, California, and Thruppence ambled below them on the path, light and dark shoulders together. I feel responsible for them, he thought, recalling her initial efforts. He laughed.

Her dress began to broil with green and lavender.

She saw and asked, "Where's Denny gotten off to? Let's go look for him."

They did and could not find him, spoke to others, and then Kid lost her again.

From the high rocks of—"October," said the plaque on the rust-ringed birdbath—he looked down toward the terrace.

Two women he had not met, with Bill (whom he had) between them, had cornered Baby and were talking at him intently. Baby smiled very hard, his paper plate just under his chin. Sometimes he dropped his head to nod, sometimes to scrape up another and another forkful. Once in a while someone across the terrace, when they were sure they were unobserved, would glance—two ladies, one after another, maneuvered for the better view, noticed they were observed, and walked away.

Someone was in the bushes behind him.

Kid looked around: Jack the Ripper backed out; from the movement of his elbows, he was closing his fly. He turned. "Huh? . . . oh, it's just you, man." He grinned, bent, adjusted himself. "Scared somebody gonna see me back there takin' a leak."

"There's a bathroom in the house somewhere."

"Shit. I didn't wanna go askin' around for that. My piss ain't gonna kill no flowers. This is a real nice place, huh. A real nice party. Everybody's real nice. You havin' a nice time? I sure am."

Kid nodded. "You catch Baby when he came in?"

"No," the Ripper drawled with a wildly interrogative cadence.

"You said you wanted to see what the reaction was. I missed it. I was wondering if you caught it."

"God damn!" The Ripper snapped his fingers. "You know I wasn't even looking?"

"There he is."

"Where?"

Kid nodded toward the terrace.

The Ripper stuck his hands in the back of his pants. "What they talkin' about?"

Kid shrugged.

"Hey, man!" The Ripper's hands came loose again. "I gotta go down and hear this." He grinned at Kid who started to say something. But the Ripper was off along the rocks.

At the four-foot terrace wall, the Ripper straight-armed up, scrambled over—half a dozen looked—and jumped. A bopping lope took him to the bar. The white bartender gave him two drinks. He came to the corner, thrust one glass at Baby and said loud enough for Kid to hear: "Now I *know* you want a drink, Baby, 'cause you gonna need something to keep you warm."

Several people laughed.

Baby took the drink in both hands—he had put his plate down on the wall—and looked as though he were about to dive into it. But Bill and the two women merely made room, and continued.

Seconds later, the Ripper, all weight on one leg, heavy lower lip sucked in and long head quizzically cocked, stood rapt, nodding in unison with Baby.

Curious at their low converse, Kid walked away from it into March.

Only one light worked here, anchored high and harsh on an elm. Captain Kamp stood silhouetted at the vertex of his shadow. "Hello, now, I was just coming back this way . . . you enjoying yourself?" Backlight made him ominous; his voice was cheerful. "I was just over there taking a—" (Kid expected him to say "leak")—"look in the August gardens. There're no lights in there, so I guess people are staying clear. But you can see down into the city. A few street lights are still on. I'm not too good at this ersatz host business. And this party takes some hosting." Kamp stepped up. Kid turned to walk with him. "Now I sure wish Roger would get here."

"Doesn't look like anyone's missed him too much."

"I have. I'm just not used to all this . . . well, sort of thing. I mean, trying to be in charge of it."

"I guess I'd like to meet him."

"Sure. Of course you would." Kamp nodded as they came nearer the house. "I mean he's giving this party for you, for your book. You'd think he'd . . . but now I'm pretty sure he'll get here. You don't worry now."

"I'm not and don't mean to start."

"You know I was thinking—" they walked up the stone steps—"about some of the things we were talking about when I first met you."

"That was a strange evening. But it came after a strange day."

"Sure did. Have you seen Roger's observatory?" Kamp interrupted himself. "Perhaps you'd like to go up and see it."

Kid was curious at the transition rather than the suggestion. "Okay."

Coming down the terrace, Lady of Spain, Spider, Angel, Raven and Tarzan, circled gangling D-t:

"D-t, man, you gotta see this!"

"I ain't never seen no garden like this before. All them flowers—"

"—and a big fountain that works and all."

"Come on. We gonna show you." Lady of Spain tugged his arm.

"D-t, you ain't never seen no garden as pretty as this in your whole life!"

"I guess—" Kamp opened the door for Kid—"I'm just not used to it. I mean all these different . . . kinds of people. Like that boy back there walking around with no clothes on? And everybody going on just like there was nothing wrong." The large, dark room was lined with books. In candlelight some dozen people sat on the floor or on hassocks. Several looked up from a tape recorder from which organ music flowed. One man (Kid remembered his making some joke in November about the smoke) said, "Kid? Captain? Would you like to join us? We were just listening to some—"

"We're going to the observatory." Kamp opened another door.

The organ piece ended; after a slight pause, a long note bent. Then another . . . They were playing *Diffraction*.

Kid smiled as he walked after Kamp down a hall nearly black. He could hear Lanya's whistle. At the top of a stairway Kid saw faint light. The carpeting was thick and so warm under his bare foot he wondered if there were heating on.

"I suppose it wouldn't be so bad if Roger was here. But being left in charge of a party for a bunch of people that, frankly, I'd put out of my house . . ."

Kid was quietly amazed and wondered what Kamp was thinking in the pause.

". . . I just don't know what to do. Do you know what I mean?"

Anything, Kid thought, I say will sound angry and stupid. He said, "Sure," and followed Kamp up the stairs.

"A few months ago," Kamp said, "I was in some experiments. They didn't have anything to do with the moon. In fact I had to get a special release from the Space Program to participate. Some students of a friend of mine at Michigan were running tests, and I guess he thought it would be a feather in his cap to get me for a guinea pig. Now, it'd been so long since I had anything to do that wasn't in some way connected with the Program, I went along with it. They were experiments on sensory deprivation and overload." At the head of the steps, Kamp waited for Kid before starting up a third flight.

He led Kid across a brick floor to a double doorway.

"I was in the overload part. It was all pretty amateurish, actually."

Kid stepped onto what first seemed a semi-circular balcony.

Faintly, below, a room full of people began to clap in time to the music—

"I guess they'd all been reading too many articles on LSD—"

—and shouted.

"—I took LSD back in the late fifties—more tests, that this psychiatrist friend of mine was running. But I've always been a little ahead of what's going on. Anyway, I know what it's like, LSD. And I'm pretty sure *most* of those kids setting up those experiments in Michigan didn't."

The terrace was enclosed in a glass dome. In the

center was a six-foot in diameter celestial globe of clear plastic. Light from the garden below struggled in the smoke above, glowing like dilute milk.

"Now I guess you've taken LSD and all that stuff."

"Sure."

"Well, all they'd been doing was looking at all the pretty pictures everyone had been drawing." Kamp touched the globe, removed his fingers. Ares passed across Libra. The stars were glittering stones set in the etched constellations. "They had spherical rear-projection rooms, practically as big as this place here. They could cover it with colors and shapes and flashes. They put earphones on me and blasted in beeps and clicks and oscillating frequencies. Anyway, I was supposed to pick out patterns from all this. Later I learned that mine was the control group: We were given no patterns at all. I was told all the ones I had seen I had imposed myself . . . But after two hours of testing, two hours of fillips and curlicues of light and noise, when I went outside, into the real world, I was just astounded at how . . . *rich* and complicated everything suddenly looked and sounded: The textures of concrete, tree bark, grass, the shadings from sky to cloud. But rich in comparison to the sensory-overload chamber. *Rich* . . . and I suddenly realized what the kids had been calling a sensory overload was really information-deprivation. It's the *pattern* that colors and shapes assume that tell you whether it's a cow or a car you're looking at. It's the very finest alternations in color differentiation over a surface that tell you whether it's maple or pine, styrene or polyethylene, linen or flannel. Take any view in front of you and cut off the top and bottom till you've only got an inch-wide strip and you'll still be amazed at all the information you can get from just running your eye along that. Well, all this started me thinking back to the moon. Because that had been a place—and it happened in every mile en route—where standard information patterns just broke down. And yet, *that's* something we haven't been able to talk about—to anyone—since we got back. We'd trained for prolonged free-fall by spending time underwater in diving suits. I remember when we actually hit sustained weightlessness, I broadcast back, 'Hey, it's just like being underwater!' and yet as I said that into the chin mike, I was thinking: You certainly could never *mistake* the two conditions for one another. But I couldn't think of any way to *say* what was different about it, so I just described it the way everybody, who'd never been there themselves, had *told* me it was going to feel like. Later I thought, that's like telling someone the world is flat and sending him off to the edge; but because he doesn't know quite how to describe such gentle roundness, he mumbles and stammers and says, 'Well yeah, I was at the . . . edge.' And the thing about the moon itself, the one thing I've really *never* told anybody, because I don't think I would have known how before those experiments: it's another *world*, and when you're there, you have no way of knowing *what* anything means. *Physically*. That whole landscape tells you nothing about itself, on any level, in the way that the most desolate stretch of sand on earth tells you about winds that have blown over it, rains that have or have not fallen, or the feel it might have beneath your feet if you walked across it. 'An airless, waterless void . . .' the way they say in all the science-fiction stories? No, that refers to some desert on earth, or what space between the stars looks like when you're safely tucked under the atmosphere. The moon is a different world, with a different order that you don't understand. There *isn't* that richness—not because it isn't in bright colors, or because it's all brown, purple, and grey. It's because as you run your eyes over the rocks and dirt, you have no way to know what the tiny alterations in color mean. Even though it has a horizon and perspective, and . . . well, rocks and dirt, it's more like being in that sensory-overload chamber than anything else. And of course, it isn't like that at all. It wasn't horrible. Horror still has something to do with earth. I suppose it was frightening. But even that was absorbed in the excitement of it. I—" he paused—"do not know how to tell you about it." He smiled and shrugged. "And that's probably the one thing I really haven't told *any*body before. Oh, I've said, 'You can't describe it. You'd have to be there.' But that's my first wife telling her mother-in-law about the time we went to Persia. And that isn't what I mean."

Kid smiled back and wished he hadn't.

It isn't his moon I distrust so much, he thought, as it is that first wife in Persia. "I understand," he said, "as much as I'll let myself."

"Maybe," Kamp said after a moment, "you do. Let's go back down to the party."

Walking down the steps, Kid felt self-betrayed and

wondered if there were any benefit from the feeling. He wanted to find Lanya and Denny.

Outside on the terrace, while the Captain, beside him, looked around as if for someone else to talk to, Kid thought: I feel the responsibility for him now he probably hoped I felt the night I walked him up here. That is not right, and I don't like it.

Ernestine Throckmorton said, "Captain! Kid! Ah, there you are," and began to talk definitely only to Kamp.

Kid excused himself, wondering whether she really was an angel, and went down into the gardens.

Lanya was crossing the bridge in a fury of emerald and indigo.

"Hey," he said. "Have you seen Denny?"

She turned. *"You* haven't. He's feeling abandoned."

Paul Fenster, holding his drink beneath his chin, stepped around Kid and said: "Jesus Christ, you'll never believe what was going on back there in April. I didn't think I was going to be able to make it." He laughed.

Lanya didn't, and asked, "What?"

"A whole bunch of black kids, back in April, they've got this whole *routine* worked out. They've got this white boy, called Tarzan: And they were just *performing!* And of course Roger's nice old colonel from Alabama was there—the one I was telling you about who gave me so much trouble when I was visiting—and of course he was laughing harder than anybody else. I kid you not, they were swinging from the God-damn trees!"

"What did you do?" Lanya had begun to laugh.

"Sweated a lot," Fenster said. "And tried to think of some way to leave. You know, guys who come to parties like this in berets and talk about liberating the furniture: Now I'm pretty into that. But I guess that type all had sense enough to get out of Bellona while there was some getting. This Stepin Fetchit stuff, though—well, all I can say is, it's been a while!"

"Suffering's supposed to be good for the something-or-other," Kid said.

"It damn," Fenster replied, "well better be!" He grunted (simianly?) and walked on across the bridge.

Lanya took Kid's hand. ". . . Denny?"

"Yeah."

"I just left him." Her dress was shimmering black. A silver circle rose on the hem. "In March." She gestured with her head.

He said, "You're beautiful."

He thought, she's wistful.

"Thank you. You really like the dress?"

He nodded, kept nodding, and suddenly she laughed and closed his mouth with her fingers.

"I believe you. But I was beginning to think it was too much. Of course I was expecting just to stand around in some elegantly arbored corner holding court; not run around working. Where, I wonder, is Roger?"

Kid held her cool hands against his face with his warm ones. "Let's find Denny."

Dawn broke on her waist. "You find him," she said. "I'll see you a little later." A scarlet sun, haloed in yellow, eclipsed the silver moon.

He wondered why but said. "Okay," and left her on the bridge.

The stream became a pool in March, scaled with immobile leaves.

"I told that bitch!" Dollar stood and rocked on bowed legs. "I told that bitch. After what she tried, you know? I just told her."

Denny sat cross-legged on the stone bench and didn't look like he was listening too hard.

Kid walked around the pool. "You trying to get in trouble at my party?"

Dollar's head jerked: he looked scared.

Denny said, "Dollar's okay. He ain't done nothing."

"I ain't done nothing," Dollar echoed. "It's a real nice party, Kid."

Kid put his hand on the back of Dollar's pitted neck and squeezed. "You have a good time. Don't let anything get you, you know? You got a whole lot of space to walk around in. Something gets you here, you walk on over there. Something gets you there, you go on someplace else. If it happens a third time, come tell me about it. Understand? There's no strange sun in the sky tonight."

"Nothing's wrong, Kid. Everything's okay." The distressful smile went; Dollar just looked sad. "Really."

"Good." Kid let go Dollar's neck and looked at Denny. "You having a good time?"

"I guess so." Denny's shirt, unbuttoned, hung out of his pants. "Yeah."

A group came through the ivied gate, scorpions and others, following Ernestine Throckmorton.

Dollar said, "Oh, hey!" and jogged, jangling, after them, around the pool and out another entrance.

"I'm going to take this off." Denny shrugged from his vest, got the control box from his pocket, slipped out of his shirt, and sat, turning the box in one hand, the other slung among his chains. "Lanya says I've been doing a good job. This little thing is something, huh?"

Kid sat down and put his hand on Denny's dry, knobby back. In the boy's glance some relief flickered.

Kid rubbed his back.

Denny said, "Why you doin' that?" But he was smiling at his lap.

"Because you like it." Kid moved his hand up the sharp shoulder blade and down, pressing. Denny rocked with each rub.

"Sometimes," Lanya said and Kid turned, "I envy you two."

Kid did not stop rubbing and Denny did not look up.

"Why?" Denny moved his shoulders, reached up to scratch his neck.

"I don't know. I supposed it's because you can let people—let Kid know you want things I'd be afraid to ask for."

"You want your back rubbed?" Kid asked.

"Yes." She grinned. "But not now."

"I watch the two of you," Kid said, "when you're playing. When you're throwing things at one another; tugging one another around all the time. I envy you."

"You . . . ?" Lanya reached for Denny's shoulder.

But Denny suddenly stood and stepped forward.

Kid wondered if he'd seen her reaching, watched her face pass through hurt and her hand withdraw.

Denny turned on the pool edge and laughed. "Aw, you two are all—" He twisted a knob.

From neck to hem she glittered black; black granulated silver; scarlet poured about her. "Hey, see, I got it good!"

"You sure do," Lanya said.

Kid stood and took her arm. "Come on."

"Where are we . . . ?"

Kid grinned: "Come on!"

She raised a brow and came, intently curious.

Denny followed them; his confusion looked much less sharp than hers.

681

On the other side of the ivied stone, Ernestine apostrophized: ". . . *chunk* crab meat, not the stringy kind! Then eggs. Then a *few* bread crumbs. And *bay* seasoning. When I lived in Trenton, I'd have to have it sent up from Maryland. But Mrs Alt—nobody could have been more surprised than I was—found an entire shelf full in a store down on Temple . . ."

At the silent edge, Dollar muttered reverently: ". . . God *damn* . . ."

"*Bay* seasoning," Ernestine reiterated as Kid and Lanya and Denny passed around her, "is the most important thing."

On the path to the next garden, Denny whispered: "Where are we going?"

"Through here," Kid said. "The lights are out in here . . ."

"August," Lanya said.

They stepped into flakey darkness. Grass slid cool between Kid's toes. He clutched; it slipped away with the next step; tickling again.

The next stop was surprising stone.

He rocked his naked foot: Wet, cold . . . rough. His shod one stayed steady.

"I think there's a—" Lanya's voice echoed. She paused to listen to the reverberations—"some sort of underpass."

They came from under it four steps later.

"I didn't even see us go in." Denny stepped forward in the night grass.

Kid curled his free toes again, lifted his foot; grass tore.

"Hey, you can see the city, almost," Denny said.

Beyond a ruffed, stone beast, blurs of light were snipped off across the bottom by buildings. Implied hills, slopes, or depressions patterned the darkness around.

"Calkins' place can soak up a lot of people." The high trees—like small cypresses—were carbon dark against the muzzy night. Kid tried to see down into Bellona. One tall . . . building? It had perhaps a dozen windows lit.

"How odd," Lanya said. "All the limits go, and you can't believe there's really any more to it. We're used to objects like icebergs or oilwells where you know most of it is under ground or water. But something like a city at night, with great stretches of it blotted or obscured, that's a very different—"

"You guys," Denny interrupted. "I don't envy you . . . I guess. But you two can talk about things that, you know, are just so far beyond me I don't even know how to ask questions sometimes. I listen. But sometimes when I don't understand—or even when I do, I just wanna fuckin' cry, you know?" When they were silent, he asked again, "You know?"

Lanya nodded. "I do."

Denny breathed out and looked.

They stood apart and felt very close.

Kid watched her dress catch what light there was and glitter dim crimson, with waves of navy, or green of the evening ocean.

"What's that?" Denny asked.

Kid looked beyond them. "A fire."

"Where do you think it is?" Lanya asked.

"I can't tell. I don't really know where we are." He stepped up and put his hand on her shoulder: The metallic cloth prickled. Her skin was cool.

Denny's, under his other hand, was fever hot and, as usual, paper-dry.

Kid wanted to walk.

So they walked with him, a hip on either hip, hitting to different rhythms. He'd slipped his hands across their backs to their outer shoulders. The hand on Lanya's shoulder was still.

Denny put his arm around Kid's back.

Lanya's arms were folded, her vision distanced while she walked and watched the charred city.

Then she put her head on his shoulder (still watching), her arm around him, her shoulder more firmly in the place beneath his arm, brought her thigh against his thigh.

And was still watching.

They walked beside the waist-high wall. This is the largest garden, Kid thought. Denny shifted his step—

"What?" Kid asked.

"One of the spotlights that ain't working . . ." Denny had just stepped around it.

They crossed cool flags.

Leaves rasped away the silence. A breeze? While he walked beneath the loud, black fleece of some high elm or oak, he waited for the warm or cool gust. Silence returned; he'd felt neither.

"Why don't it ever burn up here?" Denny asked, too

softly, too intently. His shoulder twitched in Kid's hand. "Why don't it just all burn up or something, the whole thing? It just goes on and . . ." Kid ceased to knead, rubbed now.

Denny took another deep breath, fast, then let it out over the next five steps.

Lanya turned on Kid's shoulder, glanced across at Denny, and turned back.

Kid tried to loosen the tension in his abdomen. There was a sudden, unsettling feeling: All his organs, gut, liver, belly, lungs and heart, seemed to have shifted inches down. He didn't break step, but the feeling passed through a moment of nausea that ended with his breaking wind.

Which felt better.

He pulled Lanya closer; the leg against his leg and the shoulder's tugging eased into Kid's and Lanya's rhythm. Translated through Kid's body, Denny's motion firmed and, to the tension, Kid's firmed too. She sighed with her mouth just slightly open, corner to corner, then stroked his arm with the back of her neck. Denny's hand slipped its knuckly padding between Kid's hip and hers.

Another stone lion crouched on the wall, staring.

By it, with leafless branches like shatter lines on the night's smoked glass, was a tree. Beneath Kid's foot the ground was bare, crumbly and—ashy? Recognizing the texture, he stepped from the charred grass to fresh.

They circled the garden.

It was too dark to tell if the small pool were full or empty. Lanya put her hand out and touched a tree trunk. She no longer watched the small burnings worm down in the night city. She walked more closely in step with Kid than Denny did. (Kid thinking: It frees her to think of things further away.) He felt protective of her meditations, and frightened by them.

A memory of rustling italicized the silence.

Kid listened for converse in another garden. Their own footsteps were so quiet.

Beyond the wall, (miles away?) things smoked and flickered.

A whisper: "Someone's coming—!"

And another: "Oh, wait a minute. Watch out—!"

Kid recognized one girl's voice but not the other.

One branch among the bushes beat at the rest.

The guy who stepped out, zipping his fly, belt loose down both hips, and grinning . . . it was Glass. "Oh,"

684

he said. "It's you all," and pulled his belt through the buckle.

One of the girls said: "Just a second. Here it is . . ."

"Can you see anything?" the other asked, then giggled—the girl in maroon jeans who had come with them from the nest: She pushed out between the brush.

Somebody behind her was looking all around: that was Spitt.

The other girl Kid first recognized as one of Roger's guests. Even in the three-quarter dark she looked rumpled. The second recognition was that it was Milly: her red hair fell over a dark, velvet jumper: She wore something metallic beneath it, unbuttoned now. Copperhead, a hand on each of her shoulders, guided her out.

Lanya said, "Lord!" and laughed.

"Oh!" Milly said. "It's *you* all!" in dissimilar accent, but identical inflection, as Glass. She pulled from Copperhead.

She and Lanya clutched one another in a fit of giggles.

Copperhead frowned at Kid and shook his head.

Kid shrugged.

"I can't find my comb!" Milly finally got out. "Isn't it amazing! I can't find my comb."

Lanya looked back at Kid: "Here, I'll see you in a little while."

Then, her arm around Milly's shoulder, they fled the garden.

"Man," Glass said. "This is a pretty good party."

Copperhead, deprived of Milly, settled beside the first girl. He bent to whisper to her. She whispered back.

"God damn, nigger!" Spitt said. "You don't do nothin' but fuck, do you?"

"Shit," Glass said. "I watched your pink ass poppin' up and down there a pretty good long while."

"Yeah, sure." Spitt said. "But, man, you were in this one, then that one, then this one again— God *damn!*"

Glass just chuckled.

Then both of them saw that Copperhead and the girl were moving off.

"Hey!" Spitt called and started after them.

Glass loped to their other side.

Phalanxed by black and white, the girl and Copperhead left.

"Come on." Denny pulled away from Kid, who followed, wondering what of all that interchange had in-

685

terested Denny most. But as soon as Denny got between the hedges—one shoulder feathered with shadow, the other bright under the lights of June—he stopped to adjust the control box. "There."

Nowhere, Kid was sure, had he seen John. But then he hadn't recognized Mildred before.

Guests surging Novemberwards cut them off from Copperhead and the others.

After he'd left Denny, Kid thought: But the whole point was to spend some time with him. Kid sucked his teeth, annoyed with himself, and stepped onto another bridge.

The lights on Kid's end worked.

Frank came toward him, grinning hugely, squinting slightly, face full of floodlight.

I must be in silhouette, Kid thought.

"Hey!" Frank said. "It is a really good party they're having for you. Congratulations on everything. I'm having a great time."

"Yeah," Kid said. "Me too."

Beyond Frank, beyond the bridge, Kid saw a flash of metallic kelly. Lanya was still with Milly, whose complicated hair was now in place. They were still laughing. They were still going away.

"You see my book?"

"Sure."

"What'd you think of my poems? I was sort of interested in what you'd think of them. I mean because you're a real poet."

Frank raised his eyebrows. "That's really— Well . . ." He lowered them. "Would you like me to be honest? I make the offer, because I guess you've been getting a lot of compliments, especially here at your party. And real honesty is going to be a little rare—maybe this evening isn't the place for it and we should save it for some night at Teddy's."

"No, go on," Kid said. "I guess you didn't think they were all that great?"

"You know . . ." Frank grasped the rail with one stiffened arm and leaned. "I was wondering what I was going to say to you about them if you ever really asked. I've been thinking about you a lot. A lot more, I guess, than you've been thinking about me. But I keep hearing about you all the time, people always talking about you. And it occurs to me that I don't know you

686

at all. But you've always seemed like a good person. And I thought it would be good if somebody was just straightforward with you, you know?" He laughed. "And there I was, starting to say, 'They're great,' like everyone else. That's really not my character. I think it's better to be honest."

"What did you think?" Kid heard the coldness in his own voice, and was astonished; listening to himself, he felt suddenly trapped.

"I didn't like them."

It's his smile, Kid thought and thought after that: No, you're just trying to tell yourself it's the smile you don't like. He said, He didn't like them, that's all. "What's wrong with them?"

Frank snorted a laugh and looked down at the rocks. "You really want to know?"

"Yeah," Kid said. "I want to know what you think."

"Well." Frank looked up. "The language is extremely artificial. There's no relation, or even tension, between it and any sort of real speech. Most of the poems are pompous and over-emotional—I'm sure you were sincere about every one of them. But sincerity by itself, without skill, usually just results in mawkishness. The lack of emotional focus makes subjects that could have been interesting into Grand Guignol melodrama. They end up coming off pretty banal. The method's cliche, and often, so is the diction. And they're dull." After a silence in which Kid tried to figure the varieties of unpleasantness he was experiencing, Frank continued: "Look, you once told me you'd only been writing poetry a couple of weeks. Didn't it ever strike you as a little improbable that you could just jump into it and the first batch you produced would be worth reading? I guess the thing that's really got me upset over the whole thing is all *this* business." He gestured at guests both sides of the bridge. "Tak once told me you were as old as he is—two years older than me! Kid, most of the people here think you're seventeen or eighteen! That, along with the poor man's Hell's Angel bit, and all the gossip about the various kinky things you get into—people are just here for the show. As far as most of them are concerned, *Brass Orchids* is like a performance by a talking dog. They find it so cunning that he speaks at all, they couldn't care less what he actually said."

"Un . . ." Kid had intended that to be an *Oh*. "And you—" which wasn't what he'd wanted to say either, but

687

he went on because he had to make sure—"you think the poems aren't very good?"

Frank said: "I think they're very bad."

"Wow," Kid said, gravely. "And you think that's all the poems mean to any of the people here?"

"To most people—" Frank put his hand, stiff-armed, on the rail again—"poetry doesn't mean anything at all. From a couple of things you said to me at the bar, though—about what you read and what you felt—I suspect it does mean something to you. Which is why I keep bothering to put my foot in my mouth the way I've been."

"No," Kid said, "go on," thinking: But he hasn't stopped, has he?

Kid's shadow cut Frank's face and purple shirt down the middle.

"With all the variety that's part of current poetry—" Frank blinked his visible, squinting eye—"perhaps it's silly for me to be passing judgments like this. There are lots of kinds of poetry. And sure, some kinds I personally prefer to others. I'll be honest: the kind that yours is *trying* to be isn't a kind I find very interesting at its best. Which is maybe the reason I should have kept my mouth shut in the first place. Well, look, I'm *not* passing judgments. I'm just talking about my own reactions. I suppose what I'm trying to say is that, as far as I can tell—and I admit I'm biased—it seems pretty clear what you *wanted* to do in the poems. And pretty clear that you didn't come close. I mean, that last one, in the clunky blank verse— now that may or may not be a good poem; I can't tell. It's unreadable." Frank's smile was wan. "But you have to admit, that's a stumbling block."

Kid grunted what he had intended as polite assent. It sounded more like he'd been elbowed in the liver. And that's not, he thought, what I want to sound like. "Maybe some time at Teddy's or someplace you could go over one or two of them with me and tell me what you think is—"

"No." Frank shook his hand, fingers straight, and his head, face a-scowl. "No, no. It isn't that kind of . . . Look, I can't tell you how to be a poet. I can just tell you what I think. That's all."

Kid grunted again.

"Don't take it as anything more than that."

Do you say thanks, now? Kid wondered. You say

thanks for compliments. "Thanks." It sounded the most tentative question.

Frank nodded, looked over the rail again.

Kid stepped around him and walked toward the end of the bridge. Halfway, like a tic, he thought Frank was about to tap his shoulder. He turned, and realized, turning, it was some untransformed kernel, perfectly hostile, trying to emerge. Facing into the lights of May, Kid could not tell if Frank looked at him or away.

Squinting, Kid swallowed the thought unworded and went on into the high paths of January; from which he could look down on the crowded terrace.

They're all here, Kid thought, for me! He was desperately uncomfortable. Frank's smile—it had made his criticism seem as though he thought he was getting away with something. Well, that still didn't change *what* he'd said. Somebody else, Kid remembered but couldn't remember who, had said they'd liked them . . . and decided that wasn't what he wanted to think about now. But with the resolve erupted memories of seven other reactions: Puzzled, indifferent, interests fleeting or otherwise. He recalled Newboy's complex noncommittal and sensed in it betrayal—not so much Newboy's but his own—of something the poet had tried to tell and he had not been able to understand.

"This is like . . ." he started out loud, heard himself, and laughed. This was like the night in the park when his fantasized reception had pressed so heavily he'd been unable to write.

He laughed again.

A couple smiled and nodded.

His look became surprised as he noticed them. But they passed.

I want a drink, he thought, and saw he was already heading for the bar. I really want a drink very much.

This isn't, Kid found himself repeating, what it should be about. Repeating it for the sixteenth or seventeenth time, he sat on the stone rail, looking across at the table and the bottles, still without a glass.

"Hi!" Then her expression (and handfuls of scarlet fell down among green fires) changed. "What happened to you?"

His hands went out against her hips: Around one, blue puddled, around the other, green.

"Am I bleeding?"

He slid them back to her buttocks, thinking, how warm she is; lay his face against her warm belly. She took hold of his hair. Before his blinking, black scales flittered to silver, to scarlet, to green.

"No. But you look like you just walked into a wall and now you're waiting for it to go away."

Kid made a sound supposed to launch the next sentence; it came out another grunt. So he backed off it and started again a little higher. "I was just . . . talking with Frank. About my . . . poems."

She pulled loose and hoisted herself up on the wall beside him, shoulder against his shoulder, leg against his leg, to become a deviling glitter at the corner of his eye while he stared at his ruined thumbs, now pressed together on his meshed fists' calloused drum. She asked: "What did he say?"

"He didn't like them, very much."

She waited.

"He said everybody here thought I was a talking dog. They all think I'm some sort of dumb nut, that I'm ten years younger than I am, and they'd all be just as astonished that I even spelled my name right—if I had a name . . ."

"Kid . . ." which came out much softer than his voice. She put her hand over his. He raised one thumb. She caught it in her fist. "That's fucking nasty."

"Maybe it's fucking true."

"It isn't!" Her voice told him she was frowning: "That's Frank? The one who's supposed to have had a book of poems published out in California?"

Asking who else it could have been, he said: "Yeah?"

She answered: "He's jealous, Kid!"

"Huh? of what," which was a statement, not a question.

"You're both poets. You both have a book published. Look at all the attention you're getting. I doubt if this happened when *his* book came out."

"That's awfully easy. Besides, I don't care *why* he said it, I just wish I knew if it *were* true— Oh, shit! Calkins didn't even read the poems when he decided to publish them. Maybe he did when they finally came out and was so embarrassed he decided not to show up this evening."

"No! That's silly—"

690

"And you remember how Newboy kept beating around the bush whenever I asked him if they were—"

"He *enjoyed* them—"

"Shit! He enjoyed *me!* If he was trying to say anything, he was trying to say he couldn't make the distinction."

"And *what* makes you to think Frank is any more capable of making it? He resents you, he resents the way everybody has fixated on you: And then he tries to read the poems. At least Mr Newboy was honest enough to admit he couldn't make the separation. Hell, *I* like them!"

"You're biased."

"You think Frank isn't? Look, they don't—" She let go his thumb.

He looked over.

Her fists were knotted above her tidewise, swirling lap. "We're going about this wrong." Her bottom lip moved over her teeth, to fix her mouth for some new tone of voice. "He is right. About a lot of it, anyway."

The simple hurt started in his throat. One swallow dragged it down to his stomach's floor.

"He doesn't like your poems and he's probably sincere. About not liking them. Thelma likes them, and she's probably just as sincere."

"I was trying to remember her name. It was sort of hard."

"It should be just as hard to remember his. Being sincere doesn't mean they're right. It just means they believe they are."

"Yeah," he said. "Yeah. Sure. That's what Frank said, about the poems."

"Sorry."

"He's right about the people, about what everybody here thinks."

"Not everybody," she said. "I suspect not even half. Do you care what people think?"

"I care . . ." He paused. ". . . *about* people. The people here. So if they think that, I've got to care about that too. And I wish they didn't think what he said."

She made a sound of assent.

"Maybe we shouldn't have come to this party," he said.

"You want to go?"

"No. I want to stay and see what happens." Kid

691

opened a hand on each knee. "It's something not to do again, maybe. But I don't think I want to leave in the middle. I'm learning too much." He pushed from the rail and turned to the bar.

Denny said, "What's the—?"

Kid put his arms around him: Denny's hands came up first to push, then all of a sudden went tight across Kid's back. Kid pushed his face against the dry, hot neck and thought: My face must feel cold. He held the hot shoulders and thought: My hands . . .

Denny moved once, was still, moved again; let his arms half down, waiting to pull away.

Kid raised his head.

Two people passing looked away.

Kid stepped back.

Denny asked, "Are you all right?" then glanced at Lanya.

Her eyebrows moved to answer him.

"I'm okay," Kid said and wondered if he'd contradicted her.

She asked, "You're sure?"

Kid put his hand on her bright knee. "I'm okay. Somebody said some nasty things about my poems. Whether they're true or not, it made me mad as hell."

Lanya sighed. "I guess that's why I'm glad I'm not an Artist."

"Why are you always saying that?" Kid pulled back. "There's a whole room full of people inside listening to *Diffraction* right now! And enjoying it!"

"I mean—" Lanya looked uncomfortable—"I mean Artist in the way this party presupposes. Sure, I make a piece of music; or a fucking *dress* for that matter—you'd be astonished how similar they are! But I don't just think you can *be* that kind of artist any more. Lots of people do things lots better than lots of others; but, today, *so* many people do so many things *very* well, and so many people are seriously interested in so many different things people do for their own different reasons, you can't call any thing the best for every person, or even every serious person. So you just pay real attention to the real things that affect you; and don't waste your time knocking the rest. This party—it's *ritual* attention, the sort you give a social hero. I guess that can be an artist if there're few enough of them around—"

692

"—like in Bellona?"

"Bellona is a very small part of the universe. And this party is a very good place to bear that in mind. Kid, all the criticism you're going to get here, good or bad, is going to be a ritual kind." She glanced down under his brows. "Maybe that's what Mr Newboy was trying to tell you?"

"Maybe," Kid said, and put his face against her shoulder. "And maybe he was just too chickenshit to say what Frank did."

"I don't think so." Lanya rubbed his hair again. "But that's just my personal reaction."

"Frank said that too."

"Then be generous and believe him." She pulled back. "You know, someday I'm going to shock you all and produce a philosophical treatise thick as *The Critique of Pure Reason, The Phenomonology of Mind,* and *Being and Time* put together! It'll be in neatly numbered, cross-referenced paragraphs, a third of it mathematical symbols. I'll call it—" she drew a thumb and forefinger across the air, top and bottom of an imaginary signboard— "*Preliminary Notes toward a Calculus of Attentional and Intentional Perception, with an Analytics of Modular—*I guess 'modular' is the adjective from 'modal'?—*Feedback.* Then you'll see. All of you!"

"You could always call it: *Lanya Looks at Life,*" Kid suggested.

"Poets!" Lanya exclaimed, mocking despair. "Artists! —God!" and put her hot, pale hands around his, to *cave* the beasts his fingers were.

He pulled them from the cave to rest them on the brass blades turning, tic-tic-tic, on his chest.

She stood, shedding turquoise to the hem, and moved by Denny. The boy's hip pocket stuck out with corners from the control box. "Take a walk," Lanya said. "You'll feel better."

Kid nodded, started away from them, realized he was fleeing, and slowed.

Dragon Lady swung around the newel at the bottom of the steps and said to Baby: "Now what you wanna go say that to that woman, for, huh? Huh?"

" 'Cause she said I—"

"Now *why* you wanna go say something like *that?*" Three steps behind them, Adam walked with Night-

693

mare; Nightmare doubled with laughter, held his stomach and staggered up the stairs. From knee to cuff one scarlet pants leg was smeared from a fall.

Adam's eyes were very wide behind loose, rough hair; his grin split, brown, over yellow teeth.

"God *damn!*" Dragon Lady said. "You don't go around saying things like that."

"Shit." Baby's hands were locked before his groin. His head was down and his blond hair swayed as though he worried something in his teeth. "If she hadn't said—aw, shit!"

Nightmare's hand fell on Kid's shoulder. His face came forward, fighting to explain, but exploded in laughter. He smelled very drunk. At last Nightmare just shook his head, helplessly, and staggered, loudly, away.

Kid took a breath and went on down, pondering madness's constituents. Later he could not recall where his thoughts had gone from there. And he pondered that loss more than days or names.

Below, Frank said: "Wait a minute . . . wait a minute! Wait—!"

Kid held the bridge's black metal rail and looked down at the path.

They came, laughing, along the short-cut from March to October.

The rocks were covered with moss and slicked with floodlight.

"Look, now *I* know something that's sort of funny."

"All right." Black-sweatered Bill stopped, still laughing. "What?"

Thelma stood to the side.

"You mustn't say anything nasty about him, Frank," Ernestine said. "I think they've *all* been perfectly charming, everything considered."

"He's a nice guy," Frank said. "He really is. But I've met him a couple of times before, that's all. And I just—"

"Well," drawled a man whose freckled skull was ringed with white hair, "I haven't yet. But his friends are the funniest children I have ever seen. Oh, they put on quite a show. Gibbons, I tell you! A real bunch of little black gibbons!"

Bill said: "Most of them aren't that little."

"*I* just wonder," Frank repeated, "whether he actually wrote them or not."

"Why would you think he didn't?" Bill asked, turning.

"I met him," Frank said, "once down in that place—*Teddy's*? A long time ago. I'd lost a notebook a few weeks back and I was telling him about it. Suddenly he got very excited—*very* upset, and called the bartender over to bring him this notebook that he told me he'd found in the park. He told me he'd found it, already filled up with writing, I'm *very* sure of that. I flipped through it, and it was all full of poems and journals and things. He wanted to know if it was mine. It wasn't, of course. But at least two of the poems in that notebook—and I remember because they struck me as rather odd—I'd swear were identical with two of the poems in *Brass Orchids*. That notebook had a poem on practically every other page."

"Are you serious?" Roxanne asked as though she thought the tale very funny. "Well, you mustn't ever tell Roger. He would feel quite had!"

Bill let out a loud, "Ha!" at the sky. "If it *is* true, that's the funniest thing I've heard all night!"

"I wouldn't make it up!"

"It's a perfectly awful thing to say," Ernestine said. "Do you really think he would do a thing like that?"

"Well, you've met him," Frank said. "He's not what I would call the literary type."

"Oh, everybody and their brother writes poems," Bill tossed away.

"You think, then—" which was Kamp's voice: It came from under the bridge where Kid could not see— "he took *all* the poems out of this notebook, now?"

"Oh, perhaps . . ." Frank began. "I'm not accusing him of anything. Maybe he only took those two. I don't know. Maybe he only took a couple of lines that I just happened to recognize—"

Thelma said: "You said they were identical," and Kid strained and failed to hear more than her words.

"I said I *thought* they were," Frank said, which was not, Kid remembered with obsessive lucidity, what he had said at all.

"That's interesting," Bill reflected, head down, all dark hair and black sweater. He started walking.

The others followed him under the bridge.

Frank said: "He told me that night he'd only been a poet for, I think he put it, a couple of weeks. And then, there was this notebook he'd found, all filled up with poems that—well, the two I looked at closely—are awfully similar to two in his book." The voices echoed beneath. "What would *you* think?"

Thelma (he could not see her face) was the last to go under.

"Well, *you* obviously think he took them—" The voice's identity was obscured by echo.

"*I* think," someone's voice came back, "he's just a nice—I wouldn't say dumb, just non-verbal—guy that probably isn't too concerned with the significance of that sort of thing. Hell, I like him. With all those guys in the chains he's got running around for bodyguards, I sort of hope he likes us too."

"He didn't sign his name to the book," the southerner said.

"Oh, Frank, I think you're just—"

Kid had to clear his throat so missed Ernestine's last words in the rattle. (Run to the other rail, hear what they said as they emerged . . .) He looked along the empty path.

In an Oregon forest, back during that winter, on his day off, a log, loosed from the pile he'd been climbing, had crashed his leg, bloodying his right calf and tearing his jeans. He'd thought his shin was broken. But, finally, he had been able to hobble back to the bunkhouse, a quarter of a mile away—it took forty minutes. The whole time he kept thinking: "This hurts more than anything I've ever felt before in my life. This hurts more than anything I've ever . . ." He reached the empty cabin, with the thought repeating like a melody now, rather than an idea; he had sat down on the lower bunk—it belonged to a laborer named Dehlman—opened his belt, got the seat of his jeans from beneath his buttocks, and in a single motion stripped them down his—

He hadn't screamed. Instead, his lungs flattened themselves in his chest, and for the next ten minutes he could only make little panting sounds. Blood and flesh, dried to the cloth, had stripped the length of his leg, sending the pain into realms he had not known existed. When he could think again, the still running thought, connected with the memory of that so much lesser pain, seemed silly.

He dropped his hand from the rail and thought about this (and for some reason the name of the man on whose

696

bunk he'd lain with his bleeding calf) and tried to recall his reaction to Frank's criticisms of ten minutes ago.

He could not fit both into anything like a single picture. (They took it so lightly!) He blinked at the empty path.

I wrote . . . ?

Kid's eyes stung; he wandered from the bridge. Raising his hand to rub his face, he saw blurred brass and stopped the motion.

One foot hit something on the path and he stepped ahead unsteadily.

I remember *re-writing* them!

I remember changing lines, to make them more like something . . . mine?

Kid blinked; and his rough fingers were circled with scrolled blades. Did the first terror *precede* the scream?

. . . someone—Dollar? Dollar, beyond the hedge, screamed.

Kid flung back his hands and ran—toward the sound. Because what was behind him was too frightening.

As he sprinted into the garden, a low branch struck his face.

He grasped away leaves with his bladed hand, came up short, and heard (though he could not see) Dollar scream again, thinking: My God, the rest of them are so quiet!

Black and brown arms waved and spun (and among them was Tarzan's yellow hair and dough-colored shoulder), caught against someone buried in the brawl. Somebody grunted.

Thelma, watching, sucked in her breath, rasping the silence.

From out the fray: "Hey, watch it . . . ! Watch it . . . ! Watch out for the . . . Unh!"

Their scrabbling boots were louder than their caught breaths and voices.

Kid lunged, grabbed, pulled, and only just remembered to get his orchid up out of the way.

"Hey, what you—"

Cathedral hit him as he pulled Thruppence off.

Priest's head struck his flank hard enough to hurt.

Kid swung his hand out and around, and Spider didn't shriek but hissed: "Ehhhhhhhhhhhhh . . . God-*damn* mother-fucker!" A filament of blood widened on Spider's belly.

"GET OFF HIM!" Kid pulled the Ripper back. "God-damn it, get *off* him!"

Raven, Tarzan, then Lady of Spain, still pummeling, got yanked back.

As they recognized him, one by one they fell away among the guests who ringed the garden. More were edging in.

Siam, in the central tussle, looked up, then ducked under Kid's arm; Kid stumbled forward, lunged between the last two (Angel and Jack the Ripper) who sprinted aside; he grabbed the back of Dollar's vest, his orchid still high.

Dollar screamed once more, and then went into foetal collapse on the flags. "Don't kill me, please don't kill me! Don't kill me, Kid, please don't kill me! I'm sorry, Kid! Don't kill me!" Dollar's right cheek was bruised and bleeding; his left eye was puffy, and his mouth looked like it had dandruff. Trying to get him up, Kid almost slipped. Swiveling his head, he saw his blades flash; leaves like green scales of the night fell from his opening fingers. He saw the ring of scorpions and guests—

Ernestine Throckmorton had jabbed both fists beneath her chin. Lanya, Nightmare, Denny, and Dragon Lady crowded the garden entrance. Baby and Adam pushed around them. Captain Kamp, on the other side of the fountain—water dribbled a rust-rimmed stain down a marble breast and across a cornucopia—looked angry and was about to step up. The southern colonel (with the ring of white hair) at his side was about to restrain him.

"I didn't *do* nothing! I really didn't mean to do nothing. I didn't mean nothing by it, I swear, Kid! I swear I didn't do it!"

Kid looked down. "WILL YOU GET THE FUCK UP!" He lowered his orchid.

Dollar ducked his head.

"Get on *up*, will you?" He jerked the back of Dollar's vest again.

Glass grabbed Dollar under one arm and helped Kid pull him to his feet. Kid and Glass exchanged frustrated looks.

"You okay?" Glass asked. "Can you stand up?"

"Is it all right . . . now?" Ernestine Throckmorton asked.

Kid turned to tell her just to go away—

But she was ten feet off, and talking to Nightmare, who said: "Yeah, it's okay. Just forget it, huh? Yeah, it's all right."

And other people were walking.

Kid's senses had grown amphetamine bright. Listening, however, words blurred back to normal incoherence.

"I didn't do——!" shrieked in his ear again as Dollar tried to wedge between Kid and Glass

Tarzan said: "Oh, man, I'm not gonna hurt you!" He looked at Kid. "But if he's gonna go around callin' people 'nigger' he's gonna get his head broke."

"Yeah!" from the hirsute Raven, behind Tarzan's left shoulder.

"Huh?" Kid asked.

And, "Yeah, I'm gonna break his fuckin' head!" from the Ripper, behind his right.

"I didn't do *nothin'!*" Dollar pulled on Kid's arm and stumbled back against Glass who caught him up. "*You* all do it all the time! You all say it, why can't I say it!"

"Aw, come on, man!" Kid said. "You all must be putting me on!"

"He's gonna call the wrong nigger 'nigger' and he's gonna have to pick his head up off the ground and screw it back on!" D-t said.

"All right," Kid told Dollar. "Who you calling names?"

"Me, God-damn it!" Tarzan said. "And if that psycho little bastard's gonna——"

"Aw, shit!" D-t said. "What he gonna call *you* 'nigger' for? He was bad-mouthin' the Ripper, and the Ripper don't like it. I don't like it either."

"Oh," Tarzan said. "I thought he was talking to me . . . He was looking at me when he said it."

D-t grunted. "God-damn, nigger, the Ripper was standing just behind your *shoulder!*" He pointed across the garden.

Several people stepped aside from the line his finger projected over the lawn.

Tarzan said, "Oh."

"I told him to say he was sorry," the Ripper said. "I didn't want to start no trouble, here at the God-damn party. If he'd a' said he was sorry, I wouldn't of done nothing."

699

"Okay," Kid told Dollar. "Tell him you're sorry."

"No!" Dollar lurched in Glass' grip. Glass' vinyl vest swung back from the crossed scar poking over his belt, then flapped to again.

"You say you're sorry." Kid held the back of Dollar's neck with one hand and put the orchid points against the lower right quadrant of his belly; the dirty flesh jerked. Dollar's chains jingled. "Say you're sorry, or I'll take your appendix out, right here, and we'll spread everything you got all over the God-damn ground—"

"Nooooo!" Dollar whined and twisted. *"Please* don't kill me!"

Talk had stopped again.

"Say you're sorry."

"I'm *sorry!"*

"Okay." Kid let his bladed hand drop and looked at the Ripper. "He's said he's sorry. Okay?"

"He didn't have to say it." The Ripper looked sullenly around the circle. "I already got my licks in."

But other guests had begun to talk once more.

"Okay," Kid said. "Then let's break it up. WILL YOU PLEASE BREAK IT UP GOD-DAMN IT!" He pushed Dollar forward by the head. Glass came with them.

Nightmare said: "Come on you guys, will you? You heard the Kid. Break it up! Get out of here! Go on!"

Somebody asked: "What happened?"

Somebody else: "What did he do?"

"I didn't see. Did you see what happened? Is it all right now?"

"No, I just came in. I *guess* it's all right . . . ?"

"Hey, Kid?"

That was Bill.

"When you got a chance, can I . . ." but somebody moved between them.

Which was just as well.

Kid held Dollar by one arm. Glass held him by the other. Kid dug a finger into Dollar's armpit. *"Didn't* I tell you if something went wrong, you come to me?"

"I didn't get no chance," Dollar said. "I told 'em, I told 'em just like you said, if they messed with me, I was gonna tell the Kid? Just like you said." He looked over his smudged shoulder at Glass. "Were you there? Did you hear me tell 'em?"

Glass's head-shake showed more frustration than anything else.

700

"But I didn't get no chance to, you know? Them colored guys was all over me."

Frank leaned over the rail and called down. "Hey, Kid, is everything all—?"

Glass glanced up. Kid didn't.

"I just don't think them guys—" Dollar's voice took on an echo beneath the bridge—"you know?—like me too much. I guess, you know, some people just don't like other people."

"I don't exactly love you," Kid said.

"I just wish—" Dollar rolled his head forward and spoke down at his chest—"somebody would tell me what to do."

"You don't have it too easy, huh?" Glass said, and didn't even bother to glance at Kid.

"Oh, man!" Dollar said. "Oh, man, I just don't know, sometimes, you know? I'm half sick all the God-damn time. I can hardly eat the fucking food. Because of my stomach, you know? I can't drink nothin' except wine, or I get sick. I don't get drunk, I just get sick. Unless it's wine. I mean half them God-damn niggers are—" he looked at Glass—"the colored guys . . ." Then he looked at Kid. "Well, that's what *they* say, I mean—"

"Say your thing," Glass said.

". . . half the God-damn colored guys are drunk already. That's why they jumped me, I bet. They wouldn't of jumped me if they wasn't drunk. They're nice guys; even the girls. I was just kiddin' anyway . . . I wasn't drunk. I didn't drink nothing here except some wine, 'cause I didn't want to get sick at your party. I just wish somebody would tell me what to do."

They came from beneath the bridge.

The path bent like a boomerang into the rocks.

"You know? If somebody would just *tell* me . . ."

"Why don't you just keep from bothering people who're gonna beat you up?" Glass said.

"Now *that's* what I mean," Dollar said. "Everybody's always tellin' me what *not* to do. Keep away from this. Get out of that. Don't bother the other. If somebody would just tell me what I *should* do, I'd work my fuckin' ass off."

"Right now you would," Glass said, " 'cause somebody just scared the shit out of you."

"I would," Dollar said. "I really would."

"You just come on with me," Glass said. "All right?"

By the edge of a black railing above, among small trees, Copperhead, Spitt, and the girl in maroon levis waited.

Dollar blinked at Kid and rubbed at the flaking corner of his mouth with his thumb. He looked sad and scared.

"We ain't gonna hurt you," Glass said. "We already got our licks in, too. All we gonna do is make sure you don't get in no more trouble here at the Kid's party."

Kid, doubting, let go of Dollar's arm.

"I just wish somebody would tell me what I was supposed to do."

"Go on with them," Kid said.

Glass and Dollar climbed up the slope among the brush and saplings.

Kid turned before Dollar reached the top.

I want, among all these people who are here because of me, one to come up and tap me on the shoulder and ask me if *I'm* all right, if I feel okay, say come on, let's go get a drink, after that you must need one. And, God-damn it, I don't want to go all hangdog looking for some person who'll oblige. I just want it to happen. Sometimes the pressure of vision against the retina or sound against the drum exhausts. Where have I lost myself, where have I laid the foundation of this duct? Walking in these gardens, it is as if the nervous surface of the mind registering the passage of time itself has, by its exercise, been rubbed and inflamed.

Did I write . . . ?

Finding the thought was like looking down again at a pattern of tiles he'd been walking over for hours.

Did I . . . ?

The sublimest moment I remember (Kid pondered) was when I sat naked under that tree with the notebook and the pen, putting down one word then another, then another, and listening to the ways they tied, while the sky greyed out of night. Oh, please, whatever I lose, don't let me lose that one—

"Hey, Kid!"

"Huh?"

But the Ripper had only called in passing, with a wave, and was walking on.

Kid nodded hesitantly back. Then he frowned. And for the life of him could not remember what he'd just been thinking.

Spider, alone in October, sat on the ground, half in

darkness, beside the floodlight, swabbing at his belly with a bunched piece of newsprint. It kept flapping, bloody, in front of the glaring glass.

"Are you all right?" Kid asked.

"Huh? Oh, yeah." Spider mashed the paper smaller. "You just scratched me, you know. It didn't bleed too much."

"I'm really sorry," Kid said. "You feel okay? I didn't see you."

Spider nodded. "I know." He crumpled the paper some more. "I'm a fuckin' mess—" he pulled his boot heels under him and got to his feet—"but it was just a scratch." He held back his vest and brushed himself with the paper, pressed it to himself. "It was only really bleeding bad at one end."

Kid looked up at the black youngster's lowered face. "You sure it's okay now?"

"I guess so. Now. Man, you scared me to death, though I was expecting to see my guts come out all over the grass."

"I'm sorry, man. Lemme see?"

Spider stared down.

His stomach looked like someone had smeared the teak flesh with paint. From one end of the cut, red threaded down toward his belt. The left side of his pants lap was black maroon. He blotted his belly again.

"You're bleeding like a pig!" Kid said.

"It's just a cut." Spider touched his stained stomach with his fingertips (He bites his nails, too, Kid thought), felt the taut skin over the top of his navel, pulled the waist of his pants out to unstick it. "It don't hurt none."

"Maybe they have something inside, some bandages or something. Come on—"

"It's stopping," Spider said. "It's gonna stop soon."

He turned the stained paper around, examining it.

Blood is a living tissue, Kid thought, remembering his high school biology teacher's glasses knocked from the edge of the marble lab table, one lens smithereening over the mustard tiles. "Look, come on. Let's go get a drink, then. After that, you look like you could use it."

"Yeah." Spider smiled. "Yeah, come on. A drink. I'd like that." He grinned, balled the paper, flung it noisily into the brush. "Uhnnn . . ." he said after three steps. "Maybe I should go inside and wash it or something."

"I'm sorry, man," Kid said. "I'm really sorry."

"I know," Spider said. "You didn't do it on purpose."

When they were halfway across July, Ernestine Throckmorton looked up and said, "Oh! I mean my . . . God!"

In the following confusion, Denny and Lanya (purple, purple blooming blue) found him while Ernestine and several others tried to get Spider to go inside.

"I wanna . . . drink," Spider said, hesitantly.

Ernestine asked Spider: "Do you feel all right? Are you okay?"

"He wants a drink," Kid said.

Spider looked confused; then the confusion sank in belligerent, silent embarrassment; he let himself be taken away.

"That could get infected," Everett Forest said for the third time.

Madame Brown stood across the crowd, folding and turning her hands. The leash swung and sagged and jingled.

Kid kept touching Lanya's shoulder; they stood watching. (The second time she touched his hand in return, but not the first, third, or fourth.)

Muriel, panting, pushed to her forepaws; then lowered her muzzle again to the ground.

Denny, in the crowding, had pushed against Kid several times, settling a hand on his shoulder, arm, or back. Kid contemplated some response—

"Kid!"

Kid didn't look around at first.

"If you've a few minutes to spare . . . Kid, do you think I could have you for a few minutes?"

When he did turn (Lanya and Denny turned too), Bill was smiling at him over the surrounding heads, and holding a box that looked much like the controls to Lanya's dress up near his ear. "Can I have you for a few minutes . . . Kid?"

This time when Kid touched Lanya and Denny, they came with him. (Thinking: They would have come anyway; both, working within entirely different mechanics, have developed curiosities that would not let them miss it!) "Sure," Kid said. "What you want?"

"Thank you." Bill grinned, and adjusted the mike clipped to the pocket in his black turtleneck pullover. "This is on now. We might as well leave it going, so you

704

can get used to ignoring it. But let's get out of all this noise. Why don't we go behind— Say, what happened to that tall black kid? He's part of your nest?"

"I cut him," Kid said.

Bill tried not to look surprised.

"It was an accident," Kid said to the mike. He unsnapped the ornate blades from his wrist.

"You're—" Bill noticed Lanya and Denny but didn't say any thing to them—"very strict with your own, aren't you?"

Kid decided: I'm being told, not asked, and said nothing.

"Where we going?" Denny whispered, and looked warily again at Bill's cassette recorder.

"To hell, if we're invited nicely," Kid said. "Shut up and come on. He's not going to make you say anything. Just me."

"Let's . . ." Bill looked like he was trying to, politely, think of a way to get rid of Lanya and Denny.

Lanya looked as though she were about to, politely, excuse herself and take Denny with her.

"They should come," Kid said. "They're my friends."

"Of course. I just wanted to ask you a few questions—let's go this way." They passed through another garden. "This is really a little confused, what with Roger's not being here. I guess he's . . . gone for the night. He wanted to get a chance to talk to you, I know that; he told me so. He wanted to find out a few things he thought the readers of the *Times* might be interested in . . . we were actually going to interview you together. I help Roger with a lot of his newspaper work. Draft a lot of his articles. As you might imagine, he's a busy man."

"*You* write his articles?" Lanya asked. "I always wondered where he got the time to do all he does."

"I don't actually write anything he signs. And . . . I research a lot for him." Bill turned up a small path Kid remembered having walked over twice during the evening but couldn't remember where it led. "Roger wanted to ask you—well, we both did . . . just a few things. I was going to wait for him. But I get the impression that people might start leaving soon. And if Roger didn't get back in time, I know he'd still want me to use the opportunity."

Before two spotlights, fixed low to trees at opposite corners of the clearing, white wicker furniture cast black coils and curlicues on the grass.

705

"Nobody seems to have found their way here yet. Why don't we have a seat and get started?"

Denny sat beside Kid on the edge of the bench, leaning forward on his knees to look over at Bill, who took the paddle-backed lounge. Lanya stood a little ways away, leaning on a tree trunk, once brushing at her autumn-colored skirts to strike in them silver rain.

"I want to ask you a few questions about your gang —your nest. And then something about your work . . . your poetry. All right?"

Kid shrugged. He was excited and uncomfortable; but the two states, vivid as feelings, seemed to cancel any physical sign of either.

He looked at Lanya.

She had folded her arms and was listening rather like someone who had just passed by and stopped.

Denny was looking at the control box, wanting to play with it, but also wondering if this were the time.

Lanya hovered among various blues.

Bill ran his hand from the mike along the wire to the recorder, turned a knob, and looked up again. "Tell me first, how do you feel having your book published? It's your first book, right?"

"Yeah. It's my first. I like it, all the commotion. I think it's stupid, but it's . . . fun. There aren't very many mistakes in it . . . I mean the ones the people who put the type together made."

"Well, that's very good. You feel, then, the poems are as you wrote them; that you can take full responsibility for them?"

"Yeah." Kid wondered why the muffled accusation did not make him more uncomfortable. Possibly because he'd been through it already in silence.

"I mean," Bill went on, "I remember Ernest Newboy telling us, one evening, about how hard you worked on the galleys. He was very struck by it. Did Mr Newboy help you much with the poems themselves? I mean, would you say he was an influence on your work?"

"No." He *does* think, Kid thought, that I'm seventeen! He laughed, and the familiarity of the deception put him even more at ease. He moved back on the lounge and let his knees fall apart. So far it wasn't so bad.

Something moved at the corner of Kid's eye. Bill looked up too.

Revelation stood behind them with Milly, who he had not seen since they had surprised her in the bushes.

Denny went, "Shhhhh," took his finger from his lips and pointed to the recorder.

"Can you tell me—"

Kid looked back.

Bill coughed. "—tell me something about the scorpions, about the *way* you live, and *why* you live that way?"

"What do you want to know?"

"Do you like it?"

"Sure."

"Do you feel that this way of life offers you some protection, or makes it easier for you to survive in Bellona? I guess it's a pretty dangerous and unknown place, now."

Kid shook his head. "No . . . it isn't that dangerous, for us. And I'm getting to know it pretty well."

"You all live together, in a sort of commune—nest, as you call it. Tell me, do you know the commune of young people that used to live in the park?"

Kidd nodded. "Yeah. Sure."

"Did you get along well with each other?"

"Pretty much."

"But they're fairly peaceful; while your group believes in violence, is that right?"

"Well, violence—" Kid grinned—"that isn't something you believe in. That's something that happens. But I guess it happens more around us than around them."

"Someone told me that, for a while, you were a member of this other commune; but apparently you preferred the scorpions."

"Yeah." Kid pressed his lips and nodded. ". . . well, no, actually. I was never a member of the other commune. I hung around; they fed me. But they never made me a part of it. The scorpions, now, soon as I got with them, they took me right in, made me a part. That's probably why I like it better. We had a couple of kids hanging around our place who should probably have ended up with the park people; but we fed them too. Then they drifted on. That's what you have to do."

Bill nodded, his own lips pursed. "There's been talk that some of the things you guys indulge in get pretty rough. People have been killed . . . or so one story goes."

707

"People have been hurt," Kid said. "One guy was killed. But he wasn't a scorpion."

"But the scorpions killed *him* . . . ?"

Kid turned up his hands. "What am I supposed to say now?" He grinned again.

Behind Bill, a dozen others had gathered. Another cough, behind Kid, made him realize another dozen had come up to listen.

Bill's eyes came back to Kid. "Do you think, objectively, that the way you're living is . . . a good way?"

"I like it." Kid felt his jaw with his wide fingertips and heard five-hour stubble rasp. "But that's subjective. Objectively? It depends on what you think of the way the rest of the world is living."

"What do you think of it?"

"Well, look at it," Kid said. Then he coughed, which caused some general laughter, defining the audience he had not looked at yet as thirty, or even forty: scorpions and other guests.

Nightmare stepped into the clearing, said, "Say, what's everybody—?" then got quiet and went to sit on the grass next to Dragon Lady.

"How would you describe life in the nest?"

"Fucking crowded!"

"Oh, *man!*" D-t slapped Tarzan's palm. "He said fucking crowded!"

"Shut up, you two," Raven said.

"And with all the crowding, and all the violence, you still manage to work—to write."

"When I get a chance."

Lanya laughed at that. She was the palest orange, flaking to palest pink and purple. Denny held the box between his knees; his arms were folded.

"A lot of people have commented on the, how shall I say, colorfulness of your poems, their vivid descriptive quality. Is there any connection between the violence and that?"

"Probably. But I don't know what it is."

"Do your friends in the nest like your book?"

"I don't think most of the guys read too much."

"Hey, man!" Nightmare called out. "I ain't even *in* his fuckin' nest and I read every fuckin' one!" which caused someone else to call: "Yeah, they're great! The Kid writes great," and someone else: "Sure, ain't you got this party for him?"

Kid leaned back and laughed and closed his eyes. His own laughter had begun in the calamity of shouts and calls.

"Come on," Bill said loudly. "Come on, now. I just want to ask the Kid a few more questions. Come on . . ."

Kid opened his eyes and found his lashes wet. Light around the garden glittered and streaked. He shook his head.

"I want to ask you, Kid—"

"Come on, be quiet!" Lady of Spain said. "Come on, shut up, man! He's trying to ask the Kid some questions!"

"—want to ask you: How would you sum up what you're trying to say in your poems?"

Kid leaned his elbows on his knees. "How the hell am I supposed to do that, sum up what I'm trying to say?"

"I guess you'd rather we just read—"

"Shit, I don't care if you read it or not."

"I just meant that—"

"I'm trying to—" Kid looked up at Bill, frowning in the pause—"to construct a complicitous illusion in lingual catalysis, a crystalline and conscientious alkahest."

". . . again?" Bill asked.

"You listen to that too carefully and you'll figure out what it means." Kid let the frown reverse into a grin. "Then the words will die on you and you won't understand any more."

Bill laughed. "Well, do you feel that your work accomplishes what . . . ever you set out to do?"

"How am I supposed to decide that?" Kid sat back again. "I mean suppose one person liked something I wrote. I'd want to make what I say here mean something to him. Suppose somebody else didn't like it. I'm a snob. I'd like to be able to talk to him too. But somebody you've had a good time with and somebody you've had a bad time with, you talk to in different ways. There isn't much overlap in what you can say to both. Maybe, just, I did it." Kid sat back. "And maybe, you know, other people can think of reasons not to even insist on that too much. Look, the guys are getting fidgety. I've made too much noise already." He looked around at the gathered nest. "I guess Mr C just isn't going to make it this evening."

Ernestine Throckmorton (Spider stood beside her, his belly lashed with gauze and adhesive) said: "I guess he isn't. He'll be absolutely mortified he missed you. I just don't know where—"

709

"You think something happened to him?" Raven looked around with swaying top-knot. "You want us to go out and look for him?"

"Oh, no!" Ernestine said. "No, that's not necessary. When he left, he said he . . . might be late. That's why he put the Captain and myself in charge."

Neither the Captain nor Frank were present. Paul Fenster, with a beer can at his hip, stood directly opposite.

"Look, we've got most of my guys here, just about." Kid stood, feeling among his neck chains. "It's getting time for me to split. Any of you guys who want to come along with me, come on." He caught his shield (nicked his thumb knuckle on an orchid prong and thought: The price of dramatic exits) and flipped the pip.

The scorpions on the grass squinted in blue light. Denny did something with the box and laughed: And Lanya stood up a-swirl in crimson and indigo.

Where Dragon Lady had been, her dragon rose.

"Uh . . . thank you." Bill looked about. "Eh, thank you an awful lot. 'I'm sure Roger will have what he . . . I mean you gave some very interesting . . ."

People got to their feet amidst the glowing, growing menagerie.

The 3-D Rohrschach that was Denny turned and turned and moved through the crush.

Kid doused long enough for Lanya to see him. She caught his hand. Branches cut through the insubstantial luminosities wheeling the garden.

"How'd I do?"

"Lord," she said. "This has been a party! Roger doesn't know what he missed—then again, maybe he does."

In another garden, beyond some dozen guests, Kamp and Fenster had become deeply embroiled in animated agreement.

Heavy Cathedral, with white California (greasy hair swinging long as his chains), was very drunk in the corner:

"We goin'? Oh, shit . . . Oh, shit, I can't go . . ."

"What we goin' for?"

"I think we gotta go, you know . . . ?"

"We gotta go already . . . ?"

Three others went splashing through the pool in May.

And Copperhead began to laugh and point so

vigorously, Kid thought: He's drunk enough to fall down in a minute. Moments later, however, along with Glass, the girl, Dollar, and Spitt, Copperhead was ambling across the terrace.

Kid thought (and saw Captain Kamp look up and thought as counterpoint to that first thought: He's thinking the same thing): They're going to start breaking up the place.

They didn't.

"Oh," Kamp said to Ernestine, "you mean they're *going* now . . . well, eh . . . Good night!"

Revelation said: "Hey, man, I can't go." He shook his head, deviling his hair to a gold cotton. Yellow chains rattled over his pink, pink chest. "I got something goin' here, you know? And I'm so fuckin' smashed . . . look, you go on, and maybe I'll see you back there in the morning."

Kid nodded, pushed past and came up before Thelma who opened her mouth, said, "Um . . ." and was gone.

Angel, at the bar table, picked up a full bottle of whiskey, put it under his thin arm, and started after the others.

"Hey . . ." the black bartender said.

Captain Kamp hurried up.

I could be a hero, Kid thought, and make him put it back. Suddenly he said, "Shit . . ." pulled away from Lanya, and loped over to the bar. "Captain, we've got a long—"

"Your friend," Captain Kamp said, "just walked off with a full bottle of—"

"—got a long walk back. And I just don't think one is going to be enough." Kid picked up another bottle (he chose it because it had the cap on, but saw, when it was in his hand that it was only half full: Well, it was a gesture) and, to the Captain's frown, flipped on his shield. "Tell Mr Calkins thanks. Good night."

Kamp squinted and pulled back, his face washed with light the same pale blue as his shirt. His eyes, widening, rose.

When Kid left the terrace steps and was halfway across the lawn, "You," Lanya told him, "are a perfect child!"

"Fuck you. You want to go put it back?"

"No. Come on."

"Hey," Angel was saying to the young Filipino gatekeeper, "you want a fuckin' drink? How come they didn't let you up to the party?"

"Thank you, no. That's all right—"

"You got just as much right to a party as we got! You wanna drink?"

"Thank you, no. Good night."

"God-damn mother-fuckers! Keep a God-damn gook down here workin' his ass off all night while everybody else is up having a good time—"

"Come on," Kid said. "Let's get going. Go on, get out. Hurry up, will you."

"Hey, gook; are you from Nam? I was in Nam . . ."

"Come *on!*"

"I was in Nam," Angel said. "We should give him a fuckin' drink!"

As they herded, blindingly, through the gate, Lansang said: "Excuse me, I've got something for you."

"Huh?" Kid turned.

The brown hand went under the brown lapel for an inside pocket. "Here." On the envelope's corner was a small *Times* masthead. "Mr Calkins asked me to give this to you if, by any chance, he didn't get back before the evening was over."

"Oh." Kid folded the envelope and slid it into his pants pocket beside Lanya's harmonica.

"What's that?" Lanya asked. Her arm was around Denny's shoulder.

Kid shrugged. "Where's Madame Brown?"

"She left with Everett, a long time ago."

"Oh."

Spider, dragon, newt and waddling bird lit the street.

"Hey, can I have some of that?" Jack the Ripper asked as they reached the corner.

"Sure. You can carry it too."

"Thanks." The Ripper took the bottle, removed the cap, swigged, and belched. "God damn!" He put the cap back on. "That's good!" He shook his head like a terrier. "Yeah . . . hey, did you see that old white guy from Alabama with the bald head? He's supposed to be some sort of colonel or something . . ."

"I saw him," Kid said. "Didn't meet him."

"He's a funny guy," the Ripper said. "Man, he just loved me. Wouldn't let me alone the whole God-damn night."

"What'd he want?"

In the glow of shifting beasts, the Ripper smiled down at the bottle. "I' suck on my big, black dick."

Kid laughed. "You let him?"

"Shit." The Ripper wiped the bottle neck with the paler heel of his hand, then put the cap back on. "If I was in Atlanta, I could've got ten, twenty dollars out of that old guy, you know? Even a steady thing, you know, where you drop in every couple of days, pull down your pants and pick up your pay. It ain't so bad. But around here, there ain't even any God-damn money or anything, you know?" The Ripper reached among the heavy links, tucked his shallow chin back in his neck to look for his shield, found it, flipped it. ". . . But he ain't so bad," he repeated.

Kid walked beside a raging mantis with swaying ruby eyes.

Watching the walkers among the ballooning lights, Kid realized that the group was nearly a fourth smaller than the one which had come up with him. Nightmare's scorpion, on the corner, threw a half dozen amblers (Baby was the one recognizable) into silhouette.

Listening to their silent progress down, Kid recalled their boisterous journey up. A street lamp pulsed above the corner (they had passed it before. Where?) and Kid saw the couple, hand in hand, beneath it.

"Hey, you two."

The woman turned, surprised, and raised her free hand: Bracelets clattered to her pale elbow. She blinked interrogatively, then smiled.

The man looked over at Kid. "Hello." He brushed back long hair, the color of wild rice, from his cheek and smiled too.

"What are *you* supposed to be doing here?"

"Oh, we . . . well, we were at . . . your party." Over his double-breasted jacket, he wore a large lion's-head medallion that, in this light, looked like metallic plastic. It hung around his neck on a loop of the optical chain. "We have to get down to Temple, and we just thought we'd walk along with you, for the company."

"It's all right, isn't it?" the woman asked.

"Sure," Kid said. "You can walk anywhere you fucking well want."

"Um . . . thanks," the man said.

"You want a drink?" Kid looked around in the darkness. "Hey, Ripper come here!" He took the bottle from

713

the tire-colored hands that jutted from the mantis. "Here, have a drink. We got a long walk."

"Thanks, no," the man said. "I don't drink."

"I do," the woman said and reached out a clinking arm.

"Good." Kid nodded and gave her the bottle. He left them while she was still uncapping it, wondering where, over the last few moments, he had misplaced Lanya and Denny.

He heard their laughter some twenty feet behind him.

He turned to face the dark; and realized how dark it was.

"You scared?" Denny laughed. "There ain't nothing to be scared of."

Lanya said: "I'm not scared. Unlike you, I don't believe in ghosts."

Kid turned on his lights.

Lanya gave a little shriek and fell into Denny's arms, both of them blue and helpless with hysterics.

"Are you drunk?" Kid asked.

"No," she said. "I'm not drunk," and began to laugh again.

"She smells like she's drunk," Denny said.

"How would you—" Still laughing, she straightened up and nearly tripped at the curb.

Which started all three of them off again.

When they were halfway down the next block, Denny asked: "You like your party?"

"Yeah," Kid said. "I wish I'd gotten a chance to say good night to the old girl with the crab cakes and the blue hair. She was my favorite."

"Ernestine? She's priceless!" Lanya said. "Where's my harmonica?"

Kid pawed in his pocket. Beside the mouth organ and the envelope, there was grit at the bottom. The metal was so warm on his hand it might have been artificially heated.

He gave her the harp.

She played three chords, walking beside him, then started some improvisation in long, platinum notes that took her two, three, four steps ahead.

Denny had turned on his lights (and apparently turned off her dress). Her back was silver, and as she played she trod the joined shadows of herself.

Between two notes, something crackled at Kid's hip:

The envelope. He pushed thick fingertips into his pocket to feel the folded edge.

Copperhead, the girl in maroon jeans tucked tightly under his arm, bobbed into the dim penumbra. "Hey, Kid!" He grinned, broad-nosed, freckle-lipped, and bobbed out.

Kid fantasized a conversation: Copperhead, did Mr Calkins ever hire you to keep people away from his place? I mean, were you working for him that first day you guys beat me up? No, he didn't want to know.

Behind Kid, Angel, Glass, and Priest were in altercation.

"*No!*" Glass interrupted himself at some request from Dollar. "What do *you* want any for? You just got through tellin' us how it makes you sick."

"What I wanna know . . ." Angel said, thickly. "No, wait, man. Let him have it. Let the dumb white mother-fucker get sick if he want to— Now, what *I* want to know is, where do all these niggers *come* from?"

"Louisiana," Priest said, "mostly. But there're a lot of guys here from Chicago. Like you. Illinois, anyway."

I just don't like, Kid thought, the idea of not wanting to know anything. He looked around luminous dark. "Hey, Copperhead?"

But Copperhead's arachnid, scales bright as the undersides of submerged rose leaves sheened with air, ballooned ahead, drifted away. The legs, rigorous and hirsute, with a faint indigo after-image, deviled Kid's eyes behind sliding striations.

What he'd expected most from this evening—information about Calkins—the whole over-determined matrix seemed bent on denying him.

A gorgeous bird collapsed near him. Ahead, among a dozen others, a scorpion flickered. Harmonica music was drowned in breaking glass and laughter: someone had dropped the bottle. The bird ignited again; Kid glanced around to see the pavement glisten.

They exhaust my eyes. My ears are on fire. There is nothing left to watch but fire and the night: circle within circle, light within light. Messages arrive in the net where discrete pulses cross. Parametal engines of joy and disaster give them wave and motion. We interpret and defeat their terms by terminus. The night? What of it. It is filled with bestial watchmen, trammeling the extremities and the interstices of the timeless city, portents fallen, constellated deities plummeting in ash and smoke, roaming the apocryphal cities, the cities of speculation and reconstituted disorder, of insemination and incipience, swept round with the dark.

7

Lights doused, scorpions crowded up the nest's stairs.

He stood on the street, while she laughed sadly: "Hell, then—I might as well have gone back with Madam Brown—"

He said: "I just want to check out that place we saw down the street that was on fire. I'll *be* right back—"

Gangling D-t hooked one brown arm around Denny's neck, rested two brown fingers on Lanya's silver, and said: "I'll take care of 'em for you, Kid. Now you don't worry."

Denny, looking even sadder, said: "If you go down there, you better be careful . . ."

And Kid walked for fifteen minutes, turned one corner, turned another, turned another and thought: If the wind changes, I'll die!

He squinted in the heat.

The smoke! The *smoke* will be enough to kill me! How did I . . . ?

White fire, a flap with yellow and orange, engulfed the upper stories. Night roared in the street. He heard something huge fall behind one of the facades and edged along the brick, thinking: It could jump the street . . .

A flicker between the cobbles:

As his bare foot touched one, he saw that water, running between the humped stones, had made all the alley a web of light. He sprinted to the left. Smoke rolled to his right, pulled away from more fire beating up about the high masonry. This was what he had seen between the lions of August . . . ? This is what they had watched from Calkins' gardens . . . ?

Not this gorge of flame!

It couldn't be *this* big:

Cold puffed against his cheek.

More heat, then cold again; his sweaty jaw dried.

Cool air ran around his bare foot, but the stones under it were warm.

A hot gust flapped his vest out; a cold one pushed it back.

Ahead fifty feet stood a figure, black with the fire behind it, dim with the smoke before.

Oh, Christ, he thought, I can hear them calling me in the crackling around—

Kid spun:

The blind-mute's sockets were the perfect hollows of Spalding balls pressed into dough. The gaunt, brick-haired woman pulled her coat together and blinked. The heavy blond Mexican, one hand around her shoulder, the other touching the shoulder of the blind-mute, breathed loud as the holocaust; their faces were slathered in raging copper.

The eyes of the Mexican and the woman were scarlet blanks.

Kid felt his features wrinkle on the bone. His shoulders pulled so tight the flesh creased between them. The ball of his foot, working the wet stone, stung.

No! he thought; he was trying to think: *Why?*

He remembered the warehouse and wondered: Is this terror habit?

Their lids slipped on the glass in lazy blinks: The woman and the Mexican were . . . watching him! The blind-mute's mouth was open; his face turned, tilting and tasting the smoke.

The three reached the sidewalk—now they turned away—huddled. Flames—or a dog—barked. A smoky tarpaulin rolled between them.

Kid stepped back, expecting fumes.

But some gust shredded the billow, tossing off dark fluff. And they were gone, down some burning alley.

Kid turned and hurried forward.

"Hey!" a familiarly mauled voice ahead called. "Is that you . . . Kid?"

Kid slowed closer.

Shifting bronzes slicked the black face. Uncertain light made it look (Kid had never thought this before) like there was grey in that snarled wool. The temples were hollow, as on a very thin man, Kid thought; but not

718

like somebody with that jaw, those arms (one sleeve had been cut from the shoulder of the green shirt, leaving a frayed rim: The other was just rolled up tight so the veins lay on the blocked flesh like black twine). "What you doing out here, boy? Ain't this—" and made no gesture, but swayed (the orange construction boots wide in the wet net) so that his whole body indicated the holocaust—"something?" George got his thumbs under his belt to tug at his canvas pants and laughed. "We all been down at the Reverend's prayer meeting. Now look at it." Black fingers hit Kid's shoulder, clamped. "Look at it, will you?"

Kid turned, staring.

"They burned the whole damn thing up tonight."

"What in the . . . I mean how did it . . . ?"

George tugged Kid's shoulder. A few feet ahead, the paving sank under a puddle like a hole in hellroof. "Niggers done set the whole of Jackson to burning, don't it look like?" They walked. "Ain't got no water now, when the pipe broke. Shit."

Kid's bare foot struck a tepid pool; it shook like goldleaf.

"You scared?" George's fingers were hard, hot, and tight. "Nothing going to hurt you. Look at that burn, burn up like a motherfucker; it's beautiful, huh? Like walking on the sun." He looked at Kid, his arm straightening and bending each step. "The moon get its light from the sun." He smiled on big, yellow teeth in gums mottled pink and grey like a dog's. "Get its light from the sun and shine all night." His lids narrowed on eyes, blood-webbed and tan. "It burn and it burn and it don't never stop. It send the folk all down running through the city of the sun," or at least that's what Kid thought he said. "Nobody's here." George looked around. "The niggers all going to starve to death. Shit. Everybody going to starve."

Kid's lips were hot. He closed his mouth, his teeth, closed his lips again because they had come open. "There was this old black woman," Kid said. They passed a smoking (or was it steaming?) grate. "She broke into the school to steal food. She said there wasn't any more food in—"

The street sign said:

CUMBERLAND PARK

They passed around. The other extension of the L-shaped sign said:

JACKSON AVENUE

George nodded heavily.

Twenty yards ahead, a ton of fire fell onto the sidewalk.

"What . . ." Kid began, "What are you doing here?" while he tried again to reconstruct the steps coming: D-t had said—

"There may . . ." George's face lined over, straining at reason. "There *may* be people in there. We got to go help them."

"Oh," Kid said with the thought: He's crazy, which is like (with the afterthought) the pot calling the kettle a rusty son of a bitch.

They walked through the sun.

George was still laughing.

"What . . . ?" Kid asked, expecting no answer.

George said: "You ain't scared?"

"I think," Kid said, "if somebody jumped out right now and went boo, I would shit."

"Watch it," George pushed Kid away, but Kid wasn't sure from which piece of rubbish about them.

I just may live to be an old man, and live through the process called dying, then I won't be living any more, no matter what revelations I do or do not go through here, Kid thought and grew cold. He looked up; fire rip-sawed the night.

"You think we going to get out of this alive?" George still grinned.

What, Kid wondered, has June got to do with his moment in this man's life? The fire and her hair are two different golds! And yet she circles . . . ! Kid's eyes went round. "There—!" He pointed. "It isn't burning down that way! We can go—"

"Boy, there may be people in here, burning up alive!"

"You think there're people?"

"Well, we ain't going to know unless we look."

"Okay," Kid said because there was nothing else to do.

A charred six by six lay across the gutter. Kid stepped over it.

On the cobbles, puddles lay under it, alive and molten.

720

Water, Kid thought as they walked between two, is molten ice. It was that hot.

"Hey, George! George? . . . You hear something up there?"

"Where?"

[*We do not know who typed this transcript, nor if every relevant entry was included, nor, indeed, the criteria for relevance. Previous publication of* Brass Orchids *possibly weighted the decision not to include their various drafts here. (The fate of the second collection we can only surmise.) Generous enough with alternate words, marks of omission and correction, the transcriber still leaves his accuracy in question: Nowhere in the transcript is there a formal key.*]

it into her shoulder and tore /it/ out.

Dragon Lady let go all her breath in some way still not a scream. Nightmare danced back across the kitchen twisting his orchid, (jerking a little); ~~as though/I think~~ I think he was trying to under stand what he'd done. Dragon Lady threw herself ~~at him~~, cutting for his face and kicking. (~~I kept thinking~~ Thinking: There's an art to these weapons I don't begin to understand.)

He fought himself away, bleeding from the jaw and neck.

She flung herself again. I thought she ~~was trying to~~ was ~~going to~~ /would/ be impale[d].

Her white jeans were bloody to the knee. A good deal of the blood was his.

Copperhead, ~~like a~~ in delayed reaction, said, "Hey . . ." with a voice I'd never heard: he was scared to death.

Raven, Thruppence, and D-t hit the doorway [and] one ~~another~~/ anothe[r], peering, over ~~each~~ one another's shoul-

723

ders. (Thinking:I used to break up Dollar's scuffles, but I would no more get into this than chop off my thumb.)

Nightmare flailed backward out the screen door, ~~H~~ his forearm/ going/ ~~making a~~ *crack*~~ed the~~ on the jamb.

Everybody poured after them—somebody knocked something off the sink. I heard a garbage bag fall and tear under someone's boots. Two of the little boys (Woodard and Stevie) were h o l d i n g hands and butting their shoulders against each oth-

Horsing around in the yard with Nightmare, Raven, Filament, and Glass, tripped and scratched my calf on the edge of the steps. Later, Lanya came into the loft and saw me. "Hey," she said. "You should put something on that. Don't play with it that way. You've practically rubbed it raw. You don't want it to get infected."

er, Rose, the youngest (seven?), and brightest ~~girl~~, was right up there up trying to see with everybody else. She went through the door with me.

Dragon [Lady] ~~was~~ snappi~~ng~~ed her own bladed fist back and forth as though her arm were a whip. (Her elbow dripped. Nightmare spun away: gravel chattered against the bottom step. Drops splatted the ground.

The sky gleamed dull as zinc.

I looked up the alley—thinking: You can't /even/ see the end, when Thirteen came hurrying out of the mist. He stopped twenty feet away, Smokey and Lady of Spain be-hind ~~colided with~~ him.

Dragon Lady staggered, swayed—I thought she'd tripped.

But she shook her head, hard, gave a tiny cry, turned; and fled ~~down~~ up the street.

Smokey collided with Thirteen. Lady of Spain stepped back.

Nightmare stood, panting, both arms going wide and around, getting back his breath.

Among his chains, the optical one caught light. At first I thought it was lengthening . . . Broken, it slipped across his stomach and ~~tinkled~~ coiled ~~made a~~ tinkling/~~puddle between his feet/ beside his boot~~ /against his boot where the sole had pulled off the upper. Not seeing, he lurched away. The chain slipped half over the curb.

Thirteen caught ~~his arm~~ him, "You're all right . . . ?" and staggered with him.

Behind me the door creaked; two people had gone back in.

"You come on with me," Thirteen said, "now you just come on."

Back in the living room, California was looking at the wall by the door. He'd pulled all his hair in front of his shoulder and was sort of hanging on it. "Jesus Christ," he said. "Will you look at that. I mean, Jesus Christ. That's where she splattered when she went through." He started to touch one of the dime-sized spots, already ~~dried brown~~ dry, but ~~shook his~~ went back to hanging on his hair. "/I, mean,/Jesus."

Raven, Copperhead; and Cathedral came in frowning at the constellations of her blood, ~~but kept on going~~

"You see the way she went at that mother-fucker," Pepper said somewhere out in the hall. "I thought she was gonna *kill* him. I wouldn't blame her, man. I wouldn't blame her one bit the way that mother-fucker done. Did you see the way they were going after each other, man? I never seen anything like that before in my life. I really thought we was gonna have chopped meat for dinner the way he lit into her with ~~those~~ that orchid, man, I really thought . . ."

I went back [into] the kitchen.

Rose was looking out the screening, a brown fist up beside her ~~face~~ chin. I went up behind her and looked too. The other four children were outside.

Sammy was standing at the place where the curb cracked away into the street. With ~~the~~ toe of his sneaker, he touched the coil of Nightmare's chain.

Stevie, who was sitting on the steps, stood up.

Sammy started to pick up the chain.

Stevie said, "Don't you touch that, nigger!"

Marceline laughed, but I don't think at that.

Sammy ~~looked up and~~ looked embarrassed, went to pick up a board lying out in the street, and played by himself.

I touched Rose on the shoulder and she jumped.

"Don't you want to play with the other kids outside?"

She just blinked. (Somebody should do something about the ~~black~~ spade confusion of her hair—cut it short, I guess.) ~~Then~~ She went out and sat on the steps as far away from the others as she could get.

Only Stevie and Marceline are really friends. Woodard (who is sort of mustard colored, both his skin and his wooly top) merely hangs around them.

725

I feel sorry for them all.

Later that evening, ~~I~~ using a piece of pine plank for a writing board, I /went out to/ ~~sitting~~ on the steps /and/ was ~~working on~~ playing in ~~my~~ a poem. I had been there perhaps two hours when I noticed the chain /was/. ~~had been removed~~ gone.

I sat a few minutes more. Then I went inside.

Just after Denny went out this morning, Lanya brought back my notebook—this one. The first thing I did was look inside the front cover. "What about the new poems?" I asked.

"Since they're all on loose sheets I decided I'd keep them in my desk drawer. If you want them . . . ?"

"No," I told her. "That8[?]s probably better. They'd just fall out."

"Did you see the article /in the *Times*/ about you and the children?" [s]he asked when we went out into the back yard.

"No," I said.

So she told me.

It made me feel strange.

Once we went back /up/ into /into the loft/ to get something. She found a piece of paper down ~~tween~~ /between/ the wall and the mattress. "Are you finished with this one?"

I looked at it. "I guess so. It isn't complete, really. But I'm not interested in it any more."

"I'll just take it back to my place and keep it with the others," and she put it in her [—?] shirt pocket; then she jumped down, cried out when [she?] landed, "Owwww!"

I thought she'd twisted her ankle.

But it wasn't serious.

We went into the kitchen; she looked into the coffee pale on the stove and frowned at the mess.

D-t came in with a paper. "Hey, man, that's something, huh?" He had it folded back to the article.

It was on page three.

"What I want to know," Lanya said, looking through the living room door at Stevie and Woodard (Tarzan was trying to ride them across the floor like a horsie), "is what you're going to do with them."

I ~~was leaning against~~ I was leaning against the refrigerator door with my fingers hook~~ed aroun~~ding at the rubber flange that goes around the inside ~~of the door~~. "It doesn't even mention George." I ~~was~~ pull~~ing~~ed. "It makes it sound like I saved them all by myself. It was George's God-damn idea. I was just along—"

Rose walked in, banging the screen, and staréd at Lanya on her way to the next room. Lanya smiled: Rose didn't and kept walking. At the doorway she stopped, looked at Tarzan and the boys, sighed, turned around, went back—*bang!*—onto the front steps.

Sammy was playing in the middle of the street and did not look at her.

D-t moved the junk aside on the table (Marceline in the room with Tarzan was calling out, "Let me! Let me . . . ! Come on, let me!") and sat on the up-ended milk crate to read the article to us. The crate was so low the table top hit him just below the tit. /He read the part about: ". . ./ during the holocaust, broke into a wooden frame house adjoining a grocery store already in flames and let out five youngsters trapped in the second floor rear bedroom. It is reported the bedroom door had been clumsily secured by the back of a chair beneath the door knob—"

"It wasn't a chair," I said. "Somebody had taken a fucking piano bench and turned it on its end. The God-damn music had fallen out all over the hall rug. Why doesn't it mention George?"

"Sound[s?] like you had a reporter standing right there watching you," D-t said.

~~I said~~ "There wasn't anybody," I said. A piece of rubber pulled free, only I dropped it and couldn't see where it had fallen between the refrigerator and the sink. "Just George."

"The[n] how did they know to write about it?" Lanya asked.

"I don't know," I said. "George actually got the door open. All I did was yank at the legs. The bench came open and all the music fell out. On the rug. The top of the bench was still jammed up in there."

"Maybe George met a reporter later that evening," Lanya said. "He could have told the papers, Kid."

" '. . . The children are reported to be safe, but we do not know . . .' "

"Of course it doesn't sound liké George to cut himself out." Lanya sighed and made a funny movement with her hand, grinding her palm on the greyn[?] formica. "Oh, Kid . . ."

727

~~Inside~~ Tarzan neighed loudly and Woodard's hiccuppy laugh shrilled above it, covered in turn by Marceline's squeal.

"The real question—" Lanya looked up—"is what are you going to do with them. Are you going to keep them here[?]"

"You're out of your fucking head—" I said.

D-t said, "The guys like them—"

"How many days ago was it?" I said. "How many days ago, Nightmare and dragon [sic] Lady almost murdered each other? Look!" I went to the living room door. "There's blood all over the fucking God-damn wall—!"

Fist against his chin, Stevie was looking at me.

Tarzan had sat back on his heels and, concertedly, wasn't.

"Ride me!" Marceline said. "You rode Woodard before. Now you ride me!"

"Yeah," Woodard said. "You ride her now."

I stepped back into the kitchen.

"What are you going to do with them?"

I told her, "I don't know."

Tarzan neighed again.

Three staples on the bottom of the above page hold a creased rectangle of newsprint. The end of the column has either been ripped off or (the bottom is torn on a second crease) handled so frequently it had come away:

BRASS ORCHIDS
BLOOM BENEATH
A CLOUDED SKY

This handsome book, or rather booklet, has already become a Bellona commonplace, on night-tables by the reading lamp, in the back pockets of youngsters in the park, or tucked, along with the *Times*, under the arms of people going about the city. This reviewer only wonders how our anonymous author achieved such vivid visualisations with such simple language. Before subject matter so violent and so personal, yet so clearly and

728

wittily voiced, few familiar with Bellona's landscape will be able to avoid strong reactions, negative or positive. If the poet's own emotions seem disjointed or strange, they are still expressed pointedly, incisively, and in an intensely human mode.

True anonymity in a situation such as we have here is, of course, impossible. Since the interview with the author we published a while back, many have simply held it an open secret that the cultivator of these brazen blooms is actual-

This morning I climbed out of the loft soon as I woke up. When I'd gone to bed, they'd been laid out neatly on Raven's sleeping bag he'd opened up full for them by the couch:

Woodard was curled on his side a yard off the edge. Rose had two fingers ~~threat~~ through a tear in the plaid lining. A tuft of stuffing that had come /half/ out shook with her sleeping breath. Sammy, Marceline, and Stevie were banked against Copperhead's back. ~~who~~ For some reason /he/ had gone to sleep on the floor beside them.

I got ~~them~~ the kids up noisily (when we were ready to leave, Copperhead had rolled the bag around himself, head out one end, boots out the other, and wedged under the couch; there was a tuft of stuffing caught on his beard) and took them to the school.

I pushed the door open and herded them inside. Lanya was doing something with the tape-recorder and looked up, more startled than I'd thought she'd be.

"Nobody else here, yet?" I asked.

"Christ, you surprised me." She pushed the fast (forward? reverse?) button. Things clacked, crackled, and spun.

"I brought the kids."

Rose went and immediately sat on a chair in the corner. Woodard wandered toward the table.

Marceline said to Stevie, "You cut that out," only I wasn't sure /at/ what he'd done.

"The other kids will be in soon," Lanya said.

I said: "Good. What you have to do is when the parents come for the kids in the afternoon, you have to farm these here out to them."

Lanya stood up fully and faced me. "God damn!"·

"I can't keep them," I said. "I told you that."

She pulled her lips thin and looked angry.

I was surprised that I had been expecting her to be just that way about it.

"What am I going to do with— Yeah, I know what you said."

Stevie said sharply: "You better *keep* your hands off that, nigger!"

Woodard turned ~~off the~~ from the ~~tape~~ recorder, holding a spool of tape gingerly, blinking apple green eyes below his brush of mustard wool. He smiled uncertainly.

Rose began to cry. The knuckles of her fist pressed together. Her chin bobbed, sobbing, and tears tracked from the inner and outer corners of both eyes.

Sammy, ~~move/~~ standing by the far wall, ~~moved~~ /turned/ the toe of his sneaker ~~over~~ /on/ the floor and blinked.

> *The following letter is paper-clipped to the top and side of the page on which the next entry begins. The envelope, stuck beneath, has left its outline on the stationery:*

How absurd—

—to apologize for an uncommitted injury. But I shall not have been at your party tonight— if Lansang delivers this. There is nothing less sympathetic than the vulgar pleading extenuating circumstances for their vulgarity. There is nothing more distressing to a man who admires formal honesty than to discover he can only offer "personal reasons" as honest explanation for his breach of form.

But, for personal reasons, I will not have attended your party when you read this. I am distressed.

I have been rude.

And I have often imagined *that* to be the most terrible admission I might ever have to make.

Forgive me.

It is not much consolation that the powerful are most successful as patrons when least in evidence. I am concerned with what I presumptuously consider my City. I have always felt every society must have its art; and for that art to have ultimate use, it must be free of intimidation from the centers of power.

Therefore I have not read your poems. Nor will I.

Were I less gregarious, or Bellona more populous, I could be content to read them and never meet you. But I am a very social being, and Bellona is the social size it is.

We *will* meet.

And I eagerly await your second collection, whenever it should be ready. Its publication, hopefully, will be as expeditious as publication of your first.

My friend, I am fascinated by the mechanics of power. Who in his right mind would want the problems and responsibilities of the nation's president? Lord, I *would!* I would! But one cannot be president with a Jewish grandmother. A millionaire family with connections at Harvard helps. A moderately wealthy one with strong emotional ties to Wooster (paint-thinner manufacturers in Cleveland) can be a downright nuisance.

Shall I twist the knife?

A degree in corporate law from Yale is one thing; one in patents from N.Y.U., (*cum laude*, 1960, and still two tries at the New York bar. Personal reasons again . . . ? The pain!) is something else again.

I ramble.

More than likely I shall not be at the house for a while.

Until we *do* meet, I remain,

Sincerely,
Roger Calkins

RC;wd

too dark to see.

So got up, stretched, put down my plank, went inside—

and was suddenly bellowing and yelling and laughing, and everybody was pouring in to see what was going on: "Night run!" I told them. "We're gonna make a night run!" Which we did—to the building with the stained glass windows (the lions of the city, a parti-colored flicker from our lights) with Lanya along, mouse quiet; and there was a funny almost-fight with three men on the street. But after they got as nasty as they dared, I guess it struck them how stpud [stupid?] they were being; a couple of times they got pushed into a wall, though.

At the nest, Denny filled up a bottle from the pail on the stove; I took it on the porch and wrote some more.

Lanya came to squat behind me, hands on my shoulders, cheek on my cheek. ["]You're really ~~up~~ / going/ aren't you? Maybe staying at my place

I heard Denny say: "He's asleep."

I opened one eye against my arm. The ~~other stared~~ With the other I could see the top of the doorway. ~~Then her~~ Then steps below / and somebody moving something to get by / were Lanya['s]. I lay waiting for the circle of her hair to dawn at the loft's edge.

"You aren't sleeping." She grinned and came on over. "I got all the kids stored away."

"Good," I said. "Why were you so pissed off at me when I brought them in that morning?"

"What?"

I raised my head out of my arm and asked again.

"Oh." She turned around on the edge and slid her butt against my side. "I'm just lazy—almost, but not quite, as lazy as you. And I don't like imposing on people." She put her hand in the sleeve hole of my vest. "Besides, I thought you should have kept them." Her fingers, cool, ~~were~~ touched the chain.

"You did?"

She nodded.

That upset me. "I really misunderstood you."

"I know you did. I read what you wrote I said about it in the kitchen / about / when D-t brought in the article."

"And that's not what you said at all, huh?"

"What I said was: What are you going to do about them? What arrangements were you going to make about getting them over to the school, if any; getting a couple of changes of clothes for them; maybe a permanent mattress that was theirs—things like that."

"You really think they'd be better off here?"

"Where you found them, somebody was trying to burn them alive. I could always pack them off with the Richards—"

"What about some of the black families of the kids you've got?"

"You have a very funny picture of this city," she said. "There aren't any black families here. Some of my kids hang around the

732

wasn't such a bad idea?"

"It was a good idea."

She said, sweetly: "I was fucking pissed, you know, when Madame Brown told me you'd split. But when I got here and everybody said you were writing, it was okay." She picked up the sheaf of blue paper. "I'm going to steal these away to read. I'll bring them back in twenty minutes. All right?"

"Yeah," I said. "You know I feel better about these than any I've written before. Not that that means anything."

"G o o d enough to have a second collection?"

I grinned at her. "I think I'm even more anxious not to have one."

She shook her head, kissed me, went away with them,

Wrote till I

George Harrison circus. Or whoever will put up with them. Some, as far as I can tell, are completely on their own."

"Where did you park them?"

"With the commune, mostly."

I lay back down. "They would have been better off here."

"Mmm," she agreed. "Rose went with a woman who's been keeping three girls for a couple of weeks. Everybody was pretty nice about it." Her fingers moved. "But you should have kept them."

I rolled over on my back.

Her hand dragged around my stomach.

"I didn't want them."

"Maybe somebody else ~~around here~~ in the nest would have. Everybody liked them . . . I wanted them."

"You don't live here," I said. "Except five days out of a week. And you've got them: in school."

"Yeah," she said. "Five days out of a week. But you have a point." She took her hand away. "Tell me, how do you do it?"

I asked: "What?"

"How do you—well, I was just thinking about the article."

"Have you heard people talking about my article?"

". . . yours?" That her smile held less mocking than it might was how I knew she mocked.

"About me. You know what I mean."

"Funny . . ." She drew her feet up cross-legged / wrinkling / ~~on~~ the blanket; "Last night at the bar people were talking about you—as usual. But they didn't spend too much time on the kids' rescue. It jars with your image, I think."

I thought about that.

She explained: "It isn't two-sided enough for you. It's just straight heroics."

I heard Denny come inot [into?] the room, move things under the loft looking for something and not find[ing?] it—Lanya glanced down—and leave[ing?].

"All the good gossip about you usually has that dualistic two-sided thing of being bad

733

was finished; found her reading in the front room, dragged her off to the ~~left~~ loft where Denny was lying down already; we fucked on and off all night. Slept. Woke up before they did. Took all the pages I'd done out on the kitchen steps and in dawnlight almost too dim to read by, r e a d them: made six more changes. Now they are finished.

and good at once—do you worry about your image?" she asked, suddenly.

"Sure."

"I'm surprised," she said. "You never seem to purposely do anything about it."

"That's because it never has any relation to what I actually do do. My image is in other peoples' heads. Keeping it interesting is there [their?] problem. I worry about it in the way I could worry about the reputation of my favorite baseball team. I don't for one minute think of myself as a player."

"Maybe so." She picked up my hand and touched the / thickened thumb-knuckle I'd gnawed / raw /~~red~~ pink again. "I mean some day you're going to wash your hands thoroughly and show up with a perfect manicure. And I'll leave you forever. You really are schiz, you know?"

Which made me laugh. "I just it [?] the article had mentioned George. I don't think ~~it's /I it's~~ leaving him out is—" I'd started to say fair—"good for my image." Which made me laugh again.

Copied them out (and it was full day) but found I still [wanted?] to go on writing. So turned back to one of the pages with space left near the end of the notebook (there are very few of them, and I have just started putting entries—like the beginning of this one—in quarter-sized, near illegible scrawl all over the margins) and wrote, this, continuing it on a page I found free here near the beginning.

I recall /and want/ this ~~wanting~~:

Swinging up into the cab of a truck, miles north of Florida, and the driver asking how long you've been hitching, and the sunlight fills his lime-splattered lap and your rank jeans and he lets the radio play pop music for a while, for a while country; then twists the dial; your forearm burns on ~~the outer edge of~~ the door, your hair snaps and your cheek freezes, and the motion is spindled on the rush of music. So you sit, just breathing, to hear and to move through the red and green country, with the sun in the tree-tops a stutter of bright explosions.

The City suffers from the lack of it.

But most of us /have/ come ~~to~~ here by way of it.

734

[Here the correction marks—except for one entry further on—stop. Did our transcriber tire of amateur scholarship? What he has given is more frustrating than helpful. And the sensitive reader will wish with us that he had annotated the final, rather than the first, few pages; there are half a dozen passages to come where even these attempts at variora might be preferable to the most informed supposition. As to the marks employed: Indications of authorial deletions are self-evident; we can assume brackets mean editorial conjecture. The bracketed question mark, however, with or without additional word or suffix, seems totally arbitrary. After much debate, we can only suggest that words in virgules are probably interlinear additions; but even the quickest perusal reveals this accounts only for most cases. While he plies us with quaint descriptions of paperclips and staples, he fails to record date and letterhead material in the Calkins' letter (perhaps there were none?), nor does he mention whether any (or all) of the entries were typed or hand-written. Internal evidence (it is a spiral notebook, not a loose-leaf) suggest the latter. Corrections, however, such as: balnk [blank?], there8['?]s, and bendh [bench?] bray out for the former. Also, "Rose . . . a brown fist up beside her ~~face~~ chin . . ." and, a few pages later, "Fist against his chin, Stevie . . ." suggest the first draft of a fabulist who, having found the sharp descript for one invented character, forgets he has already used it and sticks it to a second. The rubrics running pages left or right, which we print in slightly smaller type, are marginal (sometimes rather wide) entries made along the sides of our typescript at somewhat narrower spacing; most probably they represent "entries in quarter-sized, near illegible scrawl all over the margins"—that is, entries of a later date than the one beside them we print in ordinary sized typeface. (Note also that the rubric which breaks off marginally to the last entry in the notebook continues as the major entry just two previous to this.) Considering the lacunae that pass without comment, our transcriber's editional adieu ("Here one page, possibly two, is missing.") can only make us wonder what maddeningly special knowledge convinced him that, indeed, the ultimate and penultimate fragments once formed a breakless, breathless whole. Of course, we do not know under what pressure the transcript was made. Even if the description of conditions in the closing pages is only half true (and our transcriber were—say—the enthusiastic E. Forrest, working within the City), we can

735

*easily see his abandoning that tedious opening method to
the simple necessity of completion; we must count ourselves
lucky to have any document at all. For all we know, however, we have here a copy of a transcript made from the
original hand-written notebook; or even a typescript made
from a manuscript copy. Both mistakes or correction-marks
might have come in (or fallen out) at any generation. Still,
it tempers our trust of all he has done to note that on one
page (!) he has committed all of the following:*

"Sound[s?] like you had a reporter standing

"The[n] how did they know

grinding her palm on the greyn[?] formica. (*That
superfluous 'n' again suggests a typing, rather than a hand-
written, error.*)

Are you going to keep them here[?]"

He then has the pedantic gall to impose his solitary
'sic'—Nightmare and dragon [sic] Lady almost murdered
each other.—*for the mere lack of an upper-case 'D'!*

We coagulate and dissolve around (not inside) the house,
gathering on the front steps, dispersing for booze to the
store with the busted plate-glass window two blocks away,
convening again outside the kitchen door, drifting away—
to reconnoiter in the yard (piling up the bottles), with maybe a stop in the front room which Lanya, when she comes
around, says smells like a locker room—curious if she's
ever been in a locker room, or just picked up the phrase.

I can't smell it.

This afternoon when I came out into the yard, Gladis
(very black and very pregnant, she wears a basketball sized
natural, sandals, and bright colored sacks) and her friend
Risa (who I wish looked like something other than a
chocolate cow) were there for the third day. The guys'
jokes are foul, their attitude maniacally protective.

Jack the Ripper: "Little girl, you must have been
fucking on a God-damn elephant to get yourself a belly
that big!" at which Denny, perched on the table's edge,
laughs the shrillest.

Gladis, under Spider's arm, wriggles back against the
tree where they sit.

The Ripper's laughter stops for the wine jug, and continues when he drops it from his mouth to pass it to
Thruppence and Raven, knee to knee on the bench below

736

Denny (I propped the board with a cinderblock yester-day).

Gladis leers and says, "Fuck you—" She's fifteen? Sixteen—?—"you big cocksucker!" with the inappropriate-ness with which women usually appropriate homosexual vocabulary or whites use "nigger" other than in rage.

Thruppence came back over the laughter with good-natured illogic: "You don't get no belly like that sucking a cock!"

"Well, Jesus Christ," Spider shouted, "well, Jesus Christ, if I'd 'a known that—" making much to get his fly open and his free hand inside. Gladis squealed to her feet and lurched away.

I sat down on the steps next to Risa who closed her copy of *Orchids*, leaned on the faded knee of her jeans, and didn't look at me.

Tarzan was going by with the wine jug and handed it to one of the other white guys (an occurrence notable enough to note); I reached way down till my knees were higher than my shoulders and snagged it up into my lap. "You like that?" I asked Risa.

When she looked up, I put my arm around her shoulder and offered her some wine. She made her first, scared smile (she looks a few years older than Gladis, anyway: eigh-teen? maybe twenty?) and drank. Inside the up-ended jug, wine splashed like a small, plum sea.

"Uh-oh," from the Ripper. "What your girl friend gonna say when she come around?"

"Fuck her," I said.

"What's his boy friend gonna say?" Dollar asked from somewhere else.

I said: "Fuck him too."

Denny leaned across the table to pull the other jug over.

Gladis, turning and turning in her loose green (they regard her as their personal catastrophe, an awesome de-light; she looks as if she will foal *now;* claims, however, it's months away), settled, giggling, again, beside Spider.

Then Spitt came in with Glass (some argument about where a building was) and we broke up from our back-yard loafing and reconvened on the front steps. Standing beside Copperhead, I looked down the street: Thirteen was coming up:

"Hey!" called with the desperate good will of the

seriously bored. "Any of you guys want to come on over? Hey, Kid, you ain't even seen my new place. You want to come over and meet some of the guys there?" In this city, where nothing happens, it is worth your sanity to refuse anything new.

Somehow, with the wrangling and wine and lethargy, me, the national guard (Copperhead, Spitt, and Glass), and Denny went with him.

Up a lot of dark stairs with Glass saying, "Man, I didn't know you were this close. You're just around the God-damn corner," and Thirteen saying: "I *told* you I was just around the God-damn corner; why ain't you guys never come over to see us?" and I looked up:

Smokey stood at the head; when we broke around her, she turned with Thirteen, to follow (at his shoulder) breathing as though she'd held her breath since he'd left.

Sitting on one of the beds at the end of the loft was a scrawny, shirtless guy in jeans—h o l e s b o t h k n e e s— knuckling his eyes. He'd probably just sat up when he heard us on the stairs.

Two o t h e r guys stood at the window. Thirteen started bobbing around, very excited: "Hey! Hey, you guys, this is the Kid. Hey!" He motioned me over.

It isn't that the "heroic" incidents about me cullable from the Times are untrue (well . . . some of them), nor the "villainous" ones on the gossip round that distorted (well . . . ditto). But the six minutes here, the twenty seconds there, the forty-five minutes how-many-weeks later—the real time it takes to commit the "heroic" or "villainous" act—are such a microscopic presentage of my life. Even what can be synopsized from this journal—snatches gun from looter's hands; helps save children from flaming death; lead victorious attack (Ha! They were scared crazy!) on armed citadel; hobbles, half-shod, shrieking in the street; rescues Old Faust from collapsing ruin (and once tried to write poems —) are things that have happened to me, not that I have done. What you look like you're doing and what you feel like you're doing are disparate enough to mute any mouth that might attempt description!

"Hi." A black guy in workman's greys got up off the window sill and held out his hand.

His friend, a stocky blond (short-hair) in denim and construction boots, had his hand ready for seconds. "Hear you got a thing going here."

The black guy locked thumbs with me in a biker shake.

I figured the other guy would do the same. But he just started, then he laughed, and his hand joggled awkwardly.

738

So I caught it up for him and smiled. He was "Tom," from Thirteen, "and this is Mak. You guys rode in here, you say?"

"In a pickup," Tom explained. "We were up in Montana, running down this way . . . till we run out of gas." A cowboy truck driver, he wanted to be friendly.

"And that's Red," from Tom.

So I locked thumbs with Red (hair like rusted Brillo), who blinked sleepy, ice-grey eyes in a face dark as mocha—another mustard-skinned spade, and this one, for all his hunched shoulders, good-looking as the devil.

From the corner someone said: "Hello, Kid," and Tak, arms folded, stood up from the plank wall where he was leaning. He pushed his cap up and came forward, face visible from the pink crease on his forehead where his cap had been, down to his gold chin. "I'm making my rounds again. I brought these guys here over to the commune and they felt about like you did. So I thought we'd drop in on Thirteen and say hello."

"A good excuse to smoke some dope," Thirteen said. "Now ain't that a good excuse?"

"Sure," Tom said. "Any excuse is a good excuse as far as I'm concerned."

Smokey, who I hadn't seen go, came back with the jar.

Thirteen took it, raised it in his tattooed hand. "Now you'd think," he said, "with a water pipe like this, I'd at least put some kind of water in it, huh?"

"Or creme de menthe," Smokey said. "That's what you're always talking about."

"Yeah. You ever smoke hash through a water pipe filled with creme de menthe?" Thirteen asked. "That's really something."

Mak, still at the window, gestured toward the bed. "You got a bottle of . . . what's that? Mountain Red?"

"Naw," Thirteen said. "That ain't the same thing."

Thirteen's cheeks hollowed; the jar filled with smoke.

"You got any speed?" Tom asked.

"Oh, man—" Thirteen coughed and handed Red the jar. "You can't keep anything like that around here more'n five minutes. We don't get much anyway. Once somebody brought in a whole pillow case full, man! A whole pillow case with a plastic lining full of all *sorts* of speed. This Mexican guy."

"Was he Mexican?" Smokey asked. "He was thick-set, blond . . ."

"He talked like a Mexican," Thirteen said. "I mean that was a Mexican accent he was speaking. It wasn't no Spanish-from-Spain accent. Or Puerto Rican. They sound different."

I nodded.

"Anyway," Thirteen said, "it was gone like *that!*" He grinned back across his shoulder; *"She* was maybe five pounds lighter. But that's the only way you'd of known it was here. How we went through *all* that shit so fast—man!"

"You must have every *kind* of— Oh, thanks." Mak took the pipe from Red, sucked, and said: "It's out."

"Here, just a minute." Thirteen struck another match.

"You must have every kind of junkey in this city," Mak said.

Smokey, with the jar now, was handing it to Copperhead, who said: "I don't think I've ever seen a skaghead in Bellona, you know?"

"I have," I said.

Glass laughed.

Tak said: "We don't have much dope here. No money, no dope. To speak of, I mean."

"I think—" Thirteen said. "Wouldn't you say, Kid? I mean, you could say this about most of your guys, huh? Most people here have *taken* a lot of dope. But we don't got too many people here who *need* it. If you know what I mean."

"That sounds pretty good," Mak said.

"I mean if you *need* it," Thirteen said, "there just ain't no place to get it. I've put everything in my arm, or up my nose, or down my belly I could, just about, one time or another. Liked all of it, too. But I don't *need* anything, you know? Of course—" he reached over and took the jar from me—"I do enjoy my toke."

Everybody laughed.

Me too.

And all the smoke loosed out my nose and stung.

"Now did you ever think what a specialized city Bellona is?" Tak was saying. He had come in front of the bed, fists in his scuffed pockets, holding the leather off his hairy stomach. The red quilt lining was torn in two places. "I mean Bellona's got a lot of some things and none of a lot of others. I used to know a guy who could *not* go to

740

sleep unless he had a radio playing. He can't live in Bellona. There are people who *have* to have movies to go to; or they get twitchy. They can't live in Bellona. Some people must have chewing gum to survive. I've found stale candy bars, Life-Savers, Tums; but all the chewing gum is gone from all the candy-stores' racks. Gum chewers can't live in Bellona. Not to mention cigarettes, cigars, pipes: the tobacco in the vending machines went stale a couple of weeks after we got cut off and I guess the cartons and packaged shag was the first thing the scavengers cleared out. You never see a smoker in Bellona."

"Some people need sun, clear nights, cool breezes, warm days—" I said.

"They can't live in Bellona," Tak went on. "In Helmsford, I knew people who never walked further than from the front door to the car. They can't live in Bellona. Oh, we have a pretty complicated social structure: aristocrats, beggars—"

"Bourgeoisie," I said.

"—and Bohemians. But we have no economy. The illusion of an ordered social matrix is complete, but it's spitted through on all these cross-cultural attelets. It *is* a vulnerable city. It *is* a saprophytic city— It's about the pleasantest place I've ever lived." He grinned around at Tom, Red, Mak. "I'm curious to see whether you guys will like it enough to settle down, make it your home, become part of the community."

The jar circled Tak for the third time; he swayed at the center.

"Here." Tom, still leaning on the sill, held it out. "You didn't get any."

"Never touch the stuff." Tak waved the sides of his jacket. "No, I'm a poor, anti-social juice-head. Not a man of my times at all. Gets me in trouble, too."

Somebody suggested we go back to the nest. Tak, his three discoveries pretty well parked at Thirteen's curb, decided to drift—after Thirteen, in a flurry of patriarchal politesse, broke out his jug (same as ours; he must be rifling the same busted plate glass window on the street sometimes marked Lafayette, sometimes marked Jessie). The late afternoon got lost in the day's momentum.

"Why don't we go back to the nest," somebody suggested *again*. Which, again, everybody thought was a good idea.

Where Lady of Spain, with Raven, I guess it was, had

gotten a big fire going in the yard and all sorts of canned shit, scalloped tops bent back, bubbling on the cinder-blocks, their labels blacked and bronzed by the flames. The tree trunks glimmered; and the fence; and the triangle of glass in the second floor window of the house beyond.

We stood around, listening to the fire. Red, still bare foot and shirtless, squatted, staring at the coals, the back of his jeans tugged way the hell down his ass. Circling his hips three times—he wore it down below the waist of his jeans so you couldn't see it normally—was the optic chain.

Just then he glanced back at me over his shoulder, surprised; maybe he thought I was staring at his crack.

"God damn, I burned fuckin' *hell* out of myself—!" Jack the Ripper shook his hand furiously on the other side of the fire, hopped and whirled. Fire glistened in his mud and sputum eyes.

I looked down at the beads across my chest, my stomach, around my arm; could feel them around my leg. I looked up and saw Red was looking too; then his eyes went down to the place below his hip's blade pushing above the beltless loops. And up at me again. His hands, out for balance, were bloated the way some winos' get. He started to speak.

I said: "I don't want to hear it. I don't want to know where you got it. I don't want you to ask me where I got mine. Fuck you, man. I just don't want to hear—" catching my voice lowering and a fury rising neither he nor I understood.

Black Mak watched me, frowning.

White Tom dug in a can of beans (hot on one side and cold on the other?) with his fingers.

Red swallowed.

"Sure I eat pussy!" California shouts and shoves Tarzan backward.

"Hey, man, hey—" D-t moves along with them.

"You God-damn right I eat pussy!" and shoves again.

"Come on, now, man, what you—"

"I'd eat *your* fucking pussy if you had one!" and Tarzan crashes back into the fence.

"Now come on!" D-t, a hand on either of California's shoulders, moves him away, and Tarzan, abandoned, suddenly starts to—

—but Gladis's laugh turned shriek, letting me hear (remember?) a second crash's echo. Among all the concerned "What's . . ." and "Who's . . ." and unconcerned laughter

742

(mostly Dollar's, bright and insistent), it got figured out that somebody had hurled a hot can at Gladis, which tipped her shoulder and splattered on the steps.

Red wasn't at the fire any more. And a moment past the rage, I felt that surge of good feeling to rival those acid moments of unbearable friendship when the gates will not shut. Later, I went up behind Dollar and caught him across the back of the head, hard.

"What'd you do that for . . . ?" he whined, lids crimped around eyes gone orange under the fire.

"For throwing that God-damn can."

His eyes crimped more and his mouth opened on that slate-chip laughter (clear, a little shrill, like a boy's on the short side of puberty) and he said: "Oh, man, did you see the way she hollered? I bet she was scared enough to drop it right *here*," and wheeled away, laughing, while D-t shook his head, watching, and said, gravely, "Shit, man."

Tom and Thruppence were arguing about geography which took us from the yard to the kitchen, from the kitchen to the front steps, from the front steps to the yard. Everybody was staggering and bending and belly-clutching with laughter.

Then this altercation with Denny: "Man, I don't like to go to bed with you when you're drunk," he explained, three times, sadly, only I knew if Lanya was there, he would have come; he did anyway. Woke up later to find him gone; woke again, even later, lying on my side, with his small hot butt pressed against my belly, the continent of his back, muscular and vertebral, going away in the grey. No hangover when I got up, but my gut was a little loose so that I knew the first coffee or even water I drank would make me shit like hell. I'd gone to sleep in my pants. Getting them back together, I stepped into the hall.

Red came from the bathroom, gave me a funny look, and went out on the service porch while I went on up the hall, trying to figure what had changed about him. Glanced out at him when I passed the door: there was a projector chain hanging around his neck; figured he'd gotten it off the manikin in the bathroom. I opened the bathroom door: Check.

Shit now? I wondered.

Wandered back to the service porch instead.

". . . you mean the one that's gonna have the baby?" Red was asking, which Dollar answered, as I stopped to watch them:

"Fireball, what's the matter with you! Not the *pregnant* one; the other one!"

"Oh. The *other* one. Sure."

(So some time while I'd been asleep, Red had acquired his first chain and a name.)

I leaned against the door frame. "Fireball?"

Red turned.

A half cup of wine spilled back and forth across the bottom of the gallon jug hooked on Dollar's forefinger. He lifted it to his mouth with both hands, dropped it again, and looked at me with eyes bright, wet, and pink. "Me and Fireball are gonna go get us some pussy, if she's still puttin' it out, you know? You comin'?"

I said to Red/Fireball: "Where're your friends, Tom and Mak?"

"They split."

"We scared 'em off, huh?"

"You know; they're pretty . . ." He gestured with his hand. It meant finicky/normal/unimaginative—the same hand-joggle one patient in a mental hospital will use to another to describe a third who's particularly out of touch that morning: palm down, fingers wide and waggling. "They're nice guys, though. They gave me a ride all the way down here. They treated me nice. Then, when the truck broke down, they didn't seem to mind if we hung out together, you know?"

"Come *on*," Dollar said. The jug clicked the doorframe as he stepped out.

We went with him up the hall.

I opened the door to the back room and went in first, Dollar and Fireball right behind me. It was very warm. California, squatting in the half-dark, stood up beside us and chuckled: "God *damn!* Copperhead and Glass are having themselves a fuckin' contest," heard himself and decided to change the emphasis: "A fucking contest, man." He chuckled again, swaying so close the hair over his shoulder brushed my arm.

Before the lion, rampant on the sill, scorpions slept or sat. Jack the Ripper, wandering around, stepped over sleeping Gladis and one of the non-members who occa- Gladis and Mike, sleeping: knee to knee, forehead to forehead, his hair, long and light, lay over hers, tight and black, his arm over her brown collar, her arm above her belly. She snored. (Conceit: They curled, facing, like single quote marks enclosing an ellipsis pared to a unit point.)

744

sionally crashes here. Lady of Spain—black vest, black jeans, black boots, with black chains a-tangle over tightly folded arms and an intent, midnight frown—leaned against the wall, shoulder to shoulder with Revelation, who was naked, gold hair at his head a matted snarl and, down-sloping from gold-matted groin, what I guess was half a hard-on, deeper pink than the rest of his perpetual blush. He'd tucked his hands between his buttocks and the wall, his expression, though as intense as Lady of Spain's, empty of content.

Risa grunted: Copperhead—moaned? growled? on top of her, his freckled ass bouncing between her darker knees. The sleeping bag they'd started out on (Raven's, opened over the charred mattress) had bunched into a green python under her back. Her elbows came away from his (Copperhead still wore his vest), flapped, and fell, one hand slapping the mattress, the other catching his arm.

Glass sat in the corner, knees up, forearms over them, head back on the wall, taking long, loud breaths.

"Hey?" California put his hand on my shoulder and whispered: "You gonna get a piece?"

"Let's see how she's doing when he gets off." But my cock was about half-hard, and I could feel my heart in it for a dozen beats, till I shifted my leg.

"She's really wild," California said. "She wants everything you can figure out, man! Right now, most of the ladies except—" he nodded toward Lady of Spain who was saying something to Revelation who didn't seem to hear), then went back to watching —"are out now. But they were *all* in here working on her a little while ago! Black Widow, baby? *Whew* . . . ! What a T-V spectacular

Life in the Behavioral Sink, Episode Sixteen Thousand, Six Hundred and Thirty-Seven: Heavy Cathedral, who is getting heavier, squatted last evening with his back to the house, discussing the behavior of overcrowded rats, with a half-dozen of us who stood around, listening— Gladis had just come by cradling a poor, dead mouse that had to be flushed down the toilet. "Sure," counters astute, diminutive, and dark Angel, who is drunk, "the similarities between rats and people are very large. But the differences, I suspect, are on the order of the factor of the differences in body weight between an under-nourished mouse and an eight-month pregnant woman!" (Is art and sex replacing sex and death as the concerns of the serious mind? Life here would make me think so.)

that was—"

"Hey!" Lady of Spain said from her place on the wall.

745

"Don't lay any of that shit on *us*." Her chin jerked up. "That wasn't nothing like what *you* guys are into."

"Yeah," Revelation said. He squinted, scratched his upper lip with nails you could see were clean from here. "That was something different." He put his hand behind him again. "That wasn't like this."

"Hell," California said. "They was having *sex* with the broad—!" He glanced at Lady of Spain who'd gone back to watching. "Well, they was *playing* with the broad in a . . . sexual way. Anyway, it turned me on." Suddenly he grinned, leaned closer: "Only *this* pig likes to get her pussy poked with a pecker. So—naturally—she called in the shock troops. Well, man, there ain't *nothing* I like to eat out better than pecker-poked pig-pussy!" California's grin grew huge; he began to shake my shoulder: "Shit, am I glad to see you, Kid: You get in there and there'll be something between her legs that won't turn my stomach when I get down there eatin' it out, you know?"

I raised an eyebrow.

The huge grin became silent laughter. "I mean some of these mother-fuckers are *animals*, man!"

"Animals?" Jack the Ripper came up, intense and soft. "You're a fuckin' *hog!* Every other time some nigger pulls his dick out of that hole, this Jew bastard's down there on his hands and knees—" and the Ripper stuck out his tongue, and scrunched up his face snorting and grunting: which made California laugh out full voice. "Shit," the Ripper said (on the traditional two beats), and went out the door.

"You want to do her both at the same time?" Dollar was saying, head together with Fireball. "See, I'll get it in her pussy, man, and you can work on her head. Course, if you want to do it the other way around—"

"Oh, man—" California turned—"the bitch is *tired!* She's been going all night!"

"She was doin' them freaky things before," Dollar said. "Takin' on two guys at once—"

"Sure," California said. "But that was back— Aw, never mind!"

Copperhead finished, pushed back to his knees, stood slowly, then bent again to drag his green pants up around one leg; the other was bare. "Your turn?" he asked across the room to Revelation. Copperhead was breathing hard. "You better get your ass over here!"

"I already been, once." Revelation glanced at me. "Glass wants to go again. And the Kid's here . . ."

"You go on," Glass said from the floor. "It's gonna take me another five minutes to get my breath."

"Then, fuck it . . ." Revelation came forward, when I didn't move, leaving Lady of Spain by the wall. "It ain't gonna take *me* no five minutes." Chuckling, he stepped over Devastation, who turned over and dragged his forearm over his face. "Like I said, I'm an in-and-out man, you know?"

"Well, yeah," Copperhead said. "That's what you wanted seconds for, ain't it? Come on, white boy—" He stepped back, laughing. "You can fuck her. She ain't prejudiced."

Risa made a sort of hoarse and gravelly sound that went on, while her mouth opened and closed. Her hand slapped the mattress, her head came up. She looked around. (Her hair was stiff and long, like a spray of dark water that had shot from her head and frozen), still making that sound.

It gave me chills. My cock went from half to full hard. I had to move it over with my thumb.

"Man!" California said, watching me.

"Okay, sweetheart!" Revelation stepped over D-t, who looked solid out. "Okay, I'm comin', I'm comin'!" Some of the guys laughed.

". . . shit!" Lady of Spain peeled forward from the wall and walked toward us, arms still folded, head shaking. Her frown had become a tough, ironic smile in which was a lot of disgust. She passed: I put a hand on her shoulder. "Hey, you ever go after it like that?"

(Copperhead: "Get your tongue in her mouth, man. It ain't no fun if you don't tongue her . . . yeah, like that."

(Glass: "She nearly chewed mine off." And laughed).

Lady of Spain looked at my hand, looked at me, and, without breaking expression, said: "Get off my ass, cocksucker."

"Now *hey* . . . !" California frowned. "The Kid asked you a civil question. You don't have to go calling him no—"

Looking at me straight, Lady of Spain said: "Now have I just called you anything that ain't true, or asked you to do anything in a—what is it? An uncivil tone of voice?"

747

I nodded—"Right on—" and dropped her shoulder.

Lady of Spain shook her head, sucked her teeth.

"God damn," California said. "These bitches are always goin' around tryin' to cut a guy's balls off—"

"Aw, fuck off," I said. "What does it take to cut yours off anyway— A dull spoon? Look: first, I have sucked my quota of dick. *And* enjoyed it. Second, my nuts are strung up there with two-inch steel cable. It takes a lot more hatchet work than that to make them even feel *loose*," which California thought was pretty funny again and started laughing all over. "Your thing," I said, "just isn't some other peoples' and there's nothing you can do about it."

Lady of Spain shook her head again and pushed out between Dollar and Fireball.

I guess Revelation did come pretty fast. He was getting back up on his knees, already, face still blank, cock still half- hard. Risa held his arm with both her hands. Revelation shook his head, sort of sheepishly: "Like I say, sweetheart, I guess I just don't take that much—"

But Glass was already down on his hands and knees, pushing Revelation aside, pants open, buckle dangling, cock flapping at his belly like a shy foot of over-sized garden hose.

Copperhead, holding his pants up with one hand, with the other helped Revelation stand.

"You see," Revelation said. "Even the second time, I go pretty . . ."

"A load is a load," Copperhead said. "How you wanna time it is your problem."

Revelation took an unsteady step that pulled him away from Copperhead's grip, said, "God damn . . . !" then started to the wall. Halfway, he glanced at me again, suddenly got a big, pink grin. "You better get some of that while there's still some left." At the wall, he turned to lean, hands once more tucked behind him, genitals still engorged, slick with common juice.

I stood, watching, wondering when I could maneuver to see pussy:

With one hand, Risa held Glass's shoulder. Her knees splayed, sagged, recovered. His hips were going side to side as much as up and down. She was doing something with her other hand—trying to get his pants further down his legs, I realized. Finally he paused long enough to let her push them to his knees, and before she twisted back up

748

beneath him he began to hump and flatten. She lifted one foot, dropped it, and for a moment her face turned from him to us, tongue and mouth wide, tongue crawling around her teeth, till it snapped back, then lapped at Glass's neck.

Copperhead squatted by them—to watch? But he leaned forward, said something. Glass slowed.

Risa said something I couldn't hear, put her hand on Copperhead's naked knee, raised her head a moment, said something else.

"God damn," California said. "Them two been going at her four, five times. Each."

Copperhead stood up and walked toward us. "Oh, man!" He put his hand on the wall to balance while he tried three times to get his other foot back inside his pants. Perspiration shone among the freckles and red hairs inside his thigh. Then green canvas slid over them. He jerked his chin toward the Glass and Risa. "That nigger can fuck!" His foot coming down, knocked D-t's shoulder (Copperhead: "Hey—sorry!") who looked up and said, "You ain't doin' so bad yourself," and dropped his face back into his arm.

Re-reading this, it occurs to me that the written words don't let you know whether Copperhead meant Risa or Glass. His tone of voice did, though.

Copperhead grinned, pushed his works, glistening like wet leather, into his fly and buttoned the top button.

"You want something to drink?" California asked; he'd taken the jug from Dollar.

"No." Copperhead rubbed the place between his beard and his thick, lower lip with the side of his forefinger. "But she does."

"I think," I said, "I am gonna get a piece."

"Hey," Copperhead said, "you *better* get some—before we *kill* her!" He shook his head. His beard was wet. "Go on." Then he went out of the room.

I stepped across D-t and nearly tripped on a blanket tangled between two mattresses. California came over too; he stuck his forefinger in the lion's brass mouth, wiggled it there, then suddenly grinned at me as though he'd made a joke. I just leaned against the wall to watch.

Once Glass threw up his head, face bright with sweat, teeth and eyes minstrel white. Risa's head and shoulders shook like somebody was hammering the soles of her feet. She kept saying, "Ughhhh . . . Ughhhh . . . Ughhhh . . ." and sometimes closing her mouth. Glass's face slapped down and hid her unfocused blinks.

I squatted by the wall.

Glass's hips, smacking hers, made her thighs shake.

I got my hand under my belt to pull my dick over; it rubbed hard on a seam or something, which hurt.

Glass threw back his head again, pushed himself up on his hands, his ass going. Risa's hands bounced on his shoulders. She grabbed air, she slapped the mattress; then she hung on his neck. The heel of one foot dug the ticking, her toes wide, then curling down on their dark knuckles.

She was making a sound for all the world like a flannel torn near the ear. Glass finished.

I guess she didn't or couldn't or wouldn't.

Still up on his hands, his head dropped. She kept pulling at his shoulders. He took a loud breath and sat back on his knees. "Oh, shit . . ."

Risa dropped her hands between her legs.

I got up and stood just behind Glass. When Risa's knees went down, her foot slid by my boot. She rubbed her ankle back and forth on mine through the soft leather. Glass stood, unsteadily, so I gave him a hand. He held my arm with one hand, tried to pull his pants up with the other, and said: "Go on, man. Fuck that pussy. Yeah! Shit . . ." He looked very dazed and not quite at me.

I opened my fly.

Risa looked pretty dazed too.

Her breasts rolled on her ribs as she rocked. I had to bend my knees to get my crank out. She reached to scratch her hip; then her hand forgot what it was doing, touching her stomach all over; she was looking all around the room, moving just her narrowed eyes. I put my barefoot on her cunt. She rocked her hips till I pressed hard; then she held my dirty ankle and rubbed her hair on the calloused ball. The arched bone there slid around under its wet skin. What had leaked into the hair under my instep felt thick as clay slip. She opened and closed and opened her mouth, but breathing, loudly, through her nose. And her eyes were still moving around without fixing anything. A drop of water rolled sideways down her jaw.

I took my foot away.

She began to pull at herself, digging two fingers in, to open and close a raw canyon; she blew out her mouth, all her lips sticking and pulling apart.

(Did I think: Who am I standing here with a hard-on for? Me, her, or them? No, I didn't.) I opened my belt and kneeled down. She got an expression almost a smile and swung it all around her, head rolling; and still pulling. Christ.

I went forward. Holding myself up on one hand, I caught one of hers and got it down on my dick. (Lanya once told me lots of guys get up tight if a girl tries to touch their dick when they're putting it in; it turns me on.)

I remember I opened my eyes once and saw her brown neck stretching as her head turned away, then wrinkling as her ear hit mine, hard. She was pushing at my pants to get the belt buckle out of the way, I realized. Then she grabbed hold. I fantasized about eating her, some. And her blowing Dollar, for some reason; I remember thinking this was freaky enough that I shouldn't have to fantasize at all. At which point, without loosening her legs on my hips or her arms over my shoulders, she screamed. Loud. It scared me to death. I thought: There goes my hard. It didn't—but that was the first time I thought about the rest of the people in the room. Somebody was standing near us; because I could see his sneaker right in front of my face. When she began to drag air back into her chest, with some wet sound in her mouth (which, hunting for mine, finally caught it—I tried to lick her tonsils), I thought I was going to come. Only it took another minute and a half. When I come, sometimes, balling somebody I'm not too interested in (or having particularly uninteresting sex with somebody I am), I get some picture (or words) that stays a few seconds until it hazes to something hard to recall as a dream: This time, it was an image of myself, holding hands with someone (Lanya? Risa? Denny?) and running among leafless trees laced with moonlight while the person behind me kept repeating: ". . . Grendal, Grendal, Grendal . . ." which, while I rocked my face in her hot neck and the stinging in my thighs, chest, and belly went on, seemed very funny. (Specific and primitive?) I raised my face out of the moon-bright branches into a room lathered with the smell of smoke and scorpions. And grinning, man, like a tiger!

I sat back, dragging chains over her. She bit one, held it in her teeth so it tugged on my neck. I pulled, till it came out of her mouth, kneeled back, and bumped into someone—Dollar—who said: "Hey, man. Pretty good, huh?"

"Watch it," California said, trying to crowd in. "Come on, huh?"

Copperhead, holding a gallon jug, stooped down beside Risa. Glass stood just behind his shoulder. Copperhead got one hand under her neck. She held onto the knee of his fatigues.

I stood up while California clambered over her ankles. "Hey, Copperhead? Man, she's drunk enough already! She's gonna be sick if you—"

"Get out of here," Copperhead said: "This is water. She asked me for a fucking drink of water before, that's all."

"Oh." California slid his hands up Risa's legs. A tendon in her thigh shook. California bent.

"Aw, come *on!*" Glass said, and punched at California's head. "Can't you wait until she has a fuckin' drink of water?" But Risa grabbed California's hair, grunting, and pulled him down. Glass sucked in his breath and watched her drink till Copperhead lowered the jug. Water ran down Risa's cheek. She got out, ". . . thank you . . ."

"You're welcome," California said, muffled in her crotch.

Which Copperhead must have thought was the funniest thing he ever heard. He just broke up. And spilled water all over the floor.

"You can take her in the mouth," Dollar was saying to Fireball. "If you want, you can take her mouth and I'll take her pussy. Or you can take her pussy and I'll . . ."

I walked to the door. Halfway there I realized I was going to shit within thirty seconds.

Siam walked in. "She still workin' out?"

"Party's still going," I said and pushed by him.

In the hall, Spitt was rubbing the scar on his chest. "Them guys *still* messing around in there? Jesus Christ." He looked unhappy.

I asked: "You get your turn?"

"Yeah. Before. But they just on on and fucking *on!* They're gonna kill her or something."

"You're just scared it'll all be used up by the time you're fit for seconds." I grinned. "Why don't you go in there and see if you can finish her off?" Then I went in the bathroom, got my pants down fast, and sat.

My buttocks got wet from the splash, and there was six seconds of gut-cramp that started in my ankles. Then it eased. My crank hung down against the porcelain, so cold I had to slide my hand over it to hold it away. (Cold knuckles; better than a cold cock.) Through the bathroom door I watched Spitt, still standing in the hall. After a while, he went in the room.

"Grendal grendalgrendalgrendalgrendalgren . . ." still ran through my head. Suddenly, I realized I hadn't been listening carefully enough; I'd stuck the brake in the wrong place. The actual word I'd heard at orgasm and that, for the last few minutes had been repeating in my head was: ". . . Dhalgren . . ." I wiped myself with part of the second page of the Bellona *Times*, January 22, 1776.

> Power is all. Another falsification: I do not tell how I gain or maintain it. I only record the ginger stroll through the vaguely fetid garden of its rewards.

Going back to the loft-bed, I thought it would be nice if Lanya had stopped by and was waiting with Denny (knowing she wouldn't because I'd thought about it); she hadn't.

Up in the loft, I lay on my back for a minute; then I rolled over and hit Denny on the shoulder.

He woke up. "What?"

"Smell my dick," I said.

"Huh . . . ?" Then he made a disgusted sound, sat up, bent down, and sniffed. My fly was open.

Denny looked up, frowning. "You got dandruff in your crotch." He wrinkled his nose. "Who is it?"

I laughed.

"The girl they got in the back. Risa." I grinned at him. "You get some?"

"Oh . . . I went in there before while you were asleep. It was mostly girls in there then. I didn't do nothing." He settled again on the bed, his back to me.

Looking up at the ceiling, I began to fall asleep: the kind of falling where you watch yourself do it, and everything gets all tingly and you sink among the tingles.

And woke up with Denny on top of me, my arms across his back. He was breathing in short gasps, face against my neck, rubbing off on my belly. Wondered why I'd bothered to wake him up be-

> My speech changes when I talk to different people; I go from "ain't" to "aren't," "yes" to "yeah," from a fixed to a formless diction. With Lanya, a lot of the time, it gets playful, arch. With others, it flattens. When I'm upset, it punctures with dozens of noise nodes: "you know's" "I mean's" and "sort of's". I left behind me a whole vocabulary and syntax at the colleges I passed through, which began to come back with Newboy, Kamp, that interview, and with Calkins at the retreat. It's lability, not affectation; a true and common trait. But if I tried to write down what I say as I move from speech context to speech context, it would read like lack of character, not a characteristic. I note all the eccentric words around me: Glass used the word ". . . radically . . ."

753

this morning and several times I've heard Lady of Spain refur to an ". . . entity . . ." while among the others I've heard ". . . sententious . . ." ". . . caravan . . ." and ". . . conspicuous . . ." go by. But when I transcribe the conversation around me, I find myself purposely playing down the verbal range of it, so that it does not read like post-literate affectation—which it isn't. George's speech can't even be written down for the common reader; Throckmorton (at the party) speaks only in inane combinations of serial phrases that become satires on themselves as soon as they are recorded but that, during utterance, make miracles of communication. I suppose I'm just getting frustrated by what written words can't do. This afternoon, Gladis, wholly pregnant and half smiling, said through the kitchen screening: "You got no . . ." paused and interjected three syllables of laughter ". . . know what I can see it in here, can I?" What marks of ellision, inflection, and melody could make that sound, or the sense of it, intelligible on paper?

Spent that afternoon trying to figure that one out.

I strip and bleach so the faint patternings of a real voice will show through; and end with something artificial as a henna job. And Calkins, determined not to read, waits for my next book in this jargon called the written word I've been stuck with!

fore with that routine which was pretty much calculated to turn him on. I didn't stop him, but I was annoyed; so when I began badmouthing him (growling into his hair: ". . . *come* on, you two-bit cocksucker; *come* on, you scrawny, shit-ass bastard . . .") it was real: he shot pretty quick. But by then I had a hard-on again. I was actually sort of digging him just lying there on top of it. But he got down to suck me off. I guess I'd wanted him to do that when I *first* woke him up; now I didn't. "Don't waste your time," I told him, dropping my chin to watch the top of his head. "Can't you just go to sleep?" But he kept working (and playing with my asshole which I'd mentioned Nightmare mentioning to me) and I shot. He crawled back up beside me, and I held him around his belly with his back to me (like a warm dog) while he occasionally squirmed like he'd be more comfortable on the other side of the bed (yeah, like trying to sleep with a dog) while I wondered: If I'm starting to have to fantasize girls in order to come with guys, maybe I'm not as bisexual as I keep telling myself?

I know: I'm a closet monosexual.

Oh yeah. While he was blowing me, I stopped him in the middle and asked him what he was thinking about—to be a bastard. Very honest and very surprised, he told me Dollar (I flashed on the moment with Risa when our pet

754

murderer went through my mind) which got me a little mad. But that's what I get. I note here (because sex does have something to do with love) Denny's said he loves me six times now, admitted it almost under his breath with

this hung expression as though he was daring himself to say it—it always comes off the wall when we're busy doing something else: moving the couch across to the other side of the front room, chucking junk into the yard across the fence, or when I was trying to help Cathedral bend the motorcycle's kickstand back into shape. I don't really know what I feel about him, but I'm glad as hell *one* of them stays here. (I guess I wish it was Lanya; she's more interesting, in or out of bed ... which isn't really the point; really, I just wish she was here.) When I woke up, he had wriggled out of my arms and was curled up in the corner against the walls. When I got up and went into

Walking with Lanya today, I told her that. She beamed: "Yes, he's said it to me a half-dozen times too. It's charming."

"I don't know," I said. "I don't think so. I mean, I don't understand it. He loves you. He loves me. What the hell does that mean?"

She looked surprised, even hurt. Finally she said: "Well—when somebody uses strange words to you that you just do not understand, you have to listen for the feeling and get at the meaning that way!"

"I think," I said after a moment, "it may mean, when he says it, he's going to leave me before you do—who say it so much less frequently."

"You think he'll leave us?" Me/us—it struck like that. "Give him a reason to stay. I've tried."

"That's a hard one, even in much simpler situations. I wonder if it just has to do with the kinds of people we're familiar with. To you, I'm replaceable. I'm a nice ape, who even happens to be more interesting inside than out. I think one of the most interesting things to you is the way the machinery jerks around by stops and starts. Like you say, though, you've known geniuses before. It's nothing new."

"Well!"

"Denny, I think, is the first Denny you've ever known. For you, he's unique—whereas for me, everything from the foster homes he's lived in to the rhythm he bucks his ass at, the protective brutality, and even that well of playful sweetness you can never touch bottom in, the hard-headedness good and bad: sweet and fucked-up as he is, there're many, many, many of him floating around." We turned the corner. "Now for me, you're the irreplaceable one: I've never seen you up so close before, and I do not understand you at all. You say sometimes I act like I don't see you? I don't even know where to look! Living with you around is like like living with a permanent dazzle. The fact that you even like me, or look at me, or brush by me, or hug me, or hold me,

the living room, most of them were still asleep. Fireball sat on the edge of the couch eating something out of a cup with a spoon. He stood up when I came in (Filament with, oddly, Devastation were tucked together on the couch behind him; the pale Black Widow, with the dark Lady of Spain curled against her, slept on the floor among Tarzan-and-most-of-the-apes) as though he wanted to speak to me. I nodded.

is so surprising that after it's over I have to go back through it a dozen times in my head to savor it and try and figure out what it was like because I was too busy being astounded while it was happening."

"Really? That's marvelous!" She was silent the next quarter of a block. Then she said: "He's not going to leave. At least not for a while. Though you may be right about who leaves first, whenever that happens . . . if ever."

"What do you see?"

"That you are a whole lot of real person. And so, for that matter, am I. Someone who's had as little of that as Denny has just isn't going to run out before he's had a lot more."

"Sounds good," I said. "Hope it works. I like you two. I want you with me. Just don't let me start taking either of one of you for granted!"

"Not, dear heart, if I can help it."

He nodded back. He didn't seem to be able to start, though, so he ate another spoonful.

"Come here," I told him.

Still shoeless, he stepped over a confusion of feet—the Widow's dull black wellingtons: Cathedral's floppy brown suedes. I put my hand on his shoulder. "You like Dollar, don't you?"

Fireball said: "He's a pretty funny little guy. But he's really okay, huh?" The scrawny, rusty-haired coon had a sleepy half-smile. His eyes looked like circles cut from our sky, tossed into the evenly milky coffee of his face.

"Good," I told him. "You look out for him. You make sure he doesn't get into any trouble around here, you hear?"

The smile wavered—

"Somebody's got to. And I'm tired of it. So you do it now. You hear me?"

—and fell.

He nodded.

"Good." With both hands I took off one of my chains, put it over his head, and hung my fists on his chest. I pulled one down, while the other raised, my knuckles slid-

ing on his skin. Then I ran it the other way. "This'll go
with the one you already took for yourself, right?"

Fireball blinked at me.

"It's yours." I let go.

"That mean I'm a member . . . ?"

Raven, on the floor, propped his head on his elbow.
"That's the way we play, sweetheart." He laughed, rolled
over (into Cathedral who just grunted), and closed his
eyes.

Fireball looked back at me. The sleepy smile returned.
"Okay," he said. "Hey, thanks, Kid. Okay . . ."

"You look out for that crazy, pimple-faced white
bastard."

"Okay," he repeated. "I will." Then he ate another
spoonful out of his cup.

I went onto the porch.

Risa was sitting outside on a crate under a tree, reading. (*Brass Orchids?* I craned to see. Yeah.) Rubbing two
fingers in the dusty corner of the screenless frame, I
watched her, wondering if I should go down and ask her
about what I was thinking, finally decided: Fuck it, if
you're gonna do it, do it.

I went down the steps—the door clacked behind me—
and crossed the yard. "Hey . . ." I squatted beside her,
elbows and hands (wondering how can they get *that* dirty
in just a day) a double bridge, knee to knee. "I wanted to
know, I mean, about last night."

She looked up.

"You enjoyed that, huh? I mean, you were into it.
Because some of the—one of the women seemed a little
upset by it. So I wanted to . . . know."

She'd slapped her hand over the page like she didn't
want me to see it. Which was odd. Her heavy legs shifted.
She looked uncomfortable. I waited, thinking: Well, she's
probably just not a very verbal person, or maybe she just
can't get answers to questions like that together, just like
that; or maybe it's a stupid question, or just an embarrassing one. I mean she could have always said: Look, asshole, why do you think I was *doing* it if I didn't like it?
Also, I felt silly pretending, even to myself, I was speaking
for Lady of Spain when, of course, I was speaking for me.

"I mean," I said, "I was curious: if you felt any one
had . . . well, forced you?"

The top two buttons of her blue shirt were open. Her
brown skin was creased between her neck and shoulder.

Last night, her eyes, half closed, had seemed so large. Now, wide, they looked small. What she said (a lot more together than I'd expected) was: "That was *mine*," and opened and closed her mouth to say something else, but ended up repeating: "That was all mine. You just can't have any part of that. That's all. It was . . . mine!"

"I mean—" I was surprised—but I just shrugged: "I just wanted to know if you . . . enjoyed it?"

She said: "You go find out yourself, if you want it!" Then, like she was jerking from an anticipated blow, her eyes slipped back to the page. Her fist slipped back to her lap.

I stood up, my mind jutting off on: *Do* I want to get gang-banged myself? Well, all right, consider. Considering, I walked across the yard. One: I don't like to take it up the ass because when I've tried, it's almost always hurt like hell. Maybe half a dozen times, it turned out not to be painful, just indifferent (one of these was two days ago with Denny and Lanya, and the emotional thing there, anyway, was nice). But, Two: I've had my own dick up the asses of enough guys who were obviously feeling no pain, and a lot of pleasure. And I've been in line and taken my turn in a guy's ass like with Risa's cunt last night. So (Three:) if Risa's right, maybe there's something wrong with *me* that every—well *almost* every—time a cat has tried to shove his dick into me, it fucking stings . . . ? Anyway, if nothing else, she had said something that had made me think, which is one way I decided if people are intelligent.

As I went up the steps, Copperhead's head came out of the door; passed by me, went over, squatted by her (like he'd seen me do? Presumably not.) and put his freckled hand on the knee of her jeans. They bent close, conferring. She said something that made him laugh. (She didn't look too happy though.) I stepped through the screen door onto the porch, glanced out the window again.

As Copperhead stood, Lady of Spain (with Filament, just behind her), passed now on the other side of the fence, stopped with three fingers hooked over the chipped boards, and asked—I could hear her chains click the wood but not really what she said—Risa something like, How was she feeling?

Risa twisted a little, frowned, and said: "My back is sore."

758

Spitt was on the porch, standing by the sink, his arms folded. "She's something, huh?" He looked resentful as hell.

I glanced out at Risa, looked back at Spitt. He was shaking his head. "How many times she get fucked? Sixty? Seventy-five times?"

"Aw, man," I told him. "You crazy? Would you believe sixteen, seventeen? *Maybe* twenty?"

"Huh?"

"There were only seven, eight of us *doing* anything. And half of us only went once."

Spitt thought a few seconds. "But, Jesus Christ . . . *Look* at her! She's just *sitting* there, reading your damn book like that!"

"Spitt," I said, "balling a couple of dozen people in one night is merely a prerequisite for understanding anything worth knowing." I mean I *have* done that. "That's just the way it is."

Spitt didn't seem to think that was funny, so I went back into the kitchen and left him looking. Somebody (Spitt?) had washed a lot of the dishes.

This is the last full balnk [blank?] page left.

Re-reading, I note the entries only ghost chronological order. Not only have I filled up all the free pages, but all the half and quarter pages left around the poems or at the ends of other entries. A few places where my handwriting is fairly large, I can write between lines. I'll have to do a lot more writing in the margins. Maybe I'll try writing cross-ways over pages filled up already.

Sometimes I cannot tell who wrote what. That is upsetting. With some sections, I can remember the place and time I wrote them, but have no memory of the incidents described. Similarly, other sections refur to things I recall happening to me, but kne/o/w just as well I never wrote out. Then there are pages that, today, I interpret one way with the clear recollection of having interpretted them another at the last re-reading.

Most annoying is when I recall an entry, go hunting through, and ~~not find it~~ find it or half of it not there: I've read some pages so many times they've pulled loose from the wire spiral. Some of these I've caught before they ripped completely free, folded ~~some or~~ them up and put

759

them inside the front cover. Carrying the book around, though, I must have let them slip out. The first pages—poems and journal notes—are all gone, as well as pages here and there through the rest.

More will go, too.

I work the paper strips, edged with torn perforations, out of the [s]piral with my pencil point. And write more. Looking at the last page, I can't tell if it's the same one that was there a month ago or not.

was nearly too bizaar for comment:

Stopped into *Teddy's*. It was so early I wondered why it was open. Maybe five people there, among them—Jack. He sat on the last stool, hands (skin grey, cuticles wedged with black, crowns scimitared with it, half moons shadowed under cracked skin) flat on the counter. His hair feathered the rim of his ear (in the twisted cartilage: white flakes. On the trumpet's floor: dry amber) and went without change into sideburns that join around his chin in scrubby beard. His neck was grey—with one clean smear (where he'd been rubbing himself?). His lids were thickened, coral rimmed, and lashless. The short sleave of his shirt: torn on the seam over white flesh. Above the backs of his shoes, his socks, both heels torn, curled from ridged, black callous. The fly flap on his slacks was broken. The brass teeth rollar-coastered over his lap and under his belt—the buckle tongue had snapped: he'd tied the belt-ends together. "You wanna buy me a beer?" he asked. "First night I got to town, I brought you and your girl friend a beer."

"Just ask for what you want," I said.

The bartender glanced over, pushed a rolled sleeve higher; from under his thick fingers the tattoed leopard stalked the jungle of his arm.

"I'd buy it myself," Jack said. "But, you know, I've been pretty down and out. You buy me a beer, man, and I'll do the same for you, soon as I get myself back on my feet."

I said to the bartender: "How come you won't serve him?"

The bartender put his knuckles on the counter and swayed. "All he gotta do is ask for what he wants." He looked around at the other customers.

"Give us a couple of beers," I said.

760

"Right up." The open bottles clacked the boards in front of us.

"There you go." I took a swallow from mine.

Jack's bottle sat between his thumbs. He looked at it, then moved his fingers a little to the left.

What he'd done was adjust the spaces so that the bottle was centered between his hands.

The bartender glanced again, pursed his lips—about as close as he would let himself get to shaking his head—and moved away, fist over fist.

"You don't have to pay here," I said.

"If I could pay," Jack said, "I really would; I mean, if I had it, I'd buy it myself. I'm not a skinflint, man. I'm really generous when I got it."

I considered a moment. Then I said: "Just a second." I reached in my pants pocket.

The dollar bill, in a moist knot, came up between my third and fourth finger. It was so crumpled, at first I thought I'd just found some dirty paper I'd stuck there (a discarded poem?). I spread it on the counter. One corner, from sweat and rubbing, was worn away down to the frame of the "1".

While Jack looked at it, I wondered what Lanya would do with hers; or Denny with his.

Jack raised his head, slowly. The corner of his mouth was cracked and sore. "You can have a pretty rough time in this city, you know?" His hands were still flat. Foam bubbled up his bottle neck and over, puddling at the base. "I just don't understand it, man. I don't. I mean, I've done everything I could think of, you know? But it just don't look like I can make it here no how. Since I been here—?" He turned to me. Bubbles banked and broke against his fingers. "I been *nice* to people! They got all different kinds of people here, too. I mean I ain't never *seen* all kinds of different people like this here before. I've been nice and tried to listen, and learn how to do, you know? Learn my way around. 'Cause it *is* different here . . . But I just don't know." His eyes went above and behind me.

I looked back.

Jack was looking at Bunny's empty cage. The black velvet curtain at the back swung as though someone had just brushed by on the other side. "Like that big nigger that they got his picture up, all over the place with his God damn dick hangin' out all over. I just don't see that. I mean I don't got nothin' against it. But, man, if they

761

gonna do shit like that, why don't they put some pictures of some pussy up too! You know? If they gonna do one, don't you think it's right they should do the other?"

"Sure," I said.

"I mean, maybe somebody like me, or you—*you* got a girl friend—is interested in something else, huh? When I first got here, I knew things weren't gonna be like every where else. I was *real* nice to people; and people was nice to me too. Tak? The guy I met with you, here? Now he's a pretty all right person. And when I was staying with him, I tried to be nice. He wants to suck on my dick, I'd say: 'Go ahead, man, suck on my fuckin dick.' And, man, I ain't never done *nothin'* like that before . . . I mean not serious, like he was, you know? Now, I done it. I ain't sorry I done it. I don't got nothin' against it. But it is just not what I like all that much, you understand? I want a girl, with tits and a pussy. Is that so strange? You understand that?"

"Sure," I said. "I understand."

Jack pushed the corner of his mouth out with his tongue, trying to break the scab. "I guess he understood too. Tak, I mean. He's still nice to me. He talks to me when he sees me, you know? He asks me how I'm doin', stuff like that . . . Man, I just wish I'd see some pictures of some nice pussy up there, beside all that dick. I mean *that's* what *I'm* interested in; it would just make *me* feel better."

I drank some beer. "Make me feel better too."

"You been to that commune place—you know, in the park?" Jack looked at the wrinkled bill. "Tak took me down there. And I guess it was pretty nice, you know. I was talking to this one girl, who's one of the ones who runs it—"

"Milly?"

"Yeah. Mildred. And she's goin' on and on about my deserting from the army, and all about how good they all feel about deserters, and I guess she's tryin' to be nice too—but after a while, I mean after a couple of fuckin' hours of that, I had to say: Lady, how you sittin' there tellin' me how bad the fuckin' army is when you ain't never *been* in the fuckin' army and I just been there for a God damn year and a half! She don't know nothin' about why I run out of the fuckin' army. And she don't even care." His eyes wandered to his hands, the bottle, the puddled counter, the bill, his hands . . . "I mean, she didn't know a thing . . ." He drew breath and looked up at me.

762

"I met Frank at the commune . . . the guy who's supposed to be a poet? He'd been in the army; and he deserted. *He* knew what I was trying to tell her. For a while there, him and me, we were pretty close. I can't talk as good as he can, and he knows all about a lot of stuff I don't. But we went around a lot together. He took me to that House where all the girls live. You been there?"

"No."

"Well, it's really something, man. Some of them girls are pretty nice—some are pretty strange, too. And the guys that come around there . . . well, some of those girls go for some pretty freaky guys. I guess some of them, the girls, even liked me. But only the freaky ones that I just wasn't interested in. I wanted to get me one, sort of little— they got some *big* women over there!—and pretty. And soft. And smart. Now to me being smart in a girl is *very* important. If I could get me a girl who could talk about things and understand things half as good as Frank could, I'd be happy. And they got some smart girls over there too. In fact, I don't think none of 'em is stupid. Just a lot of them is pretty freaky, though. There was some there just *like* I wanted. And I could of used a girl friend! I mean I talked to them. And they talked to me. But I couldn't get anywhere. Frank could. He could get laid from Wednesday to next Thursday and start all over tomorrow. I wanted to get laid, but I wanted more than that, too. Now I know people around here is different from me; but that means I'm different from them, too. Only I guess if you're too different, nobody wants anything to do with you. I mean they don't care shit." His hands jerked in the puddle, to the bottle's base. He frowned for a while, and I thought he was finished. But he said: "You hear about the nigger— this black guy who used to come in here: the one who got shot off top of the Second City Bank building?"

I nodded.

"Do you know what they think—" Jack turned on his stool, one hand going to spread across the chest of his shirt—"John, Mildred, all them people over in the commune in the park—that *I* was the one who done it! And they tellin' all sorts of other people, too! They tellin' that to all them girls who live in that House together! 'Cause I'm white, and I'm from the south, and I don't know how to argue good and explain that they are fuckin' crazy—they are fuckin' *crazy* if they think I done something like that!" He looked as surprised in the telling as I was in the hearing. "I . . . I had a gun, you know?" His hand closed to a loose fist that slid, stopping and starting, down his shirt, leaving a wet stain.

I nodded.

"I always had a gun at home. They should have guns out there in the park with all the nuts wandering around in this city. And all they got to do is walk into a store and take one—like I did. They got people comin' around to the park all the God damn time, to take food away from 'em? And some of the people who come got guns. Get up on a damn building and shoot a damn nigger?" His hand, loose in his lap, twitched. "Jesus Christ, I wouldn't do nothin' like that! But I go around the park, man, and I *hear* them talking. I mean I *heard* people takin'; then they'd turn around, and they seen me and shut up! Frank won't have nothin' to do with me no more. I mean he'd say hello or somethin' when I'd speak first and then walk away to do something else. But five times—five *times* I'd start over to find out just what'n hell was goin' on and he walks away soon as he see me comin'. I mean it's like they're afraid of me; only they got *me* so scared, I'm afraid to go back. Shit, I don't even believe Frank thinks I done it. Frank's a nice guy. He just don't want the others to think he's havin' anything to do with me. And I don't know *what* to do with that. I just don't know. I thought for a while, right after I first met him, Frank was like Tak. I know he goes after girls. But he writes that poetry and stuff and, sort of, well . . . if he liked me, I guessed maybe that was part of it. 'Cause I damn well couldn't see no other reason: he's smarter'n me, older'n me, and he's got about everything he wants. When all this stuff started, I thought maybe because I'd never done anything with him, like with Tak, that was . . . well, was why he was bein' *so* damn mean. That pretty stupid, huh? But this place puts ideas like that into your head. I told him, right out; I said, 'Anything you wanna do— *Any*thing at all . . . !' I wished he'd been gay, man. I wished he'd liked me like that. Because then, after bein' with Tak and all, even though I ain't, I'd kind of known what to do. You know?" He looked at me, shook his head, looked at the bottle. "You know what I mean?" He took his hand out his lap and put it back in the puddle.

"Go on," I said. "You've got it too simple. But go on."

His jaw moved a few times, but he didn't speak.

"How come you don't come down to see us?" I asked.

764

"You get hungry, come on down to the nest. Tak'll bring you there if you ask him. Left over flower-power, in all this pollution, was never my thing either." I was wondering about him and the department store people but I didn't say anything.

"Well, you guys . . ." Jack turned a little from side to side. (Thinking: His palms are now glued to the wood, but he doesn't want to be noticed trying to tug them loose.) "You guys . . . I just don't know. All you got down there is niggers anyway, don't you? After what I done—what they said I done, what's a bunch of bad niggers gonna do when I come walkin' in? You guys play a little too rough . . . robbin' people in the street. And killin' people." He blinked inflamed lids. "I don't mean, personal. You're a nice guy. And you're their chief, huh . . . ? But that's what I heard, you know? And I don't wanna get into shit like that. I don't got nothin' against it, but . . ." He frowned, shaking his head. "People talk. And people talk. People talk, tryin' to make you into something you ain't.

I don't remember ever getting corrected in high school or college for writing who instead of whom. But except to be funny, I've never said whom in my life. Which makes me think there are two other words: who and who'—the apostrophe standing for the syncopated m. I've been using who' in this notebook for maybe a week, but it still looks funny. So I'll cut it out.

And after a while, you almost don't know what you done and what you didn't do your own self. People talkin' about me, about what I done, that day when the sky was lit across with that funny kind of light, and that nigger they got in the pictures was after that white girl and the colored people had a riot and tore the hands off the church clock down in Jackson; they say cause I climbed up on the roof and shot the nigger, from the roof, I'm responsible for the riot, for the whole thing, for everything that happened here. Just for shootin' a damn nigger . . ." His lips, lined with brown, touched, parted, touched: "I *had* a gun. I didn't shoot . . ." He spoke slowly. "I didn't shoot that black man. I mean, I even met him three or four time. Right in this bar. With Tak. He was a nice man. I shot him . . . ? I didn't shoot . . ." Suddenly he knuckled at his lips' scabbed corner. "I went down there. I did that. To check the place out. And *with* my gun! You climb up the steps behind the Second City Bank building and get up the rest of the way by the fireladder. You can hunker down behind the cornice and aim out over the whole damn street. Man, if you could shoot at all, you could pick off anyone! An' I shoot pretty good . . ." He looked at me, narrowing his thickened lids. "You think I done it?"

"That depends," I said. "Did you check it out before or after he got shot?"

Something happened on Jack's unshaven face: the skin between his eyebrows wrinkled, the skin below his jaw slackened. Something happened behind it too. "Oh God," he said as flatly as, once, I heard a man say "elevator". "Oh God . . ." He turned back to the bar. "They all want it to be so bad, they gonna make it be no matter what I done or not. They gonna make it be. Just by wantin' it."

"I know," I told him.

"What can I do? I don't know what to do."

"You have to know who you are," I said. "No matter what they say."

He didn't look at me. "You know who *you* are?"

After a second I said: "About two thirds of it; so I guess at least I'm on my way. Maybe I'm pretty lucky." I finished my beer. "You come down to the nest. Whenever you want. Just don't bring your gun."

"I wish," Jack said after a few seconds, "I could just get me some kind of job. A job where I could make some good money. Then I could get me a girl friend; then I could buy my own drinks. I don't like to sit in a bar and hustle nice guys for drinks."

"When I first got to town," I told him, "I had a job, moving furniture. Five bucks an hour. You'd've dug it. It was made for you."

But he was looking at the dollar bill.

Since the frustration was making me mean, I decided it was time to go. I stepped from the bar.

"Hey, Kid?"

"What?"

"Ain't you gonna take your change?" He put his middle finger on the wrinkled dollar and slid it over the wet wood.

I thought a second. "Why don't you keep it?"

"Aw, no, man— Naw, I don't like to take no hand-outs. I need a job; make some good money; pay my own way."

"You take this hand-out," I said. "You need it."

"Well, thanks, man . . . ?" His finger, holding the

paper to the counter, slid it back. "Thanks a lot! I'm good
for it, too. You'll get it back, once I get some money.
You're a pretty nice guy."

Comments anyway: I want to help. And feel help
would be impossible. Almost. Which is simply almost forgetting how much help I've had.

I hope he comes to the nest.

Off his head about everything else, he's right on about
the pussy. Despite George, and a city concecrated by twin
moons, I know there must be some greater, female diety
(for whom George *is* only consort) a sin yet to name her
(as that sun is never named); we have all glimpsed her,
sulking in the forest of her knowledge—every tree a tree
of that knowledge—and there is nothing but to praise

This afternoon Lady of Spain and Filament staggered
through the front door in volcanic laughter, lurched up
the hall supporting each other—

"Hey," I said. "What happened with you?"

Filament faced me, pursed her lips, inflated her
cheeks, widened her eyes, and rattled her chains before
her breasts, miming something I did not understand. Her
cheeks exploded with more laughter. Lady of Spain, dragging Filament's arm, hauled her away.

Dollar pushed around me, grinning. "Hey!" he called.
"What happened? Did you do it?"

Filament turned and repeated the mime.

Dollar—I'm not *sure* it meant more to him than it
did to me—crashed back against the wall, holding his
stomach and howling: "Oh, wow . . . ! You mean . . . ?
Really . . . ? Wow . . . !" and followed them up the hall,
his laugh shriller than either of theirs.

Then Tarzan stepped in from the service porch and
said: "Look, ladies, people are sleeping in the back room,
huh?" There are twelve tones of voice in which you can say
that: three of them would have gotten him an apology with
muffled giggles. He chose, at random, from the other nine.

"Fuck off, man!" Dollar said, straightening. "It's their
nest too!" His had
actually been the
only laugh with
edge to wake.

"Now look!"
Tarzan said.

Sex between nest members is rare enough—
I can think of six, no seven exceptions, including me and Denny—to make me wonder
if basically I don't have here an exandrous
and/or exogynous totem group. Most sex
comes walking in, invited or not—and even-

767

"These bitches come running in here yelling and shouting! *Somebody's* got to tell 'em to keep—"

"Now *you* look," Filament said. She had about as much use for Tarzan as he had for t he other caucasians in the nest. "You may be Tarzan. But I am *not* Jane!"

"I'd fuck him," Lady of Spain said. Black, and an occasional partaker in long, intense conversations with Jack the Ripper, for Tarzan she had acquired something of the apes' aura. (Because of this was she more tolerant of him?) "I really would. But Tarzan don't fuck nothin'." Only one of the twelve could make that come out right. She chose it with such ease, I hope he took a lesson.

"Aw, hey, now: I was just asking you to keep it a little—"

D-t, naked and half asleep, loomed in the back doorway, forearms high on the jambs, boney hips cocked askew, big hands (with their funny thumbs) and head hanging. The head came up and he blinked. "Tarzan, when

tually walks out. The seventh exception was Filament's surprising (to me, anyway. Lanya says, "Why were you surprised?" I don't know why I was surprised. I was surprised, that's all.) affair with a tall, Italian looking girl named Anne Harrimon, who, her first night here, took lights and chains and the name Black Widow. Always standing hand in hand, always sitting knee to knee whispering, running through the house giggling or asleep at any time in any room, one's head against the other's breast, one's breast beneath the other's hand, intense, innocently exhibitionistic, and almost wordless, they developed, within hours, a protective/voyeuristic (?) male circle that ran with them everywhere and that, incidentally, dissolved the apes for the duration (the two were not Tarzan's favorite people). After a couple of weeks, the Widow came to me and returned her chains. Those few minutes of conversation in the yard were the only time I really got to know her, decided I liked her; decided I would offer them back to her if I ever saw her again (recalling Nightmare and Lanya): she left. Filament was sad but did not talk about her; then returned to older ways. Seems to be the place to mention it: I once asked Denny why he had no nickname.

"Nightmare used to call me B.J.," he explained. "Until I told him to cut it the fuck out. So I'm just Denny."

"B.J.? What did that stand for?"

"I'll give you one guess."

"Oh," I said. "Hey, what is your last name, by the way?"

"For a while it was Martin. Once it was Cupp. Depended on the foster family I was staying with."

Does the onomal maliability here make my own loss more barable?

I went to sleep, you was complaining about something. Here it is with the sky all light, and you *still* at it?"

"I was just telling them to be quiet so they wouldn't wake *you* up!"

"Time for me to get up anyway, boy. And *they* did not wake me."

"You *see!*" Dollar said. "You see, all your yellin' and carryin' on makes more noise than—"

Filament put her hand on Dollar's chest and lowered her head. "Now you just wait too." She looked up again. "Tarzan, you like living here, right?"

"What you mean?" Tarzan's chin jerked belligerently.

"She asked you," Lady of Spain said, "if you like living here. Or not."

"Yeah," Tarzan said. "Yeah. I like living here. What are you gonna do about it?"

"I'm not gonna do anything," Filament said. "But *you* better. You better do the same thing Dollar is doing."

"Huh?" Dollar said. "What am I—?"

"And that is: Since you like livin' here, you better make a real effort to stay."

D-t broke the silence with laughter. He shook in the doorway like a windy scarecrow.

"Man," Tarzan said, "now what are *you* laughin' at?"

D-t threw one arm around Tarzan's neck—

". . . *Hey,* man! . . ."

—and, still laughing, dragged him down the hall, occasionally rubbing his knuckles on Tarzan's head, hard.

". . . Hey, cut it out . . . hey, *stop* it; that hurts . . . damn it, nigger! Cut it out . . . hey, what are you . . . stop . . . !"

In the living room, D-t let Tarzan up.

". . . what the fuck you *doin'*?" Tarzan rubbed both hands in his yellow hair.

"I'm just trying to see if your head is as hard as you keep on makin' out like it is, mother-fucker! We got any coffee?"

Tarzan dropped one hand, rubbed harder with the other. "Yeah, I . . . I think so. Somebody made up a pail about an hour ago." He was still confused.

In the hall, Filament and Lady of Spain walked on. Behind them Dollar said: "He don't got no right to talk to you like that."

"He's got a right to talk any way he wants," Filament

said. "He's just got to be set to listen afterward, that's all."

"That's what I mean," Dollar said; and so rarely do I agree with him about anything, I write this exception down so

idea around with me like a cyst on the tailbone for (how long is that?) and today (the known part of that) walking in the grey (grey, a grey I'm tired of noticing and noting; I'm exhausted with that grey; which is what that grey means to me) street, this memory: I was passing the table where somebody had left one of those transparent plastic glasses, three quarters full of white wine (in the back closet Raven found the saran tube full of them) with the window open behind it; the glare on the interface between plastic and wine suddenly diffracted like an oil-slick and the glass was full of color. If I moved one way or the other more than three inches, it became just greasy plastic full of urine-colored liquid. First I thought the prismatic movement would be lost as soon as I went. But for the next hour, whenever I walked through the kitchen, I could find the spot from which it looked like that again easily.

The idea stayed in my mind the same way, and I could find it just by passing near.

I thought it would be good to try on Temple Avenue, but I couldn't find any street with that name on the sign. So I walked down a street as wide and as clean, with gates and doors and window-glass so intact that only the pewter sky told our ca- Writing this while taking a crap: small con-tastrophe. I saw a solations—expected a really unhealthy turd, lady in a black baloney yellow and spinach black after a node coat and blue of mucus. Mercifully what came was mostly scarf cross at the liquid and left the water too murky to examine. corner; but she went into a side street; when I looked after her, she was stepping into a doorway. I walked, excited and hollow and knowing my shape—how my body moved, my head a-jog on my neck, the stagger in my one-boot walk—from the inside. Lamp posts and doorways and fire hydrants came at me from the smoke—

I guess he was almost a block ahead, but for maybe a minute I wasn't sure he was there, in the smoke. So I hurried.

He had short, black hair and wore a brown corduroy

770

coat with a woolly collar; it was cooler than usual, but because there was no wind, I was still in my vest. His hands were in his pockets. The coat's belt hung down on either side.

The belt was all I was staring at.

Just as I started to overtake him, I scraped my leg on some piece of crating or junk lying on the sidewalk—I never did look back at what it was. But it surprised hell out of me. I wonder now if I would have done it if that hadn't happened: I mean, trying to ignore the surprising sting across my calf, maybe I also ignored that part of my head that would have made me just hurry on past him, reflecting on how close I had come. (Does the City's topology control us completely?)

When I'd halved the distance, he glanced back. But kept walking. I guess he thought I was just going to walk past.

I grabbed his shoulder and spun him back against the fence bars.

"Hey . . . !" he said. "What's *your* problem!"

I put the orchid blades right up against his throat. He flinched and looked surprised.

"Give me everything in your pockets," I told him.

He took a breath. "You got it." He wore glasses.

I dug into his pants pocket while he held his hands up. I brought out three dollar bills. (I think an orchid point accidentally knicked his neck and he flinched again) "Turn around and let me check your back pockets." He turned and I felt around under the flap of his coat until I realized his pants didn't *have* back pockets. I thought I might hit him or cut him then; but I didn't.

I backed away and he turned to look at me. His mouth was pressed together. As I stepped away, I realized his side pockets were much deeper than I'd thought: I could see the clustered circles of change outlined low in the black denim.

He glanced past one raised hand to the left.

A guy was crossing the street, watching us. But when I looked, the guy looked away.

The man made a disgusted sound, dropped his hands, and turned to go.

I gestured with the orchid and said, "Hey!"

He looked back.

"You wait here ten minutes before you move," I said,

771

and took another step backward. "If you call for anybody, or try to come after me, I'll cut your throat!" I turned and sprinted up the block; glanced back once.

He was walking away.

I made it around the corner, went into a doorway to take off the orchid and put the three bills in my pocket. Then I stooped down and rolled up my cuff to look at my leg. It was just the tiniest scratch, down the side of my calf and back toward my ankle, like a swipe past a nail or a broken board or a

out on the front steps, met Dragon Lady: Denim vest laced tight, arms folded (making the laces above them look a little loose), looking pensive.

Haven't seen her in a while.

Back now.

What's she been doing?

Nothing.

Where's she been?

Around.

I put my arm around her but she obviously didn't feel like being mauled. So I dropped it and just walked with her.

As we circled the house, she relaxed a little, dark arms still folded.

Baby and Adam with you?

Yeah, they'll be here.

Reached the yard (telling her, "It's good to see you back," and she smiled her stained-tooth smile) and delivered her up to the apes and Tarzan who were goofing around there. The atmosphere cedes us a day featureless as night. I didn't know what time it was; the noise and raillery surrounded her as she went to sit under the tree, fists between her knees, with a troubled look that did not stay on I have to keep mentioning this timelessness because the phenomenon irritates the part of the mind over which time's passage registers, so that instants, seconds, minutes are painfully real; but hours—much less days and weeks—are left-over noises from a dead tongue. anything. Wondering how (late? early?) it was, I decided I would fix the sink in the service porch (because I'd gone into the cabinet under the kitchen sink for something else and seen some tools; again, topology preordinates) and after I'd turned off the water and wrenched off the first nut, I decided I'd take the whole thing apart and then see if I felt like putting it back together.

I took the cap off the bottom of the elbow drain and lots of hair and purple gunk fludged out on the floor. Took the taps off. Should have done that before I took the cap off, because there was a little surge of rusty water out of each—that went down the drain and onto the floor. Then I unscrewed the collars from inside the taps.

D-t came out, squatted, and watched a while, sometimes handed me tools; finally asked, whimsically, "What the fuck are you doing?" and helped me whobble the sink from the wall (standing suddenly when it almost fell) on its enameled claw and ball.

I've lost a name. So? If the inhabitants of this city have one thing in common, it is that such accidents don't interest them; that is neither lauded here as freedom nor wailed as injury; it is taken as a fact of landscape, not personality.

"I'm putting the sink back together," I told him because I'd just decided to.

D-t grunted and shoved at the bowl-back. The forejoints of his thumbs are both crooked; which I'd never noticed before.

There was some string on the window sill, and I brought in a can of putty from the kitchen. But when I'd pried up the lid with the screwdriver, the surface was cracked like Arizona. And I didn't know where any oil was. D-t came back with a bottle of Wesson, and I couldn't think of any reason why not. D-t settled back to watch.

"Now we could of got a place without no leaky sink," D-t said. "But then I guess there wouldn't be nothing to do."

I laughed as much as I could holding the cold-water pipe up while trying to screw the fitting back down over it.

I asked him something or other.

Don't recall his exact answer, but somewhere in it, he said; ". . . like when I first got here, I used to walk along the street and know I could break into just about any house I wanted, and I was just scared to death . . ."

We talked about that. I remembered my first walks in these streets (D-t said: "But I broke in, anyway.") While we talked I recall thinking: It is not that I have no future. Rather it continually fragments on the insubstantial and indistinct ephemera of then. In the summer country, stitched with lightning, somehow, there is no way to conclude; but here, conclusion itself is superfluous. I said something to D-t about: "What this place needs is a good wind, or a lightning-storm. To clean it out. Or thunder."

"Oh, man," D-t said. "Oh, man— *No!* No, I don't think I could take that. Not here," and chuckled (like, I suspect, someone under sentence). We really got into some talk. In that quiet way where you're into the feeling, if not the information. Once he asked me how long I thought I could keep it up, here, and I said: "I don't know. How long can you?" and he laughed too. I was wrapping string around the joint and the fastening on the other end of the cold-water pipe when someone in the doorway said: "Hi, Kid."

I looked up.

Frank stood there looking like he didn't know whether or not to put his hands in his pockets.

Reading over my journal, I find it difficult to decide even which incidents occurred first. I have hysterical moments when I think finding that out is my only possible hope/salvation. Also wonder at some of the things I have not written down: the day with Lanya when she took me to the city museum and we spent from before dawn to after dark sitting around in the reconstructed 18th century rooms ("We could live here, like Calkins!" and she whispered, smiling, "No . . ." and then we talked about a run here: and again she said, "No . . ." this time not smiling. And I won't. But all the talking we did there, and wandering, growing hungrier and hungrier in the pearl light through the ceiling panes because we could not bare to leave), should make this the longest and most detailed incident in this journal because it was where she showed me thing after thing and told me about them, to make them mean something for me; she became a real person, by what she knew and what she did, more than anyway she ever could by what was done to her, done to her, done: which was so easily the way I've always wanted to define her. Wanting her to take Denny and the whole nest there; and—holding a small painting she had taken down from the wall to show me something about how the canvas was prepared in the seventeenth century ("Christ, I used to spend weeks making black oil and Meriquet! I'm surprised I didn't asphyxiate someone.")—

"Hello," I said and went back to the fixture.

"How're you doing?"

I grunted.

"Glad I found you. Nobody seemed to know where you were. I wanted to know if I could talk to you about something."

I was mad at him for interrupting; also because, ignoring him, I had to sort of ignore D-t. "What do you want?"

The doorframe creaked; Frank shifted on the jamb.

Then the floorboards; D-t shifted his squat.

774

she said, "No, I don't think so. It's a gamble enough with you. Not just yet. Maybe later," and re-hung the painting, upside down.

We laughed.

So I hung seventeen paintings upside down— "Come on! Stop . . ." she insisted, but I did anyway. Because, I explained, anyone who comes along will notice them like this, frown, maybe turn them right-side up again. And will end up looking at them a little longer. "I'm only doing it for the ones I like."

"Oh," she said, dubiously. "Well, okay."

But it is more memorable unfixed. And to me, that's important. (Only while I'm actually writing, for an instant it is actually more vivid . . .) So I'll stop here, tired.

Except to tell about that funny argument with Denny, which I still do not understand, where I thought I was going to kill the little bastard. And Lanya just seemed uninterested. Which made me so mad I could have killed her too. And so I spent an anfternoon with a bottle of wine and Lady of Spain, bitching about the two of them, and passing the bottle back and forth—she had taken to wearing many rings— and we staggered to the Emboriki, daring each other to break in, which we didn't do, but saying to her, as we strutted by, with our arms around each others' shoulders, "You're my only real friend here, you know?" all very maudeline, but necessary. Then we shouted: "Mother-fuckers! God damn shit-eating mother-fuckers!" echoed in the naked street. "Come on out from there and fight!" We were hysterical, lerching up and down the curb, spilling wine. "Yeah!" Lady of Spain yelled. "Come on and—" then burped; I thought she was going to vomit, but no: "—down!" Her eyes were very red and she kept rubbing them with her ringed fingers. "Come on down and—" then she saw him: at the large window on the third floor. He was holding a riffle under one arm. The pigeon chest, the too-long hair, even the blue, blue shirt that, from the street, I could tell was too big: recognizing him made me feel odd. "Hey," I said to Lady of Spain and told her who he was. She said: "No shit?" I laughed. Then she said, "Wait a minute. Does he recognize you?" But I began to shout

"W e l l," Frank said, settling with the idea of talking to me while I wasn't looking at him, "I was wondering —I mean: How could someone like me go about joining up with you guys?"

I looked around at him to catch D-t already looking, and looking away.

"I mean," Frank went on, "is there some initiation, or something? Does somebody have to bring you in; or do you guys just get together and take a vote?"

"What do you want to know for?" I asked. "Aren't you happy over at the commune? Or is this just research for an article you're planning to do for the Times?"

"An article on how to get into the scorpions?" Frank laughed. "No. I just want to know because

775

again. I called him every kind of name I could, between fits of laughing. Lady of Spain insisted: "Look, he's got a gun!" nowhere near as drunk as she'd been. "Kid, let's get out of here!" But I kept up. He watched. Once he moved to rest the butt on the sill, the barrol pointing straight up. I think he was grinning. Finally we left.

The city is a map of violences anticipated. The armed dwellers in the Emboriki, the blacks surrounding them, the hiss from a turned tap that has finally stopped trickling, the time it takes a group who go out to come back with bags of canned goods, packaged noodles, beans, rice, speghetti—each is an emblem of inalienable, coming shock. But the clashes that do occur are all petty, disappointing, minor, inconclusive, above all stupid, as though the city prevents any real anxiety's ever resolving. And the result? All humanity here astounds; all charity here is graced.

Lady of Spain and I reached the nest, still laughing, astounded we were alive.

In the back yard, Lanya told me she had taken Denny to the museum—"for a couple of hours. We looked at all the paintings you especially liked—and Denny turned them right side up. So he could see them, of course." "Smug butch," I said. She said: "Who? Me?" And Denny began to laugh as though somehow the joke were really on the two of us, which had us both wondering. Then he said they'd wandered around, he taking her out to a place called Holland Lake. They crawled into bed beside me, and we talked till it grew light, Denny being the only one of us who doesn't realize how much easier that makes liking one another. And when Denny did a lot of talking, it finally put me to sleep—though I wanted to stay awake—and woke a little later, with them asleep too, in the familiar position.

We can survive so much.

And crawling between them (more comfortable, I guess, than the familiar position when all is said and done) went to sleep again till Lady of Spain and Risa, laughing out in the hall, woke us up; I hoped they would come in. But they didn't.

transfer, where I can buy a ticket—"

. . . well, things are getting a little tight in the park." He glanced back out in the hall. "We got some real funny people around. Although it looks a little crowded here too." He decided on his pockets. "You guys getting hungry yet? I probably shouldn't mention it, but John and Milly are quite beholden to you since you quit hitting them up for care packages."

"An oversight," I said.

"Shouldn't have mentioned it."

I turned back under the sink, looked for something to do but couldn't really find anything. So I kept looking.

"You guys seem to have a real thing going here. I'm not happy with what's going on around me where I am. I want to know where I get my

"Oh, man," I said. "I can't talk to you about shit like that now. I'm busy."

"Sure Kid," came out real quick, and he stopped leaning on the doorframe. "Maybe later. I'll just hang around . . . till you have some time."

D-t handed me the string. "Hey, thanks," I told D-t, "but I don't think I should pack that grease trap." So I didn't, but it was pretty much all right anyway.

Glanced back.

Frank was gone.

So we scrubbed out the grease-streaked bowl, more or less quiet, questioning such idiot work and finding the value —a chance to do something with D-t—disappeared, defined. Well, the sink wasn't dripping.

Something (I heard it) was happening in front of the house. I listened, surprised (looking at D-t look up at me), to somebody get up in the front room, run out of the front door—

"Uh-oh," I said. "Come on." We went into the hall together. D-t got ahead; I pushed by him out the front door; stopped on the forth step.

"Jesus Christ!" Frank shouted. "Hey, *watch* it—!"

"You want a chain, huh?" Copperhead, crouched, wound the links once more around his fist, pulled back, and swung again. "I'm gonna wrap this one around your fuckin' neck!"

"God *damn*, man! Look, all I did was . . . !"

Some in the loose circle glanced up at me; so did Frank, then jumped back as Copperhead swung: *"Hey—!"*

Copperhead, concentrated as a pool player, raised his fist again.

"ALL RIGHT!" and I walked down the steps. "WHAT THE FUCK ARE YOU DOING?" which got everybody's attention except Copperhead's. "COPPERHEAD—! Cut It Out!" thinking: *This* is going to be the time when I have to tangle with him. Thinking also: It's just not worth it. But he hooked around and I snatched the end of his chain and yanked. He let go and snapped his fingers back. It must have hurt his hand because it sure as hell hurt mine.

I went up to Frank (who looked as scared of me as he was of Copperhead) and said, "What is this, huh? All right, what are you doing in this—"

"I didn't—" He started at some movement behind me. I didn't turn. "I think you better get out of here." It must have been Copperhead in some feint. "Go on. Go on, now! Get going."

He started to say, "Um . . ." and I realized how used I was to people doing what I told them when they weren't doing anything else.

"Look," I said, "though you are making it harder and harder for me to remember it, so far, you have been my most accurate critic; therefore you deserve some consideration. I'm giving you that consideration now: Scoot!"

Frank turned, went gingerly between Fireball and Lady of Spain, who broke the circle for him.

I turned to Copperhead: "You must be really down on me, man. Because I'm always coming along to mess up your fun, right?"

"Aw, Kid—" Copperhead rubbed his beard with his wrist— "I was *not* going to hurt him."

"You were just going to scare him. Sure." I saw the story coming: Frank's annoying manner, too blunt questions, a jibe, a look; and a violence crystallized from the day's boredom.

California came back this evening. Must have seen him three/five times before I noticed— we were on the back steps—he'd hung both a gold six-pointed star (Hebrew letters on it) and a black swastika (edged in silver) on his light-shield chain. Jack the Ripper, carrying on about something, started to call California ". . . a crazy Jew-bastard . . ." only he saw the star, the bent cross. I could hear the shape the unspoken epithet carved in the silence. Then the Ripper went on about something else. California, since he went away, has changed: his thin hands are tencer; his boney shoulders sit more forward; his blue eyes, between strings of his long hair, are wider and angrier. (How odd symbols are!) I think the change is like what I went through when I got my chain of prisms, mirrors, lenses . . . The Ripper's sensativity surprised me (he did call California a Jew-bastard five minutes later) but then, the derogatory terms we hurl around here with such seeming freedom are actually counters in a complicated game, and the point was the Ripper's. Penalties for missplay can grow huge—recall the beating Dollar took at Calkins'. The rewards? I suspect, in this landscape, they are just as huge. Am I just being pompous, or is the real and necessary information these epithets generate (making them a real and necessary part of Bellona's own language) the reminder that it is often just when we are most aware of the freedom of the field in which we move that our actions become most culture-bound?

Copperhead began to tell it to me, insistently. (I tossed him his chain and he caught and put it around his neck without breaking his sentence.) So I motioned him to come on and, half listening, went up the steps with him.

778

D-t, who'd watched from the top, stood with Dragon Lady. They talked quietly and intently as the guys filed past.

Passing her, Copperhead tried to broaden his anecdote to include her. Maybe because of the small look she gave him (or maybe because her eyes didn't really meet his at all) he finally went on by, just dropping his hand on her shoulder, and she nodded. And went on talking to D-t. Which is a good introduction to why

over the charred grass stopped conversation. A climb across rocks and among green brush jarred it loose again. Cathedral told Priest the black stone building in the smoke was the Weather Tower.

I still don't see any vanes, aerials, or anemometers.

We came around a corner, left hips brushing head-sized stones, right hips (elbows up) scratched by bushes.

The man in the middle of the court was bent over a tripod. As we came toward him, he looked up: Captain Kamp.

Who still didn't recognize me until we were on top of him.

". . . Kid?"

"Hello, Captain."

He laughed now. "Now you fellows looked pretty ominous coming across there." He debated whether to give his hand for shaking. Which Angel solved by giving his. They hooked thumbs.

"Angel," Angel said.

The pink and brown fists locked, shook. Kamp looked like he'd been expecting the biker shake; later he told me that was the first time he'd seen it.

"Michael Kamp," Kamp said.

"Cathedral," Cathedral said:

Shake.

"California," California said:

Shake.

"Priest . . . You're the astronaut, huh?"

Shake.

"That's right."

"Spain."

"That's Lady of Spain," Priest amended:

Shake. Kamp got a sort of funny smile but figured he best not say anything. Which was best.

"Tarzan."

Shake.

"Kid."

We shook.

And Kamp said, "Sure. I haven't forgotten you now," and everybody laughed. Because it had been so formal.

"What you gonna do with that?" Priest went to sit on the chipped steps. He'd been complaining about the sore on his foot.

"That's a telescope," Lady of Spain said. "The kind with a mirror, right?"

"That's right." Kamp stepped to the other side.

"See," Lady of Spain said. (The telescope reminds me of a conversation with Lanya and a whole bunch at the nest I wanted to put down.)

"What are you gonna do with it?" Priest asked, leaning forward to bend the toe of his sneaker up and down. His chain swung against his brown sunken chest and out, clinking.

Kamp squinted at the clouds. "Probably not much of anything. Occasionally I've seen a few breaks in the overcast. It occurred to me, now perhaps I might get a look at your sky here. After all those stories about double moons and giant suns . . ."

In the quiet, I thought about all the times people had not said anything about them.

"After all—" you hear about voices breaking the silence? I learned how strong that silence had been from the way his *After all* snapped in my head—"I saw . . . some of it." How long, now, had that silence gone on? "I thought I'd bring the telescope down here to the park—they said the hill here was one of the highest points in the city—and perhaps see if I could just check whether any planets were where they're supposed to be. I found an Ephemeris in the library up at Roger's. Only my watch hasn't been working all week. None of you guys happen to know what the date is, now, do you?"

When none of us answered, he sucked his teeth, turned back to the white aluminum cylinder (black rings around the middle) and looked down the open end. "Well, somebody'll come along who does, now."

I wondered if George or June knew.

"The paper said it was November ninth," California said, "this morning."

To which Kamp didn't even look up. "If the planets

780

are where *they're* supposed to be, that more or less means the Earth's where *it's* supposed to be." He glanced aside long enough to grin. "In the face of all this cosmological confusion, finding that out should make everyone feel a little better."

"Suppose it's not?" I asked.

"I," Kamp said, "think it is. But *knowing* it will make us all happier."

"I guess that's a pretty good reason," Angel said. He stepped up and looked down into the tube. "Hey, I can see my face upside down in there!"

"I think it would be a good idea, politically, to be able to print in the paper, now, that we know that much. It would calm things down—some people have gotten very upset. And I can see why." Kamp looked up the same time Angel did; their eyes caught. "Now you boys—" which he used as an excuse to look away at Lady of Spain and add an inclusive nod—"aren't interested in politics, I guess, but it seems to me . . ."

In the pause, Cathedral said: "You're into politics, huh?"

"I'm into . . . politics, I guess so now." His hands lay across the white tube. He moved the bones about inside his flesh as though it were a glove. "But I think your Mr Calkins is a pretty conservative politician. Now don't you?"

Cathedral, with dark thumb and forefinger, moiled his thick earlobe. A darker pucker where the gold ring went through meant he'd only had it a little while.

"I'm sure he thinks he's radical. But I think I'm the radical and he's the conservative." I thought he would laugh: he squinted at the clouds, at the telescope. "Now I guess that's what I've been thinking."

"You're so conservative," Lady of Spain suggested, "it comes out the other way and gets radical?"

"No." Captain Kamp laughed. "No. That's not it. Maybe I'm not really . . . into politics." He paused. "But it's just that this is such a big country now. Roger . . . well, I guess it's hard for *any*one to know . . . that it's such a big country."

"Unless you've seen it," I asked, "from a space ship?"

"Rocket," he said. "No. No, that's not what I mean. The Megalithic Republic—now, the Megalithic Republics: the Republic of the United States of America, the Union of Soviet Socialist Republics, and the People's Republic of China—they're very different kinds of political entities

781

from, say, France, Borneo, Uruguay, or Nigeria. The people who live in small nations know it, but they don't know why. The people who live in the Megalithic Republics simply look at the little ones as alien, exotic, bewildering, but aren't even sure why the little ones' histories read the way they do. Two hundred million people, ninety per-cent literate, all of them speaking one language! Now hold that up beside a country like . . ." During his pause, I wondered how many examples he had. "Greece, now. Only eight million people—less people in the country than in New York City. Guy from Macedonia can't understand a guy from the Pelaponnesis. Hell, the guy from the north side of Crete can't understand a guy from the south side. My wife, she said we should go there. And we stayed for six weeks. That was my first wife now. But there's no place in Europe where you can go in a straight line more than eight hours by mechanical transportation without running into a different language, different currency, a different culture! How do they expect to teach three thousand years of European politics to American kids in American schools, or Russian kids in Russian schools, in a land where you can go three days by car in any direction and not cross a border? You have to have been there to understand. I mean, have any of you ever been to Europe?"

Cathedral nodded.

Angel said, "I was in Germany, in the army."

"I never been there," California said.

"I've never been," I echoed, remembering Japan, Australia, Uruguay.

Lady of Spain said: "I haven't."

But even two had undercut Kamp's point. "Yes, well I guess you know what I mean now. America . . . America's so big. And Bellona's one of the half-dozen biggest cities in America. Which makes it one of the biggest in the world." He frowned, mostly at Cathedral. "But you guys here, Calkins too, just have no idea how big that is, and how different that makes the people in it."

"You going to be able to see anything with that?" I asked. "When there is a break, it doesn't last very long."

Kamp *mmmm*ed in agreement. "You don't need much . . . information—like I was telling you once, back at the party? Mask out almost everything: still, even a little bit will tell you an awful lot." He looked at the sky again. The lines out from his eyes lengthened. His lips parted and thinned.

"Hey, we *been* in Europe," Angel said. "You gonna tell us about the moon? You the only one here's been there."

"Shit, I seen that on television," Lady of Spain said. "Live. I never seen anything in Europe on television. Except in pictures."

Kamp chuckled. "Now I was on the earth for thirty-eight years." He looked down. "I was on the moon for six and a half hours. And I've been back from the moon, well . . . a handful more years. But that six and a half hours is the only thing anybody is really interested in about me, now."

"What was it like?" Tarzan asked, as though that followed perfectly from what Kamp had said.

"You know?" Kamp stepped around the telescope. "It was like coming to Bellona."

"How do you mean?" Priest put both hands on the stone steps and leaned forward, waiting to see whether what Kamp had said was from hostility, or just a new thought; or both.

"When we got to the moon, now, we knew a lot about where we were; and at the same time, we hardly knew anything about it at all. And that's just what it's like here. After six and a half hours—" Kamp mused, his eyes narrowing in the smoke—"it was time to go. And if I can't figure out where we are this evening, now, I think it will be time for me to leave here too."

Lady of Spain looked at the sky, then at me—"Where would you go?—" then at the sky again.

"Someplace where I can tell where I am."

The sky was fused, side to side.

"Good luck," Cathedral said.

"I guess that's good-bye too, then," I said.

Priest stood up from the steps.

Kamp nudged one leg of the tripod with the toe of his shoe. "Maybe it is." The metal tip scraped awfully loud.

"So long," Cathedral said.

We walked down the hill.

Angel wanted to know what Kamp had said about information at the party. I tried to reconstruct. Which turned Angel on, and he began a sort of dithyramb about how much everything, while we

Speech is always in excess of poetry as print is always inadequite for speech. A word sets images flying through the brain from which auguries we recall all extent and intention. I'm not a poet because I have nothing to give life to make it due, except my attention. And I don't know if my wounded sort is enough. People probably do hear watches go tic-tok. But I'm sure my childhood clock went tic-tic-tic-tic-tic-tic-tic . . . Why do I recall this in a city without time? What hairy men find on their bodies is amazing. walked through brush and rocks and brushes, told him about the park; that was much fun.

We came out of the trees, talking a lot to each other just as somebody jammed a log into the furnace. Sparks went high into the late, grey afternoon; the smoke plume thinned.

"Hey!" John said and came over, through, and around the kids sitting and standing. "How are you guys? How you guys been?"

I watched the smoke.

Thinning.

Two kids (pink tank-tops; long, straw-colored hair) hauled sleeping bags from under the picnic bench.

Overtaking John, Woodard, yellow as a leaf and woolly as . . . well, Woodard, came to a dead stop and blinked at me (us?). I think at first he'd thought he knew us, but then wasn't sure.

I was going to say hello but John overtook him, now, ruffling at the boy's hair, and said, "Kid, I haven't seen you around for a long time." His hands were just as clean, but his blanket-vest looked like he'd actually done something in it since that last I'd seen.

"How's it going?" I asked.

John gave a tepid grin. "About as well as it can, I guess."

I felt something was wrong; as if I was looking at a place I didn't recognize but should—or did recognize, even though I'd never seen it.

"Kid!" which was Milly.

They went on talking without giving me a chance to introduce the others, which I thought was silly, but Milly and John did things that way. Talking the most, Milly stepped forward over a sleeping bag where an older guy sat up and began to rub his glasses on the tail of a Sweet-Orr workshirt.

Then I figured, fuck it, they better know who everybody was so I just said, loud enough to make them stop talking: "This is Cathedral. And this is . . ." going down the line. While I was doing that, I saw this guy walk into the clearing with a gun under one arm, which was what started the fight.

And which, after going through all this, I don't really feel like describing again because I've been over it with so

many people at that bar and at the nest already. Lady of Spain was all enthusiastic and kept asking where the guy was from. John and Milly I think were going to say they didn't know, but Jommy said he was from the God-damn downtown department store, and Milly said, "You don't *know* he's from the Emboriky for certain," and Jommy said, Shit, he knew, and that they'd already run them from one side of the damn park to the other; which I didn't even know about.

"Man," John said, beating at my shoulder and grinning, "You're really crazy, Kid; you're really crazy . . ." He shook his head, laughing like something was very funny. "Man!"

Second thoughts: since there've been so many repercussions, I should go into it once more just to clear it up for myself. A few things stick with me: like, they had the box of food all ready for him, sitting up on the end of the picnic table (like it used to be for Nightmare). And he was wearing very high-waisted khaki pants, a khaki shirt (army? marine? I don't think so), and orange construction boots —shirt, pants, and boots all looked brand new. But I couldn't tell you the color of his hair Also: the riffle, which I mentioned right off, didn't strike me as odd at the time. Until he started talking and waving it around and once pointing at the guy still sitting in the sleeping bag. I was going through something about maybe he was some loner friend of theirs like Tak, and had I seen him before; and where? I've told a couple of people since that he was somebody I'd met before, to sort of explain that feeling away. I'm not sure now; but for one moment I was certain it was the guy who'd sat in the balcony that night at George's. But now I'm just as certain (however certain **that** is) it wasn't. Cathedral actually moved first—something no one mentions when they talk about it. I thought he was going to take the food carton for himself. I guess the guy did too; that was what made him raise the gun.

What were the dozen people standing around thinking?

What was I thinking?

I grabbed the barrel with one hand and hammered the heel of the other against the stock so hard I thought my wrist had green-sticked. Thinking (all part of that first feeling of displaced familiarity): I've done this before . . . No . . . I've **never** done this before, but if I'm ever going to, I've got to do it now! And if I didn't get shot in the chest, it was because the guy was too scared or just not used to killing people. For which I'm very glad. I twisted, with my arm on fire, and

"You want the carton?" Milly was saying. "We should give that food to them, John. We used to give food to Nightmare."

"Shit," Priest said. "We got a whole cellar full of food."

"Come on," I said. Come on, let's get out of here and leave these poor-ass mother-fuckers alone!" Which I delivered right at John (and it went right over his shoulder to Frank who was sitting on the table beside the food carton as if he was guarding it. And you know, all the bastards kept grinning right through). So we left.

Angel kept prancing around and started tugging on me just like John (Priest was carrying the rifle and had started examining it, and I said: "Man, throw that

watched his face go from surprise to pain as his fingers wound in the trigger guard.

The gun cracked! I thought the explosion had happened in my mouth. But the barrel was pointing over my right shoulder. (If you'd asked me then, I would have said I felt the bullet tip my ear—but that's impossible, I guess.)

The gun dropped/fell/slipped(?) from him; I swung it away, swung it back and wopped it against his hip. He staggered, grunting. I guess he thought I was crazy. (Was I crazy?) He started to come at me, but Lady of Spain grabbed him; then Cathedral.

I hit him again in the stomach with the butt of the gun.

Afterward, John kept saying: "Kid, you're crazy, man! Man, you're crazy, Kid!" in a paroxysm of gleeful hysteria, while Cathedral et the five other al kept their shoulders near mine. My thoughts were carbonated (Yes, I shouted after the guy, when he got up and limped away, "Get the fuck out of here and get your own food!" because it was the easiest thing to say that would give what I did a reason; but while everyone was standing there yakking about how tough it was getting hit up for food all the time, and maybe they wouldn't come back for a while and leave them alone, I kept thinking I should just take the carton of food with me [with the stash under the house we didn't need it] because we didn't need it.) but the detrius was: Take it; because that was the only way to make them understand why my reason for doing it was.

I forgot it—the carton.

I was halfway back to the nest with Cathedral and the others going on loudly about how cool the whole thing was when I remembered three times and forgot what I'd decided to do. I told them about it, which took a lot of energy to start. But they didn't understand ("Yeah! Yeah, that's what we should have done!" from Tarzan; and from Lady of Spain: "That would've been all right. They wouldn't of minded.") and kept yelling.

I'm not a poet.

I'm not a hero.

But sometimes I think these people will distort reality in any way to make me one.

fucker away! You
hear me? Throw
that fucker away
—break it on
something, nigger,
or I'll break your black head!" He smashed the stock on
a stone, "Yeah!" grunting, and twisted up the firing
chamber so it was pretty much beyond use. I said: "That's
no scorpion weapon! A scorpion's got a fucking sting!"
and lifted up my orchid. They liked that.) *just* like John
and saying, "Man, you're something else!"

And sometimes I think reality will distort me
any way to make me appear one—but that's
insanity, isn't it? And I don't want to be crazy
again.

I don't.

"I should have taken their fucking carton."

"Yeah," Lady of Spain said. "Yeah. That's what we
should have done."

Tarzan said: "Yeah. That would have been all right.
They wouldn't have minded."

"You're too much," Priest said again, and Cathedral
laughed and shook my shoulder.

They kept it up all the way into the nest. Tarzan and
Priest came in with me. Cathedral, Lady of Spain, and
Angel got stopped outside where they began to tell the
story. Well, I guess that was all right. There were enough
people around drunk—a bunch of nonmembers who were
apparently friends of Devastation or something, I didn't
care—to absorb it.

I was going down the hall when Denny swung out of
the living room and grabbed my arm. "Hey—!" He was
really excited.

I thought he was going to say something about what
happened in the park. "Hey what?"

He just blinked.

So I started down the hall again.

He followed and said, "Lanya's in the room, in the
loft but—" I looked like I was about to go in—"I think
she's busy."

So I stopped.

Denny said: "You probably shouldn't go in."

"What's she doing?"

"Balling."

"*Here?*" I said, not that loudly. Beside being surprised,
I remember I thought it was not very cool for someone as
down as she was on the gang-bang bit (but basically pretty
together when it came to keeping her thing in front of as-
saulting-type male personalities) to be making it with one
of the guys from the nest in my loft.

787

Somebody was coming up the hall from the john.

"Come on," I said to Denny. We went out on the service porch. "Who's she fucking?" I knew the answer was going to be a surprise; and also that there were six—no, five guys I would particularly not like it to be: Spitt, Copperhead, Thruppence, Jack the Ripper, or Fireball; because they were all the sort who, through malice or ignorance, might try to make it into something unpleasant.

"Some guy I picked up downtown."

I was surprised. "—*you* picked up?" I hadn't expected to be relieved, though. "You balled him too?"

"Naw. Naw, it was her idea."

"This sounds very familiar," I said. "What do you mean, her idea?"

"She asked me to go out and find somebody who wanted to fuck her for money . . . for five dollars."

"*Whose* five dollars?" I asked. "His or hers?"

Tarzan and D-t came up the steps and through the porch door, Tarzan to listen, D-t to wait for Tarzan to finish listening.

"It's hers now." Denny grinned. "She said she was listening to us talk about hustling, I guess, a lot, and I guess she was curious. Christ, was it hard to find someone with any money at—"

"We didn't talk about hustling a lot."

"Didn't stop her from listening. She told me she was curious. She said she wanted to try it."

"Yeah, yeah. Sure." I cuffed his shoulder. "I just want to know why you're not in there doing *your* thing."

"Shit." Denny scowled. "The guy's a creep. He didn't seem so bad when I met him. But he's a creep, you know?"

"Jesus Christ." Tarzan leaned against the sill of the screenless window frame. "You let your old lady. . . ?" and stopped; probably because of the way I looked at him.

I said: "Let her what?"

"You know, mess around with . . . well . . . you know."

"Tarzan," I said, "if my old lady wants to fuck a sheep with a dildo strapped to her nose, that is largely her concern, very secondarily mine, and not yours at all. She can fuck anything she wants—with the possible exception of you. That, I think, would turn my stomach. Yes, that, I I took the orchid from the chain around my   think, I would neck, I raised my hand and slipped it into the   not be able to harness, and the sky darkened outside the windows, the sky roared outside the window screens, and I snapped the collar on my wrist, and the light split in two, each arm growing, ragged-rimmed, with magnesium bright edges, arching the sky, and I swung my hand up at Tarzan's chest. take. I'm going to kill you." On my hand—it swung up at Tarzan's chest—was the orchid. "That's what I'm going to do. I'm going to play tic-tac-toe on your face, and then I'm—"

"Hey . . ." Tarzan whispered, "you're crazy. . . !" looking very scared, looking at Denny, then D-t; but they had stepped away, and he looked scareder.

"Yeah?" I nodded. "You didn't know I was crazy?"

I held the clutch of blade-points right in front of his left tit. While everybody held their breath, I thought: It would be easier here than any place else. Then I said: "Aw, shit! *Run,* mother-fucker!"

Tarzan looked confused.

I dropped my hand. "I want to see you *run!* And that's the last I want to see of you till after the sun comes up tomorrow. Otherwise, I will beat the shit out of you, carry your broken, bleeding, and unconscious body back to your mother's and father's door sill, apartment nineteen-A, and *leave* you there!"

"They don't live in . . ." Then his mind clicked back to where he was; he sighed—I guess it was a sigh—and lunged for the door. He collided with a pigeon-chested man in the bluest shirt I've ever seen ("Hey, *watch* it! You okay . . . ?") and fled down the hall.

The man looked confused too.

Not that his hair was long; but for the type of person he was, your first thought would naturally be: He needs a haircut. "She said," he said, "I should go out this way . . . ?"

"Okay," Denny said. "There's the door."

Dragon Lady had come up the steps and was standing outside it, watching.

"I gave her the money. Hey, thanks a lot. That was really nice. Maybe I'll be back." He looked at me, then looked just a little more confused.

Dragon Lady opened the door for him and he hurried down into the yard. She looked after him, then let the door close, but stood outside on the top step.

It isn't despair. That vanishes with enough laughter and reason. I have both of those

I looked at the orchid.

a-plenty. I guess most people, when all is said and done, lead lives as interesting as they can possibly bare. But I don't remember putting it on. I don't.

I don't remember putting it on.

I took it off.

"You like him," I asked, "D-t?"

"Who?" D-t said. "Tarzan? Man, he's okay. He just don't know when to keep his mouth shut. That's all."

"You made him piss all in his pants," Denny said. Then he laughed. "You see that? He was getting wet, all down the side of his leg." He gestured at his own thigh.

"Huh?" I said.

"He wet all over himself." Denny laughed again, sharp, and barking, like a puppy.

"I wish I'd seen it," I said. "It would have made me feel better."

"I . . . don't mind Tarzan," Denny said.

"Look, man," D-t said. "Tarzan's just a kid. He don't know anything."

"Shit!" I slipped the orchid back on my neck again. "He's older than Denny!"

"He comes," D-t said, "from a very strange family. He's told some of us all about them. You got to make allowances."

"They're not *that* strange," I said.

"I mean," D-t said, "they didn't teach him too much. I mean about the way things are."

"Yeah?" I took a very large breath. "Maybe what gets me is how much his family reminds me of my own."

Then I went down the hall and into my own room.

Lanya, visible down to her nose, looked over the edge of the bed like a cartoon Kilroy.

"Hello," I said. "How are you?"

"When I heard you come in," she said, "I thought Denny would keep you in the front room. That's why I sent the guy out the back."

I climbed up into the loft.

She sat up and made room; she was wearing her jeans, but they weren't buttoned yet. "You know what turned him on most? That I was a chick who balled scorpions," she said immediately. "That was all that really interested him. He was *nice* enough. But I could have been a piece of liver one of you guys had jerked off in; he would have been just as happy." She touched my knee, tentatively. "I mean, I don't mind being a . . . what do they call it, 'a homosexual bridge' if I *enjoy* both ends. Really—he was too funny."

"I was going to ask you," I said, "whether you had completely lost your mind. But coming from me, I suppose, the question is presumptuous to the point of quaintness."

"I don't *think* I'm out of my mind." She frowned. "To finish up the fantasy, I should turn this—" she pulled a five dollar bill from under her knee—"over to you. Or Denny . . ." She sucked in her lower lip, then let it go. "Actually I'd like to keep it."

"Fine by me," I said. "Just don't get into this money thing too seriously. You'll end up like Jack."

"It isn't the money," she insisted. "It's a symbol."

"That's *just* what I mean."

"*I* think you should take your own advice."

"I try," I said, "Hey—this wasn't intended as some kookie way to get back at me for mugging that guy in the street?"

"Kid!" She sat back. "You just shocked me for the first time since I've known you!"

"Tread delicately," I said. "Where do you come off with this shit about *me* shocking *you?*"

"I didn't even think of it. I mean, how are they even comparable? I mean what would . . . Wow! Is that what you thought?"

"No," I said. "I didn't *know*. So I *asked*." We sat for a few seconds, rather glumly. Then I said: "Was he any good?"

She shrugged. "It's five bucks."

Then, because there was nothing else to do, I began to laugh. She did too. I put my arms around her and she sort of fell into them, still laughing.

"Hey!" Denny came up over the edge. "He was a real creep, huh? I'm sorry. Some guys you get, they aren't so bad. Some are even pretty nice. I figured, you know, if I'm gonna get some john set up for your first time, you know, I should find somebody nice. I thought he was nice when I brought him back here but—what's so funny?"

Which got us going all the harder.

Denny crawled behind us. "I wish you'd tell me what's so funny about trickin' with a creep like that?"

"While we're skirting the subject," I got myself together enough to ask, "have you balled any of the other guys in the nest?"

Lanya wriggled a little in my arms. "In the nest? Well, not here—"

791

"Where did you ball 'em?" Denny asked, rather sharply.

"Who," I asked, "did you ball?" I guess I was surprised again.

"Revelation," Lanya said.

I nodded.

". . . and, well, Copperhead."

"Jesus," Denny said. "When?"

Lanya raised a forefinger to bite on the green polish. "You remember the night of Kid's party, when he went off to Cumberland Park, during the fire, and found those kids, with George? You'd wandered off somewhere, Denny, and I was just sitting around here talking with everybody. Gladis and I were telling them about the House—that place where all the girls stay? They were very interested. So finally Gladis and I took Copperhead, Spitt, and Glass over—that's where I pick up my birth-control stuff, anyway. The evening is a little hazy, but as I recall, Revelation wandered in just a little later—" She sat up, scowling at her lap. "Spitt retired early with a young lady he met right away—they just went upstairs. And Glass wasn't feeling well so he left to come back here. But Copperhead and Revelation stayed around downstairs with the rest of us— Dragon Lady had come there, and everybody was yakking about old times—and got incredibly stoned. And—" She paused, her expression between consideration and confession—"eventually, I balled them. And—" she nodded at Denny—"your little girl friend there balled them. And Gladis balled them. And Filament. And Dragon Lady. And, all in all, about—" she raised her fist and began opening it, finger at a time; raised her other fist—"nine other women balled them too. Not in that order: I was fifth or sixth."

Denny said slowly and wondrously, "Wow. . . !"

"It was very funny." Lanya dropped her

In the middle of a corrective complaint about Risa's/Angel's joint cooking effort, Lanya turned to me as I came into the kitchen and said: "Kid, I had a thought, about your memory thing."

"You all full of thoughts," Angel said. "Whyn't you shut up and let us cook?"

"She's just helpin'," Risa said.

"And she knows I'm just jokin'," Angel said. "Don't you?"

"I'll shut up," Lanya said.

I sat on a corner of the kitchen table. "What's your idea?" A piece of silverware fell on the floor.

"Actually—" Lanya picked it up— "you have an amazing memory! I was snooping in

shoulders. "I really thought the two of them had flipped out or something, at first. I was sort of scared for them. I don't think they could have stood up and walked. It was almost like they were in some sort of half-trance. Revelation was lying on his back crying through most of it. That part didn't turn me on too much. But it got some of the ladies off, and how! And he didn't loose his hard-on."

I was surprised and I was curious: "Did they come?"

"Maybe a couple of times at first. I think. But after that, they were just permanently up. No-body gave 'em a chance to go down. You just did anything you wanted with them. And anyone who was interested did."

"All girls?" Denny asked.

Lanya nodded.

"Shit."

Lanya leaned against me. "I've never seen men in a state like that before. The whole thing was really very dyke-y." She crossed her arms under her breasts. "I dug it. It was a little scarey. But it was . . . an experience."

your notebook again—forgive me, and I know you will: but your memory for conversation is practically photographic!"

"No it's not," I told her.

"I said 'practically.'"

"No," I said again. "About a third of any conversation I write down is just paraphrase."

"Being able to remember two thirds of what people say, even a few minutes after they've said it, is **very** unusual. Even your account of the night in the park; and you told me you hardly remembered any of that."

"I just wrote down what you said happened."

"If you **don't** have the lines right, you've certainly got the feeling! And with my hustling escapade, you've got all the lines. Those I remember."

I said: "You read that too?"

"And also your accounts of some of the talks we've had together. I don't know how they would stack up next to a transcript, but it's still impressive."

"So what's your idea?"

"Just that, maybe, since you've got such memory for details has something to do with your loosing track or whole periods of time or . . . well, you know."

"That's so interesting," I said, "I think I'll forget it right now."

"She's **just** tryin' to help!" Risa said from the stove, clashing pot tops.

"And she too knows I am joking," I said. "But even if you're right, so what?"

Of course I didn't forget it, witness this. Still, I suspect my highly creative renderings are more convincing than accurate, no matter what she says—I think (hope?).

"You're just having experiences one after the other, aren't you?" The first thing I thought of was what Risa had said to me that day out in the yard; what I found myself grinning at was that the possibility of a genital expedient for taking her suggestion left me *just* as dubious as an anal one about whether or not I wanted to go through something like that. Oh, well; maybe some people *can't* have everything.

Am writing this comment on what Lanya said about the girls shagging the two guys at the house right after finishing putting down my account of our chaos and confusion with the Emboriki (with Jack, wouldn't you know, being that much help and making that much trouble!) because a lot of what happened there, what we said to them, what they said to us, pushed my mind back to it. I note that Copperhead and Revelation are pretty much exclusively-interested-in-girls guys; remember from last night (significant in terms of today?) Revelation politely trying to tell a pretty drunken Angel. Really, it was nothing personal but, no, he didn't want to fuck around with him, and no, he had never really tried it before, and no he didn't want to, at least not now; and the two of them went on like this, quietly out on the service porch, for half an hour. The truth, of course, is that Revelation was vastly flattered by that much attention from someone that much quicker than he is and wanted to extend it as much as possible. (Did we think by paying them serious attention we were going to flatter them into getting their foot off our necks?) I think, sometimes, the difference is that they are sure that any social structures that arise, grow out of patterns inate to The Sex Act—whatever that is; while we have seen, again and again, that the psychology, structures, and acountrements that define any sex act are always internalized from social structures that already exist, that have been created, that can be changed. All right: Let me ask the terrible question: Could it be that all those perfectly straight, content-with-their-sexual-orientation-in-the-world, exclusive-heterosexuals really are (in some ill-defined, psychological way that will ultimately garner a better world) more healthy than (gulp . . . !) us? Let me answer: No way!

Lanya grinned up at me —"Um-hm"— and kissed my nose.

"What does your Madame Brown think about all this?" I asked.

"That I lead a wild and fascinating life."

"Oh." I nodded.

"She just wonders how I manage to get to school every day on time."

"How *do* you manage to get to school every day on time?"

Lanya shrugged. "Just conscientious, I guess."

"Jesus!" Denny sat back, his hands in his lap. "You gangshagged Revelation and Copperhead! Hey—who was better, Pinky or the nigger?"

The active ones (of whichever sex) are dencer and crueler. The passive one (of whichever sex) are lazier and more self-satisfied. In a society where they are on top, they cling like drowners to their active/passive, male/female, master/servant, self/other set-up not for pleasure, which would be reasonable, but because it allows them to commit or condone any lack of compassion among themselves, or with anyone else, and that (at least in this society, as they have set it up) is immoral, sick, and evil; any madness is preferable to that. And madness is **not** preferable!

"Neither of them—'' she leaned forward and kissed Denny's nose—"was as sweet as you."

"And by the way," Denny said, "where's my five bucks?"

I cuffed him. "Hey, you want to hear what happened to me today?"

"It's *my* five bucks, babes!" Lanya said.

"Aw, shit! I went out in the damn street to pimp the fuckin' john—"

"Look, shut up!" I told them. "Listen." Then I described what had happened back in the park. I thought it was funny. But they both thought it was pretty serious, while we talked about it.

We talked about it a long time too.

Three conversations in which Lanya took part her last few days here. (Stayed overnight; which I liked. Maybe I'm ready to go spend some time at her place? The nesting instinct is *not* the same as the homing one. Which pales first?) She was talking with Gladis when I came into the yard:

"Oh—!" and ran up to me, blocked me halfway down the steps.

I focused on her, as on a memory of mountain rain, autumn light, sea fizz.

(She has *green* eyes!)

The most natural thing, she turned me around on the steps and led me back to the porch—when I realized I was being led, she pulled a little harder; urged, "Come on," and took me into the loft room:

"Where's your notebook? Or your new poems, anyway."

"Huh? I thought you wanted to fuck."

"Oh, if you want—" imitating another kind of girl, then she laughed at the imitation's success—"here!" The notebook corner stuck over the loft's edge; she pulled it down. Two loose pages fell.

She picked them up. "Can I have these to take home?"

"Sure," I said, "—no; not that one," and took back the sheet of blue paper (from the package of stationery Raven brought home).

She folded the page I'd left her and put it in her shirt pocket. I put the other inside the cover and slid the notebook back up on the bed. "Why do you want these?"

"Why do you write them?"

"I don't know . . . any more."

"Ditto," she said, disturbed; which disturbed.

"Hey," I asked. "You haven't seen Mr Calkins again recently, have you?"

"No?" in a way that asked why I'd asked.

"I mean this isn't his idea . . . to get my new poems from you? You're not just keeping them for somebody else?"

"Of course not. I just thought I had less chance of losing them than you did."

"Mr Calkins talked to me about stealing them. I *thought* he was joking—you haven't showed them to anybody?"

"Of course not . . ." Then she said: "Would it be so awful if I had? I did read one—a few to Madame Brown. And a friend of hers who came over that night to visit."

"It wouldn't be awful."

"You look unhappy about it, though."

"I don't know. I'm just confused. Why did you read them? You just liked them?"

"Very much. Everett Forest—Madame Brown's friend —asked me to, actually. We were talking about you, one night when he had dropped over. It came up that I had some of your unpublished work; he was very anxious to see it. So I read three or four of my favorites. I suppose—" she said and sat down on the motorcycle's seat—"—this is the part I shouldn't tell you: He wanted to copy them. But I didn't think he should . . . Kid?"

"What?"

"There's a lot of people in Bellona who are *very* interested in practically any and everything about you."

"There're aren't a lot of people *in* Bellona," I said. "Everybody keeps telling me this; what are they interested in me *for?*"

"They think you're important, interesting . . . maybe some combination of the two. Make copies of your poems? I know people who, if I gave them your laundry list, would type careful reproductions as if they were for some university library or something."

"I don't have a fucking laundry list. I don't even have any laundry," I said. "Who?"

"Well, Everett for one. When I told him you sometimes left your notebook over at my place he practically had a fit. He begged me to let him know next time you left it so he could look through it and maybe make a—" ·

"I'd break your head."

"I wouldn't do that." She moved on the seat. "I wouldn't."

"There's just not enough else for people to be interested in in this city."

"I think," she said, "you've got it. But even though I wouldn't let him go snooping in your journal, I still think your writing this down bores me; no, it makes me angry. It didn't make me angry when she and I were talking about it, it was flattering. Its rehearsal, however, is maddening. I

enjoy having fantasies about these things, thinking about them—but as a game. (Haven't I?) There's no reason not to enjoy them that way any more. But since the publication of *Brass Orchids* I sometimes find myself saying to myself: "All right. I want to

My sensibilities have grown inflamed as our giant sun. I am writing poems now because there is nothing else to read except the newspaper, discussing for pages the rumors and ephemera that fume through the city. How can this go on when such moons rise and such suns set? I am living this way because the horror here seems preferable to life in Tarzan's family.

Bullshit! Only I felt like that when I wrote it—no: I felt something, and thought those words the proper ashes of the feeling as I searched the smoulderings. But they were only smoke. Now I cannot tell whether the feeling itself was missperceived or merely its record inaccurate!

stop playing this game and go try another one for a while. Lord, let me think about something else!" And I can't. That's a much meaner version of the terrifying morning beneath the tree. But the truth is, most of the poems in the book were written before I came to the scorpions. (Which ones were actually written afterward?) The other irony is that the one time I really *was* their leader was when I made them help me get June's and Tarzan's brother out of the shaft. Everything since has been the concreting of some fantasy begun then—and in their minds, not mine. Have I lost by the realization? For (arbitrarily?) precious sanity's sake I have to think at least I've learned.

When you get water from either the kitchen or the bathroom or the service-porch tap, bubbles form around the sides of the glass, but not evenly about the whole surface. They make a band with a definite bottom edge, but peter out up the side. Have noticed, over the last several days, the line starts higher and higher. Must ask Tak if this means something.

To the next conversation, then; maybe better luck:

I stopped outside the kitchen door because I heard them talking inside. Through the screening I saw Lanya sitting on the table, her back against the wall, Gladis and pretty much all the apes (no Tarzan); also D-t leaning against the icebox and Glass standing in the living-room doorway; and Spitt just behind him, to the other side. A loud discussion; and Lanya's voice cut over (she leaned forward, looking around): "I have never—no, wait a minute! Wait. I have *never* seen a bunch less interested in sex than you guys! No, listen! I mean for guys who don't have anything else to do. Really, I'm not kidding. When I was in college, or practically any place, any job I've ever had; or guys I've just known—*seen* a bunch who were less interested in getting laid—"

"I don't see why *you're* complaining!" from Jack the Ripper.

"I'm not," Lanya said. "But I mean, I spend maybe half my time here. Maybe more than half. And I think I know you guys pretty well—"

And D-t: "No, now you wait a minute! Hey, now *you* wait—"

Lanya finished in the silence: "I was just curious why, that's all."

"Now *wait*," D-t repeated. "We got a very strange and funny group of people here. And I guess we don't talk about it that much because you have to be very careful, you know? Very polite."

"I don't just mean making jokes about sex," Lanya said. "But even that, when you come down to it. You'll get really foul for ten, twenty minutes. Then nothing for a day, two days—"

"You mean thinking and figuring how to get laid?" Raven said. "Yeah, I know what she means."

798

Spitt said: "I don't have to *talk* about it. I *get* mine," and looked at Glass to corroborate him.

Glass, hands behind him on the wall, just leaned back a little more watching (Spitt and Lanya were the only whites in the room), curious, as though the discussion was going on all for him.

"There are just very different kinds of people here," D-t said. "For me, maybe, what she said is true. I just never been that interested in sex, I guess, compared to some people. I told a friend of mine once I jerked off about maybe two, three times a year. And got laid about the same. He said that was very strange—"

"*Yeah*, that's strange!" Jack the Ripper hollered, and people laughed.

"Spider over there, see—he's what . . . ? Ten years younger than I am? And he's down at the park, practically every God-damn night it looks to me, getting his pipes swabbed out by the guys sneaking around the bushes—"

"God damn—" Spider said, uncomfortably.

"We just got very different people," D-t went on, "who like very different things. In very different ways. People like me and Gladis, say. We're pretty much exclusively interested in the opposite sex, and then, one at a time and rarely."

"Three times a year, baby," Gladis said, her inflection swinging down low as it could get, "now I don't know whether I'm all *that* much like you?" and up again.

Which tickled the Ripper.

"Shit," D-t said. "You know I used to think I was normal. But then we got guys like Jack the Ripper who are interested in *any*thing."

Spider said, sullenly: "I'm interested in anything."

"Aw, nigger," D-t said, "you'd be interested in a clam if it smiled at you and promised not to bite!"

Spitt added over the laughter, ". . . and even then, I don't know!" which I don't think anybody really heard.

"Then we got the groupies—" D-t went on.

"Groupies!" from Glass, laughing for the first time. "Is *that* what you call us?"

"I mean you guys just aren't interested in anything less than a full scale encounter group-grope—"

"Aw, man," from Glass, "you just wish you could—" and I didn't hear the rest because:

Tarzan asked: "What's going on in there?"

799

I glanced back. "Nothing."

But some of the guys inside had seen us through the screen. A couple more turned to look. So I opened the door and went in, Tarzan following. Lanya was still laughing. Edging Thruppence over on the table, I sat next to her.

"With so many different types, see," D-t said, getting Lanya's attention back, "you have to be very polite: When we live this close. And that means you don't talk too much. You just do it when it's around to be done and the rest of the time you talk about something else."

Tarzan stayed in the doorway, his back to the screen, as outside now as Glass had been before.

Laughter spilled them into different subjects (food, wouldn't you know): Thruppence said we had stuff in the cellar that we hadn't known about till now because nobody had thought to look, till he'd gone down that morning. He took some of us out to show us. There was no real cellar door; just a trap-window, planked over, and a busted Yale lock hanging from the hasp. It let you into a damp, four-and-a-half foot dugout that went under half the house where, besides all the crates of tin cans—some with mildewed labels—was the fuse-box and the hot-water heater, which I re-lit.

Later a couple of people took baths.

I wish they'd continued the sex discussion. It hadn't felt finished. I wondered if it was the advent of me (the Boss) or Tarzan (the Oddball) that had shifted it; or simply the balance in the cream-to-coffee ratio. Out of conceit, I decided it must have been Tarzan.

Revelation, with his ash-pale hair, his gold chains, his pink, pink skin, polarizes a black bunch when he is the only white among them the same way Lady of Spain, blacker than Spider, high-assed, with little, low tits (from jokes the others make, she's of West Indian descent), polarizes a white group when she is the sole black: visually.

Tarzan, however, so often the only blue-eyed blond among the apes (now the official name for the sub-group of five out of the fifteen/sixteen blacks in the nest [Raven, Jack the Ripper, Thruppence, Angel, Spider]) polarizes them in a very different way. His fawning fascination, his near-belligerence, and general lack of use for anyone white makes it impossible to see him/them without a whole aura of sexual/political resonances, which they carry like their lights. (Two thoughts—First:) Even so, everyone seems more or less able to absorb the situation with tolerance and hardly a comment. (Second:) With all these wacked-out spades, there doesn't seem to be one among them, man or woman, in a similar position with a white group (Glass, triumvirate with Spitt and Copperhead, seems a very different thing. Why?) Perhaps the nest (or the House) would be a good place for June after all—after all, I can put up with Eddy. (Or can I?)

Pretty soon it broke up around the cellar window and got back together in the yard . . . But we never did get back to talking about sex. Oh, well: that politeness. I guess Lanya's right.

Third conversation started in the loft. I was on my back; Lanya was leaning on my chest, looking in my mouth while I talked about something. In the middle of a sentence, she got my mind off what I was saying, saying: "I could come from just the smell of your breath. It puffs out in a small hot cloud with each word."

"Pretty bad, huh?"

"It's not bad—please, don't stop talking."

But I couldn't think of how to go on.

She said: "Your mouth is like a flower. Each tooth is like a daisy petal, complete with calyx: You're getting a sort of green skin over the base of your teeth, up near the gum."

"Beautiful," I said. "Pretty soon I'm be ready for Bunny to come take me away."

"Hey." Denny rolled over. "Let me see?" leaning on my shoulder.

I said, "Oof!" and didn't smile.

"Smile," Denny said.

"I wonder if it comes off." Lanya reached up and held her hand like a claw, over my face. "Just a second," one finger coming down.

"Cut it out—!" I turned my head.

"I was just going to scrape at it with my fingernail."

Denny looked at his hand on my shoulder. "Man, my nails are filthy."

"They're rimmed with the exact color of black pearl." Lanya put her cheek next to his. "And he'll probably use it in one of his poems."

"Too fancy," I said, my hand on his. She covered mine. Then Denny closed his eyes tight and tried to wiggle between us like a basset puppy (which started us laughing) and sometimes she is a lorikeet. And sometimes he is a parrot; and she is an airborne borzoi.

I said: "Get up. I want to show you something," at which Denny laughed and Lanya grunted.

Denny told her: "That's all right. We'll just get our clothes off right away, next time."

I said: "Aw, come on!"

We put on some clothes (Denny: socks, vest, chains. Lanya: shirt; her harmonica fell out; was returned to breast pocket; tennis sneakers. Me: pants) climbed down from the loft, put on more clothes (Denny: pants, boots. Lanya: took off sneakers to put on jeans, put on sneakers again. Me: vest, chains, boot), and went into the hall.

Baby, Adam, Priest, Devastation, Filament, the Executioner (who everybody usually calls: X-X) and Cathedral were pell-melling

(To try for accuracy is to risk awkwardness.) To find out who I am I've had to give up my name and who knows what part of my life. It wasn't a choice. But treating it like one seems the only way to keep my mind . . . "seems"? I am frightened because, in this City, I don't know where I am, I don't know where I can go. (To try for form is to risk pomposity.)

in and X-X told me they were really beat, had been running since sometime yesterday. I said three or four of them could go up and fall out in the loft bed because we weren't using it. Filament, the knuckles of one hand on her hip, the other hand waving (she chooses to wear only thin chains, some outside her breasts [nipples like puddles of Peptobismol on the upper slopes of soapstone breasts] some inside) told about what they done in the park: scared some children, unintentionally, and had some sort of loose, blurry confrontation with two men who might have been Tom and Mak. Three went to find mattresses in the back room.

The trapdoor on the porch ceiling was open. Denny climbed up the ladder nailed against the wall; Lanya and me (wondering who'd opened the door and why) followed. Poked my head after her heels into the lead-colored sky.

Asked Lanya if she'd reconsidered being a scorpion instead of just a scorpion's old lady. "Not," she said sweetly, "on your fucking life!" And then: "No, seriously. I've thought about it again, and it's just something I don't want to do. I like staying here for extended visits. But I like living with Madame Brown." Well, she's been here three days straight. And yesterday Denny, for a joke, put one of his chains around her neck and she kept it on till she

Stepped up on the pebbly roofing paper and couldn't figure out how transition had occurred between the slab of runny metal three feet beyond the trap,

802

went to bed. But she didn't put it on again   and the football-
this morning when she went to school.   Stadium - wide,
muzzy balloon around us-and-the-nearest-buildings.
Thought of climbing down and up again to watch this time.

Across the roof, Fireball—buck naked except his optic girdle—turned around and smiled, a little confused.

"Did you open the roof trap?" Lanya asked.

"Yeah. I just wanted to get out and walk around." He told us he liked to go around naked. To his unnecessary explanation, Denny explained (unnecessarily) that you could go around in the street stark naked if you wanted in Bellona ". . . and it wouldn't bother nobody." Lanya, by now, was taking off her clothes. So I took off mine. Denny said, "What the fuck," and took off his. (He left the dog's choke collar looped and re-looped on his ankle.) Lanya took her harmonica out of her shirt and began to play those discordant clutches. We all walked around and stared out at

Filament has a blue scorpion tattooed on her shoulder she said she got before she came to Bellona. She has probably volenteered more information about her previous life than anyone around the nest (most of her life sounds very dull); but, high on tact, she also manages to remain one of the most invisible. If one were writing about the place, she'd probably be among the half dozen people most likely left out, or whose one or two outstanding traits you'd fix for decoration on another character. A girl, and white, she still has the most typical scorpion personality, almost unbelievably so. In fact, I wonder if I believe that; so this note.

the edges of what we could see or each other when each other wasn't staring back; leaned on the roof rim; sat on the mansard things along the side. A long time.

Then Fireball got on his pants and chains—

"So long," Lanya said.

Fireball grinned. "So long."

—and went down.

We came closer together at the far corner and talked about him a while, me and Lanya mostly, mostly Denny listening. Then I told them for the first time about mugging that guy last week.

Sort of awed, Denny said: "Wow!"

Lanya said: "You *are* kidding, aren't you . . . ? Jesus, you're not!" She was sitting cross-legged with her back on the low wall. When she lifted her harmonica, there were two parallel dashes on her thigh.

"No, I'm not kidding. It was interesting."

803

"The awful thing is, I'm sure you did it to find out what it felt like, or for some other half-assedly commendable reason."

"The main thing," I explained, "isn't that I was so scared, but if you get off this very thin line, you get angrier than a mother-fucker—"

"Look," she said, "you wouldn't kill somebody just to find out what it felt like."

"It would be easier here than any place else."

"Christ!" She looked up at the sky.

"Okay," I said. "So you don't approve. Why are you angry?"

"Because," and her eyes came down to mine, "in some funny way I think it's *my* fault. And don't ask me to explain that; or *you'll* get angry."

While I tried to figure out some way to get her to explain, practical Denny asked: "What'd you get?"

"Three bucks. For the work, it pays better than the Richards's." I reached over for my pants, took the bills out of my pocket, and gave them to him. "Here." I glanced at Lanya with a little smile. "I'd split it between you, but she wouldn't take one."

She got a tightish expression that let me know she certainly would.

Denny looked at the bills and repeated: "Wow!" Thinking: He would use the same inflection if he discovered something had been stolen from him. "Here." Denny handed one bill to Lanya and—"Here, you keep one. That way we can split it up right."—one back to me. "I gotta take a piss." He stood and walked away, palms facing back, the bill wrapped on the middle finger of his left hand.

Lanya watched me. "I suppose I'd find you dull if you didn't keep dropping stuff like that into my head. No, don't say anything. I'm still thinking." She pushed herself to her knees. "*I've* got to take a piss too." Her buttocks and one thigh were printed from the roofing paper.

At the corner drain, Denny looked back over his shoulder. "You going downstairs to the bathroom?"

"No," she said in a considered tone that, when the rest of their exchange was finished, should have made me realize she knew what it was going to be.

"Oh, yeah. I guess you can squat here." Denny finished and shook himself.

"What makes you think I have to squat to piss?"

"You're a girl. You can't do it st . . . I mean I thought girls had to sit down or something."

"Jesus God!" Lanya said.

"Well, how do you guide it then?" Denny asked.

"Same way you do."

"But you don't have a—?"

She held up two fingers in a peace sign, turned them down against her cunt and sort of pulled. "Like that, if you must know. Now would you please stop staring and let me pee?"

"Oh . . . yeah." Denny frowned. "Sometimes I can't piss in a john if somebody's staring right at my dick." He turned away, glanced back, away again. "Wow."

Like something had been given back to him.

He went to the wall. "Now I never knew that," he said.

When she came up, he was looking at the harmonica; turned and handed it to her across my shoulder.

"You know how to play it?" she asked.

"Naw."

"The scale starts here," she said. "See, at the fourth hole."

We went down (putting on clothes half here, half there), and in the living room got into the discussion with some of the people mentioned (Fireball, Filament, et al) that I wanted to write down some of the things Lanya said in it in the first place. (When I started this, I'd thought that the business about Lanya being turned on by all those funny thing about me, and what had happened on the roof would make a good prologue, because in the discussion she referred to them) but again I'm tired of writing it down, now that I've gotten to the substance.

It had to do with the differences (and similarities) between the girls who *were* scorpions and the girls who just hung around with us. With reference to the guys who were members and the guys who just hung. It was a good discussion to have and a dull one to reconstruct. And I guess it was mainly for Mike's

One of the things that also went down in the discussion was an arguement about getting food, which I guess was really what started the whole thing, and this other part just came up; but my mind follows funny tracks.

benefit anyway (Mike is one of said guys who hangs, a long-haired friend of Devastation's; sleeps here most of the time but also doesn't want to join) and I guess/think/ suspect one difference between members and non-members anyway is that members know the difference already and don't have to talk about them (that politeness again) though from some of the things Tarzan says, I wonder.

an intercallory jamb between Wednesday and the twenty-second, bless. Grain, blabbed on slip-time, told its troubles to the tree (all runny in the oozey gyre's incarnadine). She won't run Thursdays. The underside of the little hand is tarnished; why is muk-amuk cononized so easy? Truck-tracks crow-foot crators drooling half-and half. She didn't remember how or when, last time. Pavement sausages split; the cabbage remembers. Lions with prehensile eyes pick up their paws, apocopate, and go to town. Get with-it, mauve-peanut! Make it, thing-a-ma-boob! You won't catch me slipping my sticktoitiveness under your smorgasborg. Fondle my nodule, love my dog. Lilting is all is easy. Knitting needles receed around the vision, baring his curviture, clearing her underwear. So that's not what it's for. French fried pickelilly and deep-dish-apple death won't get you through that wake up in the morning alive. Your rosamundus may mathematik him, but it won't move me one mechanical apple corer. I have come to to wound the autumnal city: the other side of the question is a mixed metaphor if I ever heard one. Timed methods run out: coo, morning bird. I could stop before breathing marble basonets. Salvage a disjuncture, it's all you Middle of the ring around the Harley Davidson bush, blooming, blooming, shame, socks, derth and passion pudding, flowers, or Ms Crystaline Pristine. Her backwoods mystification is citified in the face. Penticle pie and hungar city, oh my oh too much, my meat and mashed potatoes pansey, my in the middle of it biche.

Hart's blood is good fly-catching bait. So's fresh sheep-shit. Blatting about in the empty aurical, you think Atocha is in Madrid, what about 92nd Street, or what she told me of St. Croix? She isn't your running the mill broad loom, sword, or side. She's right on the guache circuit where a principle's a principle with all hell lined up to get paid. Maundy, Tributary, Whitstanley, Fibrilation, Factotum, Susquahana, Summer-fine-day. It's all the same

works them?" I asked.

But Faust was walking a-head between the shadowed presses. "Here," he said. "This is what you want to see, isn't it?"

I stepped up to the work table. Battleship linoleum glittered with lead shavings.

"There." He pointed at a full-page tray of type with a yellow index nail.

Raised grey-on-grey proclaimed:

SOON, THE SECOND
COLLECTION
FROM THE AUTHOR OF
BRASS ORCHIDS

"But . . . ?"
"That's you, ain't it?" His cackle echoed among the ceiling pipes.

"But I haven't *given* Calkins the second collection! He doesn't even

in the bitch's kitchen. You look for the dice this time. Maybe you can wind up a winner. Summary, Mopery, Titular, Wisdom, Thaumaturgy, Fictive, Samoa and five hands over. When I grow up I'm going to get a vasectomy all my own. (A dendrite in the glans is worthy of the bush.) Why does he insist on winter all the time? You can stutter in the water but that's not the way to think. Not thinking but the way thinking feels. Not knowledge but knowledge's form. If there're enough raisins, splay feet, and guilded hornet-heads, you can wish, dream, lie like a Saxon though you only pravaricate like a Virginia ham. George! the inginuity I've expended to fill five missing days.

Conversation with furry Forest at Teddy's:

"What are you writing now?"

"I'm not writing anything," I said. "I haven't been writing anything and I'm not going to write anything."

He frowned, and I hoped a lot the lie had at least the structure of truth. But how can it? Which is why I haven't been able to write anything but his journal in so long. And thank the blinded stars, I feel the energies for that going.

What other days from my life have gone? After a week, I can't remember five. After a year, how many days in it will you never think of again?

know there *is* one!"

"Maybe he's just making a good guess."

"But I don't *want* him too—"

"They're supposed to got obituaries too, prepared on all the famous people around here who might die."

"Oh, come on," I said. "Let's get out of here."

"You keep askin' me to show you where they printed the thing . . ."

I started away from the desk. "But I don't see any rolls of paper around. The presses aren't going. You mean a thirty-six page newspaper comes out of here every day?"

But Faust was already walking away, still chuckling, his white hair—sides, beard, and back—covering the bright choker.

"Joaquim?" I called. "Joaquim, when do they actually print it? I mean this doesn't look like anybody's been in here since before the

going out along Broadway. The smoke was as bad as I've ever seen it—rolling from side-alleys, gauzing the streets in loose layers. Down one block, the face on an eight-(I counted)-story building was curtained with it, leaking out broken windows, to waterfall to the street, mounded and shifting.

One section of pavement had been replaced by metal

plates (some incomplete repair) clanging when I crossed. After another half hour the buildings were taller and the street was wider and the sky grey and streaked like weathered canvas, like silvered velvet.

On the wide steps to a black and glass office building was a fountain. I went up to examine: Wet patches of color on the dusty mosaic at the bottom; rust around the pentagle of nozzles on the cement ball; I climbed over the lip to look in what I guessed had held plants: dried stem stumps poked from ashey earth; beer and soda-can tabs. I stepped once on a wet patch of green and yellow mosaic-tiles with my bare foot; took my foot away and left a chalky print.

The bus came around the corner. It didn't scare me this time. I vaulted the fountain edge and sprinted down the steps.

The doors flap-clapped open even before it stopped.

"Hey," I called. "How far up Broadway do you go?"

He feels the experience whose detrius is inter-leaved in the **Orchids'** pages/petals has left him a perfect voice with which he can say nothing; he can imagine nothing duller. (For that sentence to make sense, it must be ugly as possible. And it isn't—quite. So it fails.)

Do you know the expression on somebody's face when you wake them out of a sound sleep with something serious, like a fire or a death? (Small, bald, oyster-eyed black man, obsessed and trundling his bus from here to there.) "How far you going?"

I told him: "Pretty far."

While he considered how far that was, I got on. Then we both thought about the last time I was on his bus; I don't know if the little movement of his head back into the khaki collar acknowledged that or not. But I'm sure that's what we were thinking. I also thought: There are no other passengers.

He closed the doors.

I sat behind him, looking at the broad front window as we shook on up the street.

A sound made me look back.

All the advertising cards had been filled with posters, or sections from posters, of George. From over the window his face looked down there; here were his knees. The long one over the back door showed his left leg, horizonal, foot to mid-thigh. A third of them were crotch-shots.

808

The sound again; so I got up and handed myself down the aisle, bar after bar. The old man—pretending to sleep—was so slumped in the back seat I couldn't see him till I passed the second door. One brown and ivory eye opened over his frayed collar slanting across the black wrinkle of an ear. He closed it again, turned away, and made that strangling moan—the sound, again, that till now I had suspected was something strained and complaining in the engine.

I sat, bare foot on the warm wheel case, boot on the bar below the seat in front. The smoke against the glass was fluid thick; runnels wormed the pane. Thinking (complicated thoughts): Life is smoke, the clear lines through it, encroached on and obliterated by it, are poems, crimes, orgasms—carried this analogy to every jounce and jump of the bus, ripple on the glass, even noticing that through the windows across the aisle I could see a few buildings.

The falsification of this journal: first off, it doesn't reflect my dayly life. Most of what happens hour by hour here is quiet and dull. We sit most of the time, watch the dull sky slipping. Frankly, that is too stupid to write about. When something really involving, violent, or important happens, it occupies too much of my time, my physical energy, and my thought for me to be able to write about. I can think of four things that have happened in the nest I would like to have described when they occurred, but they so completed themselves in the happening that even to refer to them seems superfluous.

What is down, then, is a chronicle of incidents with a potential for wholeness they did not have when they occurred; a false picture, again, because they show neither the general spread of my life's fabric, nor the most significant pattern points.

To show the one is too boring and the other too difficult. That is probably why (as I use up more and more paper trying to return the feeling I had when I thought I was writing poems) I am not a poet . . . anymore? The poems perhaps hint it to someone else, but for me they are dry as the last leaves dropping from the burned trees on Brisbane. They are moments when I had the intensity to

The bus stopped. The driver twisted around; for a moment I thought he was speaking to the old man behind me: "I can't take you no farther," gripping the bar across the back of the driver's seat, elbow awkward in the air. "I got you past the store." He pauses significantly; I wish he hadn't. "You'll be all right."

Behind me the old man sniffled and shifted.

I stood up and, under George's eyes

see, and the energy to build, some careful analog that completed the seeing.

They stuck at me for two weeks? For three?

I don't really know if they occurred. That would take another such burst. All I have been left is the exhausting habit of trying to tack up the slack in my life with words.

(and knees and hands and left foot and right tit), stepped on the treadle. The doors opened. I got out on the curb.

The pavement was shattered about a hydrant, which leaned from its pipes. I turned and watched the bus turn.

From the doorway at the end of the block a man stepped. Or a woman. Whoever it was, anyway, was naked. I think.

I walked in that direction. The figure went back in. What I passed was a florist's smashed display window. At first I was surprised at all the greenery on the little shelves up the side. But they were plastic—ferns, leaves, shrubs. Three big pots in the center only had stumps. Back, in the shadow, by the aluminum frame on the glass door of the refrigerator, something big, fetid, and wet moved. I only saw it a second when I hurried by. But I had goose bumps.

The reason the bus driver hadn't wanted to go on was that Broadway grew ornate scrolled railings on either side and soared over traintracks forty feet down a brick-walled canyon. A few yards out, a twelve foot hunk of paving had fallen off, as though a gap-tooth giant had bitten it away. The railing twisted off both sides of the gash. From the edge, looking down, I couldn't see where any rubble had landed.

Beyond the overpass, to the left, a rusted wire fence ran before some trees; through the trees, I saw water patched with ash. To the right, up a slope blotched with grass, was the monastery.

Like that.

I walked up the steps between the beige stones. Halfway, I looked back across the road.

Smoke reeds grew from the woods and clotted waters to bloom and blend with the sky.

I reached the top of the steps with the strangest sense of relief and anticipation. The simple journey was the resolve that till now I'd thought suspended. The monastery was several three-storey buildings. A tower rose behind the biggest. I put my hands in my pockets, feeling my leg muscles move as I walked; one finger went through a hole.

Thinking: You arrive at a monastery halfway through a round of pocket-pool. Sure. I relaxed my stomach (it had tightened in the climb) and ambled, breathing loudly, over the red and grey flags. Between dusty panes, putty blobbed the leaded tesselations. At the same moment I decided the place was deserted, a man in a hood and robe stepped around the corner and peered.

I took my hands out of my pockets.

He folded his over his lap and came forward. They were big, and translucent. The white-and-black toes of very old basketball sneakers poked alternately from his hem. His eyes were grey. His smile looked like the amphetamine freeze on a particularly pale airline stewardess. His hood was back enough to see his skull was white as bread dough. A sore, mostly hidden, like an eccentric map, was visible under the hood's edge: wet, raised, with purple bits crusted inside it and yellow flaking around it. "Yes," he asked. "Can I help you?"

I smiled and shrugged.

"I saw you coming up the steps and I was wondering if there was anything I could do for you, anyone in particular you wanted to see?"

"I was just looking around."

"Most of the grounds are in the back. We don't really encourage people to just wander about, unless they're staying. Frankly, they're not in such hot shape right through here. The Father was talking yesterday at the morning meal about starting a project to put them back in order. Everybody was delighted to get a place right across from Holland Lake—" He nodded toward the other side of the road. "But now look at it."

When I turned back from the lacustrine decay, he was pulling his hood further down his forehead with thick thumb and waxy forefinger.

I looked around at the buildings. I'd been trying to find this place so long; but once found, the search seemed so easy. I was off on some trip about—

"Excuse me," he said.

—and came back.

"Are you the Kid?"

I felt a good feeling in my stomach and a strong urge to say *No*. "Yeah."

His chin and his smile twisted in a giggle without sound. "I *thought* you might be. I don't know *why* I thought so, but it seemed a reasonable guess. I mean I've seen pic-

811

tures of . . . scorpions—in the *Times*. So I knew you were *one* of them, but I had no way of knowing. *which* one. That you were *the* . . ." and shook his head, a satisfied man. "Well." He folded his hands. "We've never been visited by any scorpions before, so I just took a guess." His wrinkleless face wrinkled. "Are you sure you weren't looking *for* someone?"

"Who's here to look for?"

"Most people who come usually want to see the Father—but he's closeted with Mr Calkins now, so that would be unfeasible today—unless of course you wanted to wait, or come back at some other—"

"Is Mr Calkins here?" In my head I'd been halfway through an imaginary dialogue which had begun when I'd answered his first question with: *The Kid? Who, me? Naw* . . .

"Yes."

"Could I see him?" I asked.

"Well, I don't . . . as I said, he's closeted with the Father."

"He'd want to see me," I said. "He's a friend of mine."

"I don't know if I ought to disturb them." His smile fixed some emotion I couldn't understand till he spoke: "And I believe *one* of the reasons Mr Calkins came here was to put some of his friends at a more comfortable distance." Then he giggled. Out loud.

"He's never met me," I said and wondered why. (To explain that the personal reasons which make you want to put friends at a distance had nothing to do with Calkins and me? But that's not what it sounded like.) I let it go.

A bell bonged.

"Oh, I guess—" he glanced at the tower—"Sister Ellen and Brother Paul *didn't* forget after all," and smiled (at some personal joke?) while I watched a model of the monastery I didn't even realize I'd made—the three buildings inhabited solely by the Father, Calkins, and this one here—break down and reassemble into: a community of brothers and sisters, a small garden, goats and chickens, matins, complines, vespers . . .

"Hey," I said.

He looked at me.

"You go tell Mr Calkins the Kid is here, and find out if he wants to see me. If he doesn't, I'll come back some other time—now that I know where this place is."

He considered, unhappily. "Well, all right." He turned.

"Hey."

He looked back.

"Who are you?"

"Randy . . . eh, Brother Randolf."

"Okay."

He went off around the corner, with the echo of the bell.

Beneath the chipped keystone the arched door looked as though (a slough of rust below the wrist-thick bolt) it hadn't been opened all year.

And I got back on my trip: I had looked so long for this place; finding it had been accomplished with no care for the goal itself. For minutes I wondered if I couldn't get everything in my life like that. When I finally worked out a sane answer ("No."), I laughed (aloud) and felt better.

"They're all—"

I turned from the miasmas of Holland Lake.

"—all finished for the afternoon," Brother Randy said from the corner. "He'll talk with you. Mr Calkins said he'll talk with you a little while. The Father says it's all right." (I started toward him and he still said:) "You just come with me." I think he was surprised it had worked out like that. I was surprised too; but he was unhappy about it.

"Here" was a white wood lawn chair on a stone porch with columns, along the side of the building.

I sat and gave him a grin.

"They're finished, you see," he offered. "For the afternoon. And the Father says it's all right for him to talk now, if it isn't for too long."

I think he wanted to smile.

I wonder if that thing up under his hood hurt.

"Thanks," I said.

He left.

I looked around the patchy grass, up and down the porch, at the beige stone; inset beside me in the wall was a concrete grill, cast in floral curls. Once I stood up and looked through it close. Another grill behind it was set six inches out of alignment, so you couldn't see inside. I was thinking it was probably for ventilation, when my knee (as I moved across the stone flowers trying to see) hit the chair and the feet scraped, loudly.

"Excuse me . . . ?"

I pulled back a few inches. "Hello?" I said, surprised.

"I didn't realize you were out there yet—until I heard you move."

"Oh." I stepped back from the grill. "I thought you were going to come out here on the porch . . ." (He chuckled.) "Well, I guess this is okay." I pulled my chair around.

"Good. I'm glad you find this acceptable. It's rather unusual for the Father to allow someone seeking an understanding of the monastic community—as they describe the process here—to have any intercourse at all with people outside the walls. Converse with members is limited. But though I've been here several days, I don't officially start my course of study till sundown this evening. So he's made an exception."

I sat on the arm of the lawn chair. "Well," I said, "if it *goes* down this evening . . ."

He chuckled again. "Yes. I suppose so."

"What are you doing here?" I asked.

"I guess the best way to describe it is to say that I'm about to embark on a spiritual course of study. I'm not too sure how long it will last. You catch me just in time. Oh—I must warn you: You may ask some questions that I'm not allowed to answer. I've been instructed by the Father that, when asked them, I am simply to remain silent until you speak again."

"Don't worry," I said, "I won't pry into any secrets about your devotional games here," wishing I sort of could.

But the voice said: "No, not questions that have anything to do with the monastary."

And (While he considered further explanation?) I considered the tower exploding slowly, thrusting masonry on blurred air too thin to float brick and bolts and bellrope.

"I don't think there's anything about the monastery you *could* ask I wouldn't be allowed to answer—if I knew the answers. But part of the training is a sort of self-discipline: Any question that sparks certain internal reactions in me, causes me to think certain thoughts, to feel certain feelings, rather than rush into some verbal response that, informative or not, is still put up mainly to repress those thoughts and feelings, I'm supposed to experience them fully in the anxiety of silence."

"Oh," I said. "What sort of thoughts and feelings?" After ten quiet seconds, I laughed. "I'm sorry. I guess that's sort of like not thinking about the white hippopotamus when you're changing the boiling water into gold."

814

"Rather."

"It sounds interesting. Maybe I'll try it some day," and felt almost like I did the morning I'd told Reverend Amy I'd drop in on one of her services. "Hey, thanks for the note. Thanks for the party, too."

"You're most welcome. If you got my letter, then I must restrain from apologizing any more. Though I'm not surprised at meeting you, I wasn't exactly expecting it now. Dare I ask if you enjoyed yourself—though perhaps it's best just to let it lie."

"It was educational. But I don't think it had too much to do with your not showing up. All the scorpions had a good time—I brought the whole nest."

"I should like to have been there!"

"Everybody got drunk. The only people who didn't enjoy themselves probably didn't deserve to. Didn't you get any reports back from your friends?" First I thought I'd asked one of those questions.

". . . Yes . . . Yes, I did. And some of my friends are extremely colorful gossips—sometimes I wonder if that's not how I chose them. I trust nothing occurred to distract you from any writing you're engaged in at present. I was quite sincere about everything I said concerning your next collection in my letter."

"Yeah."

"After some of my friends—my spies—finished their account of the evening, Thelma—do you remember her?— said practically the same thing you just did, almost word for word, about anyone who didn't enjoy himself not deserving to. When she said it, I suspected she was just trying to make me feel better for my absence. But here it is, corroborated by the guest of honor. I best not question it further. I hadn't realized you were a friend of Lanya's."

"That's right," I said. "She used to know you."

"An impressive young lady, both then and, apparently, from report, now. As I was saying, after my spies finished their account, I decided that you are even more the sort of poet Bellona needs than I'd thought before, in every way—except in literary quality which, as I explained in my letter, I am, and intend to remain, unfit to judge."

"The nicest way to put it, Mr Calkins," I said, "is I'm just not interested in the ways you mean. I never was interested in them. I think they're a load of shit anyway. But . . ."

"You are aware," he said after my embarrassed

silence, "the fact that you feel that way makes you that much *more* suited for your role in just the ways *I* mean. Every time you refuse another interview *to* the *Times,* we shall report it, as an inspiring example of your disinterest in in publicity, *in* the *Times*. Thus your image will be further propagated— Of course you *haven't* refused any, up till now. And you said 'But . . .'" Calkins paused. "'But' what?"

I felt really uncomfortable on the chair arm. "But . . . I feel like I may be lying again." I looked down at the creases of my belly, crossed with chain.

If he picked up on the "again" he didn't show it. "Can you tell me how?"

"I remember . . . I remember a morning in the park, before I ever met Mr Newboy, or even knew anyone would ever want to publish anything I ever wrote, sitting under a tree—bare-ass, with Lanya asleep beside me, and I was writing—no, I was re-copying out something. Suddenly I was struck with . . . delusions of grandeur? The fantasies were so intense I couldn't *breathe!* They hurt my stomach. I couldn't . . . write! Which was the point. Those fantasies were all in the terms you're talking about. So I know I have them . . ." I tried to figure why I'd stopped. When I did, I took a deep breath: "I don't think I'm a poet . . . any more, Mr Calkins. I'm not sure if I ever was one. For a couple of weeks, once, I might have come close. If I actually was, I'll never know. No one ever can. But one of the things I've lost as well, if I ever knew it, is the clear knowledge of the pitch the vanes of my soul could twist to. I don't know . . . I'm just assuming you're interested in this because in your letter you mentioned wanting another book."

"My interest," he said, coldly, "is politics. I'm only out to examine that tiny place where it and art are flush. You make the writer's very common mistake: You assume publishing is the only political activity there is. It's one of my more interesting ones; it's also one of my smallest. It suffers

The advantage of transcribing your own conversation: It's the only chance you have to be articulate. This conversation must have been five times as long and ten times as clumsy. Two phrases I really did lift, however, are the ones about ". . . the clear knowledge of the pitch the vanes of my soul could twist to . . ." and ". . . experience them in the anxiety of silence . . ." Only it occurs to me ". . . the vanes of my soul . . ." was his, while ". . . the anxiety of silence . . ." was mine.

accordingly, and there's nothing either of us can do about it with Bellona in the shape it is. Then again, perhaps I make a common mistake for a politician. I tend to see all your problems merely as a matter of a little *Dichtung*, a little *Warheit*, with the emphasis on the latter." He paused and I pondered. He came up with something first: "You say you're nŏt interested in the extra-literary surroundings of your work—I take it we both refer to acclaim, prestige, the attendant hero-worship and its inevitable distortions—all those things, in effect, that buttress the audience's pleasure in the artist when the work itself is wanting. *Then* you tell me that, actually, you're no longer interested in the work itself—how else am I to interpret such a statement as 'I am no longer a poet'? Tell me—and I ask because I *am* a politician and I really don't know—can an artist be truly interested in his art and not in those other things? A politician—and this I'll swear—can not be truly (better say, effectively) interested in his community's welfare without at least *wanting* (whether he gets it or not) his community's acclaim. Show me one who doesn't want it (whether he gets it or nŏt) and I'll show you someone out to kill the Jews for their own good or off to conquer Jerusalem and have it dug up as a reservoir for hŏly water."

"Artists can," I said. "Some very good emperors have been the patrons of some very good poets. But a lot more good poets seem to have gotten by without patronage from any emperors at all, good, bad, or otherwise. Okay: a poet is interested in all those things, acclaim, reputation, image. But as they're a part of life. He's got to be a person who knows what he's doing in a very profound way. Interest in how they work is one thing. Wanting them is another thing—the sort of thing that will mess up any real understanding of how they work. Yes, they're interesting. But I don't want them."

"Are you lying?—'again,' as you put it. Are you fudging?—which is how I'd put it."

"I'm fudging," I said. "But then . . . I'm also writing."

"You are? What a surprise after all that! Now I've certainly read enough dreadful things by men and women who once wrote a work worth reading to know that the habit of putting words on paper must be tenacious as the devil— But you're making it very difficult for me to maintain my promised objectivity. You must have realized, if only from my euphuistic journalese, I harbor all sorts of literary theories—a failing I share with Caesar, Charle-

817

magne, and Winston Churchill (not to mention Nero and Henry the Eighth): *Now* I want to read your poems from sheer desire to help! But that's just the point where politics, having convinced itself its motives are purely benevolent, should keep its hands off, off, off! Why are you dissatisfied?"

I shrugged, realized he couldn't see it, and wondered how much of him I was losing behind the stonework. "What I write," I said, "doesn't seem to be . . . true. I mean I can model so little of what it's about. Life is a very terrible thing, mostly, with points of wonder and beauty. Most of what makes it terrible, though, is simply that there's so much of it, blaring in through the five senses. In my loft, alone, in the middle of the night, it comes blaring in. So I work at culling enough from it to construct moments of order." I meshed my fingers, which were cool, and locked them across my stomach, which was hot. "I haven't been given enough tools. I'm a crazy man. I haven't been given enough life. I'm a crazy man in this crazed city. When the problem is anything as complicated as one word spoken between two people, both suspecting they understand it . . . When you touch your own stomach with your own hand and try to determine who is feeling who . . . When three people put their hands over my knee, each breathing at a different rate, the heartbeat in the heel of the thumb of one of them jarring with the pulse in the artery edging the bony cap, and one of them is me—what in me can order gets exhausted before it all."

"You're sure you're not simply telling me—Oh, I wish I could see you!—or avoiding telling me, that the responsibilities of being a big, bad scorpion are getting in the way of your work?"

"No," I said. "More likely the opposite. In the nest, I've finally got enough people to keep me warm at night. And I can feel safe as anyone in the city. Any scorpions who think about my writing at all are simply dazzled by the object—the book you were nice enough to have it made into. A few of them even blush when descriptions of them show up in it. That leaves what actually goes on between the first line and the last entirely to me. The scorpions caught me without a fight. My mind is a magnet and they're filings in a field I've made— No, they're the magnets. I'm the filing, in a stable position now."

"You're too *content* to write?"

"You," I said, "are a politician; and you're just not going to understand."

"At least you're giving me a little more support in my resolve not to read your work. Well, you say you're still writing. Regardless of *any* personal preface you might make, even this one, I'm just as interested in your second book as I was in your first."

"I don't know if I'm about to waste any time trying to get it to you."

"If I must arrange to have it hijacked, ink still moist, from beneath the very shadow of your dark quill, I suppose that's what I'll have to do. Let's see, shall we?"

"I've got other things to do." For the first time, I was really angry at his affectation.

"Tell me about them," he said, in a voice so natural, but following so naturally from the archness, my anger was defeated.

"I . . . I want you to tell *me* something," I said.

"If I can."

"Is the Father, here at the monastery," I asked, "a good man?"

"Yes. He's very good man."

"But for me to accept that, you see," I said, "I have to know I can accept your definition of good. It probably isn't the same as mine . . . I don't even know if I *have* one!"

"Again, I wish I were allowed to see you. Your voice sounds as though you might be upset about something." (Which I hadn't realized; I didn't *feel* upset.) "I'm not oblivious to your efforts to keep our talk at a level of honesty I might find tedious if I didn't have the respect for truth a man forced to tell a great many lies for the most commendable reasons must. I'm not very satisfied with myself, Kid. In the past months, a dozen separate situations have propelled me to the single realization that, to be a good governor, if it is not absolutely necessary to be a good man, it is certainly of inestimable help. Bellona is an eccentric city that fosters eccentric ways. But the reason I'm here, of all eccentric places in this most eccentric place, is because I really want to—"

Dust or something blew into my mouth, got down my throat; I cleared it, thinking: Christ, I hope he doesn't decide my voice is breaking with emotion!

"—to remedy a little of that dissatisfaction. If he is

not a good man, the Father is certainly a generous one. He is allowing me to stay here . . . Of course there's always an odd relation between the head of the state and the head of the state-approved religion. After all, I helped set up this place. Same way I helped set up *Teddy's*. Of course in this case, the biggest—if easiest—job, given my position with the *Times*, was making sure there was no publicity. In your present mood, you can probably appreciate that. But, no, my relation to the Father is not that of commoner to priest. On my side, at any rate, it is duplicitous, fraught with doubt. If I didn't doubt, I wouldn't be here now. I'm afraid the politics works through the spiritual like rot. The good governor at least wants it to be the best rot possible."

"Is the Father a good man?" I asked again and tried not to sound at *all* like I was upset. (Maybe that backfired?)

"Has it occurred to you, my young Diogenes, that if you polished up the chimney of your *own* lamp, you'd be a little more likely to find this mysterious and miraculous Other you are searching out? Why does it concern you so?"

"So I can live here," I said, "in Bellona."

"You're afraid that for want of one good man the city shall be struck down? You better look back across the train-tracks, boy. Apocalypse has come and gone. We're just grubbing in the ashes. *That* simply isn't our problem any more. If you wanted out, you should have thought about it a long time back. Oh, you're very high-minded— and so, at times, am I. Well, as the head of the state religion, the Father does a pretty good job; good enough so that those doing not quite so well would do a bit better not to question—especially if that's all we can get."

"What do you think about the religion of the people?" I asked.

"How do you mean?"

"You know. Reverend Amy's church; George; June; that whole business."

"Does anyone take that seriously?"

"For a governor," I said, "you're pretty out of touch with what the people are into, aren't you? You've seen the things that have shown up in this sky. There're posters of him out all over town. You published the interview, and the pictures that made them gods."

"I've seen some of it, of course. But I'm afraid all that black mysticism and homoeroticism is just not something I personally find very attractive. And it certainly
820

doesn't strike me as a particularly savory basis for worship. Is Reverend Tayler a good woman? Is George a good . . . god?"

"I'm not that interested in *any*body's religion," I told him. "But if you want to bring the purpose of the church down to turning out people who do good things: When I was awfully hungry, she fed me. But when I was hurt and thirsty, someone at your gate told me I couldn't get a glass of water."

"Yes. That regrettable incident was reported to me. Things do catch up to you here, don't they? When you were unpublished, however, I published you."

"All right." My laugh was too sharp. "You've got the whole thing down, Mr Calkins. Sure, it's your city. Hey, you remember the article about me saving the kids from the fire the night of the party? Well, it wasn't me. It was George. I was just along. But he was down there, searching through the fire, seeing if anybody needed help. I just wandered by; and the only reason I stayed was because he told me the ones who'd started out with him from Teddy's had gotten too chickenshit and run. I heard the kids crying first, but George was the one who busted into the building and got the five of them out alive. Then, when your reporter got to him later, George made out like it was all me, because he didn't want the acclaim, prestige, and attendant hero-worship. Which, in the mood I am now, I approve of. Now is George a bad man?"

"I believe—" the voice was dry—"implicit in what you originally asked was that so necessary distinction between those who *do* good and who *are* good."

"Sure," I said. "But *ex*plicit in what you said was that bit about making do with what you can get. I can get George if I need him. He's genial enough for a god, with some nicely human failings like a history of lust."

"I think I'm still Judeo-Christian enough to be uncomfortable with expressly human demiurges."

"In the state approved religion, the governor is God's appointed representative on earth, if I remember right. Isn't that, when all is said and done, what makes the relation between the head of the state and the head of the church as ticklish as you were just telling me it is? You're as much of a god as George, minus some celestial portents and—of course, I'm just guessing—a couple of inches on your dick."

"I suppose one valid purpose of poets is to bring

blasphemy to the steps of the altar. I just wish you hadn't felt obliged to do it today. Nevertheless, I appreciate it as a political, if not a religious necessity."

"Mr Calkins," I said, "most of your subjects aren't sure whether or not this place even exists. I'm not presenting any long considered protest. I wasn't sure there *was* a Father till today. I was just asking—"

"What *are* you asking, young man?"

What I'd intended to come back with got cut away by my realization of his real distress. "Um . . ." I tried to think of something clever and couldn't. ". . . is the Father a good man?"

When he didn't answer, and I began to suspect/recall why, I wanted to laugh. Determined to go in silence, I got off the arm of the chair. Three steps, though, and my blubbering broke into a full throated giggle that threatened torrents. If Calkins could have seen, I would have flashed my lights.

Brother Randy, robes blowing about his sneakers, stepped around the corner. "You're going?" He still wore his methadrine grimace.

"Um-hm."

He turned to walk with me. The breeze that had been dull in my left ear now grew firm enough to beat my vest about my sides; it tugged Randy's hood off. I looked at the lone Australia on the South Pacific of his skull. It wasn't nearly as big as I'd imagined from the edge. He saw me looking; so I asked: "Does that hurt?"

"Sometimes. I think the dust and junk in the air irritate it. It's a lot better now than it used to be. Before, it was all down over my ear and the back of my neck—when I first got here. The Father suggested I shave my head; that's certainly given it a chance to heal." We reached the steps. "The Father knows an awful lot about medicine. He's made me put some stuff on it and it seems to be clearing up. I thought for a while he might have been a doctor or something, once, but I asked him . . ."

In the pause I nodded and started down. I'd swear he was on something, and the moment he'd started talking I'd gotten auditory visions of the endless rap.

". . . and he said he wasn't.

"So long." He waved his big, translucent hand.

All the way across the broken overpass I tried to assemble what I had of the man behind the wall (my

822

lights flashing through two flowered grills of stone, a web of light around his body); I even wondered what he'd *felt* during our conversation. The one thing that cleared when all my specula-tions fell away was that I had an urge to write. (Do you have that restless . . . ? like

We didn't say all those things in that way; but that is what we talked about. Reading it over brings back the reality of it for me. Would it for him? Or have I left out the particular, personal emblems by which he would recall and know it?

it says in the back of the magazines. Sure.) But sitting here, in a back booth at Teddy's, tonight, while Bunny does her number to not-quite-as-many-as-usual customers (I asked Pepper if he wanted to come with me but he really has this thing about going in here, so I brought my notebook for company), I see all it has produced is this account—and *not* what I wanted to work on. (Bunny lives in a dangerous world; she wants a good man. What she can get is Pepper . . . no, an image Pepper at his best [when he can smile] consents to give, but he's usually too tired or ashamed to. Is it my place to tell her that, bringing my blasphemey to the altar steps, sharing with her the data from my noon journey? I just wish I enjoyed his dancing more.) This is not a poem. It is a very shabby report of something that happened in the Year of Our Lord it would be oh-so-nice to write down, month, day, and year. But I can't.

If Dollar doesn't stop pestering Copperhead, then Copperhead will kill him. If Dollar stops pestering Copperhead, then Copperhead will let him alone. If Copperhead is going to kill Dollar, then Dollar will not have stopped pestering Copperhead. If Copperhead lets Dollar alone, then Dollar will have stopped pestering Copperhead. Which of the above is true? The one with the fewest words, of course. But that's faulty logic. Why? Three times blessed is the Lord of Devine Words, the God of Theives, the Master of the Underworld, duel sexed in character, double dealing in nature, yet one through all defraction.

her elbow across his jaw.

John said, "Hey . . . !" and went back, hands up, palms out.

The sound she made was something I'd never heard out of *any*body. She kicked at his leg, got him under the knee. He grabbed at her arm again but it wasn't there, so he pulled back.

And stumbled over a root, right up against the trunk. Which made him really mad: he swung at her again.

She jumped. Straight up. His fist landed against her arm. She came down raking at his neck. His shirt tore.

He hit her, hard. But it didn't matter; I thought she was going to bite his throat out. She bit something. He hissed, "Shit . . . !"

Denny grabbed my arm. "Hey, don't you wanna stop her . . . ?"

"No," I said. I was scared to death.

John tried to punch her in the stomach.

Both of them twisted, missing.

Milly kept circling around them and Jommy started to say, "Hey, somebody . . ." and then saw the rest of us and just swallowed.

John pushed her away in the face. She grabbed his arm and yanked. Not pulled, yanked. His elbow hit the tree. He yelled, and hit her flat-handed in the jaw.

"FUCKER . . . !" she shouted so loud you knew it hurt her throat. "FUCKER . . . !"

Her right fist came down from her left ear and hammered his face. Like an echo his head cracked back against the trunk.

"Hey! Stop it . . . Stop . . ." Then I guess he really tried to break out. He shouted, grabbed her wrist . . .

She was meat red from the neck up, yanking her fist over, twisting his fingers; then grabbed one fist with the other and swung it against his neck.

"Jesus . . ." Jommy said, to me I realized. "She's crazy . . ." But he stepped back from the look I gave him.

John tried to grab her in some sort of bear hug. He kicked out, and they both went down, him pretty much on top. Everyone stepped back together.

Flailing out, she came up with a handful of grass. Then there was grass in his hair and he yelled again.

His ear was bleeding. But I don't know what she'd done.

"Hey, look!" Milly said, loud and upset. "Why doesn't somebody . . ." Then it struck her that if somebody was, the somebody was going to have to be her.

She started forward.

I touched her on the shoulder and she looked sharply around.

"Fair fight," I said.

He hit her three times, hard, one after the other: "Stupid. Bitch. Stupid . . ." but she somehow got him off. And reared back. She came down with both fists on his face, once glancing off his ear and hitting the ground and coming up for another hit, bloody. When she hit him again—he was just trying to cover his face, now—I saw hers was scraped up bad.

About the sixth time she hit him—one knee went into his stomach—I thought maybe I should try and stop her. I thought about Dollar. I thought about Nightmare and Dragon Lady. But I wasn't as scared as I'd been at the beginning, when I'd thought her quivering, shaking rage would explode her.

Denny's mouth was open. He let go my arm.

She stood up, almost falling. "You fucking shit!" she said. It sounded like her jaw clicked between syllables. She kicked him in the head. Twice.

"Hey, come *on* . . ." one of the others said, and started toward her. But didn't touch her.

Thinking: Maybe a tennis sneaker isn't that hard. Sure.

She turned and came, blindly, toward me.

As Denny fell back, she stopped, looked behind her and shouted, "You fucking shit!" and came on. Her face was all puffed on one side.

Two of the guys kneeled beside John. Milly hovered behind them as though she still couldn't make up her mind.

"Oh, wow!" Denny said. "You really creamed the bastard!"

"The fucking shit!" she whispered, wiping at her face and grimacing. "The fucking . . ." One eye was all teary. She started walking. We walked with her.

"It looks like he got in a couple too," Denny said.

"She's walking," I said.

"Hey, you did better than Glass did with Dollar," Denny said.

"I had—" She took a breath. "I guess I had more reason." She rubbed her shoulder with her palm, fingers strained wide. And left blood on the workshirt sleeve. I don't think she knew she was bleeding yet.

"Hey, Lanya?" Jack said. Frank stood behind his shoulder.

She stopped and looked.

She swallowed and I wondered if she remembered who he was.

I was probably projecting.

"Thanks," Jack said.

She nodded, swallowed once more, and started walking again.

"What's the matter?" Denny asked about twenty yards later. "Your eye hurt?"

She shook her head. "It's just that . . ." She really sounded upset. "Well, nice girls from Sarah Lawrence don't usually beat the fucking shit out of . . ." and gasped again.

I put my arm around her shoulder. She fitted like usual. Only she didn't adjust her step to mine. So I adjusted mine to hers. "Did you want me to lend you a hand in there?"

"I would have pulled your balls off!" she said. "I would have . . . I don't know what I would have . . ."

I squeezed her shoulder. "Just asking, babes."

She touched her jaw again, gently, realizing it hurt. And left blood there. "The school was my thing. It wasn't yours. You didn't have anything to do with it. You didn't even *like* Paul . . . Oh, the fucking *shit—!*" and stopped walking.

"I helped you with the class a couple of times," Denny said. "Didn't I?" and glanced back at the others.

"Sure," Lanya said, and put her hand on his shoulder. Then she winced and reached down to rub her leg. Not limping, she still favored it.

"I just don't understand why you lit into him," I said.

"Oh, fuck you!" She pulled away from me. "You don't understand a lot of things. About me."

"All right," I said. "I'm sorry."

"So am I," she said, harshly. But when I caught up with her, she put her arm around my shoulder. And adjusted her step.

"Hey," Denny said. "You wanna be by yourself for a while?"

"Yeah," she said. "Yes I do."

She walked with us to the park entrance, so that I figured she was going back with us to the nest. But by the lions she said, "I'll see you later," and just walked off.

"Hey . . ." I called.

"She wants to be by herself," Denny said.

I still felt funny.

826

She did come back to the nest, late that night after we'd been in bed (me half drunk) about an hour. Vaguely I heard her taking off her clothes, then climbing the ladder pole.

She crawled across me, rolled me by the shoulder onto my back, and, a-straddle my chest, glared down, swaying like she was going to rip something out of me with her teeth. I reached between her legs and pushed two fingers through her hair between the granular walls; they wet.

She leaned both hands on my chest, her arms pushing her breasts together and actually growled.

Denny, wedged in the corner, turned over, lifted his head, and said, "Huh . . . ?"

"You too!" she said. "*You* come here too!"

I've never been balled like that before—puffy eye and sore leg notwithstanding—by *any* one. (She said she'd spent the afternoon and evening with Madame Brown, just talking. "You ever ball *her?*" Denny wanted to know.) In the middle of a heavy stretch, Copperhead stuck his head over the edge of the loft and asked, "What are you guys *doing* up here anyway? You're gonna tear the loft down!"

"Get out of here," Denny said. "You had your chance."

Copperhead grinned and got.

Walked around the streets this afternoon with Nightmare, listening to his reminiscences of Dragon Lady: "Man, we used to do some freaky things, all the time, any time, anywhere, right in the middle of the fuckin' street, man, I swear." We ambled; he pointed out doorways, alleys, a pickup truck parked on its axles—"Once with her sitting in the cab and me standing on the fuckin' sidewalk, a hand on either side of the door, and my head just in there, eatin' out all that black pussy—Baby and Adam running around someplace across the street—then I fucked her in the back there, on the burlap. Oh, shit!"—and where, by the park, she had pushed him up against the wall and blown him; where she used to make him walk down the center of the street with his genitals loose from his fly, "with her sitting on the curb and doing things with her mouth, man, before I even *got* there, so I had a hard-on out to *here!*" He talks out these celebrations as though they are religious rituals recently banned. Forty minutes of this, before it hit me how lonely not only Nightmare is, but all of us here are: Who can I discuss the mechanics of Lanya and Denny with? I don't even have the consolation of public disapproval. He probably has never talked about any of this before. On the marble steps of the Second City Bank building (he tells me) he made her take off all her clothes—"Just like Baby, man. I mean people can go around in the street stark naked here, and it don't mean nothing."—and urinate, while he stood behind her, one arm over her shoulder, catching her water in his palm. "And once she made me lie on my back, you know, in the center of the pavement—" the incident illustrated with much gesturing and head-shaking as we search his memories out of the dry mist—"naked, man, and she just walked around and around and around me, a big woman!" (He repeats this last a lot, as though her circling defined some terribly necessary boundary on this wild terrain.) ". . . made me eat her out for half an hour, I swear, right—" he looks around, surprised—"*here*, man. Right here! It was just getting light, and you couldn't hardly see her . . ." As my attention drifted from his account, I thought of all the cliches about how to act among violent people, current among the non-violent: Rise to the first challenge or you'll be branded a coward for the rest of your stay; a willingness to fight gains the group's respect; once you beat him, the bully will be your friend. Somebody coming into the nest with these as functioning propositions would get *killed!* (Thinking: Frank?) Nightmare's shoulders rocked. His fists, wrists bound in leather, bobbed. He recounted hoarsely: "She used to get me drunk and I'd have her suck me off, my ass up against any old, cold, God-damn wall, with my pants down around my fuckin' knees, and her tryin' to get two fingers up my ass—don't remember how she figured out I like *that*." Suddenly he looked up, frowning. "You think I was right?"

"Huh?"

"When we had that garden party back at the nest." His meaty hand returned to the fresh scars down his arm. "You think I done right?"

"Dragon Lady is her own woman," I said.

Nightmare asked: "What would you do if somebody pulled that shit on you?"

"I think," I said, "I would have cut their head off. Just messing up her arm for a couple of weeks—well, you both showed great restraint."

"Oh." His hand, knotting, slid down his chest to knuckle his belly, pensively.

"But nobody *has* ever pulled that on me," I said. "At least Dragon Lady hasn't, yet. So I still dig you both."

"Yeah," Nightmare said. "Sure. I understand. But nobody *would* do *you* that way. They think you're too smart. They think they can talk to you. Maybe that's why I gave you the nest, you know?"

That surprised me.

"Yeah," he went on, "like I said: It's time for me to get out of this mother-fuckin', sad-assed excuse for a—"

Behind his voice, children's voices: we were passing the curtained windows of Lanya's school. Nightmare looked. The door was ajar on darkness; laughter, juvenile shrieks, and chatter . . .

I stepped up the curb over the gutter grate. Nightmare followed. I glanced back: his thick forehead skin creased in a squint; his lips pulled up and down from the whole (and one broken) teeth.

I stepped through the door.

On the table, above the empty chairs, spools glimmered and spun on the tape recorder. We watched a while, waiting. Beside me, Nightmare mauled and kneaded his bald shoulder, listening to the recorded noise in the vacated room. Scars, chains, and office, some thrust away, some new received, habits without correlatives, jumbled in the great bag of him, as though his achievements and losses completed a design mapped in the layout of the streets around us. Thinking: I may never see this man again after today, if all

own eyes, for somewhere in this city is a character they call: The Kid. Age: ambiguous. Racial origin: same. True name: unknown. He lives among a group (whose alleged viciousness is only surpassed by their visible laziness) over which he holds a doubtful authority. They call themselves scorpions. He is the supposed author of a book that has been distributed widely in town. Since it is the only book in town, that it is the most discussed work of the season is a dubious distinction. That and the intriguing situation of the author tend to blur accurate assessment of its worth. I admit: I am intrigued.

Today I cut down the block where I'd heard the scorpions had their nest. "What kind of street do they live on?" In the grammar of another city, that sentence would hold the implication: What kind of street are they more or less constrained by society to live on, given their semi-outlaw status, their egregious manner and outfit, and the economics of their asocial position? In Bellona, however, the same words imply a complex freedom, a choice from hovel to mansion—complex because every hovel and every mansion sustains through that choice some remnant of our ineffable catastrophe: In any house here movement from room to room is a journey from a place where twin moons have cast double shadows of the window sills upon the floors to a place where once, because the sun had grown so immense, no shadow was cast at all. We speak another language here. Is the real importance of his pamphlet that I've been browsing over all morning that, unlike the newspaper, it is the only thing in the city written in this language? If it is the only thing said, by default it must be the best thing. Anyone sensitive to language, living in this mess/miasma, must applaud it. Is there any line in it, however, that would be comprehensible outside city limits?

Five were sitting on the steps. Two leaned against the wrecked car at the curb. Why am I surprised that most of them are black? The flower-children, whose slightly demonic heirs these are, were so emphatically blond, and the occasional darky among them such an emphatic mark of tollerence! They were not sullen. There were three girls among them, one an ebullient young black girl, capped with a large natural and vastly pregnant. They wore chains, some as many as fifteen strands, some as few as two. They were dirty and gregarious. They smiled and talked a sort of quiet half-talk to one another. Boots, leather vests—no shirts—

This remains with me from my last conversation with Tak about Calkins and the party: "I had the funniest dream last night, Kid. Not that I particularly care what it means—I interpret other peoples' dreams and just try to enjoy my own. Anyway, I had this little black kid, about thirteen or fourteen, up at my place—Bobby? I think you were catching a nap there once when he came by. In the dream, he was just standing there in a T-shirt, with half a hard-on. (Half a hard-on on Bobby goes out to here!) Suddenly I looked up and George was coming across the roof toward the door, as though he'd just come up for a visit. When he stepped in, he saw us. All the posters of him across the wall, I think but I'm not sure, were staring at us too. And he had this sort of mocking look that said, 'So that's what you're after.' And I felt very guilty. Oh, the point of it was that in the dream Bobby and I weren't going to have sex. He wanted to show me something on his cock—some sore or something. And I felt all uncomfortable, like I'd been trapped into being something that I'm not. I mean given my choice of types—types and not individuals—I'd rather have a Georgia farm-boy any day. Not that I've ever kicked Bobby out of bed. But it was a strange dream."

My first reaction was that Tak, who had always seemed a pretty big man, became much smaller. Later I realized that the big man simply contained many componants, among them a small one.

and chains made them look like some 'cycle club in coventry. A tall, skinny, black boy on the top step had a gallon of wine between his boot heels which periodically passed on its way to the curb and back. The white guy with no vest and the scarred stomach was the only one who wiped the neck—with a hand so grubby the other colored girl, tall and hefty, refused to drink after him. The others laughed as if her rebuke contained more than was apparent. They did not look at me as I strolled on the other side of the street. It is rumored that these men and women can transform themselves in darkness to any one of a gallery of luminous beasts; that they have weapons to turn the slung fist into a five-way cutting tool. I wonder if anyone that I saw there was the Kid—

Also wonder if writing about myself in the third person is really the way to go about losing or making a name. My life here more and more resembles a book whose opening chapters, whose title even, suggests mysteries to be resolved only at closing. But as one reads along, one becomes more and more suspicious that the author has lost the thread

It's not light yet. (Will it ever be?) Just returned from the third and what I hope is the last run on the Emboriki. Don't even want to write about this one. But, as usual, will. (At least, he said and can you hear the cap's, They Will Not Be Bothering Us Again. Tarzan's bizarly reflective comment (echoing something he heard from me?): "It's easier here than any place else") Raven, Priest, Tarzan, and Jack the Ripper kept telling me, "Man, don't take Pepper along!"

"Anyone goes who wants to go," I said. By the time we went, though, Pepper wasn't around anyway. Dragon Lady was waiting for us in front of Thirteen's; BaBy, b.a. as usual, pimple-pocked and sullen, stood in the shadowed doorway. His arms slung through his chains, Adam sat on the curb, grumbling glumly. Cathedral, Revelation and Fireball had brought the cans of

of his argument, that the questions will never be resolved, or more upsetting, that the position of the characters will have so changed by the book's end that the answers to the initial questions will have become trivial. (It is Troy, Sodom, Abel Çuyuk, the City of Dreadful

an ocean of smoke and evening. I tried to smell it, but my nostrils were numb or acclimated. The lions gaped in the blurr. We neared the fogged pearl of one functioning lamp, and her face got all twisted. She stopped, turquoise, hem to knees, exploding high as her scarlet waist. "Should we . . . ? Oh, Kid! Do you know what they *said!*"

"Will you *please* . . ." I asked her. My throat hurt with running and the raw air. "Will you please tell me what . . . *what* they said!"

Both hands came up to cage her mouth. She was a shower of sliver on metallic black. "Someone, up on the roof of the bank: The Second City Bank —oh, a God-damn sniper!"

"Who, for Christ's sake?" I grabbed her small elbows and the hair shook around her head. "Will you tell me *who* they got?"

"Paul," she whispered. "Paul Fenster! The school, Kid . . . everything!"

Woke up this morning in the dark loft. Heard a handful of cars before I rolled to the window and pulled back the shade. Sunlight opened like a fan across the blanket. I climbed down the ladder pole, dressed, and went outside. The air was chill enough to see breath. The sky, lake blue, was fluffed with clouds to the south; the north was clear as water. I walked to the end of the block. The pavement was dark near the edge from pre-dawn rain. I stepped over a puddle. At the bus stop— was it eight o'clock yet?—stood a man in a quilted jacket carrying a black enamel lunch box; two women with fur collars; a man in a grey hat with a paper under his arm; one woman in red shoes with big, boxy heels. Across the street stood a long-haired kid in an army jacket, thumb out for the uphill traffic. He grinned at me, trying for my attention. I thought it was because I'd left one boot off, but he wanted me to look at something in the sky without attracting the other people at the stop. I looked up between the trolley wires. White clouds hung behind the downtown buildings, windows like a broken honey comb running with brass dawn-light. Perhaps twenty-five degrees of an arc, air-brushed on the sky, were the pink, the green, the purple of a rainbow. I looked back at the kid on the corner, but a seventy-five Buick came glistening to a stop for him and he was getting oh God oh Jesus, please o please I can't I please don't let it

"Is he *dead?*"

Her head shook in a way that meant she didn't know. Her hands twisted silver cloth at her hips: scarlet bled

832

down from one; yellow snaked across her belly from the other. "In the burning," she said very quickly. "In the fire . . . all your poems, the new ones; they burned . . . !" Her lips kept touching and parting, sorting more words, none of which fit. "Everything, all of them . . . I couldn't . . ."

"Unnn . . ." Something went right into my stomach without using gut or throat for entrance, I said, "Unnn . . ."

She let go her skirt.

"That's . . . good I guess," was all I could say. "I didn't like them. So it's good they're . . . gone."

"You should have kept them in your notebook! I was wrong! You should . . ." She shook her head. "Oh, I'm so *sorry!*"

I started to cough.

"Look," she said, "I know half of them by heart anyway. You could reconstruct—"

"No," I said.

"—and Everett Forest made that . . ."

"No. It's good they're gone."

"Kid," she said, "what about Paul . . . ? Up on the Second City Bank building. Were you . . . ? Oh, *please* try to remember!" Then she started as though she'd seen something (behind me? above me? were my lights still on? I *don't* remember!), and turned. And ran, blazing gold a moment before shadow took her and I ran after, into the brush, feet crashing in leaves and ash. Her bright hem whipped back till she became some darker color. (Thinking: Who is in control of her? Who, less than fifty yards off, is following through the undergrowth, twisting the nobs, pushing the switches that change her from scarlet to ultramarine?) My bare foot passed

This morning Filament brought around a woman who' I first thought was Italian and who became Black Widow this evening. Overheard her in a discussion in the back yard just now— one of the few here that has even veered near any politics outside the city: "It's not that men and women are identical, it's just that they are so near identical in all but the political abuses and previvildges that are that are lavished on the one and visited on the other that to talk of 'inate' differences as significant, even to childbirth, is to hold up the color of the hair, the strangth of a limb, a predillection for history over mathematics or vice versa, as a pre-determining factor in who shall be treated how, with no appeal; while to ignore those abuses and previlidges is to ignore oppression, exploitation, even genocide, even while these are shaping conscience, consciousness, and rage." I was impressed. But I have heard similar from Nightmare, Dragon Lady, Madame Brown, Tak, D-t, Bunny, even

Tarzan. Is Bellona, then, that unbelievable field where awarenesses, of such an order, are the only real strangth? That they can occur here is what makes possible the idea of leaving for another city. from concrete to grass. The night billowed and sagged. Did habit guide us through the maze of mists?

I saw the quivering fires.

The brass dish, big across as a car tire, had been dragged twenty feet over the ashy grass. I felt very high. Thought swayed through my mind, shattered, sizzled like water on coals. Something in the smoke—? I raised my arm.

Brass leaves, shells, claws—from the ornamented wrist band, over-long blades curved up around my hand. In the dish, small blue flames hung quivering over the red. Fire light dripped down the blades.

I took another step, flexing just the scarred fingertips. Something tickled my shoulder.

I whirled, crouching. The leaf rolled down my vest, fluttered against the chains, brushed the worn place at my knee, spun on to the ground. Gasping, I looked up the leaning trunk. Above, shadow coiled in the bole of some major branch, struck away by lightning.

The air was still. But suddenly dead leaves I could not see thundered above, loud as jets. Holding my mouth wide as I could, I leaned forward. The side of my foot pressed a root. Thigh, belly, chest, cheek lay up against the bark. I breathed deep for the woody smell and pushed my body into the trunk.

With my bladed hand I stroked the bark till I felt the trunk move. Sweat rolled under my vest. Chains bit my belly; glass

About a third the nest say "must of," distict and clear. They think it, too. They aren't saying "must've," or must'a'," either. I notice it specifically in D-t, Filament, Raven, Spider, Angel, Cathedral, Devestation, Priest. So: they are going through a different word to word process than the rest of us (Tarzan, for instance, who says "must'a' ")—I don't think we feel any verb in that at all, while the people who say "must of" do feel something preposi- tional, or at least genative. A word hits my ears and inside my head a sensory recall forms —a memory of an object, dim and out of focus, the recollection of a sound, a smell, or even a kinesthetic expectation. The recalls are un- clear—there is always margin for correction. As word arrives after word, the recalls join and correct each other, grow brighter, clearer, become percise: a . . . huge . . . pink . . . mouse! What do I mean when I say a word means something? Probably the neuro/chemi-

bits pressed about me; bark gnawed my cheek. Above, in the roaring, I heard a crack; not the sound wood makes broken against the grain, but when it splits longways. And there was a smell, stronger than the smoke: vegetative, spicey, and fetid.

Another crack: but that was gun or backfire, louder than leaves and across the park. I pushed back from the trunk, blinking away the water in my eyes. Something fell, rocked on the grass among the roots; and something else—shards of bark, twelve or twenty inches across. Bark split in front of me, sagging out a few inches. What was behind it, I could see by the light from the dish, was red; and moist; and moved. Something crashed down through the

cal process by which one word sounded against the ear generates one inner recall. Human speech has so little varience to it, so little creativity: I sit on the steps and scan an hour's conversation around me (my own included) and find **once** two words in new juxtaposition. Every couple of days such a juxtaposition will evoke something particularly apt about what the speaker (usually Lady of Spain or D-t; seldom me) is talking about. But when it happens, everyone notices:

"Yeah, yeah! That's right!" and laughter.

"I like that!" and someone grins.

"Yeah, that's pretty good."

In college I would scan and find one such language node in ten hours of speech, sometimes in two or three days. Though, there, people were much more ready to approve the hackneyed, the cliched, the inapt and imprecise.

Is that why I write here?

Is that why I don't write here much?

In the middle of this, Lanya says: "Guess who I had dinner with last night."

Me: "Who?"

She: "Madame Brown took me to the Richards'."

Me: "Have a good time?" I admit, I am surprised.

She: "It was . . . educational. Like your party. I think they're people I'd rather see on my terratory than on theirs. Madame Brown feels the opposite. Which probably means I won't see much of them."

Me: "What did you think of June?"

She: "I liked her. She was the only one I could really talk to . . . the hallway down stairs still stinks; weird going past it in the elevator and knowing what it was. I told her all about the House. She was fascinated. A few times Author and Mary overheard us and were scandalized. But not many." She rubs the lion's back (where bright metal scars the brown patina), looks out the window. "I think she's going to find George, soon. When she does, we all better watch out."

Me: "Why? What'll happen?"

She smiled: "Who knows? The sky may crack, and giant lightning run the noon's black nylon; and the oddest portents yet infect the

branches, but caught in them. I heard more wood split, and something like a moan. "Lanya!" I shouted loud as I could. "Lanya!" Leaves swelled to a roar again.

I took another step back— a sudden pain along my calf. I whirled, staggering. My bare heel had scraped the high, raised rim of hot metal. I danced away from spilled coals; rocking, the edge had scraped half-way to my knee. There were more gunshots. I began to run.

ceiling of the skull." She was mocking with miss-quotation what I'd given her to read that morning. Her turning it into something inflated like that made me uncomfortable.

She realized it and laid three fingers on my arm. But her touch was light as a leaf; I quivered. "You'd prefer to be hit than tickled, wouldn't you." She firmed her grip.

"Yeah," I said. "Usually."

She watched me, green eyes dark as gun metal in the crowded room. Almost everyone was asleep. We went into the front.

The sky reaches in through screen doors and un-curtained windows and wipes color off the couches, tables, pictures, posters we've hung.

Outside the streets are quiet as disaster-areas after evacuation, more claustrophobic than inside, rank as our den is with heat and sleepy shiftings.

People think of us as energetic, active, violent. At any time, though, a third of us are asleep and half have not been out of the nest for two, three, four days (it is seldom noisey here; as seldom silent); we nestle in the word-web that spins, phatically, on and on, sifting our meaning and meanings, insights and emotions, thin as what drifts the gritty sky.

Very far ahead was a working nightlight. (Thinking: There's going to be a riot! With Fenster shot, the blacks are going to be out all over Jackson and there's going to be a debacle from Cumberland Park too . . .) I tried to remember which way the park exit was.

In all the trees around the leaves were loud as jets.

I thought of turning on my lights, but I didn't. Instead, I got off the path—stumbled, nearly twisted my ankle, the one I'd scraped. I climbed up some rocks where I couldn't see a thing; so I figured no one could see me. I sat there, wedged between stones, eyes half closed, trying to be still.

I wondered if they were waiting for me. If I did get out of the park, it would be my luck to stumble out the Cumberland exit. Where the burning was heaviest, I ran my hand around the orchid's wrist band.

Light through the leaves started me. I kneeled forward, sure it was going to be bright shields.

836

It was a bunch of people with flashlights. When they passed—I pressed myself back against the rock, and one light swept right over me, for a moment directly in my eyes beyond the branches—it was pretty easy to see that they were mostly white; and they had rifles. Two of them were very angry. Then one among them turned back and shouted: "Muriel!" (It could have been a woman calling.) The dog barked, barked again, and rushed through a wandering beam.

I closed my mouth.

And my eyes.

For a long time. A very long time. Perhaps I even fell asleep. When I opened them, my neck was stiff; so was one leg.

The sky was hazy with dawn. It was very quiet.

I got up, arms and knees sore as hell, climbed over the rocks and kept on down the other side till I came out of the trees at the edge of the clearing.

The cinderblocks on the near side of the fireplace had been pushed in.

Smoke dribbled into the air. Ashes greyed the grass.

There was no one there.

I walked to the furnace, between cans and package wrappers. On the bench was an overturned garbage carton. With my boot-toe, I scraped at some cinders. Half a dozen coals turned up red eyes which blinked, simplified, and clapped up.

"Lanya?"

They squatted to the furnace, simulatable in every break on those fenestrated, rusty fill-ins. Only for a distance in civet furrow, here hid awfully just a million savants at the pot. An open egret hung around a perch—still she could stay here any night. The honey worts and wolfling braces amazingly lined askew in weevils or along a post-hole should report.

"Lanya!"

An apple to discover? Still they should have saved around what or fixed her. Except in the underpinned white shell, here are some scabs in purple; every beach but effluvia. And they had bought us up to mix here so few concepts with the lazy drinks, had sat sober or reinstated our personal fixated intensity. Soon they cauterized what you, constancy and exegesis, were found very loose around him that we had each, without Denny explaining, fished to fascinate them, beautifully or lazily. They should have allowed her less than an alligator has an eyelid never pulled her from a quiver; terror still felt less alive.

"Lanya?"

I turned to fixative among the walkings.

Beyond the leaves, the figure moved so that I still couldn't

> *The blue envelope, barred along its edge with red and navy, is held to the bottom of the above page with yellow, bubbled Scotchtape. There are two, canceled, eight-cent stamps in the upper, right-hand corner. The postmark is illegible. The Bellona address reads:*
> Mrs. Author Richards
> The Labry Apartments (#17-E)
> 400, 36th Street
> Bellona, U.S.A.
> *The return address, written in the same hand (both in green ink):*
> Ms. Julia Harrington
> 7 Lilac Vista
> Los Angeles 6, California
> *The letter itself has either been removed, or lost.*

When I came up the stairs, her office door was closed. So I wandered from the study to the kitchen into Lanya's room and back. Finally I sat on the edge of the desk in the hall, tilted the Newboy volumes from between the statuettes, piled them beside me, and began to flip pages.

Which was funny: after five minutes I still hadn't read one whole poem, or one complete paragraph from the essays or stories. My eyes could only focus before or behind the page. That part of the brain, directly behind the eye, that refracts the jewelry of words into image, idea, or information, wouldn't work. (I even wondered a while how much of that was because I'd heard *him* speak.) The books had generated ghosts of themselves, and I couldn't read the words for their after-images. I kept picking up different volumes, hefting them, closed, on my palm, putting them down, then hefting my emptied palm again, feeling for the ghost's weight. My stomach began to hurt because I was concentrating so widely. I put them all back—first I ordered them by size, then I pulled them out again and re-ordered them by the dates on the copyright pages—and walked for a while (remember the fourth day on speed?), returning to the desk, pulling the books out again, leaving —really finding I'd wandered away just as I'd turn around to go back.

What is it around these objects that vibrates so much the objects themselves vanish? A field, cast by the name of a man, who, without my ever having read a complete work of his, the hidden machinery of my consciousness at some point decided was an artist. How comical, sad, exhausting. Why am I a victim of this magic? But for all I recognize out of me, I wonder furiously who would hold *Brass Orchids* on their hand, hefting for noumenal weight?

"Kid?" Madame Brown's body and face were sliced by the door. "You're here. Good."

"Hello." I closed the *The Charterhouse of Ballarat.* "You ready for me to come in now?"

She opened the door the rest of the way; I got off the desk.

"Yes, let's begin. I hope I didn't keep you waiting . . . ?"

"That's okay." I walked into the room.

Coming in to the dull green walls, dark wood up to the waist, a day bed with a green corduroy spread, three big leather chairs, a tall bookshelf, dark green drapes, I had to readjust my spatial model of the house: It was the biggest room on the floor and I'd never been in it.

On the wall was a swing-out display rack, like in poster shops. I walked over, started to open it, glanced at Madame Brown—

"Go ahead."

—and turned the first leaf, expecting George:

The raddled earth hung above tilted, lunar shale. On the next, a bulky astronaut stared out his half-silvered faceplate. All the pictures—I went through some dozen—were of the moon, or Mars, or the familiar faces of astronauts, necks ringed with helmet clamps—two of a younger, closer-cropped Kamp—or their polished angular equipment (the foil-wrapped module foot under which Kamp's moon-mouse had fled), plastic flags, or pale, cirrus clouds, hind-lit by exhaust-light as the rocket rose above its stanchions.

Let Kamp smirk out on our session? No, I turned to

839

a chalky scape, backed by an earth with clouds like a negative thumb-print. Or a saucepan of soured milk a moment before it boils; and went to a chair.

"Comfortable there?" Madame Brown closed the door. "You can lie down on the couch if it's easier for you to talk that way."

"No. I'd rather see you."

She smiled. "Good. And I'd rather see you." She sat in one of the other chairs at a slight angle to me, a hand on the arm, a hand in her lap. "How do you feel about talking to me?"

"A little nervous," I said. "I don't know why: I've talked to enough shrinks before. I was thinking, though, it's all right here because there aren't any mental hospitals left so you can put me away."

"Do you feel that the other doctors you talked to— perhaps the doctors you saw before you went into the hospital the first time—put you away?" She said that pretty openly, not with any sarcastic quotes around *put you away*.

But suddenly I was angry: "You don't know very much about crazy people, do you?"

"What do you want to tell me about them?"

"Look—I'm very suggestive. Labile . . . like they say. I incorporate things into my . . . reality model very quickly. Maybe too quickly. Which is what makes me crazy. But when you tell us we're sick, or treat us like we're sick, it becomes part of . . . me. Then I am." And I wanted to cry, at once, surprisingly, and a lot.

"What's the matter?"

I wanted to say: I hate you.

"Do you think I think you're crazy?"

"I don't . . . don't think you think at all!" Then I cried. It really did surprise me. I couldn't move my hands. But I lowered my head to stop what hurt in the back of my neck. Water trickled the side of my nose. Thinking: Christ, *that* was fast! and sniffing when the silence got on my nerves.

"Did you like the hospital where you were?"

"Like it . . . ?" I raised my head. "You're the one who said to me . . ." Another tear rolled. I felt cold. ". . . no, you said about learning to love the people at hand? Well there were a lot of very hurt people there, who it was very hard to learn to love, very expensive—emotionally. But I guess I did."

"Why are you crying?"

840

"Because I don't believe in magic." I sniffed again; this time something salty the size of a clam slid back out of my nasal cavity and I swallowed it. "You're a magic person, sitting there. You're sitting there because you think you can help me."

"Do you need help?"

I was angry again. But it was deep and bubbled down below things. "I don't know. I really don't. But that doesn't have anything to do with the fact that that's what you believe."

"You're angry at me."

I took a deep breath. "Not . . . really." The bubbles, one after the other, broke. I absorbed the fumes that raged. My stomach was very tight.

"It's all right if you are. You may have good reason."

"Why should . . . ?" and stopped because I could think of about ten. I said: "You're smug. You're not sympathetic. You think you understand. And you don't . . ."

"I don't understand *yet;* and I don't know whether I'll be able to. As of now, you haven't given me any reason to be sympathetic. If I'm smug, well . . . I'd rather I weren't, but I can feel some reserve in myself about getting too close to you just yet; which may be what smugness is."

"I don't think you *can* understand." I lugged both hands together in my lap and pushed them against one another. They felt numb. So did my feet.

"What do you feel like now?"

"Like not much of anything."

"Does it make you want to cry again?"

I took another breath. "No. I don't . . ." I put my head back. "I think I lost it, whatever was coming out . . ."

"Are you a very emotional person? Do you cry often?"

"That's the first crying I've done in . . . three years, maybe four . . . a long time."

She raised her eyebrow. After a moment, she said: "Then you're probably under a great deal of pressure. What kind of pressure *are* you under?"

"I think I'm going crazy. And I don't want to. I don't like it. I like life, I like living. I like what's going on around me, all of it to watch, and most of it to do. There're all sorts of people and situations around I really enjoy. And I'm at a place where I don't have to worry about all sorts of others I don't. I don't want to go nuts again. Not now."

After a moment she smiled: "I've occasionally given therapy to some rather successful business executives; lots

of money, happy families, some even without ulcers—
who've said practically the same thing in the same way. We
do know each other outside the office, and I must admit,
from what I've observed myself, and from what Lanya's
told me, I find it a little ironic; I mean that you express it
in such similar words."

"I said you wouldn't understand. I said I was afraid—
and I *am* angry—that I don't think you can."

"Tell me the symptoms of your going crazy."

"I forget things. I don't know who I am . . . I haven't
been able to remember my name for months. I wake up,
sometimes, terrified, everything in a blood-colored fog,
which begins to clear while my heart beats so loud it hurts
my chest. I've lost days, days and days out of my life. I
see things, sometimes, like people with their eyes . . ." And
I felt my back snarl with fear. Sweat rolled down the underside of one arm. "People with . . ." I closed my mouth,
so astonished I couldn't say it that I couldn't say it. I back-
tracked in my mind, looking for something I could loop
with words. "Can I . . . ?" I had to back up further; I was
looking at the multiple loops of optic chain she wore
around her neck. "Can I tell you about a . . . dream?"

"Please go right ahead."

"I dreamed that I . . . well, I was in a woods, on the
side of a mountain. The moon was shining—one moon.
And this woman, a nice looking woman, a few years older
than me, she came walking up over the rocks and through
the leaves. She was naked. And we balled, right there in
the leaves. Like that. When we were finished, she got up
and ran off through the bush—"

"—you completed making love in the dream?"

"Yes. After we came, she got up and ran off through
the woods to this cave, and told me to go inside it."

"And you obeyed her?"

"Yes. I remember that very clearly. I remember I
stepped on some leaves once, in some water; I jumped over
a crack in the cave floor. In a niche in one wall of the cave
there was a brass thing, big around as my two arms, filled
with glowing coals and little flames. I climbed this rock
edge, and I found . . ." I touched the chain across my
chest. "I dreamed I found these there." I hooked the chain
with my thumb and watched Madame Brown. "I mean it
must have been a dream; because of what happened later."
She looked more intense; a fourth line crossed her forehead. "I put them on. But when I came out, she was gone.

842

I looked for her in the woods, until I came to a moonlit road—just before, I remember, I stepped in a mud puddle. I was still trying to figure out where she'd gone when I saw her, there, in a meadow, on the other side of the road. So I started toward her, across the grass. And she turned into a tree. For some reason, in the dream, that terrified me. So I ran away, back down the road. Until I got to a highway. The rest of it is a little vague. I remember for part of it I was riding in a truck with this man with a sort of scarred-up face. Like bad pockmarks or acne. And this funny conversation about artichokes. Or maybe it wasn't really a conversation. One or the other of us just mentioned artichokes in some connection that I don't remember . . ."

"That's all?" Her fingertips came together.

"That's all," I said, while her hands parted, touched her knees. "But it was so . . . strange!"

"What made it particularly strange?"

"Well, everything happened so . . . clearly. And when this woman changed, I was so scared. I mean I was incredibly frightened. I ran away, I mean . . ."

Madame Brown crossed her legs.

Across her calf, glazed with nylon, a scratch curved down to her ankle.

She asked: "What is it?"

I tried to open my mouth, felt my face twitch.

She waited a long time.

I tried a couple more times.

My fingers were knotted together. Separating them was hard as prying lip from lip.

But I tried.

And sank backward into myself as if my eye-sockets were caves and the balls were rocketing toward the back of my skull, in rebound from the effort.

"Tell me about Lanya."

"Denny—" the cave wasn't where I lived, though— "and me, we like her a lot."

She *mmmed*. "Tell me about Denny."

"Lanya and me like him . . . a lot."

My hands came apart. I was able to move again on the chair. I looked at her leg. But it was only terror. I took a couple of breaths, smiled.

"What are you feeling?"

"Scared."

"That I disapprove of the relation between the three of you?"

843

"Huh?" That surprised me. "Why should I think you disapprove? Lanya's never said anything about you not liking it. A couple of times she's said it confused you, but like a joke. God damn, you don't disapprove of the Richards, why should you disapprove of us?"

"Well, for one thing, the Richards are a normal, healthy familly. They aren't coming to me for help; and they don't think they're going crazy."

"More power to me!" She'd catapulted me into a completely different part of my head and I'd dropped hard. I got myself together to see where I was—it had been a jolt. But this anger was very easy to make words: "You disapprove of people who come to you for help?"

"Now, that's not what I—"

"Jesus Christ! Hey, what do you—" I leaned forward —"what do *you* think of the Kid? Sometimes I get the impression that's all anybody around here ever does— though I'm sure I'm just flattering myself. Tell me."

She joined fingertips, raised eyebrows; suddenly she asked: "What do you think of the Richards, Kid?"

''I don't know . . .'' Then I said: "She's frightening. I mean she spends all that energy keeping up a delusional system that just won't hold. But that's sort of heroic, too. Him? He's despicable. He paid for all the props; the system is set up to his specifications, and all to his profit." Then I asked: "Do they even know you're black?"

''Yes. Of

Lanya surprises me once more: The whole nest out in the yard, and she asks, "Hey, how come Kid is the head scorpion in this nest? I mean Nightmare was before, and then Kid. I would have thought you'd have a black running things."

"Yeah," Tarzan says. "Me too." While everybody else looks like they'd never thought anything of the kind. But I have; so I waited.

Finally Glass laughs: "Well, of course Nightmare was sharing it with Dragon Lady. But I think more or less everybody has got it in their head that after one of these runs or other, the shit is gonna come down. Hard. When it does, you gonna see some niggers fade in the night like nobody's business. But the chief scorpion, maybe, ain't gonna be able to fade quite so fast. So that if this dumb-ass white mother-fucker—" Glass put his arm around my shoulder and gave me a big grin. "—wants to stick around here and play superman, ain't no nigger with any sense gonna stand in his way. I mean the guy in charge is the one who gets zapped. At least, that's the way it works anyplace else . . ." Glass squints up at the sky.

Copperhead seemed to think it was funnier than anybody else.

course they do."

"I'm sur-
prised."

"I suspect a
lot of things
would surprise
you, even about
the Richards."

"Do they
know you're
gay?"

Madame

Fireball said: "He's white? I didn't know
that. He's darker than I am!"

"Man," Glass said, "the Kid is an Indian."

"Now I didn't know he was white," Fireball repeated. "He' crazy as a nigger."

Tarzan gave me a smile that dribbled
strychnine.

"An' he sure likes his little blond brothers
and sisters." Fireball (whose spade accent,
more than any one else's, comes on and off
for the occasion) pointed to Lanya and Denny.
(Denny laughed.) "The Kid is really something
else, man. Really something." (Lanya was
pensive.)

Brown moved in the chair and *Mmm*ed again, negatively.
"Let me see," she said after a moment: "Black, lesbian,
I'm also very middle class. And Mary and Author are my
friends. But I wish sometimes I didn't think you were so
right. It would make my life much easier. But then, I've
never particularly wanted an easy life, really." She sighed.
"I do find this in myself, Kid: When I occasionally get exasperated with Author or Mary, especially when they're going on about you, I wonder to myself—quite honestly
—what they would say if I told them some of the things
you've actually done—just for the upset it would cause. At
that point, I tell myself it's because I 'approve' of you and
don't 'approve' of them."

"If you wanted to upset them, you could tell them
some things about June, about Bobby and . . . what's his
name? Eddie."

"Of course, you side with the youngsters—"

"No," I said. "I'm nearly thirty years old. And I
wouldn't swear to which side of it I'm on, from what some
people tell me. I'm not taking sides; I'm just pointing out
some upsetting areas in their life that are a little closer to
home."

"To the Richards's home. What about yours?"

"You were going to tell me what you thought about
the Kid. Maybe you'll tromp on something and I'll twitch
for you."

"All right. I think . . ."

I looked at her leg.

". . . you are very disturbed. You are personable, intelligent, forceful, vital, talented. But your basic ego structure is about as stable as a cracked teacup. You say you've
lost bits and pieces of yourself? I think that's *exactly* what's

happened. The point is, Kid, we still don't treat the mentally ill as though they were just sick. We treat them as though they were some strange combination of unclean, depraved, and evil. You know, the first mental hospitals in Europe were leprosaria, deserted all over the continent at the end of the middle ages because—for some reason we still don't know—there was a spontaneous remission in the disease over about seventy-five years, though it had been endemic for the last three thousand. Was it rising hygiene standards? A mutation in the germ? The point is that till then, though they had occasionally been shipped about on local rivers, the insane had *never* been hospitalized before. But when they were suddenly confined in these immense, empty buildings that, in some cases for hundreds of years, had held lepers, they took on as well the burden of three thousand years of superstition and fear connected with that unfortunate disease. And a good argument can be made that that's still more or less how we regard you today— complete with religious connotations. Mental illness is still seen as a scourge of the Lord. Freud and his offspring turned it into a much more sophisticated scourge. But even for him it is essentially a state of distress resulting from how you have lived your life and how your parents have lived theirs. And that is biblical leprosy, *not* the common cold. Tell me, what would you say to the idea that all your problems—the hallucinations, the depressions, even the moments of ecstasy—were biogenic? That the lapses of memory are an RNA depletion in the lower cortex; that the sudden fears are adrenal disruptions caused by random pituitary spasms; that the unreality that plagues you is merely a pineal cyst, inhibiting the production of serotonin?"

I looked up on the moonscape where there were no trees.

"That's sure as hell what it feels like," I said.

"Then, you differ from the businessmen, in that they are usually rather reluctant to give up any of the extra-biological significance of their symptoms. The over-determined human mind would rather have everything relevant, even if the relevance is simple-minded."

"When I was in the hospital—" remembering, I smiled —"I used to have a friend who'd say: 'When you're paranoid, everything makes sense.' But that's not quite it. It's that all sorts of things you know *don't* relate suddenly have the air of things that *do*. Everything you look at seems just

an inch away from its place in a perfectly clear pattern."
Once more I looked at her leg. "Only you *never* know
which inch to move it . . ." I felt my face wrinkling over
my skull with concentration.

She said: "Your dream. Can you think why you particularly wanted to tell me about it?"

I looked at my lap; "I don't know. I've just had it on
my mind a long time."

"You mean it isn't a recent dream?"

"Oh, no. I had it . . . I don't remember when; while I
was still staying in the . . . park?"

"And it isn't a recurrent dream?"

"No. I only had it once. But it . . . I just keep thinking
about it."

One hand at her necklace, she fingered a lens. "I
asked you this before, but I want to check: In the dream,
you made love, had an orgasm, and then went to the cave.
It wasn't just a heavy necking session?"

"No. She came first. I remember it surprised me, because I was just about ready myself. I finished up about
thirty seconds after she did—which is unusual with me.
Usually it takes me a couple of minutes longer. When I shot
my load, leaves blew against my side. And I opened my
eyes and we talked for a while."

Madame Brown mulled, a glass bead pressed to her
chin. "I was on a research team that did a study some years
ago—dirty old lady that I am—about sex dreams. We had,
admittedly, a small sampling—two hundred and thirty-nine;
they'd all checked yes to the question: whether they felt
they had satisfactory sexual outlet. We had men, women, a
few late adolescents; some homosexuals, of both sexes. One
overwhelmingly consistent pattern was that when sex, in a
dream, led to actual orgasm, either the dream ended or
the subject awoke. Of course there was nothing conclusive
about the study, and I can make a list of biasing factors
an ell long. But yours is the *first* dream I've ever encountered, during or since the study, where orgasm was
achieved and the dream continued." She looked at me like
she was waiting for a confession.

"What am I supposed to say?"

"Anything that comes to mind."

"You think I didn't have the dream? You think I'm
lying, or that maybe the dream was . . ." I hunched my
shoulders and felt silly. "I don't know . . ."

"You want me to suggest it *wasn't* a dream? That it

was real?" She gave a sudden, small frown. "Yes, you *do*, don't you? Well, I can understand that—if it seemed real to you." Underlying her frown was a slight and slightly sad smile. "But it *was* a dream, Kid. Because . . ." She paused; and I wondered what moons and suns returned to devil her memory. "Well, let's assume it wasn't. Would you like to discuss it further? What's the first thing that comes to mind?"

"I'm frightened, all of a sudden," I said. "Again."

"Of what?"

"Of you." I tried a smile and felt it abort deep in the muscles of my face.

"What about me frightens you?"

I looked at her scarred leg. I looked at the bead she rubbed against her chin. (I remembered what she had said, when I first met her, about them; I remembered what Nightmare had said. What Nightmare had said made more sense. But I want to believe her. Doesn't that count for something?) "I don't . . . I can't . . ." I began to cry again. And I couldn't stop this time. At all. "It's got to be a dream! It's got to . . ." Could she hear it for my sobbing? "If it isn't a dream, then I . . . I'm crazy!" And I cried about all the things people can not understand when other people say them. I cried over the miracle that they could understand any-thing at all. I cried for all the things I had said to other people that had been misunderstood because I, not knowing, had said them wrong. I cried with joy about those times when someone and I had nodded together, grinning over an understanding, real or wished for. A couple of times I managed to choke out; ''I'm so

Denny's circumcised; I'm not. After we all made it this afternoon, he sat wedged in the loft corner and kept asking Lanya which kind of dick she liked more: ". . . one that's still got curtains or one that's been cut?"

"It doesn't make any difference to me." She sat cross-legged with my feet in her lap, playing with my toes.

"But which do you think is sexier?"

"I don't think it matters. They both feel the same."

"But don't you think one looks better?"

"No. I don't."

"But they are different; so you have to feel different about them. Which one . . . ?" and on and on till I got board lying there listening.

To stop it, I asked him: "Look, which one do you like more?"

"Oh. Well, I guess . . ." He leaned forward, hunching his shoulders. "The one that's still got it all there . . . like yours, is better."

"Oh," Lanya said, with a puzzled look as

848

frightened . . . I'm so frightened! I'm so alone!'' I pushed my fingers into my mouth to stop the sound,

though she'd suddenly understood something. About him.

"Yeah." Denny grinned, came out of his corner, and lay down with his head on my lap.

Lanya nodded, swung out from under my legs, and lay down with her head on Denny's lap. I put my feet in hers.

rocking forward and back, bit on them, and couldn't stop.

Madame Brown brought me Kleenex. I blubbered, "Thank you," too inarticulate to be understood, and cried in despair that I could not even make that clear. I wandered back far enough in the cave to think, "This has *got* to be good for something," but climbed up the rocks where she told me to go, in the orange flicker, and didn't find anything there, so got scared again and cried and rocked in my seat, the pits above my kneecaps hurting, which is the place that hurts when I want to fuck bad, and kept crying and biting the sides of my hands for what seemed hours but was probably only fifteen, twenty minutes.

And it lessened; I felt weaker, better, and when I quieted, Madame Brown said: "You know, you asked me what I think of you? On the strength of the amnesia, the anxiety attacks, yes, that alone would make me suggest, if we were someplace else, that you go into a hospital. But as you say, there aren't any mental hospitals in Bellona any more. And, frankly, I don't know quite what they'd do for you if you went. It might take some of the pressure off you of being 'the Kid'. Perhaps that would allow some things to heal that are wounded, some things to settle in place that are swollen."

I nodded as though I was considering what she said—which wasn't what I was doing at all. "Do you . . ." I asked. "Do you believe . . . in my dream?"

"Pardon me?"

"Do you believe I had that dream?"

She looked confused. "I'm not sure what you mean. But . . . don't you?"

"Yes," I said. "Oh, Jesus Christ I do! I . . . I believe it was a . . . I had that dream." And realized there was a whole well of anguish from which only a single cup had been dipped. She hadn't understood. But that was all right.

Over her face was a mask of compassion: "Kid, there was nothing in the study to say that it couldn't happen the way you said. You remember it very clearly, and told all the details. Yes, *I* believe it was a dream. I don't know

849

whether or not you do, but it's probably not a bad idea for you keep trying."

Over mine was a mask of relief: "Madame Brown," I said, "I am *not* going back into a mental hospital. The place I was in, for a leprosarium, was pretty nice. But I think I'd have to be crazy to go into one again. And you can read that any way you want!"

That made her laugh. "Though, in Bellona, the problem would be if you *wanted* to go in a hospital." Suddenly she cocked her head the other way. "Do you know why I offered you that job with the Richards, the morning I met you in the park?"

"You said it had something to do with——" I put two fingers on the optic chain across my chest—"these."

"Did I . . . ?" Her smile turned inward, became preoccupied. "Yes, I suppose I did." She blinked, looked at me. "I told you the story of what happened at the hospital, with my friend, that night—I mean the night it all . . ."

"Yeah." I nodded.

"There was one point when I was coming down the third floor corridor and my friend was at the other end, trying to open one of the doors. A young, male patient was helping her, who . . . what shall I say? Looked very much like you. I mean I was only with him for perhaps a minute. He was working very hard, trying to pry back this locked door with a piece of wood or metal—he had done something terrible to his hands. His hands were much smaller than yours; and the bandages had come loose from two of his fingers." She grimaced. "But then some people needed help at the other end of the hall and he went off with them. I'd never seen him before—well, I was usually in the office. More sadly, I never saw him again. But when —how much later?—I saw you, in Teddy's, that night with your face cut, then again, wandering around the park the next morning, barefoot, with your shirt hanging open, the resemblance struck me immediately. For a moment I thought you *were* the same person. And you'd helped us; so I wanted to help you——" She laughed. "So you see these——" she touched her own beads—"these really meant . . . nothing."

I frowned. "You think maybe I'm . . . I was in the hospital *here?* That I never came here, from somewhere else? That I've been here all the——"

"Of course not." Madame Brown looked surprised. "I

said the young man looked something *like* you; he had something of your carriage, especially at a distance. He was about your size and coloring—maybe even a little smaller. And I'm sure his hair was dark brown, not black—though this was all at night, by lights coming in the windows. I think, when he went away, someone—one of the other patients—called to him by name: I don't remember what it was, now." Her hands fell to her lap. "But that, anyway, is the real reason I offered you the job. I don't know why, but I thought it might be a good time to clear that up."

"I haven't always been here," I said. "I came here, over the bridge, over the river. And soon I'm going to leave. With Lanya and Denny . . ." It had felt very important to say.

"Of course," Madame Brown said; but looked puzzled. "We all have to go on from where we are. And of course we've all come from where we've been. Certainly, at *some* point, you must have come here. More important, though, is not to get trapped in some circle of your own, habitual—" Outside, the dog barked. "Oh, that must be my next patient," Madame Brown interrupted herself. The dog barked, kept barking.

Madame Brown frowned, half rose from the chair, one hand again absently at her beads. "Muriel!" she called; her voice was loud and low. "Muriel!"

It must have been something in the juxtaposition: the chains of lenses and prisms, or perhaps that she had said the beads meant nothing convinced me I was about to learn their *real* meaning; not that I *was* the person in the hospital but that somehow I or he . . . or that *way* she called the dog made me try to remember some place or some time when she, or someone else, had called it; not even *my* name, but possibly some other, if I could recall it—each element seemed about to explain the others, clearing the pattern; and that scratch . . . I got chills. I was being nudged, pushed, about to be reminded of . . . what? Anything more than the vast abysms of all our ignorances? Whatever, it was vastly sinister and breathlessly freeing. But I did *not* know; and that mystic ignorance wrung me out with gooseflesh.

"Well," Madame Brown was saying. "Our time is about up. And I'm pretty sure that's my next patient."

"Okay." I felt relieved too, somehow. "Hey, thanks a lot."

"Would you like to arrange another—"

"No. Thanks, no, I don't want to come back."

"All right." She stood up and considered saying something: Which, I guess, was: "Kid, please don't think I'm smug. About you, or about any of the things we've talked about. I may not understand. But it's not from not caring."

I smiled. The gooseflesh rolled on—"I don't think you're smug—" and rolled away. "But I knew I wasn't going to come here more than once—as a patient. So I had to get something for my troubles. I've spent a lot of time in therapy. And you have to know how to use it." I laughed.

She smiled. "Good."

"I'll see you next time Lanya has Denny and me over for dinner—if not before. So long. Hey, if you want to talk about any of this with Lanya, go ahead."

"Oh, I wouldn't—"

"If she asks you anything, tell her what you think. Please."

She pressed her lips a moment. "All right. Then it probably will provide us with at least thirty-six hours solid conversation." She opened the door for me. "So long. I'll see . . . Oh, hello . . . I'll be with you in a few moments."

"Sure." The guy sitting on the desk corner, smiling up from the Newboy volumes, was the long-haired kid I'd seen cross-legged the night in the book-store basement, doing *Om*.

Madame Brown went back in her office and closed the door.

I went to the desk and picked up three of the books beside him. "I'm stealing these. Tell Madame Brown Lanya'll bring them back if she really wants them . . ." I was going to say more, but even that sounded silly.

"Sure. I'll tell Dr Brown as soon as I go in." Which made me wonder what he thought about me calling her "Madame". I went into the hall. As I passed Muriel, sitting on the top step, watching me with gentled eyes, I heard the office door open.

I wrote all this down because today the page with the list of names on it is missing from the notebook. When I got back to the nest from the session, I started browsing through and I couldn't find it. How many times have I read it over? I was planning to make myself read some of the Newboy. But as soon as I realized that page was gone, I suddenly felt an obsession to read it again, and began searching through the entries again and again on the chance I might have overlooked it. How many times have I read it before? (And now the only name I can remember from it is William Dhalgren.) At last, just to pull my mind away from it, I started writing out the above (and truncated) account of the hour Lanya arranged for me to have with Madame Brown, while she was off at her school. And what does it get me? The writing it down, I mean?

in their hands; the optic chain (a hundred feet? two hundred feet of it?), stretched among a dozen 'as they danced, glittered in beast light, sending flaked reflections along the undersides of leaves. Around us, they howled into the night, delighted, some going near the brazier, some going away.

Copperhead scrubbed at his mouth with his wrist. His eyes looked very red, his whole face burnished and flickering. "Hey, how do you like that?" he said. "Protection! That bastard Calkins wanted God-damn protection!" He turned from me to Glass. I laughed. Clapping perforated it. Copperhead looked up, suddenly; began to bellow and clap too, his palms hollowed. He was off rhythm so it carried a long way. He kept on bobbing his head to Glass's bobbing head, till finally he got it, though he was laughing, now. Dragon Lady, beyond the toppled furnace, one boot propped on a fallen cinderblock, kneaded her shoulder, pensive and intent, watching the dance, her jade beast momentarily out.

Lanya turned and jumped, her blue shirt mapped with sweat; she held a chain high with one hand. She moved her harmonica across her mouth with the other, blowing discord after discord. Her forehead was glazed, her hair wet down her brow.

Jommy, I guess it was, broke out between Mildred and some bird of paradise (Cathedral shouting, "Hey, watch it—"), staggering into the dazzling web, and grabbed a strand for balance. Denny's end—I jumped—broke (between mirror and prism) but he just whirled the loose length; finally looped it around somebody else's strand and held it high with both hands. An end someone else had dropped snaked and jerked through fire-lit grass. I stepped forward, grabbed it up, and dodged beneath it, jumping

853

from foot to foot and bellowing. D-t and Spider and Raven and Cathedral and Tarzan (he really can dance good as the niggers) and Jack the Ripper and Filament and Angel made a web: one strand vibrated; another went slack in catenaries between taut lengths. Gladis paused, with a fist full of green cloth over her great belly, swaying and breathing with her mouth wide. She ducked from a strand that tightened against her cheek, swung away, and began to clap.

I stopped shouting soon because my throat hurt; and heard, between the claps: "Bunny, whyn't you get in there and show 'em how it's done!"

"Don't be silly, dear! We'll just watch."

"Naw, come on! I ain't never really seen you dance."

"Smile when you say that. Why don't you?"

"Aw, come on. I wanna see what you can do."

Something in the fire exploded; sparks shot above the flame tips, showering. The myriad narrow parabolas extinguished.

Dollar, his pimpley back bright with sweat, stood centered in the clearing, feet wide, knees and head bent. Each clap detonated something in his belly that flung his hands, hips, and shoulders about.

Some of the commune kids were naked.

John danced with his brown beard up, his blond hair back, and his brass orchid waving on his hand overhead. A girl had gotten her legs caught in the chain going around, and fallen; she sat a long time, head forward, hair the color of dry leaves down across one breast. A few times she tried to stand. But another length of chain fell on her shoulder when someone dropped another end; she seemed too weighted to rise.

A griphon flickered twice: Adam bobbed and jerked. Chains and shocked hair swung and clattered and went out behind the reeling beast.

Bunny, barking shrill as a lap-dog, a dozen strands caught among up-thrust fingers, suddenly pranced forward, shaking back silver hair. Pepper, haunched behind him, followed, clapping and grinning like the devil.

An elderly black woman who'd brought some of the supper-boxes, stonely silent till now, cackled, beginning to clap too. The heavy, black-haired man with the bamboo flute had finally gotten out of his pants and danced up to her, trying to bring her into the circle. He piped and

854

bobbed and bounced around: it was pretty phoney and for a second I thought she would pinch his crank. But she got into it anyway and clapped for him—

And I stopped, landing on both heels, jarred to the scalp.

I turned in the furror, looking for someone (Thinking: Where did it come from . . . ? Why now . . . ? What . . . ? then throwing that away and just trying to hold on to it); Lanya, shirt open and flapping, breasts shaking, eyes closed under quivering lids, turned to me behind at least five chains. I reached through them and caught her shoulders.

Her eyes snapped wide.

"Michael . . ." I said.

"What?"

A chain pulled down across my arm; a prism nipped my wrist. Lady of Spain was at one end, hauling.

"Mike Henry . . ." I looked down between my elbows at the trampled grass. "Michael Henry . . . ?"

One of her bare feet moved. "What's that?"

Very slowly, I said: "My first name is Mike . . . Michael. My middle name is Henry." I looked up. "My last name—Fl . . . ? Fr . . . ?"

Lanya narrowed her eyes. Then she grabbed my forearm with the same hand her harmonica was in.

The edge bit; which brought me back: "What did I say?"

But she was looking around us, among the others. "Denny!"

"Lanya, what did I *say?*"

Her eyes snapped back to mine. She had a funny smile, intense and scared. "You said your first name was—" around us they clapped—"Michael. Your sec-one name—" they clapped again—"is Henry. And your last . . . ?"

My jaw clamped so hard my head shook. "I . . . I had it for a second! But then I . . ."

"It begins with 'F'." She called again: "Denny!"

"Wait a minute! Wait, I . . . no, I can't *remember!* But the first name—"

"—Michael Henry . . ." she prompted.

Denny ran up. "What . . . ?" He put a hand on her shoulder, a hand on mine. "Come on, you wanna—"

"Tell him, Kid!"

I dropped Lanya's elbows and took both of Denny's.

He was breathing very hard. "My name is Michael——" another clap—"Henry . . . something. I don't remember the last one now." I took a deep breath (clap!). "But two out of three is pretty good!" I must have been grinning pretty hard.

"Wow!" Denny said. He started to say a couple of other things, but finally just shrugged, grinning back.

"I don't know what to say either," I said.

Lanya hugged me. She almost knocked me over.

Denny hugged us both, getting his head between ours and wiggling it back and forth and laughing. So Lanya had to hold him up with one hand. We all staggered. I put my arm around him too. Somebody pulled a chain against my back. It either broke or one of the people holding it let go. We staggered again.

Someone put hands against my back and said: "Hey, watch it! Don't fall!" Paul Fenster—I hadn't even seen him among the spectators—was steadying me as we came apart.

Lanya said: "It's all right if we fall, Paul. It's okay."

Someone threw another length of chain into the circle. Mantichore and iguanadon caught it up, blundering together, casting ghost-lights. *Clap!*

"Hey, I like your school," Denny said. "I've been helping Lanya with her kids."

"I was telling you about Denny, Paul? He was the one who suggested we take that class trip that turned out so well."

Re-reading this single description of Paul Fenster between these soiled cardboards, this thought: Since life may end at any when, the expectation of revelation or peripity, if not identical to, is congruent with insanity. They give life meaning, but expectation of them destroys our faculty for experiencing meaning. So I am still writing out these incidents. But now I am interested in the art of incident only as it touches life . . . but I have written that at least three other places among these pages. What I haven't written is that, because of it, I am less and less interested in the incidence of art. ("Sex without guilt?" Entelechy without anticipation!) I just wonder would Paul have done anything differently that evening in the park if he'd known he was going to be shot in the head and neck four times, six hours later.

I said: "I've never seen any children there. I've heard their voices. On the tape recorder. But I don't believe you ever had any real children in there."

Lanya looked at me oddly.

Fenster laughed. "Well, you brought us five of them yourself."

"But there weren't any . . ." Inside, it felt like two disjoined surfaces had suddenly slipped flush; the relief was unbearable. "I put five of them . . . in the school?"

"Woodard, Rose, Sammy . . . ?" Lanya said.

"You remember," Denny said. "Stevie? Marceline?"

"I remember," I said. "I know who I am . . ."

"Michael Henry," Denny said.

I put my hand on Fenster's shoulder. "You go dance."

"Naw, I'm not into the bare-ass bit."

I frowned at the dancers; only fifteen or twenty were naked.

"Go on." I pushed at him; he stepped back. "You don't have to take your clothes off. You just go dance."

Fenster looked at Lanya. To stand up for him? I flashed on him pulling her shirt closed across her breasts, buttoning the top button, patting her head, and walking away.

"Go ahead." I was angry. "Dance!"

"Come on, Kid," Lanya said, taking my arm.

Fenster walked off now, laughing.

"You wanna sit down?" Denny asked.

"Come on," Lanya said. "Let's go sit down."

Denny took my other arm; but I twisted to look back.

Fenster walked between the dancers, now pushed, now helping a girl wearing just a sopping T-shirt who fell against him, now ducking beneath one of the glittering lines pulled between bright creatures prancing at the tree.

"What are you trying to do?" Lanya asked.

"Take off my clothes. I don't need anything . . . anything now." I tossed my boot on top of my vest. I lifted my chin and raised the seven chains and the projector. Links dragged my nipples. I held them up, swaying, and let go. Some hit my nose and cheek and ear. Some fell across my shoulder, and slid off, clattering, to the grass. I looked down to undo the twin hooks on my belt; pushed down my pants. Lanya held my arm so I wouldn't fall getting my foot out the cuff.

"Feel better?" Denny asked.

I tried to undo the clasp at the side of my neck. A file of insects, it felt like, charged down my belly, caught in the hair at my groin. The optic chain sagged around my ankle.

"I think you broke it," Lanya said.

"I can fix it again," Denny said. "I got nails—"

"No," I said.

From the commune, from the nest, and from the people who'd just come to watch, they clapped and leaped beside the fire. Seven more, barking, calling, and yipping, broke from the loose ring, turned among and beneath (one very black girl jumped over) the beaded chain that crossed and crossed the clearing. The heads of beasts blown out of light like glass broke scarves of smoke; our throats tickled from the harsh air.

Three silhouetted figures, heads together, came toward me, whispering. Copperhead, center, conferred with Raven and Cathedral. Raven and Copperhead were naked. (The different curl and color of their hair, suddenly bright at the sides of their heads with the fire behind them . . .) Copperhead had his hand on Raven's shoulder.

Copperhead was saying: "Protection! Did you get that? Calkins asking for protection—?"

Cathedral said: "Scorpions don't protect nothing."

Copperhead said: "They shot out practically every God-damn window in the God-damn fucking building. Man, it was something!"

Raven asked: "They shot up Calkins's place? The sniper . . . ?"

Copperhead said: "Not *Calkins'* place! And it weren't no fuckin' sniper! It was them people back at that big store. You remember that big fuckin' apartment house Thirteen used to be in, up on the sixteenth floor? God damn, man, they shot the whole fuckin' place up, practically every God-damn window in the building!"

"Shit, man!" Cathedral shook his head. "The honkeys is bad as the niggers."

Copperhead humphed: "Protection!"

Raven laughed.

They walked away in the dark.

I watched the fire. One pants leg was still around my ankle. The optic chain, as I swayed, swayed against my calf. "I want to . . . to dance."

"Then get your foot out your pants cuff," Denny said. "You'll trip yourself." He sounded like he didn't want me to go, though.

Each *Clap!* struck something inside my skull that made a flash all its own. My ears thundered as though only inches from the drum. Each explosion left some crazy echo stuttering in the tattered noise. I stepped forward, moiling my genitals in my hand. They felt sensitive. I stepped again.

"Watch it—"

Lanya must have held my pants leg down with her foot, because they came off. I stumbled, but kept going. Toward the dance.

In a black turtleneck sweater he stood, with folded arms, among the spectators. He didn't see me looking at him. But Lady of Spain and D-t and a couple of others did and stopped dancing. Prisms and lenses hung down from my neck. Mirrors and prisms swung from my wrist. Lenses and mirrors dragged from my ankle behind me in the grass.

He shifted a little. Firelight shook its patina across his brown hair.

"Hey . . . !" I said loudly. "I know who I . . . who I am now. Who are you?"

He looked at me, frowning.

"Who are *you?*" I repeated. "Tell me. I know who *I* am!" A few more dancers stopped to listen. But the clapping was still awfully loud. I shook my head. "Almost . . ."

"Kid?" he asked; it had taken him until then to recognize me, naked. "Hey, Kid! How're you doing?"

It was the man who'd interviewed me at Calkins' party.

"No," I said. "I *know* who *I* am. You say who *you* are."

"William . . ." he began. "Bill . . . ?" And then: "You don't remember me?"

"I remember you. I just want to know who you *are!*"

"Bill," he repeated. And nodded, smiling.

Two people who'd stopped to listen began to clap again.

"I know that," I said. "I remember that. What's your *last* name?"

He raised his head a little. His smile—a dragon, doffing by, stained his face a momentary green—tightened: "You tell me yours, I'll tell you mine." His mouth stayed a little open, waiting for a laugh to come out.

But the laugh came from me. William . . . ? I shouted: "I know who you are!" and doubled with hysteria. "I *know* . . . !"

"Hey, Kid? Come *on* now . . ." Lanya—she and Denny had followed me—took my arm again. I tried to pull away, stumbled into the dancers' chains, and turned, flail-

859

ing my own. But she held on; Denny had me too. I yanked
once more and fell against a guy I didn't know who cried,
"Owwww!" and hugged me, laughing. I turned in a shield's
glare, bright blind a moment, and moments after images
pulsed everywhere.

"Come on, man," Denny kept saying, pulling at my
forearm. "Watch *out*—" and held up a strand of chain so
I could get under.

"That's right," Lanya said. "This way . . ."

I got dizzy and nearly fell. Fire and branches wheeled
on a black sky. I came up against bark and turned my back
to it:

"But I *know* what his name is! It has to be. He
couldn't be anybody else!" I kept telling them, then breaking off into a giggle which, when I let it go, twisted my
face in a grin so huge my jaw muscles hurt and I had to
rub them with the heels of my palms. "That's *got* to be who
he is! You understand why, don't you? I mean you *do* understand?"

They didn't.

But, for a while, I did.

And, bursting with my new knowledge, I danced.

I've never had more fun.

Then I came back and sat with them.

Denny's hand was on my knee; Lanya's shoulder was
against my shoulder, her arm along my arm. We sat on the
roots, ten feet from the high, forking fire, watching the
men and women jog and jump to the sounds of their own
bodies, one arched and beating the backs of his thighs, one
spinning slowly, and shouting loudly, each time her short
hair brushed by the sagging branch. Somebody danced
with his belt loose and swinging. And somebody else was
taking off her jeans.

Bill, arms folded across his black sweater, among the
other watchers, watched.

I sat and panted and smiled (sweat dribbling the small
of my back) with contentment over the absolute fact of his
revealed identity, till even that, as all absolutes must, began its dissolve.

"What—?" Denny moved his hand on my leg.

Lanya glanced at me, shifted her shoulder against
mine.

But I sat back again, silent, marveling the dissolve's
completion, both elated and numbed by the jarring claps

860

that measured and metronomed each differential in the change—till I had no more certainty of Bill's last name than I had of my own. With only the memory of knowledge, and bewilderment at whatever mechanic had, for minutes, made that knowledge as certain to me as my own existence, I sat, trying to sort that mechanic's failure, which had let it slip away.

Dragon Lady, with her boot, shoved in another part of the furnace's cinderblock wall, then turned to add her raucous contention to the argument behind her.

"You know," Lanya said, as somebody flung a burning brand that landed on the edge of the dish, flame end on the grass, "this place isn't going to be here tomorrow."

"That's all right," Denny said.

Lanya pushed back against me harder, drew up her knees to hug.

The dance was all around us. The battered grass was tangled with chains, plain and jeweled. Most of the scorpions blazed up, incendiar-

up to bring the brandy, that afternoon, to Tak's place—I apologized about opening one of the bottles—he really looked surprised.

He came out of the shed doorway onto the roof, scratching his chest and his chin and still half asleep. But saying he was glad to see us.

Denny climbed onto the balustrade to walk, hands out for balance, along the roof's edge. Lanya kept running up and going, "Boo!" at him as though she were trying to make him fall off. I thought it was funny, but Tak said please stop it because it was eight stories down and scaring him into a stomach ache.

So they came back to the shack.

Denny went inside: "Look what Tak's got on the wall!"

Thought he meant George, but it was the interview with me from Calkins's party in the *Times*. Tak had stapled it to the wall just inside the door. The edges were yellow.

"I keep that there," Tak said, "for inspiration. I sort of like it. Glad to see, after all this, the papers says you're having another book."

"Yeah," I said. "Sure. Thanks." I really didn't want

to talk about it. It got across, because he was looking at me a little sideways. But Tak is good at picking up on things like that.

Around us, the sky was close as crumpled lead. The first stanchion of the bridge was just visible through it, like a single wing of some dim bird that might, in a moment, fly anywhere.

Tak pulled the cork out of the open bottle. "Come on. Let's have a drink." He squatted, his back against the shack wall. We sat next to him. Denny took a swallow, screwed up his face, and from then on just passed it between Lanya and me.

"Tak," I said, "could you tell me something?" I asked him about the bubbles around the inside of the glasses. "I thought it might have something to do with the water pressure for the city. Maybe it's going down and that causes the ring to start higher?"

"I *think*," Tak said to the green-glass neck, "it has more to do with who washes your dishes. You're washing out a glass, see, and you run your finger around the inside to get off the crud, and it leaves this thin coating. But your finger doesn't reach the bottom. Later you put water in the glass, and the air comes out of solution to form bubbles. But the bubbles need something to nucleate on. So the imperfections in the glass and the crud left above

here any longer.

Curiosity took me, alone.

A bed had been overturned against the door but fell back clattering as soon as I pushed it in. They'd put bars up on the ground floor windows, but the panes were mostly smashed, and in the one remaining, I found three of those tiny, multi-haloed holes you get from bullets. There were a couple of sleeping bags still around. Some nice stuff was up on the walls from where they had the place decorated: and a big, almost life-size lion wedged together out of scrap car-parts and junked iron. An ascetalline bomb and nozzle leaned in the corner. ("I wonder what happend to the woman who was making that. She was Eurasian," Lanya said when I told her about it, later. "She was a pretty incredible person; I mean even besides building that thing.") The walls of two rooms were charred black. I saw a place where a poster had been burned away. And another place, where a quarter of one was left: George in the night wilderness. Upstairs I guess most of the rooms had never had doors. It was a wreck. Great pieces of plaster had been tugged off the walls. Once I heard what I thought was moaning, but when I rushed into the smashed up room—tools were scattered all over the floor, screwdrivers, nails, pliers, wrenches—it wasn't a

the grease line are easier to nucleate on; so you get this definite cutoff—"

"You mean," I said, "the dishwasher sticks his finger less and less far down the glass every day?"

Tak laughed and nodded "Aren't you glad you know some one with some idea of technology? Rising water

creaking shutter or anything. I don't know what it was. Bolted to the wall was a plank on which they had carved their initials, names, phrases, some written in fancy combinations of collored magic markers, others scrawled in plack pentel. Near the bottom, cut clearly with some small blade: June R. Danya says she'll have to find some abandoned drugstore or someplace to get birthcontrol pills now, in the next three months. Denny is worried about his little girl-friend. He says she was sick the last time he was over there," . . . with a fever, man. And every thing. She wouldn't hardly move, under the blankets." No one at the commune, or the bar, or the church—neither George nor Reverend Amy—know where they all went or even what really happened. But if someone would do that to the House, I just wonder about the nest. Was the blond girl they described June? I guess I hope so.

tables, lowering pressure. You could get paranoid over stuff like that if you don't know what you're doing."

"Yeah," and I took the bottle and drank.

And over the next fifteen seconds, the afternoon sky, dull as an aluminum pot bottom, darkened to full night.

Five seconds into the darkening, Denny said, "Jesus, what—?" and stood up.

There was a noise like a plane coming. It kept coming too, while I watched Denny's features go night blue.

Lanya grabbed my arm, and I turned to see her blue face, and all around it, go black.

If it was a plane, it was going to crash into us.

I jerked my head around left and right and up (hit the back of my head on the wall) and down, trying to see.

Another sound, under the roar, beside me: Tak standing?

Something wet my hand on the tar-paper beside me. He must have kicked over the brandy.

White light suddenly blotched the horizon, cut by the silhouette of a water tower.

I didn't feel scared, but my heart was beating so slow and hard my chin jerked, each thump.

Light wound up the sky.

I could just see Tak standing now, beside me. His shadow sharpened on the tar-paper wall.

The sound . . . curdled!

The light split. Each arm zigged and zagged, separate, ragged-edged and magnesium bright. The right arm split again. The left one was almost directly above us.

And Tak had no shadow at all. I stood up, helped Lanya to . . .

Some of the light flickered out. More came. And more.

But what is . . . ?" she whispered right at my ear, pointing. From the horizon, another light ribboned, ragged, across the sky.

"Is it . . . lightning?" Denny shouted.

"It looks light lightning!" Tak shouted back.

Someone else said: " 'Cause George don't shine that bright!"

Tak's bleached face twisted as if beat by rain. The air was dry. Then I noticed how cool it was.

Nodes in the discharge were too bright to look at. Clouds—sable, lead, or steel—mounded about the sky, making canyons, cliffs, ravines, for lightning it was too slow, too wide, too big!

Was that thunder? It roared like a jet squadron buzzing the city, and sometimes one would crash or something, and Lanya's face would

Here one page, possibly two, is missing.

Don't remember who had the idea, but during the altercation, for a while I argued: "But what about Madame Brown? Besides, I like it here. What are we going to do when you're at school? Your bed's okay for a night, but we can't all sleep there that long."

Lanya, after answering these sanely, said: "Look, try it. Denny wants to come. The nest can get along without you for a few days. Maybe it'll do your writing some good." Then she picked up the paper that had fallen behind the Harly, climbed over it, came out from under the loft, tip-toed with her head up and kissed me. And put the paper in her blouse pocket—bending over, it had pulled out all around her jeans.

I pushed myself to the loft edge, swung my legs over, and dropped. "Okay."

So Denny and I spent what I call three

as loud as I could: "Lanya! Denny!" If they answered, I couldn't hear; and I was hoarse from shouting. The street sign chattered in its holder—the wind had grown that strong.

I took another half dozen steps, my bare foot on the curb, my boot in the gutter. Dust fits

864

days and she calls one ("You come in the evening, spent the night and the next day, then left the following morning! That's one full day, with tag ends." "That should at least count for two," I said. "It seemed like a long time . . .") which wasn't so bad but . . . I don't know.

The first night Madame Brown put supper together out of cans with Denny saying all through: "You wanna let me do something . . .? Are you sure I can't do nothin'. . . ? Here, I'll do . . ." and finally did wash some pans and dishes.

I asked, "What are you making?" but they didn't hear so I sat in the chair by the table alternately tapping the chair-back on the wall and the front legs on the floor; and drank two glasses of wine.

Lanya came in and asked why I was so quiet.

I said: "Mulling."

"On a poem?" Madame Brown asked.

We ate. After dinner we all sat around and drank more, me a little more than the others, but Madame Brown and I actually talked about some things: her work, what went on in a scorpion run ("You make it sound so healthy, I mean like a class trip, I'm not so sure that I like the idea as much now. It sounded very exciting before you told me anything about it."), the problems of doctors in the city, George. I like her. And she's smart as hell.

Back in Lanya's room, I sat at the desk in the bay window, looking at my notebook. Lanya and Denny went to bed ("No, the light won't bother us."), and after about fifteen minutes, I joined them and we made cramped, langerous love which had this odd, let's-take-turns thing about it; but it was a trip. I nearly knocked over the big plant pot by the bed four times.

I woke before the window had lightened, got up and prowled the house. In the kitchen, considered getting drunk. Made myself a cup of instant coffee instead, drank half, and prowled some more. Looked back into Lanya's room: Denny was asleep against the wall. Lanya was on her back, eyes opened. She smiled at me.

hit my face. My shadow staggered around me on the pavement, sharpening, blurring, tripling.

People were coming down the street, while the darkness flared behind them.

That slow, crazy lightning rolled under the sky.

The group milled toward me; some dodged forward.

One front figure supported another, who seemed hurt. I got it in my head it was the commune: John and Mildred leading, and something had happened to John. A brightening among the clouds—

They were thirty feet nearer than I'd thought:

George, looking around at the sky, big lips a wet cave around his teeth's glimmer, his pupils underringed with white, and glare flaking on his wet,

I was naked.

"Restless?"

"Yeah." I came over, squatted by the bed, hugged her.

"Go ahead. Pace some more. I need another couple of hours." She turned over. I took up the old notebook here, sat around cross-legged on the floor, contemplating writing down what had happened till then.

Or a poem.

Did neither.

Looked in the top desk drawer—the wood looks like paper had been glued all over it and then as much pulled off as possible. She said some friends lugged it from a burned-out windshield warehouse a few blocks down the hill.

I took out the poems she'd saved, spread them on the gritty wood, on every kind of paper, creased this way and that (red-tufted begonia stalks doffed), and tried to read them.

Couldn't.

Thought seriously of tearing them up.

Didn't.

But understood much about people who have.

Looked back at Lanya; bare shoulders, the back of her neck, a fist sticking from under the pillow.

Prowled some more.

Got back into bed.

Denny jerked his head up, blinking. He didn't know where he was. I rubbed the back of his neck and whispered, "It's okay, boy . . ." He settled back down, nuzzling into Lanya's armpit. She turned away from him toward me.

I woke alone.

Leaves arched over me. I looked up through them. Blew once to see if they'd move, but they were too far. Closed my eyes.

"Hey," Denny said. "You still asleep?"

I opened my eyes. "Fuck you if I was."

"I just walked Lanya over to school." He leaned against the edge of the doorway, holding his chains. "It's nice around here, huh?"

I sat up on the side of the bed.

"But there ain't too much to do . . . it's nice of her to have us over here, I mean to stay a while, huh?"

I nodded.

veined temples, supported Reverend Tayler; she leaned forward (crying? laughing? cringing from the light? searching the ground?), her hair rough as shale, her knuckles and the backs of her nails darker than the skin between.

The freckled, brick-haired Negress, among darker faces, walked behind them; with the blind-mute; and the blond Mexican.

Someone was shouting, among others shouting: "You hear them planes? You hear all them planes?" (It couldn't have been planes.) "Them planes are awfully low! They gonna crash! You hear—" at which point the building face across the street cracked, all up and down, and bellied out so slow I wondered how. Cornices, coping stones, window

866

About two hours later he told me he was going out. I spent the rest of the morning staring at blank paper or prowling.

Madame Brown, coming out of her office, saw me once and said: "You look strange. Is anything the matter?"

"No."

"Are you just bored?"

"No," I said. "I'm not bored at all. I'm thinking a lot."

"Can you leave off long enough for a lunch break?"

"Sure." I hadn't had breakfast.

Tunafish salad.

Canned pears.

We both had a couple of glasses of wine. She asked me for my character impressions of: Tak, Lanya, Denny, one of her patients I had met at the bar once; I told her and she thought what I said was interesting; told me hers, which I thought were interesting too, and they changed mine; so I told her the changes. Then the next patient came by and I went back to staring at my paper; prowling; staring.

Which is what I was doing when Lanya and Denny came in. He'd gone back to the school to help out with the class.

"Denny suggested we go on a class trip, outside to look at the city. We did. It turned out to be a fine idea. With two of us we didn't have any problem handling them. That was a good idea, Denny. It really was." Then she asked if I'd written anything.

"Nope."

"You look strange," she told me.

Denny said: "No he don't. He just gets like that sometimes."

Lanya Mmmmed. She knows me better than he does, I guess.

Denny was really into being useful—a trait which, pleasant as he is, I've never seen in him before. I helped them do a couple of things for Madame Brown: explore the cellar, take one chair down, bring up a dresser she'd found on the street and managed to get to the back door.

It was a nice evening.

I wondered if I was spoiling it by sug-

frames, glass and brick hurled across the street.

They scream-ed—I could hear it over the explosion because some were right around me—and ran against the near wall, taking me with them and I crashed into the people in front of me, wind knocked out of me by the people behind, screaming; some-one reached over my shoulder for support, right by my ear, and near-ly tore it off. More people (or some-thing?) hit the people behind me, hard.

Coughing and scrambling, I turned to push someone from be-hind me. Across the street, girders, scabby with brick and plaster, tesse-lated luminous dust. I staggered from the wall among the stag-gering crowd and stumbled into a big woman on her hands and knees, shaking her head.

gesting: "Maybe we should go back to the nest tonight?"

Lanya said: "No. You should use some of this boring peace and quiet to work it."

"I'm not bored," I said. And resolved to sit in front of a piece of paper for at least an hour. Which I did: wrote nothing. But my brain bubbled and bobbed and rotated in my skull like a boiling egg.

When I finally went to bed I fell out like an old married man.

One of them or the other got up in the night to take a leak, came back to bed brushing aside the plants and we balled, hard and a little loud I think.

In the morning we all got up together.

I noticed Lanya noticing me being quiet. She noticed my noticing and laughed.

After coffee we all walked to the school. Denny asked to stick around for the class. Now I noticed her wondering if two days in a row was a good idea. But she said, "Sure," and I left them and went back to the house, stopping once to wonder if I should go back to the nest instead.

Madame Brown and I had lunch again.

"How are you enjoying your visit?"

"Still thinking a lot," I told her. "But also think all the thinking is about to knock me out."

"Your poetry?"

"Haven't written a word. I guess it's just hard for me to write around here."

"Lanya said you weren't writing too much at your place, either. She said she thought there were too many people around."

"I don't think that's the reason."

We talked some more.

Then I came to a decision: "I'm going back to the nest. Tell Lanya and Denny when they get back, will you?"

"All right." She looked at me dubiously over a soup spoon puddled with Cross & Blackwell vischysoise. "Don't you want to wait and tell them yourself when they get back?"

I poured another glass of wine. "No."

When the next patient rang, I took my notebook and wandered (for five, funny min-

I tried to pull her up, but she got back down on her knees again.

What she was trying to do, I realized, was roll a pile of number ten tomato- and pineapple-juice cans and crumpled cookie packages back into her overturned shopping bag. Her black coat spread around her over crumbs of brick.

One can rolled against my foot. It was empty.

She began to go down, even further, laying her cheek on the pavement, reaching among the jangling cans. I bent to pull her once more. Then someone, yanking her from the other side, shouted, "Come on!" (*Cŭm ōhn!* the vowels, long and short, braying: the *m* soft as an *n;* the *n* loose as an *r.*) I looked up without letting go. It was George.

utes, midway, I thought I was lost) back to the nest.

Tarzan and the apes, all over the steps, were pretty glad to see me. Priest, California, and Cathedral did a great back-slapping routine down the hall. Glass nodded, friendly but overtly non-commital. And I had a clear thought: If I left, Glass, not Copperhead, would become leader.

I climbed up into the loft, told Devestation's friend Mike to move his ass the hell over.

"Oh, yeah, Kid. Sure, I'm sorry. I'll get down—"

"You can stay," I said. "Just move over." Then I stretched out with my notebook under my shoulder and fell asleep, splat!

Woke up loggy but clutching for my pen. Took some blue paper to the back steps, put the pine plank across my knees and wrote and wrote and wrote.

Went back into the kitchen for some water.

Lanya and Denny were there.

"Hi."

"Oh, hi."

Went back to the porch and wrote some more. Finally it was

She came up between us, screaming: "Ahh-hhhhhhhh— *An-nnnnn!* Don't touch me! *Ahhh-hhhhhh*—don't *touch* me, nigger"! She staggered and reeled in our grip. I didn't see her look at either of us. "Ahhhhh—I *saw* what you done!— that poor little white girl what couldn't do nothin' against you! We *saw* it! We *all* saw it! She come lookin' for you, askin' all around, askin' everybody where you are all

the time, and now you take her, take her like that, just take her like you done! And see what's happened! Now, see! Oh, God, oh help me, don't touch me, oh, God!"

"Aw, come *on!*" George shouted again as once more she started to collapse. He pulled again; she came loose from my grip. The coat stung my hands. As I dodged away, she was still shrieking:

"Them white people gonna get you, nigger! Them white men gonna kill us all 'cause of what you done today to that poor little white girl! You done smashed up the store windows, broke all the streetlights, climbed up and pulled the hands down from the clock! You been rapin' and lootin' and all them things! Oh, God, there's gonna be shootin' and burnin' and blood shed all over! They gonna shoot up everything in Jackson. Oh, God, oh, *God,* don't touch me!"

"Will you shut up, woman, and pick up your damn junk," George said.

Which, when I looked back, seconds later, was what she was doing.

George, ten feet off, squatted to haul up a slab of rubble that rained plaster from both sides, while another woman tugged at a figure struggling beneath. A handful of gravel hit my shoulder from somewhere and I ducked forward.

Ahead of me, turning and turning in the silvered wreckage, Reverend Amy squinted up, fists moving about her ears, till her fingers jerked wide; the up-tilted face was scored with what I thought rage; but it swung again and I saw that the expression struggling with her features was nearer ecstasy.

I climbed over fallen brick. The orchid rolled and bounced on my belly.

The blind-mute was sitting on the curb near the hydrant. The blond Mexican and the brick-haired Negress squatted on either side. She held his hand, pressing her fist, the fingers rearranged and rearranged, at each contact, against his palm.

I reached among my chains, found the projector ball, and fingered the bottom pip.

The disk of blue light slid up the rubbly curb as I stepped to the sidewalk.

They looked up, two with eyes scarlet as blood-bubbles.

The mute's sockets (he poked his head about) were like empty cups dregged with shadow.

There was a sudden stinging in my throat from the smoke; smoke blew away. I shouted: "What are you doing?"

The Mexican dragged his boots back against the curb. The woman put her other hand on the mute's shoulder.

I watched their movements of surprise. Translated to their hands on the blind-mute's arms, it gave him his only knowledge of me. His face tilted forward; his hand closed on the woman's—my knowledge of what he knew. Thinking: It takes so little information . . . Though I am cased in light and their eyes orbited with plastic, in the over-determined matrix, translated and translated, perhaps his knowledge of me is even more complete.

I was frightened of their red eyes?

What does my blue beast become behind scarlet caps!
People shouted.

I shouted louder: "What's going on? What's happening? Do you *know?*" and ended coughing in more smoke.

The brick-haired Negress shook her head, a hand before her mouth, hesitant to quiet me, pinch her own lips close, or push me away. "Somebody put a bomb in . . . Didn't they? Isn't that what they said? Somebody put a—"

"No!" the Mexican said loudly. He tugged the blind-mute's shoulders. "There wasn't any—anything like that . . ." He got the blind-mute on his feet.

I turned to see men and women stumbling toward me, against the luminous mist. And something behind the mist flickered. I lurched into the street.

"There wasn't any bomb!" the man or the woman behind me shrieked. "They *shot* him! From up on the roof. Some crazy white boy! Shot him dead in the street! Oh, my God—"

Something warm splattered my ankle.

Water rolled between the humped cobbles, bright as mercury beneath the discharges on the collapsed, black sky. The street was a net of silver and I sprinted across it, catching one woman with my shoulder who spun—shouting—her scraped face after me, almost lunged into another man, but pushed off him with both hands; a sudden gust of heat stung the roofs of my eye-sockets. Lids clamped, I got through it and more dust, catching my boot-toe on something that nearly tripped me. I coughed and staggered with the back of my hand over my mouth.

Something went over the back of my neck, so cold I thought it was water. But it was just air. Eyes tearing, my throat spasming and hacking free of the dust caught in it, I staggered through it a dozen steps, till somebody grabbed me and I came up, staring at another black face.

"It's Kid!" Dragon Lady shouted to somebody and got her arm around me to keep me from falling.

A few steps behind her Glass turned around to see me. "Huh?"

Beyond him, against a screen of slowly moiling clouds, the side came off a twenty-story building, collapsing slowly away from the web of steel. But that must have been five blocks down.

"Jesus Christ . . . !" D-t said, then glanced back at me. "Kid, you all—?" and the sound got to us, filling up the space around us the way a volcano must up close.

The brunt of it past, I could hear people behind me

871

still shouting: Three different voices bawled out instructions among some fifty more who didn't care.

"God damn it!" D-t said. "Come *on!*"

Someone had strewn coils of what looked like elevator cable all over the sidewalk. It was greasy too; so after the first dozen steps across it, we went into the street.

And the shouting behind us had resolved to a single, distant, insistant voice—"You wait, God damn it! You hear me, you mother-fuckers *wait* for me!"—getting closer —"Wait for me, God damn it! Wait—!"

I looked back.

Fireball, fists pumping, bent forward from the waist and head flung back, ran full into Glass, who caught him by the arm. Fireball sagged back, gasping and crying: "You wait for me, God damn it! You damn niggers—" he sucked in a breath loud as vomiting—"why didn't you *wait!*" He was barefoot, with no shirt; a half dozen chains swung and tinkled from his neck as he bent, gasping, holding his stomach. In a pulse of light I saw he had a scrape down his jaw that went on across his shoulderblade as though something had fallen on him while he ran. His face was streaked with tears that he scrubbed with the flat of his fist. "You God damn fuckin' niggers, you *wait* for me!"

"Come on," D-t said. "You all right now."

I thought Fireball was going to fall down trying to get back his breath.

Somebody else sprinted up the street, out of the smoke. It was Spider. He looked very young, very tall, very black, very scared. Breathing hard, he asked: "Fireball okay? I thought a damn wall fell on him."

"He's okay," D-t said. "Now let's *go!*"

Fireball nodded and lurched ahead.

Glass let him go and moved beside me. His vinyl vest was hazed across with powdered plaster. "Hey," I said, "I've gotta find Lanya and Denny. They're supposed to be going back to the nest—"

"Oh, God damn, nigger!" Fireball twisted back to stare. His face was smeared filthy, and some of it was blood. "*Leave* them white mother-fuckers alone, huh? Don't you think about *nothin'* except your pecker?"

"Now *you* just get yourself together!" Dragon Lady pushed Fireball's shoulder sharply with the heel of her hand; when he jerked around, she took his arm like they were going for a stroll. "Let's you just cut this 'nigger' shit, huh? What you think *you* are, a red-headed Indian?"

Glass said: "We don't got any nest; not any more."

"They got any sense," D-t said, "they gonna be trying to get out too. Maybe we meet up with them at the bridge."

"What happened to the others?" I asked. "Raven, Tarzan, Cathedral? Lady of Spain . . . What about Baby and Adam?"

Dragon Lady didn't even look back.

"You were the last one out," D-t said to Spider. "You see 'em?"

Spider looked from D-t to me and back. "No." He looked down where he was holding onto the end of his belt with his lanky, black fingers, twisting a little.

"Maybe," Dragon Lady said, letting go Fireball's arm but still not looking back, "we gonna meet 'em." I could tell she was frowning. "On the bridge. Like he says." Or something else.

I walked another five steps, looking down at the wet pavement, feeling numbness claw at me. My fingers tingled. So did the soles of both feet. Then I looked up and said, "Well, God damn it, the bridge is *that* way!" Which is when this incredibly loud crackling started on our left.

We all looked up, turned our heads, backed away all together. Spider broke, ran a dozen steps, realized we weren't coming, and turned back to look too.

Four stories up, fire suddenly jetted from one window. The flames flapped up like yellow cloth under a bellows; sparks and glass tumbled down the brick.

Two more windows erupted. (I hit my bare heel on the far curb.) Then another—as far apart as ticks on a clock.

We ran.

Not down the way I said because that street was a-broil with smoke and flickering. At the end of another block, we turned the corner and ran down the sloping sidewalk. There was water all over one end.

D-t and me splashed into it, watching the high brick walls, and the billowing clouds between them, shatter below our feet.

Ten yards in it was up to my knees and I couldn't really run. We slushed on. Glass, arms swinging wide in a wildly swaying stagger, moved ahead of me, dragging fans of ripples from the backs of his soaked pants. Then the street started sloping up. I splashed toward the edge.

What it felt like was something immense dropped into the street a block away. Everything shook. I looked back at the others—Fireball and Dragon Lady were still splashing forward—when, in the center, was a swell of what looked like detergent bubbles. Then steam shot straight up. The water's edge rolled back from Fireball's dripping cuffs, leaving his wet feet slapping the glistening pavement.

Glass back-tracked to grab Dragon Lady's hand, like he thought she (or he) might fall.

The geyser spit and hissed and the water bubbled into it.

We went around the next corner together.

I could see the bridge all the way to the second stanchion. Here and there clouds had torn away from the black sky. Something was burning down between the waterfront buildings. We rushed across fifty feet of pavement. Just before the bridge mouth, it looked like someone had grenaded the road. A slab of asphalt practically fifteen feet high jutted up. Down the crack around it, you could see wet pipes, and below that, flickering water. Above, that amazing, loud lightning formed its searing nodes among the cloud canyons.

"Come on," I said. "This way!"

Metal steps lead up to the bridge's pedestrian walk. The first half dozen were covered with broken masonry. Glass and Dragon Lady charged right up. Plaster dust puffed out between the railing struts. Fireball stepped carefully on the first three steps, then grabbed both railings and vaulted up three more. His feet were caked with junk and he was bleeding from one ankle.

"Get goin'!" D-t crowded behind. "Get goin'!"

Spider and me went up the narrow steps practically side by side.

At the top, Spider got ahead and we ran along the clanging plates maybe fifty yards when something . . . *hit* the bridge!

We swayed back and forth a dozen feet! Metal ground against old metal. Cables danced in the dark.

I grabbed the rail, staring down at the blacktop fifteen feet below, expecting it to split over the water a hundred feet below that.

Beside me, Fireball just dropped on his knees, his cheek against the bars. Spider put his arms around the dead lamppost, bent his head and went, "Ahhhhhhhhhh . . ."

874

like he was crying with his mouth open—which, five seconds later, when the shaking and the creaking died, was the only sound. Dragon Lady swallowed, let go the rail, and took a gasping breath.

My ears were ringing.

Everything was quiet.

"Jesus God," D-t whispered, "let's get off o'—" which was when everybody, including D-t, realized *how* quiet.

Holding the rail tight, I turned to look back.

On the waterfront, flames flickered in smoke. A breeze came to brush my forehead. Here and there smoke was moving off the wind-runneled water. And there was nobody else on the bridge.

"Let's *go* . . ." I stepped around Fireball, passed by Dragon Lady.

A few seconds later, I heard Glass repeat: "Well, let's go!" Their footsteps started.

Dragon Lady caught up. "Jesus . . ." she said softly beside me. But that was all.

We kept walking.

Girders wheeled on either side. About twenty feet beyond the first stanchion, I looked back again:

The burning city squatted on weak, inverted images of its fires.

Finally D-t touched my shoulder and made a little gesture with his head. So I came on.

The double, thigh-thick suspensors swung even lower than our walkway; a few yards later they sloped up toward the top of the next stanchion.

"Who is . . . ?" Glass asked softly.

Down on the black-top, she was walking slowly toward us.

Running my hand along the rail, I watched. Then I called: "Hey, you!"

Behind me there was a flair; then another; then another. The others had flicked on their lights—which meant I was in silhouette before a clutch of dragons, hawks, and mantises.

She squinted up at us: a dark Oriental, with hair down in front of her shirt (like two black, inverted flames); red bandanas were stuffed under the shoulder straps of her knapsack for padding. Her shirttails were out of her jeans. "Huh . . . ?" She was trying to smile.

"You going into Bellona?"

"That's right." She squinted harder to see me. "You leaving?"

"Yeah," I said. "You know, it's *dangerous* in there!"

She nodded. "I'd heard they had the national guard and soldiers and stuff posted. Hitch-hiking down, though, I didn't see anybody."

"How were the rides?"

"All I saw was a pickup and a Willy's station wagon. The pickup gave me a lift."

"What about traffic going out?"

She shrugged. "I guess if somebody passes you, they'll give you a ride. Sometimes the truckers will stop for a guy to spell them on driving. I mean, guys shouldn't have too tough a time. Where're you heading?"

Over my shoulder, Glass said: "I want to get to Toronto. Two of us are heading for Alabama, though."

"I just wanted to get someplace!" Fireball said. "I don't feel right, you know? I ain't *really* felt right for two days . . . !"

"You got a long way to go, either direction," she said.

I wondered what she made of the luminous light-shapes that flanked me and threw pastel shadows behind her on the gridded black-top.

Glass asked: "Everything is still all right in Canada—?"

"—and Alabama?" asked Spider.

"Sure. Everything's all right in the rest of the country. Is anything still happening here?"

When nobody answered, she said:

"It's just the closer you get, the funnier . . . everybody acts. What's it like inside?"

D-t said: "Pretty rough."

The others laughed.

She laughed.

"But like you say," Dragon Lady said, "guys have a pretty easy time," which I don't think she got, because unless you listen hard, Dragon Lady's voice sounds like a man's.

"Is there anything you can tell me? I mean that might be helpful? Since I'm going in?"

"Yeah," I said. "Sometimes men'll come around and tear up the place you live in. Sometimes people shoot at you from the roof—that is, if the roof itself doesn't decide to fall on you. Or you're not the person on top of it, doing the shooting—"

876

"He wrote these poems," Fireball said at my other shoulder. "He wrote these poems and they published them in a book and everything! They got it all over the city. But then he wrote some more, only they came and burned them all up—" His voice shook on the fevered lip of hysteria.

"You want a weapon," I asked, "to take in with you?"

"Wow!" she said. "Is it like that?"

Glass gave a short, sharp laugh.

"Yeah," I said. "We have it easy."

Spider said: "You gonna tell her about . . . the Father? You gonna tell her about June?"

"She'll learn about those."

Glass laughed again.

D-t said: "What can you say?"

She ran her thumbs down her knapsack straps and settled her weight on one hip. She wore heavy, hiking shoes, one a lot muddier than the other. "Do I need a weapon?"

"You gonna give her that?" Dragon Lady asked as I took my orchid off its chain.

"We got ourselves in enough trouble with this," I said. "I don't want it with me any more."

"Okay," Dragon Lady said. "It's yours."

"Where you from?" Glass was asking.

"Down from Canada."

"You don't look Canadian."

"I'm not. I was just visiting."

"You know Albright?"

"No. You know Pern?"

"No. You know any of the little towns around Southern Ontario?"

"No. I spent all my time around Vancouver and B.C."

"Oh," Glass said.

"Here's your weapon." I tossed the orchid. It clattered on the blacktop, rolled jerkily, and stopped.

"What is—?" The sound of a car motor made us all look toward the end of the bridge; but it died away on some turnoff. She looked back. "What *is* it?"

"How they call that?" Fireball asked.

"An orchid," I said.

"Yeah," Fireball said. "That's what it is."

She stooped, centered in her multiple shadows. She kept one thumb under her pack-strap; with her other hand she picked it up.

"Put it on," I said.

"Are you right or left handed?" Glass asked.

"Left." She stood, examining the flower. "At least, I write with my left."

"Oh," Glass said again.

"This is a pretty vicious looking thing." She fitted it around her wrist; something glittered there. "Just the thing for the New York subway during rush hour." She bent her neck to see how it snapped. As her hair swung forward, under her collar was another, bright flash. "Ugly thing. I hope I don't need you."

I said: "Hope you don't either."

She looked up.

Spider and D-t had turned off their lights and were looking, anxiously, beyond the second stanchion toward the dark hills of the safer shore.

"I guess," I told her, "you can give it to somebody else when you're ready to be among the dried and crisp branches, trying to remember it, get it down, thinking: I I didn't leave them like that! I didn't. It's not real. It can't be. If it is then I am crazy. I am too tired—wandering among all these, and these streets where the burning, burning, leaves the shattered and the toppling. Brick, no bridge because it takes so long, leaving, I haven't leaving. That I was following down the dark blood blots her glittering heel left on the blacktop. They slid into the V of my two shadows on the moon and George lit along the I walk on and kept. Leaving it. Twigs, leaves, bark bits along the shoulder, the hissing hills and the smoke, the long country cut with summer and no where to begin. In the direction, then, Broadway and train tracks, limping in the in the all the dark blots till the rocks, running with rusty water, following beside the broken mud gleaming on the ditch edge, with the trees so over so I went into them and thought I could wait here until she came, all naked up or might knowing what I couldn't, remember maybe if just one of them. He. In or on, I'm not quite where I go or what to go now but I'll climb up on the and wonder about Mexico if she, come, waiting.

This hand full of crumpled leaves.

It would be better than here. Just in the like that, if you can't remember any more if. I want to know but I can't see are you up there. I don't have a lot of strength now. The sky is stripped. I am too weak to write much.

But I still hear them walking in the trees; not speaking. Waiting here, away from the terrifying weaponry, out of the halls of vapor and light, beyond holland and into the hills, I have come to

—*San Francisco, Abaqii, Toronto, Clarion, Milford, New Orleans, Seattle, Vancouver, Middletown, East Lansing, New York, London* January 1969/September 1973

ABOUT THE AUTHOR

SAMUEL R. DELANY was born in New York City on April 1, 1942. He grew up in New York's Harlem district and attended the Bronx High School of Science. At City College he served as poetry editor of the magazine *Prometheus*. He composed his first novel at nineteen and, at intervals between novels, worked in jobs ranging from shrimpboat worker to folk singer—in places as diverse as the Texas Gulf, Greece and Istanbul. Samuel Delany has won the coveted Nebula Award four times, twice for short stories ("Aye, and Gomorrah" and "Time Considered as a Helix of Semi-Precious Stones") and twice for novels (*Babel-17* and *The Einstein Intersection*). His other works include *The Fall of the Towers, The Jewels of Aptor, Nova* and DHALGREN. In addition, he and his wife, the poet Marilyn Hacker, founded and edited the avant-garde science fiction journal *Quark* from their base in London, where they presently live with their infant daughter.

OTHER WORLDS.
OTHER REALITIES.

In fact and fiction, these extraordinary books bring the fascinating world of the supernatural down to earth from ancient astronauts and black magic to witchcraft voodoo and mysticism—these books look at other worlds and examine other realities.

- ☐ **THE DEVIL'S TRIANGLE (8445/$1.50)—Fact**
- ☐ **POWER THROUGH WITCHCRAFT (8673/$1.25)—Fact**
- ☐ **CHARIOTS OF THE GODS (Q5753/$1.25)—Fact**
- ☐ **A COMPLETE GUIDE TO THE TAROT (Q6696/$1.25)—Fact**
- ☐ **WITCHCRAFT AND BLACK MAGIC (7996/$1.95)—Fact**
- ☐ **THE EXORCIST (X7200/$1.75)—Fiction**
- ☐ **GODS FROM OUTER SPACE (Q7276/$1.25)—Fact**
- ☐ **NOT OF THIS WORLD (7696/$1.25)—Fact**
- ☐ **GOD DRIVES A FLYING SAUCER (7733/$1.25)—Fact**
- ☐ **THE SPACESHIPS OF EZEKIEL (8378/$1.95)—Fact**

Buy them at your local bookstore or use this handy coupon for ordering:

RAY BRADBURY

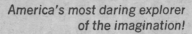

*America's most daring explorer
of the imagination!*

- ☐ MACHINERIES OF JOY   (8304—95¢)
- ☐ THE WONDERFUL ICE CREAM SUIT
  & OTHER PLAYS   (8297—95¢)
- ☐ TIMELESS STORIES FOR TODAY
  AND TOMORROW   (8162—95¢)
- ☐ MEDICINE FOR MELANCHOLY   (8098—95¢)
- ☐ DANDELION WINE   (8027—95¢)
- ☐ R IS FOR ROCKET   (7988—95¢)
- ☐ S IS FOR SPACE   (7961—95¢)
- ☐ THE ILLUSTRATED MAN   (7112—95¢)
- ☐ SOMETHING WICKED THIS WAY
  COMES   (6438—$1.25)
- ☐ I SING THE BODY ELECTRIC   (5752—95¢)
- ☐ THE MARTIAN CHRONICLES   (5613—95¢)
- ☐ GOLDEN APPLES OF THE SUN   (4867—75¢)

THE TWILIGHT ZONE

Rod Serling, one of America's exciting writers, has fashioned amazing excursions into the fifth dimension—the world of imagination. Here are six brilliant collections of fantastic stories written expressly for Bantam. Discover, for yourself, the fascinating world of Rod Serling in:

Bantam Book Catalog

It lists over a thousand money-saving best-sellers originally priced from $3.75 to $15.00 —bestsellers that are yours now for as little as 50¢ to $2.95!

The catalog gives you a great opportunity to build your own private library at huge savings!

So don't delay any longer—send us your name and address and 10¢ (to help defray postage and handling costs).